A MATTER OF HONOUR

&

NOT A PENNY MORE, NOT A PENNY LESS

D0784886

ALSO BY JEFFREY ARCHER

Jeffrey Archer is a master storyteller, the author of eleven novels which have all been worldwide bestsellers. *Not a Penny More, Not a Penny Less* was his first book, and it achieved instant success. Next came the tense and terrifying thriller *Shall We Tell the President?*, followed by his triumphant bestseller *Kane and Abel*. His first collection of short stories, *A Quiver Full of Arrows*, came next, and then *The Prodigal Daughter*, the superb sequel to *Kane and Abel*. This was followed by *First Among Equals*, considered by the *Scotsman* to be the finest novel about parliament since Trollope, the thrilling chase story *A Matter of Honour*, his second collection of stories, *A Twist in the Tale*, and the novels *As the Crow Flies* and *Honour Among Thieves*. *Twelve Red Herrings*, his third collection of stories, was followed by the novels *The Fourth Estate* and *The Eleventh Commandment*. A collected edition of his short stories was published in 1997, followed by another collection, *To Cut a Long Story Short*. His latest novel, *Sons of Fortune*, was published by Macmillan in 2002.

Jeffrey Archer was born in 1940 and educated at Wellington School, Somerset, and Brasenose College, Oxford. He represented Great Britain in the 100 metres in the early sixties, and entered the House of Commons when he won the by-election at Louth in 1969. He wrote his first novel, *Not a Penny More, Not a Penny Less*, in 1974. From September 1985 to October 1986 he was Deputy Chairman of the Conservative Party, and he was created a Life Peer in the Queen's Birthday Honours of 1992. He is married with two children.

JEFFREY ARCHER

A MATTER OF HONOUR

&

NOT A PENNY MORE, NOT A PENNY LESS

PAN BOOKS

A Matter of Honour first published 1986 by Hodder and Stoughton Ltd.
First published by Pan Books 2003
Not a Penny More, Not a Penny Less first published 1976 by Jonathan Cape Ltd.
First published by Pan Books 2003

This omnibus edition published 2004 by Pan Books
an imprint of Pan Macmillan Ltd
Pan Macmillan, 20 New Wharf Road, London N1 9RR
Basingstoke and Oxford
Associated companies throughout the world
www.panmacmillan.com

ISBN 0 330 43900 6

Copyright © Jeffrey Archer 1976, 1986

The right of Jeffrey Archer to be identified as the
author of this work has been asserted by him in accordance
with the Copyright, Designs and Patents Act 1988.

All rights reserved. No part of this publication may be
reproduced, stored in or introduced into a retrieval system, or
transmitted, in any form, or by any means (electronic, mechanical,
photocopying, recording or otherwise) without the prior written
permission of the publisher. Any person who does any unauthorized
act in relation to this publication may be liable to criminal
prosecution and civil claims for damages.

1 3 5 7 9 8 6 4 2

A CIP catalogue record for this book is available from
the British Library.

Printed and bound in Great Britain by
Mackays of Chatham plc, Chatham, Kent

This book is sold subject to the condition that it shall not,
by way of trade or otherwise, be lent, re-sold, hired out,
or otherwise circulated without the publisher's prior consent
in any form of binding or cover other than that in which
it is published and without a similar condition including this
condition being imposed on the subsequent purchaser.

A MATTER OF HONOUR

To Will

PART ONE

THE KREMLIN
MOSCOW

May 19, 1966

CHAPTER ONE

THE KREMLIN, MOSCOW
May 19, 1966

"It's a fake," said the Russian leader, staring down at the small exquisite painting he held in his hands.

"That isn't possible," replied his Politburo colleague. "The Tsar's icon of St George and the Dragon has been in the Winter Palace at Leningrad under heavy guard for over fifty years."

"True, Comrade Zaborski," said the old man, "but for fifty years we've been guarding a fake. The Tsar must have removed the original some time before the Red Army entered St Petersburg and overran the Winter Palace."

The head of State Security moved restlessly in his chair as the cat and mouse game continued. Zaborski knew, after years of running the KGB, who had been cast as the mouse the moment his phone had rung at four that morning to say that the General Secretary required him to report to the Kremlin – immediately.

"How can you be so sure it's a fake, Leonid Ilyich?" the diminutive figure enquired.

"Because, my dear Zaborski, during the past eighteen months, the age of all the treasures in the Winter

3

Palace has been tested by carbon-dating, the modern scientific process that does not call for a second opinion," said Brezhnev, displaying his new-found knowledge. "And what we have always thought to be one of the nation's masterpieces," he continued, "turns out to have been painted five hundred years after Rublev's original."

"But by whom and for what purpose?" asked the Chairman of State Security, incredulous.

"The experts tell me it was probably a court painter," replied the Russian leader, "who must have been commissioned to execute the copy only months before the Revolution took place. It has always worried the curator at the Winter Palace that the Tsar's traditional silver crown was not attached to the back of the frame, as it was to all his other masterpieces," added Brezhnev.

"But I always thought that the silver crown had been removed by a souvenir hunter even before we had entered St Petersburg."

"No," said the General Secretary drily, his bushy eyebrows rising every time he had completed a statement. "It wasn't the Tsar's silver crown that had been removed, but the painting itself."

"Then what can the Tsar have done with the original?" the Chairman said, almost as if he were asking himself the question.

"That is exactly what I want to know, Comrade," said Brezhnev, resting his hands each side of the little painting that remained in front of him. "And you are the one who has been chosen to come up with the answer," he added.

For the first time the Chairman of the KGB looked unsure of himself.

"But do you have anything for me to go on?"

"Very little," admitted the General Secretary, flicking open a file that he removed from the top drawer of his desk. He stared down at the closely typed notes headed 'The Significance of the Icon in Russian History'. Someone had been up all through the night preparing a ten-page report that the leader had only found time to scan. Brezhnev's real interest began on page four. He quickly turned over the first three pages before reading aloud: "'At the time of the Revolution, Tsar Nicholas II obviously saw Rublev's masterpiece as his passport to freedom in the West. He must have had a copy made which he then left on his study wall where the original had previously hung.'" The Russian leader looked up. "Beyond that we have little to go on."

The head of the KGB looked perplexed. He remained puzzled as to why Brezhnev should want State Security involved in the theft of a minor masterpiece. "And how important is it that we find the original?" he asked, trying to pick up a further clue.

Leonid Brezhnev stared down at his Kremlin colleague.

"Nothing could be more important, Comrade," came back the unexpected reply. "And I shall grant you any resources you may consider necessary in terms of people and finance to discover the whereabouts of the Tsar's icon."

"But if I were to take you at your word, Comrade General Secretary," said the head of the KGB, trying to disguise his disbelief, "I could so easily end up spending far more than the painting is worth."

"That would not be possible," said Brezhnev, pausing for effect, "because it's not the icon itself that I'm after." He turned his back on the Chairman of State Security and stared out of the window. He had always disliked not being able to see over the Kremlin wall and into Red Square. He waited for some moments before he proclaimed, "The money the Tsar might have raised from selling such a masterpiece would only have kept Nicholas in his accustomed lifestyle for a matter of months, perhaps a year at the most. No, it's what we believe the Tsar had secreted *inside* the icon that would have guaranteed security for himself and his family for the rest of their days."

A little circle of condensation formed on the window pane in front of the General Secretary.

"What could possibly be that valuable?" asked the Chairman.

"Do you remember, Comrade, what the Tsar promised Lenin in exchange for his life?"

"Yes, but it turned out to be a bluff because no such document was hidden . . ." He stopped himself just before saying "in the icon".

Zaborski stood silently, unable to witness Brezhnev's triumphant smile.

"You have caught up with me at last, Comrade. You see, the document was hidden in the icon all the time. We just had the wrong icon."

The Russian leader waited for some time before he turned back and passed over to his colleague a single sheet of paper. "This is the Tsar's testimony indicating what we would find hidden in the icon of St George and the Dragon. At the time, nothing was discovered in the icon, which only convinced Lenin that it had been a pathetic bluff by the Tsar to save his family from execution."

Zaborski slowly read the hand-written testimony that had been signed by the Tsar hours before his execution. Zaborski's hands began to tremble and a bead of sweat appeared on his forehead long before he had reached the last paragraph. He looked across at the tiny painting, no larger than a book, that remained in the centre of the Chairman's desk.

"Not since the death of Lenin," continued Brezhnev, "has anyone believed the Tsar's claim. But now, there can be little doubt that if we are able to locate the genuine masterpiece, we will undoubtedly also be in possession of the promised document."

"And with the authority of those who signed that document, no one could question our legal claim," said Zaborski.

"That would undoubtedly prove to be the case, Comrade Chairman," replied the Russian leader. "And I also feel confident that we would receive the backing of the United Nations and the World Court if the Americans tried to deny us our right. But I fear time is now against us."

"Why?" asked the Chairman of State Security.

"Look at the completion date in the Tsar's testimony and you will see how much time we have left to honour our part of the agreement," said Brezhnev.

Zaborski stared down at the date scrawled in the hand of the Tsar – June 20, 1966. He handed back the testimony as he considered the enormity of the task with which his leader had entrusted him. Leonid Ilyich Brezhnev continued his monologue.

"So, as you can see, Comrade Zaborski, we have only one month left before the deadline, but if you can discover the whereabouts of the original icon, President Johnson's defence strategy would be rendered virtually useless, and the United States would then become a pawn on the Russian chessboard."

CHAPTER TWO

APPLESHAW, ENGLAND
June 1966

"And to my dearly beloved and only son, Captain Adam Scott, MC, I bequeath the sum of five hundred pounds."

Although Adam had anticipated the amount would be pitiful, he nevertheless remained bolt upright in his chair as the solicitor glanced over his half-moon spectacles.

The old lawyer who was seated behind the large partners' desk raised his head and blinked at the handsome young man before him. Adam put a hand nervously through his thick black hair, suddenly conscious of the lawyer's stare. Then Mr Holbrooke's eyes returned to the papers in front of him.

"And to my dearly beloved daughter, Margaret Scott, I bequeath the sum of four hundred pounds." Adam was unable to prevent a small grin spreading across his face. Even in the minutiae of his final act, father had remained a chauvinist.

"To the Hampshire County Cricket Club," droned on Mr Holbrooke, unperturbed by Miss Scott's relative misfortunes, "twenty-five pounds, life membership."

9

Finally paid up, thought Adam. "To the Old Contemptibles, fifteen pounds. And to the Appleshaw Parish Church, ten pounds." Death membership, Adam mused. "To Wilf Proudfoot, our loyal gardener part time, ten pounds, and to Mrs Mavis Cox, our daily help, five pounds."

"And finally, to my dearly beloved wife Susan, our marital home, and the remainder of my estate."

This pronouncement made Adam want to laugh out loud because he doubted if the remainder of Pa's estate, even if they sold his premium bonds and the pre-war golf clubs, amounted to more than another thousand pounds.

But mother was a daughter of the Regiment and wouldn't complain, she never did. If God ever announced the saints, as opposed to some Pope in Rome, Saint Susan of Appleshaw would be up there with Mary and Elizabeth. All through his life 'Pa', as Adam always thought of him, had set such high standards for the family to live up to. Perhaps that was why Adam continued to admire him above all men. Sometimes the very thought made him feel strangely out of place in the swinging sixties.

Adam began to move restlessly in his chair, assuming that the proceedings were now drawing to a close. The sooner they were all out of this cold, drab little office the better, he felt.

Mr Holbrooke looked up once more and cleared his throat, as if he were about to announce who was to be left the Goya or the Hapsburg diamonds. He pushed his half-moon spectacles further up the bridge of his nose and stared back down at the last paragraphs of his late client's testament. The three surviving members of the Scott family sat in silence. What could he have to add? thought Adam.

Whatever it was, the solicitor had obviously pondered the final bequest several times, because he delivered the words like a well-versed actor, his eyes returning to the script only once.

"And I also leave to my son," Mr Holbrooke paused, "the enclosed envelope," he said, holding it up, "which I can only hope will bring him greater happiness than it did me. Should he decide to open the envelope it must be on the condition that he will never divulge its contents to any other living person." Adam caught his sister's eye but she only shook her head slightly, obviously as puzzled as he was. He glanced towards his mother who looked shocked. Was it fear or was it distress? Adam couldn't decide. Without another word, Mr Holbrooke passed the yellowed envelope over to the Colonel's only son.

Everyone in the room remained seated, not quite sure what to do next. Mr Holbrooke finally closed the thin file marked Colonel Gerald Scott, DSO, OBE, MC, pushed back his chair and walked slowly over to the widow. They shook hands and she said, "Thank you," a faintly ridiculous courtesy, Adam felt, as the only person in the room who had made any sort of profit on this particular transaction had been Mr Holbrooke, and that on behalf of Holbrooke, Holbrooke and Gascoigne.

He rose and went quickly to his mother's side.

"You'll join us for tea, Mr Holbrooke?" she was asking.

"I fear not, dear lady," the lawyer began, but Adam didn't bother to listen further. Obviously the fee hadn't been large enough to cover Holbrooke taking time off for tea.

Once they had left the office and Adam had ensured his mother and sister were seated comfortably in the back of the family Morris Minor, he took his place behind the steering wheel. He had parked outside Mr Holbrooke's office in the middle of the High Street. No yellow lines in the streets of Appleshaw — yet, he thought. Even before he had switched on the ignition his mother had offered matter-of-factly, "We'll have to get rid of this, you know. I can't afford to run it now, not with petrol at six shillings a gallon."

"Don't let's worry about that today," said Margaret consolingly, but in a voice that accepted that her mother was right. "I wonder what can be in that envelope, Adam," she added, wanting to change the subject.

"Detailed instructions on how to invest my five hundred pounds, no doubt," said her brother, attempting to lighten their mood.

"Don't be disrespectful of the dead," said his mother, the same look of fear returning to her face. "I begged your father to destroy that envelope," she added, in a voice that was barely a whisper.

Adam's lips pursed when he realised this must be *the* envelope his father had referred to all those years ago when he had witnessed the one row between his parents that he had ever experienced. Adam still remembered his father's raised voice and angry words just a few days after he had returned from Germany.

"I have to open it, don't you understand?" Pa had insisted.

"Never," his mother had replied. "After all the sacrifices I have made, you at least owe me that."

Over twenty years had passed since that confrontation and he had never heard the subject referred to again. The only time Adam ever mentioned it to his sister she could throw no light on what the dispute might have been over.

Adam put his foot on the brake as they reached a T-junction at the end of the High Street.

He turned right and continued to drive out of the village for a mile or so down a winding country lane before bringing the old Morris Minor to a halt. Adam leapt out and opened the trellised gate whose path led through a neat lawn to a little thatched cottage.

"I'm sure you ought to be getting back to London," were his mother's first words as she entered the drawing room.

"I'm in no hurry, mother. There's nothing that can't wait until tomorrow."

"Just as you wish, my dear, but you don't have to worry yourself over me," his mother continued. She stared up at the tall young man who reminded her so much of Gerald. He would have been as good-looking as her husband if it wasn't for the slight break in his nose. The same dark hair and deep brown eyes, the same open, honest face, even the same gentle approach to everyone he came across. But most of all the same high standards of morality that had brought them to their present sad state. "And in any case I've always got Margaret to take care of me," she added. Adam looked across at his sister and wondered how she would now cope with Saint Susan of Appleshaw.

Margaret had recently become engaged to a City stockbroker, and although the marriage had been postponed, she would soon be wanting to start a life of her own. Thank God her fiancé had already put a down-payment on a little house only fourteen miles away.

After tea and a sad uninterrupted monologue from his mother on the virtues and misfortunes of their father, Margaret cleared away and left the two of them alone. They had both loved him in such different ways although Adam felt that he had never let Pa really know how much he respected him.

"Now that you're no longer in the army, my dear, I do hope you'll be able to find a worthwhile job," his mother said uneasily, as she recalled how difficult that had proved to be for his father.

"I'm sure everything will be just fine, mother," he replied. "The Foreign Office have asked to see me again," he added, hoping to reassure her.

"Still, now that you've got five hundred pounds of your own," she said, "that should make things a little easier for you." Adam smiled fondly at his mother, wondering when she had last spent a day in London. His share of the Chelsea flat alone was four pounds a week and he still had to eat occasionally. She raised her eyes and, looking up at the clock on the mantel-piece, said, "You'd better be getting along, my dear, I don't like the thought of you on that motorbike after dark."

Adam bent down to kiss her on the cheek. "I'll give you a call tomorrow," he said. On his way out he stuck his head around the kitchen door and shouted to his sister, "I'm off and I'll be sending you a cheque for fifty pounds."

"Why?" asked Margaret, looking up from the sink.

"Just let's say it's my blow for women's rights." He shut the kitchen door smartly to avoid the dishcloth that was hurled in his direction. Adam revved up his BSA and drove down the A303 through Andover and on towards London. As most of the traffic was coming west out of the city, he was able to make good time on his way back to the flat in Ifield Road.

Adam had decided to wait until he had reached the privacy of his own room before he opened the envelope. Lately the excitement in his life had not been such that he felt he could be blasé about the little ceremony. After all, in a way, he had waited most of his life to discover what could possibly be in the envelope he had now inherited.

Adam had been told the story of the family tragedy by his father a thousand times – "It's all a matter of honour, old chap," his father would repeat, lifting his chin and squaring his shoulders. Adam's father had not realised that he had spent a lifetime overhearing the snide comments of lesser men and suffering the side-long glances from those officers who had made sure they were not seen too regularly in his company. Petty men with petty minds. Adam knew his father far too well to believe, even for a moment, that he could have been involved in such treachery as was whispered. Adam took one hand off the handlebars and fingered the envelope in his inside pocket like a schoolboy the day before his birthday feeling the shape of a present in the hope of discovering some clue as to its contents. He felt certain that whatever it contained would not be to anyone's advantage now his father was dead, but it did not lessen his curiosity.

He tried to piece together the few facts he had been told over the years. In 1946, within a year of his fiftieth birthday, his father had resigned his commission from the army. *The Times* had described Pa as a brilliant tactical officer with a courageous war record. His resignation had been a decision that had surprised *The Times* correspondent, astonished his immediate family and shocked his regiment, as it had been assumed by all who knew him that it was only a matter of months before crossed swords and a baton would have been sewn on to his epaulette.

Because of the colonel's sudden and unexplained departure from the regiment, fact was augmented by fiction. When asked, all the colonel would offer was that he had had enough of war, and felt the time had come to make a little money on which Susan and he could retire before it was too late. Even at the time, few people found his story credible, and that credibility was not helped when the only job the colonel managed to secure for himself was as secretary of the local golf club.

It was only through the generosity of Adam's late grandfather, General Sir Pelham Westlake, that he had been able to remain at Wellington College, and thereby be given the opportunity to continue the family tradition and pursue a military career.

After leaving school, Adam was offered a place at the Royal Military Academy, Sandhurst. During his days at the RMA, Adam was to be found diligently studying military history, tactics, and battle procedure while at weekends he concentrated on rugby and squash, although his greatest success came whenever he completed the different cross-country courses he encountered. For two years, panting cadets from Cranwell and Dartmouth only saw his mud-spattered back as Adam went on to become the Inter-Services champion. He also became the middleweight boxing champion despite a Nigerian cadet breaking his nose in the first round of the final. The Nigerian made the mistake of assuming the fight was already over.

When Adam passed out of Sandhurst in August 1956, he managed ninth place in the academic order of merit, but his leadership and example outside the classroom was such that no one was surprised when he was awarded the Sword of Honour. Adam never doubted from that moment he would now follow his father and command the regiment.

The Royal Wessex Regiment accepted the colonel's

son soon after he had been awarded his regular commission. Adam quickly gained the respect of the soldiers and popularity with those officers whose currency was not to deal in rumour. As a tactical officer in the field he had no equal, and when it came to combat duty it was clear he had inherited his father's courage. Yet, when six years later the War Office published in the *London Gazette* the names of those subalterns who had been made up to Captain, Lieutenant Adam Scott was not to be found on the list. His contemporaries were genuinely surprised, while senior officers of the regiment remained tight-lipped. To Adam it was becoming abundantly clear that he was not to be allowed to atone for whatever it was his father was thought to have done.

Eventually Adam was made up to captain, but not before he had distinguished himself in the Malayan jungle in hand-to-hand fighting against the never-ending waves of Chinese soldiers. Having been captured and held prisoner by the Communists, he endured solitude and torture of the kind that no amount of training could have prepared him for. He escaped eight months after his incarceration only to discover on returning to the front line that he had been awarded a posthumous Military Cross. When, at the age of twenty-nine, Captain Scott passed his staff exam but still failed to be offered a regimental place at the staff college, he finally accepted he could never hope to command the regiment. He resigned his commission a few weeks later; there was no need to suggest that the reason he had done so was because he needed to earn more money.

While he was serving out his last few months with the regiment, Adam learned from his mother that Pa only had weeks to live. Adam made the decision not to inform his father of his resignation. He knew Pa would only blame himself and he was at least thankful that he had died without being aware of the stigma that had become part of his son's daily life.

When Adam reached the outskirts of London his mind returned, as it had so often lately, to the pressing problem of finding himself gainful employment. In the seven weeks he had been out of work Adam had already had more interviews with his bank manager than with prospective employers. It was true that he had another meeting lined up with the Foreign Office, but he had been impressed by the standard of the other candidates he had encountered on the way, and was only too aware of his lack of a university qualification. However, he felt the first interview had gone well and he had been quickly made aware of how many ex-officers had joined the service. When he discovered that the chairman of the selection board had a Military Cross, Adam assumed he wasn't being considered for desk work.

As he swung the motorbike into the King's Road Adam once again fingered the envelope in his inside jacket pocket hoping, uncharitably, that Lawrence would not yet have returned from the bank. Not that he could complain: his old school friend had been extremely generous in offering him such a pleasant room in his spacious flat for only four pounds a week.

"You can start paying more when they make you an ambassador," Lawrence had told him.

"You're beginning to sound like Rachmann," Adam had retorted, grinning at the man he had so admired during their days at Wellington. For Lawrence – in direct contrast to Adam – everything seemed to come so easily – exams, jobs, sport and women, especially women. When he had won his place at Balliol and gone on to take a first in PPE, no one was surprised. But when Lawrence chose banking as a profession, his contemporaries were unable to hide their disbelief. It seemed to be the first time he had embarked on anything that might be described as mundane.

Adam parked his motorbike just off Ifield Road, aware that, like his mother's old Morris Minor, it would have to be sold if the Foreign Office job didn't materialise. As he strolled towards the flat a girl who passed gave him a second look: he didn't notice. He took the stairs in threes and had reached the fifth floor, and was pushing his Yale key into the lock when a voice from inside shouted, "It's on the latch."

"Damn," said Adam under his breath.

"How did it go?" were Lawrence's first words as he entered the drawing room.

"Very well, considering," Adam replied, not quite sure what else he could say as he smiled at his flatmate. Lawrence had already changed from his City clothes into a blazer and grey flannels. He was slightly shorter and stockier than Adam with a head of wiry fair hair, a massive forehead and grey thoughtful eyes that always seemed to be enquiring.

"I admired your father so much," he added. "He always assumed one had the same standards as he did." Adam could still remember nervously introducing Lawrence to his father one Speech Day. They had become friends immediately. But then Lawrence was not a man who dealt in rumours.

"Able to retire on the family fortune, are we?" asked Lawrence in a lighter vein.

"Only if that dubious bank you work for has found a way of converting five hundred pounds into five thousand in a matter of days."

"Can't manage it at the present time, old chum –

not now Harold Wilson has announced a standstill in wages and prices."

Adam smiled as he looked across at his friend. Although taller than him now, he could still recall those days when Lawrence seemed to him like a giant. "Late again, Scott," he would say as Adam scampered past him in the corridor. Adam had looked forward to the day when he could do everything in the same relaxed, superior style. Or was it just that Lawrence was superior? His suits always seemed to be well-pressed, his shoes always shone and he never had a hair out of place. Adam still hadn't fathomed out how he did it all so effortlessly.

Adam heard the bathroom door open. He glanced interrogatively towards Lawrence.

"It's Carolyn," whispered Lawrence. "She'll be staying the night . . . I think."

When Carolyn entered the room Adam smiled shyly at the tall, beautiful woman. Her long, blonde hair bounced on her shoulders as she walked towards them, but it was the faultless figure that most men couldn't take their eyes off. How did Lawrence manage it?

"Care to join us for a meal?" asked Lawrence, putting his arm round Carolyn's shoulder, his voice suddenly sounding a little *too* enthusiastic. "I've discovered this Italian restaurant that's just opened in the Fulham Road."

"I might join you later," said Adam, "but I still have one or two papers left over from this afternoon that I ought to check through."

"Forget the finer details of your inheritance, my boy. Why not join us and spend the entire windfall in one wild spaghetti fling?"

"Oh, have you been left lots of lovely lolly?" asked Carolyn, in a voice so shrill and high-pitched nobody would have been surprised to learn that she had recently been Deb of the Year.

"Not," said Adam, "when considered against my present overdraft."

Lawrence laughed. "Well, come along later if you discover there's enough over for a plate of pasta." He winked at Adam – his customary sign for "Be sure you're out of the flat by the time we get back. Or at least stay in your own room and pretend to be asleep."

"Yes, do come," cooed Carolyn, sounding as if she meant it – her hazel eyes remained fixed on Adam as Lawrence guided her firmly towards the door.

Adam didn't move until he was sure he could no longer hear her penetrating voice echoing on the staircase. Satisfied, he retreated to his bedroom and locked himself in. Adam sat down on the one comfortable chair he possessed and pulled his father's envelope out of his inside pocket. It was the heavy, expensive type of stationery Pa had always used, purchasing it at Smythson of Bond Street at almost twice the price he could have obtained it at the local W. H. Smith's. 'Captain Adam Scott, MC' was written in his father's neat copperplate hand.

Adam opened the envelope carefully, his hand shaking slightly, and extracted the contents: a letter in his father's unmistakable hand and a smaller envelope which was clearly old as it was faded with time. Written on the old envelope in an unfamiliar hand were the words 'Colonel Gerald Scott' in faded ink of indeterminate colour. Adam placed the old envelope on the little table by his side and, unfolding his father's letter, began to read. It was undated.

My dear Adam,
Over the years, you will have heard many expla-

nations for my sudden departure from the regiment. Most of them will have been farcical, and a few of them slanderous, but I always considered it better for all concerned to keep my own counsel. I feel, however, that I owe you a fuller explanation, and that is what this letter will set out to do.

As you know, my last posting before I resigned my commission was at Nuremberg from November 1945 to October 1946. After four years of almost continuous action in the field, I was given the task of commanding the British section which had responsibility for those senior ranking Nazis who were awaiting trial for war crimes. Although the Americans had overall responsibility, I came to know the imprisoned officers quite well and after a year or so I had even grown to tolerate some of them – Hess, Doenitz and Speer in particular – and I often wondered how the Germans would have treated us had the situation been reversed. Such views were considered unacceptable at the time. 'Fraternisation' was often on the lips of those men who are never given to second thoughts.

Among the senior Nazis with whom I came into daily contact was Reichsmarshal Hermann Goering, but unlike the three other officers I have previously mentioned, here was a man I detested from the first moment I came across him. I found him arrogant, overbearing and totally without shame about the barbaric acts he had carried out in the name of war. And I never once found any reason to change my opinion of him. In fact, I sometimes wondered how I controlled my temper when I was in his presence.

The night before Goering was due to be executed, he requested a private meeting with me. It was a Monday, and I can still recall every detail of that encounter as if it were only yesterday. I received the request when I took over the Russian watch from Major Vladimir Kosky. In fact Kosky personally handed me the written request. As soon as I had inspected the guard and dealt with the usual paperwork, I went along with the duty corporal to see the Reichsmarshal in his cell. Goering stood to attention by his small low bed and saluted as I entered the room. The sparse, grey-painted, brick cell always made me shudder.

"You asked to see me?" I said. I never could get myself to address him by his name or rank.

"Yes," he replied. "It was kind of you to come in person, Colonel. I simply wish to make the last request of a man condemned to death. Would it be possible for the corporal to leave us?"

Imagining it was something highly personal I asked the corporal to wait outside. I confess I had no idea what could be so private when the man only had hours to live but as the door closed he saluted again and then passed over the envelope you now have in your possession. As I took it, all he said was, "Would you be good enough not to open this until after my execution tomorrow." He then added, "I can only hope it will compensate for any blame that might later be placed on your shoulders." I had no idea what he could be alluding to at the time and presumed some form of mental instability had overtaken him. Many of the prisoners confided in me during their last few days, and towards the end, some of them were undoubtedly on the verge of madness.

Adam stopped to consider what he would have done in the same circumstances, and decided to read on to discover if father and son would have taken the same course.

However, Goering's final words to me as I left his cell seemed hardly those of a madman. He said quite simply: "Be assured. It is a masterpiece; do not underestimate its value." Then he lit up a cigar as if he was relaxing at his club after a rather good dinner. We all had different theories as to who smuggled the cigars in for him, and equally wondered what might also have been smuggled out from time to time.

I placed the envelope in my jacket pocket and left him to join the corporal in the corridor. We then checked the other cells to see that all the prisoners were locked up for the night. The inspection completed, I returned to my office. As I was satisfied that there were no more immediate duties I settled down to make out my report. I left the envelope in the jacket pocket of my uniform with every intention of opening it immediately after Goering's execution had been carried out the following morning. I was checking over the orders of the day when the corporal rushed into my office without knocking. "It's Goering, sir, it's Goering," he said, frantically. From the panic on the man's face, I didn't need to ask for any details. We both ran all the way back to the Reichsmarshal's cell.

I found Goering lying face downwards on his bunk. I turned him over to find he was already dead. In the commotion that immediately followed I quite forgot Goering's letter. An autopsy a few days later showed that he had died from poisoning; the court came to the conclusion that the cyanide capsule that had been found in his body must have been implanted in one of his cigars.

As I had been the last to see him alone and privately, it took only a few whispers before my name was linked with his death. There was, of course, no truth in the accusation. Indeed I never doubted for one moment that the court had delivered the correct verdict in his case and that he justly deserved to be hanged for the part he had played in the war.

So stung was I by the continual behind-the-back accusations that I might have helped Goering to an easy death by smuggling in the cigars that I felt the only honourable thing to do in the circumstances was to resign my commission immediately for fear of bringing further dishonour to the regiment. When I returned to England later that year, and finally decided to throw out my old uniform, I came across the envelope again. When I explained to your mother the details of the incident she begged me to destroy the envelope as she considered it had brought enough dishonour to our family already, and even if it did point to whoever had been responsible for helping Goering to his suicide, in her opinion such knowledge could no longer do anyone any good. I agreed to comply with her wishes and although I never opened the envelope I could never get myself to destroy it, remembering the last sentence Goering had uttered about it being a masterpiece. And so finally I hid it among my personal papers.

However, since the imagined sins of the father are inevitably visited upon the next generation, I feel no such qualms should influence you. If there is therefore anything to be gained from the contents

25

of this envelope I make only one request, namely that your mother should be the first to benefit from it without ever being allowed to know how such good fortune came about.

Over the years, I have watched your progress with considerable pride and feel confident that I can leave you to make the correct decision.

If you are left in any doubt about opening the envelope yourself, destroy it without further consideration. But if you open it only to discover its purpose is to involve you in some dishonourable enterprise, be rid of it without a second thought.

May God be with you.
Your loving father,

Gerald Scott

Adam read the letter over once again, realising how much trust his father had placed in him. His heart thumped in his chest as he considered how Pa's life had been wasted by the murmurings and innuendoes of lesser men – the same men who had also succeeded in bringing his own career to a premature halt. When he had finished reading the missive for a third time he folded it up neatly and slipped it back into its envelope.

He then picked up the second envelope from the side table. The words 'Colonel Gerald Scott' were written in a faded bold script across it.

Adam removed a comb from his inside pocket and wedged it into the corner of the envelope. Slowly he began to slit it open. He hesitated for a moment before extracting two pieces of paper, both yellowed with age. One appeared to be a letter while the other seemed to be a document of some sort. The crest of the Third Reich was embossed at the head of the letterpaper above the printed name of Reichsmarshal Hermann Goering. Adam's hands began to tremble as he read the first line.

It began, *Sehr geehrter Herr Oberst Scott:*

CHAPTER THREE

As the black Chaika limousine drove out under the Spasskaya Bashnya and on to Red Square, two Kremlin guards in khaki uniforms sprang to attention and presented arms. A shrill whistle sounded which ensured that Yuri Efimovich Zaborski would experience no delays on his route back to Dzerzhinsky Square.

Zaborski touched the corner of his black felt hat in automatic acknowledgment of the salute although his thoughts were elsewhere. As the car rumbled over the cobbled stones, he didn't even glance at the long snake-like queue that stretched from Lenin's Tomb to the edge of Red Square. The first decision he had to make would undoubtedly be the most important: which of his senior operatives should be charged with the task of heading the team to find the Tsar's icon? He continued to ponder the problem as his driver took him across Red Square, passing the grey façade of the GUM department store away to his left before driving along Neitsa Kuibysheva.

Within moments of leaving his leader, the Chairman of State Security had formed in his own mind a shortlist of two. Which of those two, Valchek or Romanov, should be given the nod still taxed him. In normal circumstances he would have spent at least a week making such a decision but the General Secretary's deadline of June 20 left him with no such freedom. He knew he would have to make the choice even before he reached his office. The driver cruised through another green light past the Ministry of Culture and into Cherkasskiy Bolshoy Pereulok lined with its imposing block-like, grey buildings. The car remained in the special inside lane that could be used only by senior Party officials. In England, he was amused to learn that they had plans for such a traffic lane – but it would only be for the use of buses.

The car came to an abrupt halt outside KGB head-quarters. It hadn't helped that they had been able to cover the three kilometre journey in less than four minutes. The driver ran round and opened the back door to allow his master to step out but Zaborski didn't move. The man who rarely changed his mind had already done so twice on the route back to Dzerzhinsky Square. He knew he could call on any number of bureaucrats and academics to do the spade work but someone with flair was going to have to lead them and be responsible for reporting back to him.

His professional intuition told him to select Yuri Valchek, who had proved over the years to be a trusty and reliable servant of the State. He was also one of the Chairman's longest serving heads of department. Slow methodical and reliable, he had completed a full ten years as an agent in the field before confining himself to a desk job.

In contrast, Alex Romanov, who had only recently become head of his own section, had shown flashes of brilliance in the field but they had been so often outweighed by a lack of personal judgment. At twenty-nine, he was the youngest and, without question, the most ambitious of the Chairman's select team.

Zaborski stepped out on to the pavement and walked towards another door held open for him. He strode across the marble floor and stopped only when he reached the lift gates. Several silent men and women had also been waiting for the lift but when it returned to the ground floor and the Chairman stepped into the little cage, none of them made any attempt to join him. Zaborski travelled slowly up towards his office, never failing to compare it unfavourably with the speed of the one American elevator he had experienced. They could launch their rockets before you could get to your office, his predecessor had warned him. By the time Zaborski had reached the top floor and the gates had been pulled back for him, he had made up his mind. It would be Valchek.

A secretary helped him off with his long black coat and took his hat. Zaborski walked quickly to his desk. The two files he had asked for were awaiting him. He sat down and began to pore over Valchek's file. When he had completed it, he barked out an order to his hovering secretary: "Find Romanov."

Comrade Romanov lay flat on his back, his left arm behind his head and his opponent's right over his throat preparing for a double knee-thrust. The coach executed it perfectly and Romanov groaned as he hit the floor with a thud.

An attendant came rushing over to them and bent down to whisper in the coach's ear. The coach reluctantly released his pupil who rose slowly as if in a daze, bowed to the coach and then in one movement of right arm and left leg took the legs from under him and left him flat on the gymnasium floor before making his way quickly to the off-the-hook phone in the office.

Romanov didn't notice the girl who handed him the

phone. "I'll be with him as soon as I have had a shower," was all she heard him say. The girl who had taken the call had often wondered what Romanov looked like in the shower. She, like all the other girls in the office, had seen him in the gymnasium a hundred times. Six foot tall with that long, flowing blond hair – he resembled a Western film star. And those eyes, 'piercing blue' the friend who shared her desk described them.

"He's got a scar on his . . ." the friend confided.

"How do you know that?" she had asked, but her friend had only giggled in reply.

The Chairman meanwhile had opened Romanov's personal file for a second time, and was still perusing the details. He began to read the different entries that made up a candid character assessment which Romanov would never see unless he became Chairman:

Alexander Petrovich Romanov. Born Leningrad, March 12, 1937. Elected full Party member 1958.
Father: Peter Nicholevich Romanov, served on the Eastern Front in 1942. On returning to Russia in 1945 refused to join Communist Party. After several reports of anti-State activities supplied by his son he was sentenced to ten years in prison. Died in jail October 20, 1948.

Zaborski looked up and smiled – a child of the State.

Grandfather: Nicholai Alexandrovich Romanov, merchant, and one of the wealthiest landowners in Petrograd. Shot and killed on May 11, 1918, while attempting to escape from the forces of the Red Army.

The Revolution had taken place between the princely grandfather and the reluctant comrade father.

Alex, as he preferred to be known, had nevertheless inherited the Romanov ambition so he enrolled for the Party's Pioneer organisation at the age of nine. By the age of eleven, he had been offered a place at a special school at Smolensk – to the disgust of some of the lesser Party workers who considered such privileges should be reserved for the sons of loyal Party officials, not the sons of those in jail. Romanov immediately excelled in the classroom, much to the dismay of the Director who had been hoping to disprove any Darwinian theories. And at fourteen he was selected as one of the Party's élite and made a member of the Komsomol.

By the age of sixteen, Romanov had won the Lenin language medal and the junior gymnastics prize and despite the Director's attempts to undermine young Alex's achievements, most members of the school board recognised Romanov's potential and ensured that he was still allowed to take up a place at university. As an undergraduate he continued to excel in languages, specialising in English, French and German. Natural flair and hard work kept him near the top of every subject he specialised in.

Zaborski picked up the phone by his side. "I asked to see Romanov," he said curtly.

"He was completing his morning work-out at the gymnasium, Chairman," replied the secretary. "But he left to change the moment he heard you wanted to see him."

The Chairman replaced the phone and his eyes returned to the file in front of him. That Romanov could be found in the gymnasium at all hours came as no surprise: the man's athletic prowess had been acknowledged far beyond the service.

During his first year as a student, Romanov had continued diligently with his gymnastics and even gone on to represent the State side until the university coach had written in bold letters across one of his reports, "This student is too tall to be considered for serious Olympic competition." Romanov heeded the coach's advice and took up judo. Within two years, he had been selected for the 1958 Eastern Bloc games in Budapest and within a further two years found other competitors preferred not to be drawn against him on his inevitable route to the final. After his victory at the Soviet games in Moscow the Western press crudely described him as 'The Axe'. Those who were already planning his long-term future felt it prudent not to enter him for the Olympics.

Once Romanov had completed his fifth year at the university and obtained his diploma (with distinction), he remained in Moscow and joined the diplomatic service.

Zaborski had now reached the point in the file at which he had first come across the self-confident young man. Each year the KGB were able to second from the diplomatic service any person they considered to be of exceptional talent. Romanov was an obvious candidate. Zaborski's rule, however, was not to enlist anyone who didn't consider the KGB to be the élite. Unwilling candidates never made good operatives and sometimes even ended up working for the other side. Romanov showed no such doubt. He had always wanted to be an officer of the KGB. During the next six years he carried out tours at their embassies in Paris, London, Prague and Lagos. By the time he had returned to

Moscow to join the headquarters staff he was a sophisticated operative who was as relaxed at an ambassadorial cocktail party as he was in the gymnasium.

Zaborski began to read some of the comments he himself had added to the report during the last four years – in particular how much Romanov had changed during his time on the Chairman's personal staff. As an operative, he had reached the rank of major, having served successfully in the field before being appointed head of a department. Two red dots were placed by his name indicating successful missions. A defecting violinist attempting to leave Prague and a general who had thought he was going to be the next head of a small African state. What impressed Zaborski most about his protégé's efforts was that the Western press thought the Czechs were responsible for the first and the Americans for the second. Romanov's most significant achievement, however, had been the recruitment of an agent from the British Foreign Office whose parallel rise had only assisted Romanov's career. Romanov's appointment as head of a department had surprised no one, himself included, although it soon became clear to Zaborski that he missed the raw excitement of field work.

The Chairman turned to the last page, a character assessment, in which the majority of contributors were in accord: ambitious, sophisticated, ruthless, arrogant but not always reliable were the words that appeared with regularity in almost every summation.

There was an assertive rap on the door. Zaborski closed the file and pressed a button under his desk. The doors clicked open to allow Alexander Petrovich Romanov to enter the room.

"Good morning, Comrade Chairman," said the elegant young man who now stood to attention in front of him. Zaborski looked up at the man he had selected and felt a little envy that the gods had bestowed so much on one so young. Still, it was he who understood how to use such a man to the State's best advantage.

He continued to stare into those clear blue eyes and considered that if Romanov had been born in Hollywood he would not have found it hard to make a living. His suit looked as if it had been tailored in Savile Row – and probably had been. Zaborski chose to ignore such irregularities although he was tempted to ask the young man where he had his shirts made.

"You called for me," said Romanov.

The Chairman nodded. "I have just returned from the Kremlin," he said. "The General Secretary has entrusted us with a particularly sensitive project of great importance to the State." Zaborski paused. "So sensitive in fact that you will report only to me. You can hand-select your own team and no resources will be denied you."

"I am honoured," said Romanov, sounding unusually sincere.

"You will be," replied the Chairman, "if you succeed in discovering the whereabouts of the Tsar's icon."

"But I thought . . ." began Romanov.

CHAPTER FOUR

Adam walked over to the side of his bed and removed from the bookshelf the Bible his mother had given him as a Confirmation present. As he opened it a layer of dust rose from the top of the gold-leaf-edged pages. He placed the envelope in Revelation and returned the Bible to the shelf.

Adam strolled through to the kitchen, fried himself an egg and warmed up the other half of the previous day's tinned beans. He placed the unwholesome meal on the kitchen table, unable to put out of his mind the slap-up meal Lawrence and Carolyn must now be enjoying at the new Italian restaurant. After Adam had finished and cleared his plate away, he returned to his room and lay on the bed thinking. Would the contents of the faded envelope finally prove his father's innocence? A plan began to form in his mind.

When the grandfather clock in the hall chimed ten times, Adam lifted his long legs over the end of the bed and pulled the Bible back out of the bookshelf. With some apprehension Adam removed the envelope. Next, he switched on the reading light by the side of the small writing desk, unfolded the two pieces of paper and placed them in front of him.

One appeared to be a personal letter from Goering

to Adam's father, while the other had the look of an older, more official document. Adam placed this second document to one side and began to go over the letter line by line. It didn't help.

He tore a blank piece of paper from a notepad that he found on Lawrence's desk and started to copy down the text of Goering's letter. He left out only the greeting and what he assumed to be a valediction – *'hochachtungs-voll'* – followed by the Reichsmarshal's large, bold signature. He checked over the copy carefully before replacing the original in its faded envelope. He had just begun the same process with the official document, using a separate sheet of paper, when he heard a key turning, followed by voices at the front door. Both Lawrence and Carolyn sounded as if they had drunk more than the promised bottle of wine, and Carolyn's voice in particular had ascended into little more than a series of high-pitched giggles.

Adam sighed and switched off the light by the side of the desk so they wouldn't know he was still awake. In the darkness he became more sensitive to their every sound. One of them headed towards the kitchen, because he heard the fridge door squelch closed and, a few seconds later, the sound of a cork being extracted – he presumed from his last bottle of white wine, as they were unlikely to be so drunk that they had started on the vinegar.

Reluctantly he rose from his chair, and circling his arms in front of him, he made his way back to the bed. He touched the corner of the bedstead and quietly lowered himself on to the mattress, then waited impatiently for Lawrence's bedroom door to close.

He must have fallen asleep because the next thing he remembered was the tick of the hall clock. Adam licked his fingers and rubbed them over his eyes as he tried to get accustomed to the dark. He checked the little luminous dial on his alarm clock: ten past three. He eased himself off the bed gingerly, feeling more than a little crumpled and weary. Slowly he groped his way back towards the desk, banging his knee on the corner of a chest of drawers during his travels. He couldn't stop himself cursing. He fumbled for the light switch, and when the bulb first glowed it made him blink several times. The faded envelope looked so insignificant – and perhaps it was. The official document was still laid out on the centre of the table alongside the first few lines of his handwritten duplicate.

Adam yawned as he began to study the words once more. The document was not as simple to copy out as the letter had been, because this time the hand was spidery and cramped, as if the writer had considered paper an expensive commodity. Adam left out the address on the top right hand corner and reversed the eight digit number underlined at the head of the text, otherwise what he ended up with was a faithful transcript of the original.

The work was painstaking, and took a surprisingly long time. He wrote out each word in block capitals, and when he wasn't certain of the spelling he put down the possible alternative letters below; he wanted to be sure of any translation the first time.

"My, you do work late," whispered a voice from behind him.

Adam spun round, feeling like a burglar who had been caught with his hands on the family silver.

"You needn't look so nervous. It's only me," said Carolyn, standing by the bedroom door.

Adam stared up at the tall blonde who was even more attractive clad only in Lawrence's large unbuttoned pyjamas and floppy slippers than she had been when he had seen her fully dressed. Her long, fair hair now dropped untidily over her shoulders and he began to understand what Lawrence had meant when he had once described her as someone who could turn a matchstick into a Cuban cigar.

"The bathroom is at the end of the corridor," said Adam, a little feebly.

"It wasn't the bathroom I was looking for, silly," she giggled. "I don't seem able to wake Lawrence. After all that wine he's passed out like a defeated heavyweight boxer." She sighed. "And long before round fifteen. I don't think anything will rouse him again until morning." She took a step towards him.

Adam stammered something about feeling rather whacked himself. He made sure his back shielded her from any sight of the papers on the desk.

"Oh, God," said Carolyn, "you're not queer, are you?"

"Certainly not," said Adam, a little pompously.

"Just don't fancy me?" she asked.

"Not that exactly," said Adam.

"But Lawrence is your chum," she said. Adam didn't reply.

"My God this is the sixties, Adam. Share and share alike."

"It's just that . . ." began Adam.

"What a waste," said Carolyn, "perhaps another time." She tiptoed to the door, and slipped back out into the corridor, unaware of her German rival.

The first action Romanov took on leaving the Chairman's office that morning was to return to his *alma mater* and hand-pick a team of twelve researchers. From the moment they had been briefed they proceeded to study in pairs on four-hour shifts, so that the work could continue night and day.

The early information had come in almost by the hour and the researchers had quickly been able to establish that the Tsar's icon had remained in his private quarters at the Winter Palace at Petrograd until as late as December 1914. Romanov studied religiously a photo of the small delicate painting of St George and the Dragon. St George in tiny mosaic patterns of blue and gold while the dragon was in fiery red and yellow. Although he had never shown any interest in art, Romanov could well understand why people could be moved by the little masterpiece. He continued to read details of the icon's history, but still couldn't work out why it was so important to the State. He wondered if even Zaborski knew the reason.

A royal servant who had testified before the People's Court a year after the Revolution claimed that the Tsar's icon had disappeared for a few days in 1915 after the visit of Ernst Ludwig, Grand Duke of Hesse. At the time, the inquisitors had taken scant interest in the misplaced icon because it was still on the wall of the Tsar's study when they had stormed the Winter Palace. What concerned the court more was why, in the middle of a fierce war with the Kaiser's Germany, the Grand Duke of Hesse should want to visit the Tsar at all.

The Professor of History at the university had immediately been asked for his opinion. The great academic was puzzled by the request, as the KGB had never shown any interest in the nation's past history before. Nevertheless, he briefed Romanov on everything that was known of the incident. Romanov pored over his report once again. The Grand Duke, it was thought, had been on a secret visit to his sister Alexandra, the Tsarina. Historians now believed that it had been his intention to secure a cease-fire between Germany and Russia, in the hope that Germany could then concentrate her war efforts on the British and the French.

There was no proof that the Tsar made any promises on behalf of his people but the Grand Duke, it seemed, did not return to Germany empty-handed. As the reports of the proceedings of the People's Court showed, another palace servant had been instructed to wrap up the Tsar's icon and pack it with the Grand Duke's belongings. However, no one on the palace staff could properly explain to the court how a few days later the icon reappeared in its rightful place on the wall of the Tsar's private study.

Romanov's chief researcher, Professor Oleg Konstantinov, having studied the professor's notes and the other researchers' contributions, had underlined his own conclusion in red ink.

"The Tsar must have replaced the original painting with a brilliant copy, having handed over the real icon for safe-keeping to his brother-in-law, the Grand Duke."

"But why," asked Romanov, "when the Tsar had a palace full of Goyas, El Grecos, Titians and Rubens did he bother to smuggle out one icon and why does Brezhnev want it back so badly?"

Romanov instructed the professor and his twenty-four researchers to turn their talents to the Royal House of Hesse in the hope of tracing what had then happened to the Tsar's icon. Within ten days, they possessed between them more information about the Grand Duke and his family than any professor at any university had managed to gather in a lifetime. As each file appeared on his desk Romanov laboured through the night, checking every scrap of information that might give him a lead to the whereabouts of the original painting. He came to a dead end when, after the Grand Duke's death, the painting had been left to his son who was tragically killed in a plane crash. Nothing had been seen or heard of the icon after that day.

By the beginning of the third week, Romanov had reached the reluctant conclusion that there was nothing new on the whereabouts of the icon to be discovered. He was preparing his final report for the Chairman of the KGB when one researcher, Comrade Petrova, whose mind did not work in parallel lines, stumbled across an article in the London *Times* of Wednesday, November 17, 1937. Petrova bypassed the research leader and handed the relevant photocopy to Romanov personally, who, over the next few hours, read the news item so often that he came to know it off by heart.

In keeping with the Thunderer's tradition, the foreign correspondent remained anonymous. The article carried the dateline 'Ostend, November 16, 1937'.

It read:

Grand Duke George of Hesse and four members of his family were tragically killed this morning when a Sabena aircraft carrying them from Frankfurt to London crashed in thick fog over the Belgian countryside.

The Grand Duke had been on his way to England to attend the wedding of his younger brother, Prince Louis, to the Hon. Joanna Geddes. The young prince had been waiting at Croydon Airport to greet his family when the news was broken to him. He immediately cancelled his original wedding plans and announced they would be rescheduled with a small private service in the Chapel at Windsor.

The Times went on:

Prince Louis, who succeeds his brother as the Grand Duke of Hesse, will leave for Ostend with his bride later today in order that they can accompany the five coffins on their journey back to Germany. The funerals will all take place in Darmstadt on November 23.

It was the next paragraph that the researcher had circled boldly.

Some of the late Grand Duke's personal belongings, including several wedding presents for Prince Louis and his bride, were scattered for miles in the vicinity of the crashed aircraft. The German Government announced this morning that a senior German general has been appointed to lead a team of salvage experts to ensure the recovery of any family possessions that still belong to the Grand Duke's successor.

Romanov immediately called for the young researcher. When Anna Petrova arrived a few minutes later she gave no impression of being overawed by her head of department. She accepted that it would be hard to make any impression on him with the clothes she could afford. However, she had put on the prettiest outfit she possessed and cut her hair in the style of an American actress called Mia Farrow whom she had seen in one of the few films not banned by the authorities. She hoped Romanov would notice.

"I want you to scour *The Times* every day from November 17, 1937 for six months, and also check the German and Belgian press during the same period in case you come across anything that would show what the salvage experts had discovered." He dismissed her with a smile.

Within twenty-four hours Comrade Petrova barged back into Romanov's office without even bothering to knock. Romanov merely raised his eyebrows at the discourtesy before devouring an article she had discovered in the Berlin *die Zeit* of Saturday, January 19, 1938.

"The investigation into the crash last November of the Sabena aircraft that was carrying the Hesse royal family to London has now been concluded. All personal possessions belonging to the family that were discovered in the vicinity of the wreckage have been returned to the Grand Duke, Prince Louis, who, it is understood, was particularly saddened by the loss of a family heirloom that was to have been a wedding gift from his brother, the late Grand Duke. The gift, a painting known as the 'Tsar's Icon', had once belonged to his uncle, Tsar Nicholas II. The icon of St George and the Dragon, although only a copy of Rublev's masterpiece, was considered to be one of the finest examples of early twentieth-century craftsmanship to come out of Russia since the Revolution."

Romanov looked up at the researcher. "Twentieth-century copy be damned," he said. "It was the fifteenth-century original and none of them realised it at the time – perhaps not even the old Grand Duke himself. No doubt the Tsar had other plans for the icon had he managed to escape."

Romanov dreaded having to tell Zaborski that he could now prove conclusively that the original Tsar's icon had been destroyed in a plane crash some thirty years before. Such news would not ensure promotion for its messenger, as he remained convinced that there was something far more important than the icon at stake for Zaborski to be so involved.

He stared down at the photograph above the *Zeitung* report. The young Grand Duke was shaking hands with the general in charge of the salvage team which had been successful in returning so many of the Prince's family possessions. "But did he return them all?" Romanov said out loud.

"What do you mean?" asked the young researcher. Romanov waved his hand as he continued to stare at the pre-war, faded photograph of the two men. Although the general was unnamed, every schoolboy in Germany would have recognised the large, impassive, heavy-jowled face with the chilling eyes which had become infamous to the Allied powers.

Romanov looked up at the researcher. "You can forget the Grand Duke from now on, Comrade Petrova. Concentrate your efforts on Reichsmarshal Hermann Goering."

When Adam woke his first thoughts were of Carolyn. His yawn turned into a grin as he considered her invitation of the night before. Then he remembered. He jumped out of bed and walked over to his desk: everything was in place exactly as he had left it. He yawned for a second time.

It was ten to seven. Although he felt as fit as he had been the day he left the army some seven weeks before, he still completed a punishing routine of exercise every morning. He intended to be at his peak when the Foreign Office put him through a physical. In moments he was kitted out in a singlet and a pair of running shorts. He pulled on an old army tracksuit and finally tied up his gym shoes.

Adam tiptoed out of the flat, not wanting to wake Lawrence or Carolyn – although he suspected she was wide awake, waiting impatiently. For the next thirty-four minutes he pounded the pavement down to the Embankment, across Albert Bridge, through Battersea Park to return by way of Chelsea Bridge. Only one thought was going through his mind. After twenty years of gossip and innuendo was this going to be the one chance to clear his father's name? The moment he arrived back at the flat, Adam checked his pulse: 150 beats a minute. Sixty seconds later it was down to 100, another minute 70, and before the fourth minute was up it was back to a steady 58. It's the recovery that proves fitness, not your speed, his old Physical Training Instructor at Aldershot had drummed into him.

As Adam walked back through to his room there was still no sign of Carolyn. Lawrence, smart in a grey pinstripe suit, was preparing breakfast in the kitchen while glancing at the sports pages of the *Daily Telegraph*.

"The West Indies made 526," he informed Adam forlornly.

"Have we begun our innings?" shouted Adam from the bathroom.

"No, bad light stopped play."

Adam groaned as he stripped for the shower. He was ready for his morning game of finding out how long he could last under the freezing jets. The forty-eight needles of ice cold water beat down on his back and chest, which made him take several deep intakes of breath. Once you survive the first thirty seconds you could stay under for ever, the instructor had assured them. Adam emerged three minutes later, satisfied but still damning the PTI from whose influence he felt he would never escape.

Once he had towelled himself down Adam walked back to his bedroom. A moment later he had thrown on his dressing-gown and joined his friend in the kitchen for breakfast. Lawrence was now seated at the kitchen table concentrating hard on a bowl of cornflakes, while running a finger down the Foreign Exchange rates in the *Financial Times*.

Adam checked his watch: already ten past eight. "Won't you be late for the office?" he asked.

"Dear boy," said Lawrence, "I am not a lackey who works at the kind of bank where the customers keep shop hours."

Adam laughed. "But I will, however, have to be shackled to my desk in the City by nine thirty," Lawrence admitted. "They don't send a driver for me nowadays," he explained. "In this traffic, I told them, it's so much quicker by tube."

Adam started to make himself breakfast.

"I could give you a lift on my motorbike."

"Can you imagine a man in my position arriving at the headquarters of Barclays Bank on a motorbike? The Chairman would have a fit," he added, as he folded the *Financial Times*.

Adam cracked a second egg into the frying pan.

"See you tonight then, glorious, unwashed and un-employed," jeered Lawrence as he collected his rolled umbrella from the hat stand.

Adam cleared away and washed up, happy to act as housewife while he was still unemployed. Despite years of being taken care of by a batman he knew exactly what was expected of him. All he had planned before his interview with the Foreign Office that afternoon was a long bath and a slow shave. Then he remembered that Reichsmarshal Goering was still resting on the table in the bedroom.

"Have you come up with anything that would indicate Goering might have kept the icon for himself?" asked Romanov, turning hopefully to the researcher.

"Only the obvious," Anna Petrova replied in an offhand manner.

Romanov considered reprimanding the young girl for such insolence, but said nothing on this occasion. After all, Comrade Petrova had proved to be far the most innovative of his team of researchers.

"And what was so obvious?" enquired Romanov.

"It's common knowledge that Hitler put Goering in charge of all the art treasures captured on behalf of the Third Reich. But as the Führer had such fixed personal opinions as to what constituted quality, many of the world's masterpieces were judged as 'depraved' and therefore unworthy to be put on public view for the delectation of the master race."

"So what happened to them?"

"Hitler ordered them to be destroyed. Among those works condemned to death by burning were such masters as Van Gogh, Manet, Monet – and especially the young Picasso who was considered unworthy of the blue-blooded Aryan race Hitler was grooming to rule the world."

"You are not suggesting Goering could have stolen the Tsar's icon," asked Romanov, staring up at the ceiling, "only then to burn it?"

"No, no. Goering was not that stupid. As we now know, he didn't always obey the Führer's every word."

"Goering failed to carry out Hitler's orders?" said Romanov in disbelief.

"Depends from which standpoint you view it,"

Petrova replied. "Was he to behave as his lunatic master demanded or turn a blind eye and use his common sense?"

"Stick to the facts," said Romanov, his voice suddenly sharp.

"Yes, Comrade Major," said the young researcher in a tone that suggested she believed herself to be indispensable, at least for the time being.

"When it came to it," Petrova continued, "Goering did not destroy any of the denounced masterpieces. He held some public burnings in Berlin and Düsseldorf of lesser known German artists, who would never have fetched more than a few hundred marks on the open market in the first place. But the masterpieces, the real works of genius, were moved discreetly over the border and deposited in the vaults of Swiss banks."

"So there's still an outside chance that having found the icon . . ."

"He then had it placed in a Swiss bank," added Petrova. "I wish it were that simple, Comrade Major," said the researcher, "but unfortunately Goering wasn't quite as naïve as the newspaper cartoonists of the time made him out to be. I think he deposited the paintings and antiques in several Swiss banks and to date no one has ever been able to discover which banks or the aliases he used."

"Then *we* shall have to do so," said Romanov. "Where do you suggest we start?"

"Well, since the end of the war many of the paintings have been found and restored to their rightful owners, including the galleries of the German Democratic Republic. Others, however, have appeared on walls as far-flung as the Getty Museum in California and the Gotoh in Tokyo, sometimes without a fully satisfactory explanation. In fact, one of Renoir's major works can currently be seen hanging on the walls of the Metropolitan Museum in New York. It undoubtedly passed through Goering's hands although the curator of the museum has never been willing to explain how the gallery came into possession of it."

"Have all the missing pictures now been found?" asked Romanov anxiously.

"Over seventy per cent, but there are still many more to be accounted for. Some may even have been lost or destroyed, but my guess is that there are still a large number that remain lodged in Swiss banks."

"How can you be so certain?" demanded Romanov, fearful that his last avenue might be closing.

"Because the Swiss banks always return valuables when they can be certain of a nation's or individual's right of possession. In the case of the Grand Duke of Hesse and the Tsar's icon there was no proof of ownership, as the last official owner was Tsar Nicholas II and he, as every good Russian knows, Comrade, had no successors."

"Then I must do exactly what Goering did and retrace his steps by going direct to the banks. What has been their policy to date?" asked Romanov.

"That differs from establishment to establishment," said Petrova. "Some banks wait for twenty years or more and then try either by extensive research or advertising to contact the owner or their next of kin. In the case of the Jews who lost their lives under the Nazi regime, it has often proved impossible to trace a legitimate owner. Although I have been unable to prove it, I suspect they kept the rewards and split the proceeds among themselves," said Petrova. "Typical capitalists."

"That is neither fair nor accurate, Comrade," said Romanov, glad to show that he had also been doing some research. "Because that is another of the great myths perpetrated by the poor. In fact, when the banks have been unable to discover the rightful owner of any treasure left with them they have handed it over to the Swiss Red Cross to auction."

"But if the Tsar's icon had ever been auctioned we would have heard about it by now through one of our agents?"

"Precisely," said Romanov. "And I've already checked through the inventory of the Red Cross: four icons have been disposed of during the last twenty years and none of them was St George and the Dragon."

"Then that can only mean some unscrupulous bankers have disposed of the icon privately once they felt sure no one was going to make a claim."

"Another false premise, I suspect, Comrade Petrova."

"How can you be so certain?" the young researcher asked.

"For one simple reason, Comrade. The Swiss banking families all know each other intimately and have never in the past shown any propensity for breaking the law. Swiss justice, in our experience, is as tough on corrupt bankers as it is on murderers, which is precisely why the Mafia was never happy about laundering its money through the established banks. The truth is that Swiss bankers make so much money dealing with honest people that it has never been in their best interests to become involved with crooks. There are remarkably few exceptions to this rule, which is the reason so many people are willing to do business with the Swiss."

"So, if Goering stole the Tsar's icon and deposited it in a Swiss bank vault, it could be anywhere in the world by now?" said Petrova.

"I doubt it."

"Why?" sighed Petrova, a little peeved that her deductions were now proving wide of the mark.

"Because for the past three weeks I have had heaven knows how many operatives combing Europe for the Tsar's icon. They have spoken to nearly every major curator, keeper, dealer and crook in the art world and yet they still haven't come up with a single lead. And why not? Because the only people who have seen the icon since 1917 were the Hesses and Goering, which leaves me with only one hope if it was not destroyed when the Grand Duke's plane crashed," said Romanov.

"Namely?" asked Petrova.

"That while the rest of the world is under the illusion that the original still hangs in the Winter Palace, it has, for the past twenty years, been lodged in a Swiss bank waiting for someone to claim it."

"A long shot," said the researcher.

"I am quite aware of that," said Romanov sharply, "but don't forget that many Swiss banks have a twenty-five-year rule before disclosure, some even thirty. One or two even have no deadline at all as long as enough money has been deposited to cover the housing of the treasure."

"Heaven knows how many banks there might be who fall into that category," sighed Petrova.

"Heaven knows," agreed Romanov, "and so might you by nine o'clock tomorrow morning. And then it will be necessary for me to pay a visit to the one man in this country who knows everything about banking."

"Am I expected to start straight away, Comrade Major?" the researcher asked coyly.

Romanov smiled and looked down into the girl's green eyes. Dressed in the dull grey uniform of her trade, no one would have given her a second look. But in the nude she was quite magnificent. He leaned over until their lips nearly met.

"You'll have to rise very early, Anna, but for now just turn out the light."

CHAPTER FIVE

It took Adam only a few more minutes before he had checked over both documents again. He put the original back in the faded envelope and replaced it in the Bible on his bookshelf. Finally he folded his duplicated copy of Goering's letter into three horizontal pieces and cut it carefully along the folds into strips which he placed in a clean envelope and left on his bedside table. Adam's next problem was how to obtain a translation of the document and Goering's letter without arousing unnecessary curiosity. Years of army training had taught him to be cautious when faced with an unknown situation. He quickly dismissed the German Embassy, the German Tourist Board and the German Press Agency as all three were too official, and therefore likely to ask unwanted questions. Once he was dressed he went to the hall and began to flick through the pages in the London E—K Directory until his finger reached the column he had been searching for.

German Broadcasting
German Cultural Institute
German Federal Railway
German Hospital
German Old People's Home

His eye passed over 'German Technical Translations' and stopped at a more promising entry. The address was given as Bayswater House, 35 Craven Terrace, W2. He checked his watch.

Adam left the flat a few minutes before ten, the three pieces of the letter now safely lodged in the inside pocket of his blazer. He strolled down Edith Grove and into the King's Road, enjoying the morning sun. The street had been transformed from the one he had known as a young subaltern. Boutiques had taken the place of antiquarian bookshops. Record shops had replaced the local cobbler, and Dolcis had given way to Mary Quant. Take a fortnight's holiday, and you couldn't be sure anything would still be there when you returned, he reflected ruefully.

Crowds of people spilled out from the pavement on to the road, staring or hoping to be stared at, according to their age. As Adam passed the first of the record shops he had no choice but to listen to 'I Want to Hold Your Hand' as it blared into the ears of everyone within shouting distance.

By the time Adam reached Sloane Square the world had almost returned to normal – Peter Jones, W. H. Smith's and the London Underground. The words his mother sang so often over the kitchen sink came back to him every time he walked into the square.

> And you're giving a treat (penny ice and cold meat)
> To a party of friends and relations,
> They're a ravenous horde, and they all came aboard
> At Sloane Square and South Kensington stations.

He paid a shilling for a ticket to Paddington and, installed in a half-empty carriage, once again went over his plan. When he emerged into the open air at

Paddington he checked the street name and, once he was sure of his bearings, walked out on to Craven Road until he came to the first available newsagent and then asked the directions for Craven Terrace.

"Fourth road on the left, mate," said the shopkeeper, not bothering to look up from a pile of *Radio Times* on which he was pencilling names. Adam thanked him and a few minutes later found himself standing at the end of a short drive, looking up at the bold green and yellow sign: The German Young Men's Christian Association.

He opened the gate, walked up the drive and strode confidently through the front door. He was stopped by a porter standing in the hallway.

"Can I help you, guv'nor?"

Adam put on an exaggerated military accent and explained that he was looking for a young man called Hans Kramer.

"Never 'eard of 'im, sir," said the porter, almost standing to attention when he recognised the regimental tie. He turned to a book that lay open on the desk. "'E isn't registered," he added, a Woodbine-stained thumb running down the list of names in front of him. "Why don't you try the lounge or the games room?" he suggested, gesturing with the thumb to a door on the right.

"Thank you," said Adam, not dropping the plummy tones. He walked smartly across the hall and through the swing doors – which, judging from the lack of paint on the base, looked as if they had been kicked open more often than they had been pushed. He glanced around the room. Several students were lounging about reading German papers and magazines. He wasn't sure where to start, until he spotted a studious-looking girl on her own in a corner, poring over a copy of *Time* magazine. Brezhnev's face stared out from the cover. Adam strolled over and took the empty seat beside her. She glanced sideways at him and couldn't hide her surprise at his formal dress. He waited for her to put the paper down before asking, "I wonder if you could assist me?"

"How?" enquired the girl, sounding a little apprehensive.

"I just need something translated."

She looked relieved. "I will see if I can help. Have you brought something with you?"

"Yes I have, I hope it isn't too difficult," Adam said. He took the envelope from his inside pocket and extracted the first paragraph of Goering's letter.

Then he put the envelope back in his pocket, took out a little notebook and waited expectantly. He felt like a cub reporter.

She read the paragraph over two or three times, then seemed to hesitate.

"Is anything wrong?"

"Not exactly," she replied, still concentrating on the words in front of her. "It's just that it's a little bit old-fashioned so that I might not be able to give you the exact sense."

Adam breathed a sigh of relief.

She repeated each sentence slowly, first in German and then in English as if wanting to feel the meaning as well as just translating the words.

"Over the last . . . past year we have come to know . . . each other somewhat . . . no, no," she said, "quite well." Adam wrote each word down as the girl translated them.

"You have never disguised — perhaps a better meaning is 'hidden' —" she added, "your distaste for the National Socialist Party."

She raised her head and stared at Adam. "It's only out of a book," he assured her. She didn't look convinced but nevertheless continued. "But you have at every time ... no, at all times, behaved with the courtesy of an officer and a gentleman."

The girl looked up, even more puzzled, as she had now reached the last word.

"Is that all?" she asked. "It doesn't make sense. There has to be more."

"No, that's it," said Adam, quickly taking back the sheet of paper. "Thank you," he added. "It was most kind of you to help."

He left the girl and was relieved to see her shrug resignedly and return to her copy of *Time*. Adam went in search of the games room.

When he swung the door open he found a young man in a World Cup T-shirt and brown suede shorts. He was tapping a table tennis ball up and down listlessly.

"Care for a game?" said the boy, not looking at all hopeful.

"Sure," said Adam, removing his jacket and picking up the table tennis bat at his end of the table. For twenty minutes Adam had to play flat out to make sure he lost 18–21, 21–12, 17–21. As he replaced his jacket and congratulated his opponent he felt sure he had gained the young man's confidence.

"You put up good fight," said the German. "Give me good game."

Adam joined him at his end of the table. "I wonder if you could help me with something?" he said.

"Your backhand?" said the young man.

"No, thank you," said Adam, "I just need a paragraph of German translated." He handed over the middle paragraph of the letter. Once again, the would-be translator looked puzzled.

"It's from a book, so it may seem a little out of context," Adam said, unconvincingly.

"Okay, I try." As the boy began to study the paragraph, the girl who had already translated the first section came into the games room. She made her way towards them.

"This hard to make out, I am not good translation for," the young man said. "My girlfriend better, I think. I ask her. *Liebling, kannst Du dies für den Herrn ins Englische?*" Without looking at Adam he passed the second paragraph over to the girl who immediately said, "I knew there was more."

"No, no, don't bother," said Adam, and grabbed the piece of paper away from the girl. He turned back to the boy and said, "Thank you for the game. Sorry to have bothered you," and walked hurriedly out into the corridor, heading for the front door.

"Did you find 'im, sir?"

"Find him?" said Adam.

"Hans Kramer," said the porter.

"Oh, yes, thank you," said Adam. As he turned to leave he saw the young boy and his girlfriend were following close behind.

Adam ran down the drive and hailed a passing taxi.

"Where to?" said the cabbie.

"The Royal Cleveland Hotel."

"But that's only just round the corner."

"I know," said Adam, "but I'm already late."

"Suit yourself, guv," said the cabbie, "it's your money."

As the cab moved off Adam peered out of the back window to see his table-tennis opponent in conversation with the porter. The girl stood alongside them, pointing to the taxi.

Adam only relaxed when the cab turned the corner and they were out of sight.

In less than a minute the taxi had drawn up outside the Royal Cleveland. Adam handed the cabbie half a crown and waited for the change. Then he pushed through the revolving doors of the hotel and hung around in the foyer for a few moments before returning to the pavement again. He checked his watch: twelve thirty. Easily enough time for lunch, he thought, before going on to his interview with the Foreign Office. He headed across the Bayswater Road into the park at a brisk pace, knowing he couldn't hope to find a pub until he reached Knightsbridge.

Adam recalled the table tennis match. Damn, he thought. I should have thrashed him. At least that would have given him something else to think about.

Romanov's eye ran down the list of the fourteen banks. There was still an outside chance that one of them might be in possession of the Tsar's icon, but the names meant nothing to him. It was another world, and he knew he would now have to seek advice from an expert.

He unlocked the top drawer of his desk and flicked through the red book held only by the most senior ranking officers in the KGB. Many names had been scratched out or overwritten as regimes came and went but Aleksei Andreovich Poskonov had remained in his present position as Chairman of the National Bank for nearly a decade, and only Gromyko the Foreign Secretary had served in any office longer. Romanov dialled a number on his private line and asked to be put through to the Chairman of Gosbank. It was some considerable time before another voice came on the line.

"Comrade Romanov, what can I do for you?"

"I urgently need to see you," said Romanov.

"Really." The gravelly tones that came from the other end of the line sounded distinctly unimpressed. Romanov could hear pages being flicked over. "I could manage Tuesday, say eleven thirty?"

"I said it was urgent," repeated Romanov. "It concerns a State matter that can't wait."

"We are the nation's bankers and do have one or two problems of our own, you might be surprised to hear," came back the unrepentant voice. Romanov checked himself and waited. There was more flicking of pages. "Well, I suppose I could fit you in at three forty-five today, for fifteen minutes," said the banker. "But I must warn you that I have a long-standing engagement at four."

"Three forty-five it is then," said Romanov.

"In my office," said Poskonov. The phone went dead.

Romanov cursed out loud. Why did everyone feel obliged to prove their manhood with the KGB? He began to write down the questions he needed answered in order to put his plan into operation. He couldn't afford to waste even a minute of his allocated fifteen. An hour later he asked to see the Chairman of the KGB. This time he was not kept waiting.

"Trying to play the capitalists at their own game, are we?" said Zaborski, once Romanov had outlined his intentions. "Be careful. They've been at it a lot longer than we have."

"I realise that," said Romanov. "But if the icon is in the West I'm left with little choice but to use their methods to get my hands on it."

"Perhaps," said the Chairman. "But with your name such an approach could be misunderstood."

Romanov knew better than to interrupt the brief silence that ensued. "Don't worry, I'll give you all the backing you need – although I've never had a request quite like this one before."

"Am I allowed to know why the icon is so important?" Romanov enquired.

The Chairman of the KGB frowned. "I do not have the authority to answer that question, but as Comrade Brezhnev's enthusiasm for the arts is well known you must have been able to work out that it is not the painting itself that we are after."

What secret can the painting hold? thought Romanov, and decided to press on. "I wondered if . . ."

The Chairman of the KGB shook his head firmly.

Bugs don't have eyes, thought Romanov, but you know what that something is, don't you?

The Chairman rose from his desk and walked over to the wall and tore another page from the calendar. "Only ten days left to find the damn thing," he said. "The General Secretary has taken to phoning me at one o'clock every morning."

"One o'clock in the morning?" said Romanov joining in the game.

"Yes, the poor man can't sleep, they tell me," said the Chairman, returning to his desk. "It comes to all of us in time – perhaps even you, Romanov, and maybe earlier than you expect if you don't stop asking questions." He gave his young colleague a wry smile.

Romanov left the Chairman a few minutes later and returned to his office to go over the questions that did need to be answered by the Chairman of Gosbank. He couldn't help becoming distracted by thoughts of what could possibly be the significance of such a small painting, but accepted that he must concentrate his efforts on finding it and then perhaps the secret it contained would become obvious.

Romanov reached the steps of Neglinnaya 12 at three thirty because he knew he needed more than the fifteen minutes he had been allocated if he was to get all his questions answered. He only hoped Poskonov would agree to see him immediately.

After announcing himself at the reception desk he was accompanied by a uniformed guard up the wide marble staircase to the first floor, where Poskonov's secretary was waiting to greet him. Romanov was led to an anteroom. "I will inform the Chairman of the bank that you have arrived, Comrade Romanov," the secretary said, and then disappeared back into his own office. Romanov paced up and down the small anteroom impatiently, but the secretary did not return until the hands on the clock were in a straight line. At three fifty, Romanov was ushered into the Chairman's room.

The young major was momentarily taken aback by the sheer opulence of the room. The long red velvet curtains, the marble floor and the delicate French furniture wouldn't, he imagined, have been out of place in the Governor's rooms at the Bank of England. Romanov was reminded not for the first time that money still remained the most important commodity in the world – even in the Communist world. He stared at the old stooped man with the thinning grey hair and bushy walrus moustache who controlled the nation's money. The man of whom it was said that he knew of one skeleton in everyone's cupboard. Everyone's except mine, thought Romanov. His check suit might have been made before the Revolution and would once again be considered 'with it' in London's King's Road.

"What can I do for you, Comrade Romanov?" enquired the banker with a sigh, as if addressing a tiresome customer who was seeking a small loan.

"I require one hundred million American dollars' worth of gold bullion immediately," he announced evenly.

The chairman's bored expression suddenly changed. He went scarlet and fell back into his chair. He took several short, sharp breaths before pulling open a drawer, taking out a square box and extracting a large white pill from it. It took fully a minute before he seemed calm again.

"Have you gone out of your mind, Comrade?" the old man enquired. "You ask for an appointment without giving a reason, you then charge into my office and demand that I hand over one hundred million American dollars in gold without any explanation. For what reason do you make such a preposterous suggestion?"

"That is the business of the State," said Romanov. "But, since you have enquired, I intend to deposit equal amounts in a series of numbered accounts across Switzerland."

"And on whose authority do you make such a request?" the banker asked in a level tone.

"The General Secretary of the Party."

"Strange," said Poskonov. "I see Leonid Ilyich at least once a week and he has not mentioned this to me," the chairman looked down at the pad in the middle of his desk, "that a Major Romanov, a middle-ranking" – he stressed the words – "officer from the KGB would be making such an exorbitant demand."

Romanov stepped forward, picked up the phone by Poskonov's side and held it out to him. "Why don't you ask Leonid Ilyich yourself and save us all a lot of time?" He pushed the phone defiantly towards the banker. Poskonov stared back at him, took the phone and placed it to his ear. Romanov sensed the sort of tension he only felt in the field.

A voice came on the line. "You called, Comrade Chairman?"

"Yes," replied the old man. "Cancel my four o'clock appointment, and see that I am not disturbed until Major Romanov leaves."

"Yes, Comrade Chairman."

Poskonov replaced the phone and, without another word, rose from behind his desk and walked around to Romanov's side. He ushered the young man into a comfortable chair on the far side of the room below a bay window and took the seat opposite him.

"I knew your grandfather," he said in a calm, matter-of-fact tone. "I was a junior commodity clerk when I first met him. I had just left school and he was very kind to me but he was just as impatient as you are. Which was why he was the best fur trader in Russia and thought to be the worst poker player."

Romanov laughed. He had never known his grandfather and the few books that referred to him had long ago been destroyed. His father talked openly of his wealth and position which had only given the authorities ammunition finally to destroy him.

"You'll forgive my curiosity, Major, but if I am to hand over one hundred million dollars in gold I should like to know what it is to be spent on. I thought only the CIA put in chits for those sort of expenses without explanation."

Romanov laughed again and explained to the Chairman how they had discovered the Tsar's icon was a fake and he had been set the task of recovering the original. When he had completed his story he handed over the names of the fourteen banks. The banker studied the list closely while Romanov outlined the course of action he proposed to take, showing how the money would be returned intact as soon as he had located the missing icon.

"But how can one small icon possibly be that important to the State?" Poskonov asked out loud, almost as if Romanov were no longer in the room.

"I have no idea," replied Romanov truthfully and then briefed him on the results of his research.

There was an exasperated grunt from the other chair when Romanov had finished. "May I be permitted to suggest an alternative to your plan?"

"Please do," said Romanov, relieved to be gaining the older man's co-operation.

"Do you smoke?" asked the banker, taking a packet of Dunhill cigarettes from his coat pocket.

"No," said Romanov, his eyebrows lifting slightly at the sight of the red box.

The old man paused as he lit a cigarette. "That suit was not tailored in Moscow either, Major," the banker said, pointing at Romanov with his cigarette. "Now, to business – and do not hesitate to correct me if I have misunderstood any of your requirements. You suspect that lodged in one of these fourteen Swiss banks" – the Chairman tapped the list with his index finger – "is the original Tsar's icon. You therefore want me to deposit large amounts of gold with each bank in the hope that it will give you immediate access to the head of the family, or chairman. You will then offer the chairman the chance to control the entire hundred million if they promise to co-operate with you?"

"Yes," said Romanov. "Bribery is surely something the West has always understood."

"I would have said 'naïve' if I hadn't known your grandfather, though to be fair it was he who ended up making millions of roubles, not me. Nevertheless, how much do you imagine is a lot of money to a major Swiss bank?"

Romanov considered the question. "Ten million, twenty million?"

"To the Moscow Narodny Bank perhaps," said Poskonov. "But every one of the banks you hope to deal with will have several customers with deposits of over a hundred million each."

Romanov was unable to hide his disbelief.

"I confess," continued the chairman, "that our revered General Secretary showed no less incredulity when I informed him of these facts some years ago."

"Then I will need a thousand million?" asked Romanov.

"No, no, no. We must approach the problem from a different standpoint. You do not catch a poacher by offering him rabbit stew."

"But if the Swiss are not moved by the offer of vast amounts of money, what *will* move them?"

"The simple suggestion that their bank has been used for criminal activity," said the chairman.

"But how . . ." began Romanov.

"Let me explain. You say that the Tsar's icon hanging in the Winter Palace is not the original but a copy. A good copy, painted by a twentieth-century court painter, but nevertheless a copy. Therefore why not explain to each of the fourteen banks privately that, after extensive research, we have reason to believe that one of the nation's most valuable treasures has been substituted with a copy and the original is thought to have been deposited in their bank? And rather than cause a diplomatic incident – the one thing every Swiss banker wishes to avoid at any cost – perhaps they would, in the interests of good relationships, consider checking in their vaults items that have not been claimed for over twenty years."

Romanov looked straight at the old man, realising why he had survived several purges. "I owe you an apology, Comrade Poskonov."

"No, no, we each have our own little skills. I am sure I would be as lost in your world as you appear to be in mine. Now, if you will allow me to contact each of the chairmen on this list and tell them no more than the truth – a commodity I am always obliged to trade in although I imagine your counterparts are not so familiar with – namely that I suspect the Tsar's icon is in *their* bank, most of them will be disinclined to hold on to the masterpiece if they believe in so doing a crime has been perpetrated against a sovereign state."

"I cannot overstress the urgency," said Romanov.

"Just like your grandfather," Poskonov repeated. "So be it. If they can be tracked down, I shall speak to every one of them today. At least that's one of the advantages of the rest of the world waking up after us. Be assured I shall be in touch with you the moment I have any news."

"Thank you," said Romanov, rising to leave. "You have been most helpful." He was about to add, as he normally did in such circumstances, I shall so inform my Chairman, but he checked himself, realising the old man wouldn't have given a damn.

The chairman of Gosbank closed the door behind him and walked over to the bay window and watched Romanov run down the steps of the bank to a waiting car. I couldn't have supplied you with the one hundred million in gold bullion at this particular time, even if the General Secretary had ordered me to, he thought to himself. I doubt if I have ten million dollars' worth of gold left in the vaults at this moment. The General Secretary has already ordered me to fly every available ounce to the Bank of New York – so cleverly was his ploy disguised that the CIA had been informed about the deposit within an hour of its arrival. It's hard to hide over 700 million dollars in gold, even in America. I tried to tell him. The chairman watched Romanov's car drive away. Of course if, like your grandfather, you read the *Washington Post* as well as *Pravda*, you would already have known this. He returned to his desk and checked the names of the fourteen banks.

He knew instantly which of the fourteen had to be phoned.

Adam stepped out of Tattersalls Tavern on the corner of Knightsbridge Green and headed past the Hyde Park Hotel towards the Royal Thames Yacht Club. It seemed a strange place for the Foreign Office to hold an interview, but so far everything connected with the application had been somewhat mysterious.

He arrived a few minutes early and asked the ex-Royal Marines sergeant on the door where the interviews were taking place.

"Sixth floor, sir. Take the lift in the corner," he pointed ahead of him, "and announce yourself at reception."

Adam pressed a button and waited for the lift. The doors opened immediately and he stepped in. A rather overweight, bespectacled man of roughly his own age who looked as if he never turned down the third course of any meal followed him at a more leisurely pace. Adam touched the sixth button, but neither man spoke on their journey up to the sixth floor. The large man stepped out of the lift in front of Adam.

"Wainwright's the name," he informed the girl on the reception desk.

"Yes, sir," said the girl, "you're a little early, but do have a seat over there." She gestured towards a chair in the corner, then her eyes moved on to Adam and she smiled.

"Scott," he informed her.

"Yes, sir," she repeated. "Could you join the other gentleman? They will be seeing you next." Adam went over and picked up a copy of *Punch* before settling down next to Wainwright, who was already filling in the *Telegraph* crossword.

Adam soon became bored with flicking through endless issues of *Punch* and took a more careful look at Wainwright. "Do you by any chance speak German?" Adam asked suddenly, turning to face the other interviewee.

"German, French, Italian and Spanish," Wainwright replied, looking up. "I assumed that was how I managed to get this far," he added somewhat smugly.

"Then perhaps you could translate a paragraph from a German letter for me?"

"Delighted, old fellow," said Adam's companion, who proceeded to remove the pair of thick-lensed glasses from his nose, and waited for Adam to extract the middle paragraph of the letter from his envelope.

"Now, let me see," Wainwright said, taking the little slip of paper and replacing the glasses. "Quite a challenge. I say, old fellow, you're not part of the interviewing team by any chance?"

"No, no," said Adam, smiling. "I'm in exactly the same position as you – except I don't speak German, French, Italian or Spanish."

Wainwright seemed to relax. "Now let me see," he repeated, as Adam took out the small notebook from his inside pocket.

"'During the past year you cannot have failed to . . . notice that I have been receiving from one of the guards a regular, regular . . . regular supply'," he said suddenly, "yes, 'supply of Havana cigars. One of the few pleasures I have been allocated' – no, 'allowed', better still 'permitted' – 'despite my . . . incarceration'. That's the nearest I can get," Wainwright added. "'The cigars themselves have also served another purpose'," Wainwright continued, obviously enjoying himself, "'as they contained tiny capsules . . .'"

"Mr Scott."

"Yes," said Adam, jumping up obediently.

"The Board will see you now," said the receptionist.

"Do you want me to finish it off while they're finishing you off, old chap?" said Wainwright.

"Thank you," Adam replied, "if it's not too much trouble."

"Far easier than the crossword," Wainwright added, leaving on one side the little unfilled half-matrix of squares.

Alex Romanov was not a patient man at the best of times, and with the General Secretary now ringing up his chief twice a day, these were not the best of times.

While he waited for results of the chairman of Gosbank's enquiries he re-read the research papers that had been left on his desk, and checked any new intelligence that had been sent back by his agents in the field. Romanov resented the scraps of information the chairman of Gosbank must have been receiving by the hour, but he made no attempt to pester the old man despite his time problem.

Then the chairman of the bank called.

On this occasion Romanov was driven straight over to the State Bank at Neglinnaya 12 and ushered up to the finely furnished room without a moment's delay. Poskonov, dressed in another of those suits with an even larger check, was standing to greet him at the door.

"You must have wondered if I had forgotten you," were Poskonov's opening words as he ushered Romanov to the comfortable chair. "But I wanted to have some positive news to give you rather than waste your time. You don't smoke, if I remember correctly," he added, taking out his packet of Dunhill cigarettes.

"No, thank you," Romanov said, wondering if the chairman's doctor realised how much the old man smoked.

The chairman's secretary entered the room and placed two empty glasses, a frosted flask and a plate of caviar in front of them.

Romanov waited in silence.

"I have, over the past two days, managed to talk to the chairmen of twelve of the banks on your original list," Poskonov began, as he poured two vodkas, "but I have avoided making contact with the remaining two."

"Avoided?" repeated Romanov.

"Patience, Comrade," said Poskonov, sounding like a benevolent uncle. "You have longer to live than I so if there is any time to be wasted it must be yours."

Romanov lowered his eyes.

"I avoided one of the chairmen," Poskonov continued, "because he is in Mexico showing President Ordaz how not to repay their loan to Chase Manhattan while at the same time borrowing even more dollars from the Bank of America. If he pulls that off I shall have to recommend to the General Secretary of the Party that he is offered my job when I retire. The second gentleman I have avoided because he is officially in Chicago, closing a major Eurobond deal with Continental Illinois, while in fact he is booked in at the St Francis Hotel in San Francisco with his mistress. I feel certain you would agree, Comrade Major, that it would not advance our cause to disturb either of these gentlemen at this precise moment. The first has enough problems to be going on with for the rest of the week, while the second may well have his phone tapped – and we wouldn't want the Americans to discover what we are searching for, would we?"

"Agreed, Comrade," said Romanov.

"Good. Anyway as they both return to Switzerland early next week we have quite enough to be going on with for now."

"Yes, but what –" Romanov began.

"It will please you to know," continued Poskonov, "that of the twelve remaining chairmen all have agreed to co-operate with us and five have already phoned back. Four to say they have run a thorough check on the possessions of customers who have been out of contact with the bank for over twenty years, but have come up with nothing that remotely resembles an icon. In fact, one of them opened a deposit box in the presence of three other directors that had not been touched since 1931 only to discover it contained nothing but a cork from a 1929 bottle of Taylor's port."

"Only a cork?" said Romanov.

"Well, 1929 was a vintage year," admitted the chairman.

"And the fifth?" enquired Romanov.

"Now that, I suspect, may be our first breakthrough," continued Poskonov, referring to the file in front of him. He adjusted his spectacles with the forefinger of his right hand before continuing. "Herr Dieter Bischoff of Bischoff et Cie" – he looked up at his guest, as if Romanov might have recognised the name – "an honourable man with whom I have dealt many times in the past – honourable, that is, by Western standards of course, Comrade," added the chairman, obviously enjoying himself. "Bischoff has come up with something that was left with the bank in 1938. It is unquestionably an icon, but he has no way of knowing if it is the one we are looking for."

Romanov leapt up from his seat in excitement. "Then I had better go and see for myself," said Romanov. "I could fly out today," he added. The chairman waved him back into his chair.

"The plane you require does not leave Sheremtyevo airport until four thirty-five. In any case, I have already booked two seats on it for you."

"Two?" enquired Romanov.

"You will obviously need an expert to accompany you, unless you know considerably more about icons than you do about banking," Poskonov added. "I also took the liberty of booking you on the Swissair flight. One should never fly Aeroflot if it can be avoided. It has managed only one aviation record consistently every year since its inception, namely that of losing the most passengers per miles flown, and a banker never believes in going against known odds. I have fixed an appointment for you to see Herr Bischoff at ten o'clock tomorrow morning – unless, of course, you have something more pressing to keep you in Moscow, Comrade?"

Romanov smiled.

"I note from your file that you have never served in Switzerland," said the old man, showing off. "So may

I also recommend that you stay at the St Gothard while you are in Zurich. Jacques Pontin will take excellent care of you. Nationality has never been a problem for the Swiss, only currency. And so that brings my little investigation up to date, and I shall be in touch again as soon as the two itinerant chairmen return to Switzerland next Monday. All I can do for the moment however, is wish you luck in Zurich."

"Thank you," said Romanov. "May I be permitted to add how much I appreciate your thoroughness."

"My pleasure, Comrade, let's just say that I still owe your grandfather a favour, and perhaps one day you will find you owe me one, and leave it at that."

Romanov tried to fathom the meaning of the old man's words. There was no clue to be found in Poskonov's expression and so he left without another word. But as Romanov walked down the wide marble staircase, he considered the banker's sentiment again and again because throw-away lines were never delivered to an officer of the KGB.

By the time Romanov had returned to Dzerzhinsky Square, his secretary informed him that Herr Bischoff's assistant had telephoned from Zurich to confirm his appointment with the chairman at ten o'clock the following morning. Romanov asked him to call the manager at the St Gothard Hotel and book two rooms. "Oh, and confirm my flight with Swissair," he added before walking up two floors to see the Chairman and brief him on the meeting he had had with the head of the National Bank.

"Thank God for that," were Zaborski's first words. "With only nine days left at least you've given me something to discuss with the General Secretary when he calls at one tomorrow morning."

Romanov smiled.

"Good luck, Comrade. Our Embassy will be alerted to your every need. Let us fervently hope that you will be able to return the masterpiece to the walls of the Winter Palace."

"If it is in that bank, it will be in your hands by tomorrow night," said Romanov, and left the Chairman smiling.

When he walked into his own office he found Petrova waiting for him.

"You called for me, Comrade?"

"Yes, we're going to Zurich." Romanov looked at his watch. "In three hours' time. The flight and the rooms are already booked."

"In the names of Herr and Frau Schmidt, no doubt," said his lover.

CHAPTER SIX

When Adam emerged from the interview he felt quietly confident. The chairman's final words had been to ask him if he would be available for a thorough medical in a week's time. Adam had told them he could think of nothing that would stop him attending. He looked forward to the opportunity of serving in the British Foreign Service.

Back in the waiting room Wainwright looked up and handed him back his piece of paper.

"Thank you very much," said Adam, trying to look casual by slipping it into his inside pocket without looking at the results.

"What was it like, old chap?" his companion asked cautiously.

"No trouble for a man who has German, French, Spanish and Italian as part of his armoury," Adam assured him. "Best of luck, anyway."

"Mr Wainwright," said the secretary, "the Board will see you now."

Adam took the lift to the ground floor and decided to walk home, stopping on the corner of Wilton Place to buy a bag of apples from a barrow boy who seemed to spend most of his time on the lookout for the police. Adam moved on, going over in his mind the Board's questions and his answers – a pointless exercise he decided, although he still felt confident the interview had gone well. He came to such a sudden halt that the pedestrian behind only just stopped himself bumping into Adam. What had attracted his attention was a sign which read: 'The German Food Centre'. An attractive girl with a cheerful smile and laughing eyes was sitting at the cash register by the doorway. Adam strode into the shop and went straight over to her without attempting to purchase a single item.

"You have not bought anything?" she enquired with a slight accent.

"No, I'm just about to," Adam assured her, "but I wondered, do you speak German?"

"Most girls from Mainz do," she replied, grinning.

"Yes, I suppose they would," said Adam, looking at the girl more carefully. She must have been in her early twenties, Adam decided, and he was immediately attracted by her friendly smile and manner. Her shiny, dark hair was done up in a pony tail with a big red bow. Her white sweater and neat pleated skirt would have made any man take a second look. Her slim legs were tucked under the chair. "I wonder if you would be kind enough to translate a short paragraph for me?"

"I try," she said, still smiling.

Adam took the envelope containing the final section of the letter out of his pocket and handed it over to her.

"The style is a bit old-fashioned," she said, looking serious. "It may take a little time."

"I'll go and do some shopping," he told her, and started walking slowly round the long stacked shelves. He selected a little salami, frankfurters, bacon, and some German mustard, looking up now and then to see how the girl was progressing. From what he could make out, she was only able to translate a few words at a time, as she was continually interrupted by customers. Nearly twenty minutes passed before he saw her put the piece of paper on one side. Adam immediately went over to the cash register and placed his purchases on the counter.

"One pound two shillings and sixpence," she said. Adam handed over two pounds and she returned his change and the little piece of paper.

"This I consider a rough translation, but I think the meaning is clear."

"I don't know how to thank you," said Adam, as an elderly woman joined him in the queue.

"You could invite me to share with you your frankfurters," she laughed.

"What a nice idea," said Adam. "Why don't you join me for dinner tonight?"

"I was not serious," she said.

"I was," smiled Adam. Another person joined the queue and the old lady immediately behind him began to look restive.

Adam grabbed a leaflet from the counter, retreated towards the back of the store, and began to scribble down his name, address and phone number. He waited for the two customers in front of him to pay, then handed over to her a 'once in a lifetime' Persil offer.

"What's this?" the girl asked innocently.

"I've put my name and address on the centre page," Adam said. "I will expect you for dinner at about eight this evening. At least you know what's on the menu."

She looked uncertain. "I really was only joking."

"I won't eat you," said Adam. "Only the sausages."

She looked at the leaflet in her hand and laughed. "I'll think about it."

Adam strolled out on to the road whistling. A bad

morning, a good afternoon and – perhaps – an even better evening.

He was back at the flat in time to watch the five forty-five news. Mrs Gandhi, the new Prime Minister of India, was facing open revolt in her cabinet and Adam wondered if Britain could ever have a woman Prime Minister. England were 117 for seven in their first innings, with the West Indies still well on top. He groaned and turned off the television. Once he had put the food in the fridge he went into his bedroom to assemble the full text of the Goering letter. After he had read through all the little slips of paper he took out his notepad and began to copy out the translations in order: first, the paragraph supplied by the girl from the YMCA, then Wainwright's handwritten words from the notepad, and finally the section of the letter translated by the lovely girl from Mainz. He read the completed draft through slowly a second time.

Nuremberg
October 15, 1946

Dear Colonel,

Over the past year, we have come to know each other quite well. You have never disguised your distaste for the National Socialist party, but you have at all times behaved with the courtesy of an officer and a gentleman.

During the year you cannot have failed to notice that I have been receiving from one of the guards a regular supply of Havana cigars – one of the few pleasures I have been permitted, despite my incarceration. The cigars themselves have also served another purpose, as each one contained a capsule with a small amount of poison. Enough to allow me to survive my trial, while ensuring that I shall cheat the executioner.

My only regret is that you, as the officer in charge of the watch during the period when I am most likely to die, may be held responsible for something to which you were never a party. To make amends for this I enclose a document in the name of one Emmanuel Rosenbaum which should help with any financial difficulties you face in the near future.

All that will be required of you –

"Anyone at home?" shouted Lawrence. Adam folded up the pieces of paper, walked quickly over to the bookcase and inserted them alongside the original letter in the Bible seconds before Lawrence put his head round the door.

"Bloody traffic," said Lawrence cheerfully. "I can't wait to be appointed chairman of the bank and be given that luxury flat on the top floor, not to mention the chauffeur and the company car."

Adam laughed. "Had another hard day at the office, darling?" he mimicked, before joining him in the kitchen. Adam started removing food from the fridge.

"Guess who's coming to dinner," said Lawrence as each new delicacy appeared.

"A rather attractive German girl, I hope," said Adam.

"What do you mean, 'hope'?"

"Well, it could hardly have been described as a formal invitation so I'm not even certain she'll turn up."

"If that's the situation I may as well hang around in case she gives you the elbow and you need someone to help you eat that lot."

"Thanks for the vote of confidence, but I think you'll

find it's your turn to be missing, presumed dead. Anyway, what about Carolyn?" said Adam.

"Carolyn was yesterday's girl, to quote the esteemed Harold Wilson. How did you come across your *gnädiges Fräulein*?"

"She was serving at a food store in Knightsbridge."

"I see. We're down to shop assistants now."

"I have no idea what she is or even what her name is, come to that," said Adam. "But I am hoping to find out tonight. As I said, your turn to disappear."

"*Natürlich*. As you see, you can rely on me to provide a helping hand if you need anything translated."

"Just put the wine in the fridge and lay the table."

"Are there no serious jobs for a man of my accomplishments to be entrusted with?" chuckled Lawrence.

When eight o'clock chimed, the table was set and Adam had everything ready on the boil. By eight thirty both of them stopped pretending and Adam served up two plates of frankfurters, salami and lettuce with a baked potato and sauerkraut sauce. He then hung up his Goons apron behind the kitchen door and took the chair opposite Lawrence, who had begun pouring the wine.

"Oh, *mein liebes Mädchen*, you look ravishing in that Harris tweed jacket," said Lawrence, raising his glass.

Adam was just about to retaliate with the vegetable spoon when there was a loud knock on the front door. The two men stared at each other before Adam leaped to open it. Standing in the doorway was a man well over six foot with shoulders like a professional bouncer. By his side, dwarfed by him, was the girl that Adam had invited to dinner.

"This is my brother, Jochen," she explained. Adam was immediately struck by how beautiful she looked in a dark blue patterned blouse and pleated blue skirt that fell just below the knee. Her long dark hair, now hanging loose, looked as if it had just been washed and shone even under the forty watt light bulb that hung in the hall.

"Welcome," said Adam, more than a little taken aback.

"Jochen is just dropping me off."

"Yes, of course," said Adam. "Do come in and have a drink, Jochen."

"No, I thank you. I have a date as well, but I will pick up Heidi at eleven o'clock, if all right by you?"

"Fine by me," said Adam, at last learning her name.

The giant bent down and kissed his sister on both cheeks. He then shook hands with Adam before leaving them both on the doorstep.

"I am sorry to be late," said Heidi. "My brother did not get back from work until after seven."

"It was no problem," said Adam, leading her into the flat. "If you had come any earlier I wouldn't have been ready for you. By the way, this is my flatmate, Lawrence Pemberton."

"In England the men also need a chaperone?" said Heidi.

Both men laughed. "No, no," said Lawrence. "I was just on my way out. Like your brother, I already have a date. As you can see the table is only laid for two. I'll be back around eleven, Adam, just to make sure you're safe." He smiled at Heidi, put on his coat and closed the door behind him before either could object.

"I hope I don't drive him away," said Heidi.

"No, no," said Adam, as she took Lawrence's place at the table. "He's already late for his girlfriend. Charming girl called Carolyn, a social worker." He quickly topped up her wine, pretending it hadn't already been poured.

"So I am going to eat my own sausages, after all," she said, laughing. And the laughter didn't stop for the rest of the evening, as Adam learned about Heidi's life in Germany, her family and the holiday job she had taken while on vacation from Mainz University.

"My parents only allow me to come to England because my brother is already in London; it is to help my languages course. But now, Adam, I would like to know what you are doing when you are not picking up girls in food stores."

"I was in the army for nine years and I'm now hoping to join the Foreign Office."

"In what capacity, if that is the right expression?" Heidi asked.

"It's the right expression, but I'm not sure I know the right answer," said Adam.

"When someone says that about the Foreign Service it usually means they are a spy."

"I don't know what it means, to be honest, but they're going to tell me next week. In any case, I don't think I'd make a very good spy. But what are you going to do when you return to Germany?"

"Complete my final year at Mainz and then I hope to find a job as a television researcher."

"What about Jochen?" asked Adam.

"He will join my father's law practice as soon as he is arriving home."

"So how long will you be in London?" he found himself asking.

"Another two months," she said. "If I can stand the job."

"Why do you carry on with it if it's that bad?"

"There is no better way to test your English than

impatient shoppers who speak all different accents."

"I hope you stay the full two months," said Adam.

"So do I," she replied, smiling.

When Jochen arrived back punctually at eleven o'clock, he found Adam and Heidi washing the dishes.

"Thank you for a most interesting evening," she said, wiping her hands.

"Not a good word," reprimanded Jochen. "Not interesting, I think. Lovely, happy, delightful, enjoyable perhaps, but not interesting."

"It was all those things," said Adam, "but it was also interesting."

She smiled.

"May I come and buy some more sausages tomorrow?"

"I would like that," said Heidi, "but don't hold up any sour old women this time with translation demands. By the way, you never tell me why you needed the strange paragraph translated. I have been wondering who is this Rosenbaum and what it is he left to someone."

"Next time perhaps," said Adam, looking a little embarrassed.

"And next time you can bring my sister home yourself," said Jochen, as he shook Adam's hand firmly.

After Heidi had left, Adam sat down and finished off the last glass of wine, aware that he hadn't spent such a lovely, happy, delightful, enjoyable and interesting evening for a long time.

A black limousine with dark windows and unlit number plates remained parked in the VIP area of Zurich Kloten. Fastidious Swiss policemen had twice gone up to the car and checked the driver's credentials before Major Romanov and Anna Petrova emerged from the customs hall and took their places in the back of the car.

It was already dark as the driver moved off towards the neon glow of the city. When the car drew up outside the St Gothard Hotel the only words that passed between Romanov and the driver were, "I shall return to Moscow on the Tuesday morning flight."

Jacques Pontin, the manager of the hotel, was stationed at the door waiting to greet the new arrivals; he introduced himself immediately, and as soon as he had checked them both in he banged a little bell with the palm of his hand to summon a porter to assist the guests with their bags. A moment later a young man in his early twenties, dressed in green livery, appeared.

"Suite seventy-three and room seventy-four," Jacques instructed before turning back to Romanov. "I do hope your stay will prove to be worthwhile, Herr Romanov," he said. "Please do not hesitate to call upon me if there is anything you need."

"Thank you," said Romanov as he turned to join the porter who stood sentinel-like by the door of an open lift. Romanov stood to one side to allow Anna to go in first. The lift stopped at the seventh floor and the porter led the way down a long corridor to a corner suite. He turned the key in the lock and invited the two guests to go in ahead of him. The suite was as Romanov had expected, in a different league from the finest hotels he ever experienced in either Moscow or Leningrad. When he saw the array of gadgets in the marble bathroom he reflected that even prosperous travellers to Russia, if seasoned visitors, brought their own bath plugs with them.

"Your room is through there, madam," the porter informed the researcher, and unlocked an adjoining door. Although smaller in size, the room maintained the same unassuming elegance. The porter returned to Romanov, handed him his key and asked if there would be anything else he would require. Romanov assured him there was nothing and passed over a five-franc note.

Once again the porter gave a slight bow, and closing the door behind him, left Romanov to unpack while Anna Petrova went to her own room.

Romanov started to undress and then disappeared into the bathroom. He studied himself in the mirror. Although he was vain about his looks, he was even more vain about the state of his physique. At twenty-nine, despite being six feet, he still only weighed 165 pounds on Western scales, and his muscles remained hard and taut.

By the time Romanov had returned to the bedroom, he could hear the shower beating down in the adjoining bathroom. He crept over to the door and edged it open. He could see quite clearly the outline of Anna standing in the steaming shower. He smiled and noiselessly moved back across the thick carpet, slipped under the sheets and into the researcher's bed. He waited for her to turn off the steaming shower.

Adam stepped out of the freezing shower. Within minutes he was dressed and joined Lawrence in the kitchen for breakfast.

"Still unable to charge you for hot water, am I?" Lawrence said as Adam peered over his flatmate's shoulder, trying to take in the latest Test score.

"Why can't we produce any really fast fast bowlers?" he asked rhetorically.

"Can't stay and chatter to the unemployed," said Lawrence, picking up his briefcase. "Shah of Iran wants to discuss his financial problems with me. Sorry to rush off before you've had your cornflakes but I can't afford to keep His Imperial Majesty waiting."

Left on his own, Adam boiled himself an egg and burned some toast before he turned to the newspaper to learn of the latest casualties in Vietnam and President Johnson's proposed tour of the Far East. At this rate he decided he wasn't going to win the *Daily Mail*'s 'Housewife of the Year' competition. He eventually cleared away in the kitchen, made his bed and tidied up behind Lawrence – nine years of self-discipline wasn't going to change old habits that quickly – then he settled down to plan another day.

He realised he could no longer avoid making a decision. He sat once again at his desk and began to consider how to get the official document translated without arousing further suspicion.

Almost absent-mindedly he removed the Bible from the bookshelf and extracted the letter he had read the night before. The final paragraph still puzzled him. He considered Heidi's translation once again:

All that will be required of you is to present yourself at the address printed on the top right-hand corner of the enclosed document, with some proof that you are Colonel Gerald Scott. A passport should prove sufficient. You will then be given a bequest that I have left to you in the name of Emmanuel Rosenbaum.

I hope it will bring you good fortune.

Adam turned his attention to the document. He was still quite unable to discern what the bequest could possibly be, let alone whether it was of any value. Adam mused over the fact that such an evil man could involve himself in an act of kindness hours before he knew he was going to die – an act that now left him with no choice about his own involvement.

Romanov gathered the blankets together and in one movement hurled them on to the floor to expose Anna curled up like a child, knees almost touching her exposed breasts. Anna's hand groped for a corner of the sheet to cover her naked body.

"Breakfast in bed?" she murmured hopefully.

"Dressed in ten minutes, or no breakfast at all," came back the reply. Anna lowered her feet gingerly on to the thick carpet and waited for the room to stop going round in circles before heading off towards the bathroom. Romanov heard the shower burst forth its jets. "Ahhh," came the pitiful cry. Romanov smiled when he remembered that he had left the indicator locked on dark blue.

During breakfast in the dining room they mulled over the approach he intended to take with the bank if Petrova were able to confirm that the icon was in fact Rublev's original masterpiece. He kept looking up from the table and then suddenly, without warning, said, "Let's go."

"Why?" Anna asked, as she bit into another slice of toast. Romanov rose from the table and without bothering to offer an explanation strode out of the room and headed straight for the lift. Petrova caught up with her master only moments before the lift gate closed. "Why?" she asked again, but Romanov did not speak until they were both back in his suite. He then threw open the large window that overlooked the railway station.

"Ah, it's outside your room," he said, looking to his right, and quickly walked through to the adjoining bedroom. He marched past the dishevelled double bed, jerked open the nearest window, and climbed outside. Petrova stared down from the seventh floor and felt giddy. Once Romanov had reached the bottom rung of the fire escape, he ran to a passing tram. Petrova would never have made it if she hadn't been lifted bodily on to the tram by Romanov's sheer strength.

"What's going on?" she asked, still puzzled.

"I can't be sure," said Romanov, looking out of the back of the tram. "All I do know for certain is what the local CIA agent looks like."

The researcher looked back in the direction of the hotel, but all she could see was a mass of anonymous people walking up and down the pavement.

Romanov remained on the tram for about a mile before he jumped off and hailed a passing taxi going in the opposite direction.

"Bischoff et Cie," he said as he waited for his puffing assistant to join him.

The cab headed back in the direction of the hotel, winding in and out of the morning traffic, until it came to a halt in front of a large brown granite building that filled the entire block. Romanov paid off the driver and stood in front of imposing doors made of thick glass and covered in wrought iron welded to look like the branches of a tree. By the side of the doors, carved inconspicuously into the stone and inlaid with gilt, were the words 'Bischoff et Cie'. There was no other clue as to what kind of establishment lay within.

Romanov turned the heavy wrought-iron knob and the two Russians stepped into a spacious hall. On the left-hand side of the hall stood a solitary desk behind which a smartly dressed young man was seated.

"*Guten Morgen, mein Herr*", he said.

"Good morning," said Romanov. "We have an appointment with Herr Dieter Bischoff."

"Yes, Herr Romanov," said the receptionist, checking the list of names in front of him. "Will you please take the lift to the fifth floor where you will be met by Herr Bischoff's secretary." When the two of them stepped out of the lift they were greeted by a lady in a neat plain suit. "Will you please follow me," she said, without any trace of accent. The two Russians were escorted along a picture-lined corridor to a comfortable room which more resembled the reception room of a country house than a bank.

"Herr Bischoff will be with you in a moment," the lady said, withdrawing. Romanov remained standing while he took in the room. Three black-and-white framed photographs of sombre old men in grey suits, trying to look like sombre old men in grey suits, took up most of the far wall, while on the other walls were discreet but pleasant oils of town and country scenes of nineteenth-century Switzerland. A magnificent oval Louis XIV table with eight carved mahogany chairs surrounding it dominated the centre of the room. Romanov felt a twinge of envy at the thought that he could never hope to live in such style.

The door opened and a man in his mid-sixties, followed by three other men in dark grey suits, entered the room. One look at Herr Bischoff and Romanov knew whose photograph would eventually join that of the other three grey, sombre men.

"What an honour for our little bank, Mr Romanov," were Bischoff's first words as he bowed and shook the Russian by the hand. Romanov nodded and introduced his assistant, who received the same courteous bow and handshake. "May I in turn present my son and two of my partners, Herr Muller and Herr Weizkopf." The three men bowed in unison, but remained standing while Bischoff took his seat at the head of the table.

At his gesture both Romanov and Anna sat down beside him.

"I wonder if I might be permitted to check your passport?" asked Bischoff, as if to show that the formal business had begun. Romanov took out the little blue passport with a soft cover from his inside pocket and handed it over. Bischoff studied it closely, as a philatelist might check an old stamp, and decided it was mint. "Thank you," he said, as he returned it to its owner

Bischoff then raised his hand and one of the partners immediately left them. "It will only take a moment for my son to fetch the icon we have in safe-keeping," he confided. "Meanwhile perhaps a little coffee – Russian," he added.

Coffee appeared within moments borne by yet another smartly dressed lady.

"Thank you," said Petrova, clearly a little overawed, but Romanov didn't speak again until Herr Bischoff's son reappeared with a small box and handed it over to his father.

"You will understand that I have to treat this matter with the utmost delicacy," the old man confided. "The icon may not turn out to be the one your Government is searching for."

"I understand," said Romanov.

"This magnificent example of Russian art has been in our possession since 1938, and was deposited with the bank on behalf of a Mr Emmanuel Rosenbaum."

Both visitors looked shocked.

"Nevozmozhno," said Anna, turning to her master. "He would never . . ."

"I suspect that's exactly why the name was chosen in the first place," Romanov said curtly to Anna, annoyed at her indiscretion. "Can't you see? It makes perfect sense. May I see the icon now?" said Romanov, turning back to the bank's Chairman.

Herr Bischoff placed the box in the centre of the table. The three men in grey suits each took a pace forward. Romanov looked up. "Under Swiss law we must have three witnesses when opening a box in someone else's name," explained the old man.

Romanov nodded curtly.

Herr Bischoff proceeded to unlock the metal box with a key he produced from his pocket, while his son leaned over and undid a second lock with a different key. The little ceremony completed, Herr Bischoff pushed up the lid of the box and turned it round to face his guests. Romanov placed his hands into the box like an expectant child does with a Christmas stocking, and drew out the icon. He stared at the beautiful painting. A small wooden rectangle that was covered in tiny pieces of red, gold and blue making up the mosaic of a man who looked as if he had all the worries of the world on his shoulders. The face, although sad, still evoked a feeling of serenity. The painting Romanov held in his hand was quite magnificent, as fine as any he had seen at the Winter Palace. No one in the room was quite sure what would happen next as Romanov offered no opinion.

It was Anna who finally spoke.

"A masterpiece it is," she said, "and undoubtedly fifteenth century but as you can see it's not St George and the Dragon."

Romanov nodded his agreement, still unable to let go of the little painting. "But do you know the origin of this particular icon?" Romanov asked.

"Yes," Anna replied, glad to be appreciated for the first time. "It is the Icon of St Peter, you see he holds the keys . . . painted by Dionisiy in 1471, and although it is undoubtedly one of the finest examples of his work, it is not the Tsar's icon."

"But does it belong to the Russian people?" asked Romanov, still hopeful of some reward for all his trouble.

"No, Comrade Major," said the researcher emphatically. "It belongs to the Munich Gallery, from where it has been missing since the day Hitler was appointed Reichs Chancellor."

Herr Bischoff scribbled a note on a piece of paper in front of him. At least one bank in Munich was going to be happy to do business with him in the future.

Romanov reluctantly handed back the icon to Herr Bischoff, only just managing to say, "Thank you."

"Not at all," said Herr Bischoff imperturbably, replacing the icon in the box and turning his key in his lock. His son completed the same routine with his own key and then departed with the unclaimed treasure. Romanov rose, as he considered nothing more could be gained from the meeting – although he believed he had discovered Goering's alias, or one of them.

"I wonder if I might be permitted to have a word with you in private, Herr Romanov," asked the elderly banker.

"Of course."

"It is rather a delicate matter I wish to put to you," said Herr Bischoff, "so I thought you might prefer your associate to leave us."

"That won't be necessary," said Romanov, unable to think of anything Bischoff might have to say that he wouldn't later need to discuss with Petrova.

"As you wish," said Bischoff. "I am curious to discover if there was any other reason behind your request to see me."

"I don't understand what you mean," said Romanov.

"I felt perhaps I knew the real reason you had selected this bank in particular to start your enquiry."

"I didn't select you," said Romanov. "You were only one of –" he stopped himself.

"I see," said Bischoff, himself now looking somewhat bemused. "Then may I be permitted to ask you a few questions?"

"Yes, if you must," said Romanov, now impatient to get away.

"You are Alexander Petrovich Romanov?"

"You must already believe that or we would not have proceeded this far."

"The only son of Peter Nicholevich Romanov?"

"Yes."

"And grandson of Count Nicholai Alexandrovich Romanov?"

"Is this to be a history lesson on my family tree?" asked Romanov, visibly irritated.

"No, I just wanted to be sure of my facts as I am even more convinced it would be wise for your associate to leave us for a moment," the old man suggested diffidently.

"Certainly not," said Romanov. "In the Soviet Union we are all equal," he added pompously.

"Yes, of course," said Bischoff, glancing quickly at Anna before continuing. "Did your father die in 1946?"

"Yes. He did," said Romanov, beginning to feel distinctly uncomfortable.

"And you are the only surviving child?"

"I am," confirmed Romanov proudly.

"In which case this bank is in possession . . ." Bischoff hesitated as a file was put in front of him by one of the men in grey. He placed a pair of gold, half-moon spectacles on his nose, taking as long as he could over the little exercise.

"Don't say anything more," said Romanov quietly.

Bischoff looked up. "I'm sorry, but I was given every reason to believe your visit had been planned."

Petrova was now sitting on the edge of her seat, enjoying every moment of the unfolding drama. She had already anticipated exactly what was going to happen and was disappointed when Romanov turned to speak to her.

"You will wait outside," was all he said. Petrova pouted and rose reluctantly to leave them, closing the door behind her.

Bischoff waited until he was certain the door was closed, then slid the file across the table. Romanov opened it gingerly. On the top of the first page was his grandfather's name underlined three times. Below the name were printed row upon row of incomprehensible figures.

"I think you will find that we have carried out your grandfather's instructions in maintaining a conservative portfolio of investments with his funds." Bischoff leaned across and pointed to a figure showing that the bank had achieved an average increase of 6·7 per cent per annum over the previous forty-nine years.

"What does this figure at the foot of the page represent?" asked Romanov.

"The total value of your stocks, bonds and cash at nine o'clock this morning. It has been updated every Monday since your grandfather opened an account with this bank in 1916." The old man looked up proudly at the three pictures on the wall.

"Bozhe Moi," said Romanov, as he took in the final figure. "But what currency is it in?"

"Your grandfather only showed faith in the English pound," said Herr Bischoff.

"Bozhe Moi," Romanov repeated.

"May I presume from your comment that you are not displeased with our stewardship?"

Romanov was speechless.

"It may also interest you to know that we are in possession of several boxes, the contents of which we have no knowledge. Your father also visited us on one occasion soon after the war. He appeared satisfied and assured me that he would return, but we never heard from him again. We were saddened to learn of his death. You might also prefer in the circumstances to return and investigate the boxes at another time," the banker continued.

"Yes," said Romanov quietly. "Perhaps I could come back this afternoon?"

"The bank will always be at your service, Your Excellency," replied Herr Bischoff.

No one had addressed a Romanov by his title since the Revolution. He sat in silence for some time.

Eventually he rose and shook hands with Herr Bischoff. "I will return this afternoon," he repeated before joining his companion in the corridor.

Neither uttered a word until they were back on the street outside the bank. Romanov was still so overcome by what he had learned that he failed to notice that the man he had so deftly avoided at the hotel was now standing in a tram queue on the far side of the road.

CHAPTER SEVEN

The pastor sat at the table studying the document but didn't offer an opinion for some considerable time. When he had heard Adam's request he had invited the young man into the privacy of his little office at the back of the German Lutheran Church.

It turned out to be a stark room dominated by a wooden table and several wooden chairs that didn't match. A small black crucifix was the only ornament on the blank whitewashed walls. Two of the unmatching chairs were now occupied by Adam and the pastor. Adam sat bolt upright while the man of God, clad from head to toe in a black cassock, elbows on the table and head in hands, stared down at the copy of the document.

After some considerable time, without raising his eyes, he offered, "This is a receipt, if I am not mistaken. Although I have little knowledge of such things, I am fairly confident that Roget et Cie, who must be Swiss bankers based in Geneva, have in their possession an object described herein as 'The Tsar's Icon'. If I remember my history correctly, the original can be viewed somewhere in Moscow. It appears," he continued, his eyes still fixed on the document, "that if the holder of this receipt presents himself in Geneva he will be able to claim the aforementioned icon of St George and the Dragon, deposited there by a Mr Emmanuel Rosenbaum. I confess," said the pastor, looking up for the first time, "that I've never seen anything like it before." He folded up the copy of the document and handed it back to Adam.

"Thank you," said Adam. "That has been most helpful."

"I am only sorry that my superior the Bishop is away on his annual retreat because I feel sure he would have been able to throw more light on the matter than I have."

"You have told me everything I need to know," said Adam, but couldn't resist asking, "Are icons at all valuable?"

"Once again, I must confess that I am not the best man from whom to seek such an opinion. All I can tell you is that, as with all art, the value of any object can vary from one extreme to the other without any satisfactory explanation to us normal mortals."

"Then there is no way of knowing the value of this particular icon?" asked Adam.

"I wouldn't venture an opinion, but no doubt the art auctioneers Sotheby's or Christie's might be willing to do so. After all, they claim in their advertisements that they have an expert in every field waiting to advise you."

"Then I shall put their claim to the test," said Adam, "and pay them a visit." He rose from his chair, shook hands with the pastor and said, "You have been most kind."

"Not at all," said the pastor. "I was only too pleased to assist you. It makes a change from Frau Gerber's marital problems and the size of the churchwarden's marrows."

*   *   *

Adam took a bus up to Hyde Park Corner and jumped off as it turned left into Knightsbridge. He walked through the subway and continued briskly down Piccadilly towards the Ritz. He had read somewhere that Sotheby's was in Bond Street, although he couldn't remember having ever seen it.

He walked another hundred yards before turning left, where he shortened his stride to check all the signs on both sides of the road. He passed Gucci's, Cartier's, Asprey's and was beginning to wonder if his memory had failed him and whether he should check in the telephone directory. He continued on past the Irish Tourist Board and Celines before he finally spotted the gold lettering above a little newspaper kiosk on the far side of the road.

He crossed the one-way street and entered the front door by the side of the kiosk. He felt like a boy on his first day at a new school, unsure of his surroundings and not certain to whom he should turn for advice. Most of the people who passed him went straight up the stairs and he was just about to follow them when he heard a voice say, "Up the stairs and straight through, madam. The auction is due to start in a few minutes."

Adam turned and saw a man in a long, green coat. The name 'Sotheby' was embroidered over his left-hand pocket.

"Where do I go if I want something valued?" Adam asked.

"Straight along the passage, sir, as far as you can go and you'll see a girl on the left-hand side in reception," barked his informant. Adam thanked him, presuming that the guide's former place of work could only have been on an Aldershot drill square . . . He walked along to the reception area. An old lady was explaining to one of the girls behind the counter that her grandmother had left the vase to her several years before and she wondered what it might be worth.

The girl only glanced at the heirloom before asking, "Can you come back in about fifteen minutes? By then our Mr Makepeace will have had time to look at it and will be able to give you an estimate."

"Thank you, my dear," said the old lady expectantly. The girl picked up the large ornate vase and carried it to a room in the back. She returned a few moments later to be faced with Adam.

"May I help you, sir?"

"I'm not sure," began Adam. "I need some advice concerning an icon."

"Have you brought the piece with you, sir?"

"No, it's still abroad at the moment."

"Do you have any details?"

"Details?"

"Artist's name, date, size. Or better still do you have a photograph of the piece?"

"No," said Adam sheepishly. "I only know its title but I do have some documentation," he added, handing over the receipt he had shown the pastor.

"Not a lot to go on," said the girl, studying the German transcript. "But I'll ask Mr Sedgwick, the head of our Russian and Greek Icon department, if he can help you."

"Thank you," said Adam, as the girl picked up the phone.

"Is Mr Sedgwick able to advise a customer?" the girl enquired. She listened for a moment then replaced the phone.

"Mr Sedgwick will be down in a few moments, if you would care to wait."

"Certainly," said Adam, feeling something of a fraud. While the girl attended to the next customer Adam waited for Mr Sedgwick and studied the pictures on the wall. There were several photos of items that had come under the auctioneer's hammer in recent sales. A large painting by Picasso called 'Trois Baigneuses' had been sold for fourteen thousand pounds. As far as Adam could make out the brightly coloured oil was of three women on a beach dancing. He felt confident they were women because they had breasts even if they weren't in the middle of their chests. Next to the Picasso was a Degas of a girl at a ballet lesson; this time there was no doubt it was a girl. But the painting that most caught Adam's eye was a large oil by an artist he had never heard of called Jackson Pollock that had come under the hammer for eleven thousand pounds. Adam wondered what sort of people could afford to spend such sums on works of art.

"Wonderful example of the artist's brushwork," said a voice behind him. Adam turned to face a tall, cadaverous figure with a ginger moustache and thinning red hair. His suit hung on him as if from a coathanger. "My name is Sedgwick," he announced in a donnish voice.

"Scott," said Adam, offering his hand.

"Well, Mr Scott, why don't we sit over here and then you can let me know how I can help you."

"I'm not sure you can," admitted Adam, taking the seat opposite him. "It's just that I have been left an icon in a will and I was hoping it might turn out to be valuable."

"A good start," said Sedgwick, unfolding a pair of spectacles which he had removed from his top pocket.

"It may not be," said Adam, "because I know

105

nothing about paintings and I wouldn't want to waste your time."

"You won't be wasting my time," Sedgwick assured Adam. "We sell many items for less than ten pounds, you know." Adam hadn't known and Sedgwick's gentle voice made him feel less apprehensive. "Now am I to understand you do not have a photograph of this particular icon?"

"That's right," said Adam. "The icon is still abroad, and to be honest I've never laid eyes on it."

"I see," said Sedgwick, folding up his glasses. "But can you tell me anything of its provenance?"

"A little. It is known as 'The Tsar's Icon' and the subject is St George and the Dragon."

"How strange," said Sedgwick. "Someone else was enquiring after that particular painting only last week but he wouldn't leave his name."

"Someone else wanted to know about the Tsar's icon?" said Adam.

"Yes, a Russian gentleman, if I wasn't mistaken." Sedgwick tapped his glasses on his knee. "I checked on it extensively for him but found little that wasn't already well documented. The man wondered if it had ever passed through our hands, or even if we had heard of it. I was able to explain to him that the great work by Rublev remains in the Winter Palace for all to see. One can always be certain that it's an original from the Winter Palace because the Tsar's silver crown will be embedded in the back of the frame. Since the fourteenth century many copies of Rublev's master-piece have been made and they vary greatly in quality and value; but the one he seemed interested in was a copy made for Tsar Nicholas by a court painter circa 1914. I was unable to find any trace of such an icon in any of the standard works on the subject. Do you have any documentation on your icon?" Sedgwick enquired.

"Not a lot," said Adam. "Although I do have a copy of the receipt that was left to me in the will," he added, and handed it over.

Mr Sedgwick once again unfolded his glasses before studying the paper for several moments. "Excellent, quite excellent," he said eventually. "It seems to me that, as long as Roget et Cie will release it, a copy of the Tsar's icon painted by the court painter of the time, belongs to you. But you will have to go and pick it up yourself, that's for certain."

"But is it worth all that trouble?" asked Adam. "Can you give me any idea of its value?"

"Hard to be precise without actually seeing it," Sedgwick said, returning the document.

"So what is the lowest figure I might expect to get for it?"

The older man frowned. "Ten," he said, after considerable thought. "Perhaps fifteen, but with an absolute top of twenty."

"Twenty pounds," said Adam, unable to hide his disappointment. "I'm sorry to have wasted your time, Mr Sedgwick."

"No, no, no, Mr Scott, you misunderstand me. I meant twenty *thousand* pounds."

CHAPTER EIGHT

"A little more caviar, Comrade?" enquired Petrova across the lunch table.

Romanov frowned. His pretence at 'strictly confidential information' only to be passed on at the highest level had merely elicited a knowing smile from his companion who was also not inclined to believe that her boss had a pressing appointment at the Consulate that afternoon, an appointment that he had forgotten to mention to her before.

Anna held out a spoon brimming with caviar and pushed it towards Romanov as if she was trying to feed a reluctant baby.

"Thank you – *no*," said Romanov firmly.

"Suit yourself," said the young woman before it disappeared down her own throat. Romanov called for the bill. When he was presented with the slip of paper he couldn't help thinking that for that price he could have fed a Russian family for a month. He paid without comment.

"I'll see you back in the hotel later," he said curtly.

"Of course," said Petrova, still lingering over her coffee. "What time shall I expect you?"

Romanov frowned again. "Not before seven," he replied.

"And do you have any plans for me this afternoon, Comrade Major?"

"You may do as you please," said Romanov, and left the table without further word. Once on the street, he set off in the opposite direction to the bank, but he doubted if he had fooled the researcher, who was still eyeing him suspiciously through the restaurant window; or the agent, who had waited patiently on the far side of the road for nearly two hours.

By three o'clock Romanov was once again seated in the private room on the fifth floor looked down on by the three photographs of the Herr Bischoffs, and with the fourth Herr Bischoff sitting opposite him and the fifth Herr Bischoff standing behind him.

"We are in possession of . . ." began Herr Bischoff, in the same deliberate, formal way that had dictated the pace of the morning session, ". . . five boxes which have remained unopened since your father visited us in 1945. Should it be your desire to inspect the contents . . ."

"Why else would I have returned?" asked Romanov, already made impatient by the measured voice and studied ritual.

"Indeed," said Herr Bischoff, seemingly unaware of any discourtesy. "Then all we now require is that you sign a disclaimer in order to legalise the situation under Swiss law." Romanov looked apprehensive. "It is only a formality." The Russian still didn't speak. "You can rest assured, Your Excellency, that you are not the only one of your countrymen who from time to time sits in that chair."

Herr Bischoff slid a sheet of paper across the table. There were over twenty clauses of German, all in small print. Romanov scrawled his signature between the two X's with the proffered gold pen. He made no attempt to discover what he was signing. If they hadn't stolen his grandfather's heritage already, why should they be bothering to try now, he considered.

"Perhaps you will be kind enough to accompany me," said Herr Bischoff, quickly passing the sheet of paper to his son who left immediately. He rose and led Romanov silently back to the corridor. But on this occasion they travelled down in the chairman's private lift all the way to the basement.

When the doors opened Romanov might have thought they had entered a jail had the bars not been made of highly polished steel. A man who was seated behind a desk on the far side of the bars jumped up the moment he saw the chairman and turned the lock on the steel door with a long-shafted key. Romanov followed Herr Bischoff through the open door then waited until they were both locked inside. The guard preceded them down a corridor, not unlike that of a wine cellar with temperature and humidity gauges every few yards. The light was barely bright enough to ensure that they did not lose their footing. At the end of the corridor, they found Herr Bischoff's son waiting in front of a vast circular steel door. The old man nodded and the younger Herr Bischoff placed a key in a lock and turned it. Then the chairman stepped forward and undid a second lock. Father and son pushed open the nine inch thick door but neither made any attempt to enter the vault.

"You are in possession of five boxes. Numbers 1721, 1722, 1723, 1724 . . ."

"And 1725, no doubt," interrupted Romanov.

"Precisely," said Herr Bischoff, as he removed a small package from his pocket and added, "This is your envelope and the key inside it will open all five boxes." Romanov took the envelope and turned towards the open cavern. "But we must open the bank's lock first before you proceed," said Herr Bischoff. "Will you be kind enough to follow us?" Romanov nodded and both Herr Bischoffs proceeded into the vault. Romanov ducked his head and stepped in after them. Young Mr Bischoff opened the upper lock of the five boxes, three small ones above two large ones, making a perfect cube. "Once we have left, Your Excellency," said the old man, "we shall pull the door closed, and when you require it to be opened you have only to press the red button on the side wall to alert us. But I must warn you that at six o'clock the vault locks itself automatically and it cannot be reopened until nine the following morning. However, a warning alarm will sound at five forty-five." Romanov checked the clock on the wall: three seventeen. He couldn't believe he would need over two hours to find out what was in the five boxes. The two Herr Bischoffs bowed and left.

Romanov waited impatiently for the vast door to close behind him. Once alone in the Aladdin's cave he looked around the room and estimated there must have been two or three thousand boxes filling the four walls, giving them the appearance of a library of safes. He suspected there was more private wealth in that one vault than most countries on earth could call on. He checked the numbers of his own boxes and stood waiting like an orphan who has been told there will be second helpings.

He decided to start with one of the small boxes. He turned the key and heard the lock click before pulling out the stiff drawer to discover it was full of papers. He flicked through them to find they were title deeds to many large tracts of land in Bohemia and Bulgaria – once worth millions, now controlled by the Socialist State. As he checked each document, the old saying 'not worth the paper they were written on' sprang to mind. Romanov moved to the second box which he discovered contained the bond certificates of companies once managed by His Excellency Count Nicholai Alexandrovich Romanov. The last time they had declared a profit was in 1914. He cursed the system he had been born under as he moved on to the third box which contained only one document, his grandfather's will. It took only moments to discover that it had all been left to his father and therefore he was the lawful owner of everything – and nothing.

Dismayed, Romanov knelt down to study the two larger boxes, both of which looked big enough to hold a cello. He hesitated before placing his key in the lock of the first, turning it and pulling out the vast container.

He stared down in anticipation.

It was empty. He could only presume that it had been that way for over fifty years unless his father had removed everything and there was no reason to believe that. He quickly unlocked the fifth box and in desperation pulled it open.

The box was split into twelve equal compartments. He raised the lid of the first compartment and stared down in disbelief. Before him lay precious stones of such size, variety and colour that would have made anyone who was not royal gasp. Gingerly he lifted the lid off the second compartment, to find it contained pearls of such quality that one single string of them would have transformed a plain girl into a society beauty. As he opened the third box his amazement did not lessen and he understood for the first time why his grandfather had been considered one of the most enterprising merchants of the century. And now it all belonged to Alex Romanov, an impecunious Government official who was already wondering how he could possibly enjoy such riches.

It took Romanov a further hour to go through the contents of the remaining nine compartments. When he reached the last one – almost an anti-climax, in that it contained nothing but gold coins – he felt thoroughly exhausted. He checked the clock on the wall: five thirty. He began to replace the lids on each of the compartments, but during the treasure hunt he had come across one object of such magnificence that he could not resist removing it. He paused as he held up the long heavy gold chain weighted by a medallion, also made of solid gold, that hung from it. On one side was an engraved picture of his grandfather – Count Nicholai Alexandrovich Romanov, a proud, handsome man – while on the other was a profile of his grandmother, so beautiful that she surely could have worn any of the jewellery in that treasure trove with distinction.

For some time, Romanov held the chain in his hand before finally placing it over his head and letting the medallion fall from his neck. He gave the piece one last look before tucking it under his shirt. When he had replaced the lid on the last compartment he slid the box back into place and locked it.

For the second time that day Romanov's thoughts returned to his father and the decision he must have made when faced with such a fortune. He had gone back to Russia with his secret. Had he planned to rescue Alex from the life of drudgery that was all he could look forward to? His father had always assured him that he had an exciting future but there were secrets he was too young to share and he, in turn, had

have ta...
never have learned of the a... to the authorities. His
Poskonov. But his father must
Alex would
...n for

His mind turned to the old banker. Had he known
all along or was it just a coincidence that he had been
sent by Poskonov to this bank first? Members of his
chosen profession didn't survive if they believed in
coincidence.

A false move and the State would not hesitate to send
him to the same grave as his father and grandfather. He
would have to be at his most skilful when he next came
into contact with the old banker, otherwise he might
not live to choose between power in his homeland or
wealth in the West.

"After I have found the Tsar's icon I will make my
decision," he said, quite audibly. He turned suddenly
as the alarm bell's piercing sound rang out. He checked
the clock and was surprised by how much time he had
spent in the locked room. He walked towards the vault
door and on reaching it pressed the red button without
looking back. The great door swung open to reveal
two anxious-looking Herr Bischoffs. The son stepped
quickly into the vault, walked over to the five boxes
and made safe the bank's locks.

"We were beginning to get quite worried about
the time," said the old man. "I do hope you found
everything to your satisfaction."

"Entirely," said Romanov. "But what happens if I
am unable to return for some considerable time?"

"It's of no importance," Herr Bischoff replied. "The
boxes will not be touched again until you come back,
and as they are all hermetically sealed your possessions
will remain in perfect condition."

...ept at?"

"What tempe..c question.   ...aid Herr Bischoff, some-

"Ten d...

what... they airtight?"

"Certainly," replied the banker. "And watertight, not that the basement has ever been flooded," he added quite seriously.

"So anything left in them is totally safe from any investigation?"

"You are only the third person to look inside those boxes in fifty years," came back the firm response.

"Excellent," said Romanov, looking down at Herr Bischoff. "Because there is just a possibility that I shall want to return tomorrow morning, with a package of my own to deposit."

"Can you put me through to Mr Pemberton, please?" said Adam.

There was a long pause. "We don't have a Mr Pemberton working here, sir."

"That is Barclays International in the City, isn't it?"

"Yes, sir."

"Mr Lawrence Pemberton. I feel certain I've got the right branch."

The silence was even longer this time. "Ah, yes," came back the eventual reply. "Now I see which department he works in. I'll find out if he's in." Adam heard the phone ringing in the background.

"He doesn't seem to be at his desk at the moment, sir, would you like to leave a message?"

"No thank you," said Adam, and replaced the receiver. He sat alone thinking, not bothering to switch on the light as it grew darker. If he was to carry through the idea he still needed some information which Lawrence as a banker should find easy to supply.

A key turned in the door and Adam watched Lawrence enter and switch the light on. He looked startled when he saw Adam seated in front of him.

"How does one open a Swiss bank account?" were Adam's first words.

"I can't imagine one would find it that easy if all you have to offer is next week's unemployment cheque," said Lawrence. "Mind you, they usually keep a code name for English customers," he added, as he put his copy of the *Evening News* on the table. "Yours could be 'pauper'."

"It may surprise you to learn that it was a serious question," said Adam.

"Well," said Lawrence, taking the question seriously, "in truth, anyone can open a Swiss bank account as long as they have a worthwhile sum to deposit. And by worthwhile I mean at least ten thousand pounds."

"Yes, but how would you go about getting the money out?"

"That can be done over the phone or in person, and in that way Swiss banks don't differ greatly from any bank in England. Few customers, however, would risk the phone, unless they're resident in a country where there are no tax laws to break. In which case why would they need the gnomes of Zurich in the first place?"

"What happens when a customer dies and the bank can't be sure who the rightful owner of the assets is?"

"They would do nothing but a claimant would have to prove that they were the person entitled to inherit any deposits the bank held. That's not a problem if you're in possession of the correct documentation such as a will and proof of identity. We deal with such matters every day."

"But you just admitted that it's illegal!"

"Not for those clients resident overseas, or when it becomes necessary to balance our gold deposits, not to mention the bank's books. But the Bank of England keeps a strict watch over every penny that goes in and out of the country."

"So, if I were entitled to a million pounds' worth of gold left to me by an Argentinian uncle deposited in a Swiss bank, and I was in possession of the right legal documents to prove I was the beneficiary, all I would have to do is go and claim it?"

"Nothing to stop you," said Lawrence. "Although under the law as it currently stands, you would have to bring it back to this country, and sell the gold to the Bank of England for the sum they deemed correct, and then pay death duty on that sum." Adam remained silent. "If you do have an Argentinian uncle who has left you all that gold in Switzerland, your best bet would be to leave it where it is. Under this Government, if you fulfilled the letter of the law, you would end up with about seven and a half per cent of its true value."

"Pity I haven't got an Argentinian uncle," said Adam.

"He doesn't have to be Argentinian," said Lawrence, watching his friend's every reaction closely.

"Thanks for the information," said Adam and disappeared into the bedroom.

The last pieces of the jigsaw were beginning to fit into place. He was in possession of Roget's receipt of the icon originally meant for his father; all he needed now was a copy of the will to show that the document

He could then prove that he was
~~priceless~~ – he still had no
~~Tsar's icon. He~~

letter. "If there is anything to be gained from the contents of this envelope I make only one request of you, namely that your mother should be the first to benefit from it without ever being told how such good fortune came about."

When Romanov returned to the hotel, via the Russian Consulate, he found Petrova in her room dressed in jeans and a bright pink jersey, sitting in a corner reading, her legs dangling over the side of the chair.

"I hope you had a fruitful afternoon?" he enquired, politely.

"I certainly did," Anna replied. "The galleries in Zurich are well worthy of a visit. But tell me about *your* afternoon. Did it also turn out to be fruitful?"

"It was a revelation, my little one, nothing less. Why don't we have a quiet supper in my room so I can tell you all about it while we celebrate in style?"

"What a magnificent idea," said the researcher. "And may I be responsible for ordering dinner?"

"Certainly," said Romanov.

Petrova dropped her book on the floor and began to concentrate on the extensive *à la carte* menu that had been left by Romanov's bedside table. She spent a considerable time selecting each dish for their banquet and even Romanov was impressed when it finally appeared.

Anna had chosen as an entrée gravad lax edged with dill sauce. Accompanying it was a half-bottle of Premier Cru Chablis 1958. Between mouthfuls Romanov told her of the contents of his family inheritance and as h̶ ̶.̶.̶.̶.̶.̶ ̶ only once interrupted, researcher's who wheeled in a trolley on which sat a silver salver. The waiter lifted the salver to reveal a rack of lamb surrounded by courgettes and tiny new potatoes. To accompany this particular dish, the hotel had provided a Gevrey Chambertin.

The final course, a fluffy raspberry soufflé, required in the researcher's view only the finest Château Yquem. She had selected the 'forty-nine, which only made her lapse into singing Russian folk songs which Romanov felt, given the circumstances, was somewhat inappropriate.

As she drained the last drop of wine in her glass Petrova rose and, slightly unsteady, said, "To Alex, the man I love."

Romanov nodded his acknowledgment and suggested it might be time for them to go to bed, as they had to catch the first flight back to Moscow the following morning. He wheeled the trolley out into the corridor and placed a 'Do not disturb' sign over the door knob.

"A memorable evening," smiled the researcher, as she flicked off her shoes. Romanov stopped to admire her as she began to remove her clothes, but when he unbuttoned his shirt, the researcher stopped undressing and let out a gasp of surprise.

"It's magnificent," she said in awe. Romanov held up the gold medallion. "A bauble compared with the treasures I left behind," he assured her.

"Comrade lover," Anna said in a childlike voice, pulling him towards the bed, "you realise how much I adore, admire and respect you?"

"Um," said Romanov.

"And you also know," she continued, "that I have never asked you for any favour in the past."

"But I have a feeling you are about to now," said Romanov as she lifted back the sheet.

"Only that if the gold chain is nothing more than a mere bauble, perhaps you might allow me to wear it occasionally?"

"Occasionally?" said Romanov, staring into Anna's eyes. "Why occasionally? Why not permanently, my darling?" and without another word he removed the gold chain from around his neck and placed it over the young girl's head. Anna sighed as she fingered the thick gold rings that made up the chain that Romanov didn't let go of.

"You're hurting me, Alex," she said with a little laugh. "Please let go." But Romanov only pulled the chain a little tighter. Tears began to run down her cheeks as the metal began to bite into her skin.

"I can't breathe properly," gasped the researcher. "Please stop teasing." But Romanov only continued to tighten the chain around her throat until Anna's face began to turn red as it filled with blood.

"You wouldn't tell anyone about my windfall, would you, my little one?"

"No, never, Alex. No one. You can rely on me," she choked out desperately.

"Can I feel absolutely certain?" he asked with an edge of menace now in his voice.

"Yes, yes of course, but please stop now," she piped, her delicate hands clutching desperately at her master's blond hair, but Romanov only continued to squeeze and squeeze the heavy gold chain around her neck like a rack and pinion, tighter and tighter. Romanov was not aware of the girl's hands clinging desperately to his hair, as he twisted the chain a final time. "I'm sure you understand that I must feel absolutely certain that you wouldn't share our secret – with anyone," he explained to her. But she did not hear his plea because the vertebrae in her neck had already snapped.

On his morning run along the Embankment, Adam mulled over the tasks that still needed to be carried out next.

If he took the morning flight out of Heathrow on Wednesday, he could be back in London by the same evening, or Thursday at the latest. But there were still several things that had to be organised before he could leave for Geneva.

He came to a halt on the pavement outside his block and checked his pulse, before climbing the stairs to the flat.

"Three letters for you," said Lawrence. "None for me. Mind you," he added as his flatmate joined him in the kitchen, "two of them are in buff envelopes." Adam picked up the letters and left them on the end of his bed en route to the shower. He survived five minutes of ice-cold water before towelling down. Once he was dressed he opened the letters. He began with the white one, which turned out to be a note from Heidi thanking him for dinner, and hoping she would be seeing him again some time. He smiled and tore open the first of the buff envelopes, which was yet another missive from the Foreign Office Co-ordination Staff.

Captain Scott – the rank already seemed out of place – was requested to attend a medical at 122 Harley Street at three o'clock on the following Monday, to be conducted by Dr John Vance.

Finally he opened the other brown envelope and

pulled out a letter from Lloyds, Cox and King's branch in Pall Mall, informing Dear Sir/Madam that they had been in receipt of a cheque for five hundred pounds from Holbrooke, Holbrooke and Gascoigne, and that his current account at the close of business the previous day was in credit to the sum of £272.18s.4d. When Adam checked through the account it showed that at one point he had, for the first time in his life, run up an overdraft – a situation that he knew would have been frowned upon had he still been in the army, for as little as twenty years before it was in some regiments a court-martial offence for an officer to be overdrawn.

What would his brother officers have said if he told them he was about to remove two hundred pounds from the account with no real guarantee of a return?

Once Adam had finished dressing, he rejoined Lawrence in the kitchen.

"How was the Shah of Iran?" he asked.

"Oh, very reasonable really," said Lawrence, turning a page of the *Daily Telegraph*, "considering the circumstances. Promised he would do what he could about his current financial embarrassment, but he was a bit pushed until the West allowed him to raise the price of oil."

"Where did you eventually take him to lunch?" asked Adam enjoying the game.

"I offered him a shepherd's pie at the Green Man, but the bloody fellow became quite snotty. It seems he and the Empress had to pop along to Harrods to be measured up for a new throne. Would have gone along with him, of course, but my boss wanted his wastepaper basket emptied, so I missed out on the Harrods deal as well."

"So what are you up to today?"

"I shouldn't let you in on this," said Lawrence,

peering at the photograph of Ted Dexter, the defeated English cricket captain, "but the Governor of the Bank of England wants my views on whether we should devalue the pound from $2.80 to $2.40."

"And what are your views?"

"I've already explained to the fellow that the only 240 I know is the bus that runs between Golders Green and Edgware, and if I don't get a move on I'll miss my beloved 14," said Lawrence, checking his watch. Adam laughed as he watched his friend slam his briefcase shut and disappear out of the door.

Lawrence had changed considerably over the years since he had left Wellington. Perhaps it was that Adam could only remember him as school captain and then leaving with the top classics scholarship to Balliol. He had seemed so serious in those days and certainly destined for greater things. No one would have thought it possible that he would end up as an investment analyst at Barclays DCO. At Oxford contemporaries half joked about him being a cabinet minister. Was it possible that one always expected too much of those idols who were only a couple of years older than oneself? On leaving school their friendship had grown. And when Adam was posted to Malaya, Lawrence never accepted the army report that posted his friend as missing presumed dead. And when Adam announced that he was leaving the army, Lawrence asked for no explanation and couldn't have been kinder about his unemployment problem. Adam hoped that he would be given the chance to repay such friendship.

Adam fried himself an egg and a couple of rashers of bacon. There wasn't much more he could do before nine thirty, although he did find time to scribble a note to his sister, enclosing a cheque for fifty pounds.

At nine thirty he made a phone call. Mr Holbrooke

– Adam wondered if he actually had a Christian name – couldn't hide his surprise at receiving a call from young Mr Scott. Now that my father is dead, *I* must be old Mr Scott, Adam wanted to tell him. And Holbrooke sounded even more surprised by his request. "No doubt connected in some way with that envelope," he muttered, but agreed to put a copy of his father's will in the post that afternoon.

Adam's other requirements could not be carried out over the phone, so he locked up the flat and jumped on a bus heading up the King's Road. He left the double-decker at Hyde Park Corner and made his way to Lloyds Bank in Pall Mall, where he joined a queue at the Foreign Exchange counter.

"May I help you?" asked a polite assistant when he finally reached the front.

"Yes," said Adam. "I would like fifty pounds in Swiss francs, fifty pounds in cash and a hundred pounds in traveller's cheques."

"What is your name?" she enquired.

"Adam Scott."

The girl entered some calculations on a large desk-top machine before cranking the handle round several times. She looked at the result, then disappeared for a few moments to return with a copy of the bank statement Adam had received in the morning post.

"The total cost, including our charges, will be £202.1s.8d. That would leave your account in credit with £70.16s.4d.," she informed him.

"Yes," said Adam, but didn't add that in truth it would only be £20.16s.4d. the moment his sister presented her cheque. He began to hope that the Foreign Office paid by the week, otherwise it would have to be another frugal month. Unless of course . . .

Adam signed the tops of the ten traveller's cheques

in the cashier's presence and she then handed over five hundred and ninety-four Swiss francs and fifty pounds in cash. It was the largest sum of money Adam had ever taken out at one time.

Another bus journey took him to the British European Airways terminal in Cromwell Road where he asked the girl to book him on a return flight to Geneva.

"First class or economy?" she asked.

"Economy," said Adam, amused by the thought that anyone might think he would want to go first class.

"That will be thirty-one pounds please, sir." Adam paid in cash and placed the ticket in his inside pocket, before returning to the flat for a light lunch. During the afternoon he called Heidi who agreed to join him for dinner at the Chelsea Kitchen at eight o'clock. There was one more thing Adam needed to be certain about before he joined Heidi for dinner.

Romanov was woken by the ringing of the phone.

"Yes," he said.

"Good morning, Comrade Romanov, it's Melinski, the Second Secretary at the Embassy."

"Good morning, Comrade, what can I do for you?"

"It's about Comrade Petrova," Romanov smiled at the thought of her now lying in the bath. "Have you come across the girl since you reported her missing?"

"No," replied Romanov. "And she didn't sleep in her bed last night."

"I see," said the Second Secretary. "Then your suspicions that she might have defected are beginning to look a serious possibility."

"I fear so," said Romanov, "and I shall have to make a full report of the situation to my superiors the moment I get back to Moscow."

"Yes, of course, Comrade Major."

"I shall also point out that you have done everything possible to assist me with this problem, Comrade Second Secretary."

"Thank you, Comrade Major."

"And brief me the moment you come up with any information that might lead us to where she is."

"Of course, Comrade Major." Romanov replaced the phone and walked across to the bathroom in the adjoining room. He stared down at the body hunched up in the bath. Anna's eyes were bulging in their sockets, her face contorted and the skin already grey. After throwing a towel over the dead researcher's head and locking the door, he went into his own bathroom for an unusually long shower.

He returned and sat on his side of the bed, only a towel around his waist, and picked up the phone. He ordered breakfast which arrived fifteen minutes later, by which time he had dressed. Once he had finished orange juice and croissants he returned to the phone trying to recall the name of the hotel's manager. It came back to him just as the receptionist said, "*Guten Morgen, mein Herr.*"

"Jacques, please," was all Romanov said. A moment later he heard the manager's voice, "Good morning, Herr Romanov."

"I have a delicate problem that I was hoping you might be able to help me with."

"I shall certainly try, sir," came back the reply.

"I am in possession of a rather valuable object that I wish to deposit with my bank and I wouldn't want . . ."

"I understand your dilemma entirely," said the manager. "And how can I be of assistance?"

"I require a large container in which to place the object."

127

"Would a laundry basket be large enough?"

"Ideal, but does it have a secure lid?"

"Oh, yes," replied Jacques. "We often have to drop them off down lift shafts."

"Perfect," said Romanov.

"Then it will be with you in a matter of moments," said Jacques. "I shall send a porter to assist you. May I also suggest that it is taken down in the freight elevator at the rear of the hotel, thus ensuring that no one will see you leaving?"

"Very considerate," said Romanov.

"Will a car be calling to collect you?"

"No," said Romanov. "I —"

"Then I shall arrange for a taxi to be waiting. When will you require it?"

"In no more than half an hour."

"You will find it parked outside the freight entrance in twenty minutes' time."

"You have been most helpful," said Romanov, before adding, "the Chairman of the State Bank did not exaggerate his praise of you."

"You are too kind, Herr Romanov," said Jacques. "Will there be anything else?"

"Perhaps you would be good enough to have my account prepared so that there will be no delay."

"Certainly."

Romanov put the phone down wishing he could export such service to Moscow. He only waited a moment before he dialled the first of two local numbers. On both occasions his wishes were immediately granted. As he replaced the phone for the third time there was a gentle tap on the door. Romanov went quickly over to answer it. A young porter stood in the corridor, a large laundry basket by his side. He smiled politely. Romanov merely nodded and pulled in the basket. "Please return as soon as the taxi has arrived," said Romanov. The porter bowed slightly, but said nothing.

As soon as the porter had left, Romanov locked the door and put the chain in place before wheeling the laundry basket into the main bedroom and leaving it by the side of the bed. He undid the tough leather straps and threw open the lid.

Next, he unlocked the bathroom door and lifted Petrova's stiff body in his arms before trying to cram it into the basket. Rigor mortis had already gripped the body; the legs refused to bend and the researcher didn't quite fit in. Romanov placed the naked Petrova on the floor. He held his fingers out straight and suddenly brought them down with such force on the right leg that it broke like a branch in a storm. He repeated the action on her left leg. Like the guillotine, it didn't require a second attempt. He then tucked the legs under her body. It amused Romanov to consider that, had it been he who had been murdered, Anna Petrova would never have been able to get him in the basket whatever she had tried to break. Romanov then wheeled the trolley into the researcher's bedroom and, after emptying all her drawers, including Anna's clothes, clean and dirty, her shoes, her toilet bag, toothbrush and even an old photograph of himself he hadn't realised she possessed he threw them in the basket on top of her. Once he had removed the gold medallion from around her neck and was certain that there was nothing of the researcher's personal belongings left, he covered up the body with a hotel bath towel, and sprayed it with a liberal amount of Chanel No. 5 that had been left courtesy of the hotel.

Finally he strapped the lid down securely and

wheeled the creaking basket out and left it by the outer door.

Romanov began to pack his own case but there was a knock on the door before he had finished.

"Wait," he said firmly. There was a muffled reply of "*Ja, mein Herr.*" A few moments later Romanov opened the door. The porter entered, nodded to him and began to tug at the laundry basket, but it took a firm shove from Romanov's foot before it got moving. The porter sweated his way down the corridor as Romanov walked by the side of the basket, carrying his suitcase. When they reached the rear of the hotel Romanov watched as the basket was wheeled safely into the freight elevator before he stepped in himself.

When the ground floor doors opened Romanov was relieved to be greeted by Jacques who was standing by a large Mercedes waiting for him with the boot already open. The taxi driver and the porter lifted up the laundry basket and wedged it into the boot, but Romanov's suitcase could not be fitted in as well so it had to be put in the front of the car alongside the driver's seat.

"Shall we forward your bill to the Consulate, *mein Herr*?" asked Jacques.

"Yes, that would be helpful . . ."

"I do hope everything has worked out to your satisfaction," said Jacques, as he held open the back door of the Mercedes for his departing guest.

"Entirely," said Romanov.

"Good, good. And will your young colleague be joining you?" asked the manager, looking back over his shoulder towards the hotel.

"No, she won't," said Romanov. "She has already gone on to the airport ahead of me."

"Of course," said Jacques, "but I am sorry to have missed her. Do please pass on my best wishes."

"I certainly will," said Romanov, "and I look forward to returning to your hotel in the near future."

"Thank you sir," the manager said as Romanov slipped into the back seat leaving Jacques to close the door behind him.

When Romanov arrived at the Swissair office his suitcase was checked in and he waited only moments before continuing on to the bank. Herr Bischoff's son, accompanied by another man, also clad in a grey suit, was waiting in the hall to greet him.

"How pleasant to see you again so soon," volunteered the young Herr Bischoff. His deep voice took Romanov by surprise. The taxi driver waited by the open boot while Herr Bischoff's companion, a man of at least six foot four and heavily built, lifted out the laundry basket as if it were a sponge cake. Romanov paid the fare and followed Herr Bischoff into the far lift.

"We are fully prepared for your deposition following your phone call," said Herr Bischoff. "My father was only sorry not to be present personally. He had a long-standing engagement with another customer and only hopes that you will understand." Romanov waved his hand.

The lift travelled straight to the ground floor where the guard, on seeing young Herr Bischoff, unlocked the great steel cage. Romanov and the two bankers proceeded at a leisurely pace down the corridor, while the giant carried the basket in their wake.

Standing with folded arms by the vault door was another of the partners Romanov recognised from the previous day. Herr Bischoff nodded and the partner placed his key in the top lock of the vault door without a word. Herr Bischoff then turned the second lock and together they pushed open the massive steel door. Herr Bischoff and his partner walked in ahead of Romanov and opened the top lock of all five of his boxes, while the guard placed the laundry basket on the floor beside them.

"Will you require any assistance?" asked Herr Bischoff as he handed his Russian client a personal sealed envelope.

"No thank you," Romanov assured him, but did not relax until he had seen the vast door close behind him and all four of his Swiss helpers left invisibly on the other side.

Once he felt certain he was alone, he stared down at the one large box he knew to be empty: it was smaller than he had recalled. Beads of sweat appeared on his forehead as he unlocked it, pulled it out and raised the airtight lid. It was going to be a tight fit. Romanov unstrapped the laundry basket and removed everything except the body. He stared down at the contorted face, the deep marks in the skin around the neck had turned to a dark blue. He bent over and lifted the researcher up by her waist, but as no part of the body moved other than her broken legs he had to drop her into the box head first. Even then he had to adjust her various limbs in order that the box could be shut: had Anna been even an inch taller the exercise would have proved pointless. He then stuffed the girl's belongings down at the sides of her body, leaving only the Chanel-covered towel behind in the laundry basket.

Romanov proceeded to replace the lid on the airtight box, before pushing it back securely in place and locking it. He then double-checked it could not be opened without his own personal key. He was relieved to find he could not budge it. He hesitated for a moment glancing at the second large box, but accepted that this was not the time to indulge himself: that would have to wait for another occasion. Satisfied that everything was back in place, he closed and strapped down the lid of the laundry basket and wheeled it back to the entrance of the vault. He pressed the little red button.

"I do hope you found everything in order," said the young Herr Bischoff once he had returned from locking the five boxes.

"Yes, thank you," said Romanov. "But would it be possible for someone to return the laundry basket to the St Gothard Hotel?"

"Of course," said the banker, who nodded towards the large man.

"And I can be assured that the boxes will not be touched in my absence?" he asked as they walked down the corridor.

"Naturally, Your Excellency," said Herr Bischoff, looking somewhat aggrieved at such a suggestion. "When you return," he continued, "you will find everything exactly as you left it."

Well, not exactly, Romanov thought to himself.

When they stepped out of the lift on the ground floor, Romanov spotted Herr Bischoff's father with another customer.

A Rolls-Royce accompanied by a police motorcycle whisked the Shah of Iran quickly away, and the chairman discreetly waved his farewell.

When they reached the entrance to the bank, the young Herr Bischoff bowed. "We shall look forward to seeing you again when you are next in Zurich, Your Excellency," he said.

"Thank you," said Romanov, who shook hands with the young man and walked out on to the pavement to find the anonymous black car waiting to take him to the airport.

He cursed. This time he *did* spot the agent he had seen earlier in the hotel.

CHAPTER NINE

"Kill him, sir," the corporal whispered in Adam's ear.

"Not much hope of that," muttered Adam as he bounced into the centre of the ring.

The lean, muscle-bound instructor stood waiting for him. "Let's have a few rounds and see how you make out, sir." Adam bobbed and weaved around the Physical Training Instructor looking for an opening.

Adam led with a left and received a tap on the nose for his trouble. "Keep your guard up," said the sergeant major. Adam led again, catching the instructor a full blow on the chest, but was punished with a sharp left jab into the side of his head. He wobbled and his ear tingled but this time he managed to keep his guard up when a right and left followed. "You're feeble, sir, that's your problem. You couldn't knock the skin off a rice pudding." Adam feinted with his right and then swung a left with such force that when it caught the sergeant major full on the chin he staggered and fell.

The corporal standing by the side of the ring smirked as the instructor remained on the floor. Eventually he managed to get back on his feet.

"I'm sorry," said Adam, his guard up and ready.

"Don't be sorry, you bloody fool . . . sir. You landed

a bloody good punch. A technical knockout, to be accurate, so I'll have to wait for a day or two to seek my revenge." Adam breathed a sigh of relief and lowered his guard. "But that doesn't mean you're off the hook. It's weight training for you now, sir. Beam work and floor exercises."

For the next hour the sergeant major chased, kicked, harried and badgered Adam until he finally collapsed in a heap on the floor, incapable of lifting an evening paper.

"Not bad, sir. I feel sure the Foreign Office will be able to find some niche for you. Mind you," he added, "as most of that lot are about as wet as a dishcloth even *you*'ll have a chance to shine."

"You are most flattering, Sergeant Major," said Adam from a supine position.

"Up, sir," the instructor bellowed. Adam unwillingly got to his feet as quickly as his tired body would allow.

"Don't tell me, Sergeant Major."

"It's the recovery that proves fitness, not the speed," they said in unison.

"Sad day when you left the army," said the instructor to Adam once they were back in the Queen's Club changing room. "Can't name a lot of officers who have put me on the floor." The instructor touched his chin tenderly. "That will teach me to underestimate a man who survived nine months of Chink food. So let's hope the Foreign Office doesn't underestimate you as well."

The sergeant major rose from the bench by his locker. "Same time Wednesday?"

"Can't make it Wednesday, Sergeant Major. I may not be back from a trip to Geneva."

"Swanning around Europe nowadays, are we?"

"I could manage Thursday morning if that suits you," Adam said, ignoring the jibe.

"Your check-up with the quack is next Monday, if I remember correctly."

"Right."

"Thursday at ten then, it will give you a little longer to think about my right-hook."

The Chairman of the KGB studied the report on the desk in front of him: something didn't ring true. He looked up at Romanov. "Your reason for visiting Bischoff et Cie was because they claimed to be in possession of a fifteenth-century icon that might have fitted the description of the one we are searching for?"

"That is correct, Comrade, and the chairman of Gosbank will confirm that he personally arranged the meeting."

"But the icon turned out to be of St Peter and not of St George and the Dragon."

"Also confirmed by Comrade Petrova in her report."

"Ah, yes, Comrade Petrova," said Zaborski, his eyes returning to the sheet of paper in front of him.

"Yes, Comrade."

"And later that evening Comrade Petrova mysteriously failed to keep an appointment with you?"

"Inexplicably," said Romanov.

"But which you reported to Comrade Melinski at the Embassy." He paused. "You were responsible for selecting Petrova yourself, were you not?"

"That is correct, Comrade Chairman."

"Does that not reveal a certain lack of judgment on your part?"

Romanov made no attempt to reply.

The Chairman's eyes returned to the file. "When

you awoke the next morning, there was still no sign of the girl?"

"She also failed to turn up to breakfast as arranged," said Romanov, "and when I went to her room all her personal belongings had gone."

"Which convinced you she had defected."

"Yes, sir," said Romanov.

"But the Swiss police," said Zaborski, "can find no trace of her. So I keep asking myself why would she want to defect? Her husband and her immediate family live in Moscow. They are all employed by the State, and it is not as if this was her first visit to the West."

Romanov didn't offer an opinion.

"Perhaps Petrova disappeared because she might have been able to tell us something you didn't want us to hear."

Still Romanov said nothing.

The Chairman's gaze once again returned to the file. "I wonder what it was that young Petrova wanted to tell us? Who else you were sleeping with that night, perhaps?" Romanov felt a shiver of fear as he wondered how much Zaborski really knew. Zaborski paused and pretended to be checking something else in the report. "Perhaps she could tell us why you felt it necessary to return to Bischoff et Cie a second time." Once again, Zaborski paused. "I think I may have to open an enquiry into the disappearance of Comrade Petrova. Because, Comrade Romanov, by the time you returned to the bank a third time," said the Chairman, his voice rising with each word, "every second-rate spy from here to Istanbul knew that we were searching for something." The Chairman paused. Romanov was still desperate to find out if Zaborski had any real evidence. Neither man spoke for some time. "You have always been a loner, Major Romanov, and I do not deny that at times your results have allowed me to overlook certain indiscretions. But I am not a loner, Comrade. I am a desk man, no longer allowed your freedom of action." He fiddled with the paperweight of Luna 9 on the desk in front of him.

"I am a file man, a paper man. I make reports in triplicate, I answer queries in quadruplicate, explain decisions in quintuplicate. Now I will have to explain the circumstances of Petrova's strange disappearance to the Politburo in multiplicate."

Romanov remained silent, something the KGB had taken several years to instil into him. He began to feel confident that Zaborski was only guessing. If he had suspected the truth the interview would have taken place in the basement where a less intellectual approach to questioning was carried out.

"In the USSR," continued Zaborski, now rising from his chair, "despite our image in the Western world, we investigate a suspicious death," he paused, "or defection more scrupulously than any other nation on earth. You, Comrade Romanov, would have found your chosen profession easier to follow had you been born in Africa, South America or even Los Angeles."

Still Romanov did not venture an opinion.

"The General Secretary informed me at one o'clock this morning that he is not impressed by your latest efforts, distinctly unimpressed were the exact words he used, especially after your excellent start. All he is interested in, however, is finding the Tsar's icon, and so, for the time being, Comrade, he has decided there will be no investigation. But if you ever act in such an irresponsible way again it will not be an enquiry you are facing, but a tribunal, and we all know what happened to the last Romanov that faced a tribunal."

He closed the file. "Against my better judgment and

because we are left with less than a week, the General Secretary has allowed you a second chance in the belief that you will indeed come up with the Tsar's icon. Do I make myself clear, Comrade?" he barked.

"Very clear, Comrade Chairman," said Romanov, and turning smartly on his heel quickly left the room.

The Chairman of the KGB waited for the door to close before his eyes settled back on the file. What was Romanov up to, Zaborski needed to know, suddenly realising that his own career might now be on the line. He flicked down a switch on the little console by his side. "Find Major Valchek," he ordered.

"I've never actually had champagne and caviar," admitted Adam, as he looked up at the beautiful girl who sat opposite him across the table. He loved the way she tied her hair, and the way she dressed, the way she laughed, but most of all the way she smiled.

"Well, don't get frightened, because I can't imagine caviar will ever find its place on this particular menu," teased Heidi. "But perhaps soon when you are the proud owner of the Tsar's icon, that is if Mr Rosenbau . . ."

Adam put a finger to his lips. "No one else knows about that, not even Lawrence."

"That may be wise," Heidi whispered. "He will only expect you to invest all the money you make from the sale in his boring bank."

"What makes you think I'd sell it?" asked Adam, trying to discover how much she had worked out.

"If you own a Rolls-Royce and you are out of work you do not then go and hire a chauffeur."

"But I've only got a motorbike."

"And you'll have to sell that as well if the icon turns out to be worthless," she said, laughing.

"Would you like a coffee to follow?" asked the waiter, who was already clearing their table in the hope of fitting in two more customers before the night was out.

"Yes, please. Two cappuccinos," said Adam. He turned his gaze back to Heidi. "Funnily enough," he continued as the waiter retreated, "the only time I've ever rung Lawrence at the bank the telephonist couldn't immediately locate him."

"What's so surprising about that?" asked Heidi.

"It was as if they had never heard of him," said Adam, "but perhaps I was imagining it."

"A bank that size must have over a thousand employees. You could go years without knowing everyone who worked there."

"I suppose you're right," Adam said, as two coffees were placed in front of them.

"When do you plan on going to Geneva?" Heidi asked, after she had tried a sip of the coffee and found it too hot.

"First thing Wednesday morning. I hope to be back the same evening."

"Considerate."

"What do you mean?" asked Adam.

"To choose my one day off to fly away," she said. "Not very romantic."

"Then why not come with me?" he asked, leaning across the table to take her hand.

"That might turn out to be more significant than sharing your sausages."

"I would hope so and in any case, you could be most useful."

"You do have a way with words," said Heidi.

"You know I didn't mean it that way. It's simply that I don't speak German or French and I've never

141

been to Switzerland other than on a school skiing trip – and then I kept falling over." Heidi tried her coffee again.

"Well?" said Adam, not letting go of her hand.

"The Swiss speak perfect English," she said eventually, "and should you have any problem with the bank, you can always get in touch with Lawrence."

"It would only be for the day," said Adam.

"And a waste of your money."

"Not very romantic," said Adam.

"Touché."

"Think about it," said Adam. "After the cost of your return flight I will be left with only £19,969. I don't know how I'll get by."

"You really mean it, don't you?" said Heidi, sounding serious for the first time. "But women are not impulsive creatures."

"You could always bring Jochen along with you."

Heidi laughed. "He wouldn't fit on the plane."

"Do say you'll come," said Adam.

"On one condition," said Heidi thoughtfully.

"Separate planes?" said Adam grinning.

"No, but if the icon turns out to be worthless you will let me refund the price of my ticket."

"It couldn't be worth less than thirty-one pounds, so I agree to your terms," said Adam. He leaned over and kissed Heidi on the lips. "Perhaps it will take more than one day," he said. "Then what would you say?"

"I would demand separate hotels," replied Heidi, "if it wasn't for the high cost of the Swiss franc," she added.

"You are always so reliable, Comrade Romanov. You fulfil the primary qualification for a successful banker." Romanov studied the old man carefully, looking for some sign that he knew exactly what had been awaiting him at the bank.

"And you are always so efficient, Comrade Poskonov," he paused, "the only qualification necessary in my chosen profession."

"Good heavens, we are beginning to sound like a couple of ageing commissars at an annual reunion. How was Zurich?" he asked, as he lit a cigarette.

"Like a Polish tractor. The bits that worked were fine."

"From that I assume the bits that didn't work failed to produce the Tsar's icon," the chairman said.

"Correct, but Bischoff turned out to be most helpful, as was Jacques. My every need was catered for."

"Your every need?"

"Yes," replied Romanov.

"Good man, Bischoff," said the banker. "That's why I sent you to him first." The old man slumped down into his chair.

"Was there any other reason you sent me to him first?" asked Romanov.

"Five other reasons," said Poskonov, "but we'll not bother with any of them until you have found your icon."

"Perhaps I'd like to bother now," said Romanov firmly.

"I've outlived two generations of Romanovs," said the old man raising his eyes. "I wouldn't want to outlive a third. Let's leave it at that for now, I'm sure we can come to an understanding when the spotlight is no longer on you."

Romanov nodded.

"Well, you will be pleased to learn that I have not been idle in your absence. But I fear my results also resemble a Polish tractor."

The banker waved Romanov to a seat before he reopened his file which had grown in size since he had last seen it. "Originally," the chairman began, "you presented me with a list of fourteen banks, eleven of which have now confirmed that they are not in possession of the Tsar's icon."

"I have been wondering about that – is their word to be taken at face value?" asked Romanov.

"Not necessarily," said the banker. "But on balance the Swiss prefer not to become involved rather than tell a deliberate lie. In time the liar is always found out, and I still, from this office, control the cash flow of eight nations. I may not wield what they would call financial clout but I can still put the odd spanner in the works of the capitalist monetary system."

"That still leaves us with three banks?" said Romanov.

"Correct, Comrade. The first is Bischoff et Cie, whom you have already visited. But the other two have refused to co-operate in any way."

"Why is it your influence does not extend to them?"

"The most obvious of reasons," replied Poskonov. "Other interests exert a stronger influence. If, for example, your major source of income emanates from the leading Jewish families, or alternatively the Americans, no amount of pressure will ever allow you to deal with the Soviet Union." Romanov nodded his understanding. "That being the case," continued Poskonov, "there still has to be an outside chance that one of these two banks is in possession of the Tsar's icon, and as they are never going to admit as much to Mother Russia I am not sure what I can recommend you do next."

The banker sat back and waited for Romanov to take in his news.

"You are unusually silent," Poskonov ventured, after he had lit another cigarette.

"You have given me an idea," said Romanov. "I think the Americans would describe it as a 'long shot'. But if I'm right, it will be the Russians who will get the home run."

"Baseball is a game that I've never understood but I am, however, glad to have been of some use today. Although I suspect you will still need this, whatever your long shot." Poskonov removed a single piece of paper from his file and handed it over to Romanov. On it were the words: Simon et Cie, Zurich (refused), Roget et Cie, Geneva (refused).

"No doubt you will be returning to Switzerland very soon."

Romanov stared directly at the banker.

"I wouldn't recommend you visit Bischoff et Cie on this trip, Alex. There will be time enough for that in the future."

Romanov straightened his fingers.

The old man returned his stare. "You won't find me as easy to get rid of as Anna Petrova," he added.

CHAPTER TEN

The elderly-looking man took his place at the back of the taxi queue. It was hard to estimate his height because he looked so bent and frail. A large overcoat that might have been even older than its wearer reached almost to the ground and the fingers that could only just be seen peeping through the sleeves were covered in grey woollen mittens. One hand clung on to a little leather suitcase, with the initials E.R. in black looking so worn that it might have belonged to his grandfather.

One would have had to bend down or be very short to see the old man's face – a face that was dominated by a nose that would have flattered Cyrano de Bergerac. He shuffled forward slowly until it was his turn to climb into a taxi. The operation was a slow one, and the driver was already drumming his fingers against the wheel when his passenger told him in guttural tones that he wanted to be taken to the bankers, Simon et Cie. The driver moved off without asking for further directions. Swiss taxi-drivers know the way to the banks in the same way as London cabbies can always find a theatre and New York's yellow cabs a westside bar.

When the old man arrived at his destination he took

some time sorting out which coins to pay with. He then pushed himself slowly out on to the pavement and stood gazing at the marble building. Its solidity made him feel safe. He was about to touch the door when a man in a smart blue uniform opened it.

"I have come to see –" he began in stilted German, but the doorman only pointed to the girl behind the reception desk. He shuffled over to her and then repeated, "I have come to see Herr Daumier. My name is Emmanuel Rosenbaum."

"Do you have an appointment?" she asked.

"I fear not."

"Herr Daumier is in conference at the moment," said the girl, "but I will find out if there is another partner available to see you." After a phone conversation in German she said, "Can you take the lift to the third floor?" Mr Rosenbaum nodded with obvious signs of reluctance, but did as he was bid. When he stepped out of the lift, only just before the door closed on him, another young woman was standing there ready to greet him. She asked him if he would be kind enough to wait in what he would have described as a cloakroom with two chairs. Some time passed before anyone came to see him, and the old man was unable to hide his surprise at the age of the boy who eventually appeared.

"I am Welfherd Praeger," said the young man, "a partner of the bank."

"Sit down, sit down," said Mr Rosenbaum. "I cannot stare up at you for so long." The young partner complied.

"My name is Emmanuel Rosenbaum. I left a package with you in 1938, and I have returned to collect it."

"Yes, of course," said the junior partner, the tone of his voice changing. "Do you have any proof of your identity, or any documentation from the bank?"

"Oh, yes," came back the reply, and the old man handed over his passport and a receipt that had been folded and unfolded so many times it was now almost in pieces.

The young man studied both documents carefully. He recognised the Israeli passport immediately. Everything seemed to be in order. The bank's receipt, too, although issued in the year of his birth, appeared authentic.

"May I leave you for a moment, sir?"

"Of course," said the old man, "after twenty-eight years I think I can wait for a few more minutes."

Shortly after the young man had left, the woman returned and invited Mr Rosenbaum to move to another room. This time it was larger and comfortably furnished. Within minutes the junior partner returned with another man, whom he introduced as Herr Daumier.

"I don't think we have ever met, Herr Rosenbaum," said the chairman courteously. "You must have dealt with my father."

"No, no," said Mr Rosenbaum. "I dealt with your grandfather, Helmut."

A look of respect came into Herr Daumier's eyes.

"I saw your father only on the one occasion, and was sad to learn of his premature death," added Rosenbaum. "He was always so considerate. You do not wear a rose in your lapel as he did."

"No, sir, a tiny rebellion."

Rosenbaum tried to laugh but only coughed.

"I wonder if you have any further proof of identity

other than your passport?" Herr Daumier asked politely.

Emmanuel Rosenbaum raised his head and, giving Herr Daumier a tired look, turned his wrist so that it faced upwards. The number 712910 was tattooed along the inside.

"I apologise," said Daumier, visibly embarrassed. "It will take me only a few minutes to bring your box up, if you will be kind enough to wait."

Mr Rosenbaum's eyes blinked as if he were too tired even to nod his agreement. The two men left him alone. They returned a few minutes later with a flat box about two feet square and placed it on the table in the centre of the room. Herr Daumier unlocked the top lock while the other partner acted as a witness. He then handed over a key to Rosenbaum saying, "We will now leave you, sir. Just press the button underneath the table when you wish us to return."

"Thank you," said Rosenbaum, and waited for the door to close behind them. He turned the key in the lock and pushed up the lid. Inside the box was a package in the shape of a picture, about eighteen by twelve inches, covered in muslin and tied securely. Rosenbaum placed the package carefully in his old suitcase. He then shut the box and locked it. He pressed the button under the table and within seconds Herr Daumier and the junior partner returned.

"I do hope everything was as you left it, Herr Rosenbaum," said the chairman, "it has been some considerable time."

"Yes, thank you." This time the old gentleman did manage a nod.

"May I mention a matter of no great consequence?" asked Herr Daumier.

"Pray do so," said the old man.

"Is it your intention to continue with the use of the

box? The funds you left to cover the cost have recently run out."

"No, I have no need for it any longer."

"It's just that there was a small charge outstanding. But in the circumstances we are happy to waive it."

"You are most kind." Herr Daumier bowed and the junior partner accompanied their client to the front door, helped him into a taxi and instructed the driver to take Mr Rosenbaum to Zurich airport.

At the airport, the old man took his time reaching the check-in desk, because he appeared to be frightened of the escalator, and with the suitcase now quite heavy the flight of steps was difficult to negotiate.

At the desk he produced his ticket for the girl to check and was pleased to find that the passenger lounge was almost empty. He shuffled over towards the corner and collapsed on to a comfortable sofa. He checked to be sure he was out of sight of the other passengers in the lounge.

He flicked back the little knobs on the old suitcase and the springs rose reluctantly. He pushed up the lid, pulled out the parcel and held it to his chest. His fingers wrestled with the knots for some time before they became loose. He then removed the muslin to check his prize. Mr Rosenbaum stared down at the masterpiece. 'The Cornfields' by Van Gogh – which he had no way of knowing had been missing from the Vienna National Gallery since 1938.

Emmanuel Rosenbaum swore, which was out of character. He packed the picture safely up and returned it to his case. He then shuffled over to the girl at the Swissair sales desk and asked her to book him on the first available flight to Geneva. With luck he could still reach Roget et Cie before they closed.

* * *

The BEA Viscount landed at Geneva airport at eleven twenty-five local time that morning, a few minutes later than scheduled. The stewardess advised passengers to put their watches forward one hour to Central European Time.

"Perfect," said Adam. "We shall be in Geneva well in time for lunch, a visit to the bank and then back to the airport for the five past five flight home."

"You're treating the whole thing like a military exercise," said Heidi, laughing.

"All except the last part," said Adam.

"The last part?" she queried.

"Our celebration dinner."

"At the Chelsea Kitchen again, no doubt."

"Wrong," said Adam. "I've booked a table for two at eight o'clock at the Coq d'Or just off Piccadilly."

"Counting your chickens before they're hatched, aren't we?" said Heidi.

"Oh, very droll," said Adam.

"Droll? I do not understand."

"I'll explain it to you when we have that dinner tonight."

"I was hoping we wouldn't make it," said Heidi.

"Why?" asked Adam.

"All I have to look forward to tomorrow is the check-out counter at the German Food Centre."

"That's not as bad as a work out with the sergeant major at ten," groaned Adam. "And by ten past I shall be flat on my back regretting I ever left Geneva."

"That will teach you to knock him out," said Heidi. "So perhaps we ought to stay put after all," she added, taking him by the arm. Adam leant down and kissed her gently on the cheek as they stood in the gangway waiting to be let off the plane. A light drizzle was falling out on the aircraft steps. Adam unbuttoned his raincoat and attempted to shelter Heidi beneath it as they ran across the tarmac to the Immigration Hall.

"Good thing I remembered this," he said.

"Not so much a raincoat, more a tent," said Heidi.

"It's my old army trenchcoat," he assured her, opening it up again. "It can hold maps, compasses, even an overnight kit."

"Adam, we're just going to be strolling around Geneva in the middle of summer, not lost in the Black Forest in the middle of winter."

He laughed. "I'll remember your sarcasm whenever it pours."

The airport bus that travelled to and from the city took only twenty minutes to reach the centre of Geneva.

The short journey took them through the outskirts of the city until they reached the magnificent still lake nestled in the hills. The bus continued alongside the lake until it came to a halt opposite the massive single-spouting fountain that shot over four hundred feet into the air.

"I'm beginning to feel like a day tripper," said Heidi, as they stepped out of the bus, pleased to find the light rain had stopped.

Both of them were immediately struck by how clean the city was as they walked along the wide litter-free pavement that ran alongside the lake. On the other side of the road neat hotels, shops and banks seemed in equal preponderance.

"First we must find out where our bank is so that we can have lunch nearby before going to pick up the booty."

"How does a military man go about such a demanding exercise?" asked Heidi.

"Simple. We drop in at the first bank we see and ask them to direct us to Roget et Cie."

"I'll bet your little arm must have been covered in initiative badges when you were a Boy Scout."

Adam burst out laughing. "Am I that bad?"

"Worse," said Heidi. "But you personify every German's image of the perfect English gentleman." Adam turned, touched her hair gently and leaning down, kissed her on the lips.

Heidi was suddenly conscious of the stares from passing strangers. "I don't think the Swiss approve of that sort of thing in public," she said. "In fact, I'm told some of them don't approve of it in private."

"Shall I go and kiss that old prune over there who is still glaring at us?" said Adam.

"Don't do that, Adam, you might turn into a frog. No, let's put your plan of campaign into action," she said, pointing to the Banque Populaire on the far side of the avenue.

When they had crossed the road Heidi enquired of the doorman the way to Roget et Cie. They followed his directions, once again admiring the great single-spouted fountain as they continued on towards the centre of the city.

Roget et Cie was not that easy to pinpoint, and they walked past it twice before Heidi spotted the discreet sign chiselled in stone by the side of a high wrought-iron and plate-glass door.

"Looks impressive," said Adam, "even when it's closed for lunch."

"What were you expecting – a small branch in the country? I know you English don't like to admit it but this is the centre of the banking world."

"Let's find that restaurant before our entente cordiále breaks down," said Adam. They retraced their steps towards the fountain and, as the sun was trying to find gaps between the clouds, they chose a pavement café overlooking the lake. Both selected a cheese salad and shared a half bottle of white wine. Adam was enjoying Heidi's company so much that he began to tell her stories of his army days. She had to stop him and point out that it was nearly two. He reluctantly called for the bill. "The time has now come to discover if the Tsar's icon really exists," he said.

When they had returned to the entrance of the bank Adam pushed open the heavy door, took a step inside and stared around the gloomy hall.

"Over there," said Heidi, pointing to a woman who was seated behind a desk.

"Good morning. My name is Adam Scott. I have come to collect something that has been left to me in a will."

The woman smiled. "Have you made an appointment with anyone in particular?" she asked, with only the slightest trace of accent.

"No," said Adam. "I didn't realise that I had to."

"I'm sure it will be all right," said the lady. She picked up a phone, dialled a single number and held a short conversation in French. Replacing the phone she asked them both to go to the fourth floor.

As Adam walked out of the lift, he was surprised to be met by someone of his own age.

"Good afternoon, my name is Pierre Neffe and I am a partner of the bank," said the young man in perfect English.

"I did warn you that I would be redundant," whispered Heidi.

"Don't speak too soon," replied Adam. "We haven't even begun to explain our problem yet."

M. Neffe led them to a small, exquisitely furnished room.

"I could settle down here," said Adam, taking off his coat, "without any trouble."

"We do like to make our customers feel at home," said M. Neffe condescendingly.

"You obviously haven't seen my home," said Adam. M. Neffe did not laugh.

"How can I help you?" was all the young partner offered by way of reply.

"My father," began Adam, "died last month and left me in his will a receipt for something I think you have had in your safe-keeping since 1938. It was a gift given to him by one of your customers." Adam hesitated. "A Mr Emmanuel Rosenbaum."

"Do you have any documentation relating to this gift?" enquired M. Neffe.

"Oh, yes," said Adam, digging into the map pocket of his trenchcoat. He passed over the Roget et Cie receipt to the young banker. M. Neffe studied it and nodded. "May I be permitted to see your passport, Mr Scott?"

"Certainly," said Adam, delving back into his trenchcoat and passing it to M. Neffe.

"If you will excuse me for one moment." M. Neffe rose, and left them on their own.

"What do you imagine they are up to now?" said Heidi.

"Checking first if they still have the icon, and second if my receipt is authentic. 1938 was rather a long time ago."

As the minutes ticked by, Adam started to feel disappointed, then depressed, and finally began to believe it was all going to turn out to be a complete waste of time.

"You could always take one of the pictures off the wall and put it in your trenchcoat," teased Heidi. "I'm sure it would fetch a good price in London. Perhaps even more than your beloved icon."

"Too late," said Adam as M. Neffe reappeared with another banker whom he introduced as M. Roget.

"Good morning," said M. Roget. "I am sorry that my father is not here to meet you, Mr Scott, but he has been held up in Chicago on business." He shook hands with both Adam and Heidi. "We have on file a letter from Mr Rosenbaum giving clear instructions to the bank that the box is not to be opened by any other than" – he looked at the piece of paper he had brought with him – "Colonel Gerald Scott, DSO, OBE, MC."

"My father," said Adam. "But as I explained to M. Neffe, he died last month and left me the gift in his will."

"I would be happy to accept what you say," said M. Roget, "if I might be allowed sight of a copy of the death certificate and of the will itself."

Adam smiled at his own foresight and once more searched in his trenchcoat before removing a large brown envelope with the words 'Holbrooke, Holbrooke and Gascoigne' printed in heavy black letters across the top. He took out copies of his father's death certificate, the will and a letter marked 'To Whom It May Concern' and passed them to M. Roget, who read all three documents slowly, then handed them to his senior partner, who after he had read them whispered in his chairman's ear.

"Would you object to us phoning Mr Holbrooke in your presence?" asked M. Roget.

"No," said Adam simply. "But I must warn you that he is rather curmudgeonly."

"Curmudgeonly?" said the banker. "A word I am not familiar with, but I think I can sense its meaning." He turned and spoke to M. Neffe, who swiftly left the room, only to return a minute later with a copy of the English Law Society Register, 1966.

Adam was impressed by the bank's thoroughness as M. Roget checked that the number and address on the letterhead corresponded with the number and address in the Year Book. "I don't think it will be necessary to call Mr Holbrooke," said M. Roget,. "but we have encountered one small problem, Mr Scott."

"And what is that?" asked Adam, nervously.

"Mr Rosenbaum's position is somewhat overdrawn, and the bank's rule is that an account must be cleared before any box can be opened."

Adam's pulse raced as he assumed that he hadn't brought enough money to cover this eventuality.

"The account is only 120 francs in debit," continued M. Roget, "which is the charge for housing the box over the past two years since Mr Rosenbaum's deposit ran out."

Adam breathed a sigh of relief. He took out his wallet and signed a traveller's cheque and handed it over.

"And finally," said M. Roget, "we will need you to sign a form of indemnity for the bank."

M. Roget passed over a long form containing clause after clause in tightly printed French at which Adam only glanced before passing it over to Heidi. She studied each clause carefully. M. Roget used the time to explain to Adam that it was a standard disclaimer clearing the bank of any liability concerning what might be in the box and Adam's legal claim to it.

Heidi looked up and nodded her agreement.

Adam signed on the dotted line with a flourish.

"Excellent," said the banker. "All we have to do now is go and retrieve your box."

"I suppose it could be empty," said Adam once the two of them were left alone again.

"And it could be jam-packed with gold doubloons, you old pessimist," said Heidi.

When both men returned a few minutes later, M. Neffe was carrying a flat metal box about twelve by nine inches, and some three inches deep.

Adam was disappointed by its modest size, but didn't show his feelings. M. Roget proceeded to undo the top lock with the bank's key and then handed Adam a small faded envelope with signatures scrawled across the waxed seal. "Whatever is in the box belongs to you, Mr Scott. When you have finished, perhaps you would be kind enough to let us know. Until then we shall remain outside in the corridor."

Both men left the room.

"Come on," said Heidi, "I can't wait." Adam opened the envelope and a key fell out. He fumbled with the lock which clicked and then he pushed up the lid. Inside the box was a small flat package wrapped in muslin and tied tightly with string. The knots took some undoing and then finally an impatient Adam tore off the string before slowly removing the muslin. They both stared at the masterpiece in disbelief.

The simple beauty of the golds, reds and blues left them both speechless. Neither of them had expected the icon to be so breathtaking. St George towering over the dragon, a massive sword in hand on the point of plunging it into the heart of the beast. The fire that belched from the dragon's jaw was a deep red and made a startling contrast to the gold cloak that seemed to envelop the saint.

"It's magnificent," said Heidi, eventually finding her voice.

Adam continued to hold the tiny painting in his hand.

"Say something," said Heidi.

"I wish my father had seen it, perhaps it would have changed his whole life."

"Don't forget he wanted it to change yours," said Heidi.

Adam finally turned the icon over and found on the back a small silver crown inlaid in the wood. He stared at it, trying to recall what Mr Sedgwick of Sotheby's had said that proved.

"I wish my father had opened the letter," said Adam, turning the icon back over and once again admiring St George's triumph. "Because it was his by right."

Heidi checked there was nothing else left inside the box. She then flicked down the lid and Adam locked it again with his key. He tucked the muslin round the masterpiece, tied it up firmly and slipped the little painting into the map pocket of his trenchcoat.

Heidi smiled. "I knew you'd be able to prove that you needed that coat even if it didn't rain."

Adam walked over to the door and opened it. The two bankers immediately returned.

"I hope you found what you had been promised," said M. Roget.

"Yes, indeed," said Adam. "But I shall have no further need of the box," he added, returning the key.

"As you wish," said M. Roget, bowing, "and here is the change from your traveller's cheque, sir," he said, passing over some Swiss notes to Adam. "If you will excuse me I will now take my leave of you. Monsieur Neffe will show you out." He shook hands with Adam, bowed slightly to Heidi and added with a

faint smile, "I do hope you didn't find us too cur –
mud – geonly." They both laughed.

"I also hope that you will enjoy a pleasant stay in
our city," said M. Neffe as the lift took its leisurely
pace down.

"It will have to be very quick," said Adam. "We
have to be back at the airport in just over an
hour."

The lift stopped at the ground floor and M. Neffe
accompanied Adam and Heidi across the hall. The
door was held open for them but they both stood aside
to allow an old man to shuffle past. Although most
people would have stared at his nose Adam was more
struck by his penetrating eyes.

When the old man eventually reached the woman
at the reception desk, he announced, "I have come to
see Monsieur Roget."

"I'm afraid he's in Chicago at the moment, sir, but
I'll see if his son is available. What name shall I tell
him?"

"Emmanuel Rosenbaum." The woman picked up
the phone and held another conversation in French.
When she had replaced it she asked, "Would you go
to the fourth floor, Mr Rosenbaum?"

Once again he had to take the fearsome lift, and
once again he only just got out before its great teeth
sprang back on him. Another middle-aged woman
accompanied him to the waiting room. He politely
declined her offer of coffee, thumping his heart with
his right hand.

"Monsieur Roget will be with you shortly," she
reassured the old gentleman.

He did not have to wait long before a smiling M.
Roget appeared.

"How nice to make your acquaintance, Monsieur

161

Rosenbaum, but I'm afraid you have just missed Mr Scott."

"Mr Scott?" the old man uttered in surprise.

"Yes. He left only a few minutes ago, but we carried out the instructions as per your letter."

"My letter?" said Mr Rosenbaum.

"Yes," said the banker, opening for the second time that morning a file which had remained untouched for over twenty years.

He handed a letter to the old man.

Emmanuel Rosenbaum removed a pair of glasses from his inside pocket, unfolded them slowly and proceeded to read a hand that he recognised. It was a bold script written in thick black ink.

> Forsthaus Haarhot
> Amsberg 14
> Vosswinnel
> Sachsen
> Germany
> September 12, 1946

Dear M. Roget,

I have left in your safe-keeping a small icon of St George and the Dragon in my box 718. I am transferring the ownership of that painting to a British army officer, Colonel Gerald Scott, DSO, OBE, MC. If Colonel Scott should come to claim the icon at any time please ensure that he receives my key without delay.

My thanks to you for your help in this matter, and I am only sorry we have never met in person.

> Yours sincerely,
> Emmanuel Rosenbaum

"And you say that Colonel Scott came to collect the contents of the box earlier today?"

"No, no, Monsieur Rosenbaum. The colonel died quite recently and left the contents of the box to his son, Adam Scott. Monsieur Neffe and I checked all the documents including the death eertificate and the will, and we were left in no doubt that they were both authentic and that everything was in order. He was also in possession of your receipt." The young banker hesitated. "I do hope we did the right thing, Monsieur Rosenbaum?"

"You certainly did," said the old man. "I came only to check that my wishes had been carried out."

M. Roget smiled in relief. "I feel I ought also to mention that your account had run into a small deficit."

"How much do I owe you?" asked the old man, fumbling in his breast pocket.

"Nothing," said M. Roget. "Nothing at all. Monsieur Scott dealt with it."

"I am in debt to Mr Scott. Are you able to tell me the amount?"

"One hundred and twenty francs," said M. Roget.

"Then I must repay the sum immediately," said the old man. "Do you by any chance have an address at which I can contact him?"

"No, I'm sorry I am unable to help you there," said M. Roget. "I have no idea where he is staying in Geneva." A hand touched M. Roget's elbow, and M. Neffe bent down and whispered in his ear.

"It appears," said M. Roget, "that Mr Scott was planning to return to England shortly because he had to check in at Geneva airport by five."

The old man lifted himself up. "You have been most helpful, gentlemen, and I will not take up any more of your time."

* * *

"It's flight BE 171 and your seats are 14A and B," the man behind the check-in counter told them. "The plane's on time so you should be boarding at gate Number Nine in about twenty minutes."

"Thank you," said Adam.

"Do you have any luggage that needs checking in?"

"No," said Adam. "We only spent the day in Geneva."

"Then have a good flight, sir," said the man, handing over their boarding passes. Adam and Heidi started walking towards the escalator that would take them to the departure lounge.

"I have seven hundred and seventy Swiss francs left," said Adam, thumbing through some notes, "and while we're here I must get my mother a box of decent liqueur chocolates. When I was a boy I used to give her a minute box every Christmas. I swore when I grew up if I ever got to Switzerland I would find her the finest box available." Heidi pointed to a counter that displayed row upon row of ornate boxes. Adam walked over and selected a large, gold-wrapped box of Lindt chocolates which the girl behind the counter gift-wrapped and placed in a carrier bag.

"Why are you frowning?" asked Adam after collecting his change.

"She's just reminded me that I have to be back behind a till tomorrow morning," said Heidi.

"Well, at least we've got the Coq d'Or to look forward to tonight," said Adam. He checked his watch. "Not much else we can do now except perhaps pick up some wine in the duty free."

"I'd like to find a copy of *Der Spiegel* before we go through customs."

"Fine," said Adam. "Why don't we try the paper shop over in the corner?"

"A call for Mr Adam Scott. Will Adam Scott please return to the BEA desk on the ground floor," came booming out over the public address system.

Adam and Heidi stared at each other. "Must have given us the wrong seat allocation, I suppose," said Adam, shrugging. "Let's go back and find out."

They returned downstairs and walked over to the man who had handed them their boarding passes. "I think you put a call out for me," said Adam. "My name is Scott."

"Oh, yes," said the man. "There's an urgent message for you," he said, reading from a pad in front of him. "Please call Monsieur Roget at Roget et Cie on Geneva 271279." He ripped off the piece of paper and handed it over. "The phones are over there in the far corner behind the KLM desk, and you'll need twenty centimes."

"Thank you," said Adam, studying the message, but it gave no clue as to why M. Roget should need to speak to him.

"I wonder what he can want," said Heidi. "It's a bit late to ask for the icon back."

"Well, there's only one way I'm going to find out," said Adam, passing over the bag to her. "Hang on to that and I'll be back in a moment."

"I'll try and pick up my magazine at the same time, if I can find a newspaper shop on this floor," said Heidi as she gripped the brightly coloured bag which contained the chocolates.

"Right," said Adam. "Meet you here in a couple of minutes."

"Roget et Cie. Est-ce-que je peux vous aider?"

"I am returning Monsieur Roget's call," said Adam, making no attempt to answer in French.

"Yes, sir. Whom shall I say is calling?" asked the telephonist, immediately switching to English.

"Adam Scott."

"I'll find out if he's available, sir."

Adam swung round to see if Heidi had returned to the BEA counter, but as there was no sign of her he assumed she must still be looking for a newspaper. Then he noticed an old man shuffling across the hall. He could have sworn he had seen him somewhere before.

"Mr Scott?" Adam leaned back into the box.

"Yes, Monsieur Roget, I am returning your call."

"Returning my call?" said the banker, sounding puzzled. "I don't understand."

"There was a message left at the BEA counter asking me to phone you. Urgent."

"There must be some mistake, I didn't leave any message. But now that you have rung, it might interest you to know that just as you were leaving Mr Emmanuel Rosenbaum paid us a visit."

"Emmanuel Rosenbaum?" said Adam, "but I assumed he was . . ."

"Could you assist me, please, young lady?" Heidi looked up at the old man who had addressed her in English, but with such a strong mid-European accent. She wondered why he had taken for granted that she spoke English but decided it must be the only language he felt confident conversing in.

"I am trying to find a taxi and I am already late, but I fear my eyesight is not what it used to be."

Heidi replaced the copy of *Der Spiegel* on the shelf and said, "They're just through the double doors in the centre. Let me show you."

"How kind," he said. "But I do hope I am not putting you to too much trouble."

"Not at all," said Heidi, taking the old man by the arm and guiding him back towards the door marked 'Taxi et Autobus'.

"Are you sure it was Rosenbaum?" said Adam anxiously.

"I'm certain," replied the banker.

"And he seemed happy about me keeping the icon?"

"Oh, yes. That was not the problem. His only concern was to return your 120 francs. I think he may try and get in touch with you."

"BEA announce the departure of their flight BE 171 to London Heathrow from gate Number Nine."

"I must leave," said Adam. "My plane takes off in a few minutes."

"Have a good flight," said the banker.

"Thank you, Monsieur Roget," said Adam and replaced the receiver. He turned towards the BEA counter and was surprised to find that Heidi had not yet returned. His eyes began to search the ground floor for a paper shop as he feared she might well not have heard the departure announcement. Then he spotted her walking out through the double door, helping the old man he had noticed earlier.

Adam called out and quickened his pace. Something didn't feel quite right. When he reached the automatic door he had to check his stride to allow it to slide back. He could now see Heidi standing on the pavement in front of him, opening a taxi door for the old man.

"Heidi," he shouted. The old gentleman suddenly turned and once again Adam found himself staring at the man he could have sworn he had seen at the bank. "Mr Rosenbaum?" he questioned. Then with a movement of his arm that was so fast and powerful it took Adam by surprise, the old man threw Heidi into the back of the taxi, jumped in beside her, and pulling the taxi door closed, hollered at the top of his voice, "*Allez vite*."

For a moment Adam was stunned but then he dashed to the side of the taxi and only just managed to touch the handle as it accelerated away from the kerb. The car's sudden momentum knocked Adam backwards on the pavement, but not before he saw the petrified look on Heidi's face. He stared at the number plate of the departing car: GE-7-1-2 – was all he could catch, but at least he recognised it was a blue Mercedes. Desperately he looked around for another taxi but the only one in sight was already being filled up with luggage.

A Volkswagen Beetle drew up on the far side of the concourse. A woman stepped out of the driver's seat and walked to the front to open the boot. A man joined her from the passenger's side and lifted out a suitcase, before she slammed the boot lid back into place.

On the kerb, the two of them embraced. As they did so, Adam sprinted across the road and opening the passenger door of the Volkswagen, leapt inside and slid into the driver's seat. The key was still in the ignition. He turned it on, threw the car into gear, slammed his foot on the accelerator and shot backwards. The embracing couple stared at him in disbelief. Adam jerked the gear lever out of reverse into what he hoped was first. The engine turned over slowly, but just fast enough for him to escape the pursuing man. It must be third, he thought, and changed down as he began to follow the signs to the centre of Geneva.

By the time he reached the first junction he had mastered the gears, but had to concentrate hard on remaining on the right-hand side of the road. "GE712 . . . GE712," he repeated to himself again and again, to be sure it was fixed in his memory. He checked the number plate and the passengers of every blue taxi he passed. After a dozen or so, he began to wonder if Heidi's taxi might have left the motorway for a minor road. He pressed the accelerator even harder – 90, 100, 110, 120 kilometres an hour. He passed three more taxis but there was still no sign of Heidi.

Then he saw a Mercedes in the outside lane some considerable distance ahead of him, its lights full on and travelling well above the speed limit. He felt confident that the Volkswagen was powerful enough to catch the Mercedes, especially if it had a diesel engine. Metre by metre he began to narrow the gap as he tried to fathom out why the old man would want to kidnap Heidi in the first place. Could it be Rosenbaum? But he had wanted him to keep the icon, or so the banker had assured him. None of it made sense, and he drove on wondering if at any moment he was going to wake up.

When they reached the outskirts of the city Adam hadn't woken up as he followed carefully the taxi's chosen route. By the next intersection only three cars divided them. "A red light, I need a red light," Adam shouted, but the first three traffic lights into the city remained stubbornly green. And when one finally turned red, a van suddenly pulled in front of him, lengthening the gap between them. Adam cursed as he leaped out of the car and started running towards the taxi, but the light changed back to green just before he could reach it and the Mercedes sped away. Adam sprinted back to the Volkswagen and only just managed to drive the car across the junction as the light turned red. His decision to get out of the car had lost him several crucial seconds and when he looked anxiously ahead he could only just spot the taxi in the distance.

When they reached the Avenue de France, running parallel with the west side of the lake, both cars weaved in and out of the traffic, until the Mercedes suddenly turned left and climbed up a slight hill. Adam threw his steering wheel over to follow it, and for several yards careered up the wrong side of the road, narrowly missing a post van meandering down towards him. He watched carefully as the taxi turned left again, and in order to keep in contact he veered in front of a bus so sharply that it was forced to slam on its brakes. Several passengers, thrown from their seats, waved their fists at him as the bus's horn blared.

The taxi was now only a couple of hundred yards ahead. Once again Adam began to pick up some ground when suddenly it swerved into the kerbside and screeched to a halt. Nothing seemed to happen for the next few seconds as Adam weaved his way towards the stationary taxi, skidding to a halt directly behind the Mercedes. He then leaped out of the car and ran towards the parked vehicle. But, without warning, the old man jumped out of the taxi on the far side of the car and sprinted off up a side-street carrying with him Heidi's airport shopping bag and a small suitcase.

Adam pulled the back door open and stared at the beautiful girl who sat motionless. "Are you all right, are you all right?" he shouted, suddenly realising how much she meant to him. Heidi did not move a muscle and made no reply. Adam put his arms on her shoulders and looked into her eyes but they showed no response. He began to stroke her hair and then without warning her head fell limply on to his shoulder like a rag doll and a small trickle of blood started to run from the corner of her mouth. Adam felt cold and sick and began to tremble uncontrollably. He looked up at the taxi-driver. His arms were loose by his side and his body slumped over the wheel. There was no sign of life in the middle-aged man.

He refused to accept that they were dead.

Adam kept holding on to Heidi as he stared beyond her: the old man had reached the top of the hill.

Why did he still think of him as an old man? He was obviously not old at all, but young and very fit. Suddenly Adam's fear turned to anger. He had a split second to make a decision. He let go of Heidi, jumped out of the car and started to sprint up the hill after her killer. Two or three onlookers had already gathered on the kerbside and were now staring at Adam and the two cars. He had to catch the man who was still running. Adam moved as fast as he could but the trenchcoat he was wearing slowed him down, and by the time he too had reached the top of the hill the killer was a clear hundred yards ahead of him, weaving his way through the main thoroughfare. Adam tried to lengthen his stride as he watched the man leap on to a passing tram, but he was too far behind to make any impression on him and could only watch the tram moving inexorably into the distance.

The man stood on the tram steps and stared back at Adam. He held up the shopping bag defiantly with one hand. The back was no longer hunched, the figure no longer frail, and even at that distance, Adam could sense the triumph in the man's stance. Adam stood for several seconds in the middle of the road helplessly watching the tram as it disappeared out of sight.

He tried to gather his thoughts. He realised that there was little hope of picking up a taxi during the rush hour. Behind him he could hear sirens of what he presumed were ambulances trying to rush to the scene of the accident. "Accident," said Adam. "They will soon discover it was murder." He tried to start sorting out in his mind the madness of the last half hour. None of it made sense. He would surely find it was all a mistake ... Then he touched the side of his coat, touched the package that held the Tsar's icon. The killer hadn't gone to all that trouble for £20,000 – murdering two innocent people who happened to have got in his way – why, why, *why*, was the icon that important? What had the Sotheby's expert said? "A Russian gentleman had enquired after the piece." Adam's mind began to whirl. If it was Emmanuel Rosenbaum and that was what he had killed for, all he had ended up with was a large box of Swiss liqueur chocolates.

When Adam heard the whistle behind him he felt relieved that help was at hand but as he turned he saw two officers with guns out of their holsters pointing towards him. He instinctively turned his jog into a run, and looking over his shoulder he saw that several police were now giving chase. He lengthened his stride again and, despite the trenchcoat, doubted if there were a member of the Swiss force who could hope to keep up the pace he set for more than a quarter of a mile. He turned into the first alley he came to and speeded up. It was narrow – not wide enough for even two bicycles to pass. Once he was beyond the alley he selected a one-way street. It was crammed with cars, and he was able swiftly and safely to move in and out of the slow-moving oncoming traffic.

In a matter of minutes he had lost the pursuing police, but he still ran on, continually switching direction until he felt he had covered at least two miles. He finally turned into a quiet street and halfway down saw a fluorescent sign advertising the Hotel Monarque. It didn't look much more than a guest house, and certainly wouldn't have qualified under the description of an hotel. He stopped in the shadows and waited, taking in great gulps of air. After about three minutes his breathing was back to normal and he marched straight into the hotel.

CHAPTER ELEVEN

He stood naked, staring at the image of Emmanuel Rosenbaum in the hotel mirror. He didn't like what he saw. First he removed the teeth, then began to click his own up and down: he had been warned that the gums would ache for days. Then painstakingly he shed each layer of his bulbous nose, admiring the skill and artistry that had gone into creating such a monstrosity. It will be too conspicuous, he had told them. They will remember nothing else, had come back the experts' reply.

When the last layer had been removed, the aristocratic one that took its place looked ridiculous in the centre of such a face. Next he began on the lined forehead that even moved when he frowned. As the lines disappeared, so the years receded. Next the flaccid red cheeks, and finally, the two chins. The Swiss bankers would have been amazed at how easily the sharp rubbing of a pumice stone removed the indelible number on the inside of his arm. Once more he studied himself in the mirror. The hair, short and greying, would take nature longer. When they had cut his hair and smeared that thick, mud-like concoction all over his scalp he realised how an Irishman must feel to be tarred and feathered. Moments later he stood under a warm shower, his fingers massaging deep into the roots of his hair. Black treacly water started to run down his face and body before finally disappearing down the plug hole. It took half a bottle of shampoo before his hair had returned to its normal colour, but he realised that it would take considerably longer before he stopped looking like a staff sergeant in the United States Marines.

In a corner of the room lay the long baggy coat, the shiny shapeless suit, the black tie, the off-white shirt, woollen mittens and the Israeli passport. Hours of preparation discarded in a matter of minutes. He longed to burn them all, but instead left them in a heap. He returned to the main room and stretched himself out on the bed like a yawning cat. His back still ached from all the bending and crouching. He stood up, then touched his toes and threw his arms high above his head fifty times. He rested for one minute before completing fifty press-ups.

He returned to the bathroom and had a second shower – cold. He was beginning to feel like a human being again. He then changed into a freshly ironed cream silk shirt and a new double-breasted suit.

Before making one phone call to London and two more to Moscow he ordered dinner in his room so that no one would see him – he had no desire to explain how the man who checked in was thirty years younger than the man eating alone in his room. Like a hungry animal he tore at the steak and gulped the wine.

He stared at the colourful carrier bag but felt no desire to finish off the meal with one of Scott's liqueur chocolates. Once again he felt anger at the thought of the Englishman getting the better of him.

His eyes then rested on the little leather suitcase that lay on the floor by the side of his bed. He opened it and took out the copy of the icon that Zaborski had ordered he should always have with him so that there could be no doubt when he came across the original of St George and the Dragon.

At a little after eleven he switched on the late-night news. They had no photograph of the suspect, only one of that stupid taxi-driver who had driven so slowly it had cost the fool his life, and the pretty German girl who had tried to fight back. It had been pathetic, one firm clean strike and her neck was broken. The television announcer said the police were searching for an unnamed Englishman. Romanov smiled at the thought of police searching for Scott while he was eating steak in a luxury hotel. Although the Swiss police had no photograph of the murderer, Romanov didn't need one. It was a face he would never forget. In any case, his contact in England had already told him a lot more about Captain Scott in one phone call than the Swiss police could hope to discover for another week.

When Romanov was told the details of Scott's military career and decorations for bravery he considered it would be a pleasure to kill such a man.

Lying motionless on a mean little bed, Adam tried to make sense of all the pieces that made up a black jigsaw. If Goering had left the icon to his father, and his alias had been Emmanuel Rosenbaum, then a real-life Emmanuel Rosenbaum didn't exist. But he *did* exist: he had even killed twice in his attempt to get his hands on the Tsar's icon. Adam leaned over, switched on the bedside light, then pulled the small package out of the pocket of his trenchcoat. He unwrapped it carefully before holding the icon under the light. St George stared back at him – no longer looking magnificent, it seemed to Adam, more accusing. Adam would have handed the icon over to Rosenbaum without a second thought if it would have stopped Heidi from sacrificing her life.

By midnight Adam had decided what had to be done, but he didn't stir from that tiny room until a few minutes after three. He lifted himself quietly off the bed, opened the door, checked the corridor, and then locked the door noiselessly behind him before creeping down the stairs. When he reached the bottom step he waited and listened. The night porter had nodded off in front of a television that now let out a dim, monotonous hum. A silver dot remained in the centre of the screen. Adam took nearly two minutes to reach the front door, stepping on a noisy floorboard just once: but the porter's snores had been enough to cover that. Once outside, Adam checked up and down the street but there was no sign of any movement. He didn't want to go far, so he stayed in the shadows by the side of the road, moving at a pace unfamiliar to him. When he reached the corner he saw what he was searching for and it was still about a hundred yards away.

There was still no one to be seen, so he quickly made his way to the phone box. He pressed a twenty centime coin into the box and waited. A voice said, "*Est-ce-que je peux vous aider?*" Adam uttered only one word, "International." A moment later another voice asked the same question.

"I want to make a reverse charge call to London," said Adam firmly. He had no desire to repeat himself.

"Yes," said the voice. "And what is your name?"

"George Cromer," replied Adam.

"And the number you are speaking from?"

"Geneva 271982." He reversed the last three digits:

he felt the police could well be listening in on all calls to England that night. He then told the girl the number in London he required.

"Can you wait for a moment, please?"

"Yes," said Adam as his eyes checked up and down the street once again, still looking for any unfamiliar movement. Only the occasional early morning car sped by. He remained absolutely motionless in the corner of the box.

He could hear the connection being put through. "Please wake up," his lips mouthed. At last the ringing stopped and Adam recognised the familiar voice which answered.

"Who is this?" Lawrence asked, sounding irritated but perfectly awake.

"Will you accept a reverse charge call from a Mr George Cromer in Geneva?"

"George Cromer, Lord Cromer, the Governor of the Bank of Eng –? Yes, I will," he said.

"It's me, Lawrence," said Adam.

"Thank God. Where are you?"

"I'm still in Geneva but I'm not sure you're going to believe what I'm about to tell you. While we were waiting to board our plane home a man pulled Heidi into a taxi and later murdered her before I could catch up with them. And the trouble is that the Swiss police think I'm the killer."

"Now just relax, Adam. I know that much. It's been on the evening news and the police have already been around to interview me. It seems Heidi's brother identified you."

"What do you mean *identified* me? I didn't do it. You know I couldn't do it. It was a man called Rosenbaum, not me, Lawrence."

"Rosenbaum? Adam, who is Rosenbaum?"

Adam tried to sound calm. "Heidi and I came to Geneva this morning to pick up a gift from a Swiss bank that Pa had left me in his will. It turned out to be a painting. Then when we returned to the airport, this Rosenbaum grabbed Heidi thinking she had got the painting which didn't make any sense because the damned icon's only worth £20,000."

"Icon?" said Lawrence.

"Yes, an icon of St George and the Dragon," said Adam. "That's not important. What's important is that . . ."

"Now listen and listen carefully," interrupted Lawrence, "because I'm not going to repeat myself. Keep out of sight until the morning and then give yourself up at our Consulate. Just see you get there in one piece and I'll make sure that the Consul will be expecting you. Don't arrive until eleven because London is an hour behind Geneva and I'll need every minute to arrange matters and see that the consul staff is properly organised."

Adam found himself smiling for the first time in twelve hours.

"Did the killer get what he was after?" Lawrence asked.

"No, he didn't get the icon," said Adam, "he only got my mother's chocolates . . ."

"Thank God for that and keep out of sight of the Swiss police because they are convinced it was you who killed Heidi."

"But . . ." began Adam.

"No explanations. Just be at the Consulate at eleven. Now you'd better get off the line," said Lawrence. "Eleven, and don't be late."

"Right," said Adam, "and . . ." but the phone was only giving out a long burr. Thank God for Lawrence, he thought: the Lawrence of old who didn't need to ask any questions because he already knew the answers. Christ, what had he got himself involved in? Adam checked the street once again. Still no one in sight. He quickly stole the two hundred yards back to the hotel. The front door remained unlocked, the porter asleep, the television screen still faintly humming, the silver dot in place. Adam was back on his bed by five minutes past four. He didn't sleep. Rosenbaum, Heidi, the taxi driver, the Russian gentleman at Sotheby's. So many pieces of a jigsaw, none of them fitting into place.

But the one thing that worried him most was the conversation with Lawrence – the Lawrence of old?

The two policemen arrived at the Hotel Monarque at twenty past seven that Thursday morning. They were tired, discontented and hungry. Since midnight they had visited forty-three hotels on the west side of the city, on each occasion with no success. They had checked over a thousand registration cards and woken seven innocent Englishmen who had not come anywhere near fitting the description of Adam Scott.

At eight they would be off duty and could go home to their wives and breakfasts; but they still had three more hotels to check before then. When the landlady saw them coming into the hall she waddled as quickly as possible from the inner office towards them. She loathed the police and was willing to believe anyone who told her that the Swiss pigs were even worse than the Germans. Twice in the last year she had been fined and once even threatened with jail over her failure to register every guest. If they caught her once more she knew they would take her licence away and with it her living. Her slow mind tried to recall who had booked in the previous evening. Eight people had registered but only two had paid cash – the Englishman who hardly opened his mouth, Mr Pemberton was the name he had filled in on the missing card, and Maurice who always turned up with a different girl whenever he was in Geneva. She had destroyed both their cards and pocketed the money. Maurice and the girl had left by seven and she had already made up their bed, but the Englishman was still asleep in his room.

"We need to check your registration cards for last night, madame."

"Certainly, monsieur," she replied with a warm smile, and gathered together the six remaining cards: two Frenchmen, one Italian, two nationals from Zurich and one from Basle.

"Did an Englishman stay here last night?"

"No," said the landlady firmly. "I haven't had an Englishman," she added helpfully, "for at least a month. Would you like to see the cards for last week?"

"No, that won't be necessary," said the policeman. The landlady grunted with satisfaction. "But we will still need to check your unoccupied rooms. I see from the certificate that there are twelve guest bedrooms in the hotel," the policeman continued. "So there must be six that should be empty."

"There's no one in them," said the landlady. "I've already checked them once this morning."

"We still need to see for ourselves," the other officer insisted.

The landlady picked up her pass key and waddled towards the stairs, which she proceeded to climb as if they were the final summit of Everest. She opened bedrooms five, seven, nine, ten, eleven. Maurice's room had been remade within minutes of his leaving but the old lady knew she would lose her licence the moment they entered twelve. She just stopped herself from knocking on the door before she turned the key in the lock. The two policemen walked in ahead of her while she remained in the corridor, just in case there was any trouble. Not for the first time that day she cursed the efficiency of Swiss police.

"Thank you, madame," said the first policeman as he stepped back into the corridor. "We are sorry to have troubled you," he added. He put a tick on his list next to the Hotel Monarque.

As the two policemen made their way downstairs the landlady walked into room number twelve, mystified. The bed was undisturbed, as if it had not been slept in, and there was no sign of anyone having spent the night there. She called on her tired memory. She hadn't drunk that much the previous night – she touched the fifty francs in her pocket as if to prove the point. "I wonder where he is," she muttered.

For the past hour Adam had been crouching behind a derelict coach in a railway goods yard less than half a mile from the hotel. He had a clear view for a hundred yards in every direction. He had watched the early morning commuters flooding in on every train. By twenty past eight Adam judged they were at their peak. He checked that the icon was in place and left his hideout to join the flood as they headed to work. He stopped at the kiosk to purchase a newspaper. The only English paper on sale at that time in the morning was the *Herald-Tribune*: the London papers didn't arrive until the first plane could land, but Adam had seen the *Herald-Tribune* come in on the train from Paris. He made two other purchases at the station kiosk before rejoining the scurrying crowds: a city map of Geneva and a large bar of Nestlé's chocolate.

There was still plenty of time to kill before he could present himself at the Consulate. A glance at the map confirmed that he could already see the building he had marked out as his next place of sanctuary. He steered a route towards it that allowed him to stay in contact with the largest number of people. When he arrived in the square he continued under the shop awnings round the longest route, clinging to the wall, always avoiding the open spaces. It took a considerable time but his judgment was perfect. He reached the front door as hundreds of worshippers were leaving from the early morning Communion service.

Once inside, he felt safe. Notre Dame was the main Catholic Church in the city and Adam found his bearings in a matter of moments. He made his way slowly down the side aisle towards the Lady Chapel, dropped some coins in one of the collection boxes, lit a candle and placed it in a vacant holder below a statue of the Virgin Mother. He then fell on his knees, but his eyes never closed. A lapsed Catholic, he found he no longer believed in God – except when he was ill, frightened or in an aeroplane. After about twenty minutes had passed Adam was distressed to see that there was now only a handful of people left in the cathedral. Some old ladies dressed in black filled a front pew, moving their rosary beads methodically and chanting, "*Ave Maria, gratia plena, Domine teum, Benedicta . . .*" A few tourists were craning their necks to admire the fine roof, their eyes only looking upwards.

Adam rose slowly, his eyes darting from side to side. He stretched his legs and walked over to a confessional box partly hidden behind a pillar. A small sign on the wooden support showed that the box was not in use. Adam slipped in, sat down and pulled the curtain closed.

First he took out the *Herald-Tribune* from his trench-coat pocket, and then the bar of chocolate. He tore the silver paper from the chocolate and began to munch greedily. Next he searched for the story. Only one or two items of English news were on the front page, as most of the articles were devoted to what was happening in America. "The pound still too high at $2.80?" one headline suggested. Adam's eyes passed over the smaller headlines until he saw the paragraph he was looking for. It was in the bottom left-hand corner: "Englishman sought after German girl and Swiss taxi-driver murdered." Adam read the story, and only began to tremble when he discovered they knew his name:

"Captain Adam Scott, who recently resigned his commission from the Royal Wessex Regiment, is wanted . . . please turn to page fifteen." Adam began to turn the large pages. It was not easy in the restricted space of a confessional box. ". . . for questioning by the Geneva police in connection with . . ."

"Au nom du Père, du Fils et du Saint Esprit."

Adam looked up from the paper startled and considered making a dash for it. But he allowed his long-ago training to take hold as he found himself saying automatically, "Father, bless me, for I have sinned and wish to confess."

"Good, my son, and what form has this sin taken?" asked the priest in accented but clear English.

Adam thought quickly, I must give him no clue as to who I am. He looked out through the gap in the curtain and was alarmed to see two policemen questioning another priest by the west door. He drew the curtains tight and turned to the only accent he could ever imitate with any conviction.

"I'm over from Dublin, Father, and last night I

185

picked up this local girl in a bar and took her back to my hotel."

"Yes, my son."

"Well, one thing led to another, Father."

"Another what, my son?"

"Well, I took her up to my room."

"Yes, my son?"

"And she started to undress."

"And then what happened?"

"She started to undress me."

"Did you try to resist, my son?"

"Yes, Father, but it got harder."

"And did intercourse take place?" asked the priest.

"I'm afraid so, Father. I couldn't stop myself. She was very beautiful," Adam added.

"And is it your intention to marry this girl, my son?"

"Oh, no, Father, I'm already married and have two lovely children, Seamus and Maureen."

"It is a night you must for ever put behind you."

"I'd like to, Father."

"Has this happened before?"

"No, Father, it's the first time I've been abroad on my own. I swear to it."

"Then let it be a lesson to you, my son, and may the Lord find it in his mercy to forgive you this abominable sin and now you must make your act of contrition."

"Oh my God . . ."

When Adam had completed the act of contrition the priest pronounced absolution and told him he must as penance say three decades of the Rosary.

"And one more thing."

"Yes, Father?"

"You will tell your wife everything the moment you return to Ireland or you cannot hope for atonement. You must promise me that, my son."

"When I see my wife, I will tell her everything that happened last night, Father," Adam promised, as he once again checked through the curtains. The police were no longer anywhere to be seen.

"Good, and continue to pray to our Blessed Lady to keep you from the evils of temptation."

Adam folded up his paper, pushed it in the trench-coat and bolted from the little box and took a seat on the end of a pew. He lowered his head and began to whisper the Lord's Prayer as he opened the map of Geneva and began to study the road plan. He had located the British Consulate on the far side of a large garden square by the time he reached 'Deliver us from evil.' He estimated that it was just over a mile away from the cathedral, but seven streets and a bridge had to be negotiated before he would be safe. He returned to the Lady Chapel and his knees. Adam checked his watch. It was too early to leave St Peter's so he remained head in hands for another thirty minutes, going over the route again and again. He watched a party of tourists as they were conducted through the cathedral. His eyes never left them as they began to move nearer and nearer to the great door at the west end of the aisle. He needed to time it to perfection.

Suddenly Adam rose and walked quickly down the side aisle reaching the porch only a yard behind the party of tourists. They shielded him out on to the square. Adam ducked under a shop awning at the side of the road, then walked round three sides of the square to avoid the one policeman on duty by the north corner. He crossed the first road as the light turned red and headed up a one-way street. He kept on the inside of the pavement, knowing he had to turn left at the end of the road. Two uniformed policemen came round the corner and walked straight towards him. He jumped into the first shop without looking and turned his back on the pavement.

"Bonjour, monsieur," said a young lady to Adam. *"Vous désirez quelque chose?"* Adam looked around him. Lissome mannequins in knickers and bras with suspenders and long black nylon stockings stood all around him.

"I'm looking for a present for my wife."

The girl smiled. "Perhaps a slip?" she suggested.

"Yes," said Adam, "definitely a slip. Do you have one in burgundy?" he asked, as he half turned to watch the policemen stroll past.

"Yes, I think so, but I'll have to check in the stockroom."

Adam had reached the next street corner long before she had returned with 'just the thing'.

He managed the next few minutes walk without incident and with only two hundred yards to go could already feel his heart thumping as if it was trying to escape from his body. On the final corner there was only one policeman in sight, and he seemed intent on directing traffic. Adam kept his back to the officer as he could now see the garden square that had only shown up on the map as a tiny green blob. On the far side of the road he spotted a Union Jack hanging above a blue door.

Never run the last few yards, especially when it's open ground, his sergeant had told him many times when on patrol in the Malayan jungle. He crossed the road and stood on the edge of the small park, only fifty yards away from safety. A policeman was patrolling aimlessly up the road but Adam suspected that was only because there were several consulates standing adjacent to one another. He watched the officer carefully. It took the man two minutes to reach the end before he turned and continued his leisurely walk back. Adam ducked behind a tree in the corner of the little park and selected another tree on the far side of the road only yards from the Consulate front door that would shield him from the oncoming policeman. He estimated that by walking at a speed that wouldn't attract attention he could cover the last thirty yards in under ten seconds. He waited for the policeman to reach his farthest point.

He checked the Consulate door again, relieved to see a girl go in and a man carrying a briefcase come out on to the street. There seemed to be no guard in sight as the door remained half open. He looked up at the bay window on the first floor. He could see two men staring out at the park as if waiting expectantly for someone to arrive. Lawrence had succeeded. In moments he would be safe. Adam pulled up the collar of his trenchcoat and set off as the cathedral clock behind him struck eleven. The policeman was now a few paces from reaching his farthest point but still walking in the opposite direction. Adam crossed the road at a measured stride. When he reached the centre of the row he had to stop suddenly to let a car pass by. The policeman turned to start his journey back.

For several seconds Adam remained motionless in the broad street as he stared at the tree he had selected to shield him if the policeman turned before he could reach the front door. He took a confident pace towards the British Consulate. A tall man of athletic build, his head covered in a stubble of short fair hair, stepped out to greet him.

Adam would not have recognised him but for the eyes.

PART TWO

10 DOWNING STREET
LONDON SW1

June 17, 1966

CHAPTER TWELVE

10 DOWNING STREET, LONDON SW1 *June 17, 1966*

When Sir Morris Youngfield left the Prime Minister he still was unable to work out why the possession of any icon could be that important.

Leaving Number 10 behind him, Sir Morris marched quickly into the Foreign Office courtyard and within moments was stepping out of the lift on the seventh floor. When he walked into his office, Tessa, his secretary, was laying out some papers for him.

"I want a D4 assembled immediately," he said to the woman who had served him so loyally for fourteen years. "And ask Commander Busch to join the team."

Tessa raised her eyebrows but Sir Morris ignored her silent comment as he knew he couldn't hope to get to the bottom of this one without the co-operation of the Americans. Once more Sir Morris considered the Prime Minister's instructions. Harold Wilson hadn't needed to explain that he didn't get that many transatlantic calls from Lyndon Johnson seeking his help.

But why a Russian icon of an English saint?

* * *

As Romanov moved towards him, Adam took a pace backwards from the tramlines to allow the tramcar to pass between them. When the tram had passed Adam was no longer to be seen. Romanov snarled at such an amateur trick, sprinted the twenty yards necessary to catch up with the tram and to the astonishment of the passengers, leapt on. He began checking over the faces row by row.

Adam waited for the tramcar to travel another twenty yards before he emerged from behind a tree on the far side of the road. He felt confident he could reach the safety of the Consulate door long before Heidi's killer could hope to return. He checked the other side of the road and swore under his breath. The policeman patrolling was now only a few paces from the Consulate and heading relentlessly towards it. Adam looked back at the tram which had just been passed by another heading towards him. To his dismay, he saw his adversary leap from one platform to the other with the agility of a top-class gymnast. With the policeman now only yards from the Consulate door Adam was left with no choice but to retreat and sprint back up the one-way street. After fifty yards he glanced over his shoulder. The man he knew only as Rosenbaum couldn't have looked less like a helpless old man as he started running towards him.

Adam jumped between the cars and buses and dodged around the milling pedestrians as he tried to lengthen the fifty yards' distance between them. At the first crossroad he saw a plump lady coming out of a phone box a few yards away. He changed direction quickly and leapt into the empty box, crouching into the far corner. The door slowly squelched shut. Rosenbaum came hurtling round the corner and was twenty yards past the box before he realised that Adam had shot back out and down the road in the opposite direction. Adam knew he had at least five seconds before Rosenbaum could hope to see which direction he had chosen. One and two and three and four and five, he counted as he ran along the road. He then checked right, before mounting three steps and pushing through some swing doors. He found himself in front of a small counter, behind which sat a young woman holding a small wad of tickets.

"*Deux francs, monsieur,*" said the girl. Adam looked at the little box, quickly took out two francs and made his way down the long dark passage and through another set of swing doors. He stood at the back waiting for his eyes to become accustomed to the dark. It was the first performance of the day and the cinema was nearly empty. Adam chose a seat on the end of a row that was an equal distance from both exits.

He stared at the screen, thankful that the movie had just begun, because he needed some time to formulate a plan. Whenever the screen was bright enough he checked the little red road on the map, and then using the top of his thumb as a one-inch ruler, he was able to estimate that the nearest border into France was only eight miles away at Ferney-Voltaire. From there he could travel to Paris via Dijon and be back home almost as quickly as it would take him to sit through *Exodus* a second time. Having decided on his route, the next problem for Adam was how to travel. He dismissed all forms of public transport and settled on hiring a car. He remained in his seat during the interval to double-check the routes. The moment Paul Newman reappeared on the screen, he folded up the map and left the cinema by the exit which had been least used during the past four hours.

*   *   *

195

When Sir Morris entered the room for the meeting of the 'Northern Department', he found the rest of the D4 were already assembled, and familiarising themselves with the files that had been presented to them only an hour before.

He glanced round the table at the specially selected D4, all hand-picked men but only one of them did he consider his equal. And it wasn't the old war-horse Alec Snell who had served at the Foreign Office longer than any of them and was touching his moustache nervously as he waited for Sir Morris to take his seat. Next to him sat Brian Matthews, known in the Department as the 'well-balanced man': a grammar school boy with a double first and a chip on both shoulders. Opposite him was Commander Ralph Busch, the CIA representative with a short fuse, who after five years attached to the Embassy in Grosvenor Square considered himself more British than the British, and even imitated the Foreign Office style of dress to prove it. At the far end of the table, Sir Morris's second in command, who some said was a little too young, although everyone except Tessa had forgotten that Sir Morris had held his job at the same age.

The four members of the committee stopped talking once Sir Morris had settled in his seat at the head of the table.

"Gentlemen," he began – the only lady present being Tessa, whose existence he rarely acknowledged – "the Prime Minister has given this D4 his full blessing. And he requires detailed reports to be sent to him every twelve hours, wherever he is, and at any time of the night or day if there should be any unexpected development. So, as you can see, there is no time to waste. This particular D4 has co-opted as part of its team a liaison officer from the CIA, Commander Ralph

Busch. I have worked with Commander Busch several times over the past five years and I am delighted that the American Embassy has chosen him to represent them."

The man seated on Sir Morris's right bowed slightly. At five feet nine inches, with broad, muscular shoulders and a neat black beard, he looked every inch the sailor whom Player's cigarettes were always trying to please. Indeed, a sailor wouldn't have been a bad guess because Busch had been a commander in PT boats during the Second World War.

"From the latest reports I have received," Sir Morris continued, opening the file in front of him, "it appears that Scott never reached the Consulate this morning, despite our request for the police to have no more than a token force on duty within two hundred yards of the park.

"Since our sketchy information yesterday, BEA have confirmed," said Sir Morris consulting a note in front of him, "that Scott received a call from Roget et Cie while he was at the airport. After considerable pressure from our Ambassador and Interpol we have learned from Mr Roget that the purpose of Scott's visit to the bank was to pick up an unknown bequest from a Mr Emmanuel Rosenbaum. Further checking shows that a Mr Rosenbaum arrived in Zurich yesterday morning and travelled on to Geneva in the afternoon. He left his hotel first thing this morning and has subsequently vanished from the face of the earth. None of this would be of any great significance if Mr Rosenbaum had not boarded the aeroplane to Zurich from –" Sir Morris couldn't resist a short dramatic pause "– Moscow. I think it is not unreasonable therefore to assume that Mr Rosenbaum, whoever he is, works directly or indirectly for the KGB.

"The KGB, as we know to our cost, is well serviced in Geneva, by a large number of East Europeans working under the guise of the United Nations for ILO and WHO, all with the necessary diplomatic status they need to carry out undercover work. What still remains a mystery to me is why Mr Rosenbaum should be willing to kill two innocent people for a relatively obscure icon. That brings my report up to date. But perhaps you have come up with something new," said Sir Morris turning to his Number Two.

Lawrence Pemberton looked up from his end of the table. "Since our meeting this morning, Sir Morris," he began, "I have spoken to Scott's sister, his mother and a firm of solicitors in Appleshaw who administered his father's will. It transpires that Scott was left with nothing of any real importance in the will apart from an envelope which his mother says contained a letter from Reichsmarshal Hermann Goering." There was an immediate buzz around the table until Sir Morris tapped his knuckle on the desk.

"Do we have any idea of the contents of Goering's letter?" asked Sir Morris.

"The whole letter, no, sir. But one of our examination entrants, a Mr Nicholas Wainwright, was asked by Scott to translate what we now believe was a paragraph from the letter because later Wainwright asked the examination board if it was part of his test." Lawrence extracted a piece of paper from the file in front of him and read out the paragraph:

During the year you cannot have failed to notice that I have been receiving from one of the guards a regular supply of Havana cigars – one of the few pleasures I have been permitted, despite my incarceration. The cigars themselves have also served another purpose, as each one contained a capsule with a small amount of poison. Enough to allow me to survive my trial, while ensuring that I shall cheat the executioner.

"That's all?" said Sir Morris.

"I'm afraid so," said Lawrence, "although I believe it confirms what Scott told me last night was his reason for travelling to Geneva. There is no doubt in my mind that the package he went to pick up contained the icon of St George and the Dragon left to his father by Goering."

"St George and the Dragon," said Matthews interrupting, "but that's the icon that half of the KGB have been searching for during the past two weeks and my Department has been trying to find out why."

"And what have you come up with?" asked Sir Morris.

"Very little," admitted Matthews. "But we began to assume that it must be a decoy because the Tsar's icon of St George and the Dragon hangs in the Winter Palace at Leningrad and has done so for three hundred years."

"Anything else?" asked Sir Morris.

"Only that the section leader in search of the icon is Alex Romanov," said Matthews.

Snell gave out a low whistle. "Well, at least we know we're dealing with the First Division," he said.

There was a long silence before Sir Morris offered, "One thing is clear. We have to get to Scott first and must assume that it's Romanov we're up against. So what are we doing about it?"

"As much as we can get away with," said Lawrence. "Along with the Americans we have seventeen men operatives in Geneva, all of them trying to find Scott."

"The Swiss police have a thousand doing the same job, though heaven knows whose side they imagine they're on," added Snell.

Lawrence chipped back in. "And it's been almost impossible to convince them that Scott is not in any way responsible for the two murders. So we may have to get him out without relying on their co-operation."

"But what do you imagine would be the outcome if Romanov or this Rosenbaum, who must also be part of the KGB, manages to get to Scott before we do?" asked Matthews.

"A civilian up against one of the Russians' most ruthless agents. That's all we need," said Commander Busch.

Lawrence inclined his head towards the American. "I've known Adam for most of my life. The irony of his particular predicament is that it was I who, without his knowledge, recommended that he should be interviewed for a place in the Northern Department. It was my intention that he should join us as soon as he had completed his course as a trainee. If Romanov or any of his cohorts come face to face with Scott they'd better remember that he was awarded a Military Cross when faced with a thousand Chinese."

"But if it turned out to be Romanov," asked Snell, "would Scott be able to kill him?"

"I would have said no before Rosenbaum murdered his girlfriend," said Lawrence.

"I wouldn't be confident of his chances even then," said Busch.

"Neither would I," added Matthews.

"That's because you don't know Adam Scott," said Lawrence.

Matthews lowered his eyes in order to avoid a clash with his boss. His boss. Ten years his junior. A shortlist of two and they had chosen another Oxbridge man to be Under-Secretary. Matthews knew that as far as the Foreign Office was concerned, he had gone to the wrong school and the wrong university. He should have taken his father's advice and joined the police force. There were no class barriers there, and he would probably have been a chief superintendent by now.

Sir Morris ignored the little outburst which had become fairly common since he had selected Pemberton to leapfrog the older man.

"Are we allowed to know," interrupted Snell, looking straight at Busch, "why a relatively obscure icon is of such disproportionate importance to both Russia and the United States?"

"We are as mystified as you," said the American. "All we can add to your current information, is that two weeks ago the Russians deposited gold bullion in New York to the value of over seven hundred million dollars without any explanation. We are, of course, not certain at the moment there is any connection."

"Seven hundred million dollars?" said Sir Morris. "You could buy half the countries in the United Nations for that."

"And every icon that has ever been painted," said Matthews.

"Let's get down to what we actually know, and stop guessing at what might be," said Sir Morris turning back to his Number Two. "What's the exact IA position?"

Lawrence undid a folder with a red band around it, the words 'Immediate Action' printed across the top in black. He did not need to refer to it, but still glanced down from time to time to check he had not forgotten anything. "As I have already briefed you, we have seventeen agents in the field and the Americans are flying a further twelve into Geneva today. With the Russians and the Swiss roaming the city like knights of the round table in search of the Holy Grail, I can only believe that someone will come across Scott fairly soon. One of our biggest problems, as I explained, is that the Swiss are unwilling to co-operate. As far as they are concerned, Scott is a common criminal on the run and should they get to him first they have made it clear they will not allow him diplomatic immunity.

"We, as well as the Swiss police, and undoubtedly the Russians," continued Lawrence, "have started checking out all the obvious places: hotels, guest houses, restaurants, airports, car hire companies, even lavatories, and we remain in constant touch with every one of our agents on the ground. So if Scott suddenly appears out of nowhere we should be able to go to his aid at a moment's notice." Lawrence looked up to observe that one of the team was taking down all the details. "Added to that, the Post Office are intercepting every call made to Barclays DCO from Geneva. If Scott does try to get in contact with me again at the bank or at my flat it will be put through to this office automatically," he said.

"Is he aware that you work for the Service?" asked Snell, putting a hand through his dark hair.

"No. He, like my dear mother, still thinks I'm a bank official in the International Department of Barclays DCO. But it won't be long before he works out that that's only a front. Unlike my mother, he doesn't always believe everything I tell him and after our conversation last night he is bound to have become suspicious."

"Do we have anything else to go on?" Sir Morris asked, looking up at Lawrence.

"Not a lot more at the moment, sir. We are doing

everything possible, remembering this is not a home match; but I still anticipate that the exercise will be over one way or another within twenty-four hours. Because of that I have requested overnight facilities to be set up in the building should you feel we need them. When you return after dinner you will find beds already made up in your offices."

"No one will be going out to dinner tonight," said Sir Morris.

The cinema door opened on to the busy pavement and Adam slipped into the main stream of commuters who were now returning home for dinner. As he kept walking he made certain of as little head movement as possible but his eyes never stayed still, checking everything within 180 degrees. After he had covered three blocks, he spotted a red Avis sign swinging in the afternoon breeze on the far side of the road. He safely reconnoitred the crowded crossing, but once his foot touched the far pavement he froze on the spot. Just ahead of him in the fast, jostling crowd stood a man in a raincoat. He was continually looking around, while making no attempt to walk in either direction. Was he one of Rosenbaum's men, the police, or even British? There was no way of telling whose side he was on. Adam's eyes didn't leave the man as he took out an intercom and, putting it to his mouth, whispered into it. "Nothing to report, sir. Still no sign of our man, and I haven't seen any of the KGB either."

Adam, unable to hear the words, switched into a side road and almost knocked over a boy selling papers. '*Le soldat anglais toujours à Genève*' the headline blared. Quickly he crossed another road, where he came to a stop again, this time behind a marble statue in the centre of a small patch of grass. He stared at the building in front of him but he knew there would be no point in his trying to hide there. He started to move away as a large, empty touring coach drew up and parked in front of the block. Smart blue lettering along the side of the coach proclaimed 'The Royal Philharmonic Orchestra'. Adam watched as some musicians walked out of the front door and climbed on to the coach carrying their instrument cases of assorted lengths and widths. One was even lugging a large kettle drum which he deposited in the boot of the coach. As the musicians continued to stream out of the hotel Adam decided he wouldn't get a better opportunity. When the next group came through the double doors he walked quickly forward and stepped into the middle of them before anyone could have spotted him. He then continued on past them through the open hotel door. The first thing he spotted in the crowded lobby was a double bass leaning against the wall. He glanced at the label around the neck of the unwieldy case. 'Robin Beresford.'

Adam walked over to the counter and gestured to the clerk. "I need my room key quickly – I've left my bow upstairs and now I'm holding everyone up."

"Yes, sir. What room number?" asked the clerk.

"I think it's 312, or was that yesterday?" said Adam.

"What name, sir?"

"Beresford – Robin Beresford."

The clerk handed him key 612. His only comment was: "You were three floors out."

"Thank you," said Adam. As he left the counter, he turned to check that the receptionist was already dealing with another customer. He walked smartly over to the lift which was disgorging still more musicians. Once it had emptied he stepped in, pressed the button for the sixth floor, and waited. He felt exhilarated as the lift doors eventually slid across and he was alone for the first time in several hours. When the doors opened again he was relieved to find there was no one standing in the corridor. He made his way quickly along the passage to room 612.

As he turned the key and opened the door he said firmly in as good a French accent as he could manage, "Room service", but as no one responded, he stepped in and locked the door behind him. An unopened suitcase had been left in one corner. Adam checked the label. Obviously Mr Beresford hadn't even had time to unpack. Adam checked the room, but there was no other sign of the hotel guest apart from a piece of paper on the side table. It was a typed itinerary:

'European Tour: Geneva, Frankfurt, Berlin, Amsterdam, London.

'Geneva, Bus 5.00 to Concert Hall rehearsal 6.00, Concert performance 7.30, encores 10.00.

'Programme: Mozart's Third Horn Concerto, First Movement, Brahms's Second Symphony, Schubert's Unfinished Symphony.'

Adam looked at his watch: by the time Robin Beresford had completed the 'Unfinished Symphony' he would be over the border; but he still felt safe to remain in Room 612 until it was dark.

He picked up the phone by the bed and dialled room service. "Beresford, 612," he announced, and ordered himself some dinner before going into the bathroom. On the side of the basin was propped a little plastic bag with the words 'Compliments of the Management' printed across it. Inside Adam found soap, a tiny toothbrush, toothpaste and a plastic razor.

He had just finished shaving when he heard a knock on the door and someone calling "Room service". Adam quickly covered his face with lather again and put on a hotel dressing gown before he opened the door. The waiter set up a table without giving Adam a second look. When he had finished his task he enquired, "Will you sign the bill, please, sir?"

He handed Adam a slip of paper. He signed it 'Robin Beresford' and added a fifteen per cent tip.

"Thank you," said the waiter and left. As soon as the door closed behind him Adam's eyes settled on the feast of onion soup, rump steak with green beans and potatoes, and finally a raspberry sorbet. A bottle of house wine had been uncorked and needed only to be poured. He suddenly didn't feel that hungry.

He still couldn't accept what he had gone through. If only he hadn't pressed Heidi into joining him on this unnecessary journey. A week before she hadn't even known him and now he was responsible for her death. He would have to explain to her parents what had happened to their only daughter. But before Adam could face them he still had to come up with some explanation for the things he hadn't yet begun to understand. Not least the unimportant icon. Unimportant?

After he had half finished the meal he wheeled the trolley out into the corridor and placed the 'Do not disturb' sign on the door. Once back in the bedroom he stared out of the window over the city. The sun looked as if it had another hour allocated for Geneva. Adam lay down on the bed and began to consider what had happened in the last twenty-four hours of his life.

"Antarctic is in possession of an icon of St George and the Dragon. But we know from our files of that period that that particular icon was destroyed when the Grand Duke of Hesse's plane crashed over Belgium in 1937."

"That may well be what is written in your files," said the man on the other end of the phone. "But what if your information at Langley turns out to be wrong and the icon was found by Goering but not returned to the Grand Duke?"

"But Stalin confirmed at Yalta that the icon and its contents had been destroyed in the plane crash. He agreed to make no protest while he was not in possession of the original document. After all, that was the reason Roosevelt appeared to be gaining so little at the time while Stalin was getting so much in return. Can't you remember the fuss Churchill made?"

"I certainly can because he had worked out that it wasn't Britain who was going to benefit from such a decision."

"But if the Russians have now discovered the existence of the original icon?"

"You are suggesting they might also get their hands on the original document?"

"Precisely. So you must be sure to get to Antarctic before the Russians do, or for that matter, the Foreign Office."

"But I'm part of the Foreign Office team."

"And that's precisely what we want the Foreign Office to go on believing."

"And who's been sleeping in my bed, said Mother Bear."

Adam woke with a start. Looking down at him was a girl who held a double bass firmly by the neck with one hand and a bow in the other. She was nearly six foot and certainly weighed considerably more than Adam. She had long, gleaming red hair that was in such contrast to the rest of her that it was as if the Maker had started at the top and quickly lost interest.

She wore a white blouse and a black flowing skirt that stopped an inch above the ground.

"Who are you?" asked Adam, startled.

"I'm not Goldilocks, that's for sure," parried the girl. "More to the point, who are you?"

Adam hesitated. "If I told you, you wouldn't believe me."

"I can't imagine why not," she said. "You don't look like Prince Charles or Elvis Presley to me, so go on, try me."

"I'm Adam Scott."

"Am I meant to swoon and run to your side, or scream and run away?" she enquired.

Adam suddenly realised that the girl couldn't have watched television or read a paper for at least two days. He switched tactics. "I thought my friend Robin Beresford was meant to be booked into this room," he said confidently.

"And so did I until I saw you on my bed."

"You're Robin Beresford?"

"You're quite sharp for someone who has just woken up."

"But Robin?"

"It's not my fault my father wanted a boy," she said. "And you still haven't explained what you're doing on my bed."

"Is there any hope of you listening to me for five minutes without continually interrupting?" asked Adam.

"Yes, but don't bother with any more fairy stories," said Robin. "My father was a born liar, and by the time I was twelve I could see through him like a pane of glass."

"I should have a seat if I were you," said Adam. "This may take longer than the average double bass accompaniment."

"I'll remain on my feet, if you don't mind," said Robin. "At least until the first lie."

"Suit yourself. What would you like first? The good news or the bad news?"

"Try me on the bad news," said Robin.

"The Swiss police want to arrest me and . . ."

"What for?" interrupted Robin.

"Murder," said Scott.

"What's the good news?" she asked.

"I'm innocent."

Romanov stood in the Ambassador's office and rested his fingers on the table. "I blame myself," he said very quietly, "even more than I blame any of you. I underestimated the Englishman. He's good, and if any of you are hoping to kill him before I get to him you'll have to be *very* good." No one assembled in the Ambassador's office that night was disposed to disagree with the Comrade Major. Romanov paused to study the group of men who had been flown in from several Eastern satellites at short notice. All with long records of service to the State but only one of them, Valchek, was known to Romanov personally and he worked too closely with Zaborski to be trusted. Romanov had already faced the fact that only a few of them were acquainted with Geneva. He could only pray that the British and Americans were suffering from the same problem.

His eyes swept around the room. The Swiss police had the best chance of finding Scott and they weren't being at all helpful, he thought ruefully. However, Romanov had been pleased to learn from their head man stationed in Geneva that the Swiss had also refused to co-operate with the British or the Americans.

"Comrades," he said, the moment they had all

settled, "there is no need to remind you that we have been entrusted with a vital assignment for the Motherland." He paused to check if any of the faces registered the slightest suggestion of cynicism. Satisfied, he continued, "We will therefore maintain a tight surveillance over Geneva in case Scott is still holed up somewhere in the city. My own guess is that, like all amateurs, he is, and will wait until it's dark, perhaps even first light, before he makes a run for the nearest border. The French border will be his most obvious choice. Despite going to war against the Germans twice in the past fifty years, the English have never bothered to master the German language, although a few of them can manage to speak passable French. So he's more likely to feel safe in that country. It also offers him the opportunity to cross only one border before reaching the coast.

"If he's stupid enough to try and leave by plane he will find we have the airports covered; if by train, we have the stations manned. But my guess is still that he will try to escape by motor vehicle.

"I shall therefore take five men to the French border with me while Major Valchek will take another five to Basle to cover the German crossing point. The rest of you will remain on surveillance in Geneva. Those of you who have just arrived will relieve those agents who are in the field already. And don't expect Scott to be roaming around looking like a tourist on holiday. Study your picture of the Englishman carefully and even be prepared for him to try and get away with some amateur disguise."

Romanov paused for effect. "The man who brings me the Tsar's icon need have no fear for his future prosperity when we return home." Hopeful expressions appeared on their faces for the first time as Romanov pulled out the duplicate icon from his coat pocket and held it high above his head for all to see.

"When you find the original of this your task will be completed. Study it carefully, Comrades, because no photographs are being issued. And remember," Romanov added, "the only difference between this and Scott's icon is that his has a small silver crown embedded in the back of the frame. Once you see the crown you will know that you have found the missing masterpiece."

Romanov put the icon back in his pocket and looked down at the silent men.

"Remember that Scott is good but he's not that good."

CHAPTER THIRTEEN

"You're not bad, Scott, not bad at all," said Robin, who had remained standing by the double bass throughout Adam's story. "Either you're one hell of a liar, or I've lost my touch." Adam smiled up at the massive girl, who made the bow she was holding in her right hand look like a toothpick.

"Am I permitted to see this icon, or am I just supposed to take your word for it?"

Adam jumped off the bed and pulled out the package containing the Tsar's icon from the map pocket of his trenchcoat. Robin put her double bass up against the wall and leaving the bow propped against it, lowered herself into the only chair in the room.

Adam handed the icon over to her. For some time, she stared at the face of St George without making any comment. "It's magnificent," she said at last. "And I can understand anyone wanting to possess it. But no painting could be worth the tragedy and trouble you've had to go through."

"I agree it's inexplicable," said Adam. "But Rosenbaum or whatever his real name is has been willing to kill twice to get his hands on the piece, and he's already convinced me that as long as I am in possession of the icon then I'll be the next in line."

213

Robin continued to stare at the tiny pieces of gold, red, blue and yellow that made up St George and the Dragon.

"No other clues?" she asked, looking up.

"Only the letter given to my father by Goering."

Robin turned the painting over. "What does that mean?" she asked, pointing to the tiny silver crown embedded in the wood.

"That proves it was once owned by a Tsar, according to the man from Sotheby's. And greatly enhances its value, he assured me."

"Still couldn't be worth killing for," said Robin. She handed the icon back to Adam. "So what other secret is St George keeping to himself?"

Adam shrugged and frowned, having asked himself the same question again and again since Heidi's death. He returned the silent saint to his trenchcoat.

"What was to have been your plan if you had stayed awake?" asked Robin. "Other than making the bed?"

Adam smiled. "I hoped to call Lawrence again once I could be sure he had returned home and check if he had any more news for me. If he wasn't back, or couldn't help, I was going to hire a car and try to get across the Swiss border to France and then on to England. I felt sure that between Rosenbaum and his men and the Swiss police they would have had all the airports and stations fully covered."

"No doubt Rosenbaum will have also thought that much out as well, if he's half as good as you claim," said Robin. "So we'd better try and get in touch with your friend Lawrence and see if he's come up with any bright ideas." She pushed herself up out of the chair and walked across to the phone.

"You don't have to get yourself involved," said Adam hesitantly.

"I am involved," said Robin. "And I can tell you it's far more exciting than Schubert's Unfinished. Once I've got your friend on the line I'll pass him over to you and then no one will realise who's phoning." Adam told her the number of the flat and she asked the girl on the switchboard to connect her.

Adam checked his watch: eleven forty. Surely Lawrence would be home by now? The phone didn't complete its first two rings before Robin heard a man's voice on the line. She immediately handed the receiver over.

"Hello, who is that?" asked the voice. Adam was reminded how strange he always found it that Lawrence never announced his name.

"Lawrence, it's me."

"Where are you?"

"I'm still in Geneva."

"My clients were waiting for you at eleven o'clock this morning."

"So was Rosenbaum."

"Who is Rosenbaum?"

"A six-foot, fair-haired, blue-eyed monster, who seems determined to kill me."

Lawrence did not speak for some time. "And are you still in possession of our patron saint?"

"Yes, I am," said Adam. "But what can be so important about . . ."

"Put the phone down and ring me back again in three minutes."

The line went dead. Adam couldn't fathom the sudden change in his old friend's manner. What had he missed during those months he had lodged with him? He tried to recall details that he had previously considered unimportant and that Lawrence had so skilfully disguised.

"Is everything all right?" asked Robin, breaking into his thoughts.

"I think so," said Adam, a little mystified. "He wants me to ring back in three minutes. Will that be all right with you?"

"This tour's already lost eight thousand pounds of the taxpayers' money, so what difference can a few international calls make?" she said.

Three minutes later, Robin picked up the receiver and repeated the number. In one ring Lawrence was back on the line.

"Only answer my questions," said Lawrence.

"No, I will not answer your questions," said Adam, becoming increasingly annoyed with Lawrence's manner. "I want one or two of my own answered before you get anything more out of me. Do I make myself clear?"

"Yes," said a more gentle sounding Lawrence.

"Who is Rosenbaum?"

Lawrence didn't immediately reply.

"You'll get nothing further from me until you start telling the truth," said Adam.

"From your description I have every reason to believe Rosenbaum is a Russian agent whose real name is Alex Romanov."

"A Russian agent? But why should a Russian agent want to get his hands on my icon?"

"I don't know," said Lawrence. "We were rather hoping you might be able to tell us."

"Who's we?"

Another long silence.

"Who's we?" repeated Adam. "You can't really expect me to go on believing you work for Barclays DCO."

"I work at the Foreign Office," said Lawrence.

"In what capacity?"

"I am not at liberty . . ."

"Stop being so pompous, Lawrence. In what capacity?"

"I'm the Number Two in a small section that deals in . . ." Lawrence hesitated.

"Espionage I think is the current jargon we laymen are using," said Adam, "and if you want my icon that badly you had better get me out of this mess alive because Romanov is willing to kill for it as I am sure you are aware."

"Where are you?"

"The Richemond Hotel."

"In a public phone box?" asked Lawrence, sounding incredulous.

"No, in a private room."

"But not registered in your name?"

"No, in the name of a friend. A girlfriend."

"Is she with you now?" asked Lawrence.

"Yes," said Adam.

"Damn," said Lawrence. "Right. Don't leave that room until seven a.m., then phone on this number again. That will give me enough time to get everything in place."

"Is that the best you can do?" said Adam, but the phone had already gone dead. "It looks as if I'm stuck with you for the night," he told Robin as he replaced the phone.

"On the contrary, it is I who am stuck with you," said Robin, and disappeared into the bathroom. Adam paced around the room several times before he tested the sofa. Either he had to rest his head on a cushion, balanced on the thin wooden arm, or he had to let his legs dangle over the far end. By the time Robin had come back out clad in a pair of sky-blue pyjamas he had selected the floor as his resting place.

"Not much of a chair, is it?" said Robin. "But then British Intelligence didn't warn me to book a double room." She climbed into the bed and turned out the light. "Very comfortable," were the last words she uttered.

Adam lay down flat on the bedroom floor, using the cushion from the chair as a pillow and a hotel dressing gown as a blanket. He slept intermittently, his mind switching between why the icon could be that important, how Lawrence knew so much about it, and, most immediate, how the hell were they going to get him out of the hotel alive?

Romanov waited patiently for the phone to be picked up.

"Yes," said a voice that he recognised immediately.

"Where is he?" were the only words Romanov uttered. Four words were all he received from Mentor in reply before the phone went dead.

Adam woke with a start an hour before he was due to phone Lawrence back. For nearly forty minutes he lay on the floor with only Robin's steady breathing to remind him he was not alone. Suddenly he became aware of a strange sound coming from the corridor outside – two or three steps, a pause, then whoosh, two or three steps, a pause, another whoosh. Adam raised himself up silently from the floor and crept to the door. The rhythm of Robin's breathing never faltered. Whoosh: it now sounded closer. He picked up a heavy wooden coathanger from the table by the door. He gripped it firmly in his right hand, raised it above his head and waited. Whoosh – and a newspaper shot under the door and the steps moved on. He didn't have to bend down to see that it was his photograph that dominated the front page of the international edition of the *Herald Tribune*.

Adam took the paper into the bathroom, closed the door silently, switched on the light and read the lead article. It was yesterday's story with guarded comments from his old commanding officer and embarrassed silence from his mother. He felt helpless.

He crept up to Robin hoping she wouldn't wake. He stood over her but she didn't stir. He silently picked up the phone and dragged it to the bathroom. He could only just manage to close the door behind him. He dialled the operator and repeated the number.

When the ringing stopped, he immediately said, "Is that you, Lawrence?"

"Yes," came back the reply.

"Things have become much worse now. I'm still holed up in the hotel but my picture is on the front page of every paper."

"I know," said Lawrence. "We tried to prevent it, but yet again the Swiss wouldn't co-operate."

"Then I may as well give myself up to the Swiss," said Adam. "Damn it all, I am innocent."

"No, Adam, in Switzerland you're guilty until proven innocent and you must have worked out by now that you're involved in something far more important than a double murder."

"What could be more important than a double murder when the rest of the world thinks you're the murderer?" asked Adam angrily.

"I can understand exactly how you feel, but your only chance now is to carry out my instructions to the letter and treat with suspicion every other person with whom you come in contact."

"I'm listening," said Adam.

"Just remember everything I say because I am only going to tell you once. The Royal Philharmonic Orchestra are staying in the same hotel as you. They are going on to Frankfurt at ten o'clock this morning. Leave your room at five to ten, join the orchestra in the lobby and then make your way to the front door where you'll find their coach parked. We will have a car waiting for you on the far side of the road. The car is a black Mercedes and you will see a man in grey chauffeur's uniform holding the door open for you. We have already arranged that no other car will be able to park on that side of the road between nine thirty and ten thirty, so you can't mistake it. Just get into the back and wait. There will be another man in the back with you and you will then be driven to the safety of our Consulate. Do you need me to repeat any of that?"

"No," said Adam, "but . . ."

"Good luck," said Lawrence, and the phone went dead.

By seven-thirty he had showered, while Robin remained unrepentant in a deep sleep. Adam envied her; only a twig had to break outside and he was wide awake. Two years of living in the Malayan jungle, never knowing when the Chinese would strike, never being able to sleep for more than two or three hours at a time if one wanted to stay alive, still kept its hold on him.

Robin did not stir for another thirty minutes, during which time Adam sat on the sofa and went over Lawrence's plan in his mind. At ten to eight she finally woke, even then taking several minutes before she was fully conscious. Robin blinked at Adam and a large grin appeared on her face.

"So you didn't murder me while I slept," she said.

"I don't think you'd have noticed if I had," said Adam.

"When your father is an habitual drunk and comes home at all hours of the night, you learn to sleep through anything," she explained, placing both feet firmly on the carpet. "Aren't you meant to have phoned London by now?"

"I already have."

"And what is the master plan to be?" she asked, rubbing her eyes on her way to the bathroom.

"I will be leaving with you," said Adam.

"Most of my one-night stands don't bother to stay that long," she remarked as she closed the bathroom door behind her. He tried to read the paper while the bath was filling up.

"Does that mean we're sharing a room in Frankfurt as well?" she asked a few minutes later when the bathroom door reopened, as if the conversation had never been interrupted.

"No, as soon as we're clear of the hotel I leave you at the coach and make my own way to a car on the far side of the road."

"That sounds more like the men in my life," she said. "But at least we can have a farewell breakfast," she added, picking up the phone. "I'm nuts about kippers. How about you?"

Adam didn't answer. He had begun looking at his watch every few moments. The waiter arrived with breakfast about fifteen minutes later: Adam waited in the bathroom. When he reappeared he showed no interest in the food, so Robin ate four kippers and most of the toast. Nine o'clock passed; a porter took away the breakfast trolley and Robin began to pack. The phone rang and Adam jumped nervously as Robin picked it up.

"Yes, Stephen," she said. "No, I won't need any help with my luggage. Not this time." She put the phone down. "We depart for Frankfurt at ten."

"I know," said Adam.

"We ought to make Lawrence the orchestra manager. He seems to know everything even before it's been decided." Adam had been thinking the same thing. "Well, at least I've found someone to help with my luggage for a change," added Robin.

"I'll carry the double bass for you if you like," offered Adam.

"I'd like to see you try," said Robin. Adam walked over to the large instrument that was propped up in its case against the wall. He tried the double bass from all angles but couldn't manage to do better than hold it off the floor for a few moments. Robin joined him and with one flick she had the stem on her shoulder and the instrument balanced perfectly. She walked up and down the bedroom demonstrating her prowess.

"It's a matter of skill, my puny friend," she said. "And to think I believed all those stories last night about your outrunning half the Swiss police force to spend a night with me."

Adam tried to laugh. He picked up his trenchcoat, checking the icon was zipped up. But he couldn't stop himself shaking from a combination of fear and anticipation.

Robin looked at him. "Don't worry," she said gently. "It will all be over in a few minutes' time." Then she saw the paper on the floor. "I should sue them if I were you."

"Why?" asked Adam.

"You're a lot better looking than that." Adam smiled and walked across, and just managed to get his arms round her to give her a hug.

"Thanks for everything," he said. "But now we have to go."

"You're sounding more like one of my lovers all the time," said Robin, mournfully.

Adam picked up her suitcase while Robin jerked up the stem of the double bass onto her shoulder. She opened the door and checked the corridor: two of her colleagues from the RPO were waiting by the lift, otherwise there was nobody else in sight. Robin and Adam joined the two musicians and after "Good mornings" no one spoke until the lift doors slid open. Once the doors were closed Robin's colleagues couldn't resist taking a closer look at Adam. At first Adam was anxious they had recognised him from the newspaper. Then he realised that it was who Robin had spent the night with that fascinated them. Robin gave him a lewd wink, as if she fully intended to live off this one for a long time. For his part Adam ducked behind the double bass and remained in the corner breathing deeply in and out as the lift trundled down towards the ground floor. The doors sprang open and Robin waited for her two colleagues to leave before she shielded Adam as best she could all the way across the foyer. His eyes were now fixed on the front door. He could see the bus taking up most of the road and several members of the orchestra were already clambering on. One more minute and he should be safely away. He watched as the drums were packed carefully in the large boot.

"Oh, God, I forgot," said Robin. "I'm meant to put this in the boot at the back of the bus."

"Do it later," said Adam sharply. "Just keep going until you reach the coach door." Then he saw the car on the far side of the road. He felt light with relief, almost dizzy. The car door was being held open for

223

him. Another man was seated in the back just as Lawrence had promised. Ten o'clock struck somewhere in the distance. The man dressed in chauffeur's uniform, hat pulled down over his forehead, stood by the open door. He turned towards the hotel in anticipation. Adam stared towards him as the man's eyes scanned the hotel entrance. The uniform wasn't a good fit.

"Into the bus," hissed Adam.

"With this thing? They'll kill me," said Robin.

"If you don't, he'll kill me."

Robin obeyed, despite the adverse comments as she lumbered down the aisle with her double bass screening Adam from the gaze of anyone on the far side of the road. He wanted to be sick.

Adam slumped into a seat next to Robin with the double bass between them.

"Which one?" she whispered.

"In the chauffeur's uniform."

Robin glanced out of the window. "He may be evil, but he's damned good looking," she said, inconsequentially.

Adam looked disbelieving. Robin smiled apologetically.

"Everybody's in," called a man from the front of the bus, "and I've double-checked and we seem to have one extra."

Oh, my God, thought Adam, he's going to throw me off the bus.

"My brother," shouted Robin from the back. "He's only travelling with us for part of the journey."

"Oh, that's okay then," said the manager. "Well, let's be on our way." He turned to the driver.

"He's started looking at the bus," said Robin.

"But I don't think he can see you. No, you're all right, he's now turned his gaze back to the hotel entrance."

"I didn't realise you had a brother," said the manager, who was suddenly standing beside them. The coach moved slowly out of the square.

"Neither did I until this morning," mumbled Robin, still looking out of the window. She turned and faced her boss. "Yes, I forgot to mention to you that he might be in Switzerland at the same time as the orchestra. I do hope it's not going to cause a problem."

"Not at all," said the manager.

"Adam, this is Stephen Grieg who, as you will already have gathered, is the orchestra's manager."

"Are you a musician as well?" asked Stephen as he shook Adam's hand.

"No, I can truthfully say that I have never been able to master any instrument," said Adam.

"He's tone deaf," butted in Robin. "Takes after my father. He's in tyres, actually," she continued, enjoying herself.

"Oh, really. Which company are you with?" enquired Stephen.

"I'm with Pirelli," said Adam, mentioning the first tyre company that came into his head.

"Pirelli, the company that produces those fabulous calendars?"

"What's so special about their calendars?" asked Robin innocently. "If you want one I'm sure Adam can get you one."

"Oh, that would be great," said Stephen. "I hope it won't put you to too much trouble."

"No trouble at all," said Robin, leaning over Adam conspiratorially. "Actually, to let you in on a little family secret there is a rumour at HQ that Adam will soon be joining the main board. The youngest member in the company's history, you know."

"How impressive," said the manager, taking a closer look at the orchestra's latest recruit.

"Where shall I send the calendar?" bleated out Adam.

"Oh, direct to the RPO. No need to tell you the address, is there?"

"In a brown envelope, no doubt," said Robin. "And don't worry about the year. It's not the dates that he gets worked up about."

"What time are we expecting to reach Frankfurt, Stephen?" shouted a voice from the front. "Must leave you now," said the manager. "Thanks for the promise of a calendar. Robin's right, of course – any year will do."

"Who taught you to spin a yarn like that?" asked Adam, as soon as he was out of earshot.

"My father," said Robin. "You should have heard him at his best. In a class of his own. The problem was my mother still believed every word."

"He would have been proud of you today."

"Now we've found out what you do for a living," said Robin, "may we learn what's next on the agenda for the youngest director of Pirelli?"

Adam smiled. "I've started trying to reason like Rosenbaum, and I think he'll stay in Geneva for at least an hour, two at the most, so with luck I'll get a fifty-mile start on him." He unfolded the map across the two seats.

His finger ran along the road the bus was travelling on, and it was Robin who spoke first.

"That means you could make Zurich airport before he has any chance of catching up with you."

"Perhaps," said Adam, "but that would be too much

of a risk. Whoever Rosenbaum is," he went on, abiding by Lawrence's request to be cautious by not letting Robin into his secret, "we now know for certain that he has a professional organisation behind him so I must expect the airports to be the first place he will have covered. And don't forget the Swiss police are still on the lookout for me as well."

"So why don't you come on to Frankfurt with us?" asked Robin. "I can't believe you'll have any trouble from Stephen."

"I've thought about that already but discounted it also as too great a risk," said Adam.

"Why?"

"Because, when Rosenbaum has had time to think about it," said Adam, "the one thing he'll remember is this bus. Once he's found out the direction we're heading in he's sure to come after us."

Robin's eyes returned to the map. "So you'll need to decide where and when to get off."

"Exactly," whispered Adam. "I can risk sixty to seventy miles, but not a lot further."

Robin's finger ran along the little road. "About here," she said, her finger stopping on a little town called Solothurn.

"Looks about the right distance."

"But once you're off the bus what will you do for transport?"

"I've little choice but to walk or thumb lifts – unless I pinch another car."

"With your luck, Rosenbaum will be the one person who stops to pick you up."

"Yes, I've thought about that as well," said Adam. "I would have to find a long stretch of road where I can see without being seen for about one hundred

227

yards, and then thumb lifts only from British cars or cars with British number plates."

"They taught you a trick or two in the army, didn't they?" said Robin. "But how do you intend to cross the frontier with your passport?"

"That's one of the many problems I haven't yet come up with a solution for."

"If you decide to stay with us," said Robin, "it wouldn't be a problem."

"Why?" asked Adam.

"Because whenever we cross a border they only count the number of people on the bus and the number of passports, and as long as they tally the customs officials don't bother to check everyone individually. After all, why should they? The RPO is not exactly an unknown quantity. All I would have to do is add your passport to the bundle and mention it to the manager."

"It's a clever idea but it's not on. If Rosenbaum caught up with me while I'm still on this bus then I would be left with no escape route."

Robin was silent for a moment. "Once you're on your own will you contact Lawrence again?"

"Yes. I've got to let him know what happened this morning, because whoever he's dealing with must have a direct line to Rosenbaum."

"Could it be Lawrence himself?"

"Never," said Adam.

"Your loyalty is touching," said Robin, turning to look at him, "but what you actually mean is you don't want to believe it could be Lawrence."

"What are you getting at?"

"Like my mother didn't want to believe that my father was a liar and a drunk. So she turned a blind eye to his little foibles. You know even when he dropped dead of cirrhosis of the liver, her only words were, 'strange for a man who never drank'."

Adam thought about his relationship with Lawrence and wondered if you could know someone for twenty years and really not know them at all.

"Just be wary how much you let him know," advised Robin.

They sat in silence as Adam checked the map and went over all the different possible routes he could take once he had left the bus. He decided to aim for the German border and take the long route back to England, from Hamburg or Bremerhaven, rather than the shorter, more obvious route via Calais or Ostend.

"Got it," said Robin suddenly.

"Got what?" said Adam, looking up from the map.

"How we solve your passport problem," she murmured.

Adam glanced at her hopefully. "If you let me have your passport," she explained, "I'll substitute it for the member of the orchestra who most resembles you. No one will notice anything strange at our end until we're back home in Britain on Sunday night."

"Not a bad idea, if there is anyone who remotely resembles me."

"We'll have to see what we can do," said Robin. She sat bolt upright, her eyes moving slowly from person to person. By the time she had scanned all those in the bus from front to back, a small smile appeared on her face. "There are two of our lot who bear a passable resemblance to you. One is about five years older and the other is four inches shorter, but you go on working out the safest way of escape while I carry out some research. Let me have your passport," she said. Adam handed it over and then watched Robin walk up to the front and sit next to the manager. He was chatting to the driver about the most convenient place to stop for lunch.

"I need to check something in my passport," Robin broke in. "Sorry to bother you."

"No bother. You'll find them all under my seat in a plastic bag," he said, and continued his conversation with the driver.

Robin bent down and started to shuffle through the passports as if searching for her own. She picked out the two she had considered as possible substitutes and compared the photographs. The shorter man's photo looked nothing like Adam. The older man's was at least five years out of date but could have passed for Adam as long as the officials didn't study the date of birth too carefully. She bundled up the passports, placing Adam's in the middle. She then put them back in the plastic bag and returned the bag under the manager's seat.

Robin made her way back to her seat. "Take a look at yourself," she said, slipping the passport over to Adam. He studied the photo.

"Other than the moustache, not a bad likeness, and it's certainly my best chance in the circumstances. But what will happen when you return to London and they find out my passport has been substituted?"

"You'll be back in England long before us," said Robin. "So put this one in an envelope with the calendar and send it direct to the RPO in Wigmore Street, W1, and I'll see that they return yours." Adam vowed to himself that if he ever got back to London, he would become a life subscriber to the Friends of the Royal Philharmonic.

"That seems to have solved one of your problems."

"For the moment at least," said Adam. "I only wish I could take you with me for the rest of the trip."

Robin smiled. "Frankfurt, Berlin, Amsterdam—just in case you get bored. I wouldn't mind meeting up with Rosenbaum. But this time face to face."

"He might just have met his match," said Adam.

"Can I have a last look at the icon?" Robin asked, ignoring the comment.

Adam bent down to retrieve his trenchcoat and slipped the painting out of his map pocket, careful to shield it from anyone else's view. Robin stared into the eyes of St George before she spoke again. "When I lay awake last night waiting for you to ravish me, I passed the time trying to fathom out what secret the icon held."

"I thought you were asleep," said Adam smiling. "When all along we were both doing the same thing. Anyway, did you come up with any worthwhile conclusions?"

"First, I decided your taste was for male double bass players," said Robin, "or how else could you have resisted me?"

"But what about St George and the Dragon?" asked Adam, grinning.

"To begin with I wondered if the little pieces of mosaic made up a code. But the picture is so magnificently executed that the code would have to have been worked out afterwards. And that didn't seem credible."

"Good thinking, Batman."

"No, you're Batman. So I wondered if there was another painting underneath. I remembered from my schooldays that Rembrandt and Constable often painted on the top of their paintings, either because they didn't care for their original effort or because, in the case of Rembrandt, he couldn't afford another canvas."

"If that were the answer only an expert could have

231

carried out the task of removing every piece of paint."

"Agreed," said Robin. "So I dismissed that as well. My third idea was that the crown on the back" – she turned the icon over and stared at the little piece of silver embedded in the wood – "indicates as your expert suggested that this is the original by Rublev and not a copy as you have been led to believe."

"I had already considered that," said Adam, "during my sleepless night and although it would place a far higher value on the work, it is still not enough to explain why Rosenbaum would kill indiscriminately for it."

"Perhaps someone else needs St George every bit as much as Rosenbaum does," said Robin.

"But who and why?"

"Because it's not the icon they're after, but something else. Something hidden in or behind the painting."

"That was the first thing I checked," said Adam smugly. "And I'm convinced that it's a solid piece of wood."

"I don't agree with you," said Robin as she began tapping the wood all over like a doctor examining someone's chest. "I've worked with instruments all my life, watched them being made, played with them, even slept with them, and this icon is not solid right through, though God knows how I can prove it. If something is hidden inside it was never intended to be discovered by laymen like ourselves."

"Quite an imaginative little thing, aren't you?" said Adam.

"Comes naturally," she said as she handed the icon back to Adam. "Do let me know if you ever discover what is inside," she added.

"When I get five minutes to myself I might even

spend some time on one or two of my own theories," said Adam, returning the icon to his trenchcoat pocket.

"Two more kilometres to Solothurn," said Robin, pointing out of the window at a signpost.

Adam buttoned up his coat. "I'll see you off," she said, and they both made their way up the aisle. When Adam reached the front of the coach he asked the driver if he could drop him off just before they reached the next village.

"Sure thing," said the driver without looking back.

"Leaving us so soon?" said Stephen.

"Afraid so," said Adam. "But thanks for the lift. And I won't forget the calendar." The driver pulled into a lay-by, pressed a knob and the hydraulic doors swung back.

"Bye, Robin," said Adam, giving her a brotherly kiss on the cheek.

"Goodbye, baby brother," said Robin. "Give my love to mother if you see her before I do." She smiled and waved at him as the door swung closed and the coach returned to the highway to continue its journey on to Frankfurt.

Adam was on his own again.

CHAPTER FOURTEEN

Professor Brunweld was rarely treated with any respect. It was the fate of academics, he had long ago concluded. The 'President' was all they had said and he had wondered if he should believe it. Certainly they had got him out of bed in the middle of the night and escorted him silently to the Pentagon. They wanted Brunweld's expert opinion, they had assured him. Could it be possible? After Cuba and Dallas he'd begun to believe anything was possible.

He had once read that the Pentagon had as many floors below the ground as there were above it. He could now confirm that as an established fact.

Once they had handed him the document they left him alone. They only wanted one question answered. He studied the clauses for over an hour and then called them back. It was, he told them, in his opinion, authentic and if the Russians were still in possession of their copy, also signed in 1867, then his adopted country was – what was that awful American expression? Ah, yes – in all sorts of trouble.

He began to realise how serious it was when they told him that he would not be allowed to leave the Pentagon until Monday. That didn't surprise him once he'd seen the date on the bottom of the treaty. So it was to be three days of solitude away from his demanding students and chattering wife. He would never have a better opportunity to settle down and read the collected works of Proust.

Romanov knew he couldn't risk standing by the side of the car for much longer. He was too conspicuously dressed not to be noticed by everyone who came out of the hotel. Three minutes later he thew his grey cap on the back seat and instructed Valchek to get rid of the car and then return to the Consulate.

Valchek nodded. He had already carried out Romanov's orders to kill the two British agents as if he had been asked to fix a burst water pipe. The only thing that hadn't run to plan was when Valchek tried to button up the dead chauffeur's uniform. Romanov thought he detected the suggestion of a smirk on Valchek's face when he realised who would have to be the chauffeur.

Romanov slipped into the shadows and waited for another half hour, by which time he was sure the plan must have been aborted from the London end. He hailed a taxi and asked the driver to take him to the Soviet Consulate. He didn't notice the taxi-driver's look of disbelief at his passenger's chauffeur-clad vision.

Could he really have lost Scott twice? Had he also underestimated him? Once more and Zaborski was going to require a very convincing explanation.

On his way back to the Consulate an image kept flashing across Romanov's mind, but he couldn't make any sense of it. Something had happened outside the hotel that didn't quite fit. If he could only think clearly for a moment he felt certain it would become clear to him. He kept playing the last thirty minutes over in his mind, as if rewinding the reel of an old film; but some of the frames still remained blurred.

Once Romanov was back in the Consulate Valchek handed him a large envelope which he was informed had just arrived in the diplomatic pouch from Moscow.

Romanov read over the decoded telex a second time, still unable to fathom its possible significance.

"Information has come to light concerning the late Colonel Gerald Scott, DSO, OBE, MC, that may prove useful when you make contact with your quarry. Full documentation will be with you by morning, latest, A1."

Romanov wondered what headquarters had discovered about Scott's father that could possibly prove of interest to him. It was still his avowed intention that the son would be despatched to join the father long before any further missive from Moscow had arrived.

Romanov thought of his own father and the escape route he had made possible by leaving such a fortune, and how for the sake of advancement he had betrayed him to the State. Now, for the sake of further advancement he had to kill Scott and bring home the icon. If he failed . . . He dismissed both fathers.

"Either he's very clever or he's living on an amateur's luck," Romanov said, moving into the small office that had been made available for his use. Valchek who followed him did not comment other than to ask what he should do next.

"Tell me what you saw when we were at the hotel."

"What do you mean?" asked Valchek.

"Don't ask questions," said Romanov, changing back into his own clothes, "answer them. Tell me everything you remember seeing, from the moment we drew up outside the hotel."

"We arrived at the Richmond a few minutes before ten," began Valchek, "parked the Mercedes on the far side of the road, and waited for Scott to show up. We stayed put for a few minutes after ten but Scott never materialised."

"No, no, no. Be more specific. Don't just generalise. For instance, do you remember anything unusual taking place while we were waiting?"

"Nothing in particular," said Valchek. "People continually entering and leaving the hotel – but I'm sure Scott wasn't among them."

"You are fortunate to be so certain. What happened next?" asked Romanov.

"Next? You instructed me to go back to the Consulate and wait for you to return."

"What time was that?"

"It must have been about seven minutes past ten. I remember because I checked my watch when that coach left."

"The coach?" said Romanov.

"Yes, the one that was being loaded up with musical instruments. It left about . . ."

"Instruments, that's it," said Romanov. "Now I remember what was worrying me. Cellos, violins, and a double bass that didn't go into the boot." Valchek looked puzzled but said nothing. "Ring the hotel immediately and find out who was on that bus and where they are heading." Valchek scurried away.

Romanov checked his watch: ten fifty-five. We are going to have to move, and move quickly. He pressed the intercom by the side of the phone. "I want a fast car, and more important, a superb driver." Valchek returned as Romanov replaced the receiver. "The bus was hired by the Royal Philharmonic Orchestra, who are on a European tour . . ."

"Where are they héading next?" asked Romanov.
"Frankfurt."

He strolled away from the village, having checked everything with a professional soldier's eye. The main street was deserted but for a little boy who relentlessly kicked a plastic football into a gap in the hillside which he was using as a goal. The boy turned when he saw Adam and kicked the ball towards him. Adam kicked it back and the boy took it in his arms, a wide smile appearing on his face. The smile disappeared as he watched Adam continue quickly up the hill. There were only a few old houses on the main road. On one side was a dangerous ravine with tree-covered hills rising in the distance, while on the other side stretched green fields in which cows, bells round their necks, munched happily away. It made Adam feel hungry.

He went further up the road until he came to a sharp bend in the hill. Standing on the corner he could see down the hill for about half a mile without being seen. He tested the feasibility of his plan for several minutes and soon became expert at picking out British cars or cars with British number plates as far as two or three hundred yards away. It didn't take long to work out how few foreigners bought British.

During the next twenty minutes he thumbed optimistically at seven cars with English number plates heading towards Lausanne, but they all ignored him. He had forgotten just how easy it had been for him when he was a cadet in uniform. In those days almost everyone would stop. He checked his watch: he could only risk it for a few more minutes. Three more cars refused to pull up and when a fourth slowed down it only sped away again as Adam ran towards it.

By eleven twenty Adam decided he could no longer

chance being seen on the road. He stared down the ravine, realising there was no alternative left open to him now but to travel by foot. He shrugged and began to climb down one of the steep trails that led into the valley, in the hope of meeting up with the other road that was marked clearly on the map.

He cursed when he looked at the open ground between him and safety. If only he'd started an hour earlier.

"I fear Antarctic has become expendable."

"Why?"

"Because we now know his father was involved in helping Goering to an easy death."

"I don't understand."

"No reason why you should although it's quite simple. That patriotic stiff-upper-lipped Englishman of yours is the son of the bastard who smuggled a cyanide capsule into Goering's cell at Nuremberg. His reward for services rendered turns out to be the Tsar's icon."

"But all the members of D4 are convinced that he's our only hope."

"I don't give a damn what your D4 thinks. If the father would side with the Germans during a war, why shouldn't the son side with the Russians in peace?"

"Like father, like son."

"Precisely."

"So what am I expected to do?"

"Just keep us briefed as to what the Foreign Office is up to. Our agents in Switzerland will do the rest."

"Faster!" said Romanov, aware that it was not possible as the Ambassador's driver was proving to be a consummate professional. Not once did Romanov feel that he had missed a gap, a light, a chance to overtake. In fact another five kilometres an hour on the speedometer might well have seen them over the precipice. The moment they were on the highway, with full lights blazing and the driver's hand almost lodged on the horn, the speedometer rarely fell below 130 kilometres an hour. "We must beat them to the border," he kept repeating as he thumped his fist on the leather dashboard. After they had covered one hundred kilometres in fifty-five minutes, the three men began watching ahead of them for the coach, but it was another thirty kilometres before Valchek was able to point ahead and shout, "That must be them, about a kilometre up the hill."

"Force them off the road," said Romanov, his eyes never leaving the bus. The Embassy driver swung out to overtake and once he was in front immediately cut across, forcing the coach driver to throw on his brakes and swerve into the side. Valchek waved dictatorially at the coach driver to slow down and the man stopped the vehicle just off the road on the edge of the mountain.

"Don't either of you speak. Just leave everything to me," said Romanov, "and remain near the driver in case there's trouble." Romanov jumped out of the car and ran towards the coach, his eyes already searching for anyone who might be attempting to leave it. He banged on the door impatiently until the driver pressed a knob and the big doors swung open. Romanov leapt on, with the other two following only paces behind. He took out his passport from an inside pocket, flashed it in the frightened driver's face and shouted, "Who's in charge here?"

Stephen Grieg stood up. "I am the manager of the company, and I can . . ."

"Swiss police," said Romanov. Grieg was about to ask a question when Romanov said, "When you left

241

your hotel in Geneva this morning, did you take on any extra passengers?"

"No," said Grieg. Romanov scowled. "Unless you count Robin Beresford's brother."

"Robin Beresford's brother?" enquired Romanov, his eyebrows raising interrogatively.

"Yes," said the manager. "Adam Beresford. But he only travelled with us as far as Solothurn. Then he got off."

"Which one of you is Robin?" said Romanov, staring around a sea of men's faces.

"I am," piped up a voice from the back. Romanov marched down the bus and saw the double bass case and then everything fitted into place. It always worried him when something was out of context. Yes, that was what hadn't rung true. Why hadn't she put the double bass in the boot with all the other large instruments? He stared down at the heavy-framed woman who now sat behind the monstrous instrument.

"Your brother is the one called Adam?"

"Yes," said Robin.

"Quite a coincidence."

"I don't understand what you mean," she said, trying not to sound nervous.

"The man I am looking for just happens to be called Adam as well."

"Common enough name," said Robin. "Perhaps you've never read the first chapter of the Bible?"

"Six foot one inch, perhaps two inches, dark hair, dark eyes, slim and fit. Not a convincing brother for you," added Romanov studying her frame.

Robin pushed back her red hair but didn't rise. Romanov could sense from the nervous expressions on the faces around him that it was Scott who had been on the bus.

"Where was your *brother*," he emphasised the word, "intending to go once he had left the coach?" Romanov asked, tapping his passport against his other hand, like a baton.

"I have no idea," said Robin, still not changing her expression from one of uninterested politeness.

"I will give you one more chance to co-operate with me. Where was your brother heading?"

"And I'll tell you once more, I don't know."

"If you refuse to answer my questions," said Romanov, "I shall have to arrest you."

"On whose authority?" asked Robin calmly.

Romanov considered showing her his passport but realised that this girl was sharper than either the driver or the manager.

"With the authority of the Swiss police," Romanov said confidently.

"Then no doubt you'll be happy to show me proof of your identity."

"Don't be insolent," Romanov said sharply. He towered over her.

"It is you who are insolent," said Robin, standing up. "You drive in front of our coach like a lunatic, nearly sending us down the mountain, then the three of you burst in like a bunch of Chicago mobsters, claiming to be Swiss police. I have no idea who you are or what you are, but I'll let you into two secrets. You touch me and there are forty men on this coach who will beat you and your two cronies to pulp. And even if you managed to get off this bus alive, we are members of the Royal Philharmonic Orchestra of Great Britain, and as such are guests of the Swiss Government. In a few moments when we cross the border, we will become guests of the West German Government, so you're about to get yourself on to every front page in the world. Single-handedly, you will bring a totally new meaning to the words 'diplomatic incident'." She leaned forward and pointing a finger at him said, "So I'm telling you, whoever you are, in as ladylike fashion as I can, 'piss off'."

Romanov stood staring at her for some moments and then backed away as Robin's eyes remained glued on him. When he reached the front he waved at Valchek and the chauffeur, indicating that they should leave the coach. Reluctantly they obeyed him. The coach driver closed the door the moment Romanov's foot touched the ground and he quickly moved into first gear and drove back on to the highway.

The entire orchestra turned round and gave Robin the kind of ovation normally reserved for the entrance of the leader of the orchestra.

It went unappreciated. Robin had collapsed back into her seat, shaking uncontrollably, only too aware that not one of the forty men on that coach would have lifted a finger against Rosenbaum.

Sir Morris Youngfield glanced round the table: everyone was in place despite the few minutes' notice the head of D4 had given them.

"Let's hear the latest report," said Sir Morris, looking up at his Number Two, who was once again seated at the far end of the table.

"Not clever, sir, I'm afraid," began Lawrence. "Two of our most experienced agents were selected to pick up Scott at the Richmond Hotel as planned and then take him to the safety of the British Consulate."

"So what happened?" asked Sir Morris.

"No one at our Geneva office can be certain. Our men certainly never turned up at the hotel and they haven't been seen since."

"What are the Swiss police saying?" asked Busch.

"They are not being very helpful," said Lawrence, turning to the American. "They are aware that we are not the only foreign power involved and as is their custom in such circumstances, they have no intention of being seen to favour either side."

"Bloody Swiss," said Snell with feeling.

"And where do we imagine Scott is now?" asked Matthews.

"We've also drawn a blank on that," said Lawrence. Matthews smiled at Lawrence's embarrassment. "We feel certain he must have got on the coach with the girl —" he looked down at the sheet of paper on the table in front of him "— Robin Beresford. But he wasn't on it when we were waiting for them at the border. The orchestra is due at their Frankfurt hotel in about one hour so we will be able to find out more then. The German police are being far more co-operative," Lawrence added.

"Meanwhile what else are *we* doing?" asked Sir Morris.

"Checking all the usual places as well as keeping a close eye on Romanov who, incidentally, turned up on the French border last night. One of our old hands recognised him despite the fact that he's cut his hair very short; doesn't suit him, apparently."

"So Scott could be anywhere by now?" said Matthews. "Do you think he's still in Switzerland, or managed to cross one of the borders?"

Lawrence hesitated. "I have no idea," he said without expression.

Sir Morris stared at him from the far end of the table but didn't comment.

"Do you think he'll contact you again?" asked Snell.

"Almost certainly, if he's still alive."

"If Romanov is still in Switzerland, Scott *must* still be alive," said Busch. "Because the moment he gets his hands on the icon he will head east."

"Agreed," said Lawrence, "and we have men stationed at the airport checking every flight out to the East. I therefore suggest we follow up any further leads and assemble again tomorrow at seven a.m. unless Scott contacts me before then."

Sir Morris nodded and rose to leave. Everyone stood.

"Thank you, gentlemen," he said, and walked towards the far end of the room. As he passed Lawrence, he murmured, "Perhaps you could come to my office when you have a moment."

Adam slipped and stumbled the last few yards down the ravine before finally landing with a bump on his backside. His hands were cut and bleeding in several places, his trousers torn and smeared with clay and earth. He sat still for about two minutes trying to get his breath back as he looked back up towards the road. He had taken just under an hour to cover what a stone could have managed in three seconds. Still, there had been one advantage: no one could have seen him from the road. He gazed across the valley ahead. Anyone would be able to see him now, but he had left himself with no alternative.

Judge by eye, check by map. The map wasn't much help but he estimated the distance to the far ridge to be about two more miles. At least the map had promised him there was a road, hidden from sight on the other side of the ridge. He studied the terrain – rolling green fields, no hedgerows to shield him, and then one wide, shallow river. He reckoned hc could cover the ground to the road in about twenty minutes. He checked that the icon was securely in place and then set off at an even pace.

Romanov had hardly uttered a word since the three men had been unceremoniously removed from the coach, and Valchek and the driver certainly hadn't ventured any opinions. Romanov knew the girl had called his bluff, and he couldn't afford a further diplomatic incident which would undoubtedly be reported back to his Chairman in Moscow. But Romanov would never forget the girl with the man's name.

Solothurn was about forty kilometres back in the direction they had already travelled, and the driver could have completed the journey in about twenty minutes had Romanov not insisted on slowing down as they passed every vehicle that travelled towards them. They checked the occupants of each vehicle on the other side of the road, just in case Scott had managed to thumb a lift. It was a necessary precaution in Romanov's judgment, but it meant a total time of thirty-one minutes before they arrived back in Solothurn. At least Romanov felt confident Scott wasn't heading for the German border – unless he had been very well disguised or travelled in the boot of a car.

As soon as they reached Solothurn Romanov instructed the driver to leave the car in the middle of the town while they split up to see if they could discover any clues as to the route Scott might have taken. None of the locals whom they questioned had seen anyone resembling Scott that morning, and Romanov was beginning to wonder which border he should now head for when he saw the driver kicking a football back to a little boy. Romanov ran down the hill and was about to remonstrate with him when the boy turned and kicked the ball hard at the Russian. Romanov trapped the ball automatically and kicked it firmly past the boy and into the goal. Romanov turned towards the driver and was about to shout at him when the ball reappeared at his feet. He picked it up in anger and was going to throw it back at the boy when he saw his hopeful smile. Romanov held the ball high above his head. The boy ran up and jumped towards the ball but however hard he tried he couldn't reach it.

"Have you seen any strangers this morning?" he asked in slow deliberate German.

"Yes, yes," said the boy. "But he didn't score a goal."

"Where did he go?" asked Romanov.

"Up the hill," said the boy. To the child's dismay, Romanov dropped the ball and began to run. Valchek and the driver followed after him.

"*Nein, nein,*" cried the little boy who followed after them. Romanov looked back to see the boy was standing on the spot where Adam had been thumbing lifts, pointing out over the ravine.

Romanov quickly turned to the driver. "Get the car, I need the glasses and the map." The driver ran back down the hill once again followed by the boy. A few minutes later the Mercedes drew up by Romanov's side. The driver jumped out and handed the glasses over to Romanov, while Valchek spread a map out on the car bonnet.

Romanov focused the binoculars and began to sweep the hills in the distance. It was several minutes before the glasses stopped and settled upon a brown speck climbing up the farthest hill.

"The rifle," were Romanov's only words.

Valchek ran to the boot of the car and took out a Dragunov sniper's rifle with telescopic sights. He assembled the long, slim weapon with its distinctive wooden skeleton stock and checked that it was loaded. He then raised it, moved it around until it felt comfortable nestled in his shoulder and swept the ground in front of him until he too focused on Scott. Romanov followed Adam's relentless stride with the binoculars. Valchek's arm moved with him, keeping the same pace. "Kill him," said Romanov. Valchek was grateful for the clear windless day as he kept the rifle sight in the middle of the Englishman's back, waited for three more strides, then slowly squeezed the trigger. Adam had almost reached the top of the ridge when the bullet tore through him. He fell to the ground with a thud. Romanov smiled and lowered the glasses.

Adam knew exactly what had ripped through his shoulder and where the shot must have come from. He instinctively rolled over until he reached the nearest tree. And then the pain began. Although the bullet had lost a lot of its power at such a distance, it still stung like an adder's bite, and blood was already beginning to seep through his trenchcoat from the torn muscle. He turned his head and gazed back behind him. He could see no one but he knew Romanov must be standing there waiting to take a second shot.

Turning with difficulty, he looked back up towards the edge of the hill. Only thirty yards to the safety of the ridge, but he would have to run over the top, remaining exposed for several vital seconds. Even if he made it Romanov would still be able to reach him by car within thirty minutes.

Nevertheless, that was his one chance. Slowly, very slowly, he crawled inch by inch up the ridge, thankful for the tree that he could still use as protection. One arm followed one leg, like a beached crab. Once he had covered ten yards he knew the angle would be against him and Romanov would have a flat, slow-moving target to aim at. He moved four more lengths of his body and stopped.

You can't hold a rifle up on your shoulder for ever, Adam thought. He counted to two hundred slowly.

"I suspect he's going to make a run for it," Romanov told Valchek as he raised the glasses, "which will give you about three seconds. I'll shout the moment he moves." Romanov kept the glasses trained on the tree. Suddenly Adam jumped up and sprinted as though it were the last twenty metres of an Olympic final. Romanov shouted "Now" and Valchek pulled the rifle up into his shoulder, focused on the moving man and squeezed the trigger as Adam threw himself over the ridge. The second bullet whistled by the side of Adam's head.

Romanov cursed, as he stared through the binoculars, knowing that Valchek had missed. He turned to the open map. The others joined him around the car as he began to consider the alternatives. "He should reach that road in about ten minutes," he said, putting his finger in the middle of a small red line that ran between Neuchâtel and the French border. "Unless the first bullet hit him, in which case it could take him longer. So how long will it take you to get to that border?" Romanov asked the driver.

The chauffeur studied the map. "About twenty-five, at most thirty minutes, Comrade Major," came back the reply.

Romanov turned and looked back towards the hills. "Thirty minutes, Scott, that's how long you've got to live."

When the car sped away, the little boy ran home as fast as he could. He quickly told his mother everything he had seen. She smiled understandingly. Only children always had such vivid imaginations.

* * *

When Adam looked up, he was relieved to see the road was only about a mile away. He jogged towards it at a steady pace, but found that the running caused him even more discomfort. He was anxious to stop and check the wound but waited till he reached the road. The bullet had torn through the outer flesh of his shoulder muscle leaving him in considerable pain. An inch lower and he would have been unable to move. He was relieved to see that the blood had only made a small stain on his trenchcoat. He folded a handkerchief in four and placed it between his shirt and the wound. He knew he daren't risk a hospital. As long as he could get to a pharmacy by nightfall, he felt he could take care of the problem himself.

Adam checked the map. He was now only a few kilometres from the French border, and decided, because of the wound, to cross into France as quickly as possible rather than keep to his original plan of going up through Basle and on to Bremerhaven.

Desperately he began to thumb at any car that passed, no longer bothering with the nationality of the number plates. He felt he was safe for about twenty minutes but after that he would have to disappear back into the hills. Unfortunately there were far fewer cars driving towards the French border than there had been on the Basle road, and they all ignored his plea. He feared that the time was fast approaching for him to return to the hills when a yellow Citroën drew into the side of the road a few yards ahead of him.

By the time Adam had reached the car the woman in the passenger seat had already wound down the window.

"Where – are – you – going?" asked Adam, pronouncing each word slowly and carefully.

Jeffrey Archer

The driver leant across, took a lengthy look at Adam and said in a broad Yorkshire accent, "We're on our way to Dijon. Any use to you, lad?"

"Yes, please," said Adam, relieved that his scruffy appearance had not put them off.

"Then jump in the back with my daughter."

Adam obeyed. The Citroën moved off, as Adam checked out of the back window; he was relieved to see an empty road stretching out behind him.

"Jim Hardcastle's the name," said the man, as he moved the car into third gear. Jim appeared to have a large, warm smile perpetually imprinted on his chubby red face. His dark ginger hair went straight back and was plastered down with Brylcreem. He wore a Harris tweed jacket and an open-necked shirt that revealed a little red triangle of hair. It looked to Adam as if he had given up attempts to do anything about his waistline. "And this is the wife, Betty," he said, gesturing with his elbow towards the woman in the front seat. She turned towards Adam, revealing the same ruddy cheeks and warm smile. Her hair was dyed blonde but the roots remained an obstinate black. "And sitting next to you is our Linda," Jim Hardcastle added, almost as an afterthought. "Just left school and going to work for the local council, aren't you, Linda?" Linda nodded sulkily. Adam stared at the young girl whose first experiment with make-up hadn't worked that well. The dark over-lined eye shadow and the pink lipstick did not help what Adam considered was an attractive girl probably in her late teens. "And what's your name, lad?"

"Dudley Hulme," said Adam, recalling the name on his new passport. "And are you on holiday?" he asked, trying to keep his mind off the throbbing shoulder.

"Mixing business with pleasure," said Jim. "But this part of the trip is rather special for Betty and myself. We flew to Genoa on Saturday and hired the car to tour Italy. First we travelled up through the Simplon Pass. It's a bit breathtaking after our home town of Hull."

Adam would have asked for details, but Jim didn't reckon on any interruptions. "I'm in mustard, you see. Export director for Colman's, and we're on our way to the annual conference of the IMF. You may have heard of us." Adam nodded knowingly. "International Mustard Federation," Jim added. Adam wanted to laugh, but because of the pain in his shoulder, managed to keep a straight face.

"This year they've elected me President of the IMF, the high point of my career in mustard, you might say. And, if I may be so bold as to suggest, an honour for Colman's as well, the finest mustard in the world," he added, as if he said it at least a hundred times a day. "As President I have to preside over the conference meetings and chair the annual dinner. Tonight I shall be making a speech of welcome to delegates from all over the world."

"How fascinating," winced Adam, as the car went over a pothole.

"It certainly is," said Jim. "People have no idea how many makes of mustards there are." He paused for a second and then said, "One hundred and forty-three. There's no doubt the Frogs make one or two good attempts and even the Krauts don't do too badly, but there's still nothing to beat Colman's. British is best after all, I always say. Probably the same in your line of country," said Jim. "By the way, what is your line of country?"

"I'm in the army," said Adam.

"What's a soldier doing thumbing a lift on the borders of Switzerland?"

"Can I speak to you in confidence?" asked Adam.

"Mum's the word," said Jim. "We Hardcastles know how to keep our traps shut."

In the case of Jim's wife and daughter, Adam had no proof to the contrary.

"I'm a captain in the Royal Wessex, at present on a NATO exercise," began Adam. "I was dumped off the coast at Brindisi in Italy last Sunday with a false passport and ten English pounds. I have to be back in barracks at Aldershot by midnight Saturday." When he saw the look of approbation appear on Jim's face, he felt even Robin would have been proud of him. Mrs Hardcastle turned around to take a more careful look at him.

"I knew you were an officer the moment you opened your mouth," said Jim. "You couldn't have fooled me. I was a sergeant in the Royal Army Service Corps in the last war myself. Doesn't sound much, but I did my bit for the old country." The acronym for the Corps – 'Rob All Serving Comrades' – flashed through Adam's mind. "Have you seen any action yourself, Dudley?" Jim was asking.

"A little in Malaya," said Adam.

"I missed that one," said Jim. "After the big one was over, I went back into mustard. So where's the problem in getting you back to England?"

"There are about eight of us trying to reach Aldershot, and a thousand Americans trying to stop us."

"Yanks," said Jim with disdain. "They only join wars just as we're about to win them. All medals and glory, that lot. No, I mean is there any real problem?"

"Yes, the border officials have been briefed that eight British officers are attempting to get over into

France and the Swiss love to be the ones to pull us in. Only two officers out of twelve made it back to barracks last year," said Adam, warming to his own theme. "Both were promoted within weeks."

"The Swiss," said Jim. "They're even worse than the Americans. They don't even join in a war – happy to fleece both sides at the same time. They won't pick you up, lad, believe me. I'll see to that."

"If you can get me across the border, Mr Hardcastle, I'm confident I will be able to make it all the way back to Aldershot."

"Consider it done, lad."

The fuel indicator was flashing red. "How many kilometres left when that happens?" demanded Romanov.

"About twenty, Comrade Major," said the driver.

"Then we should still make the French border?"

"Perhaps it might be safer to stop and fill up," suggested the driver.

"There is no time for safety," said Romanov. "Go faster."

"Yes, Comrade Major," said the driver, who decided it was not the occasion to point out they would run out of petrol even more quickly if he was made to push the car to its limits.

"Why didn't you fill the tank up this morning, you fool?" said Romanov.

"I thought I was only taking the Consul to lunch at the town hall today, and I had intended to fill the tank up during my lunch hour."

"Just pray for your sake that we reach the border," said Romanov. "Faster."

The Mercedes touched 140 kilometres per hour and Romanov relaxed only when he saw a sign saying they were only ten kilometres from the border. A few minutes later a smile grew on his face as they passed the five-kilometre sign, and then suddenly the engine spluttered as it tried helplessly to continue turning over at the speed the pressed-down accelerator was demanding. The indicator on the speedometer started to drop steadily as the engine continued to chug. The driver turned off the ignition and threw the gear lever into neutral. The sheer momentum of the heavy Mercedes took them another kilometre before the car slowed to a complete stop.

Romanov did not even look at the driver as he jumped out of the car and began running the last three kilometres towards the border.

"I've come up with an idea," said Jim, as they passed a signpost warning drivers that the border was only two kilometres away.

"What's that, sir?" asked Adam, who could now feel his shoulder beating like a steady tune hammered out by a child on a tin drum.

"When it comes to the time for us to present our passports, you put your arm round Linda and start cuddling her. Leave the rest to me."

Mrs Hardcastle turned round and gave Adam a much closer look as Linda went scarlet. Adam looked across at the mini-skirted pink-lipped Linda and felt embarrassed by the predicament her father had placed his daughter in. "Don't argue with me, Dudley," continued Jim confidently. "I promise you what I have in mind will work." Adam made no comment and neither did Linda. When they reached the Swiss border a few moments later, Adam could see that there were two checkpoints about one hundred yards apart. Drivers were avoiding one line of traffic in which a row was going on between a customs official and an irate lorry driver. Jim drove up straight behind the gesticulating Frenchman. "Give me your passport, Dudley," he said. Adam handed over the violinist's passport.

Why did you choose this line? Adam wanted to ask.

"I chose this line," continued Jim, "because by the time it comes for our passports to be inspected I reckon the customs officer will be only too happy to allow us through without much fuss." As if in reaction to his logic, a long queue started to form behind Jim, but still the argument raged in front of them. Adam remained alert, continually looking out of the back window, waiting for the moment when Romanov would appear. When he turned back, he was relieved to find that the lorry in front of them was being told to pull over into the side and wait.

Jim drove quickly up to the customs post. "Get necking, you two," he said.

Up until that point Adam had kept his hands hidden in his trenchcoat pocket because they were so scratched and bruised. But he obeyed Jim and took Linda in his arms and kissed her perfunctorily, one eye still open watching for Romanov. To his surprise she parted his lips and began exploring inside his mouth with her tongue. Adam thought about protesting but realised there was no way he could make it sound gallant or credible.

"The wife, the daughter and the future son-in-law," said Jim, handing over the four passports.

The customs man started to check.

"What was all the trouble about, officer?"

"Nothing for you to worry about," said the official, flicking through the passports. "I hope it hasn't inconvenienced you."

"No, no," said Jim. "They didn't even notice," he said, pointing over his shoulder and laughing.

The policeman shrugged and, handing the passports back, he said, "*Allez*," waving them on.

"Sharp as mustard Jim, that's what they call me back in Hull." He looked over his shoulder towards Adam. "You can stop that now, Dudley, thank you." Adam felt Linda release him with some reluctance.

She glanced at him shyly, then turned towards her father. "But we still have to go over the French border, don't we?"

"We have already been alerted to look out for him and I can assure you he hasn't been through this post," said the senior customs officer. "Otherwise one of my men would have spotted him. But if you want to double-check, be my guest."

Romanov went quickly from officer to officer showing them the blown-up photograph of Adam, but none of them could recall anyone resembling him. Valchek joined him a few minutes later and confirmed that Scott was not in any of the cars still waiting to be allowed over the border and that the Mercedes was being pushed into the border garage.

"Is it back to the hills, Comrade Major?" asked Valchek.

"Not yet. I want to be absolutely certain he hasn't managed to cross the border."

The senior official emerged from his post in the centre of the road. "Any luck?" he asked.

"No," said Romanov glumly. "You seem to be right."

"I thought as much. If any of my men had let the Englishman through they would have been looking for a new job by now."

Romanov nodded in acknowledgment. "Could I have missed any of your staff?"

"Doubt it – unless there's a couple of them taking a break. If so you'll find them in the bar about a hundred metres up towards the French border point."

Four customs officers and a French waitress were the only people to be found in the bar. Two of the officers were playing pool while the other two sat at a corner table, drinking coffee. Romanov took the photo out once more and showed it to the two men at the pool table. They both shook their heads in an uninterested fashion and returned to potting the multi-coloured balls.

The two Russians made their way to the bar. Valchek passed Romanov a cup of coffee and a sandwich, which he took over to the table where the other two border guards sat. One of them was telling his colleague the trouble he had had with a French lorry driver who was trying to smuggle Swiss watches over the border. Romanov pushed the photograph of Scott across the table.

"Have you seen this man today?"

Neither showed any sign of recognition and the younger one quickly returned to his story. Romanov sipped his coffee, and began to consider whether he should make a run for Basle or call for reinforcements to sweep the hills. Then he noticed that the young man's eyes kept returning to the photo. He asked once again if he had seen Scott.

"No, no," said the young officer, a little too quickly. In Moscow Romanov would have had a 'yes' out of him within minutes, but he would have to follow a more gentle approach here.

"How long ago?" Romanov asked quietly.

"What do you mean?" asked the policeman.

"How long ago?" repeated Romanov in a firmer voice.

"It wasn't him," said the officer, sweat now appearing on his forehead.

"If it wasn't him, how long ago wasn't it him?"

The officer hesitated. "Twenty minutes, maybe thirty."

"What make of vehicle?"

The young officer hesitated. "A Citroën, I think. "

"Colour?"

"Yellow."

"Other passengers?"

"Three. Looked like a family. Mother, father, daughter. He was in the back with the daughter. The father said they were engaged."

Romanov had no more questions.

Jim Hardcastle managed to keep a one-sided conversation going for over an hour.

"Naturally," he said, "the IMF holds its annual conference in a different city every year. Last year it was in Denver in Colorado, and next year it'll be at Perth in Australia, so I manage to get around a bit. But as the export man you have to get used to a lot of travel."

"I'm sure you do," said Adam, trying to concentrate on his benefactor's words while his shoulder throbbed on.

"I'm only President for a year, of course," continued Jim. "But I have plans to ensure that my fellow delegates won't forget 1966 in a hurry."

"I'm sure they won't," said Adam.

"I shall point out to them that Colman's has had another record year on the export side."

"How impressive."

"Yes, but I must admit that most of our profits are left on the side of the plate," he said, laughing.

Adam laughed as well but sensed that Mrs Hardcastle and Linda might have heard the line before.

"I've been thinking, Dudley, and I'm sure the wife would agree with me, that it would be most acceptable to us if you felt able to join the presidential table for dinner tonight – as my guest, of course." Mrs Hardcastle nodded, as did Linda with enthusiasm.

"I can think of nothing that would give me greater pleasure," said Adam. "But I fear my commanding officer might not be quite as delighted to hear I had stopped on the way back to England to take in a party. I do hope you'll understand."

"If he is anything like my old CO I certainly do," said Jim. "Still, if you should ever be Hull way, look us up." He took a card out of his top pocket and passed it over his shoulder.

Adam studied the embossed letters and wondered what 'MIFT' stood for. He didn't ask.

"Where in Dijon would you like to be dropped off?" asked Jim as he drove into the outskirts of the town.

"Anywhere near the centre that's convenient for you," replied Adam.

"Just holler when it suits you then," said Jim. "Of course, I always maintain that a meal without mustard . . ."

"Can you drop me on the next corner?" said Adam suddenly.

"Oh," said Jim, sad to be losing such a good listener. And he reluctantly drew the car up alongside the kerb.

Adam kissed Linda on the cheek before getting out of the back. He then shook hands with Mr and Mrs Hardcastle.

"Nice to have made your acquaintance," said Jim. "If you change your mind you'll find us at the hotel . . . Is that blood on your shoulder, lad?"

"Just a graze from a fall – nothing to worry about. Wouldn't want the Americans to think they'd got the better of me."

"No, no, of course not," said Jim. "Well, good luck."

As the car moved off Adam stood on the pavement watching them disappear. He smiled and tried to wave, then turning, he walked quickly down a side street looking for a shopping precinct. Within moments he was in the centre of town, relieved to find that all the shops were still open. He began to search up and down the street for a green cross above a door. Adam had to walk only fifty yards before he spotted one. He entered the shop tentatively and checked the shelves.

A tall man with short fair hair, wearing a long leather coat, stood in the corner with his back to the entrance. Adam froze. Then the man turned round, frowning at the packet of tablets he wanted to purchase, while at the same time rubbing his thick Gallic moustache.

Adam walked up to the counter.

"Do you speak English, by any chance?" he asked the dispenser, trying to sound confident.

"Passable, I hope," came back the reply.

"I need some iodine, cotton wool, a bandage and heavy Elastoplast. I fell and bruised my shoulder on a rock," Adam explained.

The dispenser quickly put the order together without showing much interest.

"This is what you require but you will find that the trade names are different," explained the dispenser. "That will be twenty-three francs," he added.

"Will Swiss do?"

"Certainly."

"Is there a hotel anywhere nearby?" asked Adam.

"Around the next corner, on the other side of the square."

Adam thanked him, handed over the Swiss notes, and then left the pharmacy in search of the hotel. The Hotel Frantel was, as promised, only a short distance away. He walked across the square and up the steps into the hotel to find several people were waiting at reception to be booked in. Adam swung his trenchcoat over his blood-stained shoulder and walked past them as he checked the signs on the wall. He then strode across the entrance hall as though he were a guest of several days' standing. He followed the sign he had been looking for which took him down a flight of stairs, to come head on with three further signs. The first had the silhouette of a man on the door, the second a woman, the third a wheelchair.

He opened the third tentatively and was surprised to find behind it nothing more than a sizeable square room with a high-seated lavatory against the wall. Adam locked himself in and let his trenchcoat fall to the ground.

He rested for a few minutes before slowly stripping to the waist. He then ran a basinful of warm water.

Adam was thankful for the endless first-aid seminars every officer had to go through, never believing they would serve any purpose. Twenty minutes later the pain had subsided and he even felt comfortable.

He picked up his coat with his right hand and tried to throw it back over his shoulder. The very movement caused the icon to fall out of the map pocket and onto the tiled floor. As it hit the ground, the sound made Adam fear that it might have broken in half. He stared down anxiously and then fell to his knees.

The icon had split open like a book.

CHAPTER FIFTEEN

When Adam returned to the Hotel Frantel an hour later few guests would have recognised the man who had crept in earlier that afternoon.

He wore a new shirt, trousers, tie and a double-breasted blazer that wouldn't be fashionable in Britain for at least another year. Even the raincoat had been ditched because the icon fitted snugly into the blazer pocket. He considered the shop had probably given him a poor exchange rate for his traveller's cheques but that was not what had been occupying his mind for the past hour.

He booked himself into a single room in the name of Dudley Hulme and a few minutes later took the lift to the third floor.

Lawrence picked the phone up even before Adam heard the second ring.

"It's me," said Adam.

"Where are you?" were Lawrence's first words.

"I'll ask the questions," said Adam.

"I can understand how you feel," said Lawrence, "but . . ."

"No buts. You must be aware by now that someone on your so-called team has a direct line to the Russians because it was Romanov and his friends who were waiting for me outside the hotel in Geneva, not your lot."

"We realise that now," said Lawrence.

"We?" said Adam. "Who are we? Because I'm finding it rather hard to work out who's on my side."

"You don't believe that . . ."

"When you get your girlfriend murdered, chased across Europe by professional killers, shot at and . . ."

"Shot at?" said Lawrence.

"Yes, your friend Romanov took a shot at me today, hit me in the shoulder. Next time we meet I intend it to be the other way round and it won't be the shoulder."

"There won't be a next time," said Lawrence, "because we'll get you out safely if you'll only let me know where you are."

The memory of Robin's words, "Just be wary of how much you let him know," stopped Adam from telling Lawrence his exact location.

"Adam, for God's sake, you're on your own; if you don't trust me who can you trust? I admit it looks as if we let you down. But it won't happen again."

There was another long silence before Adam said, "I'm in Dijon."

"Why Dijon?"

"Because the only person who would give me a lift was going to a mustard conference in Dijon."

Lawrence couldn't stop himself smiling. "Give me your number and I'll phone you back within the hour."

"No," said Adam, "I'll phone *you* back in one hour."

"Adam, you've got to show some trust in me."

"Not now that I know what it is you're all after, I can't afford to trust anybody."

Adam replaced the phone and stared down at the icon which lay open on the bed. It wasn't the signature of Stoeckle or Seward that worried him. It was the date – June 20, 1966 – that read like a death warrant.

"Goodnight, sir," said the doorkeeper as the senior civil servant left Century House that evening. "Another late night for you," he added sympathetically. He acknowledged the doorman by raising his rolled umbrella a few inches. It *had* been another late night, but at least they had caught up with Scott again. He was beginning to develop quite a respect for the man. But how they failed to pick him up in Geneva still required a fuller explanation than the one Lawrence Pemberton had supplied the D4 with that afternoon.

He set off at a brisk pace towards the Old Kent Road, conspicuous in his black coat and pin-striped trousers. He tapped his umbrella nervously before hailing a passing taxi.

"Dillon's bookshop, Malet Street," he told the driver, before getting in the back. Already seven thirty, but he still wouldn't be too late and a few minutes either way wasn't going to make that much difference. Pemberton had agreed to remain at his desk until all the loose ends were tied up and he was sure that nothing could go wrong this time. He allowed himself a wry smile as he thought how they had all accepted his plan. It had the double advantage of ensuring enough time for them to get their best men into position, while keeping Scott well out of sight in a deserted hideaway. He hoped that this was the last time they would expect him to come up with an original proposal.

"Eight shillings, guv'nor," said the taxi-driver, as he drew up outside Dillon's. He handed over the money and added a sixpenny tip. He stood staring at the window of the university bookshop, watching the reflection of the taxi as it moved off. The moment the taxi had turned the corner into Gower Street he began walking away. In moments he had reached a side road into which he turned. Ridgmount Gardens was one of those streets which even London cabbies had to think about for a few moments. He had walked only a matter of yards before he disappeared down some stone steps to a basement flat. He inserted a Yale key in the front door lock, turned it quickly, stepped inside and closed the door behind him.

During the next twenty minutes he made two telephone calls – one international, one local – and then had a bath. He emerged back on Ridgmount Gardens less than an hour later dressed in a casual brown suit, pink floral open shirt and brown brogue shoes. The parting in his hair had changed sides. He returned to Dillon's on foot and hailed another taxi.

"The British Museum," he instructed the driver, as he stepped into the back. He checked his watch: nearly ten past eight. Scott would be fully briefed by now, he thought, although his associates would be already on the way back to Dijon, as his plan had allowed for a two-hour delay.

The taxi drew up outside the British Museum. He paid and walked up the twelve steps in front of the museum, admiring the Byzantine architecture as he regularly did each week, before walking back down again to hail another taxi.

"Middlesex Hospital, please," was all he said. The taxi executed a U-turn and headed west.

Poor bastard. If Scott hadn't opened that envelope in the first place the icon would have ended up with its rightful owner.

"Shall I drive up to the entrance?" asked the cabbie.

"Yes, please."

A moment later he strolled into the hospital, checked

the board on the wall as if he were looking for a certain ward, then walked back out on to the street. From the Middlesex Hospital it always took him about three minutes at a steady pace to reach Charlotte Street, where he stopped outside a house and pressed a buzzer attached to a little intercom.

"Are you a member?" enquired a voice suspiciously.

"Yes."

On the hour Adam phoned and listened carefully to all Lawrence had to say.

"I'll take one more risk," said Adam, "but if Romanov turns up this time I'll hand over the icon to him personally and with it a piece of property so valuable that no amount of money the Americans could offer would be sufficient to purchase it back."

When Adam put the phone down Lawrence and Sir Morris played the conversation back over again and again.

"I think *property*'s the key word," said Sir Morris.

"Agreed," said Lawrence, "but what piece of property could be that valuable to both the Russians and the Americans?"

Sir Morris began slowly rotating the globe that stood by the side of his desk.

"What does that buzz mean?" asked Romanov. "We are not running out of petrol again, are we?"

"No, sir," said the chauffeur. "It's the new calling device now fixed to all ambassadorial cars. It means they expect me to check in."

"Turn round and go back to that petrol station we passed a couple of miles ago," Romanov said quietly.

Romanov started tapping the dashboard impatiently as he waited for the petrol station to reappear on the horizon. The sun was going down quickly and he feared it would be dark within the hour. They had travelled about ninety kilometres beyond Dijon and neither he nor Valchek had even seen a yellow Citroën going either way.

"Fill up again while I phone Geneva," Romanov said the moment he saw the petrol station. He ran to the phone box while Valchek still kept a watchful eye on the passing traffic.

"I am answering your signal," said Romanov when he was put through to the euphemistically titled Second Secretary.

"We've had another call from Mentor," said the Second Secretary. "How far are you from Dijon?"

The member stumbled about the dimly lit room until he came across an unoccupied table wedged up against a pillar in one corner. He sat down on a little leather stool by its side. He swivelled around nervously, as he always did when waiting for someone to bring him his usual malt whisky on the rocks. When the drink was placed on the table in front of him he sipped at it, in between trying to discover if there were any new faces spread around the dark room. Not an easy task, as he refused to put on his glasses. His eyes eventually became accustomed to the dim light thrown out by the long red fluorescent bulb that stretched above the bar. All he could make out were the same old faces staring at him hopefully; but he wanted something new.

The proprietor, noticing that a regular customer had remained on his own, came out and sat opposite him on the other little stool. The member never could get himself to look the man in the eyes.

"I've got someone who's very keen to meet you," whispered the proprietor.

"Which one?" he asked, looking up once more to check the faces at the bar.

"Leaning on the juke box in the corner. The tall, slim one. And he's young," added the proprietor. He looked towards the blaring machine. A pleasing new face smiled at him. He smiled nervously back.

"Was I right?" asked the proprietor.

"Is he safe?" was all he asked.

"No trouble with this one. Upper-class lad, right out of a top-drawer public school. Just wants to earn a bit of pocket money on the side."

"Fine." The member took a sip of whisky.

The proprietor walked over to the juke box. The member watched him talking to the young man. The boy downed his drink, hesitated for a moment, then strolled across the crowded floor to take the empty stool.

"My name is Piers," the young man said.

"Mine's Jeremy," the member said.

"A gentle name," said Piers. "I've always liked the name Jeremy."

"Would you care for a drink?"

"A dry Martini, please," said Piers.

The member ordered a dry Martini and another malt whisky. The waiter hurried away. "I haven't seen you here before."

"No, it's only my second time," said Piers. "I used to work in Soho, but it's got to be so rough lately, you never know who you might end up with."

The drinks arrived and the member took a quick gulp.

"Would you like to dance?" asked Piers.

"It's an emergency," the voice said. "Is the tape on?"

"I'm listening."

"Antarctic is in Dijon and he's discovered what's in the icon."

"And did he give them any clue?"

"No, all he told Pemberton was that he was in possession of a piece of property so valuable that no amount of money we could offer would be sufficient to purchase it back."

"Indeed," said the voice.

"The British think the important word is property," said the caller.

"They're wrong," said the voice on the other end of the line. "It's purchase."

"How can you be so sure?"

"Because the Russian Ambassador in Washington has requested a meeting with the Secretary of State on June 20 and he's bringing with him a bullion order to the value of 712 million dollars in gold."

"So where does that leave us?"

"On our way to Dijon so that we can be sure to lay our hands on that icon before the British or the Russians. The Russians obviously feel confident that it will soon be in their possession, so my bet is that they must already be on the way."

"But I've already agreed to go along with the British plan."

"Try not to forget which side you're on, Commander."

"Yes, sir. But what are we going to do about Antarctic if we get our hands on the icon?"

"It's only the icon we're after. Once that's in our possession, Antarctic is expendable."

Adam checked his watch: a few minutes after seven.

It was time for him to leave because he had decided not to carry out Lawrence's instructions to the letter.

He intended to be waiting for *them*, and not as Lawrence had planned. He locked the bedroom door and returned to reception where he paid for the use of the room and the telephone calls he had made.

"Thank you," he said to the receptionist, and turned to leave.

"Dudley." Adam froze on the spot.

"Dudley," the voice boomed again. "I almost didn't recognise you. Did you change your mind?" A hand thumped him on the shoulder – at least it wasn't the left shoulder, he thought – as he stared down at Jim Hardcastle.

"No," said Adam, wishing he possessed the guile of Robin's father. "I think I was spotted in town so I had to get a change of clothes and keep out of sight for a few hours."

"Then why don't you come to the mustard dinner?" said Jim. "No one will see you there."

"Wish I were able to," said Adam, "but I can't afford to lose any more time."

"Anything I can do to help?" said Jim conspiratorially.

"No, I've got to get to . . . I have a rendezvous just outside the town in less than an hour."

"Wish I could take you there myself," said Jim. "Do anything to help an old soldier, but I'm a bit stuck tonight – of all nights."

"Don't give it a second thought, Jim, I'll be all right."

"I could always take him, Dad," said Linda, who had slipped up by her father's side and was listening intently.

They both turned towards Linda who was wearing a tight-fitting black crêpe dress that started as low and ended as high as it dared while her freshly washed hair now fell to her shoulders. She looked up hopefully.

"You've only just got your licence, lass. Don't be daft."

"You always treat me like a child when there's something worthwhile to do," came back her immediate response.

Jim hesitated. "How far is this rendezvous?" he asked apprehensively.

"About five, maybe six miles," said Adam, "but I'll be fine. I can get a taxi easily."

"The lass is right," said Jim, and taking his car keys out of his pocket, he turned to her and added, "but if you ever let on to your mother I'll kill you." Jim took Adam by the hand and shook it furiously.

"But I'll be just fine . . ."

"I won't hear of it, lad. Never forget, that in the end we're both on the same side, and good luck."

"Thank you, sir," said Adam reluctantly.

Jim beamed. "You'd better be getting along, lass, before your mother shows up."

Linda happily took Adam by the hand and led him away to the car park.

"Which direction?" she asked, once they were seated in the car.

"The Auxerre road," said Adam, looking down at the piece of paper on which he had written the directions Lawrence had read over the phone to him.

Linda set off at a slow pace, seeming at first to be unsure of the car, but once they had reached the outskirts of the town Adam suggested that she might go a little faster.

"I'm very nervous," she said, as she put her hand on Adam's knee.

"Yes, I can tell you are," said Adam, crossing his

legs quickly. "Don't miss the turning," he added when he noticed a signpost pointing to the left.

Linda swung down off the main road on to a country lane while Adam kept his eyes peeled for the building Lawrence had described. It was another two miles before it came into sight.

"Draw into the side," said Adam, "and turn the lights off."

"At last," said Linda, sounding more hopeful, as she brought the car to a halt.

"Thank you very much," said Adam, as he touched the door handle.

"Is that all I get for risking life and limb?" asked Linda.

"I wouldn't want you to be late for the dinner."

"That dinner will be about as exciting as a dance at the Barnsley Young Conservatives."

"But your mother will be worried about you."

"Dudley, you're so up-tight."

"I wouldn't be in normal circumstances but if you stay much longer your life could be in danger," Adam said quietly.

Linda turned ashen. "You're not joking, are you?"

"I wish I was," said Adam. "Now, when I get out of this car you must turn round and go back to the hotel and never mention this conversation to anyone, especially your mother."

"I will," Linda said, sounding nervous for the first time.

"You're a fantastic girl," said Adam, and took her in his arms and gave her the longest, warmest kiss she had ever experienced. Adam then got out of the car and watched her do a five-point turn before she headed off back in the direction of Dijon.

He checked his watch: an hour and a half still to go

before they were due, and by then it would be pitch dark. He jogged over to the airfield and studied the burnt-out buildings that ran alongside the road. It was exactly as Lawrence had described it. It was like a ghost town and Adam was confident that no one else could be there yet as they still wouldn't have had enough time to carry out Lawrence's plan.

Looking across the runway, Adam spotted the ideal place to hide while he waited to see which of the two plans he had prepared would prove necessary.

Flight Lieutenant Alan Banks was thankful that the moon shone so brightly that night. He had landed the little Beaver full of combat men in far worse conditions when a runway had been lit up like the Blackpool seafront.

Banks circled the perimeter of the airfield once and studied the two runways carefully. The airport had been out of action for such a long time that none of the aircraft manuals included a detailed ground plan.

The flight lieutenant was breaking every rule in the book, including piloting an unmarked aircraft informing the French that they would be landing in Paris; not easy to explain overshooting an airport by over a hundred miles.

"I can make a landing on the north–south runway more easily," Banks said, turning to the SAS captain, who sat crouched in the back with his five men. "How near to that hangar do you want me to go?" he said, pointing out of the window.

"Stay well clear, at least a couple of hundred yards," came back the reply. "We still don't know what to expect."

The six SAS men continued to stare cautiously out of the side windows. They had been briefed to pick up a lone Englishman called Scott who would be waiting for them, and then get out fast. It sounded easy enough but it couldn't be that easy otherwise they wouldn't have been called in.

The pilot swung the Beaver round to the south and put the nose down. He smiled when he spotted the burnt-out Spitfire that had been left derelict on the corner of the runway. Just like the ones his father used to fly during the Second World War. But this one had obviously never made it home. He descended confidently and as the little plane touched down it bounced along not because the pilot lacked experience but because the surface of the runway was so badly pitted.

Flight Lieutenant Banks brought the plane to a halt about two hundred yards from the hangar and swung the fuselage round a full circle ready for that quick getaway the captain seemed so keen to execute. He pressed the button that cut the propellers' engines and turned the lights out. The whirring slowed to an eerie whisper. They were forty-three minutes early.

Adam watched the new arrivals suspiciously from the cockpit of the Spitfire some four hundred yards away. He wasn't going to make a run for it across that open ground while the moon shone so brightly. His eyes never left the little unmarked plane as he waited for some clue as to who the occupants might be. He estimated it would be another fifteen minutes before the moon would be shielded by clouds. A few minutes more passed before Adam watched six men drop out of the blind side of the aircraft and lie flat on the tarmac on their stomachs. They were correctly dressed in SAS battle kit but Adam remained unconvinced while he still recalled Romanov's chauffeur's uniform. The six soldiers made no attempt to move. Neither did

Adam as he was still uncertain which side they were on.

All six men on the ground hated the moon and even more the open space. The captain checked his watch: thirty-six minutes to go. He raised his hand and they began to crawl towards the hangar where Pemberton had said Scott would be waiting, a journey which took them nearly twenty minutes, and with each movement they made they became more confident that Pemberton's warning of an enemy waiting for them was unjustified.

At last a mass of clouds reached the moon and a shadow was thrown across the whole airfield. The SAS captain quickly checked his watch. Five minutes to go before the rendezvous was due. He was the first to reach the door of the hangar and he pushed it open with the palm of his hand. He wriggled in through the gap. The bullet hit him in the forehead even before he had found time to raise his gun.

"Move, laddies," shouted the second in command, and the other four were up in a flash, firing in an arc in front of them and running for the protection of the building.

As soon as Adam heard the Scottish brogue, he jumped out of the cockpit and sprinted across the tarmac towards the little plane whose propellers were already beginning to turn. He jumped on the wing and climbed in by the side of the surprised pilot.

"I'm Adam Scott, the man you've come to pick up," he shouted.

"I'm Flight Lieutenant Alan Banks, old chap," said the pilot, thrusting out his hand. Only a British officer could shake hands in such a situation, thought Adam, relieved if still terrified.

They both turned and watched the battle.

"We ought to get going," said the pilot. "My orders are to see you are brought back to England in one piece."

"Not before we are certain none of your men can make it back to the plane."

"Sorry, mate. My instructions are to get you out. Their orders are to take care of themselves."

"Let's at least give them another minute," Adam said.

They waited until the propellers were rotating at full speed. Suddenly the firing stopped and Adam could hear his heart thumping in his body.

"We ought to get moving," said the pilot.

"I know," replied Adam, "but keep your eyes skinned. There's something I still need to know."

Years of night marches made it possible for Adam to see him long before the pilot.

"Get going," said Adam.

"What?" said the pilot.

"Get going."

The pilot moved the joystick forward and the plane started moving slowly down the crumbling runway.

Suddenly a dark figure was running towards them firing long bursts straight at them. The pilot looked back to see a tall man whose fair hair shone in the moonlight.

"Faster, man, faster," said Adam.

"The throttle's full out," said the pilot, as the firing began again, but this time the bullets were ripping into the fuselage. A third burst came but by then the plane was going faster than the man and Adam let out a scream of delight when it left the ground.

He looked back to see that Romanov had turned around and was now firing at someone who was not wearing an SAS uniform.

"They couldn't hope to hit us now unless they've got a bazooka," said Flight Lieutenant Banks.

"Well done, well done," said Adam turning back to the pilot.

"And to think my wife had wanted me to go to the cinema tonight," said the pilot laughing.

"And what were you hoping to see?" asked Adam.

"My Fair Lady."

"Isn't it time for us to be going home?" asked Piers, removing his hand from the member's leg.

"Good idea," he said. "Just let me settle the bill."

"And I'll pick up my coat and scarf," said Piers. "Join you upstairs in a few moments?"

"Fine," he said. Catching the eye of the proprietor the member scribbled his signature in the air. When the 'account' appeared – a bare figure written out on a slip of paper without explanation – it was, as always, extortionate. As always, the member paid without comment. He thanked the proprietor as he left and walked up the dusty, creaky stairs to find his companion already waiting for him on the pavement. He hailed a taxi and while Piers climbed in the back he directed the cabbie to Dillon's bookshop.

"Not in the cab," he said, as his new friend's hand began to creep up his leg.

"I can't wait," said Piers. "It's way past my bedtime."

"Way past my bedtime," his companion repeated involuntarily, and checked his watch. The die must have been cast. They would have moved in by now: surely they had caught Scott this time and, more important, the . . . ?

"Four bob," said the cabbie, flicking back the glass.

He handed over five shillings and didn't wait for any change.

"Just around the corner," he said, guiding Piers past the bookshop and into the little side street. They crept down the stone steps and Piers waited as he unlocked the door, switched on the lights, and led the young man in.

"Oh, very cosy," said Piers. "Very cosy indeed."

Flight Lieutenant Alan Banks stared out of his tiny window as the plane climbed steadily.

"Where to now?" said Adam, relief flooding through his body.

"I had hoped England but I'm afraid the answer is as far as I can manage."

"What do you mean?" said Adam anxiously.

"Look at the fuel gauge," said Alan Banks, putting his forefinger on a little white indicator that was pointing halfway between a quarter full and empty. "We had enough to get us back to Northolt in Middlesex until those bullets ripped into my fuel tank."

The little white stick kept moving towards the red patch even as Adam watched it and within moments the propellers on the left side of the aircraft spun to a halt.

"I am going to have to put her down in a field. I can't risk going on as there are no other airports anywhere nearby. Just be thankful it's a clear moonlit night."

Without warning the plane began to descend sharply. "I shall try for that field over there," said the flight lieutenant, sounding remarkably blasé as he pointed to a large expanse of land to the west of the aircraft. "Hold on tight," he said as the plane spiralled inevitably down. The large expanse of land suddenly looked very small as the plane began to approach it.

Adam found himself gripping the side of his seat and gritting his teeth.

"Relax," said the pilot. "These Beavers have landed on far worse places than this," he went on, as the wheels touched the brown earth. "Damn mud. I hadn't anticipated that," he cursed as the wheels lost their grip in the soft earth and the plane suddenly nosedived forward. A few seconds passed before Adam realised he was still alive but upside down swinging from his seat belt.

"What do I do next?" he asked the pilot but there was no reply.

Adam tried to get his bearings and began to rock his body backwards and forwards until he could touch the side of the plane with one hand while gripping the joystick with his feet. Once he was able to grab the side of the fuselage he undid the belt and collapsed onto the roof of the plane.

He picked himself up, relieved to find nothing was broken. He quickly looked around but there was still no sign of the pilot. Adam clambered out of the plane, glad to feel the safety of the ground. He scrambled around for a considerable time before he found Alan Banks some thirty yards in front of the aircraft motionless on his back.

"Are you all right?" asked the pilot before Adam could ask the same question.

"I'm fine, but how about you, Alan?"

"I'm OK. I must have been thrown clear of the aircraft. Just sorry about the landing, old chap, have to admit it wasn't up to scratch. We must try it again some time."

Adam burst out laughing as the pilot slowly sat up.

"What next?" Banks asked.

"Can you walk?"

"Yes, I think so," said Alan, gingerly lifting himself up. "Damn," he said, "it's only my ankle but it's sure going to slow me down. You'd better get going without me. That bunch back there with the arsenal can only be about thirty minutes behind us."

"But what will you do?"

"My father landed in one of these bloody fields during the Second World War and still managed to get himself back to England without being caught by the Germans. I owe you a great debt of gratitude, Adam, because if I can get back I'll be able to shut him up once and for all. Which lot are chasing us this time, by the way?"

"The Russians," said Adam who was beginning to wonder if perhaps there was a second enemy.

"The Russians – couldn't be better. Anything less and Dad wouldn't have accepted it as a fair comparison."

Adam smiled as he thought of his own father and how much he would have liked Alan Banks. He touched the icon instinctively and was relieved to find it was still in place. The pilot's words had only made him more determined to get back to England.

"Which way?" asked Adam.

The pilot looked up at the Great Bear. "I'll head east, seems appropriate, so you'd better go west, old fellow. Nice to have made your acquaintance," and with that he limped off.

"I'm not sure how much longer I can last, Comrade Major."

"You must try to hold on, Valchek. It's imperative that you try. We cannot afford to stop now," said

Romanov. "I know that plane isn't far. I saw it falling out of the sky."

"I believe you, Comrade, but at least let me die a peaceful death on the side of the road, rather than endure the agony of this car."

Romanov glanced across at his colleague who had been shot in the abdomen. Valchek's hands were covered in blood, and his shirt and trousers were already drenched as he tried helplessly to hold himself in. He continued to clutch on to his stomach like a child who is about to be sick. The driver had also been shot, but in the back while attempting to run away. If he hadn't died instantly, Romanov would have put the next bullet into the coward himself. But Valchek was a different matter. No one could have questioned his courage. He had first taken on the British flat on their stomachs and then the Americans charging in like the seventh cavalry. Romanov had Mentor to thank for ensuring that they had been there first. But he must now quickly warn him that someone else was also briefing the Americans. Romanov, however, felt some satisfaction in having tricked the Americans into turning their fire on the British while he and Valchek waited to pick off the survivors. The last survivor was an American who fired at Valchek continually as they were making their getaway.

Romanov reckoned he had a clear hour before the French, British and Americans would be explaining away several bodies on a disused airfield. Romanov's thoughts returned to Valchek when he heard his comrade groan.

"Let's turn off into this forest," he begged. "I cannot hope to last much longer now."

"Hold on, Comrade, hold on," repeated Romanov.

"We can't be far away from Scott. Think of the Motherland."

"To hell with the Motherland," said Valchek. "Just let me die in peace." Romanov looked across again and realised that he could be stuck with a dead body within a few minutes. Despite Valchek's efforts the blood was now seeping on to the floor like a tap that wouldn't stop dripping.

Romanov noticed a gap in the trees ahead of him. He switched his lights on to full beam and swung off the road on to a dirt track and drove as far as he could until the thicket became too dense. He switched off the headlights and ran round the car to open the door.

Valchek could only manage two or three steps before he slumped to the ground, still holding on to his intestines. Romanov bent down and helped him ease himself up against the trunk of a large tree.

"Leave me to die, Comrade Major. Do not waste any more of your time on me."

Romanov frowned.

"How do you wish to die, Comrade?" he asked. "Slowly and in agony, or quickly and peacefully?"

"Leave me, Comrade. Let me die slowly, but you should go while you still have Scott in your sights."

"But if the Americans were to find you, they might force you to talk."

"You know better than that, Comrade." Romanov accepted the rebuke, then rose and after a moment's thought, ran back to the car.

Valchek began to pray that once the bastard had left someone might find him. He'd never wanted this assignment in the first place, but Zaborski needed two extra eyes on Romanov and Zaborski was not a man to cross. Valchek wouldn't talk, but he still wanted to live.

The bullet from the 9mm Makarov went straight through the back of Valchek's temple and blew away one side of his head. Valchek slumped to the ground and for several seconds his body trembled and spasmed, subsiding into twitches as he emptied his bowels and bladder on to the brown earth.

Romanov stood over him until he was certain he was dead. Valchek would probably not have talked, but this was not a time for taking unnecessary risks.

When he woke the next morning he felt the same familiar guilt. Once again he swore it would be the last time. It was never as good as he had anticipated, and the regret always lingered on for several hours.

The expense of keeping up an extra flat, the taxi fares and the club bills nearly made it prohibitive. But he always returned, like a salmon to its breeding ground. "A queer fish," he murmured out loud, and then groaned at his own pun.

Piers began to wake, and for the next twenty minutes he made his companion forget those regrets. After a moment of lying in exhausted silence the older man slipped out of bed, took ten pounds out of his wallet and left it on the dresser before going to run himself a bath. He anticipated that by the time he returned the boy and the money would have gone.

He soaked himself in the bath wondering about Scott. He knew he should feel guilty about his death. A death that, like so many others before him, had been caused by his picking up a young Pole who he had thought was safe. It was now so many years ago that he couldn't even remember his name.

But Mentor had never been allowed to forget the

name of the young aristocratic KGB officer he had
found sitting on the end of their bed when he woke the
next morning, or the look of disgust he showed for
them both.

CHAPTER SIXTEEN

Adam lay flat on his stomach in the bottom of the empty barge. His head propped on one side, he remained alert to the slightest unfamiliar sound.

The bargee stood behind the wheel counting the three hundred Swiss francs for a second time. It was more than he could normally hope to earn in a month. A woman standing on tiptoes was eyeing the notes happily over his shoulder.

The barge progressed at a stately pace down the canal and Adam could no longer see the crashed plane.

Suddenly, far off in the distance, he heard distinctly the report of what sounded like a gunshot. Even as he listened the woman turned and scuttled down the hatch like a frightened rat. The barge ploughed its course on slowly through the night while Adam listened anxiously for any other unnatural noises, but all he could hear was the gentle splash of the water against the barge's hull. The clouds had moved on and full moon once again lit up the bank on both sides of the river. It became abundantly clear to Adam as he watched the towpath that they were not moving very fast. He could have run quicker. But even if it had cost him the remainder of his money, he was grateful to be escaping. He lowered himself again and curled up in the bow of the boat. He touched the icon, something he found himself doing every few minutes since he had discovered its secret. He did not move for another half hour, although he doubted that the barge had covered more than five miles.

Although everything appeared absolutely serene, he still remained alert. The river was far wider now than when he had first leapt on the barge.

The bargee's eyes never left him for long. He stood gripping the wheel, his oil-covered face not much cleaner than the old dungarees he wore – which looked as if they were never taken off. Occasionally he took a hand from the wheel, but only to remove the smokeless pipe from his mouth, cough, spit and put it back again.

The man smiled, took both hands off the wheel and placed them by the side of his head to indicate that Adam should sleep. But Adam shook his head. He checked his watch. Midnight had passed and he wanted to be off the barge and away long before first light.

He stood up, stretched, and wobbled a little. His shoulder, although healing slowly, still ached relentlessly. He walked up the centre of the barge and took his place next to the wheel.

"La Seine?" he asked, pointing at the water.

The bargee shook his head, no. "Canal de Bourgogne," he grunted.

Adam then pointed in the direction they were moving. "*Quelle ville?*"

The bargee removed his pipe. "*Ville? Ce n'est pas une ville, c'est Sombernon,*" he said, and put the stem back between his teeth.

Adam returned to his place in the bow. He tried to find a more comfortable position to relax and, curling up against the side of the boat, rested his head on some old rope and allowed his eyes to close.

"You know Scott better than any of us," said Sir Morris, "and you still have no feel as to where he might be now, or what he might do next, do you?"

"No, sir," admitted Lawrence. "The only thing we know for certain is that he has an appointment for a medical on Monday afternoon, but somehow I don't think he'll make it."

Sir Morris ignored the comment. "But someone was able to get to Scott, even though we didn't call D4," he continued. "That icon must hold a secret that we haven't begun to appreciate."

"And if Scott is still alive," said Lawrence, "nothing is going to convince him now that we're not to blame."

"And if we're not, who is?" asked Sir Morris. "Because someone was so desperate to discover our next move that they must have taken one hell of a risk during the last twenty-four hours. Unless, of course, it was you," said Sir Morris. The Permanent Secretary rose from his desk and turned around to look out of his window on to Horse Guards Parade.

"Even if it was me," said Lawrence, his eyes resting on a picture of the young Queen which stood on the corner of his master's desk, "it doesn't explain how the Americans got there as well."

"Oh, that's simple," said Sir Morris. "Busch has been briefing them direct. I never doubted he would from the moment he joined us. What I hadn't anticipated was how far the Americans would go without keeping us informed."

"So it was you who told Busch," said Lawrence.

"No," said Sir Morris. "You don't end up sitting behind this desk risking your own skin. I told the Prime

Minister, and politicians can always be relied on to pass on your information if they consider it will score them a point. To be fair, I knew the Prime Minister would tell the President. Otherwise I wouldn't have told him in the first place. More important: do you think Scott can still be alive?"

"Yes, I do," said Lawrence. "I have every reason to believe that the man who ran across the tarmac to our waiting plane was Scott. The French police, who incidentally have been far more co-operative than the Swiss, have informed us that our plane crashed in a field twelve miles north of Dijon but neither Scott nor the pilot were to be found at the scene of the crash."

"And if the French reports on what took place at the airport are accurate," said Sir Morris, "Romanov escaped and they must have had a couple of hours' start on us."

"Possibly," said Lawrence.

"And do you think it equally possible," asked Sir Morris, "that they have caught up with Scott and are now in possession of the icon?"

"Yes, sir, I fear that is quite possible," Lawrence said. "But I can't pretend it's conclusive. However, the BBC monitoring service at Caversham Park picked up extra signals traffic to all Soviet embassies during the night."

"That could mean anything," said Sir Morris, removing his spectacles.

"I agree, sir. But NATO reports that Russian strategic forces have been placed at a state of readiness and several Soviet Ambassadors across Europe have requested formal audiences with their Foreign Secretaries, ours included."

"That *is* more worrying," said Sir Morris. "They don't do that unless they are hoping for our support."

"Agreed, sir. But most revealing of all is that the Active Measures section of the KGB, First Chief Directorate, has booked pages of advertising space in newspapers right across Europe and, I suspect, America."

"Next you'll be telling me they hired J. Walter Thompson to write the copy," growled Sir Morris.

"They won't need them," said Lawrence. "I suspect it's a story that will make every front page."

If it hadn't been for the ceaseless throbbing in his shoulder, Adam might not have woken so quickly. The barge had suddenly swung at 90° and started heading east when Adam woke up with a start. He looked at the bargee and indicated that as the river was far wider now could he ease them nearer to the bank so he could jump off. The old man shrugged his shoulders pretending not to understand as the barge drifted aimlessly on.

Adam looked over the side and despite the lateness of the hour could see the bed of the river quite clearly. He tossed a stone over the side and watched it drop quickly to the bottom. It looked almost as if he could reach down and touch it. He looked up helplessly at the bargee who continued to stare over his head into the distance.

"Damn," said Adam, and taking the icon out of his blazer pocket held it high above his head. He stood on the edge of the barge feeling like a football manager asking the referee for permission to substitute a player. Permission was granted and Adam leaped into the water. His feet hit the canal bed with a thud and knocked the breath out of his body despite the fact that the water only came up to his waist.

Adam stood in the canal, the icon still held high above his head as the barge sailed past him. He waded to the nearest bank and clambered up on to the tow-path, turning slowly round as he tried to get some feel for direction. He was soon able to distinguish the Plough again and plot a course due west. After an hour of soggy jogging he began to make out a light in the distance which he estimated to be under a mile away. His legs were soaking and cold as he started to squelch his way across a field towards the first rays of the morning sun.

Whenever he came to a hedge or gate he climbed over or under like a Roman centurion determined to hold a straight line with his final destination. He could now see the outline of a house, which as he got nearer he realised was no more than a large cottage. He remembered the expression 'peasant farmer' from his school geography lessons. A little cobbled path led up to a half-open wooden door that looked as if it didn't need a lock. Adam tapped gently on the knocker and stood directly below the light above the doorway so that whoever answered would see him immediately.

The door was pulled back by a woman of perhaps thirty, who wore a plain black dress and a spotless white apron. Her rosy cheeks and ample waist confirmed her husband's profession.

When she saw Adam standing under the light she couldn't mask her surprise – she had been expecting the postman, but he didn't often appear in a neat navy blue blazer and soaking grey trousers.

Adam smiled. "*Anglais*," he told her, and added, "I fell in the canal."

The lady burst out laughing and beckoned Adam into her kitchen. He walked in to find a man evidently dressed for milking. The farmer looked up and when he saw Adam he joined in the laughter – a warm, friendly laugh more with Adam than against him.

When the woman saw that Adam was dripping all over her spotless floor she quickly pulled down a towel from the rack above the fire and said, "*Enlevez-moi ça,*" pointing to Adam's trousers.

Adam turned towards the farmer for guidance but his host only nodded his agreement and added with a mime of pulling down his own trousers.

"*Enlevez les, enlevez les,*" the woman repeated, pointing at him, and handed him the towel.

Adam removed his shoes and socks but the farmer's wife went on pointing until he took off his trousers, and she didn't budge before he had finally removed his shirt and underclothes and wrapped the towel around his waist. She stared at the large bandage on his shoulder but then quickly picked up everything except his blazer and took them over to the sink while he stood by the fire and dried himself.

Adam hitched up the towel around his waist, as the farmer beckoned him to join him at the table, pouring a large glass of milk for his guest and another for himself. Adam sat down next to the farmer, hanging his fashionable new blazer over the back of the chair near the fire. A delicious aroma arose from the pan where the farmer's wife was frying a thick slice of bacon which she had cut from the joint hanging in the smoky recess of the chimney.

The farmer raised his glass of milk high in the air.

"Winston Churchill," he toasted. Adam took a long gulp from his own glass and then raised it dramatically.

"Charles de Gaulle," he said, and finished off the warm milk as if it had been his first pint at the local pub.

The farmer picked up the jug once more and refilled their glasses. "*Merci,*" said Adam, turning to the farmer's wife as she placed in front of him a large plate sizzling with eggs and bacon. She nodded and handed Adam a knife and fork before saying, "*Mangez.*"

"*Merci, merci,*" Adam repeated, as she cut him a thick oval slice from the huge loaf in front of im.

Adam began to devour the freshly cooked food which was the first meal he'd managed since the dinner he'd ordered at Robin's expense.

Without warning the farmer suddenly rose from his place and thrust out his hand. Adam also got up and shook it gratefully, only to be reminded how sore his shoulder still was.

"*Je dois travailler à la laiterie,*" he explained.

Adam nodded, and remained standing as his host left the room, but the farmer waved him down with a further, "*Mangez.*"

When Adam had finished the last scrap of food – he did everything except lick the plate – he took it over to the farmer's wife who was busy removing a pot from the stove in order to pour him a large, steaming cup of hot coffee. He sat back down and began to sip at it.

Adam tapped the jacket pocket almost automatically to make sure the icon was still safely in place. He pulled it out and studied St George and the Dragon. He turned it over, hesitated and then pressed the silver crown hard. The icon split in half like a book revealing two tiny hinges on the inside.

He glanced up at the farmer's wife, who was now wringing out his socks. Adam noticed his pants had already joined the trousers on the rack above the fire. She removed an ironing board from a little alcove by the side of the stove and began to set it up, showing no interest in Adam's discovery.

Once again he stared down at the inside of the open icon which was now laid flat on the table in front of him. The true irony was that the woman pressing his trousers was able to understand every word on the parchment while at the same time unable to explain the full significance to him. The complete surface of the inside of the icon was covered by a parchment which was glued to the wood and fell only a centimetre short of the four edges. Adam swivelled it round so that he could study it more clearly. The scrawled signatures in black ink at the bottom and the seals gave it the look of a legal document. On each reading he learned something new. Adam had been surprised originally to discover it was written in French until he came to the date on the bottom – June 20, 1867 – and then he remembered from his military history lectures at Sandhurst that long after Napoleonic times most international agreements remained conducted in French. Adam began to reread the script again slowly.

His French was not good enough to translate more than a few odd words from the finely handwritten scroll. Under *Etas Unis* William Seward's bold hand was scrawled across a crest of a two-headed eagle. Next to it was the signature of Edward de Stoeckle below a crown that mirrored the silver ornament embedded in the back of the icon. Adam double-checked. It had to be some form of agreement executed between the Russians and the Americans in 1867.

He then searched for other words that would help to explain the significance of the document. On one line he identified: '*Sept millions deux cent mille dollars d'or (7.2 million)*' and on another '*Sept cent douze millions huit cent mille dollars d'or (712.8 million) le 20 juin 1966.*

His eyes rested on a calendar hanging by a nail from the wall. It was Friday, June 17, 1966. If the date in the agreement were to be believed, then in only three days the document would no longer have any legal validity. No wonder the two most powerful nations on earth seemed desperate to get their hands on it, thought Adam.

Adam read through the document line by line searching for any further clues, pondering over each word slowly.

His eyes came to a halt on the one word that would remain the same in both languages.

The one word he had not told Lawrence.

Adam wondered how the icon had ever fallen into the hands of Goering in the first place. He must have bequeathed it to his father unknowingly – for had he realised the true importance of what was hidden inside it, he would surely have been able to bargain for his own freedom with either side.

"Voilà, voilà," said the farmer's wife, waving her hands as she placed warm socks, pants and trousers in front of Adam. How long had he spent engrossed in his fateful discovery? She looked down at the upside down parchment and smiled. Adam quickly snapped the icon closed and then studied the masterpiece carefully. So skilfully had the wood been cut that he could no longer see the join. He thought of the words of the letter left to him in his father's will: "But if you open it only to discover its purpose is to involve you in some dishonourable enterprise, be rid of it without a second thought." He did not need to give a second thought to how his father would have reacted in the same circumstances. The farmer's wife was now standing hands on hips, staring at him with a puzzled look.

Adam quickly replaced the icon in his jacket pocket and pulled back on his trousers.

He could think of no adequate way of thanking the farmer's wife for her hospitality, her lack of suspicion or inquisitiveness, so he simply walked over to her, took her gently by the shoulders, and kissed her on the

cheek. She blushed and handed him a small plastic
bag. He looked inside to find three apples, some bread
and a large piece of cheese. She removed a crumb from
his lip with the edge of her apron and led him to the
open door.

Adam thanked her and then walked outside into his
other world.

PART THREE

THE WHITE HOUSE
WASHINGTON DC

June 17, 1966

CHAPTER SEVENTEEN

THE WHITE HOUSE
WASHINGTON DC *June 17, 1966*

"I don't want to be the first god-damn President in the history of the United States to hand back an American state rather than be founding one."

"I appreciate that, Mr President," said the Secretary of State. "But . . ."

"Where do we stand on this legally, Dean?"

"We don't, Mr President. Abraham Brunweld, the leading authority on documents of this period, confirms that the terms of the ninety-nine year lease are binding on both sides. The lease was signed on behalf of Russia by Edward de Stoeckle and for the US by the then Secretary of State, William Seward."

"Can this agreement still be valid today?" asked the President, turning to his chief legal officer, Nicholas Katzenbach.

"It certainly can, sir," said the Attorney General. "But only if they can produce their original. If they do, the UN and the international court at The Hague would have no choice but to support the Russian claim. Otherwise no international agreement signed by us in the past or in the future would carry any credibility."

"What you're asking me to do is lie down and wag my tail like a prize labrador while the Russians shit all over us," said the President.

"I understand how you feel, Mr President," said the Attorney General, "but it remains my responsibility to make you aware of the legal position."

"God dammit, is there a precedent for this kind of stupidity by a Head of State?"

"The British," chipped in Dean Rusk, "will be facing a similar problem with the Chinese in 1999 over the New Territories of Hong Kong. They have already accepted the reality of the situation and indeed have made it clear to the Chinese Government that they are willing to come to an agreement with them."

"That's just one example," said the President, "and we all know about the British and their 'fair play' diplomacy."

"Also, in 1898," continued Rusk, "the Russians obtained a ninety-nine-year lease on Port Arthur in Northern China. The port was vital to them because, unlike Vladivostok, it is ice-free all year round."

"I had no idea the Russians *had* a port in China."

"They don't any longer, Mr President. They returned it to Mao in 1955, as an act of goodwill between fellow Communists."

"You can be damn sure the Russians won't return this piece of land to *us* as an act of goodwill," said the President. "Am I left with any alternative?"

"Short of military action to prevent the Soviets claiming what they will rightfully see as theirs, no sir," replied the Secretary of State.

"So one Johnson buys the land from the Russians in 1867 and another has to sell it back in 1966. Why did Seward and the President ever agree to such a damn cockamaney idea in the first place?"

"At the time," said the Attorney General, removing his spectacles, "the purchase price of the land in question was seven point two million dollars and inflation was then virtually unheard of. Andrew Johnson could never have imagined the Russians wanting to purchase it back at ninety-nine times its original value, or in real terms, seven hundred and twelve point eight million dollars in gold bullion. In reality, years of inflation have made the asking price cheap. And the Russians have already lodged the full amount in a New York bank to prove it."

"So we can't even hope that they won't stump up in time," said the President.

"It would seem not, sir."

"But why did Tsar Alexander want to lease the damn land in the first place? That's what beats me."

"He was having trouble with some of his senior ministers at the time over the selling off of land belonging to Russia in Eastern Asia. The Tsar thought this transaction would be more palatable to his inner circle if he presented it as nothing more than a long lease, with a buy-back clause, rather than an outright sale."

"Why didn't Congress object?"

"After Congress ratified the main treaty, the amendment was not strictly subject to approval by the House, because no further expenditure by the United States government was involved," Rusk explained. "Ironically, Seward was proud of the fact he had demanded such a high premium in the repayment clause. At the time he had every reason to believe it would be impossible to repay."

"Now it's worth that in annual oil revenue alone," said the President, looking out of the Oval Office window towards the Washington Monument. "Not to mention the military chaos it's going to create in this country if they've got their hands on their copy of the treaty. Don't ever forget that I was the President who asked Congress to spend billions of dollars putting the early warning system right across that border so the American people could sleep easy."

Neither adviser felt able to contradict their elected leader.

"So what are the British doing about all this?"

"Playing it close to the chest, as usual, Mr President. It's an English national who is thought to be in possession of the treaty at the moment and they still seem quietly confident that they will get their hands on him and the icon before the Russians, so they may yet turn out to be our saviours."

"Nice to have the British coming to *our* rescue for a change," said the President. "But have we meanwhile been sitting on our asses while they try to solve our problems for us?"

"No, sir. The CIA have been on it for over a month."

"Then it's only surprising that the Russians haven't got their hands on the icon already."

Nobody laughed.

"So what am I expected to do next? Sit and wait for the Soviets to move 712 million dollars of gold from their New York bank to the US Treasury before midnight on Monday?"

"They must also deliver their original copy of the agreement to me at the same time," said Rusk. "And they have only sixty hours left to do that."

"Where's our copy, at this moment?" asked the President.

"Somewhere deep in the vaults of the Pentagon. Only two people know the exact location. Since the

Yalta conference, our copy of the treaty has never seen the light of day."

"Why have I never been told about it before today?" asked the President. "At least I could have put a stop to so much expenditure."

"For over fifty years, we've believed the Russians' copy was destroyed at the time of the Revolution. As the years passed it became clear that the Soviets accepted this as a *fait accompli* with the final acknowledgment of this fact coming from Stalin at Yalta. Brezhnev must have come across something within the last month that convinced him that their copy had only been mislaid."

"Christ, another month and we would have had a home run."

"That is correct, sir," said the Secretary of State.

"Do you realise, Dean, that if the Russians turn up at your office before midnight on Monday with their copy, all I'll be able to do will be so much piss in a thunderstorm?"

CHAPTER EIGHTEEN

When the cottage door closed behind Adam, all he could make out was the outskirts of a small town. While it was still so early he felt safe to jog towards the '*centre ville*', but as soon as the early-morning workers began to appear on the streets, he slowed to a walk. Adam opted not to go straight into the centre of the town but to look for somewhere to hide while he considered his next move. He came to a halt outside a multi-storey car park and decided he was unlikely to find a better place to formulate a plan.

Adam walked through an exit door at ground level and came to a lift that indicated that the car park was on four floors. He ran down the steps to the lowest level, tentatively pulled back the door to the basement, and found it was badly lit and almost empty. Adam had chosen the basement as he assumed that it would be the last floor to fill up with customers. He walked around the perimeter of the floor and studied the layout. Two cars were parked in the far corner, and a thick layer of dust suggested that they had been there for some time. He crouched down behind one of them and found that he was safely out of sight to all but the most inquisitive.

He began to fantasise that someone might park a

car on that floor and leave the keys in the ignition. He checked the doors of the two cars already parked but both were securely locked. He settled back to work out a more serious plan of how he could reach the coast by nightfall.

He was deep in thought when he heard a scraping noise that made him jump. He peered round the gloomy basement, and out of the darkness a man appeared pulling behind him a plastic dustbin half full of rubbish. Adam could barely see the old man dressed in a dirty brown coat that stretched nearly to the ground and left little doubt about the height of the previous employee. He wasn't sure what he would do if the man continued to walk towards him. But as he came nearer Adam could see that he was stooped and old; the stub of a cigarette protruded from his lips. The cleaner stopped in front of him, spotted a cigarette packet, picked it up and checked to be sure it was empty before dropping it in the dustbin. After that, a sweet paper, a Pepsi-Cola can and an old copy of *Le Figaro* all found their way into the dustbin. His eyes searched slowly round the room for more rubbish, but still he didn't notice Adam tucked away behind the farthest car. Satisfied that his task was completed, he dragged the dustbin across the floor and pushed it outside the door. Adam began to relax again but after about two minutes, the old man returned, walked over to a wall and pulled open a door that Adam hadn't previously noticed. He took off the long brown coat and replaced it with a grey one that didn't look in a much better state but at least it made a more convincing fit. He then disappeared through the exit. Moments later Adam heard a door close with a bang.

The cleaner had ended his day.

Adam waited for some time before he stood up and stretched. He crept around the edge of the wall until he reached the little door. He pulled it open quietly and removed the long brown coat from its nail, then headed back to his place in the corner. He ducked down as the first of the morning cars arrived. The driver swung into the far corner in such a fluent circle that Adam felt sure it must have been a daily routine. A short dapper man with a pencil moustache, dressed in a smart pin-stripe suit, jumped out of the car carrying a briefcase. Once he had locked the car door he proceeded with fast mincing strides towards the exit. Adam waited until the heavy door swung back into place before he stood up and tried on the brown coat over his blazer. It was tight on the shoulders and a little short in the arm, but at least it made him look as if he might have worked there.

For the next hour he watched the cars as they continued to arrive at irregular intervals. Tiresomely, all the owners carefully locked their doors and checked them before disappearing through the exit with their keys.

When he heard ten o'clock strike in the distance Adam decided that there was nothing to be gained by hanging around any longer. He had crept out from behind the car that was shielding him and began to make his way across the floor towards the exit when a Rover with English registration plates swung round the corner and nearly blinded him. He jumped to one side to let the car pass but it screeched to a halt beside him and the driver wound down his window.

"All – right – park – here?" the driver asked, emphasising each word in an English accent.

"Oui, monsieur," said Adam.

"Other – floors – marked – *privé*," the man continued, as if addressing a complete moron. "Any-where?" His arm swept round the floor.

"*Oui,*" repeated Adam, "bert ay merst paak you," he added, fearing he sounded too much like Peter Sellers.

Balls, was what Adam expected to hear him reply. "Fine," was what the man actually said. He got out of the car, and handed Adam his keys and a ten franc note.

"*Merci,*" said Adam, pocketing the note and touching his forehead with his hand. "*Quelle – heure – vous – retournez?*" he asked, playing the man at his own game.

"One hour at most," said the man as he reached the door. Adam waited by the car for a few minutes but the man did not come back. He opened the passenger door and dropped the food bag on the front seat. He then walked round to the other side and climbed in the driver's seat, switched on the ignition and checked the fuel gauge: a little over half full. He revved the engine and drove the car up the ramp until he reached the first floor, where he came to a halt unable to escape. He needed a two-franc piece to make the arm swing up and let him out. The lady in the car behind him reluctantly changed his ten-franc note once she realised there was no other way of getting out.

Adam drove quickly out on to the road looking for the sign 'Toutes Directions'. Once he had found one, it was only minutes before he was clear of the town and travelling up the N6 to Paris.

Adam estimated that he had two hours at best. By then the police would surely have been informed of the theft of the car. He felt confident he had enough petrol to reach Paris; but he certainly couldn't hope to make Calais.

He remained in the centre lane of the N6 for most

of the journey, always keeping the speedometer five kilometres below the limit. By the end of the first hour Adam had covered nearly ninety kilometres. He opened the bag the farmer's wife had given him and took out an apple and a piece of cheese. His mind began to drift to Heidi, as it had so often in the past two days.

If only he had never opened the letter.

Another hour passed before he spotted him limping up a hill only a few hundred yards from the main road. A broad smile came over Romanov's face when he realised he could get to Scott long before he could hope to reach the road. When Romanov was within a few yards of him the flight lieutenant turned round and smiled at the stranger.

When Romanov left Banks thirty minutes later hidden behind a tree with a broken neck he reluctantly admitted that the young pilot officer had been as brave as Valchek – but he couldn't waste any more time trying to discover in which direction Scott was heading.

Romanov headed west.

The moment Adam heard the siren he came out of his reverie. He checked the little clock on the dashboard. He had only been driving for about an hour and a half. Could the French police be that efficient? The police car was now approaching him fast on his left but Adam maintained the same speed – except for his heartbeat, which climbed well above the approved limit – until the police car shot past him.

As the kilometres sped by, he began to wonder if it might be wiser to turn off on to a quieter road, but decided, on balance, to risk pushing on to Paris as quickly as possible.

He remained alert for further sirens as he continued to follow the signs to Paris. When he finally reached the outskirts of the city, he proceeded to the Boulevard de l'Hôpital and even felt relaxed enough to bite into another apple. In normal circumstances he would have appreciated the magnificent architecture along the banks of the Seine, but today his eyes kept returning to the rear view mirror.

Adam decided he would abandon the vehicle in a large public car park: with any luck it could be days before anyone came across it.

He turned down the Rue de Rivoli and took in at once the long colourful banners looming up in front of him. He could hardly have picked a better place, as he felt sure it would be packed with foreign cars.

Adam backed the Rover in the farthest corner of the square. He then wolfed down the last piece of cheese, and locked the car. He started walking towards the exit, but had only gone a few yards when he realised that the strolling holidàymakers were amused by his ill-fitting brown jacket which he had completely forgotten. He decided to turn back and throw the coat in the boot. He quickly took it off and folded it in a small square.

He was only a few yards away from the car when he saw the young policeman. He was checking the Rover's number plate and repeating the letters and numbers into an intercom. Adam inched slowly back, never taking his eyes from the officer. He only needed to manage another six or seven paces before he would be lost in the throng of the crowd.

Five, four, three, two, he backed, as the man continued speaking into the intercom. Just one more pace . . . *"Alors!"* hollered the lady on whose foot Adam stepped.

"I'm so sorry," said Adam, instinctively in his native

language. The policeman immediately looked up and stared at Adam, then shouted something into the intercom and began running towards him.

Adam dropped the brown coat and swung round quickly, nearly knocking the stooping lady over before sprinting off towards the exit. The car park was full of tourists who had come to enjoy the pleasures of the Louvre, and Adam found it hard to pick up any real speed through the dense crowd. By the time he reached the entrance to the car park he could hear the policeman's whistle a few paces behind him. He ran across the Rue de Rivoli, through an archway and into a large square.

By then another policeman was coming from his right, leaving him with no choice but to run up the steps in front of him. When he reached the top he turned to see at least three other policemen in close pursuit. He threw himself through the swing door and past a group of Japanese tourists who were surrounding the Rodin statue that stood in the hallway. He charged on past a startled ticket collector, and on up the long marble staircase. *"Monsieur, monsieur, votre billet?"* he heard shouted in his wake.

At the top of the staircase he turned right and ran through *The Special '66' Centuries Exhibition*, Modern – Pollock, Bacon, Hockney – into the Impressionist room – Monet, Manet, Courbet – desperately looking for any way out. On into Eighteenth Century – Fragonard, Goya, Watteau – but still no sign of an exit. Through the great arch into Seventeenth Century – Murillo, Van Dyck, Poussin – as people stopped looking at the pictures and turned their attention to what was causing such a commotion. Adam ran on into Sixteenth Century – Raphael, Caravaggio, Michelangelo – suddenly aware that there were only two centuries of paintings to go.

Right or left? He chose right, and entered a huge square room. There were three exits. He slowed momentarily to decide which would be his best bet when he became aware that the room was full of Russian icons. He came to a halt at an empty display case. *'Nous regrettons que ce tableau soit soumis à la restauration.'*

The first policeman had already entered the large room and was only a few paces behind as Adam dashed on towards the farthest exit. There were now only two exits left open for him from which to choose. He swung right, only to see another policeman bearing straight down on him. Left: two more. Ahead, yet another.

Adam came to a halt in the middle of the Icon Room at the Louvre, his hands raised above his head. He was surrounded by policemen, their guns drawn.

CHAPTER NINETEEN

Sir Morris picked up the phone on his desk.

"An urgent call from Paris, sir," said his secretary.

"Thank you, Tessa." He listened carefully as his brain quickly translated the exciting news.

"Merci, merci," said Sir Morris to his opposite number at the French Foreign Ministry. "We will be back in touch with you as soon as we have made all the necessary arrangements to collect him. But for now, please don't let him out of your sight." Sir Morris listened for a few moments before he said: "And if he has any possessions on him, please keep them guarded under lock and key. Thank you once again." His secretary took down every word of the conversation in shorthand – as she had done for the past seventeen years.

Once the police had snapped the handcuffs on Adam and marched him off to a waiting car, he was surprised how relaxed, almost friendly, they became. He was yanked into the back of the car by the policeman to whom he was attached. He noticed that there was a police car in front of him and yet another behind. Two motorcycle outriders led the little motorcade away. Adam felt more like visiting royalty than a criminal who was wanted for questioning for two murders, two car thefts and travelling under false identification. Was it possible at last that someone had worked out he was innocent?

When Adam arrived at the Sûreté on the Ile de la Cité, he was immediately ordered to empty all his pockets. One wristwatch, one apple, forty pounds in traveller's cheques, eight francs, and one British passport in the name of Dudley Hulme. The station inspector asked him politely to strip to his vest and pants. It was the second time that day. Once Adam had done so, the inspector carefully checked every pocket of the blazer, even the lining. His expression left Adam in no doubt he hadn't found what he was looking for.

"Do you have anything else in your possession?" the officer asked in slow, precise English.

Damn silly question, thought Adam. You can see for yourself. "No," was all he replied. The inspector checked the blazer once again but came across nothing new. "You must be dressed," he said abruptly.

Adam put back on his shirt, jacket and trousers but the inspector kept his tie and shoelaces.

"All your things will be returned to you when you leave," the inspector explained. Adam nodded as he slipped on his shoes, which flapped uncomfortably when he walked. He was then accompanied to a small cell on the same floor, locked in and left alone. He looked around the sparsely furnished room. A small wooden table was placed in its centre, with two wooden chairs on either side. His eyes checked over a single bed in the corner which had on it an ancient horse-hair mattress. He could not have described the room properly as a cell because there were no bars, even across the one small window. He took off his jacket, hung it over the chair and lay down on the bed. At least it was an improvement over anything he had slept on for the past two nights, he reflected. Could it have only been two nights since he had slept on the floor of Robin's hotel room in Geneva?

As the minutes ticked by, he made only one decision. That when the inspector returned, he would demand to see a lawyer. "What the hell's the French for lawyer?" he asked out loud.

When an officer eventually appeared, in what Adam estimated must have been about half an hour, he was carrying a tray laden with hot soup, a roll, and what looked to Adam like a steak with all the trimmings and a plastic cup filled to the brim with red wine. He wondered if they had got the wrong man, or if this was simply his last meal before the guillotine. He followed the officer to the door.

"I demand to speak to a lawyer," he said emphatically, but the policeman only shrugged.

"Je ne comprends pas l'anglais," he said, and slammed the door behind him.

Adam settled down to eat the meal that had been set before him, thankful that the French assumed good food should be served whatever the circumstances.

Sir Morris told them his news an hour later and then studied each of them round the table carefully. He would never have called the D4 if he hadn't felt sure that Adam was at last secure. Matthews continued to show no emotion. Busch was unusually silent while Snell looked almost relaxed for a change. Lawrence was the only one who seemed genuinely pleased.

"Scott is locked up in the Ministry of the Interior off the Place Beauvais," continued Sir Morris, "and I have already contacted our military attaché at the Embassy . . ."

"Colonel Pollard," interrupted Lawrence.

"Colonel Pollard," said Sir Morris, "who has been sent over in the Ambassador's car and will bring Scott back to be debriefed at our Embassy in Faubourg St Honoré. Sûreté rang a few moments ago to confirm that Colonel Pollard had arrived." Sir Morris turned towards his Number Two. "You will fly over to Paris tonight and conduct the debriefing yourself."

"Yes, sir," said Lawrence, looking up at his boss, a smile appearing on his face.

Sir Morris nodded. A cool lot, he considered, as he stared round that table, but the next half hour would surely find out which one of them it was who served two masters.

"Good. I don't think I shall need any of you again today," said Sir Morris as he rose from his chair.

Mentor smiled as Sir Morris left the room; his task had already been completed. So simple when you can read upside-down shorthand.

A black Jaguar bearing CD plates had arrived at police headquarters a few minutes earlier than expected. The traffic had not been as heavy as the colonel had anticipated. The inspector was standing on the steps as Pollard jumped out of the car. The policeman looked at the flapping Union Jack on the bonnet and considered the whole exercise was becoming rather melodramatic.

Pollard, a short, thickset man, dressed in a dark suit, regimental tie and carrying a rolled umbrella, looked like so many of those Englishmen who refuse to acknowledge that they could possibly be abroad.

The inspector took Pollard directly through to the little room where Adam had been incarcerated.

"Pollard's the name, Colonel Pollard. British Military Attaché stationed here in Paris. Sorry you've been put through this ordeal, old fellow, but a lot of paperwork had to be completed to get you out. Bloody red tape."

"I understand," said Adam, jumping off the bed and shaking the colonel by the hand. "I was in the army myself."

"I know. Royal Wessex, wasn't it?"

Adam nodded, feeling a little more confident.

"Still, the problem's been sorted out now," continued the colonel. "The French police have been most co-operative and have agreed to let you accompany me to our Embassy."

Adam looked at the colonel's tie. "Duke of York's?"

"What? Certainly not," said Pollard, his hand fingering his shirt front. "Green Jackets."

"Yes, of course," said Adam, pleased to have his mistake picked up.

"Now I think we ought to be cutting along, old fellow, I know you'll be relieved to hear that they won't be laying any charges."

The colonel didn't know just how relieved Adam did feel.

The inspector led them both back out into the hall where Adam had only to identify and sign for his personal belongings. He put them all in his pocket, except for the watch, which he slipped over his wrist, and his shoelaces, which he quickly inserted and tied. He wasn't surprised they didn't return Dudley Hulme's passport.

"Don't let's hang around too long, old fellow," said the colonel, beginning to sound a little anxious.

"I won't be a moment," said Adam. "I'm just as keen to get out of this place as you are." He checked his laces before following Colonel Pollard and the inspector out to the waiting Jaguar. He noticed for the first time that the colonel had a slight limp. A chauffeur held the door open for him; Adam laughed.

"Something funny, old fellow?" asked the colonel.

"No. It's just that the last chauffeur who offered to do that for me didn't look quite as friendly."

Adam climbed into the back of the Jaguar and the colonel slipped in beside him.

"Back to the Embassy," said Pollard, and the car moved off briskly.

Adam stared in horror at the flapping Union Jack.

CHAPTER TWENTY

When Adam awoke he was naked.

He looked around the sparse room but this time, unlike the French jail, he was unable to see what was behind him: his arms, legs and body were bound tightly by a nylon cord to a chair that had been placed in the middle of the room, and which made him all but immobile.

When he looked up from the chair all he could see was Colonel Pollard standing over him. The moment the colonel was satisfied that Adam had regained consciousness he quickly left the room.

Adam turned his head to see all his clothes laid out neatly on a bed at the far side of the cell. He tried to manoeuvre the chair, but he could barely manage to make it wobble from side to side, and after several minutes had advanced only a few inches towards the door. He switched his energies to trying to loosen the cords around his wrists, rubbing them up and down against the wood of the slats, but his arms were bound so tightly that he could only manage the slightest friction.

After struggling ineffectively for several minutes he was interrupted by the sound of the door swinging open. Adam looked up as Romanov strode through.

He decided he was no less terrifying at close quarters. He was followed by another man whom Adam didn't recognise. The second man was clutching what looked like a cigar box as he took his place somewhere behind Adam. Pollard followed him, carrying a large plastic sheet.

Romanov looked at Adam's naked body and smiled; enjoying his humiliation he came to a halt directly in front of the chair.

"My name is Alexander Petrovich Romanov," he announced with only a slight accent.

"Or Emmanuel Rosenbaum," said Adam, staring at his adversary closely.

"I am only sorry that we are unable to shake hands," he added, as he began circling the chair. "But I felt in the circumstances certain precautions were necessary. First I should like to congratulate you on having eluded me for so long, but as you will now realise my source in London can place a call every bit as quickly as yours."

"Your source?" said Adam.

"Don't be naïve, Captain. You must be painfully aware by now that you're in no position to be asking questions, only answering them."

Adam fixed his gaze on a brick in the wall in front of him, making no attempt to follow Romanov's circum-navigations.

"Pollard," said Romanov sharply, "put Captain Scott back in the centre of the room. He seems to have managed to move at least a foot in his getaway attempt."

Pollard did as he was bid, first spreading the plastic sheet on the floor, then manoeuvring Adam till the chair was on the centre of the sheet.

"Thank you," said Romanov. "I think you have

already met our Colonel Pollard," he continued. "That's not his real name, of course, and indeed he's not a real colonel either, but that's what he always wanted to be in life, so when the opportunity arose, we happily obliged.

"In fact the good colonel did serve in the British Army, but I fear he entered the service of King and country as a private soldier and eighteen years later left, still as a private soldier. And despite an injury to his leg – unfortunately not received from any known enemy of the Crown – he was unable to claim a disability pension. Which left him fairly destitute. But, as I explained, he always wanted to be a colonel," continued Romanov. "It was a good attempt of yours – 'The Duke of York's?' – but as the colonel had genuinely served with the Green Jackets it was the one tie he felt safe wearing."

Adam's eyes remained fixed on the wall. "Now I confess, our mistake over the Union Jack was lax but as it is impossible to fly the Russian flag upside down without everyone noticing, it was perhaps understandable. Although, in truth, Pollard should have spotted it immediately, we must be thankful that you did not until the car doors were safely locked."

Romanov stopped his endless circling and stared down at the nude body.

"Now I think the time has come for you to be introduced to our Dr Stavinsky who has so been looking forward to making your acquaintance because he hasn't had a lot of work to do lately and he fears he might be becoming a little rusty."

Romanov took a pace backward allowing Stavinsky to come and take his place immediately in front of Adam. The cigar box was still tucked under his arm. Adam stared at the diminutive figure who seemed to be sizing him up. Stavinsky must have been no taller than five feet and wore an open-necked grey shirt and a badly creased grey suit that made him resemble a junior clerk in a not very successful solicitor's office. A one-day bristle covered his face, leaving the impression that he hadn't expected to be working that day. His thin lips suddenly parted in a grin as if he had come to some conclusion.

"It is a pleasure to make your acquaintance, Captain Scott," began Stavinsky. "Although you are an unexpected guest of the Embassy you are most welcome. You could of course make our association very short by simply letting me have one piece of information. In truth" – he let out a small sigh – "I only require to know the whereabouts of the Tsar's icon." He paused. "Although I have a feeling it's not going to be that easy. Am I correct?"

Adam didn't reply.

"It doesn't come as a great surprise. I warned Comrade Romanov that after his laudatory description of you a simple series of questions and answers would be unlikely to suffice. However, I must follow the normal procedure in such circumstances. As you will find, the Russians go by the book every bit as much as the British. Now you may have wondered," added Stavinsky as if it were an afterthought, "why a man who never smokes should be seen carrying a Cuban cigar box."

Stavinsky waited for Adam's reply but none was forthcoming.

"Ah, no attempt at conversation. I see you have been through such an experience before. Well, then I must continue talking to myself for the moment. When I was a student at the University of Moscow my subject was chemistry, but I specialised in one particular aspect of the science."

Adam feigned no interest as he tried not to recall his worst days in the hands of the Chinese.

"What few people in the West realise is that we Russians were the first to pioneer, at university level, a Department of Scientific Interrogation with a full professorial chair and several research assistants. They are still without one at either Oxford or Cambridge I am told. But then the West continues to preserve a quixotic view of the value of life and the right of the individual. Now, as you can imagine, only certain members of the university were aware of the existence of such a department, let alone able to enrol as a student – especially as it was not on the curriculum. But as I had already been a member of the Perviyotdel it was common sense that I should add the craft of torture to my trade. Now I am basically a simple man," continued Stavinsky, "who had previously shown little interest in research but once I had been introduced to the 'cigar box' I became, overnight, an enthralled and retentive pupil. I could not wait to be let loose to experiment." He paused to see what effect he was having on Scott, and was disappointed to be met by the same impassive stare.

"Torture, of course, is an old and honourable profession," continued Stavinsky. "The Chinese have been at it for nearly three thousand years as I think you have already experienced, Captain Scott, and even you British have come a long way since the rack. But that particular instrument has proved to be rather cumbersome for carrying around in a modern world. With this in mind, my tutor at Moscow, Professor Metz, has developed something small and simple that even a man of average intelligence can master after a few lessons."

Adam was desperate to know what was in the box but his look remained impassive.

"With torture, as with making love, Captain Scott, foreplay is the all-important factor. Are you following me, Captain?" asked Stavinsky.

Adam tried to remain relaxed and calm.

"Still no response, Captain Scott, but as I explained I am in no hurry. Especially, as I suspect in your case, the whole operation may take a little longer than usual, which I confess will only add to my enjoyment. And although we are not yet in possession of the Tsar's icon I *am* at least in control of the one person who knows where it is."

Adam still made no comment.

"So I will ask you once and once only before I open the box. Where is the Tsar's icon?"

Adam spat at Stavinsky.

"Not only ill-mannered," remarked Stavinsky, "but also stupid. Because in a very short time you will be desperate for any liquid we might be kind enough to allow you. But, to be fair, you had no way of knowing that."

Stavinsky placed the box on the floor and opened it slowly.

"First, I offer you," he said, like a conjurer in front of a child, "a six-volt nickel-cadmium battery, made by EverReady." He paused. "I thought you would appreciate that touch. Second," he continued, putting his hand back in the box, "a small pulse generator." He placed the rectangular metal box next to the battery. "Third, two lengths of wire with electrodes attached to their ends. Fourth, two syringes, fifth, a tube of collodion glue and finally, a phial, of which more later. When I say 'finally', there are still two items left in the box which I shall not require unless it becomes necessary for us to progress to Stage Two in our little experiment, or even Stage Three."

Stavinsky placed everything in a straight line on the floor in front of Adam.

"Doesn't look a lot, I confess," said Stavinsky. "But with a little imagination I'm sure you will be able to work out its potential. Now. In order that Comrade Romanov and the colonel can enjoy the spectacle I am about to offer it is necessary to add a few details about the nervous system itself. I do hope you are following my every word, Captain Scott, because it is the victim's knowledge which allows him to appreciate the true genius of what is about to follow."

It didn't please Adam that Stavinsky spoke English so well. He could still vividly remember how the Chinese had told Adam what they were going to do to him in a language that he couldn't understand. With them, he had found it easier to allow his mind to drift during their diatribe but he still ended up in a fridge for four hours.

"Now to the practical," continued the grey figure. "By sending a small electrical impulse to the end of the synapse, it is possible to pass on a large electric message to thousands of other nerves within a fraction of a second. This causes a nasty sensation not unlike touching a live wire when the electrical power has been left on in one's home, more commonly known as an electric shock. Not deadly, but distinctly unpleasant. In the Moscow school this is known as Stage One and there is no necessity for you to experience this if you are now willing to tell me where I can find the Tsar's icon."

Adam remained impassive.

"I see you have not paid attention during my little

lecture so I fear we will have to move from the theoretical to the practical."

Adam began reciting to himself the thirty-seven plays of Shakespeare. How his old English master would have been delighted to know that after all those years of drumming the complete Shakespearean canon into a reluctant student, Adam could still recall them at a moment's notice.

Henry VI part one, Henry VI part two, Henry VI part three, Richard II . . .

Stavinsky picked up the tube of collodion glue, removed the cap and smeared two lumps of it on Adam's chest.

. . . *Comedy of Errors, Titus Andronicus, The Taming of the Shrew* . . .

The Russian attached the two electrodes to the glue, taking the wires back and screwing them to the six-volt battery, which in turn was connected to the tiny pulse generator.

. . . *Two Gentlemen of Verona, Love's Labour's Lost, Romeo and Juliet* . . .

Without warning, Stavinsky pressed down the handle of the generator for two seconds during which time Adam received a two-hundred-volt shock. For those seconds Adam screamed as he experienced excruciating pain as the volts forced their way to every part of his body. But the sensation was over in a moment.

"Do feel free to let us know how exactly you feel. You are in a soundproof room, and therefore you won't be disturbing anyone else in the building."

Adam ignored the comment and gripping the side of the chair, mumbled . . . *Richard III, Midsummer Night's Dream, King John* . . .

Stavinsky pressed the plunger down for another two

seconds. Adam felt the pain instantly the second time. The moment it was over he felt violently nauseated, but he managed to remain conscious.

Stavinsky waited for some time before he volunteered an opinion. "Impressive. You have definitely qualified to enter Stage Two, from which you can be released immediately by answering one simple question. Where is the Tsar's icon?"

Adam's mouth had become so dry that he couldn't speak, let alone spit.

"I did try to warn you, Captain Scott." Stavinsky turned towards the door. "Do go and fetch the captain some water, Colonel."

. . . *The Merchant of Venice*, *Henry IV part one*, *Henry IV part two* . . .

A moment later Pollard was back, and a bottle was thrust into Adam's mouth. He gulped half the contents down until it was pulled away.

"Mustn't overdo it. You might need some more later. But that won't be necessary if you let me know where the icon is."

Adam spat what was left of the water towards where his adversary was standing.

Stavinsky leapt forward and slapped Adam hard across the face with the back of his hand. Adam's head slumped.

"You give me no choice but to advance to Stage Two," said Stavinsky. He looked towards Romanov who nodded. Stavinsky's thin lips parted in another smile. "You may have wondered," he continued, "how much more harm I can do with a simple six-volt battery, and indeed having seen in numerous American gangster movies an execution by the electric chair you will know a large generator is needed to kill a man. But first it is important to remember that I don't want to kill you. Second, my science lessons didn't end at Stage One. Professor Metz's mind was also exercised by the feebleness of this stage and after a lifetime of dedicated research he came up with an ingenious solution known as 'M', which the Academy of Science named after him in his honour. If you inject 'M' into the nervous system, messages can be transmitted to all your nerves many times more efficiently, thus allowing the pain to multiply without actually proving fatal.

"I only need to multiply a few milli-amps by a suitable factor to create a far more interesting effect – so I must ask you once again, where is the Tsar's icon?"

... *Much Ado About Nothing, Henry V, Julius Caesar* ...

"I see you are determined that I should proceed," said Stavinsky, removing a syringe from the floor and jabbing the long thin needle into a phial before withdrawing the plunger until the barrel of the syringe was half full. Stavinsky held the needle in the air, pressed the knob and watched a little spray flow out like a tiny fountain. He moved behind Adam.

"I am now going to give you a lumbar puncture which if you attempt to move will paralyse you from the neck down for life. By nature I am not an honest man but on this occasion I must recommend you to trust me. I assure you that the injection will not kill you because, as you already know, that is not in our best interest."

Adam didn't move a muscle as he felt the syringe go into his back. *As You Like* ... he began. Then excruciating pain swept his body, and suddenly, blessedly, he felt nothing.

When he came round there was no way of telling how much time had passed. His eyes slowly focused on his tormentor pacing up and down the room impatiently. Seeing Adam's eyes open, the unshaven man stopped pacing, smiled, walked over to the chair and ran his fingers slowly over the large piece of sticking plaster that covered Adam's two-day-old shoulder wound. The touch appeared gentle, but to Adam it felt like a hot iron being forced across his shoulder.

"As I promised," said Stavinsky. "A far more interesting sensation is awaiting you. And now I think I'll rip the plaster off." He waited for a moment while Adam pursed his lips. Then, in one movement, he tore the plaster back. Adam screamed as if the bullet had hit him again. Romanov came forward, leaned over and studied the wound.

"I'm relieved to see my colleague didn't miss you completely," Romanov said before adding, "can you imagine what it will be like when I allow Mr Stavinsky to wire you up again and then press the little generator?"

". . . *Twelfth Night, Hamlet, The Merry Wives of Windsor* . . ." Adam said aloud for the first time.

"I see you wish to leave nothing to the imagination," said Romanov and disappeared behind him. Stavinsky checked that the wires were attached to the collodion glue on Adam's chest and then he returned to the generator. "I shall press down the handle in three seconds' time. You know what you have to do to stop me."

". . . *Troilus and Cressida, All's Well That Ends Well* . . ."

As the handle plunged down the volts seemed to find their way to every nerve-ending in his body. Adam let out such a scream that if they had not been in a soundproofed room anyone within a mile would have heard him. When the initial effect was over he was left shaking and retching uncontrollably. Stavinsky and Pollard rushed forward to the chair and quickly undid the nylon cords. Adam fell on his hands and knees, still vomiting.

"Couldn't afford to let you choke to death, could we?" said Stavinsky. "We lost one or two that way in the early days but we know better now."

As soon as the sickness subsided, Stavinsky threw Adam back up on to the chair and Pollard tied him up again.

"Where is the Tsar's icon?" shouted Stavinsky.

"*. . . Measure for Measure, Othello, King Lear . . .*" Adam said, his voice now trembling.

Pollard picked up another bottle of water and thrust it at Adam's lips. Adam gulped it down but it was as a tiny oasis in a vast desert. Romanov came forward and Stavinsky took his place beside the plunger.

"You are a brave man, Scott," said Romanov, "with nothing left to prove, but this is madness. Just tell me where the icon is and I will send Stavinsky away and order the colonel to leave you on the steps of the British Embassy."

"*. . . Macbeth, Antony and Cleopatra . . .*"

Romanov let out a sigh and nodded. Stavinsky pushed the plunger down once again. Even the colonel turned white as he watched Adam's reaction. The pitch of the scream was even higher and the muscles contorted visibly as Adam felt the volts reach the millions of little nerve-ends in his body. When once more he had been released, Adam lay on the floor on his hands and knees. Was there anything left in his stomach that could still possibly come up? He raised his head, only to be hurled back on to the chair and bound up again. Stavinsky stared down at him.

"Most impressive, Captain Scott, you have qualified for Stage Three."

When Lawrence arrived at Orly Airport that evening he was looking forward to a quiet dinner with his old friend at the Ambassador's residence. He was met at the barrier by Colonel Pollard.

"How is he?" were Lawrence's first words.

"I hoped you were going to tell us," said Pollard, as he took Lawrence's overnight suitcase. Lawrence stopped in his tracks and stared at the tall, thin soldier who was in the full dress uniform of the Royal Dragoon Guards.

"What do you mean?" said Lawrence.

"Simply that," said Pollard. "I followed your instructions to the letter and went to pick up Scott at the Ile de la Cité but when I arrived I was informed that he had been taken away twenty minutes earlier by someone else using my name. We contacted your office immediately but as you were already en route the Ambassador ordered me straight to the airport while he phoned Sir Morris."

Lawrence staggered and nearly fell. The colonel came quickly to his side. He didn't understand what Lawrence meant when he said, "He's bound to believe it's me."

When Adam regained consciousness, Romanov stood alone.

"Sometimes," said the Russian, continuing as if Adam had never passed out, "a man is too proud to show lack of resolution in front of the torturer or indeed one of his own countrymen, especially a traitor. That is why I have removed Stavinsky and the colonel from our presence. Now I have no desire to see Stavinsky continue his experiment to Stage Three, but I can stop him only if you will tell me where you have put the icon."

"Why should I?" said Adam belligerently. "It's legally mine."

"Not so, Captain Scott. What you picked up from the bank in Geneva is the priceless original painted by Rublev which belongs to the Union of Soviet Socialist Republics. And if that icon were to appear in any auction house or gallery in the world, we would immediately claim it as a national treasure stolen by the seller."

"But how could that be . . .?" began Adam.

"Because," said Romanov, "it is you who are now in possession of the original that the Tsar left in the safe-keeping of the Grand Duke of Hesse and for over fifty years the Soviet Union has only had a copy." Adam's eyes opened wide in disbelief as Romanov removed from the inside pocket of his overcoat an icon of St George and the Dragon. Romanov paused and then turned it over; a smile of satisfaction crossed his face as Adam's eyes registered the significance of the missing crown.

"Like you," continued Romanov, "I only have this one on loan – but you tell me where the original is and I will release you and exchange the copy for the original. No one will be any the wiser and you'll still be able to make yourself a worthwhile profit."

"Old lamps for new," said Adam with a sneer.

Romanov's eyes narrowed menacingly. "Surely you realise, Scott, that you are in possession of a priceless masterpiece that belongs to the Soviet Union. Unless you return the icon you are going to cause considerable embarrassment for your country and you will probably end up in jail. All you have to do is tell me where the icon is and you can go free."

Adam didn't even bother to shake his head.

"Then the time has obviously come to let you into some information you will be more interested in," Romanov said, extracting a single sheet of paper from an envelope he removed from his inside pocket. Adam was genuinely puzzled, quite unable to think what it could be. Romanov opened it slowly and held it up so that Adam could only see the back.

"This single sheet of paper reveals a sentence carried out in Moscow in 1946 by Judge I. T. Nikitchenko – the death sentence," continued Romanov, "pronounced on a certain Major Vladimir Kosky, the Russian guard in charge of the Soviet watch the night Reichsmarshal Hermann Goering died." He turned the paper round so Adam could see it. "As you can see, Major Kosky was found guilty of collaboration with the enemy for financial gain. It was proved he was directly responsible for smuggling cyanide into the Reichsmarshal's cell on the night he died." Adam's eyes widened. "Ah, I see I have dealt the ace of spades," said Romanov. "Now I think you will finally tell me where the icon actually is because you have an expression in England, if I recall correctly: fair exchange is no robbery. Your icon for my icon, plus the legal judgment that will finally vindicate your father's honour."

Adam closed his eyes, painfully aware for the first time that Romanov had no idea what was inside the icon.

Romanov was unable to hide his anger. He walked to the door and flung it open. "He's yours," he said.

Dr Stavinsky re-entered the room and, smiling, continued as if nothing had interrupted him. "Professor

Metz was never really satisfied with Stage Two because he found the recovery time even for an extremely brave and fit man like yourself could sometimes hold him up for hours, even days. So during his final years at the university he devoted his time to finding how he could possibly speed the whole process up. As for all geniuses the final solution was staggering in its simplicity. All he had to produce was a chemical formula that when injected into the nervous system caused an immediate recovery – a rapid analgesic. It took him twelve years and several deaths before he came up with the final solution," said Stavinsky, removing another phial from the cigar box and plunging the needle of a second syringe into the seal on the top of the phial.

"This," Stavinsky said, holding up the little phial in triumph, "when injected into your blood stream, will aid recovery so quickly that you may even wonder if you ever went through any pain in the first place. For this piece of genius Metz should have been awarded the Nobel Prize, but it was not something we felt he could share with the rest of the scientific world. But because of him I can repeat the process you have just experienced again and again, never permitting you to die. You see, I can keep this generator pumping up and down every thirty minutes for the next week if that is your desire," said Stavinsky, as he stared down at Adam's white, disbelieving face flecked with yellow specks of his vomit.

"Or I can stop immediately after I have administered the antidote the moment you let me know where the Tsar's icon is."

Stavinsky stood in front of Adam and half filled the syringe. Adam felt intensely cold, yet the shock of his torture had caused him to sweat profusely. "Sit still, Captain Scott, I have no desire to do you any permanent injury." Adam felt the needle go deep in and moments later the fluid entered his blood stream.

He could not believe how quickly he felt himself recovering. Within minutes he no longer felt sick or disorientated. The sensation in his arms and legs returned to normal while the wish never to experience Stage Two again became acute.

"Brilliant man, Professor Metz, on that I'm sure we can both agree," said Stavinsky, "and if he were still alive I feel certain he would have written a paper on your case." Slowly and carefully Stavinsky began to smear more lumps of jelly on Adam's chest. When he was satisfied with his handiwork he once again attached the electrodes to the jelly.

"Coriolanus, Timon of Athens, Pericles." Stavinsky thrust his palm down and Adam hoped that he would die. He found a new level to scream at, as his body shook and shook. Seconds later he felt ice cold and, shivering uncontrollably, he started to retch.

Stavinsky was quickly by his side to release him. Adam fell to the ground and coughed up what was left in his body. When he was only spitting, Pollard placed him back in the chair.

"You must understand I can't let you die, Captain. Now where is the icon?" Stavinsky shouted.

In the Louvre, Adam wanted to scream, but his words barely came out as a whisper, the inside of his mouth feeling like sandpaper. Stavinsky proceeded to fill the second syringe again and injected Adam with the fluid. Once again it was only moments before the agony subsided and he felt completely recovered.

"Ten seconds, we go again. Nine, eight, seven . . ."

"Cymbeline."

". . . six, five, four . . ."

"The Winter's Tale."

". . . three, two, one."

"The Tempest. Aahhhh," he screamed and immediately fainted. The next thing Adam remembered was the cold water being poured over him by the colonel before he began to retch again. Once tied back in the chair Stavinsky thrust the syringe into him once more, but Adam couldn't believe he would ever recover again. He must surely die, because he wanted to die. He felt the syringe jab into his flesh again.

Romanov stepped forward and looking straight at Adam, said, "I feel Dr Stavinsky and I have earned a little supper. We did consider inviting you but felt your stomach wouldn't be up to it, but when we return fully refreshed Dr Stavinsky will repeat the entire exercise again and again until you let me know where you have hidden the icon."

Romanov and Stavinsky left as Colonel Pollard came back in. Romanov and the colonel exchanged a few sentences which Adam could not make out. Then Romanov left the room, closing the door quietly behind him.

Pollard came over to Adam and offered him the water bottle. Adam gulped it down and was genuinely surprised how quickly he was recovering. Yet although his senses were returning to normal Adam still doubted he could survive one more time.

"I'm going to throw up again," said Adam and suddenly thrust his head forward. Pollard quickly undid the knots and watched Adam slump to his hands and knees. He threw up some spit and rested before the colonel helped him gently back into the chair. As he sat down Adam gripped both sides of the chair legs firmly, then with all the strength he could muster jack-knifed forward, swung the chair over his head, and brought it crashing down on top of the unsuspecting colonel. Pollard collapsed in a heap, unconscious, on the floor in front of Adam and never heard him utter the words, "*Henry VIII* and *Two Noble Kinsmen* – I'll bet that's one you've never heard of, Colonel. Mind you, to be fair, not everyone thinks Shakespeare wrote it."

Adam remained on his knees over the colonel's body, wondering what his next move should be. He was grateful that the soundproofed room was now working in his favour. He waited for a few more seconds as he tried to measure what was left of his strength. He picked up the water bottle that had been knocked over and drained it of its last drops. He then crawled across to the bed and pulled on his pants and socks, shoes, and his not so white shirt, followed by his trousers. He was about to put on the blazer, but found the lining had been ripped to shreds. He changed his mind and stumbled like an old man back towards the colonel, removed his Harris tweed coat and slipped it on. It was large round the shoulders but short at the hips.

Adam made his way to the door, feeling almost exhilarated. He turned the handle and pulled. The door came open an inch – nothing happened – two inches – still nothing. He stared through the crack but all he could see was a dark corridor. As he pulled the door wide open the hinges sounded to Adam like racing tyres screeching. Once he was certain that no one was going to return, he ventured into the corridor.

Standing against the wall he stared up and down the thin windowless passage, waiting for his eyes to adjust to the dark. He could make out a light shining through a pebbled pane in a door at the far end of the corridor, and began to take short steps towards it. He continued on, as if he were a blind man, creeping slowly forward until he saw another beam of light coming from under a door to his right about ten yards away from the one he needed to reach. He edged cautiously on and was only a pace away from the first door when it opened abruptly and out stepped a small man in a white tunic and blue kitchen overalls. Adam froze against the wall as the kitchen hand removed a packet of cigarettes and a box of matches from his pocket and headed away in the opposite direction. When the man reached the glazed door he opened it and walked out. Adam watched the silhouette outlined against the pebbled window, a match being struck, a cigarette being lit, the first puff of smoke; he even heard a sigh.

Adam crept past what he now assumed was a kitchen and on towards the outer door. He turned the knob slowly, waiting for the silhouette to move. The outer door also possessed hinges which no one had bothered to oil for months. The smoker turned round and smiled as Adam's left hand landed firmly in his stomach. As the smoker bent over, Adam's right fist came up to the man's chin with all the force he could muster. The smoker sank in a heap on the ground, and Adam stood over him thankful that he didn't move.

He dragged the limp body across the grass, dumped it behind a bush and remained kneeling by it while he tried to work out his bearings. Adam could just make out a high wall ahead of him with a gravelled courtyard in front of it. The wall threw out a long shadow from the moon across the tiny stones. About twenty yards . . . Summoning up every ounce of energy, he ran to the wall and then clung to it like a limpet, remaining motionless in its shadow. Slowly and silently he moved round the wall, yard by yard, until he reached the front of what he now felt sure was the Russian Embassy. The great green wooden gates at the front entrance were open, and every few seconds limousines swept past him. Adam looked back up towards the front door of the Embassy and at the top of the steps he saw a massive man, medals stretching across his formal dress jacket, shaking hands with each of his departing guests. Adam assumed he was the Ambassador.

One or two of the guests were leaving by foot. There were two armed gendarmes on the gate who stood rigidly to attention and saluted as each car or guest passed by.

Adam waited until a vast BMW, the West German flag fluttering on its bonnet, slowed as it passed through the gates. Using the car to shield him, Adam walked out into the centre of the drive, then, following closely behind, walked straight between the guards towards the road.

"Bonsoir," he said lightly to the guards as the car moved forward: he was only a yard from the road. "Walk," he told himself, "don't run. Walk, walk until you are out of their sight." They saluted deferentially. "Don't look back." Another car followed him out, but he kept his eyes firmly to the front.

"Tu cherches une femme?" a voice repeated from the shadows of a recessed doorway. Adam had ended up in a badly lit one-way street. Several men of indeterminate age seemed to be walking aimlessly up and down the kerbside. He eyed them with suspicion as he moved on through the darkness.

"Wha –?" said Adam, stepping sharply into the road, his senses heightened by the unexpected sound.

"From Britain, eh? Do you search for a girl?" The voice held an unmistakable French accent.

"You speak English," said Adam, still unable to see the woman clearly.

"You have to know a lot of languages in my profession, *chéri*, or you'd starve."

Adam tried to think coherently. "How much for the night?"

"*Eh bien*, but it's not yet midnight," said the girl. "So I would have to charge two hundred francs."

Although he had no money Adam hoped the girl might at least lead him to safety.

"Two hundred is fine."

"*D'accord*," said the girl, at last stepping out of the shadows. Adam was surprised by how attractive she turned out to be. "Take my arm and if you pass a gendarme say only, '*Ma femme*'."

Adam stumbled forward.

"Ah, I think you drink too much, *chéri*. Never mind, you can lean on me, yes."

"No, I'm just tired," said Adam, trying hard to keep up with her pace.

"You have been to party at Embassy, *n'est-ce pas?*"

Adam was startled.

"Don't be surprised, *chéri*. I find most of my regulars from the Embassies. They can't risk to be involved in casual affairs, *tu comprends?*"

"I believe you," said Adam.

"My apartment is just round the corner," she assured him. Adam was confident he could get that far but he took a deep breath when they arrived at a block of flats and first saw the steps. He just managed to reach the front door.

"I live on the top of the house, *chéri*. Very nice view," she said matter-of-factly, "but I'm afraid – how you say – no lift."

Adam said nothing, but leaned against the outside wall, breathing deeply.

"You are *fatigué*," she said. By the time they had

reached the second floor she almost had to drag Adam up the last few steps.

"I don't see you getting it up tonight, *chéri*," she said, opening her front door and turning on the light. "Still, it's your party." She strode in, turning on other lights as she went.

Adam staggered across the floor towards the only chair in sight and collapsed into it. The girl had by this time disappeared into another room and he had to make a supreme effort not to fall asleep before she returned.

As she stood in the light of the doorway Adam was able to see her properly for the first time. Her blonde hair was short and curly and she wore a red blouse and a knee-length skin-tight black skirt. A wide white plastic belt emphasised her small waist. She wore black mesh stockings and what he could see of her legs would have normally aroused him had he been in any other condition.

She walked over to Adam with a slight swing of the hips, and knelt down in front of him. Her eyes were a surprisingly luminous green.

"Would you please give me the two hundred now?" she asked, without harshness. She ran her hand along his thigh.

"I don't have any money," said Adam quite simply.

"What?" she said, sounding angry for the first time. Placing her hand in his inside pocket she removed a wallet and asked, "Then what's this? I don't play the games," handing the thick wallet over to Adam. He opened the flap to find it was jammed full of French francs and a few English notes. Adam concluded that the colonel was obviously paid in cash for his services.

Adam extracted two one-hundred francs and dutifully handed them over.

"That's better," she said, and disappeared into the other room.

Adam checked quickly through the wallet to discover a driving licence and a couple of credit cards in the colonel's real name of Albert Tomkins. He quickly looked around: a double bed that was wedged up against the far wall took up most of the floor space. Apart from the chair he was settled in, the only other pieces of furniture were a dressing table and a tiny stool with a red velvet cushion on it. A stained l lue carpet covered most of the wooden floor.

To his left was a small fireplace with logs stacked neatly in one corner. All Adam wished to do was fall asleep but with what strength was left in his body, he pushed himself up, wobbled over to the fireplace and hid the wallet between the logs. He lurched back towards the chair and fell into it as the door reopened.

Again the girl stood in the light of the doorway but this time she wore only a pink negligée, which even in his present state Adam could see right through whenever she made the slightest movement. She walked slowly across the room and once more knelt down beside him.

"How you like it, *mon cher*? Straight or the French way?"

"I need to rest," said Adam.

"For two hundred francs you sleep in any 'otel," she said in disbelief.

"I only want to be allowed to rest a few minutes," he assured her.

"*L'Anglais,*" she said, and began to try to lift Adam out of the chair and towards the bed. He stumbled and fell, landing half on and half off the corner of the mattress. She undressed him as deftly as any nurse could have done before lifting his legs up on to the bed. Adam made no effort to help or hinder her. She hesitated for a moment when she saw the shoulder wound, bewildered as to what kind of accident could have caused such a gash. She rolled him over to the far side and pulled back the top sheet and blanket. Then she walked round to the other side of the bed and rolled him back again. Finally she pushed him flat on his back and covered him with the sheet and blankets.

"I could still give you French if you like," she said. But Adam was already asleep.

CHAPTER TWENTY-ONE

When Adam eventually awoke the sun was already shining through the small window of the bedroom. He blinked as he took in his surroundings and tried to recall what had happened the night before. Then it all came back to him and suddenly he felt sick again at the memory. He sat on the edge of the bed but the moment he tried to stand he felt giddy and weak, and fell back down. At least he had escaped. He looked around the room but the girl was nowhere to be seen or heard. Then he remembered the wallet.

He sat bolt upright, gathering himself for a few moments before standing up again and trying to walk. Although he was still unsteady it was better than he had expected. It's only the recovery that counts, not the speed, he thought ironically. When he reached the fireplace he fell on his knees and searched among the logs, but the colonel's wallet was no longer there. As quickly as he could he went to the jacket hanging over the back of the chair. He checked in the inside pocket: a pen, a half-toothless comb, a passport, a driving licence, some other papers, but no wallet. He searched the outside pockets: a bunch of keys, a penknife, a few assorted coins, English and French, but that was all that was left. With a string of oaths he collapsed on to the floor. He sat there for some time and didn't move until he heard a key in the lock.

The front door of the flat swung open and the girl sauntered in carrying a shopping basket. She was dressed in a pretty floral skirt and white blouse that would have been suitable for any churchgoer on a Sunday morning. The basket was crammed with food.

"Woken up, 'ave we, *chéri? Est-ce-que tu prends le petit déjeuner?*"

Adam looked a little taken aback.

She returned his stare. "Even working girls need their breakfast, *n'est-ce pas*? Sometimes is the only meal I manage all day."

"Where's my wallet?" asked Adam coldly.

"On the table," said the girl, pointing.

Adam glanced across the room, to see that she had left the wallet in the most obvious place.

"It not necessary of you to 'ide it," she reprimanded him. "Because I'm a whore don't think I'm a thief." With this she strode off into the kitchen, leaving the door open.

Adam suddenly knew how big Tom Thumb felt.

"Coffee and croissants?" she shouted.

"Fantastic," said Adam. He paused. "I'm sorry. I was stupid."

"Not to think about it," she said. "*Ça n'est rien.*"

"I still don't know your name," said Adam.

"My working name is Brigitte, but as you 'ave not use my services last night or this morning you can call me by my real name – Jeanne."

"Can I have a bath, Jeanne?"

"The door in the corner, but don't take too long, unless you like croissants cold." Adam made his way to the bathroom and found Jeanne had provided for everything a man might need: a razor, shaving cream, soap, flannel, clean towels – and a gross box of Durex.

After a warm bath and a shave – delights Adam had nearly forgotten – he felt almost back to normal again, if still somewhat fragile. He tucked a pink towel around his waist before joining Jeanne in the kitchen. The table was already laid and she was removing a warm croissant from the oven.

"Good body," she said, turning round and scrutinising him carefully. "Much better than I usually 'ave." She put the plate down in front of him.

"You're not so bad yourself," said Adam grinning, taking the seat opposite her.

"I am 'appy you notice," said Jeanne. "I was beginning to think about you." Adam spread the roll liberally with jam and didn't speak again for several seconds.

"When 'ave you last eat?" asked Jeanne as he devoured the final scrap left on the plate.

"Yesterday lunch. But I emptied my stomach in between."

"Sick, eh? You mustn't drink so much."

"I think 'drained' might be a better word. Tell me, Jeanne," said Adam, looking up at her, "are you still available for work?"

She checked her watch. "One of my regulars is at two this afternoon, and I must be back on the streets by five. So it would 'ave to be this morning," she said matter-of-factly.

"No, no, that's not what I meant," said Adam.

"You could quickly give a girl, how do you say in England? – a complex," said Jeanne. "You not one of those weird ones, are you?"

"No, nothing like that," said Adam, laughing. "But I would be willing to pay you another two hundred francs for your services."

"Is it legal?"

"Absolutely."

"*Alors*, that makes a change. 'Ow long you need me?"

"An hour, two at the most."

"It's better than the rate for my present job. What am I expected to do?"

"For one hour I want every man in Paris to fancy you. Only this time you won't be available – at any price."

"Scott has just contacted me a few minutes ago," said Lawrence to the assembled D4.

"What did he have to say?" asked an anxious Sir Morris.

"Only that he was turning back the clock."

"What do you think he meant by that?" asked Snell.

"Geneva would be my guess," said Lawrence.

"Why Geneva?" said Matthews.

"I'm not certain," said Lawrence, "but he said it had something to do with the German girl, or the bank, but I can't be sure which."

No one spoke for some time.

"Did you trace the call?" asked Busch.

"Only the area," said Lawrence, "Neuchâtel on the German–Swiss border."

"Good. Then we're in business again," said Sir Morris. "Have you informed Interpol?"

"Yes sir, and I've personally briefed the German, French and Swiss police," added Lawrence, which was the only true word he had spoken since the meeting had begun.

Jeanne took forty minutes to get herself ready and when Adam saw the result he let out a long whistle.

"No one is going to give me a second look, even if I were to empty the till in front of them," he told her.

"That is the idea, *n'est-ce pas?*" Jeanne said, grinning.

"Now, are you sure you know exactly what you have to do?"

"I know well." Jeanne checked herself once more in the long mirror. "We 'ave rehearse like military exercise four times already."

"Good," said Adam. "You sound as if you're ready to face the enemy. So let's begin with what in the army they call 'advance to contact'."

Jeanne took out a plastic bag from a drawer in the kitchen. The single word 'Céline' was printed across it. She handed it over to Adam. He folded the bag in four, and stuffed it into his jacket pocket before walking into the corridor. She then locked the flat door behind them, and they walked down the stairs together and out on to the pavement.

Adam hailed a taxi and Jeanne told the driver "Tuileries gardens". Once they had arrived, Adam paid the fare and joined Jeanne on the pavement.

"*Bonne chance,*" said Adam as he remained on the corner, allowing Jeanne to walk twenty yards ahead of him. Although he still felt unsteady he was able to keep up at her pace. The sun beat down on his face as he watched her walk in and out of the ornate flower beds. Her pink leather skirt and tight white sweater made almost every man she passed turn and take a second look. Some even stopped in their tracks and continued watching until she was out of sight.

The comments she could hear and Adam, twenty yards behind, couldn't, ranged from "*Je payerais n'importe quoi,*" which she reluctantly had to pass up, to just plain "*Putain*", which Adam had told her to ignore. Her part had to be acted out, and for two hundred francs she would just have to suffer the odd insult.

Jeanne reached the far side of the gardens and did not look back: she had been instructed not to turn around in any circumstances. Keep going forwards, Adam had told her. He was still twenty yards behind her when she reached the Quai des Tuileries. She waited for the lights to turn green before she crossed the wide road, keeping in the centre of a throng of people.

At the end of the quai she turned sharp right, and for the first time could see the Louvre straight in front of her. She had been too embarrassed to admit to him that she had never been inside the building before.

Jeanne climbed the steps to the entrance hall. By the time she had reached the swing doors, Adam was approaching the bottom step. She continued on up the marble staircase with Adam still following discreetly behind.

When Jeanne reached the top of the stairs she passed the statue of the Winged Victory of Samothrace. She proceeded into the first of the large crowded rooms and began counting to herself, noting as she passed through each gallery that there was at least one attendant on duty in each, usually standing around aimlessly near one of the exits. A group of schoolchildren were studying 'The Last Supper' by Giovanni but Jeanne ignored the masterpiece and marched straight on. After passing six attendants she arrived in the room Adam had described to her so vividly. She strode purposefully into the centre and paused for a few seconds. Some of the men began to lose interest in the paintings. Satisfied by the impact she was making, she flounced over to the guard, who straightened up his jacket and smiled at her.

"Dans quelle direction se trouve la peinture du seizième siècle?" Jeanne asked innocently. The guard turned to point in the direction of the relevant room. The moment he turned back, Jeanne slapped him hard across the face and shouted at him at the top of her voice: *"Quelle horreur! Pour qui est-ce que vous me prenez?"*

Only one person in the Icon Room didn't stop to stare at the spectacle. *"Je vais parler à la Direction,"* she screamed, and flounced off towards the main exit. The entire charade was over in less than thirty seconds. The bemused guard remained transfixed, staring after his assailant in bewilderment.

Jeanne continued on through three centuries more quickly than H. G. Wells. She took a left turn into the sixteenth-century room as instructed and then another left brought her back into the long corridor. A few moments later, she joined Adam at the top of the marble staircase leading down to the front entrance.

As they walked back down the steps together, Adam handed her the Céline bag and was about to set off again, when two attendants waiting on the bottom step threw out their arms indicating they should halt.

"Do you wish a run for it?" she whispered.

"Certainly not," said Adam very firmly. "Just don't say anything."

"Madame, excusez-moi, mais je dois fouiller votre sac."

"Allez-y pour tout ce que vous y trouvez!" said Jeanne.

"Certainly you can search her bag," said Adam, returning to her side before Jeanne could say anything more. "It's an icon, quite a good one, I think. I purchased it in a shop near the Champs-Elysées only this morning."

"Vous me permettez, monsieur?" the senior attendant asked suspiciously.

"Why not?" said Adam. He removed the Tsar's icon

from the bag and handed it over to the attendant, who seemed surprised by the way things were turning out. Two more attendants rushed over and stood on each side of Adam.

The senior attendant asked in broken English if Adam would mind if one of the gallery's experts were to look at the painting.

"Only too delighted," said Adam. "It would be fascinating to have a second opinion."

The senior attendant was beginning to look unsure of himself. "*Je dois vous demander de me suivre,*" he suggested in a tone that was suddenly less hostile. He ushered them quickly through to a little room at the side of the gallery. The attendant put the Tsar's icon in the middle of a table that dominated the room. Adam sat down and Jeanne, still bemused, took the seat beside him.

"I'll only be a moment, sir." The senior attendant almost ran out while the two other attendants remained stationed near the door. Adam still did not attempt to speak to Jeanne although he could see that she was becoming more and more apprehensive. He shot her a little smile as they sat waiting.

When the door eventually opened, an elderly man with a scholarly face preceded the senior attendant.

"*Bonjour, monsieur,*" the man began, looking at Adam, the first man who did not show an overt interest in Jeanne. "I understand that you are English," and without giving either of them more than a glance, he picked up the icon.

He studied the painting carefully for some time before he spoke. Adam felt just a moment's apprehension. "Most interesting. Yes, yes." One of the attendants put a hand on his truncheon.

"Interesting," he repeated. "I would be so bold as

to suggest," he hesitated, "late nineteenth century, eighteen seventy, possibly eighty. Fascinating. Not that we have ever had anything quite like it at the Louvre," he added. "You do realise it's an inferior copy," he said as he handed the icon back to Adam. "The original Tsar's icon of St George and the Dragon hangs in the Winter Palace in Leningrad. I've seen it, you know," he added, sounding rather pleased with himself.

"You certainly have," said Adam under his breath as he placed the icon back in its plastic bag. The old man bowed low to Jeanne and said as he shuffled away, "Funnily enough, someone else was making enquiries about the Tsar's icon only a few weeks ago." Adam was the only person who didn't seem surprised.

"I was only –" began the senior attendant.

"Doing your duty," completed Adam. "A natural precaution, if I may say so," he added a little pompously. "I can only admire the way you carried out the entire exercise."

Jeanne stared at them both, quite unable to comprehend what was happening.

"You are kind, *monsieur*," said the attendant, sounding relieved. "Hope you come again," he added, smiling at Jeanne.

The attendant accompanied the two of them to the entrance of the Louvre, and when they pushed through the door he stood smartly to attention and saluted.

Adam and Jeanne walked down the steps and into the Paris sun.

"Well, now can I know what that's all about?" asked Jeanne.

"You were *magnifique*," said Adam, not attempting to explain.

"I know, I know," said Jeanne. "But why you need

Oscar-winning show by me when the picture was always yours?"

"True," agreed Adam. "But I had left it in their safe-keeping overnight. And without your bravura performance it might have taken considerably longer to convince the authorities that it belonged to me in the first place."

Adam realised from the look on her face that Jeanne had no idea what he was talking about.

"You know, that my first time in the Louvre?" said Jeanne linking her arm in Adam's.

"You're priceless," said Adam, laughing.

"That I'm not," she said, turning to face him. "Two hundred francs was our bargain even if it belongs to you or not."

"Correct," said Adam, taking out the colonel's wallet and extracting two hundred francs, to which he added another hundred. "A well-earned bonus," said Adam.

She pocketed the money gratefully. "I think I'll take an evening off," she said.

Adam held her in his arms and kissed her on both cheeks as if she was a French general.

She kissed him on the lips and smiled. "When you next in Paris, *chéri*, look me up. I owe you one – on the house."

"How can you be so sure?"

"Because Antarctic was willing to give Pemberton too many facts."

"What do you mean?"

"You told me that Pemberton said he would never phone back if you let him down again. Not only did he phone back but he peppered you with facts. Which way did he say he was going?"

"Back to Geneva. Something to do with the German girl and the bank."

"The girl's dead and the bank's closed for the weekend. He must be on his way to England."

"I would like to rent a car which I will be dropping off at the coast. I haven't decided which port yet," he told the girl behind the counter.

"Bien sûr, monsieur," said the girl. "Would you be kind enough to fill in the form, and we will also need your driving licence." Adam removed all the papers from his inside pocket and passed over the colonel's driving licence. He filled in the forms slowly, copying the signature off the back of the colonel's Playboy Club card. He handed over the full amount required in cash hoping it would speed up the transaction.

The girl picked up the cash and counted the notes carefully before checking the back of the licence against the signature on the form. Adam was relieved that she hadn't spotted the disparity in the dates of birth. He replaced all Albert Tomkins's documents and the wallet in his inside jacket pocket, as the girl turned round and removed an ignition key from a hook on a board behind her.

"It's a red Citroën, parked on the first floor," she told him. "The registration number is stamped on the key ring."

Adam thanked her and walked quickly up to the first floor where he handed the key over to an attendant, who drove the car out of its parking space for him.

When the attendant returned the key, Adam handed him a ten-franc note. Exactly the same sum as the other man had given him to let him know if an Englishman who fitted Adam's description tried to hire a car. What had he promised? Another hundred francs if he phoned within five minutes of seeing him.

PART FOUR

THE KREMLIN
MOSCOW

June 19, 1966

CHAPTER TWENTY-TWO

THE KREMLIN, MOSCOW
June 19, 1966

Leonid Ilyich Brezhnev entered the room, hardly allowing the other four members of the inner quorum of the Defence Council enough time to stand. Their faces were grim, resolute, no different from their public image – unlike Western politicians.

The General Secretary took his place at the head of the table and nodded to his colleagues to sit.

The last time the inner quorum of the Defence Council had been summoned to a meeting at an hour's notice had been at the request of Khrushchev, who was hoping to enlist support for his Cuban adventure. Brezhnev would never forget the moment when his predecessor had uncontrollably burst into tears because they forced him to order the Soviet ships to return home. From that moment, Brezhnev knew it could only be a matter of time before he would succeed Khrushchev as the leader of the Communist world. On this occasion he had no intention of bursting into tears.

On his right sat Marshal Malinovsky, Minister of Defence: on his left Andrei Gromyko, the young

Foreign Minister. Beside him sat the Chief of the General Staff, Marshal Zakharov, and, on his left, Zaborski. Even the seating plan confirmed Brezhnev's obvious displeasure with the Chairman of the KGB.

He raised his eyes and stared up at the massive oil painting of Lenin reviewing an early military parade in Red Square: a picture no one other than members of the Politburo had seen since it disappeared from the Tretyakov in 1950.

If only Lenin had realised the icon was a fake in the first place, Brezhnev reflected ... Yet, despite the traditional Russian pastime of blaming the dead for everything that goes wrong, he knew that Vladimir Ilyich Lenin was beyond criticism. He would have to find a living scapegoat.

His eyes rested on Zaborski. "Your report, Comrade Chairman."

Zaborski fingered a file in front of him although he knew the contents almost off by heart. "The plan to locate the Tsar's icon was carried out in an exemplary fashion," he began. "When the Englishman, Adam Scott, was caught and later ... questioned" – they all accepted the euphemism – "by Comrade Dr Stavinsky in the privacy of our Embassy in Paris, the Englishman gave no clue as to where we would find the icon. It became obvious he was a professional agent of the West. After three hours, interrogation was momentarily suspended. It was during this period that the prisoner managed to escape."

"Managed," interjected Brezhnev.

Just as he had taught his subordinates over the years, the Chairman of the KGB made no attempt to reply.

"Don't you realise," continued the General Secretary, "that we had within our grasp the opportunity to turn the very land the Americans use for their early warning system into a base for our short range missiles? If it had proved possible to retrieve our icon it would also have been possible to site those very missiles along a border less than a thousand eight hundred kilometres from Seattle – two thousand kilometres from Chicago. Not only could we have made the Americans' early warning system redundant, we could have greatly improved our ability to detect any enemy missiles while they were still thousands of kilometres from our nearest border."

The General Secretary paused to see if the Chairman of the KGB had any further explanation to offer but Zaborski kept his eyes fixed on the table in front of him. When Brezhnev began again it was almost in a whisper:

"And for such a prize we would not have had to sacrifice one life, one rocket, one tank or even one bullet – because all this was ours by right. But if we fail to locate the Tsar's icon in the next thirty-six hours we will never be given such a chance again. We will have lost our one opportunity to remove a star from the American flag."

Foreign Secretary Gromyko waited until he was certain Brezhnev had completed his statement before he enquired:

"If I may ask, Comrade Chairman, why was Major Romanov allowed to continue being involved in such a sensitive operation after it was suspected he had killed" – with this he glanced down at the papers in front of him – "Researcher Petrova?"

"Because when that situation was drawn to my attention," replied Zaborski, at last looking up, "I had only seven days left to tomorrow's deadline, and in my judgment there was *no one* who could have taken over Romanov's place at such short notice –"

There was a timid knock on the door. All the faces round the table showed surprise. The Minister of Defence had given specific orders that no one was to interrupt them.

"Come," shouted Brezhnev.

The great door inched open and a secretary appeared in the gap; the thin piece of paper in his hand shook, betraying his nervousness. The Minister of Defence waved him in as Brezhnev had no intention of turning around to see who it was. The secretary walked quickly towards them. As soon as he had deposited the telex on the table he turned, and almost ran from the room.

Brezhnev slowly unfolded his tortoise-shell glasses before picking up the missive. Once he had read through the cable, he looked up at the expectant faces in front of him. "It seems an Englishman left an icon in the Louvre and picked it back up this morning."

The blood quickly drained from Zaborski's face.

The four ministers round the table all began talking together, until Brezhnev raised the vast palm of his right hand. There was immediate silence. "I intend to continue my plans on the assumption that it will still be us who get to the Englishman first."

Brezhnev turned towards his Foreign Minister. "Alert all our Western Ambassadors to be prepared to brief the Foreign Ministers of the country in which they reside on the full implications of honouring the amendment to the treaty. Then instruct Anatoly Dobrynin in Washington to demand an official meeting with the Secretary of State to be fixed for late Monday. At the same time I want a further meeting arranged between our Ambassador at the United Nations and U Thant."

Gromyko nodded as Brezhnev turned his attention to the Chief of the General Staff. "See that our strategic forces in all zones are put at a state of readiness to coincide with the timing of the announcement of our diplomatic initiative." Malinovsky smiled. The General Secretary finally turned to the Chairman of the KGB. "Do we still have advertising space booked in every major newspaper in the West?"

"Yes, Comrade General Secretary," replied Zaborski. "But I cannot be certain they will be willing to print the statement as you have prepared it."

"Then pay every one of them in advance," said Brezhnev. "Few Western editors will withdraw a full page advertisement when they already have the money in the bank."

"But if we then don't find the icon . . ." began the Chairman of the KGB.

"Then your last duty as Chairman of State Security will be to withdraw all the advertisements," said the General Secretary of the Communist Party.

CHAPTER TWENTY-THREE

Adam wound down the car window and immediately the warm summer air flooded in. He had decided to avoid the main road to Calais in favour of the N1 to Boulogne. He still considered it possible that Romanov would have men watching at every port on the Channel coast although he doubted if Lawrence or the Americans were aware he had escaped.

Once he had cleared the outskirts of the French capital, he was confident that he could average seventy kilometres an hour the rest of the way. But what he hadn't anticipated was running into a hundred or more cyclists, daubed in their various stripes of reds, greens, blues, blacks and golds, bobbing along ahead of him. As he drifted past them Adam was able accurately to check that they were averaging 40 miles an hour.

Having followed the build-up for the forthcoming World Cup in Britain, he was also able to make out the national colours of France, Germany, Italy and even Portugal. He honked his horn loudly as he passed a group of four men quite near the front, clad in red, white and blue T-shirts with the British team van driving just ahead of them. A few moments later he had overtaken the leaders, and was able to put the car back into fourth gear.

He switched on the car radio and fiddled around for some time before he tuned in to the Home Service of the BBC. He settled back to listen to the news in English for the first time in days. The usual reports of long strikes, high inflation, and of England's chances when the second Test Match at Lord's resumed after the rest day almost made him feel he was already back home, and then he nearly swerved off the road and into a tree.

The news reader reported matter-of-factly that a young RAF pilot had been found dead in a field off the Auxerre/Dijon road after his plane had crashed in mysterious circumstances. No more details were available at the present time. Adam cursed and slammed his fist on the steering wheel at the thought of Alan Banks becoming another victim of Romanov. He tapped the icon and cursed again.

"It was foolish of you to contact me, young man," said the old banker. "You're not exactly a hero of the Soviet Union at the present time."

"Listen, old man, I don't have to be a hero any longer because I may never come back to the Soviet Union."

"Be warned: Mother Russia has extremely long finger nails."

"And because of my grandfather's foresight, I can afford to cut them off," the caller said, touching the gold medallion he wore beneath his shirt. "I just need to be sure you don't let them know where I keep the scissors."

"Why should I remain silent?" asked Poskonov.

"Because if I haven't got my hands on St George within the next twenty-four hours, I'll phone again with the details of how you can hope to collect a larger golden handshake than you could have expected from your present employers." The banker offered no comment.

The Ambassador's secretary rushed into the room without knocking. "I told you no interruptions," shouted Romanov, covering the mouthpiece with his hand.

"But we've located Scott."

Romanov slammed the phone down. In Moscow, the old Russian banker wound the tape back. Poskonov smiled and listened to Romanov's words a second time and came to the conclusion that Romanov had left him with only one choice. He booked a flight to Geneva.

"Robin?"

"Batman. Where have you got to?"

"I'm just outside Paris on my way back home," Adam said. "Are you sticking to the schedule you outlined on the bus?"

"Sure am. Why, are you still desperate to spend the night with me?"

"Sure am," said Adam, mimicking her. "But when do you get back home?"

"The orchestra is taking the ferry from Dunkerque at six thirty tonight. Can you join us?"

"No," said Adam. "I have to return by another route. But, Robin, when I reach London can you put me up for the night?"

"Sounds like an offer I can't refuse," she said, and then repeated her address to be sure he had time to write it down. "When shall I expect you?" she asked.

"Around midnight tonight."

"Do you always give a girl so much notice?"

The young KGB officer standing in the adjoining box had caught most of the conversation. He smiled when he recalled Major Romanov's words: "The man who brings me the Tsar's icon need have no fear for his future in the KGB."

Adam jumped back in the car and drove on until he reached the outskirts of Beauvais, where he decided to stop at a wayside *routier* for a quick lunch.

According to the timetable he had picked up from the Hertz counter, the ferry he wanted to catch was due to leave Boulogne at three o'clock, so he felt confident he would still make it with about an hour to spare.

He sat hidden in an alcove by the window enjoying what might have been described in any English pub as a ploughman's lunch. With each mouthful he became aware that the French ploughmen demanded far higher standards of their innkeepers than any English farm-worker was happy to settle for.

As he waited for his coffee he took out Albert Tomkins's papers from his inside pocket and began to scrutinise them carefully. He was interested to discover exactly how many weeks he had been claiming unemployment benefit.

Through the window of the inn he watched the first of the cyclists as they pedalled by. The athletes' muscles strained in their determination to remain among the leading group. As they shot through Beauvais, Adam was amused by the fact that they were all breaking the speed limit. The sight of the competitors reminded him that he was expected to attend the final part of his medical for the Foreign Office tomorrow afternoon.

Romanov read the decoded message a second time. "Scott returning Geneva. Check German girl and bank." He looked up at the senior KGB officer who had handed him the missive.

"D... Mentor think I'm that naïve?" said Romanov ...we already know from our agent in Amsterdam that he's now on his way towards the French coast."

"Then why should Mentor want to send you in the opposite direction?"

"Because it must be him who's been briefing the Americans," said Romanov coldly.

Romanov turned to the colonel who was standing by his side. "We know it can't be Dunkerque, so how many other possibilities are we left with?"

"Cherbourg, Le Havre, Dieppe, Boulogne, or Calais," replied the colonel, looking down at the map laid out on the table in front of him. "My bet would be Calais," he added.

"Unfortunately," said Romanov, "Captain Scott is not quite *that* simple. And as the motorway takes you direct to Calais, the captain will expect us to have that part of his route well covered. I think our friend will try Boulogne or Dieppe first."

He checked ...e first boat he could ...oulogne for Dover at three, ...ond Secretary ...one from Dieppe to Newhaven at

...Romanov also checked Calais and Le Havre. "Good. Calais left at twelve this morning, and as he phoned the girl after twelve he had no hope of catching that one. And Le Havre doesn't leave until seven fifteen tonight, and he won't risk leaving it that late. Assuming we can beat him to the coast, Colonel, I think Captain Scott is once again within our grasp."

* * *

Once Adam had left the *relais routier* it was only minutes before he began to catch up with the straggling cyclists as they pedalled on towards Abbeville. His thoughts reverted to Romanov. A... Abbeville. His thoughts would have the airports, stations, auto...... well covered. But even the KGB could not be in fifty places at once.

Adam took the Boulogne route out of Abbeville but had to remain in the centre of the road to avoid the bobbing cyclists. He even had to slam his brakes on once when an Italian and a British rider collided in front of him. The two men, both travelling at some speed, were thrown unceremoniously to the ground. The British rider remained ominously still on the side of the road.

Adam felt guilty about not stopping to help his fellow countryman but feared that any hold-up might prevent him catching his boat. He spotted the British team van ahead of him and speeded up until he was alongside. Adam waved at the driver to pull over.

The man ... and wou... ...looked surprised but stopped and ... leaped ... pulled up in front of him, ... to the van.

"One of your chaps has had an accident about a mile back," shouted Adam, pointing towards Paris.

"Thanks, mate," said the driver who turned round and sped quickly back down the road.

Adam continued to drive on at a sedate speed until he had passed all the leaders. Then, once again, he put the car into top gear. A signpost informed him that it was now only thirty-two kilometres to Boulogne: he would still make the three o'clock sailing comfortably.

He began to imagine what it might be like if he could survive beyond Monday. Would his life ever be routine again? Jogs in the park, Foreign Office interviews, workouts with the sergeant major and even the acknowledgment of the part he had played in delivering the icon into safe hands. The problem was that he hadn't yet decided who had safe hands.

A helicopter looking like a squat green bullfrog swept over him; now that would be the ideal way to get back to England, Adam considered. With help like that he could even make it to Harley Street in time for his medical for the Foreign Office.

He watched as the helicopter turned and swung back towards him. He assumed that there must be a military airport somewhere nearby, but couldn't remember one from his days in the army. A few moments later he heard the whirl of the blades as the helicopter flew across his path at a considerably lower level. Adam gripped the wheel of the car until his knuckles went white as an impossible thought crossed his mind. As he did so the helicopter swung back again, and this time flew straight towards him.

Adam wound the window up and crouching over the top of the steering wheel, stared into the sky. He could see the silhouetted outline of three figures sitting in the helicopter cockpit. He banged his fist on the steering wheel in anger as he realised how easy it must have been for them to trace a car signed for in the one name they would immediately recognise. He could sense Romanov's smile of triumph as the chopper hovered above him.

Adam saw a signpost looming up ahead of him and swung off the main road towards a village called Fleureville. He pushed the speedometer well over ninety causing the little car to skid along country lanes.

The helicopter likewise swung to the right, and dog-like followed his path.

Adam took a hard left and only just avoided colliding with a tractor coming out of a newly ploughed field. He took the next right and headed back towards the Boulogne road, desperately trying to think what he could do next. Every time he looked up the helicopter was there above him: he felt like a puppet dancing on the end of Romanov's string.

A road sign depicting a low tunnel ahead flashed past them and Adam dismissed the melodramatic idea of trying to make them crash; he didn't need reminding that it was he who was proving to be the novice.

When he first saw the tunnel he estimated it to be sixty or seventy yards in length. Although it was quite wide, a double-decker bus could not have entered it without the upstairs passengers ending up walking on the bridge.

For a brief moment Adam actually felt safe. He slammed on the little Citroën's brakes and skidded to a halt about thirty yards from the end of the tunnel. The car ended up almost scraping the side of the wall. He switched on his side lights and they flashed brightly in the darkness. For several seconds he watched as approaching cars slowed down before safely overtaking him.

At last he jumped out of the car and ran to the end of the tunnel where he pinned himself against the wall. The helicopter had travelled on some way, but was already turning back, and heading straight towards the tunnel. Adam watched it fly over his head, and moments later heard it turn again. As he waited, two hitch-hikers passed by on the other side, chatting away to themselves, oblivious to Adam's predicament.

He looked across desperately at the two young men

and shouted, "Were you hoping to thumb a lift?"

"Yes," they called back in unison. Adam staggered across the road to join them.

"Are you all right?" Adam heard one of them ask but he could hardly make out which one as his eyes had not yet become accustomed to the darkness.

"No, I'm not," Adam explained simply. "I drank too much wine at lunch and because of a cycle race the road is just crawling with police. I'm sure to be picked up if I go much further. Can either of you drive?"

"I only have my Canadian licence," said the taller of the two youths. "And in any case we are heading for Paris and your car is facing the opposite direction."

"It's a Hertz Rent-a-Car," Adam explained. "I picked it up on the Rue St Ferdinand this morning, and I have to return it by seven tonight. I don't think I can make it in my present state."

The two young men looked at him apprehensively. "I will give you both one hundred francs if you will return it safely for me. You see I can't afford to lose my licence, I'm a commercial traveller," Adam explained. Neither of them spoke. "My papers are all in order, I can assure you." Adam handed them over to the taller man who crossed back over the road and used the car lights to study Albert Tomkins's licence and insurance before carying on a conversation with his friend.

Adam could hear the helicopter blades whirling above the tunnel entrance.

"We don't need the hundred francs," the taller one said eventually. "But we will need a note from you explaining why we are returning the car to Hertz in Paris on your behalf." Adam pulled out the colonel's pen and, feeling remarkably sober, he bent over the hood of the car and scribbled on the back of the Hertz agreement.

"Do you want to come back to Paris with us?"

Adam hesitated fractionally. Couldn't they hear the noise too? "No. I have to get to Boulogne."

"We could drive you to Boulogne and still have enough time to take the car to Paris."

"No, no. That's very considerate. I can take care of myself as long as I feel confident that the car will be delivered back as soon as possible."

The taller one shrugged while his companion opened a rear door and threw their rucksacks on the back seat. Adam remained in the tunnel while they started up the engine. He could hear the purr of the helicopter blades change cadence: it had to be descending to land in a nearby field.

Go, go, for God's sake go, he wanted to shout as the car shot forward towards Boulogne. He watched them travel down the road for about a hundred yards before turning in at a farm entrance, reversing, and heading back towards the tunnel. They tooted as they passed him in the dark, disappearing in the direction of Paris. Adam sank down on to his knees with relief and was about to pick himself up and start walking towards Boulogne when he saw two figures silhouetted at the far entrance of the tunnel. Against the clear blue sky he could make out the outline of two tall, thin men. They stood peering into the tunnel. Adam didn't move a muscle, praying they hadn't spotted him.

And then suddenly one of them started walking towards him, while the other remained motionless. Adam knew he could not hope to escape again. He knelt there cursing his own stupidity. In seconds they would be able to see him clearly.

"Don't let's waste any more valuable time, Marvin, we already know that the limey bastard's heading back to Paris."

"I just thought perhaps . . ." began the one called Marvin in a Southern drawl.

"Leave the thinking to me. Now let's get back to the chopper before we lose him."

When Marvin was only twenty yards away from Adam he suddenly stopped, turned around and began running back.

Adam remained rooted to the spot for several minutes. A cold, clammy sweat had enveloped his body the moment he realised his latest pursuer was not Romanov. If one of them hadn't referred to him as a 'limey bastard', Adam would have happily given himself up. Suddenly he had become painfully aware of the difference between fact and fiction: he had been left with no friends.

Adam did not move again until he heard the helicopter rise above him. Peering out, he could see outlined against the arc of the tunnel the Americans heading back in the direction of Paris.

He staggered outside and put a hand across his eyes. The sunlight seemed much fiercer than a few minutes before. What next? He had less than an hour to catch the boat but no longer had any transport. He wasn't sure whether to thumb lifts, search for a bus stop, or simply get as far away from the main road as possible. His eyes were continually looking up into the sky. How long before they reached the car, and realised it was not him inside?

Cyclists began to pass him again as he jogged slowly towards Boulogne. He kept on moving, and even found enough strength to cheer the British competitors as they pedalled by. The British team van followed close behind and Adam gave it the thumbs-up sign. To his surprise the van came to a halt in front of him.

The driver wound down the window. "Weren't you the fellow who stopped me back in Abbeville?"

"That's right," said Adam. "Has your man recovered?"

"No, he's resting in the back – pulled ligament. What happened to your car?"

"Broke down about a mile back," said Adam, shrugging philosophically.

"Bad luck. Can I give you a lift?" the man asked. "We're only going as far as Boulogne on this stage, but jump in if it will help."

"Thank you," said Adam, with the relief of a bearded beatnik who has found the one person willing to stop to pick him up. The driver leaned across and pushed open the door for him.

Before climbing in, Adam shielded his eyes and once more looked up into the sky. The helicopter was nowhere to be seen – although he knew it couldn't be long before it returned. They would quickly work out that there was only one place where the switch could possibly have been made.

"My name's Bob," said the track-suited driver, thrusting out his free hand. "I'm the British team manager."

"Mine's Adam." He shook the other's hand warmly.

"Where are you heading?"

"Boulogne," said Adam, "and with luck I could still make my crossing by three."

"We should be there about two thirty," said Bob. "We have to be: the afternoon stage starts at three."

"Will your man be able to ride?" asked Adam, pointing over his shoulder.

"No, he won't be competing in this race again," said

the team manager. "He's pulled a ligament in the back of his leg, and they always take a couple of weeks to heal properly. I shall have to leave him in Boulogne and complete the last leg myself. You don't ride by any chance, do you?" Bob asked.

"No," said Adam. "Run a little, but haven't done a lot on wheels since my sister crashed the family tricycle."

"We're still in with a chance for the bronze," Bob said, as they overtook the British riders once more.

Adam gave them the thumbs-up sign and then looked over his shoulder through the back window. He was thankful to see that there was still no sign of the helicopter as they drove into the outskirts of Boulogne. Bob took him all the way up to the dockside. "Hope you get that bronze medal," said Adam as he jumped out of the van. "And thanks again. Good luck with the next stage."

Adam checked his watch: twenty minutes before the boat was due to sail. He wondered if it was too much time. He walked over to the booking office and waited in a short line before buying a passenger ticket. He kept looking round to check if anyone was watching him, but no one seemed to be showing the slightest interest. Once he had purchased his ticket he headed towards the ship and had just begun to start whistling a tuneless version of 'Yesterday' when a black speck appeared in the distance. There was no mistaking it – the sound was enough.

Adam looked up at the gangway which led to the deck of the ship now only yards away from him, and then back to the speck as it grew larger and larger in the sky. He checked his watch: the ship was due to leave in twelve minutes – still time enough for his pursuers to land the helicopter and get on board. If he

381

climbed on and the Americans followed, they were bound to discover him. But if the Americans got on and he stayed off that would still give him enough time to reach Dieppe before the next sailing . . .

Adam jogged quickly back towards the large crowd that was hanging about waiting for the start of the next stage of the road race. As he did so the helicopter swept overhead and started hovering, like a kestrel that is looking for a mouse.

"I thought you said you were desperate to be on that ship."

Adam swung round, his fist clenched, only to face the British team manager now dressed in riding gear.

"Changed my mind," said Adam.

"Wouldn't care to drive the van for us on the next stage?" said Bob hopefully.

"Where does the next stage go?" Adam asked.

"Dunkerque," said the team manager.

Adam tried to remember what time Robin had said her boat left from Dunkerque.

"Six minutes," a voice said over the loudspeaker.

"Okay," said Adam.

"Good," said the team manager. "Then follow me."

Adam ran behind the team manager as he headed towards the van.

"Quatre minutes," Adam heard clearly as Bob unlocked the van and handed him the keys. He stared towards the ship. The two Americans were emerging from the ticket office.

"Deux minutes."

Adam jumped up into the driver's seat, looked over towards the boat and watched Marvin and his colleague stride up the gangplank.

"Une minute."

"Just get the van to Dunkerque and leave the keys

at the British checkpoint. We'll see you when we get there."

"Good luck," said Adam.

"Thank you," said Bob, and ran to the starting line to join his team mates who were anxiously holding his bike.

"Trente secondes."

Adam watched the gangplank being hoisted up as the starter raised his gun.

"On your marks, set . . ."

The ship's fog horn belched out a droning note and the two Americans started their journey to Dover. A second later, the gun went off as Adam put the van into second gear and headed towards Dunkerque.

CHAPTER TWENTY-FOUR

Adam sat in the little dockside café waiting for the coach to appear. The team van had been left at the checkpoint and he was now ready to board the ship but he still needed to be sure Robin was on it. The coach trundled in with only ten minutes to spare and Adam greeted her as she stepped off.

"Just couldn't keep away from me, could you?" said Robin.

Adam burst out laughing and threw his arms almost round her.

"It's good to see you," he said.

"I thought you were going back to England by some mysterious route, you know, spy rocket or something even more exotic."

"I wanted to," said Adam, "but the Americans were sitting at the controls just as I decided to climb aboard."

"The Americans?" she said.

"I'll explain everything once we're on board," said Adam. Neither of them noticed the young agent who had trailed Robin from Berlin. He sat in a phone booth on the far side of the dock and dialled an overseas number.

"I wouldn't have believed a word of it a week ago," she said, "but for two things."

"Namely?"

"First, a senior official of the Foreign Office returned Dudley Hulme's passport to him in Amsterdam. Which reminds me to give you yours back." She rummaged around in her bag for a few moments before taking out a dark blue passport and handing it to him.

"And what's the second thing?" said Adam, taking the passport gratefully.

"I had the doubtful pleasure of coming face to face with Comrade Romanov, and I have no desire to do so again."

"I intend to meet him again," said Adam.

"Why?" asked Robin.

"Because I'm going to kill him."

Romanov and Pollard arrived in Dover a few minutes before the ferry was due to dock. They waited expectantly. Romanov stationed himself so that he could look through the customs hall window and watch the ferry as it sailed into Dover harbour. He had found the perfect spot behind a coffee-vending machine from which he could observe everyone who entered or left the customs hall, while at the same time remaining hidden from view.

"Just in case he should act out of character for a change," said Romanov, "and fails to go in a straight line, you will cover the car exit and report back to me if you notice anything unusual."

The colonel left Romanov secreted behind the coffee machine while he selected a place for himself on the dockside where he could watch the cars as they entered the customs area some fifty yards from the exit gate. If Scott did leave the ferry in a car Pollard would easily have enough time to run back and warn Romanov before Scott could hope to clear customs and reach the main gate. At least this would be the one place Scott couldn't risk hiding in the trunk. Both men waited.

The captain switched on his ship-to-shore radio to channel nine and spoke clearly into the small microphone. "This is the MV *Chantilly* calling the Dover Harbour Master. Are you receiving me?" He waited for a moment, flicked up the switch in front of him and then heard: "Harbour Master to MV *Chantilly*. Receiving you loud and clear, over."

"This is the captain speaking. We have an emergency. A male passenger has fallen out of a lifeboat on to the deck and contracted multiple injuries to his arms and legs." Adam groaned as the captain continued. "I shall need an ambulance to be standing by at the quayside to take him to the nearest hospital once we have docked. Over."

"Message received and understood, Captain. An ambulance will be waiting for you when the ship docks. Over and out."

"Everything will be all right, my dear," said Robin in a gentle voice that Adam had not heard before. "As soon as we arrive, they are going to see you are taken straight to a hospital."

"I must get back to the bridge," said the captain gruffly. "I shall instruct two stewards to bring a stretcher down for your brother."

"Thank you, Captain," said Robin. "You have been most helpful."

"It's quite all right, miss. You did say your brother?"

"Yes, Captain," said Robin.

"Well, you might advise him in future that it's in

his best interests to drink less before he comes on board."

"I've tried," said Robin, sighing. "You couldn't believe how many times I've tried, Captain, but I'm afraid he takes after my father." Adam held on to his leg and groaned again.

"Um," said the captain, looking down at the gash across Adam's shoulder. "Let's hope it turns out not to be serious. Good luck," he added.

"Thank you again, Captain," said Robin as she watched the cabin door close behind them.

"So far, so good," said Robin. "Now let's hope the second part of the plan works. By the way, your breath smells foul."

"What do you expect after making me swirl whisky round in my mouth for twenty minutes and then forcing me to spit it out all over my own clothes?"

Adam was lifted carefully on to the stretcher, then carried out on to the deck by two stewards. They waited at the head of the gangplank and placed Adam gently on the deck while a customs officer, accompanied by an immigration officer, ran up to join them. Robin handed over his passport. The immigration officer flicked through the pages and checked the photograph.

"Quite a good likeness for a change," said Robin, "but I'm afraid they may have to include this under 'unusual scars' in the next edition." She threw back the blanket dramatically and revealed the deep gash on Adam's shoulder. Adam looked suitably crestfallen.

"Is he bringing anything in with him that needs to be declared?" asked the customs official. Adam couldn't stop himself from touching the icon.

"No, I wouldn't let him buy any more booze on this

trip. And I'll be responsible for checking his personal belongings through with mine when I leave the ship."

"Right. Thank you, miss. Better see he gets off to the hospital then," said the officer, suddenly aware that a restless mob of people were waiting at the top of the gangplank to disembark.

The two stewards carried Adam down the gangplank. An attendant was on hand to check his wound. Adam waved gamely at Robin as they placed him in the ambulance.

Romanov spotted her as she came through customs. "Now I know exactly how Captain Scott hopes to get off the ship, and we will be waiting for him when he least expects it. Go and hire a car to take us to London," he barked at the colonel.

The ambulance shot out through the customs gates with its lights full on and bells ringing. By the time they had arrived at The Royal Victoria Hospital the attendant had watched his patient's remarkable recovery en route with disbelief. He was beginning to feel that the captain might have exaggerated the scale of the emergency.

Romanov stood by the gate and smiled as he watched the coach carrying the musicians emerge from the deep black hole of the ship and take its turn in the queue for customs.

As Romanov's eyes ranged up and down the coach he quickly picked out Robin Beresford. Just as he had anticipated, the double bass was propped up by her side, making it impossible to see who was seated next to her.

"You won't pull that one on me a second time," Romanov muttered, just as the colonel appeared by his side, red in the face.

"Where's the car?" the Russian demanded, not taking his eye from the coach.

"I've booked one provisionally," said the colonel, "but they'll need your international licence. I forgot Scott has got mine, along with all my other papers."

"You stay put," said Romanov, "and make sure Scott doesn't try to get off that coach." Romanov ran to the Avis desk at the same time as Adam was being wheeled into a little cubicle to be examined by the duty registrar.

The young doctor leant over his patient for several minutes. He had never seen a wound quite like it before. He examined him carefully, before making any comment. "Nasty lacerations," he said finally, cleaning Adam's shoulder wound. "Can you circle your arm?" Adam turned the arm in a full circle and straightened it again. "Good. No break, at least." He continued to clean the wound.

"I'm going to put some iodine on the open cut and it may sting a little," said the doctor. He cleaned up both elbows before placing a plaster on them.

"That didn't happen today, did it?" he asked, staring at Adam's half-healed shoulder.

"No," said Adam, without offering any explanations.

"You have been in the wars lately. I'm going to give you an anti-tetanus injection." Adam turned white. "Funny how many grown men don't care for the sight of a needle," said the doctor. Adam groaned.

"Now that wasn't so bad, was it?" he coaxed as he placed a large bandage over the top of the shoulder. "Do you have someone to collect you?" the doctor asked finally.

"Yes, thank you," said Adam. "My wife is waiting for me."

"Passable," said Adam.

"What belt are you?" demanded Terry belligerently. "Go on, tell me, a black belt, I knew it," he added, sniggering.

"I haven't been a black belt for nearly eight years," said Adam casually, "but I've been recently awarded my second Dan."

A look of apprehension came over three of the four faces.

"I was thinkin' about taking up judo myself," continued the leader, straightening his arm. "How long does it take to get any good at it?"

"I've been working at it three hours a day for nearly twelve years and I'm still not up to Olympic standard," replied Adam as he watched the dark-haired man in the duffle coat pass by the compartment again. This time he stared directly at Adam before quickly moving on.

"Of course," continued Adam, "the only quality you really need if you are thinking of taking up judo seriously is nerve, and no one can teach you that. You've either got it or you haven't."

"I've got nerve," said Terry belligerently. "I'm not frightened of nothin'. Or nobody," he added, staring straight at Adam.

"Good," said Adam. "Because you may be given the chance to prove your claim before this journey is over."

"What're you getting at?" said the 'Heil Hitler'-clad youth. "You trying to pick a fight or somethin'?"

"No," said Adam calmly. "It's just that at this moment I'm being followed by a private detective who is hoping to catch me spending the night with his client's wife."

The four of them sat still for the first time during

the journey and stared at Adam with something approaching respect.

"And are you?" asked the leader.

Adam nodded conspiratorially.

"Nice bit of skirt when you've got it in the hay?" Terry asked, leering.

"Not bad," said Adam, "not bad at all."

"Then just point out this detective git and we'll sew him up for the night," said the leader, thrusting his left hand on his right bicep while pulling up his clenched fist with gusto.

"That might turn out to be overkill," said Adam. "But if you could delay him for a little when I get off at Waterloo East, that should at least give me enough time to warn the lady."

"Say no more, squire," said the leader. "Your friend the Peeping Tom will be delivered to Charing Cross all trussed up like a British Rail parcel."

The other three youths burst out laughing and Adam was beginning to realise that it had taken Romanov only one week to turn him into a storyteller almost in the class of Robin's late father.

"That's him," whispered Adam as the duffle-coated man passed by a third time. They all looked out into the corridor but only saw his retreating back.

"The train is due to arrive at Waterloo East in eleven minutes' time," said Adam, checking his watch. "So what I suggest we do is . . . if you still think you're up to it, that is." All four of his new-found team leaned forward in eager anticipation.

A few minutes later Adam slipped out of the compartment, leaving the door wide open. He started to walk slowly in the direction opposite to that in which the man in the blue duffle coat had last been seen going. When Adam reached the end of the carriage, he turned to find the man was now following quickly behind. As he passed the open compartment the man smiled and raised a hand to attract Adam's attention but two leather-clad arms shot out and the man disappeared inside the compartment with a muffled cry. The door was slammed and the blinds pulled quickly down.

The train drew slowly into Waterloo East station.

Robin remained tense as the bus drew into Wigmore Street and came to a halt outside the RPO headquarters. A dark green Ford had been following them for at least thirty miles, and once she had become aware of it she had not dared to move from her seat.

As she dragged her double bass off the bus she looked back to see that the Ford had stopped about fifty yards down the road and turned off its headlights. Romanov was standing on the pavement looking like a caged animal that wanted to spring. Another man that Robin did not recognise remained seated behind the wheel. Adam had warned her not to turn around at any time but to walk straight into the RPO headquarters without stopping. Even so, she couldn't resist looking Romanov in the eye and shaking her head. Romanov continued to stare impassively ahead of him.

When the last musician had left the bus Romanov and 'the Colonel' searched up and down the inside of the vehicle and then finally the trunk, despite noisy protests from the driver. Robin eyed them nervously from an upstairs window, as the two of them jumped back into the green Ford and drove off. She continued watching the car until the back lights had faded away in the darkness.

* * *

The colonel swung out of Wigmore Street towards Baker Street, bringing the car to a halt opposite Baker Street station. Romanov jumped out, walked into a vacant telephone booth and started thumbing through the A–D directory. Only one Robin Beresford was listed and it was the same address as the young agent had read over to him. He dialled the number and after ten unanswered rings smiled at the realisation that she lived alone. He was not surprised.

"What now?" asked the colonel, once Romanov was back at the car.

"Where's Argyle Crescent, NW3?"

"Must be out towards Hampstead," said the colonel. "But I'll first check in the London A to Z roadmap. What's the plan?"

"Rather than waiting for Miss Beresford to come out we will be waiting for her to come in," said Romanov.

Robin slipped out of the back of the RPO headquarters about thirty minutes later. She zig-zagged around Portman Square then walked as quickly as she knew how up to the corner. She kept telling herself that Romanov was not coming back, but she found it impossible to stop herself from shaking all the same. She hailed a taxi and was relieved to see one draw up to her side almost immediately. She checked the driver and the back seat, as Adam had advised her, then climbed in.

Romanov arrived at Robin's front door a few moments after she had hailed the taxi. The name holder on the side wall indicated that Miss Beresford resided on the fourth floor.

The door itself would have proved no problem to any self-respecting petty thief in Moscow and

Romanov had secured entry within moments. The colonel quickly joined him before they proceeded silently up the dark staircase to the fourth floor.

Romanov slipped the Yale lock faster than Robin could have opened it with her own key. Once inside he quickly checked the layout of the room and assured himself no one else was in the flat.

The colonel stood around fidgeting. "Settle down, Colonel. I don't expect the lady will keep us waiting too long." The colonel laughed nervously.

The taxi drew up outside the house that Robin pointed to. She then jumped out and tipped the cabbie extra because the bewitching hour had long passed and at last she felt safe. It seemed ages since she had been home. All she was looking forward to now was a hot bath and a good night's sleep.

Adam stepped off the train at Waterloo East a little after midnight and was pleased to find the underground was still running. He had avoided going on to Charing Cross, as he couldn't be sure which side would have a reception committee waiting for him. He produced a season ticket for the West Indian on the ticket barrier and waited around on the underground platform for some time before the train eventually drew in.

There were several stations between Waterloo and his destination, and even at this time of night there seemed to be a prolonged stop at every one. Several late-night revellers got in at the Embankment, more still at Leicester Square. Adam waited nervously at each station, now aware that he must have caught the last train. He only hoped Robin had carried out his instructions faithfully. He looked around the carriage he was sitting in. It was full of night people, waiters, nurses, party returners, drunks – even a traffic warden. The train eventually pulled into his station, at twelve forty.

The ticket collector was able to give him the directions he needed. It was a relief to reach his final destination so quickly because there was no one else around to ask the way at that time of night. He moved slowly towards number twenty-three. There were no lights on in the house. He opened the swinging gate and walked straight up the path, removed the bunch of keys from his pocket, putting the Chubb one in the lock. Adam pushed open the door cautiously and then closed it noiselessly behind him.

A little after twelve ten the last train from Dover pulled into Charing Cross station. As Adam was nowhere to be seen, Lawrence instructed his driver to take him back to Cheyne Walk. He couldn't understand why the agent whom he had hand-picked hadn't reported in. When Lawrence arrived back at the flat he put the key in his lock, hoping to find Adam was already waiting for him.

CHAPTER TWENTY-FIVE

He pushed open the swinging gate and made his way slowly up the path in the pitch darkness. Once he reached the corner of the house he searched for the third stone on the left. When he located the correct stone where he always left his spare key, he pulled it up with his fingers and felt around in the dirt. To his relief the key was still in place. Like a burglar he pushed it into the lock quietly.

He crept into the hall and closed the door behind him, switched on the light and began to climb the stairs. Once he had reached the landing he switched off the hall light, turned the knob of his bedroom door and pushed.

As he stepped in an arm circled his throat like a whiplash and he was thrown to the ground with tremendous force. He felt a knee pressed hard against his spine and his arm was jerked up behind his back into a half nelson. He lay on the floor, flat on his face, hardly able to move or even breathe. The light switch flashed on and the first thing Adam saw was the colonel.

"Don't kill me, Captain Scott sir, don't kill me," he implored.

"I have no intention of doing so, Mr Tomkins,"

said Adam calmly. "But first, where is your esteemed employer at this moment?"

Adam kept his knee firmly in the middle of the colonel's back and pressed his arm a few inches higher before the colonel bleated out, "He went back to the Embassy once he realised the girl wasn't going to return to the flat."

"Just as I planned," said Adam, but he didn't lessen the pressure on the colonel's arm as he described in vivid detail everything that would now be expected of him.

The colonel's face showed disbelief. "But that will be impossible," he said. "I mean, he's bound to noti – Ahhh."

The colonel felt his arm forced higher up his back. "You could carry out the whole exercise in less than ten minutes and he need never be any the wiser," said Adam. "However, I feel that it's only fair that you should be rewarded for your effort."

"Thank you, sir," said the fawning colonel.

"If you succeed in delivering the one item I require and carry out my instructions to the letter you will be given in exchange your passport, driving licence, papers, wallet and a guarantee of no prosecution for your past treachery. But if, on the other hand, you fail to turn up by nine thirty tomorrow morning with the object of my desire," said Adam, "all those documents will be placed thirty minutes later on the desk of a Mr Lawrence Pemberton of the FO, along with my report on your other sources of income which you have failed to declare on your tax return."

"You wouldn't do that to me, would you, Captain Scott?"

"As ten o'clock chimes," said Adam.

"But think what would then happen to me, Captain

Scott, sir, if you carried out such a threat," moaned the colonel.

"I have already considered that," said Adam, "and I have come to two conclusions."

"And what are they, Captain Scott?"

"Spies," continued Adam, not loosening his grip, "at the present time seem to be getting anything from eighteen to forty-two years at Her Majesty's pleasure, so you might, with good behaviour, be out before the turn of the century, just in time to collect your telegram from the Queen."

The colonel looked visibly impressed. "And the other conclusion?" he blurted out.

"Oh, simply that you could inform Romanov of my nocturnal visit and he in return would arrange for you to spend the rest of your days in a very small dacha in a suitably undesirable suburb of Moscow. Because, you see, my dear Tomkins, you are a very small spy. I personally am not sure when left with such an alternative which I would view with more horror."

"I'll get it for you, Captain Scott, you can rely on me."

"I'm sure I can, Tomkins. Because if you were to let Romanov into our little secret, you would be arrested within minutes. So at best, you could try to escape on the Aeroflot plane to Moscow. And I've checked, there isn't one until the early evening."

"I'll bring it to you by nine thirty on the dot, sir. You can be sure of that. But for God's sake have yours ready to exchange."

"I will," said Adam, "as well as all your documents, Tomkins."

Adam lifted the colonel slowly off the ground and then shoved him towards the landing. He switched on the light and then pushed the colonel on down the stairs until they reached the front door.

"The keys," said Adam.

"But you've already got my keys, Captain Scott, sir."

"The car keys, you fool."

"But it's a hire car, sir," said the colonel.

"And I'm about to hire it," said Adam.

"But how will I get myself back to London in time, sir?"

"I have no idea, but you still have the rest of the night to come up with something. You could even walk it by then. The keys," Adam repeated, jerking the colonel's arm to shoulder-blade level.

"In my left hand pocket," said the colonel, almost an octave higher.

Adam put his hand into the colonel's new jacket and pulled out the car keys.

He opened the front door, shoved the colonel on to the path, and then escorted him to the pavement.

"You will go and stand on the far side of the road," said Adam, "and you will not return to the house until I have reached the end of the road. Do I make myself clear, Tomkins?"

"Abundantly clear, Captain Scott, sir."

"Good," said Adam releasing him for the first time, "and just one more thing, Tomkins. In case you think of double-crossing me, I have already instructed the Foreign Office to place Romanov under surveillance and put two extra lookouts near the Soviet Embassy with instructions to report the moment anyone suspicious turns up or leaves before nine tomorrow morning." Adam hoped he sounded convincing.

"Thought of everything, haven't you, sir?" said the colonel mournfully.

"Yes, I think so," said Adam. "I even found time to disconnect your phone while I was waiting for you to return." Adam pushed the colonel across the road before getting into the hire car. He wound the window down. "See you at nine thirty tomorrow morning. Prompt," he added, as he put the Ford into first gear.

The colonel stood shivering on the far pavement, nursing his right shoulder, as Adam drove to the end of the road. He was still standing there when Adam took a left turn back towards the centre of London.

For the first time since Heidi's death, Adam felt it was Romanov who was on the run.

"What a great honour for our little establishment," said Herr Bischoff, delighted to see the most important banker in the East sitting in his boardroom sharing afternoon tea.

"Not at all, my dear Bischoff," said Poskonov. "After all these years the honour is entirely mine. And kind of you to be so understanding about opening the bank on a Sunday. But now to business. Did you manage to get Romanov to sign the release form?"

"Oh, yes," said Bischoff, matter-of-factly. "He did it without even reading the standard clauses, let alone the extra three you asked us to put in."

"So his inheritance automatically returns to the Russian state?"

"That is so, Mr Poskonov, and we in return . . ."

". . . will represent us in all the currency exchange transactions we carry out in the West."

"Thank you," said Herr Bischoff. "And we shall be delighted to assist you in your slightest requirement, but what happens when Romanov returns to the bank and demands to know what has become of his inheritance?" asked the chairman of the bank anxiously.

"He will not return," the Russian banker said emphatically. "You can have my word on it. Now, I would like to see what is in those boxes."

"Yes, of course," said Herr Bischoff. "Will you please accompany me?"

The two banking chairmen took the private lift to the basement and Herr Bischoff accompanied his guest to the underground vault.

"I will unlock the five boxes now in your name with the bank's key but only you can open them with your key."

"Thank you," said Poskonov, and left Herr Bischoff to open the five locks and return to the entrance of the vault.

"Do take as long as you like," said Herr Bischoff, "but at six o'clock the great door is automatically locked until nine o'clock tomorrow morning, and nothing less than a nuclear weapon would prise it open. At five forty-five, an alarm goes off to warn you that you only have fifteen minutes left."

"Excellent," said the man who through his entire banking career had never been given a fifteen-minute warning of anything.

Herr Bischoff handed Comrade Poskonov the envelope with Romanov's key inside it.

As soon as the massive steel door had been swung closed behind him the Russian checked the clock on the wall. They had left him with over two hours to sort out what could be transported to Brazil and what would have to be left behind. A state pension and the Order of Lenin (second class) hadn't seemed much of an alternative to Poskonov.

He turned the key and opened the first of the small boxes and found the deeds to lands the State had owned for decades. He growled. The second box contained the shares of companies once brilliantly successful, now shells in every sense of the word. And to Poskonov's disappointment the third of the small boxes only held a will proving everything belonged to Romanov's father and his immediate heirs. Had he waited all these years to discover the stories the old man had told him of gold, jewels and pearls were nothing but a fantasy? Or had Romanov already removed them?

Poskonov opened the first of the large boxes and stared down at the twelve little compartments. He removed the lid of the first one tentatively, and when he saw the array of gems and stones that shone in front of him his legs felt weak. He put both hands into the box and let the gems slip through his fingers like a child playing with pebbles on a beach.

The second box produced pearls and the third gold coins and medallions that could make even an old man's eyes sparkle. He hadn't realised how long it had taken him to go through the remaining boxes but when the alarm went off he was five thousand miles away already enjoying his new-found wealth. He glanced at the clock. He had easily enough time to get everything back into the compartments and then he would return the following day and remove once and for all what he had earned from fifty years of serving the State.

When the last lid had been placed back on he checked the clock on the wall: six minutes to six. Just enough time to glance in the other box and see if he could expect the same again.

He turned the key and licked his lips in anticipation as he pulled the large box out. Just a quick look, he promised himself, as he lifted the lid. When he saw the decaying body with its grey skin and eyes hanging in their sockets he reeled backwards from the sight and, falling to the floor, clutched his heart.

Both bodies were discovered at nine the next morning.

The phone rang and Adam grabbed at it before the shrill tone could deafen him a second time.

"Your alarm call, sir," said a girl's voice gently. "It's eight o'clock."

"Thank you," Adam replied and replaced the receiver. The call had proved unnecessary because he had been sitting up in bed considering the implications of his plan for nearly an hour. Adam had finally worked out exactly how he was going to finish Romanov.

He jumped out of bed, threw back the curtains and stared down at the Soviet Embassy. He wondered how long the Russian had been awake.

He returned to the side of the bed and picked up the phone to dial the number Robin had given him. The phone rang several times before it was answered by an elderly voice saying, "Mrs Beresford."

"Good morning, Mrs Beresford. My name is Adam Scott, I'm a friend of Robin's. I was just phoning to check that she reached home safely last night."

"Oh, yes, thank you," said Robin's mother. "It was a pleasant surprise to see her before the weekend. She usually spends the night in the flat when she gets back that late. I'm afraid she's still asleep. Would you like me to wake her?"

"No, no, don't disturb her," said Adam. "I only rang to fix up a lunch date. Can you tell her I'll call back later?"

"I certainly will," she replied. "Thank you for phoning, Mr Scott."

Adam replaced the receiver and smiled. Each piece of the jigsaw was fitting neatly into place but without the colonel's help he still lacked the vital corner-piece.

Adam began to put everything Tomkins needed, including his passport, personal papers and wallet into a large envelope. He removed the icon from his jacket pocket, turned it over and carefully examined the little silver crest of the Tsar. He then flicked open the colonel's penknife and began the slow and delicate task of removing the crown.

Thirty minutes later, Adam was in the lift on the way to the hotel basement. When he stepped out, he walked across to the space where he had parked the green Cortina earlier that morning. He unlocked the door and threw the colonel's old jacket on to the seat, then locked the car, checking all the doors before taking the lift back up to the ground floor.

The manager of the men's shop in the arcade had just flicked over the 'closed' sign and Adam took his time selecting a white shirt, grey flannels and a blue blazer, trying them on in their little changing room.

At nine twenty-three he settled his bill with the Royal Garden Hotel and asked the doorman to bring the green Ford up from the parking lot. He waited by the hotel entrance.

As the minutes passed, he began to fear that the colonel wouldn't turn up. If he failed to, Adam knew that the next call would have to be to Lawrence and not Romanov.

His reverie was disturbed by a honk on a car horn; the colonel's rented car had been left by the entrance.

"Your car is waiting on the ramp," said the doorman, as he returned the keys to Adam.

"Thank you," said Adam and handed over the last of the colonel's pound notes. He dropped the wallet into the large envelope, which he sealed, before checking his watch again.

He stood waiting anxiously for another two minutes

before he spotted the colonel puffing up the slope leading to the hotel entrance.

He was clinging on to a small carrier bag.

"I've done it, Captain Scott, sir, I've done it," said the colonel, before he had reached Adam's side. "But I must return immediately or he's bound to notice it's gone."

He passed the carrier bag quickly to Adam who opened the top and stared down at the object inside.

"You're a man of your word," said Adam, "and as promised you'll find everything you need in there." He passed over his own package along with the car keys without speaking. He pointed to the hire car.

The colonel ran to it, jumped in and drove quickly down the ramp of the Royal Garden Hotel before turning left into Kensington Palace Gardens.

Adam checked his watch: nine thirty-five.

"Could you call me a taxi?" he asked the doorman.

The driver pulled the window down and gave Adam an enquiring look.

"Chesham Place, SW1. A carpenter's shop."

Adam spent twenty minutes looking around the shop while the craftsman carried out his unusual request. Adam studied the result with satisfaction, paid him two half-crowns and then walked back on to King's Road, to hail another taxi.

"Where to, guv'nor?"

"The Tower of London."

Everyone was in their place for the D4 meeting at nine thirty and Busch had gone on the attack even before Lawrence had had the chance to sit down.

"How in hell did you manage to lose him this time?"

"I must take the blame myself," said Lawrence. "We had every port from Newhaven to Harwich covered, but the moment my man saw Romanov and his henchman leave the quayside at Dover and chase off down the motorway after the coach he assumed he must have seen Scott. I had already instructed the senior immigration officer at the port," he continued, "to allow Scott to disembark without a fuss. It had been my intention to take over once he passed through customs. There seemed no reason to change that plan while we had Romanov under close surveillance. Scott then proceeded to fool both Romanov and our man at Dover."

"But we were given a second chance when Scott got on the train," persisted Busch. Lawrence stared at the American, waiting to see if he would admit that his two CIA agents had also lost Scott at Dover.

"My man was on the train," said Lawrence emphatically, "but had only the one opportunity to make contact with Scott while he was on his own, and at just that moment he was grabbed and badly beaten up by a bunch of drunken louts – teenagers, apparently – who were on their way back from a day trip to the seaside."

"Perhaps we're recruiting our agents from the wrong class of person," said Matthews, staring down at his briefing papers.

Lawrence made no attempt to reply.

"So, as far as we can tell, Scott, the Tsar's icon and Romanov are still holed up somewhere in London?" said Snell.

"It looks that way," admitted Lawrence.

"Perhaps all is not lost then," suggested Snell. "Scott may still try and get in touch with you again."

"I think not," said Lawrence quietly.

"How can you be so sure?" asked Busch.

"Because Scott knows that one of us in this room is a traitor and he thinks it's me."

"Good morning. Soviet Embassy."

"My name is Adam Scott and I need to get in contact with a Major Romanov."

"Good morning, Mr Scott. We do not have a Major Romanov working at the Embassy," came back the polite reply.

"I'm sure you don't."

"But if you would like to leave your number, I will make further enquiries."

"I'll wait. Wouldn't surprise me if you find him very quickly once he knows who it is calling."

There was a long silence at the other end, and Adam only hoped the shilling he had pressed into the call box would prove to be enough. At last there was a click, and then Adam heard a voice.

"Who is this?" said the voice, unable to mask its incredulity.

"You know very well who it is," said Adam curtly. "I want to make a deal."

"A deal?" Romanov repeated, his voice changing from one of disbelief to surprise.

"I'll swap you my icon – which as you so vividly pointed out is worthless to me – in exchange for your copy, which is not. But I also require the papers that prove my father's innocence."

"How do I know you're not setting me up?"

"You don't," said Adam. "But you're the one with nothing to lose."

The pips began to sound across the line.

"Tell me your number," said Romanov.

"738–9121," said Adam.

"I'll phone you back," said Romanov as the line went dead.

"How quickly can we find out where 738–9121 is located?" Romanov asked the local KGB operative who sat opposite him.

"About ten minutes," the aide replied. "But it could be a trap."

"True, but with nineteen hours to go before the icon has to be in America I don't have a lot of choice."

Romanov turned back to the KGB agent. "What's the traffic like in London on a Friday morning?"

"One of the busiest times in the week. Why do you ask?"

"Because I'll need a motorbike and a superb driver," was all Romanov said.

Adam could do nothing about the middle-aged lady who was now occupying his phone booth. He had nervously walked out to check the bridge when she slipped in. She must have been puzzled as to why the young man didn't use the empty box that stood next to it.

He checked his watch anxiously: ten forty-five. He knew he couldn't risk waiting a minute after eleven but was confident that Romanov would have traced where he'd made the call from long before then.

The talkative woman was another twelve minutes before she eventually put the phone down. When she stepped out of the box she gave Adam a warm smile.

Three more minutes and he would have to phone Lawrence and abort his original plan. He began to watch the Beefeaters as they patrolled under Traitors' Gate. Traitors' Gate -- how appropriate, Adam thought. He had chosen the spot because he could see clearly up and down the path leading to the drawbridge and felt he could not be taken by surprise. And in desperation there was always the moat that surrounded them on all sides.

For the first time in his life, Adam discovered exactly how long five minutes could be. When the phone rang, it sounded like an alarm bell. He picked it up nervously, his eyes never leaving the main road.

"Scott?"

"Yes."

"I can now see you clearly as I am less than one minute away. I will be standing at the end of Tower Bridge until the end of that minute. Be sure you're there with the icon. If you're not, I shall burn the papers that prove your father's innocence in front of you."

The phone went dead.

Adam was delighted that another piece of the jigsaw had fallen into place. He stepped out of the phone booth and checked up and down the road. A BMW motorcycle swerved to a halt at the end of the bridge. A rider dressed in a leather jacket sat astride the bike but only seemed interested in watching the flow of traffic as it passed by the Tower. It was the man seated behind him who stared directly at Adam.

Adam began to walk slowly towards the end of the bridge. He put a hand in his pocket to be sure the icon was still in its place.

He was about thirty yards from the end of the bridge when the second figure got off the bike and started walking towards him. When their eyes met, Romanov stopped in his tracks and held up a small, square frame. Adam did not respond in kind, but simply tapped the side of his pocket and continued walking. Both men advanced towards each other like knights of old until they were only a few paces apart. Almost simultaneously they stopped and faced one another.

"Let me see it," said Romanov.

Adam paused, then slowly removed the icon from his pocket and held it to his chest for his adversary to see St George stared at him.

"Turn it over," said Romanov.

Adam obeyed, and the Russian could not hide his delight when he saw the little silver crown of the Tsar embedded in the back.

"Now you," said Adam. Romanov held his icon away from his body, as if brandishing a sword. The masterpiece shone in the summer sun.

"And the documents," said Adam, forcing himself to speak calmly.

The Russian pulled out a package from within his jacket and slowly unfolded them. Adam stared at the official court verdict for a second time.

"Go to the wall," said Adam, pointing with his left hand to the side of the bridge, "and leave the icon and the documents on it."

It was Romanov who now obeyed as Adam proceeded to the wall on the other side of the bridge and placed his icon in the middle of it.

"Cross slowly," called Adam. The two men moved sideways back across the bridge, never getting closer than a couple of yards from each other until they had come to a halt at each other's icon. The moment the painting was within his reach, Romanov grabbed it, ran and jumped on to the motorcycle without looking back. Within seconds the BMW had disappeared into the dense traffic.

Adam did not move. Although it had only been out of his sight for just over an hour, he was relieved to have the original back. Adam checked the papers that would establish his father's innocence and placed them in his inside pocket. Ignoring the tourists, some of whom had stopped to stare at him, Adam began to relax when suddenly he felt a sharp prod in the middle of his back. He jumped round in fright.

A little girl was staring up at him.

"Will you and your friend be performing again this morning?"

When the BMW motorcycle drew up outside the Soviet Embassy in Kensington Palace Gardens, Romanov leapt off and ran up the steps and straight into the Ambassador's office without knocking. The Ambassador didn't need to ask if he had been successful.

"It worked out just as I planned. He was taken completely by surprise," said Romanov, as he handed the icon over to the Ambassador.

The Ambassador turned the painting over and saw the little silver crown of the Tsar. Any doubts that he might have had were also dispelled.

"I have orders to send the icon to Washington in the diplomatic pouch immediately. There is no time to be lost."

"I wish I could deliver it in person," said Romanov.

"Be satisfied, Comrade Major, that you have carried out your part of the operation in an exemplary fashion."

The Ambassador pressed a button on the side of his desk. Two men appeared immediately. One held open the diplomatic pouch while the other stood motionless by his side. The Ambassador handed over the icon and watched it being placed into the pouch. The two couriers looked as if they would have had no trouble in carrying out the Ambassador's desk as well, thought Romanov.

"There is a plane standing by at Heathrow to take

you both direct to Washington," said the Ambassador. "All the necessary documentation for customs has already been dealt with. You should touch down at National airport around five o'clock Washington time, easily giving our comrades in America enough time to fulfil their part of the contract."

The two men nodded, sealed the diplomatic pouch in the Ambassador's presence and left. Romanov walked over to the window and watched the official car drive the two men out into Kensington High Street and off in the direction of Heathrow.

"Vodka, Comrade Major?"

"Thank you," Romanov replied, not moving from the window until the car was out of sight.

The Ambassador went over to a side cabinet and took out two glasses and a bottle from the fridge before pouring Romanov a large vodka.

"It would not be exaggerating to say that you have played your part in establishing the Soviet Union as the most powerful nation on earth," he said as he handed over the drink. "Let us therefore drink to the repatriation of the people of Aleuts as full citizens of the Union of Soviet Socialist Republics."

"How is that possible?" asked Romanov.

"I think the time has come to let you know," said the Ambassador, "the significance of your achievement." He then went on to tell Romanov of the briefing he had received from Moscow that morning.

Romanov was thankful he had never known how much was at stake.

"I have made an appointment to see the Foreign Secretary at three o'clock this afternoon in order to brief him. We can be sure the British will only be interested in fair play," the Ambassador continued. "I am told he is not at all pleased as he had hoped to be

415

in his constituency to open some fete; the British have some strange ideas about how to keep their party system going."

Romanov laughed. "To Aleuts," he said, raising his glass. "But what is happening in Washington at this moment?"

"Our Ambassador has already requested a meeting with the American Secretary of State to be scheduled for eight this evening. He is also setting up a press conference at the Embassy to follow that meeting. It may amuse you to know that President Johnson had to cancel his visit to Texas this weekend and has requested that the networks should allow him to address 'his fellow Americans' at peak time on Monday as a matter of national importance."

"And we achieved it with only hours to spare," said Romanov, pouring himself another vodka.

"Touch and go, as the English would say. Let us also be thankful for the time difference between here and the United States because without that we would never have been able to beat the deadline."

Romanov shuddered at the thought of how close it had been and downed his second vodka in one gulp.

"You must join me for lunch, Comrade. Although your orders are to return to Moscow immediately my secretary assures me that the first plane leaving Heathrow for Moscow does not depart until eight this evening. I envy you the reception you will receive when you arrive back in the Kremlin tomorrow."

"I still need the £1000 for . . ."

"Ah, yes," said the Ambassador, "I have it ready for you." He unlocked the little drawer of his desk and passed over a slim wad of notes in a small cellophane wrapper.

Romanov slipped the tiny packet in his pocket and joined the Ambassador for lunch.

Busch barged into Lawrence's office.

"Romanov's got the icon," he shouted.

Lawrence's jaw dropped. A look of desperation appeared on his face. "How can you be so sure?" he demanded.

"I've just had a message from Washington. The Russians have requested an official meeting with the Secretary of State to be arranged for eight this evening."

"I don't believe it," said Lawrence.

"I do," said Busch. "We've always known that God-damned friend of yours, like his father, was a lousy traitor. There's no other explanation."

"He could be dead," said Lawrence quietly.

"I hope he is, for his sake," said Busch.

The phone on Lawrence's desk rang. He grabbed it as if it were a lifeline. "A Dr John Vance wants a word with you, sir," said his secretary. "He said you had asked him to call."

Vance? Vance? Lawrence recalled the name but couldn't quite place it. "Put him on," he said.

"Good morning, Mr Pemberton," said a voice.

"Good morning, Dr Vance. What can I do for you?"

"You asked me to call you after I had examined Scott."

"Scott?" repeated Lawrence, not believing what he was hearing.

"Yes, Adam Scott. Surely you remember? You wanted him to complete a medical for your department."

Lawrence was speechless.

"I've given him a clean bill of health," continued

the doctor. "Some cuts and a nasty bruise, but nothing that won't heal in a few days."

"Cuts and bruises?" said Lawrence.

"That's what I said, old chap. But don't worry about Scott. He's fit enough to start work whenever you want him. That's if you still want him."

"If I still want him," repeated Lawrence. "Mr Scott isn't there with you at this moment, by any chance?"

"No," said Vance. "Left my surgery about ten minutes ago."

"He didn't happen to tell you where he was going?" asked Lawrence.

"No, he wasn't specific. Just said something about having to see a friend off at the airport."

Once the coffee had been cleared away, Romanov checked his watch. He had left easily enough time to keep the appointment and still catch his plane. He thanked the Ambassador for all his help, left him, ran down the Embassy steps and climbed into the back of the anonymous black car.

The driver moved off without speaking as he had already been briefed as to where the major wanted to go.

Neither of them spoke on the short journey, and when the driver drew into Charlotte Street he parked the car in a lay-by. Romanov stepped out, walked quickly across the road to the door he was looking for and pressed the buzzer.

"Are you a member?" said a voice through the intercom.

"Yes," said Romanov, who heard a metallic click as he pushed the door open and walked down the dark staircase. Once he had entered the club it took a few seconds for his eyes to become accustomed to the light.

But then he spotted Mentor seated on his own at a little table near a pillar in the far corner of the room.

Romanov nodded and the man got up and walked across the dance floor and straight past him. Romanov followed as the member entered the only lavatory. Once inside, Romanov checked that they were alone. Satisfied, he led them both into a little cubicle and slipped the lock to engaged. Romanov removed the thousand pounds from his pocket and handed it over to the man who sat down on the lavatory seat. Mentor greedily ripped open the packet, leaned forward and began to count. He never even saw Romanov straighten his fingers; and when the hand came down with a crushing blow on the back of Mentor's neck he slumped forward and fell to the ground in a heap.

Romanov yanked him up; it took several seconds to gather the ten-pound notes that had fallen to the floor. Once he had all hundred, he stuffed them into the member's pocket. Romanov then undid the member's fly buttons one by one and pulled down his trousers until they fell around his ankles. He lifted the lid and placed the man on the lavatory seat. The final touch was to pull his legs as wide open as the fallen trousers would allow, the feet splayed apart. Romanov then slipped under the large gap at the bottom of the door leaving the cubicle locked from the inside. He quickly checked his handiwork. All that could be seen from the outside was the splayed legs and fallen trousers.

Sixty seconds later, Romanov was back in the car on his way to Heathrow.

Adam arrived at Heathrow two hours before the Aeroflot flight was due to depart. He stationed himself with a perfect view of the forty-yard stretch Romanov

419

would have to walk to board the Russian aircraft. He felt confident he would never reach the Aeroflot steps.

Romanov checked in at the BEA desk a little after six. He couldn't resist taking the BEA flight rather than Aeroflot even though he knew Zaborski would frown at such arrogance; he doubted if anyone would comment on this of all days.

Once he had been given his boarding card, he took the escalator to the executive lounge and sat around waiting to be called. It was always the same – the moment any operation had been completed, all he wanted to do was get home. He left his seat to pour himself some coffee and, passing a table in the centre of the room, caught the headline on the London *Evening Standard*. Exclusive. 'Johnson Texas Weekend Cancelled – Mystery.' Romanov grabbed the paper from the table and read the first paragraph but it contained no information he couldn't have already told them. None of the speculation in the paragraphs that followed even began to get near the truth.

Romanov couldn't wait to see the front page of *Pravda* the next day in which he knew the true story would be emblazoned. By Western standards it would be an exclusive.

"BEA announce the departure of their flight 117 to Moscow. Would all first class passengers now board through gate No. 23." Romanov left the lounge and walked the half mile long corridor to the plane. Romanov strolled across the tarmac to the waiting plane a few minutes after six fifty. The plane carrying the icon would be touching down in Washington in about two hours. Romanov would arrive back in Moscow well in time to see Dynamo play Spartak at the Lenin Stadium on Tuesday. He wondered if they would announce his arrival to the crowd over the loudspeakers as they always did when a member of the Politburo attended a match. Romanov walked up the steps and on board, stepping over the feet of the passenger placed next to him, thankful that he had been given the window seat.

"Would you care for a drink before take-off?" the stewardess asked.

"Just a black coffee for me," said his neighbour. Romanov nodded his agreement.

The stewardess arrived back a few minutes later with the two coffees and helped the man next to Romanov pull out his table from the armrest. Romanov flicked his over as the stewardess passed him his coffee.

He took a sip but it was too hot so he placed it on the table in front of him. He watched his neighbour take out a packet of saccharines from his pocket and flick two pellets into the steaming coffee.

Why did he bother, thought Romanov. Life was too short.

Romanov stared out of the window and watched the Aeroflot plane start to taxi out on to the runway. He smiled at the thought of how much more comfortable his own flight would be. He tried his coffee a second time: just as he liked it. He took a long gulp and began to feel a little drowsy which he didn't find that strange as he had hardly slept for the last week.

He leaned back in his seat and closed his eyes. He would now take every honour the State could offer him. With Valchek conveniently out of the way, he could even position himself to take over from Zaborski. If that failed, his grandfather had left him another alternative.

He was leaving London with only one regret: he had failed to kill Scott. But then he suspected that the

Americans would take care of that. For the first time in a week he didn't have to stop himself falling asleep . . .

A few moments later the passenger seated next to Romanov picked up the Russian's coffee cup and put it next to his own. He then flicked Romanov's table back into the armrest and placed a woollen blanket over Romanov's legs. He quickly slipped the BEA eye shades over the Russian's head, covering his open eyes. He looked up to find that the stewardess was standing by his side.

"Can I help?" she asked, smiling.

"No, thank you. All he said was that he did not want to be disturbed during the flight as he has had a very hard week."

"Of course, sir," said the stewardess. "We'll be taking off in a few minutes," she added, and picked up the two coffee cups and whisked them away.

The man tapped his fingers impatiently on the little table. At last the chief steward appeared at his side.

"There's been an urgent call from your office, sir. You're to return to Whitehall immediately."

"I had been half expecting it," he admitted.

Adam stared up at the Russian plane as it climbed steeply and swung in a semi-circle towards the East. He couldn't understand why Romanov hadn't boarded it. Surely he wouldn't have taken the BEA flight. Adam slipped back into the shadows the moment he saw him. He stared in disbelief. Lawrence was striding back across the tarmac, a smile of satisfaction on his face.

EPILOGUE

SOTHEBY'S
FOUNDED 1744

SOTHEBY'S
NEW BOND STREET,
LONDON W1

October 18, 1966

EPILOGUE

"Sold to the gentleman in the centre of the room for five thousand pounds.

"We now move on to Lot no. 32," said the auctioneer, looking down from the raised platform at the front of the crowded room. "An icon of St George and the Dragon," he declared as an attendant placed a little painting on the easel next to him. The auctioneer stared down at the faces of experts, amateurs and curious onlookers. "What am I bid for this magnificent example of Russian art?" he asked, expectantly.

Robin gripped Adam's hand. "I haven't felt this nervous since I came face to face with Romanov."

"Don't remind me," said Adam.

"It is, of course, not the original that hangs in the Winter Palace," continued the auctioneer, "but it is nevertheless a fine copy, probably executed by a court painter circa 1914," he added, giving the little painting an approving smile. "Do I have an opening bid? Shall I say eight thousand?" The next few seconds seemed interminable to Robin and Adam. "Thank you, sir," said the auctioneer, eventually looking towards an anonymous sign that had been given somewhere at the front of the room.

Neither Adam nor Robin were able to make out

where the bid had come from. They had spent the last hour seated at the back of the room watching the previous items coming under the hammer and had rarely been able to work out whose hands they had ended up in.

"How much did the expert say it might go for?" Robin asked again.

"Anywhere between ten and twenty thousand," Adam reminded her.

"Nine thousand," said the auctioneer, his eyes moving to a bid that appeared to come from the right-hand side of the room.

"I still think it's amazing," said Robin, "that the Russians ever agreed to the exchange in the first place."

"Why?" asked Adam. "Once the Americans had extracted the treaty, there was no harm in allowing the Russians to have their original back in exchange for the copy which rightly belonged to me. As an example of diplomatic ingenuity it was Lawrence at his most brilliant."

"Ten thousand from the front of the room. Thank you, sir," said the auctioneer.

"What are you going to do with all that money?"

"Buy a new double bass, get a wedding present for my sister and hand over the rest to my mother."

"Eleven thousand, a new bid on the centre aisle," said the auctioneer. "Thank you, madam."

"No amount of money can bring back Heidi," said Robin quietly.

Adam nodded thoughtfully.

"How did the meeting with Heidi's parents turn out?"

"The Foreign Secretary saw them personally last week. It couldn't help, but at least he was able to confirm that I had only been telling them the truth."

426

"Twelve thousand." The auctioneer's eye returned to the front of the room.

"Did you see the Foreign Secretary yourself?"

"Good heavens, no, I'm far too junior for that," said Adam. "I'm lucky if I get to see Lawrence, let alone the Foreign Secretary."

Robin laughed. "I consider you were *lucky* to have been offered a place at the Foreign Office at all."

"Agreed," said Adam chuckling to himself, "but a vacancy arose unexpectedly."

"What do you mean, 'unexpectedly'?" asked Robin, frustrated by how few of her questions had been answered directly in the past half hour.

"All I can tell you is that one of Lawrence's old team was 'retired early'," said Adam.

"Was that also true of Romanov?" asked Robin, still desperately trying to discover all that had taken place since they had last met.

"Thirteen thousand," said the auctioneer, his eyes returning to the lady on the centre aisle.

"After all he can't have survived for long once they discovered you had done a switch on Tower Bridge that gave the Russians back the copy while Romanov ended up presenting you with the original," said Robin.

"He's never been heard of since," admitted Adam innocently.

"And all our information leads us to believe that his boss Zaborski is soon to be replaced by someone called Yuri Andropov."

"Fourteen thousand," said the auctioneer, his eye settling on the gentleman at the front once again.

"What happened when you produced the papers proving that it was not your father who had smuggled the poison into Goering's cell?"

"Once they had been authenticated by the Russians," Adam said, "Lawrence paid an official visit to the Colonel of the Regiment and furnished him with the conclusive evidence."

"Any reaction?" probed Robin.

"They're going to hold a memorial service in Pa's memory and have commissioned some fellow called Ward to paint his portrait for the regimental mess. Mother has been invited to unveil it in the presence of all those officers who served with my father."

"Fourteen thousand for the first time then," said the auctioneer raising the little gavel a few inches in the air.

"She must have been over the moon," said Robin.

"Burst into tears," said Adam. "All she could say was 'I wish Pa could have lived to see it.' Ironic, really. If only he had opened that letter."

"Fourteen thousand for the second time," said the auctioneer, the gavel now hovering.

"How do you fancy a celebration lunch at the Ritz?" said Adam, delighted with how well the sale was turning out.

"No thank you," said Robin.

Adam looked across at his companion in surprise.

"It won't be much fun if every time I ask you a question I only get the official Foreign Office briefing."

Adam looked sheepish. "I'm sorry," he said.

"No, that wasn't fair," said Robin. "Now you're on the inside it can't be easy, so I suppose I will have to go to my grave wondering what treaty was inside that icon."

Adam looked away from the girl who had saved his life.

"Or perhaps I'll find out the truth in 1996 when the cabinet papers are released."

He turned slowly to face her.

"Alas . . ." he began as the auctioneer's hammer came down with a thud. They both looked up.

"Sold to the gentleman at the front for fourteen thousand pounds."

"Not a bad price," said Adam, smiling.

"A bargain in my opinion," replied Robin quietly.

Adam turned to her, a quizzical look on his face.

"After all," she said in a whisper, "imagine what the forty-ninth state would have fetched if it had come up for auction."

THE END

THE END

NOT A PENNY MORE, NOT A PENNY LESS

To Mary

AND THE FAT MEN

Author's Note

I acknowledge all the help I received from so many people in writing this book and wish to thank them: David Niven, Jr, who made me do it, Sir Noel and Lady Hall who made it possible, Adrian Metcalfe, Anthony Rentoul, Colin Emson, Ted Francis, Godfrey Barker, Willy West, Madame Tellegen, David Stein, Christian Neffe, Dr John Vance, Dr David Weeden, the Rev. Leslie Styler, Robert Gasser, Professor Jim Bolton, and Jamie Clark; Gail and Jo for putting it together; and my wife, Mary, for the hours spent correcting and editing.

PROLOGUE

'JÖRG EXPECT $7 million from Crédit Parisien in the No. 2 account by 6 pm tonight, Central European time, and place it with first-class banks and triple "A" commercial names. Otherwise, invest it in the overnight Euro-dollar market. Understood?'

'Yes, Harvey.'

'Place $1 million in the Banco do Minas Gerais, Rio de Janeiro, in the names of Silverman and Elliott and cancel the call loan at Barclays Bank, Lombard Street. Understood?'

'Yes, Harvey.'

'Buy gold on my commodity account until it reaches $10 million and then hold until you receive further instructions. Try and buy in the troughs and don't rush – be patient. Understood?'

'Yes, Harvey.'

Harvey Metcalfe realised that the last instruction was unnecessary. Jörg Birrer was one of the most conservative bankers in Zürich and, more important to Harvey, had over the past twenty-five years proved to be one of the shrewdest.

'Can you join me at Wimbledon on Tuesday, June

25th at 2 pm, Centre Court, my usual debenture seat?'

'Yes, Harvey.'

The telephone clicked into place. Harvey never said goodbye. He had never understood the niceties of life and it was too late to start learning now. He picked up the phone, dialled the seven digits which would give him the Lincoln Trust in Boston, and asked for his secretary.

'Miss Fish?'

'Yes, sir.'

'Remove the file on Prospecta Oil and destroy it. Destroy any correspondence connected with it and leave absolutely no trace. Understood?'

'Yes, sir.'

The telephone clicked again. Harvey Metcalfe had given similar orders three times in the last twenty-five years and by now Miss Fish had learnt not to question him.

Harvey breathed deeply, almost a sigh, a quiet exhalation of triumph. He was now worth at least $25 million, and nothing could stop him. He opened a bottle of Krug champagne 1964, imported from Hedges & Butler of London. He sipped it slowly and lit a Romeo y Julieta Churchill, which an Italian immigrant smuggled in for him in boxes of two hundred and fifty once a month from Cuba. He settled back for a mild celebration. In Boston, Massachusetts, it was 12.20 pm – nearly time for lunch.

*

In Harley Street, Bond Street, the King's Road and Magdalen College, Oxford, it was 6.20 pm. Four men, unknown to each other, checked the market price of Prospecta Oil in the final edition of the London *Evening Standard*. It was £3.70. All four of them were rich men, looking forward to consolidating their already successful careers.

Tomorrow they would be penniless.

1

MAKING A MILLION legally has always been difficult. Making a million illegally has always been a little easier. Keeping a million when you have made it is perhaps the most difficult of all. Henryk Metelski was one of those rare men who had managed all three. Even if the million he had made legally came after the million he had made illegally, Metelski was still a yard ahead of the others: he had managed to keep it all.

Henryk Metelski was born on the Lower East Side of New York on May 17th, 1909, in a small room that already slept four children. He grew up through the Depression, believing in God and one meal a day. His parents were from Warsaw and had emigrated from Poland at the turn of the century. Henryk's father was a baker by trade and had soon found a job in New York, where immigrant Poles specialised in baking black rye bread and running small restaurants for their countrymen. Both parents would have liked Henryk to be an academic success, but he was never destined to become an outstanding pupil at his high school. His natural gifts lay elsewhere. A cunning, smart little boy, he was far more interested in the control of the underground school market in cigarettes and liquor than in stirring tales of the American Revolution and the Liberty Bell. Little Henryk never believed for one moment that the best things in life were free, and the pursuit of money and power came as naturally to him as the pursuit of a mouse to a cat.

When Henryk was a pimply and flourishing four-teen-year-old, his father died of what we now know to be cancer. His mother outlived her husband by no more than a few months, leaving the five children to fend for themselves. Henryk, like the other four, should have gone into the district orphanage for destitute children, but in the mid-1920s it was not hard for a boy to disappear in New York – though it was harder to survive. Henryk became a master of survival, a schooling which was to prove very useful to him in later life.

He knocked around the Lower East Side with his belt tightened and his eyes open, shining shoes here, washing dishes there, always looking for an entrance to the maze at the heart of which lay wealth and prestige. His first chance came when his room-mate Jan Pelnik, a messenger boy on the New York Stock Exchange, put himself temporarily out of action with a sausage garnished with salmonella. Henryk, deputed to report his friend's mishap to the Chief Messenger, upgraded food-poisoning to tuberculosis, and talked himself into the ensuing vacancy. He then changed his room, donned a new uniform, lost a friend, and gained a job.

Most of the messages Henryk delivered during the early twenties read 'Buy'. Many of them were quickly acted upon, for this was a boom era. He watched men of little ability make fortunes while he remained nothing more than an observer. His instincts directed him towards those individuals who made more money in a week on the Stock Exchange than he could hope to make in a lifetime on his salary.

He set about learning how to master the way the Stock Exchange operated, he listened to private conversations, opened sealed messages and found out which closed company reports to study. By the age of eighteen he had four years' experience of Wall Street: four years which most messenger boys would have spent simply walking across crowded floors, delivering little pink pieces of paper; four years which to Henryk Metelski were the equivalent of a Master's Degree from the Harvard Business School. He was not to know that one day he would lecture to that august body.

One morning in July 1927 he was delivering a message from Halgarten & Co, a well-established brokerage house, making his usual detour via the washroom. He had perfected a system whereby he could lock himself into a cubicle, study the message he was carrying, decide whether the information was of any value to him and, if it was, immediately telephone Witold Gronowich, an old Pole who managed a small insurance firm for his fellow countrymen. Henryk reckoned to pick up an extra $20 to $25 a week for the inside knowledge he supplied. Gronowich, in no position to place large sums on the market, never let any of the leaks lead back to his young informant.

Sitting on the lavatory seat, Henryk began to realise that this time he was reading a message of considerable importance. The Governor of Texas was about to grant the Standard Oil Company permission to complete a pipeline from Chicago to Mexico, all other public bodies involved having already agreed to the proposal. The market was aware that the company had been trying to obtain this final permission for nearly a year, but the general view was that the Governor would turn it down. The message was to be passed direct to John D. Rockefeller's broker, Tucker Anthony, immediately. The granting of this permission to build a pipeline would open up the entire North to a ready supply of oil, and that could only mean increased profits. It was obvious to Henryk that Standard Oil stock must rise steadily on the market once the news had broken, especially as Standard Oil already controlled 90 per cent of the oil refineries in America.

In normal circumstances Henryk would have sent on this information direct to Mr Gronowich, and was about to do so when he noticed a rather overweight man, who was also leaving the washroom, drop a piece of paper. As there was no one else about at the time, Henryk picked it up and retreated back into his private cubicle, thinking that at best it would reveal another piece of information. In fact, it was a cheque for $50,000 made out to cash from a Mrs Rose Rennick.

Henryk thought quickly, and not on his feet. He left the washroom at speed and was soon standing outside on Wall Street itself. He made his way to a small coffee-shop on Rector Street and sat there pretending to drink a Coca-Cola while he carefully worked out his plan. He then proceeded to act on it.

First, he cashed the cheque at a branch of the Morgan Bank on the south-west side of Wall Street, knowing that in his smart uniform as a messenger at the Exchange he would easily pass as a carrier for some distinguished firm. He then returned to the Exchange and acquired from a floor broker 2,500 Standard Oil shares at $19⅞, leaving himself $126.61 change after brokerage charges. He placed the $126.61 in a Checking Account with the Morgan Bank. Then, waiting in tense anticipation for an announcement from the Governor's office, he put himself through the motions of a normal day's work, too preoccupied with Standard Oil even to make a detour via the washroom with the messages he carried.

No announcement came. Henryk could not know that the news was being held up until the Exchange had officially closed at 3 pm in order to allow the

Governor himself to buy shares anywhere and everywhere he could lay his grubby hands on them. Henryk went home that night petrified that he had made a disastrous mistake. He had visions of losing his job and everything he had built up over the past four years. Perhaps he would even end up in jail.

He was unable to sleep that night and became steadily more restless in his small open-windowed but airless room. At 1 am he could stand the uncertainty no longer, so he jumped out of bed, shaved, dressed and took a subway to Grand Central Station. From there he walked to Times Square where with trembling hands he bought the first edition of the *Wall Street Journal*. For a moment he couldn't take in the news, although it was shrieking at him in banner headlines:

GOVERNOR GRANTS OIL PIPELINE RIGHTS TO ROCKEFELLER

and a secondary headline:

HEAVY TRADING EXPECTED IN STANDARD OIL SHARES

Dazed, Henryk walked to the nearest all-night café, on West 42nd Street, and ordered a large hamburger and French fries, which he covered in ketchup and nibbled at like a man eating his last breakfast before facing the electric chair, rather than his first on the way to fortune. He read the full details of Rockefeller's coup on page one, which spread over to page fourteen, and by 4 am he had bought the first three editions of the *New York Times* and the first two editions of the *Herald Tribune*. The lead story was the same in each. Henryk hurried home, giddy and elated, and changed into his uniform. He arrived at the Stock Exchange at 8 am and went through the motions of a day's work, thinking only of how to carry out the second part of his plan.

When the Stock Exchange opened officially, Henryk went over to the Morgan Bank and requested a loan of $50,000 against the security of his 2,500 Standard Oil shares, which had opened that morning at $21¼. He placed the loan in his Checking Account and instructed the bank to issue him a draft for the $50,000 to be made out to Mrs Rose Rennick. He left the bank and looked up the address and telephone number of his unwitting benefactor.

Mrs Rennick, a widow who lived off the investments left by her late husband, lived in a small apartment on 62nd Street, which Henryk knew to be one of the most fashionable parts of New York. The call from a Henryk Metelski, asking to see her on an urgent private matter, came as something of a surprise to her, but a final mention of Halgarten & Co. gave her a little more confidence and she agreed to see him at the Waldorf-Astoria at 4 pm that afteroon.

Henryk had never been inside the Waldorf-Astoria, but after four years on the Stock Exchange there were few prominent hotels or restaurants he had not heard mentioned in other people's conversations. He realised that Mrs Rennick was more likely to have tea with him there than to see a man with a name like Henryk Metelski in her own apartment, especially as his Polish accent was more pronounced over the telephone than it was face to face.

As Henryk stood in the thickly carpeted lobby of the Waldorf, he blushed at his sartorial naïveté. Imagining that everybody was staring at him, he buried his short, amply-covered frame in an elegant chair in the Jefferson Room. Some of the other patrons of the Waldorf were amply covered too, but Henryk felt that *Pommes de Terre Maître d'Hôtel* were more likely to have caused their obesity than French fries. Vainly wishing he had put a little less grease on his black wavy hair and a little more on his down-at-heel shoes, he scratched nervously at an irritating pustule on the side of his mouth and waited. His suit, in which he felt so assured and prosperous among his friends, was shiny, skimpy, cheap and loud. He did not blend in with the décor, still less with the patrons of the hotel, and, feeling inadequate for the first time in his life, he picked up a copy of the *New Yorker*, hid behind it, and prayed for his guest to arrive quickly. Waiters fluttered deferentially with instinctive superciliousness. One, he noticed, did nothing more than circle the tearoom delicately proffering lump sugar from silver tongs in a white-gloved hand: Henryk was enormously impressed.

Rose Rennick arrived a few minutes after four, accompanied by two small dogs and wearing an outrageously large hat. Henryk thought she looked over sixty, overweight, overmade-up and overdressed, but she had a warm smile and appeared to know everyone, as she moved from table to table, chatting to the regular Waldorf-Astoria set. Eventually reaching what she had rightly assumed to be Henryk's table, she was rather taken aback, not only to find him so strangely dressed, but also looking even younger than his eighteen years.

Mrs Rennick ordered tea while Henryk recited his well-rehearsed story: there had been an unfortunate mistake with her cheque, which had been wrongly credited to his firm at the Stock Exchange on the previous day; his boss had instructed him to return the cheque immediately and to say how much they regretted the unfortunate error. Henryk then passed over the draft for $50,000, and added that he would lose his job if she insisted on taking the matter any further, as he had been entirely responsible for the mistake. Mrs Rennick had, in fact, only been informed of the missing cheque that morning and did not realise that it had been cashed, as it would have taken a few days to clear her account. Henryk's perfectly genuine anxiety as he stumbled through his tale would have convinced a far more critical observer of human nature than Mrs Rennick. Readily she agreed to let the matter drop, only too pleased to have her money returned; as it was in the form of a draft from the Morgan Bank, she had lost nothing. Henryk breathed a sigh of relief and for the first time that day began to relax and enjoy himself. He even called for the waiter with the sugar and silver tongs.

After a respectable period of time had passed, Henryk explained that he must return to work, thanked Mrs Rennick for her co-operation, paid the bill and left. Outside on the street he whistled with relief. His new shirt was soaked in sweat (Mrs Rennick would have called it perspiration), but he was out in the open and could breathe freely again. His first major operation had been a success.

He stood on Park Avenue, amused that the venue for his confrontation with Mrs Rennick had been the Waldorf, the very hotel where John D. Rockefeller, the President of Standard Oil, had a suite. Henryk had arrived on foot and used the main entrance, while Mr Rockefeller had earlier arrived by subway and taken his private lift to the Waldorf Towers. Although few New Yorkers were aware of it, Rockefeller had had his own private station built fifty feet below the Waldorf-Astoria to save him travelling the eight blocks to Grand Central Station, there being no stop between there and 125th Street. (The station remains to this day, but as no Rockefellers live at the Waldorf-Astoria, the train never stops there.) While Henryk had been discussing his $50,000 with Mrs Rennick, Rockefeller had been considering an investment of $5,000,000 with Andrew W. Mellon, President Coolidge's Secretary of the Treasury, fifty-seven floors above him.

The next morning Henryk returned to work as usual. He knew he had only five days' grace to sell the shares and clear his debt with the Morgan Bank and the stockbroker, as an account on the New York Stock Exchange runs for five business days or seven calendar days. On the last day of the account the shares were standing at $23¼. He sold at $23⅛, and cleared his overdraft of $49,625 and, after expenses, realised a profit of $7,490 which he left deposited with the Morgan Bank.

Over the next three years, Henryk stopped ringing Mr Gronowich, and started dealing for himself, in small amounts to begin with, but growing larger as he gained in experience and confidence. Times were still good, and while he didn't always make a profit, he had learnt to master the occasional bear market as well as the more common bull. His system in the bear market was to sell short – not a practice considered to be entirely ethical in business. He soon mastered the art of selling shares he didn't own in expectation of a subsequent fall in their price. His instinct for market trends refined as rapidly as did his taste for clothes, and the guile learnt in the backstreets of the Lower East Side always stood him in good stead. Henryk soon discovered that the whole world was a jungle – sometimes the lions and tigers wore suits.

When the stock market collapsed in 1929 Henryk had turned his $7,490 into $51,000 of liquid assets, having sold on every share he possessed the day after the Chairman of Halgarten & Co jumped out of one of the Stock Exchange windows. Henryk had got the message. With his newly acquired income he had moved into a smart apartment in Brooklyn and started driving a rather ostentatious red Stutz. Henryk realised at an early age that he had come into the world with three main disadvantages – his name, background and impecunity. The money problem was solving itself, and now the time had come to expunge the other two. To that end, he had made an application to change his name by court order to Harvey David Metcalfe. When the application was granted, he ceased all further contact with his friends from the Polish community, and in May 1930 he came of age with a new name, new background, and very new money.

It was later that year at a football game that he first met Roger Sharpley and discovered that the rich have their problems too. Sharpley, a young man from Boston, had inherited his father's company, which specialised in the import of whisky and the export of furs. Educated at Choate and later in Dartmouth College, Sharpley had all the assurance and charm of the Boston set, so often envied by his fellow countrymen. He was tall and fair, looked as if he came from Viking stock, and with his air of the gifted amateur, found most things came easily to him – especially women. He was in every way a total contrast to Harvey. Although they were poles apart, the contrast acted like a magnet and attracted the one to the other.

Roger's only ambition in life was to become an

officer in the Navy, but after graduating from Dartmouth he had had to return to the family business because of his father's ill-health. He had only been with the firm a few months when his father died. Roger would have liked to have sold Sharpley & Son to the first bidder, but his father had made a codicil to his will to the effect that if the firm were sold before Roger's fortieth birthday (that being the last day one can enlist for the US Navy), the money gained from the sale would be divided equally among his other relatives.

Harvey gave Roger's problem considerable thought, and after two lengthy sessions with a skilful New York lawyer, suggested a course of action to Roger: Harvey would purchase 49 per cent of Sharpley & Son for $100,000 and the first $20,000 profit each year. At the age of forty, Roger could relinquish the remaining 51 per cent for a further $100,000. The Board would consist of three voting members – Harvey, Roger and one nominated by Harvey, giving him overall control. As far as Harvey was concerned, Roger could join the Navy and need only attend the annual shareholders' meeting.

Roger could not believe his luck. He did not even consult anyone at Sharpley & Son, knowing only too well that they would try to talk him out of it. Harvey had counted on this and had assessed his quarry accurately. Roger gave the proposition only a few days' consideration before allowing the legal papers to be drawn up in New York, far enough away from

Boston to be sure the firm did not learn what was going on. Meanwhile, Harvey returned to the Morgan Bank, where he was now looked upon as a man with a future. Since banks deal in futures, the manager agreed to help him in his new enterprise with a loan of $50,000 to add to his own $50,000, enabling Harvey to acquire 49 per cent of Sharpley & Son, and become its fifth President. The legal documents were signed in New York on October 28th, 1930.

Roger left speedily for Newport, Rhode Island, to commence his Officers Training programme in the US Navy. Harvey left for Grand Central Station to catch the train for Boston. His days as a messenger boy on the New York Stock Exchange were over. He was twenty-one years of age and the President of his own company.

What looked like disaster to most, Harvey could always turn into triumph. The American people were still suffering under Prohibition, and although Harvey could export furs, he could no longer import whisky. This had been the main reason for the fall in the company profits over the past decade. But Harvey soon found that with a little bribery, involving the Mayor of Boston, the Chief of Police and the Customs officials on the Canadian border, plus a payment to the Mafia to ensure that his products reached the restaurants and speak-easies, somehow the whisky imports went up rather than down. Sharpley & Son lost its more respectable and long-serving staff, and replaced them with animals better-suited to Harvey Metcalfe's particular jungle.

From 1930 to 1933 Harvey went from strength to strength, but when Prohibition was finally lifted by President Roosevelt after overwhelming public demand, the excitement went with it, Harvey allowed the company to continue to deal in whisky and furs while he branched out into new fields. In 1933 Sharpley & Son celebrated a hundred years in business. In three years Harvey had lost 97 years of goodwill and doubled the profits. It took him five years to reach his first million and only another four to double the sum again, which was when he decided the time had come for Harvey Metcalfe and Sharpley & Son to part company. In twelve years from 1930 to 1942, he had built up the profits from $30,000 to $910,000. He sold the company in January 1944 for $7,000,000, paying $100,000 to the widow of Captain Roger Sharpley of the US Navy and keeping $6,900,000 for himself.

Harvey celebrated his thirty-fifth birthday by buying at a cost of $4 million a small, ailing bank in Boston called the Lincoln Trust. At the time it boasted a profit of approximately $500,000 a year, a prestigious building in the centre of Boston and an unblemished and somewhat boring reputation. Harvey intended to change both its reputation and its balance sheet. He enjoyed being the President of a bank – but it did nothing to improve his honesty. Every dubious deal in the Boston area seemed to emanate from the

Lincoln Trust, and although Harvey increased the bank's profits to $2 million per annum during the next five years, his personal reputation was never in credit.

Harvey met Arlene Hunter in the winter of 1949. She was the only daughter of the President of the First City Bank of Boston. Until then Harvey had never taken any real interest in women. His driving force had always been making money, and although he considered the opposite sex a useful relaxation in his free time, on balance he found them an inconvenience. But having now reached what the glossy magazines referred to as middle age and having no heir to leave his fortune to, he calculated that it was time to find a wife who would present him with a son. As with everything else that he had wanted in his life, he considered the problem very carefully.

Harvey had first run into Arlene when she was thirty-one: quite literally, when she had backed her car into his new Lincoln. She could not have been a greater contrast to the short, uneducated, overweight Pole. She was nearly six feet tall, slim and although not unattractive, she lacked confidence and was beginning to think that marriage had passed her by. Most of her school friends were already on their second divorces and felt rather sorry for her. Harvey's extravagant ways came as a welcome change after her parents' prudish discipline, which she often felt was to blame for her awkwardness with men of her own age. She had only had one affair – a disastrous failure, thanks to her total innocence – and until Harvey arrived, no one had seemed to be willing to give her a second chance. Arlene's father did not approve of Harvey, and showed it, which only made him more attractive to her. Her father had not approved of any of the men she had associated with, but on this occasion he was right. Harvey on the other hand realised that to marry the First City Bank of Boston with the Lincoln Trust could only be of long-term benefit to him, and with that in mind he set out, as he always did, to conquer. Arlene didn't put up much of a battle.

Arlene and Harvey were married in 1951 at a wedding more memorable for those who were absent than those who attended. They settled into Harvey's Lincoln home outside of Boston and very shortly afterwards Arlene announced she was pregnant. She gave Harvey a daughter almost a year to the day after their marriage.

They christened her Rosalie, and she became the centre of Harvey's attention; his only disappointment came when a prolapse closely followed by a hysterectomy prevented Arlene from bearing him any more children. He sent Rosalie to Bennetts, the most expensive girls' school in Washington, and from there she was accepted at Vassar to major in English. This even pleased old man Hunter, who had grown to tolerate Harvey and adore hs granddaughter. On gaining her degree, Rosalie continued her education at the

Sorbonne, after a fierce disagreement with her father concerning the type of friends she was keeping, particularly the ones with long hair who didn't want to go to Vietnam – not that Harvey had done much during the Second World War, except to cash in on every shortage. The final crunch came when Rosalie dared to suggest that morals were not to be decided only by length of hair or political views. Harvey missed her, but refused to admit the fact to Arlene.

Harvey had three loves in his life: the first was still Rosalie, the second was his paintings, and the third his orchids. The first had started the moment his daughter was born. The second was a love that had developed over many years and had been kindled in the strangest way. A client of Sharpley & Son was about to go bankrupt while still owing a fairly large sum of money to the company. Harvey got wind of it and went round to confront him, but the rot had already set in and there was no longer any hope of securing cash. Determined not to leave empty-handed, Harvey took with him the man's only tangible asset – a Renoir valued at $10,000.

Harvey's intention was to sell the picture quickly before it could be proved that he was a preferred creditor, but he became so entranced with the fine brushwork and the delicate pastel shades that his only desire was to own more. When he realised that pictures were not only a good investment, but that he actually liked them as well, his collection and his love grew hand in hand. By the early 1970s, Harvey had a Manet, two Monets, a Renoir, two Picassos, a Pissarro, a Utrillo, a Cézanne, as well as most of the recognised lesser names, and he had become quite a connoisseur of the Impressionist period. His one remaining desire was to possess a Van Gogh, and only recently he had failed to acquire *L'Hôpital de St Paul à St Remy* at the Sotheby-Parke Bernet Gallery in New York, when Dr Armand Hammer of Occidental Petroleum had outbid him – $1,200,000 had been just a little too much for Harvey.

Earlier, in 1966, he had failed to acquire Lot 49, *Mademoiselle Ravoux*, from Christie, Manson & Woods, the London art dealers; although the Rev. Theodore Pitcairn, representing the Lord's New Church in Bryn Athyn, Pennsylvania, had pushed him over the top, he had only whetted his appetite further. The Lord giveth, and on that occasion the Lord had taken away. Although it was not fully appreciated in Boston, it was already recognised in the art world that Harvey had one of the finest Impressionist collections in the world, almost as widely admired as that of Walter Annenberg, President Nixon's Ambassador to London who, like Harvey, had been one of the few people to build up a major collection since the Second World War.

Harvey's third love was his prize collection of orchids, and he had three times been a winner at the New England Spring Flower Show in Boston, twice beating old man Hunter into second place.

*

Harvey now travelled to Europe once a year. He had established a successful stud in Kentucky and liked to see his horses run at Longchamp and Ascot. He also enjoyed watching Wimbledon, which he considered was still the greatest tennis tournament in the world. It amused him to do a little business in Europe at the same time, giving him the opportunity to make some more money for his Swiss bank account in Zürich. He did not need a Swiss account, but somehow he got a kick out of doing Uncle Sam. Although Harvey had mellowed over the years and cut down on his more dubious deals, he could never resist the chance to take a risk if he thought the reward was likely to be big enough. One such golden opportunity presented itself in 1964 when Her Majesty's Government invited applications for exploration and production licences in the North Sea. At that time neither the British Government nor the civil servants involved had any idea of the future significance of North Sea oil, or the role it would eventually play in British politics. If the Government had known that in 1978 the Arabs would be holding a pistol to the heads of the rest of the world, and the British House of Commons would have eleven Scottish Nationalist Members of Parliament, it would surely have reacted in a totally different way.

On May 13th, 1964, the Secretary of State for Power laid before Parliament 'Statutory Instrument – No. 708 – Continental Shelf – Petroteum'. Harvey read this particular document with great interest, thinking that it might well be a means of making an exceptional killing. He was particularly fascinated by Paragraph 4 of the document, which read:

> Persons who are citizens of the United Kingdom and Colonies and are resident in the United Kingdom or who are bodies corporate incorporated in the United Kingdom may apply in accordance with these Regulations for:
>
> (a) production licence; or,
> (b) an exploration licence.

When he had studied the Regulations in their entirety, he had to sit back and think hard. Only a small amount of money was required to secure a production and exploration licence. As Paragraph 6 went on to point out:

> (1) With every application for a production licence there shall be paid a fee of two hundred pounds with an additional fee of five pounds for every block after the first ten in respect whereof that application is made.
>
> (2) With every application for an exploration licence there shall be paid a fee of twenty pounds.

Harvey couldn't believe it. How easy it would be to use such a licence to create an impression of a vast enterprise! For a few hundred dollars he could be alongside such names as Shell, BP, Total, Gulf and Occidental.

Harvey went over the Regulations again and again, hardly believing that the British Government could release such potential for so small an investment. Only the application form, an elaborate and exacting document, now stood in his way. Harvey was not a British subject, none of his companies was British and he realised he would have problems of presentation. He decided that his application must therefore be backed by a British bank and that he would set up a company whose directors would win the confidence of the British Government.

With this in mind, early in 1964, he registered at Companies House in England a firm called Prospecta Oil, using Malcolm, Bottnick and Davis as his solicitors and Barclays Bank, who were already the Lincoln Trust's representative in Europe, as his bankers. Lord Hunnisett became Chairman of the company and several distinguished public figures joined the Board, including two ex-Members of Parliament who had lost their seats when the Labour Party won the 1964 Election. Prospecta Oil issued 2,000,000 10-pence shares at one pound, which were all taken up for Harvey by nominees. He also deposited $500,000 in the Lombard Street branch of Barclays Bank.

Having thus created the front, Harvey then used Lord Hunnisett to apply for the licence from the British Government. The new Labour Government elected in October 1964 was no more aware of the significance of North Sea oil than the earlier Conservative administration. The Government's requirements for a licence were a rent of £12,000 a year for the first six years, 12½ per cent revenue tax, and a further Capital Gains tax on profits; but as Harvey's plan was to reap profits for himself rather than the company that presented no problems.

On May 22nd, 1965, the Minister of Power published in the *London Gazette* the name of Prospecta Oil among the fifty-two companies granted production licences. On August 3rd, 1965, Statutory Instrument No. 1531 allocated the actual areas. Prospecta Oil's was 51° 50′ 00″ N: 2° 30′ 20″ E, a site adjacent to one of BP's holdings.

Then Harvey sat back, waiting for one of the companies which had acquired North Sea sites to strike oil. It was a longish wait but Harvey was in no hurry, and not until June 1970 did BP make a big commercial strike in their Forties Field. BP had already spent over $1 billion in the North Sea and Harvey was determined to be one of the main beneficiaries. He was now on to another winner, and immediately set the second part of his plan in motion.

Early in 1972 he hired an oil rig which, with much flourish and advance publicity, he had towed out to the Prospecta Oil site. Having hired the rig on the basis of being able to renew the contract if he made a successful strike, he engaged the minimum number of workers allowed by the Government Regulations, and then proceeded to drill to 6,000 feet. After this drilling had been completed he released from the company's employment all those involved, but told Reading &

Bates, from whom he had rented the rig, that he would be requiring it again in the near future and therefore would continue to pay the rental.

Harvey then released Prospecta Oil shares on to the market at the rate of a few thousand a day for the next two months, all from his own stock, and whenever the financial journalists of the British Press rang to ask why these shares were steadily rising, the young public relations officer at Prospecta Oil's city office would say, as briefed, that he had no comment to make at present but there would be a press statement in the near future; some newspapers put two and two together and made about fifteen. The shares climbed steadily from 10 pence to nearly £2 under the guidance of Harvey's chief executive in Britain, Bernie Silverman, who, with his long experience of this kind of operation, was only too aware of what his boss was up to. Silverman's main task was to ensure that nobody could show a direct connection between Metcalfe and Prospecta Oil.

In January 1974 the shares stood at £3. It was then that Harvey was ready to move on to the third part of his plan, using Prospecta Oil's enthusiastic new recruit, a young Harvard graduate called David Kesler, as the fall-guy.

2

DAVID PUSHED his glasses back on to the bridge of his nose and read the advertisement in the Business Section of the *Boston Globe* again, to make sure he was not dreaming. It could have been tailor-made for him:

> Oil Company based in Great Britain, carrying out extensive work in the North Sea off Scotland, requires a young executive with experience in the stock market and/or financial marketing. Salary $25,000 a year. Accommodation supplied. Based in London. Apply Box No. 217A.

Knowing it could lead to other openings in an expanding industry, David thought it sounded like a challenge and wondered if they would consider him experienced enough. He recalled what his tutor in European affairs used to say: 'If you must work in Great Britain, better make it the North Sea. With their union problems, there's nothing else great about the country.'

David Kesler was a lean, clean-shaven young American, with a crew cut which would have been better suited to a lieutenant in the Marines, a fresh complexion and an unquenchable earnestness. David wanted to succeed in business with all the fervour of the new Harvard Business School graduate. He had spent six years in all at Harvard, the first four studying mathematics for his Bachelor degree, and the last two across the Charles River at the Business School. Recently graduated and armed with a BA and an MBA, he was looking for a job that would reward him for the exceptional capacity for hard work he knew he possessed. Never a brilliant scholar, he envied those natural academics among his classmates who mastered post-Keynesian economic theories like children learning their multiplication tables. David had worked ferociously for six years, only lifting his nose far enough from the grindstone to fit in a daily workout at the gymnasium and the occasional weekend watching Harvard Jocks defending the honour of the university on the football field or on the basketball court. He would have enjoyed playing himself, but that would have meant less time for study.

He read the advertisement again, and then typed a carefully prepared letter to the box number. A few days passed before a reply came, summoning him for an interview at a local hotel on the following Wednesday at 3.00.

David arrived at 2.45 pm at the Copley Hotel on Huntingdon Avenue, the adrenalin pumping through his body. He repeated the Harvard Business School motto to himself as he was ushered into a small private room: look British, think Yiddish.

Three men, who introduced themselves as Silverman, Cooper and Elliott, interviewed him. Bernie Silverman, a short, grey-haired, check-tied New Yorker with a solid aura of success, was in charge. Cooper and Elliott sat and watched David silently.

Silverman spent a considerable time giving David an enticing description of the company's background and its future aims. Harvey had trained Silverman carefully and he had at his well-manicured fingertips all the glib expertise needed by the right-hand man in a Metcalfe coup.

'So there you have it, Mr Kesler. We're involved in one of the biggest commercial opportunities in the world, drilling for oil in the North Sea off Scotland. Our company, Prospecta Oil, has the backing of a group of banks in America. We have been granted licences from the British Government and we have the financing. But companies are made not by money, Mr Kesler, but by people – it's as simple as that. We're looking for a man who will work night and day to help put Prospecta Oil on the map, and we'll pay the right man a top salary to do just that. If we offer you the position, you'll be working in our London office under the immediate direction of our Managing Director, Mr Elliott.'

'Where are the company headquarters?'

'New York, but we have offices in Montreal, San Francisco, London, Aberdeen, Paris and Brussels.'

'Is the company looking for oil anywhere else?'

'Not at the moment,' answered Silverman. 'We're

sinking millions into the North Sea after BP's successful strike, and the fields around us have so far had a one-in-five success ratio, which is very high in our business.'

'When would you want the successful applicant to start?'

'Some time in January, when he's completed a government training course on management in oil,' said Richard Elliott. The slim, sallow No. 2 sounded as if he was from Georgia. The government course was a typical Harvey Metcalfe touch – maximum credibility for minimum expense.

'And the company apartment,' said David, 'where's that?'

Cooper spoke:

'You'll have one of the company flats in the Barbican, a few hundred yards away from our London City office.'

David had no more questions – Silverman had covered everything and seemed to know exactly what he wanted.

Ten days later David received a telegram inviting him to join Silverman for lunch at the 21 Club in New York. When David arrived at the restaurant, he recognised a host of well-known faces at nearby tables and felt new confidence: his host obviously knew what he was about. Their table was in one of the small alcoves selected by businessmen who prefer their conversations to remain confidential.

Silverman was genial and relaxed. He stretched

the conversation out a little, discussing irrelevancies, but finally, over a brandy, offered David the position in London. David was delighted: $25,000 a year, and the chance to be involved with a company which obviously had such an exciting future. He did not hesitate in agreeing to start his new appointment in London on January 1st.

David Kesler had never been to England before: how green the grass was, how narrow the roads, how closed in by hedges and fences were the houses! It felt like Toy Town after the vast highways and large automobiles of New York. The small flat in the Barbican was clean and impersonal and, as Mr Cooper had said, convenient for the office a few hundred yards away in Threadneedle Street.

Prospecta's offices consisted of seven rooms on one floor of a large Victorian building; Silverman's was the only office with a prestigious air about it. There was a tiny reception area, a telex room, two rooms for secretaries, a larger room for Mr Elliott and another small one for himself. It seemed very poky to David, but as Silverman was quick to point out, office rent in the City of London was $30 a square foot compared with $10 in New York.

Bernie Silverman's secetary, Judith Lampson, ushered David through to the well appointed office of the Chief Executive. Silverman sat in a large black swivel chair behind a massive desk, which made him look like a midget. By his side were positioned four telephones, three white and one red. David was later to learn that the important-looking red telephone was directly connected to a number in the States, but he never actually discovered to whom.

'Good morning, Mr Silverman. Where would you like me to start?'

'Bernie, please call me Bernie. Take a seat. Notice the change in the price of the company's shares in the last few days?'

'Oh, yes,' enthused David. 'Up a half to nearly $6. I suppose it's because of our new bank backing and the other companies' successful strikes?'

'No,' said Silverman in a low tone designed to give the impression that no one else must hear this part of the conversation, 'the truth is that we've made a big strike ourselves, but we haven't yet decided when to announce it. It's all in this geologist's report.' He threw a smart, colourful document over his desk.

David whistled under his breath. 'What are the company's plans at the moment?'

'We'll announce the strike,' said Silverman quietly, picking at his India rubber as he talked, 'in about three weeks' time, when we're certain of the full extent and capacity of the hole. We want to make some plans for coping with the publicity and the sudden inflow of money. The shares will go through the roof, of course.'

'The shares have already climbed steadily. Perhaps some people already know?'

'I guess that's right,' said Silverman. 'The trouble with that black stuff is once it comes out of the ground you can't hide it.' Silverman laughed.

'Is there any harm in getting in on the act?' asked David.

'No, as long as it doesn't harm the company in any way. Just let me know if anyone wants to invest. We don't have the problems of inside information in England – none of the restrictive laws we have in America.'

'How high do you think the shares will go?'

Silverman looked him straight in the eye and then said casually, '$20.'

Back in his own office, David carefully read the geologist's report that Silverman had given him: it certainly looked as if Prospecta Oil had made a successful strike, but the extent of the find was not, as yet, entirely certain. When he had completed the report, he glanced at his watch and cursed. The geologist's file had totally absorbed him. He threw the report into his briefcase and took a taxi to Paddington Station, only just making the 6.15 train. He was due in Oxford for dinner with an old classmate from Harvard.

On the train down to the university city he thought about Stephen Bradley, who had been a friend in his Harvard days and had generously helped David and other students in mathematics classes that year. Stephen, now a visiting Fellow at Magdalen College, was undoubtedly one of the most brilliant scholars of

David's generation. He had won the Kennedy Memorial Scholarship to Harvard and later in 1970 the Wister Prize for Mathematics, the most sought-after award in the mathematical faculty. Although in monetary terms this award was a derisory $80 and a medal, it was the reputation and job offers it brought with it that made the competition so keen. Stephen had won it with consummate ease and nobody was surprised when he was successful in his application for a Fellowship at Oxford. He was now in his third year of research at Magdalen. His papers on Boolean algebra appeared at short intervals in the *Proceedings of the London Mathematical Society*, and it had just been announced that he had been elected to a Chair in Mathematics back at his alma mater, Harvard, to commence in the fall.

The 6.15 train from Paddington arrived in Oxford an hour later and the short taxi ride from the station down New College Lane brought him to Magdalen at 7.30. One of the College porters escorted David to Stephen's rooms, which were spacious, ancient, and comfortably cluttered with books, cushions and prints. How unlike the antiseptic walls of Harvard, thought David. Stephen was there to greet him. He didn't seem to have changed one iota. His suit seemed to hang off his tall, thin, ungainly body; no tailor would ever have employed him as a dummy. His heavy eyebrows protruded over his out-of-date round-rimmed spectacles, which he almost seemed to hide behind in his shyness. He ambled over to David and welcomed him, one minute an old man, the next younger than his thirty years. Stephen poured David a Jack Daniels and they settled down to chat. Although Stephen never looked upon David as a close friend at Harvard, he had enjoyed coaching him and always found him eager to learn; besides, he always welcomed an excuse to entertain Americans at Oxford.

'It's been a memorable three years, David,' said Stephen, pouring him a second drink. 'The only sad event was the death of my father last winter. He took such an interest in my life at Oxford and gave my academic work so much support. He's left me rather well off, actually . . . Bath plugs were obviously more in demand than I realised. You might be kind enough to advise me on how to invest some of the money, because at the moment it's just sitting on deposit in the bank. I never seem to have the time to do anything about it, and when it comes to investments I haven't a clue.'

That started David off about his demanding new job with Prospecta Oil.

'Why don't you invest your money in my company, Stephen. We've had a fantastic strike in the North Sea, and when they announce it the shares are going to go through the roof. The whole operation would only take a month or so and you could make the killing of a lifetime. I only wish I had some of my own money to put into it.'

'Have you had the full details of the strike?'

'No, but I've seen the geologist's report, and that makes pretty good reading. The shares are already going up fast and I'm convinced they'll reach $20. The problem is that time is already running out.'

Stephen glanced at the geologist's report, thinking he would study it carefully later.

'How does one go about an investment of this sort?' he asked.

'Well, you find a respectable stockbroker, buy as many shares as you can afford and then wait for the strike to be announced. I'll keep you informed on how things are going and advise you when I feel is the best time to sell.'

'That would be extremely thoughtful of you, David.'

'It's the least I can do after all the help you gave me with maths at Harvard.'

'Oh, that was nothing. Let's go and have some dinner.'

Stephen led David to the college dining hall, an oblong, oak-panelled room covered in pictures of past Presidents of Magdalen, bishops and academics. The long wooden tables at which the undergraduates were eating filled the body of the hall, but Stephen shuffled up to the High Table and offered David a more comfortable seat. The students were a noisy, enthusiastic bunch – Stephen didn't notice them, but David was enjoying the whole experience.

The seven-course meal was formidable and David wondered how Stephen kept so thin with such daily temptations. When they reached the port, Stephen suggested they return to his rooms rather than join the crusty old dons in the Senior Common Room.

Late into the night, over the rubicund Magdalen port, they talked about North Sea oil and Boolean algebra, each admiring the other for his mastery of his subject. Stephen, like most academics, was fairly credulous outside the bounds of his own discipline. He began to think that an investment in Prospecta Oil would be a very astute move on his part.

In the morning, they strolled down Addison's Walk near Magdalen Bridge, where the grass grows green and lush by the Cherwell. Reluctantly, David caught a taxi at 9.45 leaving Magdalen behind him and passing New College, Trinity, Balliol and finally Worcester, where he saw scrawled across the college wall, '*c'est magnifique mais ce n'est pas la gare*'. He caught the 10.00 am train back to London. He had enjoyed his stay at Oxford and hoped he had been able to help his old Harvard friend, who had done so much for him in the past.

'Good morning, David.'

'Good morning, Bernie. I thought I ought to let you know I spent the evening with a friend at Oxford, and he may invest some money in the company. It might be as much as $250,000.'

'That's fine, David, keep up the good work. You're doing a great job.'

Silverman showed no surprise at David's news, but once back in his own office he picked up the red telephone.

'Harvey?'

'Yes.'

'Kesler seems to have been the right choice. He may have talked a friend of his into investing $250,000 in the company.'

'Good. Now listen carefully. Brief my broker to put 40,000 shares on the market at just over $6 a share. If Kesler's friend does decide to invest in the company, mine will be the only large block of shares immediately available.'

After a further day's consideration, Stephen noticed that the shares of Prospecta Oil moved from £2.75 to £3.05 and decided the time had come to invest in what he was now convinced must be a winner. He trusted David, and had been impressed by the glossy geologist's report. He rang Kitcat & Aitken, a firm of stockbrokers in the City, and instructed them to buy $250,000-worth of shares in Prospecta Oil. Harvey Metcalfe's broker released 40,000 shares when Stephen's request came on to the floor of the stock exchange and the transaction was quickly completed. Stephen's purchase price was £3.10.

After investing his father's inheritance, Stephen spent the next few days happily watching the shares climb to £3.50, even before the expected announcement. Though Stephen didn't realise it, it was his own investment that had caused the shares to rise. He began to wonder what he would spend the profit on even before he had realised it. He decided not to cash in immediately, but hold on; David thought the shares would reach $20, and in any case he had promised to tell him when to sell.

Meanwhile, Harvey Metcalfe began to release a few more shares on to the market, because of the interest created by Stephen's investment. He was beginning to agree with Silverman that David Kesler, young, honest, and with all the enthusiasm of a man in his first appointment, had been an excellent choice. It was not the first time Harvey had used this ploy, keeping himself well away from the action while placing the responsibility on inexperienced, innocent shoulders.

At the same time, Richard Elliott, acting as the company spokesman, leaked stories to the press about large buyers coming into the market, which in itself occasioned a flood of small investors and kept the price steady.

One lesson a man learns in the Harvard Business School is that an executive is only as good as his health. David never felt happy without a regular medical check-up; he rather enjoyed being told he was in good shape, but perhaps should take things a little easier. His secretary, Miss Rentoul, had therefore made an appointment for him with a Harley Street doctor.

Dr Robin Oakley was by anyone's standards a successful man. At thirty-seven he was tall and handsome, with a head of dark hair that looked as if it would never recede. He had a classic strong face and the self-assurance that came from proven success. He still played squash twice a week, which helped him look enviably younger than his contemporaries. Robin had remained fit since his Cambridge days, which he left with a Rugby Blue and an upper-second-class degree. He had gone on to complete his medical training at St Thomas's, where once again his Rugby football rather than his medical skill brought him into prominence with those who decide the future careers of young men. When he qualified, he went to work as an assistant to a highly successful Harley Street practitioner, Dr Eugene Moffat. Dr Moffat was successful not so much in curing the sick as in charming the rich, especially middle-aged women, who came to see him again and again however little seemed to be wrong with them. At fifty guineas a visit that had to be regarded as success.

Moffat had chosen Robin Oakley as his assistant for exactly those qualities which he himself displayed, and which had made him so sought-after. Robin Oakley was unquestionably good-looking, personable, well-educated – and just clever enough. Robin settled very well into Harley Street and the Moffat system, and when the older man died suddenly in his early sixties, he took over his mantle with the ease with which a crown prince would take over a throne. Robin continued to build up the practice, losing none of Moffat's ladies other than by natural causes, and did remarkably well for himself. He had a wife and two sons, a comfortable country house a few miles outside Newbury in Berkshire, and a considerable saving in blue chip securities. He never complained at his good fortune and enjoyed life, at the same time being, he had to confess, a little bored with it all. He was beginning to find that the bland role of sympathetic doctor was almost intolerably cloying. Would the world come to an end if he admitted that he neither knew nor cared just what was causing the minute patches of dermatitis on Lady Fiona Fisher's diamond-studded hands? Would the Heavens descend if he told the dreaded Mrs Page-Stanley that she was a malodorous old woman in need of nothing more medically taxing than a new set of dentures? And would he be struck off if he personally administered to the nubile Miss Lydia de Villiers a good dose of what she so clearly indicated she desired?

David Kesler arrived on time for his appointment. He had been warned by Miss Rentoul that in England doctors and dentists cancel if you are late and still charge you.

He stripped and lay on Robin Oakley's couch. The doctor took his blood pressure, listened to his heart, and made him put out his tongue, an organ that seldom stands up well to public scrutiny. As he tapped and poked his way over David's body, they chatted.

'What brings you to work in London, Mr Kesler?'

'I'm with an oil company in the City. I expect you've heard of us – Prospecta Oil?'

'No,' said Robin. 'Can't say I have. Bend your legs up, please.' He hit David's knee-caps smartly, one after the other, with a patella hammer. The legs jumped wildly.

'Nothing wrong with those reflexes.'

'You will, Dr Oakley, you will. Things are going very well for us. Watch out for our progress in the papers.'

'Why?' said Robin, smiling, 'Struck oil, have you?'

'Yes,' said David quietly, pleased with the impression he was creating, 'as a matter of fact we've done just that.'

Robin prodded David's abdomen for a few seconds. 'Good muscular wall, not fat, no sign of an enlarged liver. Young man, you're in good physical shape.'

Robin left him in the examination room to get dressed and thoughtfully wrote out a brief report on Kesler for his records, while his mind dwelt on deeper things. An oil strike.

Harley Street doctors, although they routinely keep private patients waiting for three-quarters of an hour in a gas-fired waiting-room equipped with one out-of-date copy of *Punch*, never let them feel rushed once they are in the consulting room. Robin had no intention of rushing Mr Kesler.

'There's very little wrong with you, Mr Kesler. Some signs of anaemia, which I suspect are caused by nothing more than overwork and your recent rushing about. I'm going to give you some iron tablets which should quickly take care of that. Take two a day, morning and night.' He scribbled an illegible prescription for the tablets and handed it to David.

'Many thanks. It's kind of you to give me so much of your time.'

'Not at all. How are you finding London?' asked Robin. 'Very different from America, I expect.'

'Sure – the pace is much slower. Once I've mastered how long it takes to get something done here I'll be halfway to victory.'

'Do you have many friends in London?'

'No,' replied David, 'I have one or two buddies at Oxford from my Harvard days, but I haven't yet made contact with many people in London.'

Good, thought Robin, here is a chance for me to find out a little more about the oil game, and spend some time with a man who makes most of his patients look as if they had both feet in the grave. It might even shake me out of my lethargy. He continued, 'Would you care to join me for lunch later in the week? You might like to see one of our antique London clubs.'

'How very kind of you.'

7

'Excellent. Will Friday suit you?'

'It certainly will.'

'Then let's say one o'clock at the Athenaeum Club in Pall Mall.'

David returned to his City desk, picking up his tablets on the way. He took one immediately. He was beginning to enjoy his stay in London. Silverman seemed pleased with him, Prospecta Oil was doing well and he was already meeting some interesting people. Yes, he felt this was going to be a very happy period in his life.

On Friday at 12.45 pm, David arrived at the Athenaeum, a massive white building on the corner of Pall Mall, overlooked by a statue of the Duke of York. David was amazed by the size of the rooms and his commercial mind could not help wondering what price they would fetch as office space. The place appeared to be full of moving waxworks who, Robin later assured him, were in fact distinguished generals and diplomats.

They lunched in the Coffee Room, dominated by a Rubens of Charles II, and talked about Boston, London, squash, and their shared passion for Katharine Hepburn. Over coffee, David readily told Robin the details of the geologist's findings on the Prospecta Oil site. The shares had now climbed to £3.60 on the London Stock Exchange, and were still going up.

'Sounds like a good investment,' said Robin, 'and as it's your own company, it might be worth the risk.'

'I don't think there's much of a risk,' said David, 'as long as the oil is actually there.'

'Well, I'll certainly consider it most seriously over the weekend.'

They parted on the steps of the Athenaeum, David to a conference on the Energy Crisis organised by the *Financial Times*, Robin to his home in Berkshire. His two young sons were back from prep school for the weekend and he was looking forward to seeing them again. How quickly they had passed from babies to toddlers, to boys; soon they would be young men, he thought. And how reassuring to know their future was secure. Perhaps he should make that future a little more secure by investing in David Kesler's company. He could always put the money back into blue chip shares once the strike had been announced.

Bernie Silverman was also pleased to hear the possibility of a further investment.

'Congratulations, my boy. We're going to need a lot of capital to finance the pipe-laying operations, you know. Pipe-laying can cost $2 million per mile. Still, you're playing your part. I've just had word from head office that we are to give you a $5,000 bonus for your efforts. Keep up the good work.'

David smiled. This was business in the proper Harvard tradition. If you bring home the results, you get the rewards.

'When will the strike be officially announced?' he asked.

'Some time in the next few days.'

David left Silverman's office with a glow of pride.

Silverman immediately contacted Harvey Metcalfe on the red phone, and he set the routine in motion once again. Metcalfe's brokers released on to the market 35,000 shares at £3.73 and approximately 5,000 each day on to the open market, always being able to feel when the market had taken enough and thus keeping the price steady. Once again, the shares climbed when Dr Oakley invested heavily in the market, this time to £3.90, keeping David, Robin and Stephen all happy. They were not to know that Harvey was releasing more shares each day because of the interest they had caused, and that this was now creating a market of its own.

David decided to spend some of his bonus on a painting for his little flat in the Barbican, which he felt was rather grey. About $2,000, he thought, something that was going to appreciate in value. David quite enjoyed art for art's sake, but he liked it even more for business's sake. He spent Friday afternoon tramping around Bond Street, Cork Steet and Bruton Street, the home of the London art galleries. The Wildenstein was too expensive for his pocket and the Marlborough too modern for his taste. The painting he finally picked out was at the Lamanns Gallery in Bond Street.

The gallery, just three doors away from Sotheby's,

consisted of one vast room with a worn grey carpet and red faded wallpaper. As David was later to learn, the more worn the carpet, the more faded the walls, the greater the success and reputation of the gallery. There was a staircase at the far end of the room, against which some unregarded paintings were stacked, backs to the world. David sorted through them on a whim and found, to his delight, something that appealed to him.

It was an oil by Leon Underwood called *Venus in the Park*. The large, rather sombre canvas contained about six men and women sitting on metal chairs at circular tea-tables. Among them, in the foreground, was a comely naked woman with generous breasts and long hair. Nobody was paying her the slightest attention and she sat gazing out of the picture, face inscrutable, a symbol of warmth and love in indifferent surroundings. David found her utterly compelling.

The gallery proprietor, Jean-Pierre Lamanns, advanced on him, adorned in an elegantly tailored suit, as befitted a man who rarely received cheques for less than a thousand pounds. At thirty-five, he could afford the little extravagances of life, and his Gucci shoes, Yves St Laurent tie, Turnbull & Asser shirt and Piaget watch left no one, especially women, in any doubt that he knew what he was about. He was an Englishman's vision of a Frenchman, slim and neat with longish, dark wavy hair and deep brown eyes that hinted at being a little sharp. He was capable of being pernickety and demanding, with a wit that

was often as cruel as it was amusing, which may have
been one of the reasons why he had not married.
There certainly had been no shortage of applicants.
Customers, however, saw only his charming side. As
David wrote out his cheque, Jean-Pierre rubbed his
forefinger backwards and forwards over his fashionable moustache, only too happy to discuss the picture.

'Underwood is one of the greatest sculptors and
artists in England today. He even tutored Henry
Moore, you know. I believe he is underestimated
because of his dislike of journalists and the press,
whom he describes as nothing more than drunken
scribblers.'

'Hardly the way to endear oneself to the media,'
murmured David, as he handed over the cheque for
£850, feeling agreeably prosperous. Although it was
the most expensive purchase he had ever made, he
felt the picture was a good investment and, more
important, he liked it.

Jean-Pierre took David downstairs to show him
the Impressionist and Modern collection he had built
up over many years, continuing to enthuse about
Underwood. They celebrated David's first acquisition
over a whisky in Jean-Pierre's office.

'What line of business are you in, Mr Kesler?'

'I work with a small oil company called Prospecta
Oil, who are exploring prospects in the North Sea.'

'Had any success?' enquired Jean-Pierre, a little
too innocently.

'Well, between the two of us, we're rather excited

about the future. It's no secret that the company shares have gone from £2 to nearly £4 in the last few weeks, but no one knows the real reason.'

'Would it be a good investment for a poor little art dealer like myself?' asked Jean-Pierre.

'I'll tell you how good an investment I think it is,' said David. 'I am putting $3,000 in the company on Monday, which is all I have left in the world – now that I've captured Venus, that is. We'll shortly be making a rather important announcement.'

A twinkle came into Jean-Pierre's eye. To one of his Gallic subtlety, a nod was as good as a wink. He did not pursue the line of conversation any further.

'When's the strike going to be announced, Bernie?'

'I'm expecting it early next week. We've had a few problems. Nothing we can't lick, though.'

That gave David some relief, as he had taken up 500 shares himself that morning, investing the remaining $3,000 from his bonus. Like the others, he was hoping for a quick profit.

'Rowe Rudd.'

'Frank Watts, please. Jean-Pierre Lamanns.'

'Good morning, Jean-Pierre. What can we do for you?'

'I want to buy 25,000 Prospecta Oil.'

'Never heard of them. Hold on a minute . . . New

company, very low capital. A bit risky, J.-P. I wouldn't recommend it.'

'It's all right, Frank, I only want them for two or three weeks, then you can sell. I've no intention of holding on to them. When did the account start?'

'Yesterday.'

'Right. Buy this morning and sell them before the end of the account, or earlier. I'm expecting an announcement next week, so once they go over £5 you can get rid of them. No need to be greedy, but buy them in my company name, I don't want the deal traced back to me – it might embarrass the informant.'

'Right, sir. Buy 25,000 Prospecta Oil at market price and sell before the last day of the account, or sooner if instructed.'

'Correct, I'll be in Paris all next week looking at pictures, so don't hesitate to sell once they go over £5.'

'Right, J.-P. Have a good trip.'

The red telephone rang.

'Rowe Rudd are looking for a substantial block of shares. Do you know anything about it?'

'No idea, Harvey. It must be David Kesler again. Do you want me to speak to him?'

'No, say nothing. I've released another 25,000 shares at £3.90. Kesler's only got to do one more big one and I'll be out. Prepare our plan for seven days before the end of this Stock Exchange account.'

'Right, boss. You know quite a few people are also buying in small amounts.'

'Yes, just as before, they all have to tell their friends they're on to a good thing. Say nothing to Kesler.'

'You know, David,' said Richard Elliott, 'you work too hard. Relax. We're going to have enough work on our hands when the announcement's made.'

'I guess so,' said David. 'Work's just a habit with me now.'

'Well, why don't you take tonight off and join me for a spot of something at Annabel's?'

David was flattered by the invitation to London's most exclusive nightclub and accepted enthusiastically.

David's hired Ford Cortina looked somewhat out of place that evening in Berkeley Square among the double-parked Rolls Royces and Mercedes. He made his way down the little iron staircase into the basement, which at one time must have been no more than the servants' quarters for the elegant town house above. Now it was a splendid club, with a restaurant, discothèque and a small elegant bar, the walls covered in old prints and pictures. The main dining-room was dimly lit and crowded with small tables, most of them already occupied. The décor was Regency and extravagant. Mark Birley, the owner, had in the short period of ten years made Annabel's the most sought-after club in London, with a waiting list for membership of well over a thousand. The discothèque was playing in the far corner of a crowded dance floor, on which you couldn't have parked two Cadillacs. Most of the couples were dancing very close to each other – they had little choice. David was somewhat surprised to observe that nearly all of the men on the floor were about twenty years older than the girls they held in their arms. The head waiter, Louis, showed David to Richard Elliott's table, realising it was David's first visit to the club by the way he stared at all the personalities of the day. Oh well, thought David, perhaps one day they'll be staring at me.

After an exceptionally good dinner Richard Elliott and his wife joined the crowd on the dance floor, while David returned to the little bar surrounded by comfortable red settees and struck up a conversation with someone who introduced himself as James Brigsley. Even if he did not treat the whole world as such, Mr Brigsley certainly treated Annabel's as a stage. Tall, blond and aristocratic, his eyes alight with good humour, he seemed at ease with everyone around him. David admired his assured manner, something he had never acquired and feared he never would. His accent, even to David's untutored ears, was resonantly upper-class.

David's new acquaintance talked of his visits to the States, flattering him by remarking how much he had always liked the Americans. After some time, David was able quietly to ask the head waiter who the Englishman was.

'He's Lord Brigsley, the eldest son of the Earl of Louth, sir.'

What do you know, thought David, lords look like anyone else, especially when they've had a few drinks. Lord Brigsley was tapping David's glass.

'Would you care for another?'

'Thank you very much, my lord,' said David.

'Don't bother with all that nonsense. The name's James. What are you doing in London?'

'I work for an oil company. You probably know my Chairman, Lord Hunnisett. I've never met him myself, to tell you the truth.'

'Sweet old buffer,' said James. 'His son and I were at Harrow together. If you're in oil, perhaps you can tell me what to do with my Shell and BP shares.'

'Hold on to them,' said David. 'It's sensible to remain in any commodities, especially oil, as long as the British Government doesn't get greedy and try to take control of the assets themselves.'

Another double whisky arrived. David was beginning to feel just slightly tipsy.

'What about your own company?' enquired James.

'We're rather small,' said David, 'but our shares have gone up more than any other oil company in the last three months. Even so, I suspect they've nowhere near reached their zenith.'

'Why?' demanded James.

David glanced round and lowered his voice to a confidential whisper.

'Well, I expect you realise that if you make an oil strike in a big company it can only put the percentage of your profits up by a tiny amount. But if you make a strike in a small company, naturally that profit will be reflected as a considerably larger percentage of the whole.'

'Are you telling me you've made a strike?'

'Perhaps I shouldn't have said that,' said David. 'I'd be obliged if you'd treat that remark in confidence.'

David could not remember how he arrived home or who put him to bed, and he appeared rather late in the office the next morning.

'I am sorry, Bernie, I overslept after a very good evening with Richard at Annabel's.'

'Doesn't matter a bit. Glad you enjoyed yourself.'

'I hope I wasn't indiscreet, but I told some lord, whose name I can't even remember, that he ought to invest in the company. I may have been a little too enthusiastic.'

'Don't worry, David, we're not going to let anyone down and you need the rest. You've been working your ass off.'

James Brigsley left his London flat in Chelsea and took a taxi to his bank, Williams & Glyn's. James was an extrovert by nature and at Harrow his only real love had been acting; but when he had left school, his father had refused to allow him to go on the stage and insisted that he complete his education at Christ Church, Oxford, where again he took a greater interest in the Dramatic Society than in gaining a degree in his chosen subjects of Politics, Philosophy and Economics. James had never mentioned to anyone since leaving Oxford the class of degree he managed to secure, but for better or worse the fourth-class Honours degree was later abolished. After Oxford he joined the Grenadier Guards, which gave him considerable scope for his histrionic talent. This was indeed to be James's introduction to society life in London, and he succeeded as well as a personable, rich young viscount might be expected to do in the circumstances.

When he had completed his two years in the Guards, the earl gave him a 250-acre farm in Hampshire to occupy his time, but James did not care for the coarser country life. He left the running of the farm to a manager and once again concentrated on his social life in London. He would dearly have liked to go on the stage, but he knew the old man still considered Mrs Worthington's daughter's ambition an improper one for a future peer of the realm. The fifth earl didn't think a great deal of his eldest son one way and another, and James did not find it easy to persuade his father that he was shrewder than he was given credit for. Perhaps the inside information David Kesler had let slip after a few drinks would give him the opportunity to prove his old dad wrong.

In Williams & Glyn's fine old building in Birchin Lane, James was ushered into the manager's office.

'I should like to borrow some money against my farm in Hampshire,' said Lord Brigsley.

Philip Izard, the manager, knew Lord Brigsley well and was also acquainted with his father. Although he had respect for the earl's judgment, he did not have a great deal of time for the young lord. Nevertheless, it was not for him to query a customer's request, especially when the customer's family was one of the longest-standing in the bank's history.

'Yes, my lord, what sum do you have in mind?'

'Well, it seems that farmland in Hampshire is worth about £1,000 an acre and is still climbing. Why don't we say £150,000? I should then like to invest the money in shares.'

'Will you agree to leave the deeds with the bank as security?' enquired Izard.

'Yes, of course. What difference does it make to me where they are?'

'Then I am sure we will find it acceptable to advance you a loan of £150,000 at 2 per cent above base rate.'

James was not at all sure what base rate was, but he knew that Williams & Glyn's were as competitive as everyone else in such matters and that their reputation was beyond dispute.

'Thank you,' said James. 'Please acquire for me 35,000 shares in a company called Prospecta Oil.'

'Have you checked carefully into this company, my lord?' enquired Izard.

'Yes, of course I have,' said Lord Brigsley, very sharply. He was not in awe of the bank-managerial class.

In Boston, Harvey Metcalfe was briefed over the telephone by Silverman of the meeting in Annabel's between David Kesler and a nameless peer who seemed to have more money than sense. Harvey released 40,000 shares on to the market at £4.80. Williams & Glyn's acquired 35,000 of them and, once again, the remainder was taken up by small investors. The shares rose a little. Harvey Metcalfe was now left with only 30,000 shares of his own, and over the next four days he was able to dispose of them all. It had taken him fourteen weeks to off-load his entire stock in Prospecta Oil at a profit of just over $6 million.

On the Friday morning, the shares stood at £4.90 and Kesler had, in all innocence, occasioned four large investments: Harvey Metcalfe studied them in detail before putting through a call to Jörg Birrer.

Stephen Bradley had bought 40,000 shares at
$6.10
Dr Robin Oakley had bought 35,000 shares at
$7.23

Jean-Pierre Lamanns had bought 25,000 shares at
$7.80
James Brigsley had bought 35,000 shares at
$8.80
David Kesler himself had bought 500 shares at
$7.25.

Among them they had purchased 135,500 shares at a cost of just over $1 million. They had also kept the price rising, giving Harvey the chance to off-load all his own stock on to a natural market.

Harvey Metalfe had done it again. His name was not on the letterhead and now he possessed no shares. Nobody would be able to place any blame on him. He had done nothing illegal; even the geologist's report contained enough ifs and buts to pass in a court of law. As for David Kesler, Harvey could not be blamed for his youthful over-enthusiasm. He had never even met the man. Harvey Metcalfe opened the bottle of Krug Privée Cuvée 1964, imported from Hedges & Butler of London. He sipped it slowly, then lit a Romeo y Julieta Churchill, and settled back for a mild celebration.

David, Stephen, Robin, Jean-Pierre and James celebrated at the weekend as well. Why not? Their shares were at £4.90 and David had assured them all that they would reach £10. On Saturday morning David ordered his first bespoke suit from Aquascutum, Stephen tut-tutted his way through the end-of-vacation examination papers he had set his freshmen students, Robin attended his sons' prep school Sports Day, Jean-Pierre re-framed a Renoir, and James Brigsley went shooting, convinced that at last he had one in the eye for his father.

3

DAVID ARRIVED AT the office at 9 am on Monday to find that the front door was locked. He could not understand it. The secretaries were supposed to be in by 8.45.

After waiting around for over an hour, he walked to the nearest telephone box and dialled Bernie Silverman's home number. There was no reply. He then rang Richard Elliott at home: the ringing tone continued. He rang the Aberdeen office with the same result. He decided to return to the office. There must be a simple explanation, he thought. Was he daydreaming? Or was it Sunday? No – the streets were jammed with people and cars.

When he arrived back at the office a young man was nailing up a board. '2,500 sq ft to let. Apply Conrad Ritblat.'

'What do you think you are doing?' David demanded.

'The old tenants have given notice and left. We're looking for new ones. Are you interested in looking over the property?'

'No,' said David, backing away in panic. 'No, thank you.'

He raced down the street, sweat beginning to show on his forehead, praying that the telephone box would still be empty.

He flicked quickly through the L–R directory and looked up Bernie Silverman's secretary, Judith Lampson. This time there was a reply.

'Judith, in God's name, what's going on?' His voice would have left her in no doubt how anxious he was.

'No idea,' replied Judith. 'I was given my notice on Friday night with a month's pay in advance and no explanation.'

David dropped the telephone. The truth was slowly beginning to dawn on him although he still wanted to believe there was some simple explanation. Whom could he turn to? What should he do?

He returned in a daze to his flat in the Barbican. The morning post had arrived in his absence. It included a letter from the landlords of his flat:

Corporation of London,
Barbican Estate Office,
London EC2
01–628–4341

Dear Sir,
    We are sorry to learn you will be leaving at the end of the month, and would like to take this opportunity of thanking you for the payment of rent in advance.

We should be pleased if you would kindly deposit the keys at this office at your earliest covenience.

Yours faithfully,

C. J. Caselton,
Estate Manager

David stood frozen in the middle of the room, gazing at his new Underwood with sudden loathing.

Finally, fearfully, he dialled his stockbrokers.

'What price are Prospecta Oil this morning?'

'They've dipped to £3.80,' replied the broker.

'Why have they fallen?'

'I've no idea, but I'll make some enquiries and ring you back.'

'Please put my 500 shares on the market immediately.'

'500 Prospecta Oil at market price. Yes, sir.'

David put the phone down. It rang a few minutes later. It was his broker.

'They've only made £3.50 – exactly what you paid for them.'

'Would you credit the sum to my account at Lloyd's Bank, Moorgate Branch?'

'Of course, sir.'

David did not leave the flat for the rest of the day or night. He lay on his bed chain-smoking, wondering what he ought to do next, sometimes looking out of his little window over a rain-drenched City of banks, insurance companies, stockbrokers and public companies – his own world, but for how much longer? In the morning, as soon as the market opened, he rang his broker again, in the hope that they would have some new information.

'Can you give me any more news on Prospecta Oil?' His voice was tense and weary now.

'The news is bad, sir. There's been a spate of heavy selling and the shares have dropped to £2.80 on the opening of business this morning.'

'Why? What the hell's going on?' His voice rose with every word.

'I've no idea, sir,' replied a calm voice that always made one per cent, win or lose.

David replaced the receiver. All those years at Harvard were about to be blown away in a puff of smoke. An hour passed, but he did not notice it.

He ate lunch in an inconspicuous restaurant and read a disturbing report in the *London Evening Standard* by its City Editor, David Malbert, headlined 'The Mystery of Prospecta Oil'. By the close of the Stock Exchange at 4 pm the shares had fallen to £1.60.

David spent another restless night. He thought with pain and humiliation of how easily two months of good salary, a quick bonus and a good deal of smooth talk had bought his unquestioning belief in an enterprise that should have excited all business suspicion. He felt sick as he recalled his man-to-man tips on Prospecta Oil, whispered confidentially into willing ears.

On Wednesday morning, dreading what he knew he was bound to hear, David once again rang the broker. The shares had collapsed to £1 and there was no longer a market for them. He left the flat and walked over to Lloyd's Bank where he closed his account and drew out the remaining £1,345. The cashier smiled at him as she passed over the notes, thinking what a successful young man he must be.

David picked up the final edition of the *Evening Standard* (the one marked '7RR' in the right-hand corner). Prospecta Oil had dropped again, this time to 25 pence. Numbed, he returned to his flat. The housekeeper was on the stairs.

'The police have been round enquiring after you, young man,' she said haughtily.

David climbed the stairs, trying to look unperturbed.

'Thank you, Mrs Pearson. I guess it's another parking fine I forgot to pay.'

Panic had now taken over completely: David never felt so small, so lonely and so sick in his life. He packed everything he owned into a suitcase, except the painting, which he left hanging on the wall, and booked a one-way ticket to New York.

4

STEPHEN BRADLEY was delivering a lecture on group theory at the Mathematics Institute in Oxford to a class of third-year undergraduates the morning David left. Over breakfast he had read with horror in the *Daily Telegraph* of the collapse of Prospecta Oil. He had immediately rung his broker, who was still trying to find out the full facts for him. He then phoned David Kesler, who seemed to have vanished without trace.

The lecture Stephen was delivering was not going well. He was preoccupied, to say the least. He could only hope that the undergraduates would misconstrue his absentmindedness as brilliance, rather than recognise it for what it was – total despair. He was at least thankful that it was his final lecture of the Hilary term.

Stephen looked at the clock at the back of the lecture theatre every few minutes, until at last it pointed to the hour and he was able to return to his rooms in Magdalen College. He sat in his old leather chair wondering where to start. Why the hell had he put everything into one basket? How could he, normally so logical, so calculating, have been so recklessly stupid and greedy? He had trusted David, and still found it hard to believe that his friend was in any way involved with the collapse. Perhaps he shouldn't have taken for granted that someone he had befriended at Harvard must automatically be right. There had to be a simple explanation. Surely he must be able to get all his money back. The telephone rang. Perhaps it was his broker with more concrete news.

As he picked up the phone, he realised for the first time that the palms of his hands were slippery with sweat.

'Stephen Bradley.'

'Good morning, sir. I am sorry to bother you. My name is Detective Inspector Clifford Smith of the Fraud Squad, Scotland Yard. I was wondering if you would be kind enough to see me this afternoon?'

Stephen hesitated, thinking wildly for a minute that he might have done something criminal by investing in Prospecta Oil.

'Certainly, Inspector,' he replied uncertainly, 'would you like me to travel to London?'

'No, sir,' replied the Inspector, 'we'll come to you. We can be in Oxford by 4 pm, if that's convenient.'

'I'll expect you then. Goodbye, Inspector.'

Stephen replaced the receiver. What could they want? He knew little of English law and hoped he was not going to be involved with the police as well. All this just six months before he was due to return to

Harvard as a professor. Stephen was even beginning
to wonder if that would materialise.

The Detective Inspector was about 5 ft 11 in in height,
and somewhere between forty-five and fifty. His hair
was turning grey at the sides, but brilliantine toned it
in with the original black. His shabby suit, Stephen
suspected, was more indicative of a policeman's pay
than of the Inspector's personal taste. His heavy frame
would have fooled most people into thinking he was
rather slow. In fact, Stephen was in the presence of
one of the few men in England who fully understood
the criminal mind. Time and time again he had been
the man behind the arrest of international defrauders.
He had a tired look that came from years of putting
men behind bars for major crimes, only to see them
freed again shortly after and living comfortably off the
spoils of their shady transactions. In his opinion, crime
did pay. The department was so understaffed that
some of the smaller fry even got away scot-free; often
the office of the Director of Public Prosecutions would
decide it would be too expensive to follow the case
through to a proper conclusion. On other occasions.
the Fraud Squad simply did not have the back-up staff
to finish the job properly.

The Detective Inspector was accompanied by
Detective Sergeant Ryder, a considerably younger
man – 6 ft 1 in, thin in body and face. His large brown

eyes had a more innocent look against his sallow skin. He was at least a little better dressed than the Inspector, but then, thought Stephen, he probably wasn't married.

'I'm sorry about this intrusion, sir,' began the Inspector, after he had settled himself comfortably in the large armchair usually occupied by Stephen, 'but I'm making enquiries into a company called Prospecta Oil. Now before you say anything, sir, we realise that you had no personal involvement in the running of this company or indeed its subsequent collapse. But we do need your help, and I would prefer to ask you a series of questions which will bring out the points I need answered, rather than have you just give me a general assessment. I must tell you, sir, you don't have to answer any of my questions if you don't want to.'

Stephen nodded.

'First, sir, what made you invest such a large amount in Prospecta Oil?'

The Inspector had in front of him a sheet of paper with a list of all the investments made in the company over the past four months.

'The advice of a friend,' replied Stephen.

'Mr David Kesler, no doubt?'

'Yes.'

'How do you know Mr Kesler?'

'We were students at Harvard together and when he took up his appointment in England to work for an oil company, I invited him down to Oxford for old times' sake.'

Stephen went on to detail the full background of his association with David, and the reason he had been willing to invest such a large amount. He ended his explanation by asking if the Inspector thought that David was criminally involved in the rise and fall of Prospecta Oil.

'No, sir. My own view is that Kesler, who incidentally has made a run for it and left the country, is no more than the dupe of bigger men. But we would still like to question him, so if he contacts you, please let me know immediately. Now, sir,' the Inspector continued, 'I'm going to read you a list of names and I would be obliged if you could tell me whether you have ever met, spoken to or heard of any of them . . . Harvey Metcalfe?'

'No,' said Stephen.

'Bernie Silverman?'

'I've never met or spoken to him, but David did mention his name in conversation when he dined with me here in college.'

The Detective Sergeant was writing down everything Stephen said, slowly and methodically.

'Richard Elliott?'

'The same applies to him as Silverman.'

'Alvin Cooper?'

'No,' said Stephen.

'Have you had any contact with anyone else who was involved in the company?'

'No.'

For well over an hour the Inspector quizzed

Stephen on minor points, but he was unable to give him very much help, although he had kept a copy of the geologist's report.

'Yes, we are in possession of one of those documents, sir,' said the Inspector, 'but it's cleverly worded. I doubt if we'll be able to rely much on that for evidence.'

Stephen sighed and offered the two men some whisky and poured himself a donnish dry sherry.

'Evidence against whom or for what, Inspector?' he said as he returned to his chair. 'It's clear to me that I've been taken for a sucker. I probably don't need to tell you what a fool I've made of myself. I put my shirt on Prospecta Oil because it sounded like a sure-fire winner, and ended up losing everything I had without having a clue what to do about it. What in heaven's name has been going on in Prospecta Oil?'

'Well, sir,' said the Inspector, 'you'll appreciate there are aspects of the case I'm not at liberty to discuss with you. Indeed, there are some things that aren't very clear to us yet. But the game isn't a new one, and this time it's been played by an old pro, a very cunning old pro. It works something like this: a company is set up or taken over by a bunch of villains who acquire the majority of the shares. They invent a plausible story about a new discovery or super product that will send the shares up, whisper it in a few willing ears, release their own shares on to the market and let them be snapped up by the likes of you, sir, at a higher price. Then they clear off with the profit they have made, after which the shares collapse because the company has no real substance. As often as not, it ends with dealings in the shares being suspended on the stock market, and finally in the compulsory liquidation of the company. That hasn't happened yet in this case, and it may not. The London Stock Exchange is only just recovering from the Caplan fiasco and they don't want another scandal on their hands. I'm sorry to say that we can hardly ever recover the money, even if we produce enough evidence to nail the villains. They have it all stashed away all over the world before you can say Dow-Jones Index.'

Stephen groaned. 'My God, you make it all sound so appallingly simple, Inspector. The geologist's report was a fake, then?'

'Not exactly, sir. Very impressively worded and well presented, but with plenty of ifs and buts; and one thing is for certain; the DPP's office is hardly likely to spend millions finding out if there *is* any oil in that part of the North Sea.'

Stephen buried his head in his hands and mentally cursed the day he met David Kesler.

'Tell me, Inspector, who put Kesler up to this? Who was the real brains behind it all?'

The Inspector realised only too well the terrible agony Stephen was going through. During his career he had faced many men in the same position, and he was grateful for Stephen's co-operation.

'I'll answer any questions I feel cannot harm my

own enquiry,' said the Inspector. 'But it's no secret that the man we'd like to nail is Harvey Metcalfe.'

'Who's Harvey Metcalfe, for God's sake?'

'He's a first-generation American who's had his fingers in more dubious deals in Boston than you've had hot dinners. Made himself a multi-millionaire and a lot of other people bankrupt on the way. His style is so professional and predictable now we can smell the man a mile off. It will not amuse you to learn that he is a great benefactor of Harvard – does it to ease his conscience, no doubt. We've never been able to pin anything on him in the past, and I doubt if we'll be able to this time either. He was never a director of Prospecta Oil, and he only bought and sold shares on the open market. He never, as far as we know, even met David Kesler. He hired Silverman, Cooper and Elliott to do the dirty work, and they found a bright enthusiastic young man all freshly washed behind the ears to sell their story for them. I'm afraid it was a bit unlucky for you, sir, that the young man in question was your friend, David Kesler.'

'Never mind him, poor sod,' said Stephen. 'What about Harvey Metcalfe? Is he going to get away with it again?'

'I fear so,' said the Inspector. 'We have warrants out for the arrest of Silverman, Elliott and Cooper. They all beat it off to South America. After the Ronald Biggs fiasco I doubt if we'll ever get an extradition order to bring them back, even though the American and Canadian police also have warrants out for them. They were fairly cunning too. They closed the London office of Prospecta Oil, surrendered the lease and returned it to Conrad Ritblat, the estate agents, and gave notice to both secretaries with one month's pay in advance. They cleared the bill on the oil rig with Reading & Bates. They paid off their hired hands, Mark Stewart in Aberdeen, and took the Sunday morning flight to Rio de Janeiro, where there was $1 million in a private account waiting for them. Another two or three years, after they've spent all the money, and they'll undoubtedly turn up again with different names and a different company. Harvey Metcalfe rewarded them well and left David Kesler holding the baby.'

'Clever boys,' said Stephen.

'Oh, yes,' said the Inspector, 'it was a neat little operation. Worthy of the talents of Harvey Metcalfe.'

'Are you trying to arrest David Kesler?'

'No, but as I said we would like to question him. He bought and sold 500 shares, but we think that was only because he believed in the oil strike story himself. In fact, if he was wise, he would return to England and help the police with their enquiries, but I fear the poor man has panicked under pressure and made a bolt for it. The American police are keeping an eye out for him.'

'One last question,' said Stephen. 'Are there any other people who made such fools of themselves as I did!'

The Inspector gave this question long consideration. He had not had as much success with the other big investors as he had had with Stephen. They had all been evasive about their involvement with Kesler and Prospecta Oil. Perhaps if he released their names it might bring them out in some way.

'Yes, sir, but . . . you must understand that you never heard about them from me.'

Stephen nodded.

'For your own interest you could find out what you need to know by making some discreet enquiries through the Stock Exchange. There were four main punters, of whom you were one. Between the four of you you lost approximately $1 million. The others were a Harley Street doctor, Robin Oakley, a London art dealer called Jean-Pierre Lamanns, and a farmer, the unluckiest of all, really. As far as I can gather, he mortgaged his farm to put up the money. Titled young gentleman: Viscount Brigsley. Metcalfe's snatched the silver spoon out of his mouth, all right.'

'No other big investors?'

'Two or three banks burnt their fingers badly, but there were no other private investors above £10,000. What you, the banks and the other big investors did was to keep the market buoyant long enough for Metcalfe to off-load his entire holding.'

'I know, and worse, I foolishly advised some of my friends to invest in the company as well.'

'Er . . . there are two or three small investors from Oxford, yes sir,' said the Inspector, looking down at the sheet of paper in front of him, 'but don't worry –

we won't be approaching them. Well, that seems to be all. It only leaves me to thank you for your co-operation and say we may be in touch again some time in the future. In any case, we'll keep you informed of developments, and I hope you'll do the same for us.'

'Of course, Inspector. I do hope you have a safe journey back to town.' The two policemen downed their drinks and left.

Stephen could never recall if it was while sitting in his armchair looking out at the Cloisters, or later in bed that night, that he decided to employ his academic mind to carry out a little research on Harvey Metcalfe and his fellow dupers. His grandfather's advice to him, when as a small child he failed to win their nightly game of chess, floated across his mind: Stevie, don't get cross, get even. He was pleased he had given his final lecture and finished work for the term, and as he fell asleep at 3 am only one name was on his lips: Harvey Metcalfe.

5

STEPHEN AWOKE at about 5.30 am. He seemed to have been heavily, dreamlessly asleep, but as soon as he came to, the nightmare started again. He forced himself to use his mind constructively, to put the past firmly behind him and see what could be done about the future. He washed, shaved, dressed and missed college breakfast, occasionally murmuring to himself 'Harvey Metcalfe'. He then pedalled to Oxford station on an ancient bicycle, his preferred mode of transport in a city blocked solid with juggernaut lorries and full of unintelligible one-way systems. He left Ethelred the Unsteady padlocked to the station railings. There were as many bicycles standing in the ranks as there are cars in other railway stations.

He caught the 8.17 train so favoured by those who commute from Oxford to London every day. All the people at breakfast seemed to know each other and Stephen felt like an uninvited guest at someone else's party. The ticket collector bustled through the buffet car and clipped Stephen's first-class ticket. The man opposite Stephen produced a second-class ticket from behind his copy of the *Financial Times*. The collector clipped it grudgingly.

'You'll have to return to a second-class compartment when you've finished your breakfast, sir. The restaurant car is first-class, you know.'

Stephen considered the implication of these remarks as he watched the flat Berkshire countryside jolt past, and his coffee cup lurched unsampled in its saucer before he turned his mind to the morning papers. *The Times* carried no news of Prospecta Oil that morning. It was, he supposed, an insignificant story, even a dull one. Not kidnap, not arson, not even rape; just another shady business enterprise collapsing – nothing there to hold the attention of the front page for more than one day. Not a story he would have given a second thought to himself but for his own involvement, which gave it all the makings of a personal tragedy.

At Paddington he pushed through the ants rushing round the forecourt, glad that he had chosen the closeted life of a university or, more accurately, that it had chosen him. Stephen had never come to terms with London – he found the city large and impersonal, and he always took a taxi everywhere for fear of getting lost on the buses or the underground. Why didn't the English number their streets so Americans would know where they were?

'*The Times* office, Printing House Square.'

The cabby nodded and moved his black Austin deftly down the Bayswater Road, alongside a rain-sodden Hyde Park. The crocuses at Marble Arch looked sullen and battered, splayed wetly on the close grass. Stephen was impressed by London cabs: they never had a scrape or mark on them. He had once been told that cab-drivers are not allowed to pick up fares unless their vehicles are in perfect condition. How different from New York's battered yellow monsters, he thought. The cabby proceeded to swing down Park Lane to Hyde Park Corner, past the House of Commons and along the Embankment. The flags were out in Parliament Square. Stephen frowned. What was the lead story he had read over so inattentively in the train? Ah yes, a meeting of Commonwealth leaders. He supposed he must allow the world to go about its daily business as usual.

Stephen was unsure how to tackle the problem of checking Harvey Metcalfe out. Back at Harvard he would have had no trouble, first making a bee-line for his father's old friend Hank Swaltz, the business correspondent of the *Herald American*. Hank would be sure to have supplied him with the inside dope. The diary correspondent of *The Times*, Richard Compton-Miller, was by no means as appropriate a contact, but he was the only British press man Stephen had ever met. Compton-Miller had been visiting Magdalen the previous spring to write a feature on the time-honoured observance of May Day in Oxford. The choristers on the top of the College tower had sung the Miltonian salute as the sun peeped over the horizon on May 1st:

> Hail, bounteous May, that doth inspire
> Mirth and youth and warm desire.

On the banks of the river beneath Magdalen bridge where Compton-Miller and Stephen had stood, several couples had clearly been inspired.

Later, Stephen had been more embarrassed than flattered by his appearance in the resulting piece written by Compton-Miller for *The Times* diary: academics are sparing with the word brilliant, but journalists are not. The more self-important of Stephen's Senior Common Room colleagues had not been amused to see him described as the brightest star in a firmament of moderate luminescence.

The taxi pulled into the forecourt and came to a stop by the side of a massive hunk of sculpture by Henry Moore. *The Times* and the *Observer* shared a building with separate entrances, *The Times*'s by far the more prestigious. Stephen asked the sergeant behind the desk for Richard Compton-Miller, and was directed to the fifth floor and then to his little private cubicle at the end of the corridor.

It was only a little after 10 am when Stephen arrived, and the building was practically deserted. Compton-Miller later explained that a national newspaper does not begin to wake up until 11 am and generally indulges itself in a long lunch hour until about 3. Between then and putting the paper to bed, about 8.30 pm for all but the front page, the real work is done. There is usually a complete change of staff, staggered from 5 pm onwards, whose job it is to watch for major news stories breaking during the night. They always have to keep a wary eye on what is happening in America, because if the President makes an important statement in the afternoon in Washington they are already going to press in London. Sometimes the front page can change as often as five times during the night; in the case of the assassination of President Kennedy, news of which first reached England about 7 pm on the evening of November 22nd, 1963, the entire front page had to be scrapped to make way for the tragedy.

'Richard, it was kind of you to come in early for me. I didn't realise that you started work so late. I rather take my daily paper for granted.'

Richard laughed. 'That's OK. We must seem a lazy bunch to you, but this place will be buzzing at midnight when you're tucked up in bed and sound asleep. Now, how can I help you?'

'I'm trying to do a little research on a fellow countryman of mine called Harvey Metcalfe. He's a substantial benefactor of Harvard, and I want to flatter the old boy by knowing all about him when I return.' Stephen didn't care very much for the lie, but these were strange circumstances he now found himself in.

'Hang on here and I'll go and see if we have anything in the cutting room on him.'

Stephen amused himself by reading the headlines pinned up on Compton-Miller's board – obviously stories he had taken some pride in: 'Prime Minister to Conduct Orchestra at Royal Festival Hall', 'Miss World loves Tom Jones', 'Muhammad Ali says "I will be Champion Again"'.

Richard returned fifteen minutes later, carrying a thickish file.

'Have a go at that, Descartes. I'll be back in an hour and we can have some coffee.'

Stephen nodded and smiled gratefully. Descartes never had to solve the problems he was facing.

Everything Harvey Metcalfe wanted the world to know was in that file, and a little bit he didn't want the world to know. Stephen learned of his yearly trips to Europe to visit Wimbledon, of the success of his horses at Ascot and of his pursuit of Impressionist pictures for his private art collection. William Hickey of the *Daily Express* had on one occasion titillated his readers with a plump Harvey clad in Bermuda shorts and a report that he spent two or three weeks a year on his private yacht at Monte Carlo, gambling at the Casino. The Metcalfe fortune was in his opinion too new to be respectable. Stephen wrote down meticulously all the facts he thought relevant and was studying the photographs when Richard returned.

He took Stephen off to have some coffee in the canteen on the same floor. Cigarette smoke swirled mistily round the girl at the cashier's desk at the end of the self-service counter.

'Richard, I don't quite have all the information I might need. Harvard want to touch this man for quite a large sum: I believe they are thinking in terms of about $1 million. Where could I find out some more about him?'

'*New York Times*, I should imagine,' said Compton-Miller. 'Come on, we'll give Terry Robards a visit.'

The *New York Times* office in London was also on the fifth floor of *The Times* building in Printing House Square. Stephen thought of the vast *New York Times* building on 43rd Street and wondered if the London *Times* had a reciprocal arrangement, and was secreted away in their basement. Terry Robards turned out to be a wiry American wearing a perpetual smile. Terry immediately made Stephen feel at ease, a knack he had developed almost subconsciously over the years and which was a great asset when digging a little deeper for stories.

Stephen repeated his piece about Metcalfe. Terry laughed.

'Harvard aren't too fussy where they get their money from, are they? That guy has discovered more legal ways of stealing money than the Internal Revenue Service.'

'You don't say,' said Stephen innocently.

The *New York Times* file on Harvey was voluminous. 'Metcalfe's rise from Messenger Boy to Millionaire', as one headline put it, was documented admirably. Stephen took further careful notes. The details of Sharpley & Son fascinated him, as did the facts on some war-time arms dealing and the background of his wife Arlene and their daughter Rosalie. There was a picture of both of them, but the daughter was only fifteen at the time. There were also long reports of two court cases some twenty-five years past, in which Harvey had been charged with fraud but never convicted, and a more recent case in 1956 concerning a share transfer scheme in Boston. Again Harvey had escaped the law, but the District Attorney had left the jury in little doubt of his views on Mr Metcalfe. The most recent press stories were all in the gossip columns: Metcalfe's paintings, his horses, his orchids, his daughter's success at Vassar and his trips to Europe. Of Prospecta Oil there was not a word. Stephen had to admire Harvey's ability to conceal his more dubious activities from the press.

Terry invited his fellow expatriate to lunch. Newsmen always like new contacts and Stephen looked like a promising one. He asked the cabby to go to Whitfield Street. As they inched their way out of the City into the West End, Stephen hoped that the meal would be worth the journey. He was not disappointed.

Lacy's restaurant was airy and bedecked with clean linen and young daffodils. Terry said it was greatly favoured by press men. Margaret Costa, the cookery writer and her chef husband, Bill Lacy, certainly knew their onions. Over delicious watercress soup followed by *Médaillons de veau à crème au calvados* and a bottle of *Château de Péronne 1972*, Terry became quite expansive on the subject of Harvey Metcalfe. He had interviewed him once at Harvard on the occasion of the opening of Metcalfe Hall, which included a gymnasium and four indoor tennis courts.

'Hoping to get himself an honorary degree one day,' said Terry cynically, 'but not much hope, even if he gives a billion.'

Stephen noted the words thoughtfully.

'I guess you could get some more facts on the guy at the American Embassy,' said Terry. He glanced at his watch. 'No, hell, the library closes at 4 pm. Too late today. Time I got back to the office now America's awake.'

Stephen wondered if press men ate and drank like that every day. They made University dons look positively celibate – and however did they manage to get a paper out?

Stephen fought his way on to the 5.15 train to return with the Oxford-bound commuters, and only when he was alone in his room did he begin to study the results of his day's work. Though exhausted, he forced himself to sit at his desk until he had prepared the first neat draft of a dossier on Harvey Metcalfe.

Next day Stephen again caught the 8.17 to London, this time buying a second-class ticket. The ticket collector repeated his piece about leaving the restaurant car after he had finished his meal.

'Sure,' said Stephen, as he toyed with the remains of his coffee for the rest of the hour-long journey, never shifting from first-class. He was pleased with himself: he had saved £2, and that was exactly how Harvey Metcalfe would have behaved.

At Paddington he followed Terry Robard's advice and took a taxi to the American Embassy, a vast monolithic building which sprawls over 250,000 square feet and is nine storeys high, stretching the entire length of one side of Grosvenor Square. It was not, however, as elegant as the American Ambassador's magnificent official residence, Winfield House in Regents Park, where Stephen had been summoned to drinks last year, which was once the private home of Barbara Hutton before it was sold to the American government in 1946. Certainly, either of them was large enough for seven husbands, thought Stephen.

The entrance to the Embassy Reference Library on the ground floor was firmly shut. Stephen was reduced to a close study of the plaques on the wall in the corridor outside, honouring recent Ambassadors to the Court of St James. Reading backwards from Walter Annenberg, he had reached Joseph Kennedy when the doors of the library swung open, not unlike a bank. The prim girl behind a sign marked 'enquiries' was not immediately forthcoming on the subject of Harvey Metcalfe.

'Why do you require this information?' she asked sharply.

This threw Stephen for a moment, but he quickly recovered. 'I'm returning to Harvard in the fall as a professor and I feel I should know more about his involvement with the university. I'm at present a Visiting Fellow at Magdalen College, Oxford.'

Stephen's answer motivated the girl to immediate action and she produced a file within a few minutes. Though by no means as racy as the *New York Times*'s, it did put figures on the amounts Harvey Metcalfe had donated to charity and gave precise details of his gifts to the Democratic Party. Most people do not divulge the exact amount they give to political parties, but Harvey only knew about lights – no one seemed to have told him about bushels.

Having finished his research at the Embassy, Stephen took a taxi to the Cunard offices in St James's Square and spoke to a booking clerk and from there on to Claridge's in Brook Street, where he spent a few minutes with the duty manager. A telephone call to Monte Carlo completed his research. He travelled back to Oxford on the 5.15.

Stephen returned to his college rooms. He felt he now knew as much about Harvey Metcalfe as anyone, except perhaps for Arlene and Detective Inspector Clifford Smith of the Fraud Squad. Once again he stayed up into the early hours completing his dossier, which now ran to over forty typewritten pages.

When the dossier was finally completed he went to bed and fell into a deep sleep. He rose again early in the morning, strolled across the Cloisters to a Common Room breakfast and helped himself to eggs, bacon, coffee and toast. He then took his dossier to the Bursar's office where he made four copies of every document, ending up with five dossiers in all. He strolled back across Magdalen Bridge, admiring as always the trim flower beds of the University Botanic Gardens beneath him on his right, and called in at Maxwell's Bookshop on the other side of the bridge.

Stephen returned to his rooms with five smart files all of different colours. He then placed the five dossiers in the separate files and put them in a drawer of his desk which he kept locked. Stephen had a tidy and methodical mind, as a mathematician must: a mind the like of which Harvey Metcalfe had never yet come up against.

Stephen then referred to the notes he had written after his interview with Detective Inspector Smith and rang Directory Enquiries, asking for the London addresses and telephone numbers of Dr Robin Oakley, Jean-Pierre Lamanns and Lord Brigsley. Directory Enquiries refused to give him more than two numbers at any one time. Stephen wondered how the GPO expected to make a profit. In the States the Bell Telephone Company would happily have given him a dozen telephone numbers and still ended with the inevitable 'You're welcome'.

The two he managed to wheedle out of his reluctant informant were Dr Robin Oakley at 122 Harley Street, London W1, and Jean-Pierre Lamanns at the Lamanns Gallery, 40 New Bond Street, W1. Stephen then dialled Directory Enquiries a second time and requested the number and address of Lord Brigsley.

'No one under Brigsley in Central London,' said

the operator. 'Maybe he's ex-Directory. That is, if he really is a lord,' she sniffed.

Stephen left his study for the Senior Common Room, where he thumbed through the latest copy of *Who's Who* and found the noble lord:

BRIGSLEY, Viscount; James Clarence Spencer; b. 11 Oct. 1942; Farmer; *s* and *heir* of 5th Earl of Louth, *cr* 1764, *qv. Educ*: Harrow; Christ Church, Oxford (BA). Pres. Oxford University Dramatic Society. Lt Grenadier Guards 1966–68. *Recreations*: polo (not water), shooting. *Address*: Tathwell Hall, Louth, Lincs. *Clubs*: Garrick, Guards.

Stephen then strolled over to Christ Church and asked the secretary in the Treasurer's office if she had in her records a London address for James Brigsley, matriculated 1963. It was duly supplied as 119 King's Road, London SW3.

Stephen was beginning to warm to the challenge of Harvey Metcalfe. He left Christ Church by Peckwater and the Canterbury Gate, out into the High and back to Magdalen, hands in pockets, composing a brief letter in his mind. Oxford's nocturnal slogan-writers had been at work on a college wall again: 'Deanz meanz feinz' said one neatly painted graffito. Stephen, the reluctant Junior Dean of Magdalen, responsible for undergraduate discipline, smiled. If they were funny enough he would allow them to remain for one term, if not, he would have the porter scrub them out immediately. Back at his desk, he wrote down what had been in his mind.

> Magdalen College,
> Oxford.
> April 15th
>
> Dear Dr Oakley,
>   I am holding a small dinner party in my rooms next Thursday evening for a few carefully selected people.
>   I would be delighted if you could spare the time to join me, and I think you would find it worth your while to be present.
>
> Yours sincerely,
>   Stephen Bradley
>
> PS: I am sorry David Kesler is unable to join us.
> Black Tie: 7.30 for 8 pm.

Stephen changed the sheet of letter paper in his old Remington typewriter and addressed similar letters to Jean-Pierre Lamanns and Lord Brigsley. Then he sat thinking for a little while before picking up the internal telephone.

'Harry?' he said to the head porter. 'If anyone rings the lodge to ask if the college has a fellow called Stephen Bradley, I want you to say, "Yes, sir, a new Mathematics Fellow from Harvard, already famous for his dinner parties." Is that clear, Harry?'

'Yes, sir,' said Harry Woodley, the head porter.

He had never understood Americans – Dr Bradley was no exception.

All three men did ring and enquire, as Stephen had anticipated they might. He himself would have done the same in the circumstances. Harry remembered his message and repeated it carefully, although the callers still seemed a little baffled.

'No more than me, or is it I?' muttered the head porter.

Stephen received acceptances from all three during the next week, James Brigsley's arriving last, on the Friday. The crest on his letter paper announced a promising motto: *ex nihilo omnia.*

The butler to the Senior Common Room and the college chef were consulted, and a meal to loosen the tongues of the most taciturn was planned:

Coquilles St Jacques	Pouilly Fuissé 1969
Carrée d'agneau en croûte	Feux St Jean 1970
Casserôle d'artichauts et champignons	
Pommes de terre boulangère	
Griestorte with raspberries	Barsac Ch. d'Yquem 1927
Camembert frappé	Port Taylor 1947
Café	

Everything was ready; all Stephen could do now was wait for the appointed hour.

On the stroke of 7.30 pm on the appointed Thursday Jean-Pierre arrived. Stephen admired the elegant dinner-jacket and large floppy bow-tie that his guest wore, while he fingered his own little clip-on, surprised that Jean-Pierre Lamanns, who had such obvious savoir-faire, could also have fallen victim to Prospecta Oil. Stephen plunged into a monologue on the significance of the isosceles triangle in modern art while Jean-Pierre stroked his moustache. It was not a subject Stephen would normally have chosen to speak on without a break for five minutes, and he was only saved from the inevitability of more direct questions from Jean-Pierre by the arrival of Dr Robin Oakley. Robin had lost a few pounds in the past month, but Stephen could see why his practice in Harley Street was a success. He was, in the words of H. H. Munro, a man whose looks made it possible for women to forgive any other trifling inadequacies. Robin studied his shambling host, wondering whether he dared to ask immediately if they had ever met before. No, he decided; he would leave it a little and hope perhaps some clue as to why he had been invited would materialise during dinner. The David Kesler P.S. worried him.

Stephen introduced him to Jean-Pierre and they chatted while their host checked the dinner-table. Once again the door opened, and with a little more respect than previously displayed, the porter announced, 'Lord Brigsley'. Stephen walked forward to greet him, suddenly unsure whether he should bow or shake hands. Although James did not know anyone present at the strange gathering, he showed no signs of discomfort and entered easily into the conversation. Even Stephen was impressed by James's relaxed line of small talk, although he couldn't help recalling his academic results when at Christ Church and wondered whether the noble lord would in fact be an asset to his plans.

The culinary efforts of the chef worked their intended magic. No guest could possibly have asked his host why the dinner party was taking place while such delicately garlic-flavoured lamb, such tender almond pastry, such excellent wine, were still to hand.

Finally, when the servants had cleared the table and the port was on its way round for the second time, Robin could stand it no longer:

'If it's not a rude question, Dr Bradley.'

'Do call me Stephen.'

'Stephen, may I ask what is the purpose of this select little gathering?'

Six eyes bored into him demanding an answer to the same question.

Stephen rose and surveyed his guests. He walked around the table twice before speaking and then started his discourse by recalling the entire history of the past few weeks. He told them of his meeting in that very room with David Kesler, his investment in Prospecta Oil, followed soon afterwards by the visit of the Fraud Squad, and their disclosure about Harvey Metcalfe. He ended his carefully prepared speech with the words, 'Gentlemen, the truth is that the four of us are in the same bloody mess.' He felt that sounded suitably British.

Jean-Pierre reacted even before Stephen could finish what he was saying.

'Count me out. I couldn't be involved in anything quite so ridiculous as that. I am a humble art dealer, not a speculator.'

Robin Oakley also jumped in before Stephen was given the chance to reply:

'I've never heard anything so preposterous. You must have contacted the wrong man. I'm a Harley Street doctor – I don't know the first thing about oil.'

Stephen could see why the Fraud Squad had had trouble with these two and why they had been so thankful for his co-operation. They all looked at Lord Brigsley, who raised his eyes and said very quietly:

'Absolutely right on every detail, Dr Bradley, and I'm in more of a pickle than you. I borrowed £150,000 to buy the shares against the security of my small farm in Hampshire and I don't think it will be long before the bank insists that I dispose of it. When they do and my dear old pa, the fifth earl, finds out, it's curtains for me unless I become the sixth earl overnight.'

'Thank you,' said Stephen. As he sat down, he turned to Robin and raised his eyebrows interrogatively.

'What the hell,' said Robin. 'You're quite right – I was involved. David Kesler was a patient of mine and in a rash moment I invested £100,000 in Prospecta Oil as a temporary advance against my securities. God only knows what made me do it. As the shares are only worth 50 pence I'm stuck with them. I have a shortfall at my bank which they're beginning to fuss about. I also have a large mortgage on my country home in Berkshire and a heavy rent on my Harley Street consulting-room, a wife with expensive tastes and two boys at the best private prep school in England. I've hardly slept a wink since Detective Inspector Smith visited me two weeks ago.' He looked up. His face had drained of colour and the suave self-confidence of Harley Street had gone. Slowly, they all turned and stared at Jean-Pierre.

'All right, all right,' he admitted, 'me too. I was in Paris when the damned thing folded under me, so now, I'm stuck with the useless shares. £80,000 borrowed against my stock at the gallery. And what's worse, I advised some of my friends to invest in the bloody company too.'

Silence enveloped the room. It was Jean-Pierre who broke it again:

'So what do you suggest, Professor,' he said sarcastically. 'Do we hold an annual dinner to remind us what fools we've been?'

'No, that was not what I had in mind.' Stephen hesitated, realising that what he was about to suggest was bound to cause even more commotion. Once again he rose to his feet, and said quietly and deliberately:

'We have had our money stolen by a very clever man who has proved to be an expert in share fraud. None of us is knowledgeable about stocks and shares, but we are all experts in our own fields. Gentlemen, I therefore suggest we steal it back.

' – NOT A PENNY MORE AND NOT A PENNY LESS.'

A few seconds' silence was followed by uproar.

'Just walk up and take it I suppose?' said Robin.

'Kidnap him,' mused James.

'Why don't we just kill him and claim the life insurance?' said Jean-Pierre.

Several moments passed. Stephen waited until he had complete silence again, and then he handed round the four dossiers marked 'Harvey Metcalfe' with each of their names below. A green dossier for Robin, a blue one for James and a yellow for Jean-Pierre. The red master copy Stephen kept for himself. They were all impressed. While they had been wringing their hands in unproductive dismay, it was obvious that Stephen Bradley had been hard at work.

Stephen continued:

'Please read your dossier carefully. It will brief you on everything that is known about Harvey Metcalfe. Each of you must take the document away and study the information, and then return with a plan of how we are, between us, to extract $1,000,000 from him without his ever being aware of it. All four of us must come up with a separate plan. Each may involve the other three in his own operation. We will return here in fourteen days' time and present our conclusions. Each member of the team will put $10,000 into the kitty as a float and I, as the mathematician, will keep a running account. All expenses incurred in retrieving our money will be added to Mr Metcalfe's bill, starting with your journey down here this evening and the cost of the dinner tonight.'

Jean-Pierre and Robin began to protest again, but it was James who stopped the proceedings, by simply saying:

'I agree. What have we got to lose? On our own we've no chance at all: together we might just tweak the bastard.'

Robin and Jean-Pierre looked at each other, shrugged and nodded.

The four of them settled down to discuss in detail the material Stephen had acquired over the past few days. They left the college a little after midnight, each agreeing to have a plan ready for the Team's consideration in fourteen days' time. None of them was quite sure where it all might end, but each was relieved to know he was no longer on his own.

Stephen decided that the first part of the Team versus Harvey Metcalfe had gone as well as he could have wished. He only hoped his co-conspirators would now get down to work. He sat in his armchair, stared at the ceiling and continued thinking.

6

ROBIN RETRIEVED his car from the High Street, not for the first time in his life being thankful for the 'Doctor on Call' sticker which always gave him an extra degree of freedom when parking. He headed back towards his home in Berkshire. There was no doubt about it, Stephen Bradley was a very impressive man; Robin was determined to come up with something that would ensure that he played his full part.

Robin let his mind linger a little on the delightful prospect of recovering the money he had so ill-advisedly entrusted to Prospecta Oil and Harvey Metcalfe. It must be worth a try: after all, he might as well be struck off the register of the General Medical Council for attempted robbery as for bankruptcy. He wound the window of the car down a little way to dispel the last delicious effects of the claret and considered Stephen's challenge more carefully.

The journey between Oxford and his country house passed very quickly. His mind was so preoccupied with Harvey Metcalfe that when he arrived home to his wife there were large sections of the journey that he could not even remember. Robin had only one talent to offer, apart from his natural charm, and he hoped that he was right in thinking that particular talent was the strength in his armour and a weakness in Harvey Metcalfe's. He began to repeat aloud something that was written on page 16 of Stephen's dossier, 'One of Harvey Metcalfe's recurrent worries is . . .'

'What was it all about, darling?'

His wife's voice brought Robin quickly to his senses and he locked the briefcase containing the green Metcalfe dossier.

'You still awake, Mary?'

'Well, I'm not talking in my sleep, love.'

Robin had to think quickly. He had not yet steeled himself to tell Mary the details of his foolish investment, but he had let her know about the dinner in Oxford, not at that time realising it was in any way connected with Prospecta Oil.

'It was a tease, sweetheart. An old friend of mine from Cambridge has been appointed a lecturer at Oxford, so he dragged a few of his contemporaries down for dinner and we had a damn good evening. Jim and Fred from my old college were there, but I don't expect you remember them.'

A bit weak, thought Robin, but the best he could do at 1.15 in the morning.

'Sure it wasn't some beautiful girl?' said Mary.

'I'm afraid Jim and Fred could hardly be described as beautiful, even by their loving wives.'

'Do lower your voice, Robin, or you'll wake the children.'

'I'm going down again in two weeks time to . . .'

'Oh, come to bed and tell me about it at breakfast.'

Robin was relieved to be let off the hook until the morning. He clambered in beside his fragrant silk-clad wife and ran his finger hopefully down her vertebral column to her coccyx.

'You'll be lucky, at this time of night,' she mumbled.

They both slept.

Jean-Pierre had booked himself in at the Eastgate Hotel in the High. There was to be an undergraduate exhibition the next day at the Christ Church Art Gallery. Jean-Pierre was always on the look-out for new young talent which he could contract to the Lamanns Gallery. It was the Marlborough Gallery, a few doors away from him in Bond Street, that had taught the London art world the astuteness of buying up young artists and being closely identified with their careers. But for the moment, the artistic future of his gallery was not uppermost in Jean-Pierre's mind: its very survival was threatened, and the quiet American don from Magdalen had offered him the chance of redress. He settled down in his comfortable hotel bedroom, oblivious of the late hour, reading his dossier and working out where he could fit into the jigsaw. He was not going to allow two Englishmen and a Yank to beat him. His father had been relieved at Rochefort by the British in 1918 and released from a prisoner-of-war camp near Frankfurt by the Americans in 1945. Nothing was going to stop him being a full participant in this operation. He read his yellow dossier late into the night: the germ of an idea was beginning to form in his mind.

James made the last train from Oxford and looked for an empty carriage where he could settle down to study the blue dossier. He was a worried man: he was sure the other three would each come up with a brilliant plan and, as had always seemed to be the case in the past, he would be found lacking. He had never been under any real pressure before – everything had come to him so easily; now it had all gone just as easily. A foolproof scheme for relieving Harvey Metcalfe of some of his excess profits was not James's idea of an amusing pastime. Still, the awful vision of his father discovering that the Hampshire farm was mortgaged up to the hilt was always there to keep his mind on the job. But fourteen days was such a short time: where on earth should he begin? He was not a professional man like the other three and had no particular skills to offer. He could only hope that his stage experience might come in useful at some point.

He bumped into the ticket collector, who was not surprised to find James was the holder of a first-class ticket. The quest for an empty compartment was in vain. James concluded that Richard Marsh must be trying to run the railways at a profit. Whatever next?

Still more aggravating, they would probably give him a knighthood for his pains.

The next best thing to an empty compartment, James always thought, was one containing a beautiful girl – and this time his luck was in. One of the compartments was occupied by a truly stunning creature who looked as if she was alone. The only other person in the carriage was a middle-aged lady reading *Vogue*, who showed no signs of knowing her travelling companion. James settled down in the corner with his back to the engine, realising he could not study the Metcalfe dossier on the train. They had all been sworn to total secrecy, and Stephen had cautioned them against reading the dossiers in anyone else's company. James feared that of the four of them he was going to find it the most difficult to remain silent: a companionable man, he found secrets rather burdensome. He touched his overcoat pocket, the one holding the dossier in the envelope supplied by Stephen Bradley. What an efficient man he was, thought James. Alarmingly brainy, too. He was bound to have a dozen clever plans ready for consideration by the next meeting. James frowned and stared out of the window hoping some serendipitous idea would strike him. Instead he found himself studying the reflection of the profile of the girl sitting opposite him . . .

She had a shiny bob of dark brown hair, a slim straight nose and her large hazel eyes seemed fixed on the book she held in her lap. James wondered if she was as entirely oblivious of his presence as she appeared to be, and reluctantly decided that she was. His eyes slipped down to the gentle curve of her breast, softly encased in angora. He craned his neck slightly to see what sort of legs the reflection had. Damn it, she was wearing boots. He looked back at the face again. It was now looking back at him, faintly amused. Embarrassed, he switched his attention to the third occupant of the carriage, the unofficial chaperone in front of whom James lacked the courage even to strike up a conversation with the beautiful profile.

In desperation he stared at the cover of the middle-aged lady's *Vogue*. Another beautiful girl. And then he looked more carefully. It wasn't another girl, it was the same girl. To begin with, he could hardly believe his eyes, but a quick check against the genuine article left him in no doubt. As soon as *Vogue* was relinquished in favour of *Queen*, James leant across and asked the chaperone if he might be allowed to read it.

'Station bookstalls are closing earlier and earlier,' he said idiotically. 'I couldn't get anything to read.'

The chaperone agreed reluctantly.

He turned to the second page. 'Cover: Picture yourself like this . . . black silk georgette dress with chiffon handkerchief points. Ostrich-feather boa. Turban with flower, matching dress. Made to measure by Zandra Rhodes. Anne's hair by Jason at Vidal Sassoon. Photograph by Lichfield. Camera: Hasselblad.'

James was quite unable to picture himself like that. But at least he now knew the girl's name, Anne. The next time the real-life version looked up, he showed her by sign language that he had spotted the photograph. She smiled briefly at James and then returned to her book.

At Reading station the middle-aged lady left, taking *Vogue* with her. Couldn't be better, mused James. Anne looked up, faintly embarrassed, and smiled hopefully at the few passers-by walking up and down the corridor looking for a seat. James glared at them as they passed. No one entered the carriage. James had won the first round. As the train gathered speed he tried his opening gambit, which was quite good by his normal standards:

'What a super picture on the front of *Vogue* taken by my old friend Patrick Lichfield.'

Anne Summerton looked up. She was even more beautiful than the picture James had referred to. Her dark hair, cut softly in the latest Vidal Sassoon style, her big hazel eyes and faultless skin gave her a gentle look that James found irresistible. She had that slim, graceful body that all leading models need to earn their living, but Anne also had a presence that most of them would never have. James was quite stunned and wished she would say something.

Anne was used to men trying to pick her up but she was rather taken aback by the remarks about Lord Lichfield. If he was a friend, it would be offhand not to be at least polite. On a second glance she found James's diffidence rather charming. He had used the self-deprecating approach many times with great success, but this time it was perfectly genuine. He tried again.

'It must be a hell of a job being a model.'

What a bloody silly line, he thought. Why couldn't he just say to her, I think you're absolutely fantastic? Can we talk a little and if I still think you're fantastic perhaps we can take it from there? But it never worked that way. He knew he would have to go through the usual routine.

'It's bearable if the contracts are good,' she replied, 'but today's been particularly tiring.' Her voice was gentle, and the faint transatlantic accent appealed to James. 'I've been smiling my head off all day, modelling an advertisement for Close-Up toothpaste: the photographer never seemed to be satisfied. The only good thing about it was that it ended a day earlier than expected. How do you know Patrick?'

'We were fags together at Harrow in our first year. He was rather better than me at getting out of work.'

Anne laughed – a gentle, warm laugh. It was obvious he knew Lord Lichfield.

'Do you see much of him now?'

'Occasionally at dinner parties, but not regularly. Does he photograph you a lot?'

'No,' said Anne, 'the cover picture for *Vogue* was the only time.'

As they chatted on, the thirty-five-minute journey between Reading and London seemed to pass in a flash. Walking down the platform of Paddington Station with Anne, James ventured:

'Can I give you a lift home? My car is parked round the corner in Craven Street.'

Anne accepted, relieved not to have to search for a taxi at that late hour.

James drove her home in his Alfa Romeo. He had already decided that he could not hold on to that particular luxury for much longer with petrol going up and cash flow going down. He chattered merrily all the way to her destination, which turned out to be a block of flats in Cheyne Row overlooking the Thames; much to Anne's surprise he just dropped her off at the front door and said goodnight. He did not even ask for her telephone number and he only knew her Christian name. In fact, she did not have any idea what his name was. Pity, she thought as she closed the front door; he had been a rather pleasant change from the men who worked on the fringe of the advertising media, who imagined they had an automatic right to a girl's compliance just because she posed in a bra.

James knew exactly what he was doing. He had always found a girl was more flattered if he called her when she least expected it. His tactics were to leave the impression that she had seen the last of him, especially when the first meeting had gone well. He returned to his home in the King's Road and considered the situation. Unlike Stephen, Robin and

Jean-Pierre, with thirteen days to go, he still had no ideas for defeating Harvey Metcalfe. But he was hatching plans for Anne.

On waking in the morning, Stephen began to do a little more research. He started with a close study of the way the university was administered. He visited the Vice-Chancellor's office in the Clarendon Building, where he spent some time asking strange questions of his personal secretary, Miss Smallwood. She was most intrigued. He then left for the office of the University Registrar, where he was equally inquisitive. He ended the day by visiting the Bodleian Library, and copying out some of the University Statutes. Among other outings during the next fourteen days was a trip to the Oxford tailors, Shepherd and Woodward, and a full day at the Sheldonian Theatre to watch the brief ceremony as a batch of students took their Bachelor of Arts degrees. Stephen also studied the layout of the Randolph, the largest hotel in Oxford. This he took some considerable time over, so much so that the manager became inquisitive and Stephen had to leave before he became suspicious. His final trip was a return journey to the Clarendon to meet the Secretary of the University Chest, and to be taken on a guided tour of the building by the porter. Stephen warned him that he anticipated showing an American around the building on the day of Encaenia, but remained vague.

'Well, that won't be easy . . .' began the porter. Stephen carefully and deliberately folded a pound note and passed it to the porter '. . . though I'm sure we'll be able to work something out, sir.'

In between his trips all over the university city, Stephen did a lot of thinking in the big leather chair and a lot more writing at his desk. By the fourteenth day his plan was perfected and ready for presentation to the other three. He had put the show on the road, as Harvey Metcalfe might have said, and he intended to see it had a long run.

Robin rose early on the morning after the Oxford dinner, and avoided awkward questions from his wife at breakfast about his experience the night before. He travelled up to London as soon as he could get away, and on arrival in Harley Street was greeted by his efficient secretary-cum-receptionist, Miss Meikle.

Elspeth Meikle was a dedicated, dour Scot who looked upon her work as nothing less than a vocation. Her devotion to Robin, not that she ever called him that even in her own mind, was obvious for all to see.

'I want as few appointments as possible over the next fourteen days, Miss Meikle.'

'I understand, Dr Oakley,' she said.

'I have some research to carry out and I don't want to be interrupted when I'm alone in my study.'

Miss Meikle was somewhat surprised. She had always thought of Dr Oakley as a good physician, but had never known him in the past to over-indulge in research work. She padded off noiselessly in her white-shod feet to admit the first of a bunch of admirably healthy ladies to Dr Oakley's clinic.

Robin disposed of his patients with less than dignified speed. He went without lunch and began the afternoon by making several telephone calls to the Boston Infirmary and several to a leading gastro-enterologist for whom he had been a houseman at Cambridge. Then he pressed the buzzer to summon Miss Meikle.

'Could you pop round to H. K. Lewis for me, Miss Meikle, and put two books on my account. I want the latest edition of Polson and Tattersall's *Clinical Toxicology* and Harding Rain's book on the bladder and abdomen.'

'Yes, sir,' she said, quite unperturbed at the thought of interrupting her lunchtime sandwich to fetch them.

They were on his desk before he had completed his calls, and he immediately started reading long sections of them carefully. The following day he cancelled his morning clinic and went to St Thomas's Hospital to watch two of his old colleagues at work. His confidence in the plan he had formulated was growing. He returned to Harley Street and wrote some notes on the techniques he had observed that morning, much as he had done in his student days. He paused to remember the words Stephen had used: 'Think as Harvey Metcalfe would. Think for the first time in your life, not as a cautious professional man, but as a risk-taker, as an entrepreneur.'

Robin was tuning in to Harvey Metcalfe's wavelength, and when the time came he would be ready for the American, the Frenchman and the lord. But would they be willing to fall in with his plan? He looked forward to their meeting.

Jean-Pierre returned from Oxford the next day. None of the youthful artists had greatly impressed him, though he had felt that Brian Davis's still life showed considerable promise and had made a mental note to keep an eye on his future work. When he arrived back in London he started, like Robin and Stephen, on his research. A tentative idea that had come to him in the Eastgate Hotel was beginning to germinate. Through his numerous contacts in the art world he checked all the buying and selling of major Impressionist paintings over the previous twenty years and made a list of the pictures which were currently thought to be on the market. He then contacted the person who held it in his power to set his plan in motion. Fortunately the man whose help he most needed, David Stein, was in England and free to visit him: but would he fall in with the plan?

Stein arrived late the following afternoon and spent two hours with Jean-Pierre privately in his little room in the basement of the Lamanns Gallery. When he left Jean-Pierre was smiling to himself. A final afternoon spent at the German Embassy in Belgrave Square, followed by a call to Dr Wormit of the Preussischer Kulturbesitz in Berlin and a further one to Mme Tellegen at the Rijksbureau in The Hague, gave him all the information he required. Even Metcalfe would have praised him for the final touch. There would be no relieving the French this time. The American and the Englishman had better be up to scratch when he presented his plan.

On waking in the morning the last thing James had on his mind was an idea for outwitting Harvey Metcalfe. His thoughts were fully occupied with more important things. He telephoned Patrick Lichfield at home.

'Patrick?'

'Yes,' mumbled a voice.

'James Brigsley.'

'Oh, hello James. Haven't seen you for some time. What are you doing waking a fellow up at this filthy hour?'

'It's 10 am Patrick.'

'Is it? It was the Berkeley Square Ball last night and I didn't get to bed until four. What can I do for you?'

'You took a picture for *Vogue* of a girl whose first name was Anne.'

'Summerton,' said Patrick without hesitation. 'Got her from the Stacpoole Agency.'

'What's she like?'

'No idea,' said Patrick. 'I thought she was awfully nice. She just thought I wasn't her type.'

'Obviously a woman of taste, Patrick. Now go back to sleep.' James put the phone down.

Anne Summerton was not listed in the telephone directory – so that ploy had failed. James remained in bed, scratching the stubble on his chin, when a triumphant look came into his eye. A quick flip through the S–Z directory revealed the number he required. He dialled it.

'The Stacpoole Agency.'

'Can I speak to the manager?'

'Who's calling?'

'Lord Brigsley.'

'I'll put you through, my lord.'

James heard the phone click and the voice of the manager.

'Good morning, my lord. Michael Stacpoole speaking. Can I help you?'

'I hope so, Mr Stacpoole. I have been let down at the last moment and I'm looking for a model for the opening of an antique shop and I'll need a classy sort of bird. You know the kind of girl.'

James then described Anne as if he had never met her.

'We have two models on our books who I think would suit you, my lord,' offered Stacpoole. 'Pauline Stone and Anne Summerton. Unfortunately, Pauline is in Birmingham today for the launching of the new

Allegro car and Anne is completing a toothpaste session in Oxford.'

'I need a girl today,' James said. How he would have liked to have informed Stacpoole that Anne was back in town. 'If you find either of them are free for any reason, perhaps you would ring me at 735–7227.'

James rang off, a little disappointed. At least, he thought, if nothing comes of it today he could start planning his part in the Team versus Harvey Metcalfe. He was just resigning himself to that when the phone rang. A shrill, high-pitched voice announced:

'This is the Stacpoole Agency. Mr Stacpoole would like to speak to Lord Brigsley.'

'Speaking,' said James.

'I'll put you through, my lord.'

'Lord Brigsley?'

'Yes.'

'Stacpoole here, my lord. It seems Anne Summerton is free today. When would you like her to come to your shop?'

'Oh,' said James, taken aback for a second. 'The shop is in Berkeley Street, next to the Empress Restaurant. It's called Albemarle Antiques. Perhaps we could meet outside at 12.45?'

'I'm sure that will be acceptable, my lord. If I don't ring you back in the next ten minutes, you can assume the meeting is on. Perhaps you'd be kind enough to let us know if she's suitable. We normally prefer you to come to the office, but I'm sure we can make an exception in your case.'

'Thank you,' said James and put the phone down, pleased with himself.

James stood on the west side of Berkeley Street in the doorway of the Mayfair Hotel so that he could catch Anne arriving. When it came to work, Anne was always on time, and at 12.40 pm she appeared from the Piccadilly end of the street. Her skirt was of the latest elegant length, but this time James could see that her legs were as slim and shapely as the rest of her. She stopped outside the Empress Restaurant and looked in bewilderment at the Brazilian Trade Centre on her right and the Rolls Royce showrooms of H. R. Owen on her left.

James strode across the road, a large grin on his face.

'Good morning,' he said casually.

'Oh hello,' said Anne, 'what a coincidence.'

'What are you doing here all alone and looking lost?' said James.

'I'm trying to find a shop called Albemarle Antiques. You don't know it by any chance? I must have the wrong street. As you go in for knowing lords, you might know the owner, Lord Brigsley?'

James smiled:

'I am Lord Brigsley.'

Anne looked surprised and then burst out laughing. She realised what James had done and was flattered by the compliment.

They lunched together at the Empress, James's favourite eating place in town. He explained to Anne why it had been Lord Clarendon's favourite restaurant as well – 'Ah,' he had once declared, 'the millionaires are just a little fatter, and the mistresses are just a little thinner, than in any other restaurant in town.'

The meal was a triumph and James had to admit that Anne was the best thing that had happened to him for a long time. After lunch she asked where the agency should send their account.

'With what I have in mind for the future,' replied James, 'they'd better be prepared for a large bad debt.'

7

STEPHEN WRUNG James warmly by the hand the way
the Americans will and presented him with a large
whisky on the rocks. Impressive memory, thought
James, as he took a gulp to give himself a little Dutch
courage, and then joined Robin and Jean-Pierre. By
unspoken mutual consent, the name of Harvey Metcalfe was not mentioned. They chattered inconsequentially of nothing in particular, each clutching his
own dossier, until Stephen summoned them to the
table. Stephen had not, on this occasion, exercised
the talents of the college chef and the butler to the
Senior Common Room. Instead, sandwiches, beer
and coffee were stacked neatly on the table, and the
college servants were not in evidence.

'This is a working supper,' said Stephen firmly,
'and as Harvey Metcalfe will eventually be footing
the bill, I've cut down considerably on the hospitality.
We don't want to make our task unnecessarily harder
by eating our way through hundreds of dollars per
meeting.'

The other three sat down quietly as Stephen took
out some closely-typed sheets of paper.

'I'll begin,' he said, 'with a general comment. I've been doing some further research into Harvey Metcalfe's movements over the next few months. He seems to spend every summer doing the same round of social and sporting events. Most of the details are already well documented in your files. My latest findings are summarised on this separate sheet which should be added as page 38A of your dossiers. It reads:

> Harvey Metcalfe will arrive in England on the morning of June 21st on board the QE2, docking at Southampton. He has already reserved the Trafalgar Suite for his crossing and booked a Rolls Royce from Guy Salmon to take him to Claridge's. He will stay there for two weeks in the Royal Suite and he has his own debenture tickets for every day of the Wimbledon Championships. When they are over he flies to Monte Carlo to stay on his yacht *Messenger Boy* for another two weeks. He then returns to London and Claridge's to see his filly, Rosalie, run in the King George VI and Queen Elizabeth Stakes. He has a private box at Ascot for all five days of Ascot Week. He returns to America on a Pan American jumbo jet from London Heathrow on July 29th, flight No. 009 at 11.15 to Logan International Airport, Boston.'

The others attached page 38A to their dossiers, aware once again how much detailed research Stephen had undertaken. James was beginning to feel ill, and it certainly was not the excellent salmon sandwiches that were causing his discomfort.

'The next decision to be taken,' said Stephen, 'is to allocate the times during Metcalfe's trip to Europe when each plan will be put into operation. Robin, which section would you prefer?'

'Monte Carlo,' said Robin without hesitation. 'I need to catch the bastard off his home ground.'

'Anyone else want Monte Carlo?'

Nobody spoke.

'Which would you prefer, Jean-Pierre?'

'I'd like Wimbledon fortnight.'

'Any other takers?'

Again, nobody spoke. Stephen continued:

'I'm keen to have the Ascot slot myself and the short time before he returns to America. What about you, James?'

'It won't make any difference what period I have,' said James rather sheepishly.

'Right,' said Stephen.

Everybody, except James, seemed to be warming to the exercise.

'Now expenses. Have all of you brought your cheques for $10,000? I think it's wise to think in dollars as that was the currency Harvey Metcalfe worked in.'

Each member of the Team passed over a cheque to Stephen. At least, thought James, this is something I can do as well as the others.

'Expenses to date?'

Each passed a chit to Stephen again and he began to work out figures on his stylish little HP 65 calculator, the digits glowing red in the dimly-lit room.

'The shares cost us $1 million. Expenses to date $142, so Mr Metcalfe is in debt to us to the tune of $1,000,142. Not a penny more and not a penny less,' he repeated. 'Now to our individual plans. We will take them in the order of execution.' Stephen was pleased with that word. 'Jean-Pierre, Robin, myself and finally James. The floor is yours, Jean-Pierre.'

Jean-Pierre opened a large envelope and took out four sets of documents. He was determined to show that he had the measure of Stephen as well as of Harvey Metcalfe. He handed round photographs and road maps of the West End and Mayfair. Each street was marked with a number, indicating how many minutes it took to walk. Jean-Pierre explained his plan in great detail, starting with the crucial meeting he had had with David Stein, and ending with the roles the others would have to carry out.

'All of you will be needed on the day. Robin will be the journalist, James the representative from Sotheby's, and Stephen, you will act as the purchaser. You must practise speaking English with a German accent. I shall also require two tickets for the whole of Wimbledon fortnight on the Centre Court opposite Harvey Metcalfe's debenture box.'

Jean-Pierre consulted his notes.

'That is to say, opposite box No. 17. Can you arrange that, James?'

'No problem. I'll have a word with Mike Gibson, the Club referee, in the morning.'

'Good. Finally, then, you must all learn to operate

these little boxes of tricks. They are called Pye Pocket-fones and don't forget that the use and ownership of them are illegal.'

Jean-Pierre produced four miniature sets and handed three to Stephen.

'Any questions?'

There was a general murmur of approval. There were going to be no loose ends in Jean-Pierre's plan.

'My congratulations,' said Stephen. 'That should get us off to a good start. Now, how about you, Robin?'

Robin relayed the story of his fourteen days. He reported on his meeting with the specialist, and explained the toxic effects of anticholinesterase drugs.

'This one will be hard to pull off; we'll have to be patient and wait for the right opportunity. But, we must stay prepared every moment Metcalfe is in Monte Carlo.'

'Where will we be staying in Monte Carlo?' asked James. 'I usually go to the Metropole. Better not make it there.'

'No, it's all right, James, I have provisional reservations at the Hôtel de Paris from June 29th to July 4th. However, before that you are all to attend several working sessions at St Thomas's Hospital.'

Diaries were consulted, and a series of meetings agreed upon.

'Here is a copy of Houston's *Short Textbook of Medicine* for each of you. You must all read the chapter on severe cuts and bruises. I don't want any of you to stick out like sore thumbs when we're all dressed in white. You, Stephen, will come to Harley Street the week after next for an intensive medical course, as you must be totally convincing as a doctor.'

Robin had chosen Stephen because he felt that with his academic mind he would pick up the most in the short time available.

'Jean-Pierre, you must attend a gaming club every evening for the next month and learn exactly how baccarat and blackjack are played, and how to continue playing for several hours at a time without losing money. It'll help if you get hold of Peter Arnold's *The Encyclopedia of Gambling* from Hatchards. James, you will learn to drive a small van through the rush hour traffic, and you are also to report to Harley Street next week so that we can try a dry run together.'

All eyes were wide open. If they pulled that one off they could do anything. Robin could see the anxiety in their faces.

'Don't worry,' he said, 'my profession has been carried on by witch-doctors for a thousand years. People never argue when they're confronted with a trained man, and you, Stephen, are going to be a trained man.'

Stephen nodded. Academics could be equally naïve. Hadn't that been exactly what had happened to all of them with Prospecta Oil?

'Remember,' said Robin, 'Stephen's comment at the bottom of page 33 of the dossier . . . "At all times we must think like Harvey Metcalfe".'

Robin gave a few more details of how certain rocedures were to be carried out. He then answered demanding questions for twenty-eight minutes. Finally, Jean-Pierre softened:

'I thought none of you would beat me, but Robin's plan is brilliant. If we get the timing right we'll only need an ounce of luck.'

James was beginning to feel distinctly uneasy as his time drew nearer. He rather wished he had never accepted the invitation to dinner in the first place and regretted being the one to urge the others to take up Stephen's challenge. At least the duties he had been given in the first two operations were well within his scope.

'Well, gentlemen,' said Stephen, 'you've both risen admirably to the occasion, but my proposals will make more demands on you.'

Stephen began to reveal the fruits of his research during the past two weeks and the substance of his plan. They all felt rather like students in the presence of a professor. Stephen's lecturing tone was not intentional; it was a manner he had developed, and like so many academics, he was unable to switch it off in private company. He produced a calendar for Trinity Term and outlined how the university weeks worked, the role of its Chancellor, Vice-Chancellor, the Registrar and the Secretary of the University Chest. Like Jean-Pierre, he supplied maps to each member of the Team, this time of Oxford. He had carefully marked a route from the Sheldonian Theatre to Lincoln

College, and from Lincoln to the Randolph Hotel, and had drawn up a contingency plan if Harvey Metcalfe insisted on using his car, despite the one-way system.

'Robin, you must study what the Vice-Chancellor does at Encaenia. It won't be like Cambridge; the two universities do everything similarly but not identically. You must know the route he's likely to take on that day and his habits backwards. I've arranged for a room at Lincoln to be at your disposal on the final day. Jean-Pierre, you will study and master the duties of the Registrar at Oxford and know the alternative route marked on your map so that you never come face to face with Robin. James, you must know how the Secretary of the University Chest goes about his work – the location of his office, which banks he deals with and how the cheques are cashed. You must also know the routes he's likely to take on the day of Encaenia as if they were part of your father's estate. I have the easiest role on the day, because I will be myself in everything but name. You must all learn how to address each other correctly and we'll have a dress rehearsal in the ninth week of term, on a Tuesday when the university is fairly quiet. Any questions?'

Silence reigned, but it was a silence of respect. All could see that Stephen's operation would demand split-second timing and that they would have to run through it several times to cover all contingencies. But if they were convincing they could hardly fail.

'Now, the Ascot part of my plan is simple. I will

only want Jean-Pierre and James inside the Members' Enclosure. I shall need two Enclosure tickets which I'm hoping you can acquire, James.'

'You mean badges, Stephen,' corrected James.

'Oh, do I?' said Stephen. 'I also require someone in London to send the necessary telegram. That'll have to be you, Robin.'

'Agreed,' said Robin.

For nearly an hour the others asked several questions of detail in order to be as familiar with the plan as Stephen was.

James asked no questions and his mind began to drift, hoping the earth would swallow him up. He even began to wish that he had never met Anne, although she was hardly to blame. In fact, he could not wait to see her again. What was he going to say when they . . .

'James, wake up,' said Stephen sharply. 'We're all waiting.'

Six eyes were now fixed on him. They had produced the ace of hearts, diamonds and spades. But had he the ace of trumps? James was flustered and poured himself another drink.

'You bloody upper-class twit,' said Jean-Pierre, 'you haven't got an idea, have you?'

'Well, actually, I've given the problem a lot of thought, but nothing seemed to come.'

'Useless – worse than useless,' said Robin.

James was stammering helplessly. Stephen cut him short.

'Now listen, James, and listen carefully. We meet here again in twenty-one days' time. By then we must know each other's plans backwards. One error could blow the whole thing. Do you understand?'

James nodded – he was determined not to let them down in that.

'And what's more,' said Stephen firmly, 'you must have your own plan ready for scrutiny. Is that also clear?'

'Yes,' mumbled James unhappily.

'Any other questions?' said Stephen.

There were none.

'Right. We go through the three individual operations again in full.'

Stephen ignored the muttered protests.

'Remember, we're up against a man who isn't used to being beaten. We won't get a second chance.'

For an hour and a half they went through the details of each operation in the order of action. First, Jean-Pierre during Wimbledon fortnight: second, Robin in Monte Carlo: third, Stephen during and after Ascot.

It was late and they were all weary when they finally rose from the table. They departed sleepily, each with several tasks to carry out before their next meeting. Each went his separate way, but all were due to meet again the following Friday in the Jericho Theatre of St Thomas's Hospital.

8

THE NEXT TWENTY DAYS turned out to be an exacting time for all four of them. Each had to master the other plans as well as organising his own. Friday brought them all together for the first of many sessions at St Thomas's Hospital, which would have been entirely successful if James had managed to stay on his feet. It was not the sight of blood that daunted him – the sight of the knife was enough. The only virtue from James's standpoint was that he once again avoided having to explain why he had not come up with any ideas of his own.

The next week was almost full time, with Stephen in Harley Street taking a potted course in one particular field of medicine at a fairly high level.

James spent several hours driving an old van through the heavy traffic from St Thomas's to Harley Street, preparing for his final test in Monte Carlo, which he felt could only be considerably easier. He also returned to Oxford for a week, learning how the Secretary of the University Chest's office operated, and also studying the movements of the Secretary himself, Mr Caston.

Jean-Pierre, at a cost to Mr Metcalfe of $25 and a 48-hour wait, became an overseas member of The Claremont, London's most distinguished gaming club, and passed his evenings watching the wealthy and lazy play baccarat and blackjack, their stakes often reaching $1,000. After three weeks of watching he ventured to join the Golden Nugget casino in Soho, where the stakes rarely exceeded £5. By the end of the month he had played for 56 hours, but so conservatively that he was only showing a small loss.

James's overriding worry was still his personal contribution. The more he grappled with the problem, the less he came to grips with it. He turned it over and over in his mind, even when he was travelling through London at high speed. One night after returning the van to Carnie's in Lots Road, Chelsea, he drove his Alfa Romeo over to Anne's flat by the river, wondering if he dared confide in her.

Anne was preparing a special meal for James. She was aware that he not only appreciated good food, but had taken it for granted all his life. The home-made gazpacho was smelling good and the *Coq au vin* was all but ready. Lately she had found herself avoiding modelling assignments out of London as she did not care to be away from James for any length of time. She was also conscious that he was the first man for some time that she would have been willing to go to bed with – and to date he had made no efforts to leave the dining-room.

James arrived carrying a bottle of Beaune Montée

Rouge 1971 – even his wine cellar was fast diminishing. He only hoped it would last long enough for the plans to come to fruition. Not that he felt an automatic right to a part of the bounty while he failed to contribute his own plan.

Anne looked stunning. She was wearing a long black dress of some soft material that tantalised James with the reticence with which it outlined her shape. She wore no makeup or jewellery, and her heavy hair gleamed in the candlelight. The meal was a triumph for Anne, and James started wanting her badly. She seemed nervous, spilling a little ground coffee as she filtered two strong tiny cups. What was in her mind? He did not want to blunder with unwanted attentions. James had had much more practice at being loved than at being in love. He was used to adulation, to ending up in bed with girls who made him shudder in the cold clear light of morning. Anne affected him in an entirely different way. He wanted to be close to her, to hold her and to love her. Above all, he wanted her to be there in the morning.

Anne cleared away the supper, avoiding James's eye, and they settled down to brandy and Lena Horne singing 'I Get Along Without You Very Well'. She sat, hands clasped round her knees on the floor at James's feet, staring into the fire. Tentatively, he put out a hand and stroked her hair. She sat unresponsive for a moment and then bent her head back and stretched out her arm to bring his face down to hers. He responded, leaning forward and stroking her cheek and nose with his mouth, holding her head in his hands, his fingers gently exploring her ears and neck. Her skin smelled faintly of jasmine and her open mouth glinted in the firelight as she smiled up at him. He kissed her and slid his hands down on to her body. She felt soft and slight under his hands. He caressed her breasts gently, and moved down beside her, his body pressing against hers. Wordlessly, he reached behind her and unzipped her dress and watched it fall to the ground. He stood up, his eyes never leaving hers, and undressed quickly. She glanced at his body and smiled shyly.

'Darling James,' she said softly.

After they had made love, like two people in love and not as lovers, Anne settled her head on James's shoulder and stroked the hair on his chest with a fingertip.

'What's the matter, James? I know I'm rather shy. But it will . . .'

'You were beautiful. God knows, you were perfect. That's not the problem . . . Anne, I have to tell you something, so just lie back and listen.'

'You're married.'

'No, it's far worse than that.' James lay silent for a moment, lit a cigarette and inhaled deeply. There are occasions in life when revelation is made easier by circumstance; it all came out in an unco-ordinated jumble. 'Anne darling, I've made a bloody fool of myself by investing a vast sum of money with a bunch of crooks who've stolen it. I haven't even told my family – they'd be terribly distressed if they ever found out. To make matters better or worse, I've got myself involved with three other chaps who found themselves in the same predicament, and now we're all trying to get our money back. They're nice fellows, full of bright ideas, but I haven't a clue how to begin to keep my part of the bargain. What with the worry of being £150,000 down the drain and having to keep racking my brain for a good idea, I'm half frantic. You're the only thing that's kept me sane the last month.'

'James, start again, but slower this time,' said Anne.

Thus James revealed the entire history of Prospecta Oil from his meeting with David Kesler at Annabel's to his invitation to dine with Stephen Bradley at Magdalen, finally explaining why he had been driving a hired van like a maniac through the rush hour. The only detail James left out was the name of their intended victim, as he felt that by withholding that he was not completely violating his bond of secrecy with the rest of the Team.

Anne inhaled very deeply.

'I hardly know what to say. It's incredible. It's so unbelievable that I believe every word.'

'I feel better just for telling someone, but it would be terrible if the others ever found out.'

'James, you know I won't say a word to anyone. I'm just so very sorry you're in such a mess. You must let me see if I can come up with an idea. Why don't we work together without letting the others know?'

James felt better already.

She began stroking the inside of his leg. Twenty minutes later, they sank into a blissful sleep, dreaming up plans to defeat Harvey Metcalfe.

9

In Lincoln, Massachusetts, Harvey Metcalfe began to prepare for his annual trip to England. He intended to enjoy himself thoroughly and expensively. He had plans for transferring some more money from his numbered accounts in Zürich to Barclays Bank, Lombard Street, ready to buy yet another stallion from one of the Irish stables to join his stud in Kentucky. Arlene had decided not to accompany him on this trip: she did not care too much for Ascot and even less for Monte Carlo. In any case, it gave her the chance to spend some time with her ailing mother in Vermont, who still had little respect for her prosperous son-in-law.

Harvey checked with his secretary that all the arrangements for the holiday had been completed. There was never any need to check up on Miss Fish, it was simply a habit on Harvey's part. Miss Fish had been with him for twenty-five years, from the days when he had first taken over the Lincoln Trust. Most of the respectable staff had walked out on Harvey's arrival, or shortly afterwards, but Miss Fish had remained, nursing in her unalluring bosom ever fainter hopes of eventual marriage to Harvey. By the time Arlene appeared on the scene, Miss Fish was an able and completely discreet accomplice without whom Harvey could hardly have operated. He paid her accordingly, so she swallowed her chagrin at the thought of another Mrs Metcalfe, and stayed put.

Miss Fish had already booked the short flight to New York and the Trafalgar Suite on the *QE2*. The trip across the Atlantic was almost the only total break Harvey ever had from the telephone or telex. The bank staff were instructed to contact the great liner only in dire emergency. On arrival at Southampton it would be the usual Rolls Royce to London and the private suite at Claridge's, which Harvey judged to be one of the last English hotels, along with the Connaught and Browns, where his money allowed him to mix with what he called 'class'.

Harvey flew to New York in high good humour, relaxing and drinking a couple of Manhattans on the way. The arrangements on board ship were as impeccable as ever. The Captain, Peter Jackson, always invited the occupant of the Trafalgar Suite or the Queen Anne Suite to join him on the first night out at the Captain's table. At $1,250 a day for the suites it could hardly be described as an extravagant gesture on Cunard's part. On such occasions, Harvey was always on his best behaviour, although even that struck most onlookers as somewhat brash.

One of the Italian stewards was detailed to arrange a little diversion for Harvey, preferably in the shape of a tall blonde with a large bosom. The going rate for the night was $200, but the Italian could charge Harvey $250 and still get away with it. At 5 ft 7 in and 227 lb, Harvey's chances of picking up a young thing in the discothèque were slender, and by the time he had lashed out on drinks and dinner, he could have spent almost as much money and achieved absolutely nothing. Men in Harvey's position do not have time for that sort of failure and expect everything in life to have its price. As the voyage was only five nights, the steward was able to keep Harvey fully occupied, although he felt it was just as well that Harvey had not booked a three-week Mediterranean cruise.

Harvey spent his days catching up with the latest novels he had been told he must read and also taking a little exercise, a swim in the morning and a painful session in the gymnasium during the afternoon. He reckoned to lose 10 lb during the crossing, which was pleasing, but somehow Claridge's always managed to put it back on again before he returned to the States. Fortunately, his suits were tailored by Bernard Weatherill of Dover Street, Mayfair, who by dint of near-genius and impeccable skill made him look well-built rather than distinctly fat. At £300 per suit it was the least he could expect.

When the five days were drawing to a close, Harvey was more than ready for land again. The women, the exercise and the fresh air had quite revived him and he had lost all of 11 lb on the crossing.

He felt a good deal of this must have come off the night before, which he had spent with a young Indian girl who had made the *Kama Sutra* look like a Boy Scout's handbook.

One of the advantages of real wealth is that menial tasks can always be left to someone else. Harvey could no longer remember when he last packed or unpacked a suitcase, and when the ship docked at the Ocean Terminal it came as no surprise to him to discover everything packed and ready for Customs – a $100 bill for the head steward seemed to bring men in little white coats from every direction.

Harvey always enjoyed disembarking at Southampton. The English were a race he liked, though he feared he would never understand them. He found them always so willing to be trodden on by the rest of the world. Since the Second World War, they had relinquished their colonial power in a way no American business man would have ever considered for an exit from his own boardroom. Harvey had finally given up trying to understand the British way of business during the 1967 devaluation of the pound. Every jumped-up speculator on the face of the globe had taken advantage of the inside knowledge. Harvey knew on the Tuesday morning that Harold Wilson was going to devalue any time after Friday, 5 pm Greenwich Mean Time, when the Bank of England closed for the weekend. On the Thursday even the junior clerk at the Lincoln Trust knew. It was no wonder that the Old Lady of Threadneedle

Street was raped and despoiled of an estimated £1½ billion over the next few days. Harvey had often thought that if only the British could liven up their boardrooms and get their tax structure right, they might end up being the richest nation in the world, instead of a nation which, as *The Economist* had stated, could now be taken over by the Arabs with ninety days of oil revenue. While the British flirted with socialism and still retained a *folie de grandeur*, they seemed doomed to sink into insignificance. But still Harvey adored them.

He strode down the gangplank like a man with a purpose. Harvey had never learnt to relax completely, even when he was on vacation. He could spend just about four days away from the world, but if he had been left on the *QE2* any longer he would have been negotiating to buy the Cunard Steamship Company. Harvey had once met the Chairman of Cunard, Vic Matthews, at Ascot and had been baffled to hear him harking on the prestige and reputation of the company. Harvey had expected him to brag about the balance sheet. Prestige interested Harvey, of course, but he always let people know how much he was worth first.

Customs clearance was given with the usual speed. Harvey never had anything of consequence to declare on his European trips, and after they had checked two of his Gucci suitcases, the other seven were allowed through without inspection. The chauffeur opened the door of the white Rolls Royce Corniche. The vehicle sped through Hampshire and into London in a little over two hours, which gave Harvey time for a rest before dinner.

Albert, the head doorman at Claridge's, stood smartly to attention and saluted as the car drew up. He knew Harvey of old and was aware that he had come, as usual, for Wimbledon and Ascot. Albert would undoubtedly receive a 50 pence tip every time he opened the white Rolls door. Harvey didn't know the difference between a 50 pence and 10 pence piece – a difference which Albert had welcomed since the introduction of decimalisation in Britain. Moreover, Harvey always gave Albert £5 at the end of Wimbledon fortnight if an American won the singles title. An American invariably reached the finals, so Albert always placed a bet with Ladbrokes on the other finalist and won either way. Gambling appealed to both Harvey and Albert; only the sums involved were different.

Albert arranged for the luggage to be sent up to the Royal Suite, which during the year had already been occupied by King Constantine of Greece, Princess Grace of Monaco and Emperor Hailé Selassie of Ethiopia, all with considerably more conviction than Harvey. But Harvey still considered that his annual holiday at Claridge's was more assured than theirs.

The Royal Suite is on the first floor at Claridge's and can be reached by an elegant sweeping staircase from the ground floor, or by a commodious lift with its own seat. Harvey always took the lift up and walked down. At least that way he convinced himself he was taking some exercise. The suite itself consists of four rooms: a small dressing-room, a bedroom, a bathroom, and an elegant drawing-room overlooking Brook Street. The furniture and pictures make it possible for you to believe that you are still in Victorian England. Only the telephone and television dispel the illusion. The room is large enough to be used for cocktail parties or by visiting heads of state to entertain large parties. Henry Kissinger had received Harold Wilson there only the week before. Harvey enjoyed the thought of that. It was about as close as he was going to get to either man.

After a shower and change of clothes, Harvey glanced through his waiting mail and telexes from the bank, which were all routine. He took a short nap before going down to dine in the main restaurant.

There in the large foyer was the usual string quartet, looking like out-of-work refugees from Hungary. Harvey even recognised the four musicians. He had reached that time in life when he did not like change; the management of Claridge's, aware that the average age of their customers was over fifty, catered accordingly. François, the head waiter, showed Harvey to his usual table.

Harvey managed a little shrimp cocktail and a medium fillet steak with a bottle of Mouton Cadet. As he leaned forward to study the sweets trolley, he did not notice the four young men eating in the alcove on the far side of the room.

Stephen, Robin, Jean-Pierre and James all had an excellent view of Harvey Metcalfe. He would have had to bend double and move slightly backwards to have any sight of them.

'Not exactly what I expected,' commented Stephen.

'Put on a bit of weight since those photographs you supplied,' said Jean-Pierre.

'Hard to believe he's real after all this preparation,' remarked Robin.

'The bastard's real enough,' said Jean-Pierre, 'and a million dollars richer because of our stupidity.'

James said nothing. He was still in disgrace after his futile efforts and excuses at the last full briefing, although the other three had to admit that they did receive good service wherever they went with him. Claridge's was proving to be no exception.

'Wimbledon tomorrow,' said Jean-Pierre. 'I wonder who'll win the first round?'

'You will of course,' chipped in James, hoping to soften Jean-Pierre's acid comments about his own feeble efforts.

'We can only win your round, James, if we ever fill in an entry form.'

James sank back into silence.

'I must say, looking at the size of Metcalfe we ought to get away with your plan, Robin,' said Stephen.

'If he doesn't die of cirrhosis of the liver before we're given the chance,' replied Robin. 'How do you feel about Oxford now you've seen him, Stephen?'

'I don't know yet. I'll feel better when I've belled the cat at Ascot. I want to hear him speak, watch him in his normal environment, get the feel of the man. You can't do all that from the other side of the dining-room.'

'You may not have to wait too long. This time tomorrow we may know everything we need to know – or all be in West End Central Police Station,' said Robin. 'Maybe we won't even pass Go, let alone collect £200.'

'We have to – I can't afford bail,' said Jean-Pierre.

When Harvey had downed a large snifter of Rémy Martin VSOP he left his table, slipping the head waiter a crisp new pound note.

'The bastard,' said Jean-Pierre with great feeling. 'It's bad enough knowing he's stolen our money, but it's humiliating having to watch him spend it.'

The four of them prepared to leave, the object of their outing achieved. Stephen paid the bill and carefully added the sum to the list of expenses against Harvey Metcalfe. Then they left the hotel separately and as inconspicuously as possible. Only James found this difficult as all the waiters and porters insisted on saying 'Good night, my lord.'

Harvey took a stroll round Berkeley Square and did not even notice the tall young man slip into the doorway of Moyses Stevens, the florists, for fear of being spotted by him. Harvey could never resist asking a policeman the way to Buckingham Palace, just to compare his reaction with that of a New York cop, leaning on a lamp post, chewing gum, holster on hip. As Lenny Bruce had said on being deported from England, 'Your pigs is so much better than our pigs'. Yes, Harvey liked England.

He arrived back at Claridge's at about 11.15 pm, showered and went to bed – a large double bed with that glorious feel of clean sheets. There would be no women for him at Claridge's or, if there were, it would be the last time he would find the Royal Suite available to him during Wimbledon or Ascot. The room moved just a little, but then after five days on an ocean liner it was unlikely to be still for a couple of nights. He slept well in spite of it, without a worry on his mind.

10

HARVEY ROSE AT at 7.30 am, a habit he could not break, but he did allow himself the holiday luxury of breakfast in bed. Ten minutes after he had called room service, the waiter arrived with a trolley laden with half a grapefruit, bacon and eggs, toast, steaming black coffee, a copy of the previous day's *Wall Street Journal*, and the morning edition of *The Times*, *Financial Times* and *International Herald Tribune*.

Harvey was not sure how he would have survived on a European trip without the *International Herald Tribune*, known in the trade as the 'Trib'. This unique paper, published in Paris, is jointly owned by the *New York Times* and the *Washington Post*. Although only one edition of 120,000 copies is printed, it does not go to press until the New York Stock Exchange is closed. Therefore, no American need wake up in Europe out of touch. When the *New York Herald Tribune* folded in 1966, Harvey had been among those who advised John H. Whitney to keep the *International Herald Tribune* going in Europe. Once again, Harvey's judgment had been proved sound. The *International Herald Tribune* went on to absorb its faltering rival, the *New York*

Times, which had never been a success in Europe. From then on the paper went from strength to strength.

Harvey ran an experienced eye down the Stock Exchange lists in the *Wall Street Journal* and the *Financial Times*. His bank now held very few shares as he, like Jim Slater in England, had suspected that the Dow-Jones Index would collapse and had therefore gone almost entirely liquid, holding only some South African gold shares and a few well-chosen stocks about which he had inside information. The only monetary transaction he cared to undertake with the market so shaky was to sell the dollar short and buy gold, so that he caught the dollar on the way down and gold on the way up. There were already rumours in Washington that the President of the United States had been advised by his Secretary of the Treasury, George Schultz, to allow the American people to buy gold on the open market later that year or early the following year. Harvey had been buying gold for the past fifteen years: all the President was going to do was to stop him from breaking the law. Harvey was of the opinion that the moment the Americans were able to buy gold, the bubble would burst and the price of gold would recede – the real money would be made while the speculators anticipated the rise, and Harvey intended to be out of gold well before it came on to the American market. Once the President made it legal, Harvey couldn't see a profit in it.

Harvey checked the commodity market in Chicago. He had made a killing in copper a year before. Inside information from an African ambassador had made this possible – information the ambassador had imparted to too many people. Harvey had not been surprised to read that he had later been recalled to his homeland and shot.

He could never resist checking the price of Prospecta Oil, now at an all-time low of $\$\frac{1}{8}$: there could be no trading in the stock, simply because there would only be sellers and no buyers. The shares were virtually worthless. He smiled sardonically and turned to the sports page of *The Times*.

Rex Bellamy's article on the forthcoming Wimbledon Championships tipped John Newcombe as favourite and Jimmy Connors, the new American star who had just won the Italian Open, as the best outside bet. The British press wanted the 39-year-old Ken Rosewall to win. Harvey could well remember the epic final between Rosewall and Drobny in 1954, which had run to 58 games. Like most of the crowd, he had supported the 33-year-old Drobny, who had finally won after three hours of play, 13–11, 4–6, 6–2, 9–7. This time, Harvey wanted history to repeat itself and Rosewall to win, though he felt the popular Australian's chance had slipped by during the ten years when the professionals were barred from Wimbledon. Still, he saw no reason why the fortnight should not be a pleasant break, and perhaps there might be an American victor even if Rosewall couldn't manage it.

Harvey had time for a quick glance at the art reviews before finishing his breakfast, leaving the papers strewn over the floor. The quiet Regency furniture, the elegant service and the Royal Suite did nothing for Harvey's habits. He padded into the bathroom for a shave and a shower. Arlene told him that most people did it the other way round – showered and then ate breakfast. But, as Harvey pointed out to her, most people did things the other way round from him, and look where it got them.

Harvey habitually spent the first morning of Wimbledon fortnight visiting the Summer Exhibition at the Royal Academy in Piccadilly. He would then follow this with visits to most of the West End's major galleries – Agnew's, Tooths, the Marlborough, Wildenstein – all within easy walking distance of Claridge's. This morning would be no exception. If Harvey was anything, he was a creature of habit, which was something the Team were quickly learning.

After he had dressed and bawled out room service for not leaving enough whisky in his cabinet, he headed down the staircase, emerged through the swing door on to Davies Street and strode off towards Berkeley Square. Harvey did not observe a studious young man with a two-way radio on the other side of the road.

'He's left the hotel by the Davies Street entrance,' said Stephen quietly to his little Pye Pocketfone, 'and he's heading towards you, James.'

'I'll pick him up as he comes into Berkeley Square, Stephen. Robin, can you hear me?'

'Yes.'

'I'll let you know as soon as I spot him. You stay put at the Royal Academy.'

'Right you are,' said Robin.

Harvey strolled round Berkeley Square, down into Piccadilly and through the Palladian arches of Burlington House. With a bad grace, he stood and queued with the assorted humanity in the forecourt, shuffling past the Astronomical Society and the Society of Antiquaries. He did not see another young man opposite standing in the entrance of the Chemical Society, deep in a copy of *Chemistry in Britain*. Finally, Harvey made it up the red-carpeted ramp into the Royal Academy itself. He handed the cashier £5.00 for a season ticket, realising that he would probably want to return at least three or four times. He spent the rest of the morning studying the 1,182 pictures, none of which had been exhibited anywhere else in the world before the opening day, in accordance with the stringent rules of the Academy. Despite that ruling, the Hanging Committee had still had over 5,000 pictures to choose from.

On the opening day of the exhibition the month before, Harvey had acquired, through his agent, a watercolour by Alfred Daniels of the House of

Commons for £350 and two oils by Bernard Dunstan of English provincial scenes for £125 each. The Summer Exhibition was still, in Harvey's estimation, the best value in the world. Even if he did not want to keep all the pictures himself, they made wonderful presents when he returned to the States. The Daniels reminded him of a Lowry he had bought some twenty years before at the Academy for £80: that had turned out to be another shrewd investment.

Harvey made a special point of looking at the Bernard Dunstans in the Exhibition. Of course, they were all sold. Dunstan was one of the artists whose pictures always sold in the first minutes of the opening day. Although Harvey had not been in London on that day, he had had no difficulty in buying what he wanted. He had planted a man at the front of the queue, who had obtained a catalogue and marked those artists he knew Harvey could resell easily if he made a mistake and keep if his judgment were right. When the exhibition opened on the dot of 10 am, the agent had gone straight to the purchasing desk and acquired the five or six pictures he had marked in the catalogue before he or anyone other than the Academicians had seen them. Harvey studied his vicarious purchases with care. On this occasion he was happy to keep them all. If there had been one that did not quite fit in with his collection, he would have returned the picture for resale, undertaking to purchase it if nobody else showed any interest. In twenty years he had acquired over a hundred pictures by this method and returned a mere dozen, never once failing to secure a resale. Harvey had a system for everything.

At 1 pm, after a thoroughly satisfactory morning, he left the Royal Academy. The white Rolls Royce was waiting for him in the forecourt.

'Wimbledon.'

'Shit.'

'What did you say?' queried Stephen.

'S.H.I.T. He's gone to Wimbledon, so today's down the drain,' said Robin.

That meant Harvey would not return to Claridge's until at least seven or eight that evening. A rota had been fixed for watching him, and Robin accordingly picked up his Rover 3500 V8 from a parking meter in St James's Square and headed off to Wimbledon. James had obtained two tickets for every day of the Championships opposite Harvey Metcalfe's debenture box.

Robin arrived at Wimbledon a few minutes after Harvey and took his seat in the Centre Court, far enough back in the sea of faces to remain inconspicuous. The atmosphere was already building up for the opening match. Wimbledon seemed to be getting more popular every year and the Centre Court was packed to capacity. Princess Alexandra and the Prime Minister were in the Royal Box awaiting the entrance of the gladiators. The little green scoreboards at the southern end of the court were flashing up the names of Kodeš and Stewart as the umpire took his seat on the high chair in the middle of the court directly overlooking the net. The crowd began to applaud as the two athletes, both dressed in white, entered the court carrying four rackets each. Wimbledon does not allow its competitors to dress in any colour other than white, although they had relaxed a little by permitting the trimming of the ladies' dresses to be coloured.

Robin enjoyed the opening match between Kodeš and an unseeded player from the United States, who gave the champion a hard time before losing to the Czech 6–3, 6–4, 9–7. Robin was sorry when Harvey decided to leave in the middle of an exciting doubles match. Back to duty, he told himself, and followed the white Rolls at a safe distance to Claridge's. On arriving, he telephoned James's flat, which was being used as the Team's headquarters in London, and briefed Stephen.

'May as well call it a day,' said Stephen. 'We'll try again tomorrow. Poor old Jean-Pierre's heart-beat reached 150 this morning. He may not last many days of false alarms.'

When Harvey left Claridge's the following morning he went through Berkeley Square into Bruton Street and then on into Bond Street, stopping only 50 yards from Jean-Pierre's gallery. But he turned east instead of west and slipped into Agnew's, where he had an appointment with Sir Geoffrey Agnew, the head of the family firm, for news of Impressionist pictures on the market. Sir Geoffrey was anxious to get away to another meeting and could only spend a few minutes with Harvey. He had nothing worthwhile to offer him.

Harvey left Agnew's soon afterwards clutching a small consolation prize of a maquette by Rodin, a mere bagatelle at £800.

'He's coming out,' said Robin, 'and heading in the right direction.' Jean-Pierre held his breath, but Harvey stopped once again, this time at the Marlborough Gallery to study their latest exhibition of Barbara Hepworth. He spent over an hour appreciating her beautiful work, but decided the prices were now outrageous. He had bought two Hepworths only ten years before for £800. The Marlborough was now asking between £7,000 and £10,000 for her work. So he left and continued up Bond Street.

'Jean-Pierre?'

'Yes,' replied a nervous voice.

'He's reached the corner of Conduit Street and he's about 50 yards away from your front door.'

Jean-Pierre prepared his window, removing the Graham Sutherland watercolour of the Thames and the Boatman.

'He's turned left, the bastard,' said James, who was stationed opposite the gallery. 'He's walking down Bruton Street on the right-hand side.'

Jean-Pierre put the Sutherland back on the easel in the window and retired to the lavatory, muttering to himself:

'I can't cope with two shits at once.'

Harvey meanwhile stepped into an inconspicuous entrance on Bruton Street and climbed the stairs to Tooths, more hopeful of finding something in a gallery which had become famous for its Impressionists. A Klee, a Picasso and two Salvador Dalis – not what Harvey was looking for. Though very well executed, the Klee was not as good as the one in his dining-room in Lincoln, Massachusetts. Besides, it might not fit in with any of Arlene's decorative schemes. Nicholas Tooth, the managing director, promised to keep his eyes open and ring Harvey at Claridge's should anything of interest turn up.

'He's on the move again, but I think he's heading back to Claridge's.'

James willed him to turn round and return in the direction of Jean-Pierre's gallery, but Harvey strode purposefully towards Berkeley Square, only making a detour to the O'Hana Gallery. Albert, the head door-man, had told him there was a Renoir in the window, and indeed there was. But it was only a half-finished canvas which Renoir had obviously used for a practice run or had disliked enough to leave unfinished. Harvey was curious as to the price and entered the gallery.

'£30,000,' said the assistant, as if it was $10 and a snip at that.

Harvey whistled through the gap between his front teeth. It never ceased to amaze him that an inferior picture by a first-rank name could fetch £30,000 and an outstanding picture by an artist with no established reputation could only bring a few hundred dollars. He thanked the assistant and left.

'A pleasure, Mr Metcalfe.'

Harvey was always flattered by people who remembered his name. But hell, they ought to remember – he had purchased a Monet from them last year for £62,000.

'He's definitely on his way back to the hotel,' said James.

Harvey spent only a few minutes in Claridge's, picking up one of their famous specially prepared luncheon hampers of caviar, beef, ham and cheese sandwiches and chocolate cake for later consumption at Wimbledon.

James was next on the rota for the Championships and decided to take Anne with him. Why not – she knew the truth. It was Ladies' Day and the turn of Billie Jean King, the vivacious American champion, to take the court. She was up against the unseeded American, Kathy May, who looked as if she was in for a rough time. The applause Billie Jean received was unworthy of her abilities, but for some reason she had never become a Wimbledon favourite. Harvey was accompanied by a guest who James thought had a faintly mid-European look.

'Which one is your victim?' asked Anne.

'He's almost exactly opposite us talking to the man in a light grey suit who looks like a government official from the EEC.'

'The short fat one?' asked Anne.

'Yes,' said James.

Whatever comments Anne made were interrupted by the umpire's call of 'Play' and everyone's attention focused on Billie Jean. It was exactly 2 pm.

'Kind of you to invite me to Wimbledon, Harvey,' said Jörg Birrer. 'I never seem to get the chance for much relaxation nowadays. You can't leave the market for more than a few hours without some panic breaking out somewhere in the world.'

'If you feel that way it's time for you to retire,' said Harvey.

'No one to take my place,' said Birrer. 'I've been chairman of the bank for ten years now and finding a successor is turning out to be my hardest task.'

'First game to Mrs King. Mrs King leads by one game to love in the first set.'

'Now, Harvey, I know you too well to expect this invitation to have been just for pleasure.'

'What an evil mind you have, Jörg.'

'In my profession I need it.'

'I just wanted to check how my three accounts stand and brief you on my plans for the next few months.'

'Game to Mrs King. Mrs King leads by two games to love in the first set.'

'Your No. 1 official account is a few thousand dollars in credit. Your numbered commodity account'

– at this point Birrer unfolded a small piece of unidentifiable paper with a set of neat figures printed on it – 'is short by $3,726,000, but you are holding 37,000 ounces of gold at today's selling price of $135 an ounce.'

'What's your advice on that?'

'Hold on, Harvey. I still think your President is either going to announce a new gold standard or allow your fellow-countrymen to buy gold on the open market some time next year.'

'That's my view too, but I'm still convinced we want to sell a few weeks before the masses come in. I have a theory about that.'

'I expect you're right, as usual, Harvey.'

'Game to Mrs King. Mrs King leads by three games to love in the first set.'

'What are your charges on my overdraft?'

'One-and-a-half per cent above inter-bank rate, which at present is 13.25, and therefore we're charging you 14.75 per cent per annum, while gold is rising in price at nearly 70 per cent per annum. It can't go on that way; but there are still a few months left in it.'

'OK,' said Harvey, 'hold on until November 1st and we'll review the position again then. Coded telex as usual. I don't know what the world would do without the Swiss.'

'Just take care, Harvey. Do you know there are more specialists in our police force on fraud than there are for homicide?'

'You worry about your end, Jörg, and I'll worry

about mine. The day I get uptight about a few underpaid bureaucrats from Zürich who haven't got any balls, I'll let you know. Now, enjoy your lunch and watch the game. We'll have a talk about the other account later.'

'Game to Mrs King. Mrs King leads by four games to love in the first set.'

'They're very deep in conversation,' said Anne. 'I can't believe they're enjoying the match.'

'He's probably trying to buy Wimbledon at cost price,' laughed James. 'The trouble with seeing the man every day is that one begins to have a certain respect for him. He's the most organised man I've ever come across. If he's like this on holiday, what the hell is he like at work?'

'I can't imagine,' said Anne.

'Game to Miss May. Mrs King leads by four games to one in the first set.'

'No wonder he's so overweight. Just look at him stuffing that cake down.' James lifted his Zeiss binoculars. 'Which reminds me to ask, darling, what have you brought for lunch?'

Anne dug into her hamper and unpacked a crisp salad in French bread for James. She contented herself with nibbling a stick of celery.

'Getting far too fat,' she explained. 'I'll never get into those winter clothes I'm supposed to be modelling next week.' She touched James's knee and smiled. 'It must be because I'm so happy.'

'Well, don't get too happy. I prefer you thin.'

'Game to Mrs King. Mrs King leads by five games to one in the first set.'

'This is going to be a walkover,' said James. 'It so often is in the opening match. People only come to see if the champion's in good form, and I think she'll be very hard to beat this year now she's after Helen Moody's record of eight Wimbledon championships.'

'Game and first set to Mrs King by six games to one. Mrs King leads one set to love. New balls, please. Miss May to serve.'

'Do we have to watch him all day?' asked Anne.

'Yes, we must make sure he returns to the hotel and doesn't change his plans suddenly or anything silly like that. If we miss our chance when he walks past Jean-Pierre's gallery, we may not get another one.'

'What do you do if he does decide to change his plans?'

'God knows, or to be more accurate, Stephen knows – he's the mastermind.'

'Game to Mrs King. Mrs King leads by one game to love in the second set.'

'Poor Miss May, she's about as successful as you are, James. How is the Jean-Pierre operation looking?'

'Awful. Metcalfe hasn't been anywhere near the gallery. He was within 30 yards of the window today and marched off in the opposite direction. Poor Jean-Pierre nearly had heart failure. But we're more hopeful of tomorrow. So far he seems to have covered Piccadilly and the top end of Bond Street, and the one thing we can be sure of with Harvey Metcalfe is that he's thorough. So he's almost bound to cover our bit of territory at one time or another.'

'You should all have taken out life insurance for $1 million, naming the other three as beneficiaries,' said Anne, 'and then if one of you had a heart attack, the others would all get their money back.'

'It's no laughing matter, Anne. It's bloody nerveracking while you're hanging around, especially when you have to wait for him to make all the moves.'

'Game to Mrs King. Mrs King leads by two games to love in the second set and by one set to love.'

'How about your own plan?'

'Nothing. Useless. And now we've started on the others I seem to have less time to concentrate on my own.'

'Why don't I seduce him?'

'Not a bad idea, but you'd have to be pretty special to get £100,000 out of him, when he can hang around outside the Hilton or in Shepherd Market and get it for £30. If there's one thing we've learnt about that gentleman it's that he expects value for money. At £30 a night it would take you just under fifteen years to repay my share, and I'm not sure the other three would be willing to wait that long. In fact, I'm not sure they'll wait another fifteen days.'

'We'll think of something, don't worry,' said Anne.

'Game to Miss May. Mrs King leads by two games to one and by one set to love.'

'Well, well. Miss May has managed another game. Excellent lunch, Harvey.'

'A Claridge's special,' said Harvey, 'so much better than getting caught up with the crowds in the restaurant where you can't even watch the tennis.'

'Billie Jean is making mincemeat of the poor girl.'

'No more than I expected,' said Harvey. 'Now, Jörg, to my second numbered account.'

Once again the unidentifiable piece of paper that bore a few numbers appeared. It is this discretion of the Swiss that leads half the world, from heads of state to Arab sheiks, to trust them with their money. In return the Swiss maintain one of the healthiest economies in the world. The system works, so why go elsewhere? Birrer spent a few seconds studying the figures.

'On April 1st – only you could have chosen that day, Harvey – you transferred $7,486,000 to your No. 2 account which was already in credit $2,791,428. On April 2nd, on your instructions, we placed $1 million in the Banco do Minas Gerais in the names of Mr Silverman and Mr Elliott. We covered the bill with Reading & Bates for the hire of the rig for $420,000 and several other bills amounting to $104,112, leaving your present No. 2 account standing at $8,753,316.'

'Game to Mrs King. Mrs King leads three games to one in the second set and by one set to love.'

'Very good,' said Harvey.

'The tennis or the money?' said Birrer.

'Both. Now, Jörg, I anticipated needing about $2

million over the next six weeks. I want to purchase one or two pictures in London. I have seen a Klee that I quite like and there are still a few galleries I want to visit. If I'd known the Prospecta Oil venture was going to be such a success, I'd have outbid Armand Hammer at the Sotheby-Parke Bernet for that Van Gogh last year. I shall also need some ready cash for some new horses at the Ascot Blood Stock Auctions. My stud's running down and it's still one of my greatest ambitions to win the King George and Elizabeth Stakes.' (James would have winced if he could have heard Harvey describe the race so inaccurately.) 'My best result so far, as you know, was third place, and that's not good enough. This year I've entered Rosalie, my best filly for years. If I lose I'll have to build up the stud again, but I'm damn well going to win this year.'

'Game to Mrs King. Mrs King leads four games to one and by one set to love.'

'So is Mrs King, it seems,' said Birrer. 'I'll brief my senior cashier that you're likely to be drawing large amounts over the next few weeks.'

'Now I don't wish the remainder to lie idle, so I want you to purchase more gold carefully over the next few months, with a view to off-loading it in the New Year. If the market does take a downward turn, I'll phone you in Zürich. At the close of business each day you are to loan the outstanding balance on an overnight basis to first-class banks and triple "A" commercial names.'

'What are you going to do with it all, Harvey, if those cigars don't get you first?'

'Oh, lay off, Jörg. You sound like my doctor. I've told you a hundred times, next year I retire, I quit, finito.'

'I can't see you dropping out of the rat race voluntarily, Harvey. It pains me to think how much you're worth now.'

Harvey laughed.

'I can't tell you that, Jörg. It's like Aristotle Onassis said – if you can count it, you haven't got any.'

'Game to Mrs King. Mrs King leads by five games to one and by one set to love.'

'How's Rosalie? We still have your instructions to pass the accounts on to her in Boston if anything should happen to you.'

'She's well. Phoned me this morning to tell me she won't be able to join me at Wimbledon because she's tied up with her work. I expect she'll end up marrying some rich American and won't need it. Enough of them have asked her. Can't be easy for her to decide if they like her or my money. I'm afraid we had a row about that a couple of years back and she still hasn't forgiven me.'

'Game, set and match to Mrs King: 6–1, 6–1.'

Harvey, Jörg, James and Anne joined in the applause while the two women left the court, curtseying in front of the Royal Box to the President of the All England Club, His Royal Highness, The Duke of Kent. Harvey and Jörg Birrer stayed for the next match, a doubles, and then returned to Claridge's together for dinner.

James and Anne had enjoyed their afternoon at Wimbledon and when they had seen Harvey safely back to Claridge's, accompanied by his mid-European friend, they returned to James's flat.

'Stephen, I'm back. Metcalfe is settled in for the night. On parade at 8.30 tomorrow morning.'

'Well done, James. Maybe he'll bite then.'

'Let's hope so.'

The sound of running water led James to the kitchen in search of Anne. She was elbow-deep in suds, attacking a soufflé dish with a scourer. She turned and brandished it at him.

'Darling, I don't want to be offensive about your daily, but this is the only kitchen I've ever been in where you have to do the washing up before you make the dinner!'

'I know. She only ever cleans the clean bits of the flat. Her work load's getting lighter by the week.'

He sat on the kitchen table, admiring her slim body.

'Will you scrub my back like that if I go and have a bath before dinner?'

'Yes, with a scourer.'

*

The water was deep and comfortably hot. James lay back in it luxuriously, letting Anne wash him. Then he stepped dripping out of the bath.

'You're a bit overdressed for a bathroom attendant, darling,' he said. 'Why don't we do something about it?'

Anne slipped out of her clothes while James dried himself. When he went into the bedroom, Anne was already huddled under the sheets.

'I'm cold,' she said.

'Fear not,' said James. 'You're about to be presented with your very own six-foot hot water bottle.'

She took him in her arms.

'Liar, you're freezing.'

'And you're lovely,' said James, trying to hold on to every part of her at once.

'How's your plan going, James?'

'I don't know yet, I'll tell you in about twenty minutes.'

She didn't speak again for nearly half an hour, when she said:

'Out you get. The baked cheese will be ready by now and in any case I want to remake the bed.'

'No need to bother about that, you silly woman.'

'Yes, there is. Last night I didn't sleep at all. You pulled all the blankets over to your side and I just watched you huddled up like a self-satisfied cat while I froze to death. Making love to you isn't at all what Harold Robbins promised it would be.'

'When you've finished chattering, woman, set the alarm for 7 am.'

'Seven am? You don't have to be at Claridge's until 8.30.'

'I know, but I want to go to work on an egg.'

'James, you really must give up your undergraduate sense of humour.'

'Oh, I thought it was rather funny.'

'Yes, darling. Why don't you get dressed before the dinner is burnt to a cinder?'

James arrived at Claridge's at 8.29 am. Whatever his own inadequacies, he was determined not to fail the others in their plans. He tuned in to check that Stephen was in Berkeley Square and Robin in Bond Street.

'Morning,' said Stephen. 'Had a good night?'

'Bloody good,' said James.

'Sleep well, did you?' asked Stephen.

'Hardly a wink.'

'Stop making us jealous,' said Robin, 'and concentrate on Harvey Metcalfe.'

James stood in the doorway of Slater's, the furriers, watching the early morning cleaners leave for home and the first of the office staff arriving.

Harvey Metcalfe was going through his normal routine of breakfast and the papers. Just before he had gone to bed he had a telephone call from his wife in Boston and another from his daughter during breakfast the next morning, which started his day well. He decided to continue his pursuit of an Impressionist picture in some of the other galleries in Cork Street and Bond Street. Perhaps Sotheby's would be able to help him.

He left the hotel at 9.47 am at his usual brisk pace. 'Action stations.'

Stephen and Robin snapped out of their daydreaming.

'He's just entered Bruton Street. Now he's heading for Bond Street.'

Harvey walked briskly down Bond Street, past the territory he had already covered.

'Only 50 yards off now, Jean-Pierre,' said James. 'Forty yards, 30 yards, 20 yards . . . Oh no, damn it, he's gone into Sotheby's. There's only a sale of medieval painted panels on there today. Hell, I didn't know he was interested in them.'

He glanced up the road at Stephen, padded out and aged to the condition of a wealthy, middle-class business man for the third day in a row. The cut of the collar and the rimless glasses proclaimed him as West German. Stephen's voice came over the speaker:

'I am going into Jean-Pierre's gallery. James, you stay north of Sotheby's on the far side of the street and report in every fifteen minutes. Robin, you go inside and dangle the bait under Harvey's nose.'

'But that's not in the plan, Stephen,' stammered Robin.

'Use your initiative and get on with it, otherwise

all you'll be doing is taking care of Jean-Pierre's heart condition and receiving no fees. Right?'

'Right,' said Robin nervously.

Robin walked into Sotheby's and made a surreptitious bee-line for the nearest mirror. Yes, he was still unrecognisable. Upstairs, he spotted Harvey near the back of the sale room, and planted himself on a nearby seat in the row behind him.

The sale of medieval painted panels was well under way. Harvey knew he ought to like them, but could not bring himself to condone the Gothic partiality for jewellery and bright, gilded colours. Behind him, Robin hesitated but then struck up a quiet-voiced conversation with his neighbour.

'Looks all very fine to me, but I've no knowledge of the period. I'm so much happier with the modern era. Still, I must think of something appropriate to say for my readers.'

Robin's neighbour smiled politely.

'Do you have to cover all the auctions?'

'Almost all – especially when there may be surprises. In any case, at Sotheby's you can always find out what's going on everywhere else. Only this morning one of the assistants gave me a tip that the Lamanns Gallery may have something special in the Impressionist field.'

Robin beamed the whispered information carefully at Harvey's right ear and then sat back and waited to see if it had created any effect. Shortly afterwards, he was rewarded by the sight of Harvey squeezing out of his row to leave. Robin waited for three more lots to be auctioned, then followed him, fingers crossed.

Outside, James had been keeping a patient vigil.

'10.30 – no sign of him.'

'Roger.'

'10.45 – still no sign of him.'

'Roger.'

'11.00 – he's still inside.'

'Roger.'

'11.12 action stations, action stations.'

James slipped quickly into the Lamanns Gallery as Jean-Pierre once again removed from his window the Sutherland watercolour of the Thames and the Boatman, and replaced it with an oil by Van Gogh, as magnificent an example of the master's work as a London gallery had ever seen. Now came the acid test: the litmus paper was walking purposefully down Bond Street towards it.

The picture had been painted by David Stein, who had achieved notoriety in the art world for faking 300 paintings and drawings by well-known Impressionists, for which he had received a total of $864,000 and, later, four years. He was only exposed when he put on a Chagall exhibition at the Niveaie Gallery in Madison Avenue in 1969. Unknown to Stein, Chagall himself was in New York at the time for an exhibition at the museum in Lincoln Center where two of his most famous works were on display. On being informed of the Niveaie exhibition, Chagall furiously reported the pictures to the District Attorney's office as fakes. Stein had already sold one of the imitation Chagalls to Louis D. Cohen at a price of nearly $100,000, and to this day there is a Stein Chagall and a Stein Picasso at the Galleria d'Arte Moderna in Milan. Jean-Pierre was confident that what Stein had achieved in the past in New York and Milan he could now repeat in London.

Stein had continued to paint Impressionist pictures, but now signed them with his own name; thanks to his indubitable talent he was still making a handsome living. He had known and admired Jean-Pierre for several years and when he heard the story of Metcalfe and Prospecta Oil, he agreed to produce a Van Gogh for $10,000 and to sign the painting with the master's famous 'Vincent'.

Jean-Pierre had gone to considerable lengths to identify a Van Gogh that had vanished in mysterious circumstances, so that Stein could resurrect it to tempt Harvey. He had started with de la Faille's comprehensive *oeuvres* catalogue, *The Works of Vincent Van Gogh*, and selected from it three pictures that had hung in the National Gallery in Berlin prior to the Second World War. In de la Faille, they were entered under Nos. 485, *Les Amoureux* (*The Lovers*), 628, *La Moisson* (*The Harvest*), and 766, *Le Jardin de Daubigny* (*The Garden of Daubigny*). The last two were known to have been bought in 1929 by the Berlin Gallery, and *Les Amoureux* probably bought around the same time. At the start of the war, all three had disappeared.

Jean-Pierre then contacted Professor Wormit of

the Preussischer Kulturbesitz. The Professor, a world authority on missing works of art, was able to rule out one of the possibilities, *Le Jardin de Daubigny*; soon after the war it apparently had reappeared in the collection of Siegfried Kramarsky in New York, though how it got there remains a mystery. Kramarsky had subsequently sold the painting to the Nichido Gallery in Tokyo, where it now hangs. The Professor confirmed that the fate of the other two Van Goghs remained unknown.

Next Jean-Pierre turned to Madame Tellegen-Hoogendoorm of the Dutch Rijksbureau voor Kunsthistorische Documentatie. Madame Tellegen was the acknowledged authority on Van Gogh and gradually, with her expert help, Jean-Pierre pieced together the story of the missing paintings. They had been removed, along with many others, from the Berlin National Gallery in 1937 by the Nazis, despite vigorous protests from the Director, Dr Hanfstaengl, and the Keeper of Paintings, Dr Hentzen. The paintings, stigmatised by the philistinism of the National Socialists as degenerate art, were stored in a depot in the Kopenickerstrasse in Berlin. Hitler himself visited the depot in January 1938, and legalised the proceedings as an official confiscation.

What happened to the two Van Goghs after that, nobody knows. Many of the Nazi-confiscated works were quietly sold abroad by Joseph Angerer, an agent of Hermann Goering, to obtain much-needed foreign currency for the Führer. Some were disposed of in a sale organised by the Fischer Art Gallery in Lucerne on June 30th, 1939. But many of the works in the depot in the Kopenickerstrasse were simply burned, stolen, or are still missing.

Jean-Pierre managed to obtain black-and-white reproductions of *Les Amoureux* and *La Moisson*: no colour positives survive, if they were ever made. It seemed to Jean-Pierre unlikely that any colour reproductions of two paintings last seen in 1938 would exist anywhere. He therefore settled down to choose between the two.

Les Amoureux was the larger of the two, at 76 × 91 cm. However, Van Gogh did not seem to have been satisfied with it. In October 1889 (letter No. 556) he referred to 'a very poor sketch of my last canvas'. Moreover, it was impossible to guess the colour of the background. *La Moisson*, in contrast, had pleased Van Gogh. He had painted the oil in September 1889 and written of it, 'I feel very much inclined to do the reaper once more for my mother' (letter No. 604). He had in fact already painted three other very similar pictures of a reaper at harvest time. Jean-Pierre was able to obtain colour transparencies of two of them, one from the Louvre and the other from the Rijksmuseum, where they now hang. He studied the sequence. The position of the sun, and the play of light on the scene, were practically the only points of difference. Jean-Pierre was therefore able to see in his mind's eye what *La Moisson* must have looked like in colour.

Stein agreed with Jean-Pierre's final choice and he studied the black-and-white reproduction of *La Moisson* and the colour transparencies of its sister paintings long and minutely before he set to work. He then found an insignificant late-nineteenth-century French work, and skilfully removed the paint from it, leaving a clean canvas except for a vital stamp on the back which even Stein could not have reproduced. He marked on the canvas the exact size of the picture, 48.5 × 53 cm and selected a palette knife and brush of the type that Van Gogh had favoured. Six weeks later *La Moisson* was finished. Stein varnished it, and baked it for four days in an oven at a gentle 85°F to age it. Jean-Pierre provided a heavy gilt Impressionist frame and it was well ready for Harvey Metcalfe's scrutiny.

Harvey, acting on his overheard tip, could see no harm in dropping into the Lamanns Gallery. He was about five paces away when he first caught sight of the picture being taken out of the window. He could not believe his eyes. A Van Gogh, without a doubt, and a superlative one at that. *La Moisson* had actually been on display for only two minutes.

Harvey almost ran into the gallery, only to discover Jean-Pierre deep in conversation with Stephen and James. None of them took any notice of him. Stephen was addressing Jean-Pierre in a guttural accent.

'170,000 guineas seems high, but it is a fine example. Can you be sure it is the picture that disappeared from Berlin in 1937?'

'You can never be sure of anything, but you can see on the back of the canvas the stamp of the Berlin National Gallery, and the Bernheim Jeune have confirmed they sold it to the Germans in 1927. The rest of its history is well chronicled back to 1890. It seems certain that it was looted from the museum in the upheaval of the war.'

'How did you come into possession of the painting?'

'From the private collection of a member of the British aristocracy who wishes to remain anonymous.'

'Excellent,' said Stephen. 'I would like to reserve it until 4 pm when I will bring round a cheque for 170,000 guineas from the Dresdner Bank AG. Will that be acceptable?'

'Of course, sir,' replied Jean-Pierre. 'I will place a red dot on it.'

James, in the sharpest of suits and a dashing trilby, hovered knowledgeably behind Stephen.

'It certainly is a marvellous example of the master's work,' he remarked ingratiatingly.

'Yes. I took it round to Julian Barron at Sotheby's and he seemed to like it.'

James retreated mincingly to the end of the gallery, relishing his role as a connoisseur. At that moment Robin walked in, a copy of the *Guardian* sticking out of his pocket.

'Good morning, Mr Lamanns. I heard a rumour at Sotheby's about a Van Gogh which I'd always thought must be in Russia. I'd like to write a few paragraphs about the history of the painting and how you came into possession of it for tomorrow's paper. Is that OK by you?'

'I should be delighted,' said Jean-Pierre, 'although actually I have just reserved the picture for Herr Drosser, the distinguished German dealer, at 170,000 guineas.'

'Very reasonable,' said James knowingly from the end of the gallery. 'I think it's the best Van Gogh I have seen in London since *Mademoiselle Ravoux* and I'm only sorry my house won't be auctioning it. You're a lucky man, Mr Drosser. If you ever decide to sell it, don't hesitate to contact me.' James handed Stephen a card and smiled at Jean-Pierre.

Jean-Pierre watched James. It was a fine performance. Robin began to take notes in what he hoped looked like shorthand and again addressed Jean-Pierre.

'Do you have a photograph of the picture?'

'Of course.'

Jean-Pierre opened a drawer and took out a colour photograph of the picture with a typewritten description attached. He handed it to Robin.

'Do watch the spelling of Lamanns, won't you? I get so bored with being confused with a French motor car race.'

He turned to Stephen.

'So sorry to keep you waiting, Herr Drosser. How would you like us to despatch the picture?'

'You can send it to me at the Dorchester tomorrow morning, room 120.'

'Certainly, sir.'

Stephen started to leave.

'Excuse me, sir,' said Robin, 'can I take the spelling of your name?'

'D.R.O.S.S.E.R.'

'And may I have permission to quote you in my article?'

'You may. I am with my purchase very pleased. Good day, gentlemen.'

Stephen bowed his head smartly, and departed. He stepped out into Bond Street and to the horror of Jean-Pierre, Robin and James, Harvey, without a moment's hesitation, also walked out.

Jean-Pierre collapsed heavily on his Georgian mahogany desk and looked despairingly at Robin and James.

'God Almighty, the whole thing's a fiasco. Six weeks of preparation, three days of agony, and then he walked out on us.' Jean-Pierre looked at *La Moisson* angrily.

'I thought Stephen assured us that Harvey would stay and bargain with Jean-Pierre. It's in his character,' mimicked James plaintively. 'He'd never let the picture out of his sight.'

'Who the hell thought up this bloody silly enterprise?' muttered Robin.

'Stephen,' they all cried together, and rushed to the window.

'What an interesting maquette by Henry Moore,' said an impeccably corseted middle-aged lady, her hand firmly placed on the bronze loin of a naked acrobat. She had slipped unnoticed into the gallery while the three had been grumbling. 'How much are you asking for it?'

'I will be with you in a minute, madam,' said Jean-Pierre. 'Oh hell, I think Metcalfe's following Stephen. Get him on the pocket radio, Robin.'

'Stephen, can you hear me? Whatever you do, don't look back. We think Harvey's only a few yards behind you.'

'What the hell do you mean he's only a few yards behind me? He's meant to be in the gallery with you buying the Van Gogh. What are you playing at?'

'Harvey didn't give us a chance. He walked straight out after you before any of us could continue as planned.'

'Very clever. Now what am I meant to do?'

Jean-Pierre took over:

'You'd better go to the Dorchester just in case he is actually following you.'

'I don't even know where the Dorchester is,' yelped Stephen.

Robin came to his rescue:

'Take the first right, Stephen, and that'll bring you into Bruton Street, keep walking as straight as you can until you reach Berkeley Square. Stay on the line, but don't look back or you may turn into a pillar of salt.'

'James,' said Jean-Pierre, thinking on his feet for the first time in his life. 'You take a taxi immediately to the Dorchester and book room 120 in the name of Drosser. Have the key ready for Stephen the moment he walks through the door, then make yourself scarce. Stephen, are you, still there?'

'Yes.'

'Did you hear all that?'

'Yes. Tell James to book 119 or 121 if 120 is not available.'

'Roger,' replied Jean-Pierre. 'Get going, James.'

James bolted out of the gallery and barged in front of a woman who had just hailed a taxi, a thing he had never done before.

'The Dorchester,' he hollered, 'as fast as you can go.'

The taxi shot off.

'Stephen, James has gone and I'm sending Robin to follow Harvey so he can keep you briefed and guide you to the Dorchester. I'm staying put. Everything else OK?'

'No,' said Stephen, 'start praying. I've reached Berkeley Square. Where now?'

'Across the garden then continue down Hill Street.'

Robin left the gallery and ran all the way to Bruton Street until he was only 50 yards behind Harvey.

'Now about the Henry Moore,' said the well-corseted lady.

'Screw Henry Moore,' said Jean-Pierre, not even looking around.

The steel-reinforced bosom heaved.

'Young man, I have never been spoken to in . . .'

But Jean-Pierre had already reached the lavatory, and closed the door.

'You're crossing South Audley Street now, then continue into Deanery Street. Keep going, don't turn right or left and don't whatever you do look back. Harvey is still about 50 yards behind you. I'm a little more than 50 yards behind him,' said Robin. Passers-by stared at the man talking into his little instrument.

'Is Room 120 free?'

'Yes, sir, they checked out this morning, but I'm not sure if it's ready for occupancy yet. I think the maid may still be clearing the room. I'll have to check, sir,' said the tall receptionist in the morning suit, which indicated that he was a senior member of the floor staff.

'Oh, don't worry about that,' said James, his German accent far better than Stephen's. 'I always have that room. Can you book me in for one night? Name's Drosser, Herr – um – Helmut Drosser.'

He slipped a pound over the counter.

'Certainly, sir.'

'That's Park Lane, Stephen. Look right – the big hotel on the corner straight in front of you is the Dorchester. The semi-circle facing you is the main entrance. Go up the steps, past the big man in the green overcoat, and through the revolving door and you'll find reception on your right. James ought to be there waiting for you.'

Robin was grateful that the annual dinner of the Royal Society for Medicine had been held at the Dorchester last year.

'Where's Harvey?' bleated Stephen.

'Only 40 yards behind you.'

Stephen quickened his pace, ran up the steps of the Dorchester and pushed through the revolving door so hard that the other residents coming out found themselves on the street faster than they had planned. Thank God, James was standing there holding a key.

'The lift's over there,' said James, pointing. 'You've only chosen one of the most expensive suites in the hotel.'

Stephen glanced in the direction James had indicated and turned back to thank him. But James was already heading off to the American Bar to be sure he was well out of sight when Harvey arrived.

Stephen left the lift at the first floor and found that the Dorchester, which he had never entered before, was as traditional as Claridge's, its thick royal blue and golden carpets leading to a magnificently appointed corner suite which overlooked Hyde Park. He collapsed into an easy chair, not quite sure what to expect next. Nothing had gone as planned.

Jean-Pierre waited at the gallery, James sat in the American Bar and Robin loitered by the side of Barclays Bank, Park Lane, a mock-tudor building 50 yards from the entrance of the Dorchester.

'Have you a Mr Drosser staying at this hotel? I think it's room 120,' barked Harvey.

The receptionist looked through the card index.

'Yes, sir. Is he expecting you?'

'No, but I'll have a word with him on the house phone.'

'Of course, sir. If you'd be kind enough to go through the small archway on your left you will find five telephones. One of them is a house phone.'

Harvey marched through the archway as directed.

'Room 120,' he instructed the operator, who sat in his own little section, wearing the green Dorchester uniform with golden castles on the lapels.

'Cubicle No. 1, please, sir.'

'Mr Drosser?'

'Speaking,' said Stephen, summoning up his German accent for a sustained effort.

'My name is Harvey Metcalfe. I wonder if I could come up and have a word with you? It's about the Van Gogh you bought this morning.'

'Well, it's a little inconvenient at the moment. I am about to take a shower and I do have a lunch appointment.'

'I won't keep you more than a few minutes.'

Before Stephen could reply, the telephone clicked. A few moments later there was a knock on the door. Stephen's legs wobbled. He answered it nervously. He had changed into a white Dorchester dressing-gown and his brown hair was somewhat dishevelled and darker than normal. It was the only disguise he could think of at such short notice as the original plan had not allowed for a face-to-face meeting with Harvey.

'Sorry to intrude, Mr Drosser, but I had to see you immediately. I know you have just purchased a Van Gogh from the Lamanns Gallery and I was hoping that, as you are a dealer, you might be willing to sell it on for a quick profit.'

'No, thank you,' said Stephen, relaxing for the first time. 'I've wanted a Van Gogh for my gallery in Munich for many years. I'm sorry, Mr Metcalfe, it's not for sale.'

'Listen, you paid 170,000 guineas for it. What's that in dollars?'

Stephen paused.

'Oh, about $435,000.'

'I'll give you $15,000 if you release the picture to me. All you have to do is ring the gallery and tell them that the picture is now mine and that I will cover the bill.'

Stephen sat silent, not sure how to handle the situation without blowing it. Think like Harvey Metcalfe, he told himself.

'$20,000 in cash and you've got a deal.'

Harvey hesitated. Stephen's legs wobbled again.

'Done,' said Harvey. 'Ring the gallery immediately.'

Stephen picked up the telephone.

'Can you get me the Lamanns Gallery in Bond Street as quickly as possible, please – I have a lunch appointment.'

A few seconds later the call came through.

'Lamanns Gallery.'

'I would like to speak to Mr Lamanns.'

'At last, Stephen. What the hell is happening your end?'

'Ah, Mr Lamanns, this is Herr Drosser. You remember, I was in your gallery earlier this morning.'

'Of course I remember, you fool. What are you going on about, Stephen? It's me – Jean-Pierre.'

'I have a Mr Metcalfe with me.'

'Christ, I'm sorry, Stephen. I didn't . . .'

'And you can expect him in the next few minutes.'

Stephen looked towards Harvey who nodded his assent.

'You are to release the Van Gogh I purchased this morning to Mr Metcalfe and he will give you a cheque for the full amount, 170,000 guineas.'

'Out of disaster, triumph,' said Jean-Pierre quietly.

'I'm very sorry I shall not be the owner of the picture myself, but I have, as the Americans would say, had an offer I can't refuse. Thank you for the part you played,' said Stephen and put the telephone down.

Harvey was writing out a cheque to cash for $20,000.

'Thank you, Mr Drosser. You have made me a happy man.'

'I am not complaining myself,' said Stephen honestly. He escorted Harvey to the door and they shook hands.

'Goodbye, sir.'

'Good day, Mr Metcalfe.'

Stephen closed the door and tottered to the chair, almost too weak to move.

Robin and James saw Harvey leave the Dorchester. Robin followed him in the direction of the gallery, his hopes rising with each stride. James took the lift to the first floor and nearly ran to Room 120. He banged on the door. Stephen jumped at the noise. He didn't feel he could face Harvey again. He opened the door.

'James, it's you. Cancel the room, pay for one night and then join me in the cocktail bar.'

'Why? What for?'
'A bottle of Krug 1964 Privée Cuvée.'

One down and three to go.

11

Jean-Pierre was the last to arrive at Lord Brigsley's King's Road flat. He felt he had earned the right to make an entrance. Harvey's cheque had been cleared and the Lamanns Gallery account was for the moment $447,560 in credit. The painting was in Harvey's possession and the heavens had not yet fallen in. Jean-Pierre had cleared more money in two months of crime than he had in ten years of legitimate trading.

The other three greeted him with the acclaim normally reserved for a sporting hero, and a glass of James's last bottle of Veuve Clicquot 1959.

'We were lucky to pull it off,' said Robin.

'We weren't lucky,' said Stephen. 'We kept our nerve under pressure, and the one thing we've learned from the exercise is that Harvey can change the rules in the middle of the game.'

'He almost changed the game, Stephen.'

'Agreed. So we must always remember that we shall fail unless we can be as successful, not once, but four times. We must not underestimate our opponent just because we've won the first round.'

'Relax, Professor,' said James. 'We can get down

to business again after dinner. Anne came in this afternoon especially to make the salmon mousse, and it won't go down well with Harvey Metcalfe.'

'When am I going to meet this fabulous creature?' asked Jean-Pierre.

'When this is all over and behind us.'

'Don't marry her, James. She's only after our money.'

They all laughed. James hoped the day would come when he could tell them she had known all along. He produced the *boeuf en croûte* and two bottles of Echezeaux 1970. Jean-Pierre sniffed the sauce appreciatively.

'On second thoughts she ought to be seriously considered if her touch in bed is half as deft as it is in the kitchen.'

'You're not going to get the chance to be the judge of that, Jean-Pierre. Content yourself with admiring her French dressing.'

'You were quite outstanding this morning, James,' said Stephen, steering the conversation away from Jean-Pierre's pet subject. 'You should go on the stage. As a member of the British aristocracy, your talent's simply wasted.'

'I've always wanted to, but my old pa is against it. Those who live in expectation of a large inheritance must expect to have to toe the filial line.'

'Why don't we let him play all four parts in Monte Carlo?' suggested Robin.

The mention of Monte Carlo sobered them up.

'Back to work,' said Stephen. 'We have so far received $447,560. Expenses with the picture and an unexpected night at the Dorchester were $11,142 so Metcalfe still owes us $563,582. Think of what we've still lost, not of what we've gained. Now for the Monte Carlo operation, which depends upon split-second timing and our ability to sustain our roles for several hours. Robin will bring us up to date.'

Robin retrieved the green dossier from the briefcase by his side and studied his notes for a few moments.

'Jean-Pierre, you must grow a beard, starting today, so that in three weeks' time you'll be unrecognisable. You must also cut your hair very short.' Robin grinned unsympathetically at Jean-Pierre's grimace. 'Yes, you'll look absolutely revolting.'

'That,' said Jean-Pierre; 'will not be possible.'

'How are the baccarat and blackjack coming on?' continued Robin.

'I have lost $37 in five weeks, which includes my member's fee at the Claremont and the Golden Nugget.'

'It all goes on expenses,' said Stephen. 'That puts the bill up to $563,619.'

The others laughed. Only Stephen's lips did not move. He was in sober earnest.

'James, how is your handling of the van going?'

'I can reach Harley Street from St Thomas's in 14 minutes. I should be able to do the actual run in Monte Carlo in about 11 minutes, though naturally

I shall want to do some practice runs the day before. To start with I'll have to master driving on the wrong side of the road.'

'Strange how everybody except the British drives on the wrong side of the road,' observed Jean-Pierre.

James ignored him.

'I'm not sure of all the continental road signs either.'

'They are detailed in the Michelin guide that I gave you as part of my dossier.'

'I know, but I'll still feel easier when I've experienced the actual run and not just studied maps. There are quite a few one-way streets in Monaco and I don't want to be stopped going down the wrong one with Harvey Metcalfe unconscious in the back.'

'Don't worry. You'll have ample time when we're there. So, that only leaves Stephen, who's about the most competent medical student I've ever had. You're confident of your newly acquired knowledge, I hope?'

'About as confident as I am with your American accent, Robin. Anyway, I trust that Harvey Metcalfe will be in no state of mind to worry about such trivialities by the time we meet up.'

'Don't worry, Stephen. Believe me, he wouldn't even register who you were if you introduced yourself as Herr Drosser with a Van Gogh under both arms.'

Robin handed round the final schedule of rehearsals for Harley Street and St Thomas's, and once again consulted the green file.

'I've booked four single rooms on different floors

at the Hôtel de Paris and confirmed all the arrangements with the Centre Hospitalier Princesse Grace. The hotel is reputed to be one of the best in the world – it's certainly expensive enough – but it's convenient for the Casino. We fly to Nice on Monday, the day Harvey is due to arrive on his yacht.'

'What do we do for the rest of the week?' enquired James innocently.

Stephen resumed control:

'We master the green dossier backwards, frontwards and sideways for a full dress rehearsal on Friday. The most important thing for you, James, is to get a grip of yourself and let us know what you intend to do.'

James sank back into gloom.

Stephen closed his file briskly.

'That seems to be all we can cover tonight.'

'Hang on, Stephen,' said Robin. 'Let's strip you off once more. I'd like to see if we can do it in 90 seconds.'

Stephen lay down slightly reluctantly in the middle of the room, and James and Jean-Pierre swiftly and carefully removed all his clothes.

'Eighty-seven seconds. Excellent,' said Robin, looking down at Stephen, naked except for his watch. 'Hell, look at the time. I must get back to Newbury. My wife will think I have a mistress and I don't fancy any of you.'

Stephen dressed himself quickly while the others prepared to leave. A few minutes later, James stood by the front door, watching them depart one by one. As soon as Stephen was out of sight, he bounded downstairs into the kitchen.

'Did you listen?'

'Yes, darling. They're all rather nice and I don't blame them for being cross with you. They're being very professional about the whole venture, while you sounded like the only amateur. We'll have to think up something good for you to match them. We've over a week before Mr Metcalfe goes to Monte Carlo and we must use the time constructively.'

James sighed: 'Well, let's enjoy tonight. At least this morning was a triumph.'

'Yes, but not yours. Tomorrow we work.'

12

'PASSENGERS FOR flight 017 to Nice are now requested to board the aircraft at gate No. 7,' boomed the loudspeaker at Heathrow's No. 1 terminal.

'That's us,' said Stephen.

The four of them took the escalator to the first floor, and walked down the long corridor. After being searched for guns, bombs, and whatever else terrorists are searched for, they proceeded down the ramp.

They sat separately, never speaking or even looking at each other. Stephen had warned them that the flight could well be sprinkled with Harvey's friends, and each imagined himself to be sitting next to the closest of them.

James gazed moodily at the cloudless sky and brooded. He and Anne had read every book they could lay their hands on that even hinted at stolen money or successful duplicity, but they had found nothing they could plagiarise. Even Stephen, in between being undressed and practised upon at St Thomas's, was becoming daunted by the task of finding a winning plan for James.

The Trident touched down at Nice at 13.40, and

the train journey from Nice to Monte Carlo took
them a further twenty minutes. Each member of the
team made his own way to the elegant Hôtel de Paris
in the Place du Casino. At 7 pm they were all present
in room 217.

'All settled into your rooms?'

The other three nodded. 'So far, so good,' said
Robin. 'Right, let's go over the timing. Jean-Pierre,
you will go to the Casino tonight and play a few
hands of baccarat and blackjack. Try to acclimatise
to the place and learn your way around. In particular, master any variations in the rules there might be
from the Claremont, and be sure you never speak
in English. Do you foresee any problems?'

'No, can't say I do, Robin. In fact I may as well
go now and start rehearsing.'

'Don't lose too much of our money,' said Stephen.

Jean-Pierre, resplendent in beard and dinner-
jacket, grinned and slipped out of room 217 and down
the staircase, avoiding the lift. He walked the short
distance from the hotel to the famous Casino.

Robin continued:

'James, you take a taxi from the Casino to the
hospital. On arrival you will leave the meter running
for a few minutes and then return to the Casino. You
can normally rely on a taxi to take the shortest route,
but to be sure, tell the driver it's an emergency. That'll
give you the opportunity of seeing which traffic lanes
he uses under pressure. When he's returned you to
the Casino, walk the route from there to the hospital

and back. Then you can assimilate it in your own time. After you've mastered that, repeat the same procedure for the route between the hospital and Harvey's yacht. Never enter the Casino or even get close enough to the boat to be seen. Being seen now means being recognised later.'

'What about my knowledge of the Casino on the night of the operation?'

'Jean-Pierre will take care of that. He'll meet you at the door because Stephen won't be able to leave Harvey. I don't think they will charge you the 12 franc entrance fee if you're wearing a white coat and carrying a stretcher, but have it ready to be sure. When you've completed the walk, go to your room and stay there until our meeting at 11 am tomorrow. Stephen and I will also be going to the hospital to check that all the arrangements have been carried out as cabled from London. If at any time you see us, ignore us.'

As James left room 217, Jean-Pierre arrived at the Casino.

The Casino stands in the heart of Monte Carlo overlooking the sea, surrounded by the most beautiful gardens. The present building has several wings, the oldest of which was designed by Charles Garnier, the architect of the Paris Opera House. The gambling rooms, which were added in 1910, are linked by an atrium to the Salle Garnier in which operas and ballets are performed.

Jean-Pierre marched up the marble staircase to the

entrance and paid his 12 francs. The gambling rooms are vast, full of the decadence and grandeur of Europe at the turn of the century. Massive red carpets, statues, paintings and tapestries give the building an almost regal appearance and the portraits lend an air of a country home still lived in. Jean-Pierre found the clientèle were of all nationalities: Arabs and Jews played next to each other at the roulette wheel and chatted away with an ease that would have been unthinkable at the United Nations. Jean-Pierre felt totally relaxed in the unreal world of the wealthy. Robin had assessed his character accurately and given him a role he could master with aplomb.

Jean-Pierre spent over three hours studying the layout of the Casino – its gambling rooms, bars and restaurants, the telephones, the entrances and exits. Then he turned his attention to the gambling itself. He discovered that two shoes of baccarat were played in the Salons Privés at 3 pm and 11 pm, and learned from Pierre Cattalano, the head of the public relations department of the Casino, which of the private rooms Harvey Metcalfe preferred to play in.

Blackjack is played in the Salon des Amériques from 11 am daily. There are three tables, and Jean-Pierre's informant told him that Harvey always played on table No. 2, seat No. 3. Jean-Pierre played a little blackjack and baccarat, to discover any slight variations in rules there might be from the Claremont. In fact there were none, as the Claremont still adheres to French rules.

Harvey Metcalfe arrived noisily at the Casino just after 11 pm, leaving a trail of cigar ash leading to his baccarat table. Jean-Pierre, inconspicuous at the bar, watched as the head croupier first showed Harvey politely to a reserved seat, and then walked through to the Salon des Amériques to the No. 2 blackjack table and placed a discreet white card marked '*Réservé*' on one of the chairs. Harvey was clearly a favoured client. The management knew as well as Jean-Pierre which games Harvey Metcalfe played. At 11.27 pm Jean-Pierre left quietly and returned to the solitude of his hotel room where he remained until 11 am the next day. He phoned no one and did not use room service.

James's evening also went well. The taxi-driver was superb. The word 'emergency' brought out the Walter Mitty in him: he travelled through Monte Carlo as if it were nothing less than the Rally itself. When James arrived at the hospital in 8 minutes 44 seconds, he genuinely felt a little sick and had to rest for a few minutes in the Entrée des Patients before returning to the taxi.

'Back to the Casino, but much slower, please.'

The journey back along the Rue Grimaldi took just over eleven minutes and James decided he would settle for trying to cover it in about ten. He paid off the taxi-driver and carried out the second part of his instructions.

Walking to the hospital and back took just over an hour. The night air was gentle on his face, and the streets crowded with lively chattering people. Tourism is the chief source of income for the Principality, and the Monégasques take the welfare of their visitors very seriously. James passed innumerable little pavement restaurants and souvenir shops stocked with expensive trinkets of no significance that once bought would be forgotten or lost within a week. Noisy groups of holiday-makers strolled along the pavements, their multilingual babel forming a meaningless chorus to James's thoughts of Anne. On arrival back at the Casino, James then took a taxi to the harbour to locate *Messenger Boy*, Harvey's yacht, and from there once more to the hospital. He then walked the same route and, like Jean-Pierre, he was safely in his room before midnight, having completed his first task.

Robin and Stephen found the walk to the hospital from their hotel took a little over 40 minutes. On arrival Robin asked the receptionist if he could see the superintendent.

'The night superintendent is now on duty,' said a freshly starched French nurse. 'Who shall I say is asking him for?'

Her English pronunciation was excellent and they both avoided a smile at her slight mistake.

'Doctor Wiley Barker of the University of California.'

Robin began to pray that the French superintendent would not happen to know that Wiley Barker, President Nixon's physician and one of the most respected surgeons in the world, was actually touring

Australia at the time lecturing to the major universities.

'*Bonsoir, Docteur Barker. Monsieur Bartise à votre service. Votre visite fait grand honneur à notre hôpital humble.*'

Robin's newly acquired American accent stopped any further conversation in French.

'I would like to check the layout of the theatre,' said Robin, 'and confirm that we have it provisionally booked for tomorrow from 11 pm to 4 am for the next five days.'

'That is quite correct, *Docteur Barker*,' said the superintendent, looking down at a clip-board. 'The theatre is off the next corridor. Will you follow me, please?'

The theatre was not dissimilar to the one the four of them had been practising in at St Thomas's – two rooms with a rubber swing door dividing them. The main theatre was well equipped and a nod from Robin showed Stephen that it had all the instruments he required. Robin was impressed. Although the hospital had only some 200 beds, the theatre itself was of the highest standard. Rich men had obviously been ill there before.

'Will you be requiring an anaesthetist or any nurses to assist you, *Docteur Barker*?'

'No,' said Robin. 'I have my own anaesthetist and staff but I will require a tray of laparotomy instruments to be laid out every night. However, I will be able to give you at least an hour's warning before you need make any final preparations.'

'That's plenty of time. Will there be anything else, sir?'

'Yes, the special vehicle I ordered. Can it be ready for my driver at 12 pm tomorrow?'

'Yes, *Docteur Barker*. It will be in the small car park behind the hospital and your driver can pick up the keys from the reception.'

'Can you recommend an agency from which I can hire an experienced nurse for post-operative care?'

'*Bien sûr*, the Auxiliaire Médical of Nice will be only too happy to oblige – at a certain price, of course.'

'Of course,' said Robin. 'And that reminds me to ask, have all your expenses been dealt with?'

'Yes, *Docteur*. We received a cheque from California last Thursday for $7,000.'

Robin had been very pleased with that touch. It had been so simple. Stephen had contacted his bank at Harvard and asked them to send a draft from the First National City Bank in San Francisco to the hospital secretary at Monte Carlo.

'Thank you all for your help, Monsieur Bartise. You have been most obliging. Now you do understand that I am not quite sure which night I shall be bringing my patient in. He's a sick man, although he doesn't know it, and I have to prepare him for the operation.'

'Of course, *mon cher Docteur*.'

'Finally, I would appreciate it if you would tell as few people as possible that I am in Monte Carlo. I am trying to snatch a holiday at the same time as working.'

'I understand, Docteur Barker. You can be assured of my discretion.'

Robin and Stephen bade farewell to Monsieur Bartise and took a taxi back to the hotel.

'I'm always slightly humiliated by how well the French speak our language compared with our grasp of theirs,' said Stephen.

'It's all the fault of you bloody Americans,' said Robin.

'No, it isn't. If France had conquered America, your French would be excellent. Blame it on the Pilgrim Fathers.'

Robin laughed. Neither of them spoke again until they reached room 217 for fear of being overheard. Stephen had no doubts about the responsibility and risk they were taking with Robin's plan.

Harvey Metcalfe was on the deck of his yacht, sunbathing and reading the morning papers. *Nice-Matin*, irritatingly enough, was in French. He read it laboriously, with the aid of a dictionary, to see if there were any social events to which he ought to get himself invited. He had gambled late into the night, and was enjoying the sun's rays on his fleshy back. If money could have obtained it, he would have been 6 ft and 170 lb with a handsome head of hair, but no amount of suntan oil would stop his balding dome from burning, so he covered it with a cap inscribed with the words 'I'm sexy'. If Miss Fish could see him now . . .

At 11 am, as Harvey turned over and allowed the sun to see his massive stomach, James strolled into room 217 where the rest of the Team were waiting for him.

Jean-Pierre reported on the layout of the Casino and Harvey Metcalfe's habits. James brought them up to date on the result of his race through the city the night before and confirmed that he thought he could cover the distance in just under eleven minutes.

'Perfect,' said Robin. 'Stephen and I took 15 minutes by taxi from the hospital to the hotel so if Jean-Pierre warns me immediately the balloon goes up in the Casino, I should have enough time to see that everything is ready before you all arrive.'

'I do hope the balloon will be going down, not up, in the Casino,' remarked Jean-Pierre.

'I have booked an agency nurse to be on call from tomorrow night. The hospital has all the facilities I require. It'll take about two minutes to walk a stretcher from the front door to the theatre, so from the moment James leaves the car park I should have at least 16 minutes to prepare myself. James, you'll be able to pick up the vehicle from the hospital car park at 12 pm. The keys have been left in reception in the name of Dr Barker. Do a couple of practice runs and no more. I don't want you causing interest by looking conspicuous. And could you leave this parcel in the back, please.'

'What is it?'

'Three long white laboratory coats and a stethoscope for Stephen. While you're at it, better check that you can unfold the stretcher easily. When you've finished the two runs, put the vehicle back in the car park and return to your room until 11 pm. From then through to 4 am you'll have to wait in the car park until you get the "action stations" or "all clear" signal from Jean-Pierre. Everybody buy new batteries for your transmitters. I don't want the whole plan to collapse for the sake of a ten-penny battery. I'm afraid there's nothing much for you to do, Jean-Pierre until this evening, except relax. I hope you have some good books in your room.'

'Can't I go to the Princess Cinema and see François Truffaut's *La Nuit Américaine*? I just adore Jacqueline Bisset. *Vive la France.*'

'My dear Jean-Pierre, Miss Bisset's from Reading,' said James.

'I don't care. I still want to see her.'

'A frog he would a-wooing go,' said James mockingly.

'But why not?' said Robin. 'The last thing Harvey will do is take in an intellectual French film with no sub-titles. Hope you enjoy it – and good luck tonight, Jean-Pierre.'

Jean-Pierre left for his room as quietly as he had come, leaving the rest of them together in room 217.

'Right, James. You can do your practice runs any time that suits you. Just make sure you're wide awake tonight.'

'Fine. I'll go and pick up the keys from the hospital reception. Let's just hope nobody stops me for a real emergency.'

'Now, Stephen, let's go over the details again. There's more than money to lose if we get this wrong. We'll start from the top. What do you do if the nitrous oxide falls below five litres . . .'

'Station check – station check – operation Metcalfe. This is Jean-Pierre. I am on the steps of the Casino. Can you hear me, James?'

'Yes. I am in the car park of the hospital. Out.'

'Robin here. I am on the balcony of room 217. Is Stephen with you, Jean-Pierre?'

'Yes. He's drinking on his own at the bar.'

'Good luck and out.'

Jean-Pierre carried out a station check every hour on the hour from 7 pm until 11 pm, merely to inform Robin and James that Harvey had not arrived.

Eventually, at 11.16, he did show up, and took his reserved place at the baccarat table. Stephen stopped sipping his tomato juice and Jean-Pierre moved over and waited patiently by the table for one of the men seated on the left or right of Harvey to leave. An hour passed by. Harvey was losing a little, but continued to play. So did the tall thin American on his right and the Frenchman on his left. Another hour and still no movement. Then suddenly the Frenchman on the left of Metcalfe had a particularly bad run, gathered his few remaining chips and left the table. Jean-Pierre moved forward.

'I am afraid, Monsieur, that that seat is reserved for another gentleman,' said the banker. 'We do have an unreserved place on the other side of the table.'

'It's not important,' said Jean-Pierre, who backed away, not wanting to be remembered, cursing the deference with which the Monégasques treat the wealthy. Stephen could see from the bar what had happened and made furtive signs to leave. They were all back in room 217 just after 2 am.

'What a bloody silly mistake. *Merde, merde, merde.* I should have thought of reservations the moment I knew Harvey had one.'

'No, it was my fault. I don't know anything about how casinos work and I should have queried it during rehearsals,' said Robin, stroking his newly acquired moustache.

'No one is to blame,' chipped in Stephen. 'We still have three more nights, so no need to panic. We'll just have to work out how to overcome the seating problem, but for now we'll all get some sleep and meet again in this room at 10 am.'

They left, a little depressed. Robin had sat waiting in the hotel on edge for four hours. James was cold and bored in the hospital car park, Stephen was sick of tomato juice and Jean-Pierre had been on his feet by the baccarat table waiting for a seat that wasn't even available.

Once again Harvey lounged in the sun. He was now a light pink and was hoping to be a better colour towards the end of the week. According to his copy of the *New York Times*, gold was still climbing and the Deutschmark and the Swiss franc remained firm, while the dollar was on the retreat against every currency except sterling. Sterling stood at $2.42. Harvey thought a more realistic price was $1.80 and the sooner it reached that the better.

Nothing new, he thought, when the sharp ring of a French telephone roused him. He never could get used to the sound of foreign telephones. The attentive steward bustled out on deck with the instrument on an extension lead.

'Hi, Lloyd. Didn't know you were in Monte . . . why don't we get together? . . . 8 pm? . . . Me too . . . I'm even getting brown . . . Must be getting old . . . What? . . . Great, I'll see you then.'

Harvey replaced the receiver and asked the steward for a large whisky on the rocks. He once again settled down happily to the morning's financial bad news.

'That seems to be the obvious solution,' said Stephen.

They all nodded their approval.

'Jean-Pierre will give up the baccarat table and book a place next to Harvey Metcalfe on his black-jack table in the Salon des Amériques and wait for him to change games. We know both the seat numbers Harvey plays at and we'll alter our own plans accordingly.'

Jean-Pierre dialled the number of the Casino and asked to speak to Pierre Cattalano:

'*Réservez-moi la deuxième place à la table 2 pour le vingt-et-un ce soir et demain soir, s'il vous plaît.*'

'*Je pense que cette place est déjà réservée, Monsieur. Un instant, s'il vous plaît, je vais vérifier.*'

'*Peut-être que 100 francs la rendra libre,*' replied Jean-Pierre.

'*Mais certainement, Monsieur. Présentez-vous à moi dès votre arrivée, et le nécessaire sera fait.*'

'*Merci,*' said Jean-Pierre and replaced the receiver. 'That's under control.'

Jean-Pierre was visibly sweating, though had his call had no other outcome than to secure him a reserved seat, not a drop of perspiration would have appeared. They all returned to their rooms.

When the clock in the town square struck twelve, Robin was waiting quietly in room 217, James stood in the car park humming 'I Get Along Without You Very Well', Stephen was at the bar of the Salon des Amériques toying with yet another tomato juice and Jean-Pierre was at seat No. 2 on table No. 2, playing blackjack. Both Stephen and Jean-Pierre saw Harvey come through the door, chatting to a man in a loud-checked jacket which only a Texan could have worn outside his own back yard. Harvey and his friend sat down together at the baccarat table. Jean-Pierre beat a hasty retreat to the bar.

'Oh, no. I give up.'

'No, you don't,' whispered Stephen. 'Back to the hotel.'

Spirits were very low when they were all assembled in room 217, but it was agreed that Stephen had made the right decision. They could not risk the entire exercise being carefully observed by a friend of Harvey's.

'The first operation is beginning to look a bit too good to be true,' said Robin.

'Don't be silly,' said Stephen. 'We had two false alarms then, and the entire plan had to be changed at the last minute. We can't expect him just to walk in and hand over his money. Now snap out of it, all of you, and go and get some sleep.'

They returned to their separate rooms, but not to much sleep. The strain was beginning to tell.

'That's enough I think, Lloyd. A goodish evening.'

'For you, you mean, Harvey, not for me. You are one of nature's winners.'

Harvey patted the checked shoulder expansively. If anything pleased him more than his own success, it was other people's failure.

'Do you want to spend the night on my yacht, Lloyd?'

'No thanks. I must get back to Nice. I have a meeting in Paris, France, tomorrow lunch. See you soon, Harvey – take care of yourself.' He dug Harvey in the ribs jocularly. 'That's a fair-sized job.'

'Goodnight, Lloyd,' said Harvey, a little stiffly.

The next evening Jean-Pierre did not arrive at the Casino until 11 pm. Harvey Metcalfe was already at the baccarat table minus Lloyd. Stephen was at the bar looking angry, and Jean-Pierre glanced at him apologetically as he took his seat at the blackjack table. He played a few hands to get the feel, trying to keep his losses fairly limited without drawing attention to the modesty of his stakes. Suddenly Harvey left the baccarat table and stalked into the Salon des Amériques, glancing at the roulette tables as he passed more out of curiosity than interest. He detested games of pure chance, and considered baccarat and black-jack games of skill. He headed to table No. 2 seat No. 3, on Jean-Pierre's left. Jean-Pierre felt his adrenalin start pumping round and his heart-beat rise up to 120 again. Stephen left the Casino for a few minutes to warn James and Robin that Harvey had moved to the blackjack table and was now sitting next to Jean-Pierre. He then returned to the bar and waited.

There were seven punters at the blackjack table. On box No. 1, a middle-aged lady smothered in diamonds, who looked as if she might be passing time while her husband played roulette or perhaps bacca-rat. On box No. 2, Jean-Pierre. On Box No. 3, Harvey. On Box No. 4, a dissipated young man with the world-weariness that usually goes with a large unearned income. On box No. 5, an Arab in full robes. On box No. 6, a not-unattractive actress who was clearly resting, Jean-Pierre suspected, with the occupant of box No. 5; and on box No. 7, an elderly straight-backed aristocratic Frenchman in evening dress.

'A large black coffee,' Harvey drawled to the slim waiter in his smart brown jacket.

Monte Carlo does not allow hard liquor to be sold at the tables or girls to serve the customers. In direct contrast to Las Vegas, the Casino's business is gambling, not booze or women. Harvey had enjoyed Vegas when he was younger, but the older he became the more he appreciated the sophistication of the French. He had grown to prefer the formal atmosphere and decorum of this particular Casino. Although at the No. 3 table only he, the aristocratic Frenchman and Jean-Pierre wore dinner-jackets, it was frowned upon by the management to be dressed in any way that might be described as casual.

A moment later, piping hot coffee in a large golden cup arrived at Harvey's side. Jean-Pierre eyed it nervously while Harvey placed 100 francs on the table next to Jean-Pierre's 3-franc chip, the minimum and maximum stake allowed. The dealer, a tall young man of not more than thirty, who was proud of the fact that he could deal a hundred hands in an hour, slipped the cards deftly out of the shoe. A king for Jean-Pierre, a four for Harvey, a five for the young man on Harvey's left and a six for the dealer. Jean-Pierre's second card was a seven. He stuck. Harvey drew a ten and also stuck. The young man on Harvey's left also drew ten and asked the dealer to twist again. It was an eight – bust.

Harvey despised amateurs in any field and even fools know you don't twist if you have twelve or more when the dealer's card face up is a three, four, five or six. He grimaced slightly. The dealer dealt himself a ten and a six. Harvey and Jean-Pierre were winners. Jean-Pierre ignored the fate of the other players.

The next round was unwinnable. Jean-Pierre stuck at eighteen, two nines which he chose not to split as the dealer had an ace. Harvey stuck on eighteen, an eight and a jack, and the young man on the left bust again. The bank drew a queen – 'Black Jack' – and took the table.

The next hand gave Jean-Pierre a three, Harvey a seven and the young man a ten. The dealer drew himself a seven. Jean-Pierre drew an eight and doubled his stake to 6 francs and then drew a ten – vingt-et-un. Jean-Pierre did not blink. He realised he was playing well and that he must not draw attention to himself, but let Harvey take it for granted. In fact Harvey hadn't even noticed him: his attention was riveted on the young man on his left, who seemed anxious to make a gift to the management on every hand. The dealer continued, giving Harvey a ten and the young man an eight, leaving them both no choice but to stick. The dealer drew a ten, giving himself seventeen. He paid Jean-Pierre, left Harvey's stake and paid the young man. The management was happy to pay the young man occasionally, if only to keep him sitting there all night.

There were no more cards left in the shoe. The dealer made a great show of re-shuffling the four packs and invited Harvey to cut the cards before replacing them in the shoe. They slipped out again: a ten for Jean-Pierre, a five for Harvey, a six for the young man and a four for the dealer. Jean-Pierre drew an eight. The cards were running well. Harvey drew a ten and stuck at fifteen. The young man drew a ten and asked for another card. Harvey could not believe his eyes and whistled through the gap in his front teeth. Sure enough, the next card was a king. The young man was bust. The dealer dealt himself a jack and then an eight, making twenty-two, but the young man had learned nothing from it. Harvey stared at him. When would he discover that, of the fifty-two cards in the pack, no less than sixteen have a face value of ten?

Harvey's distraction gave Jean-Pierre the opportunity he had been waiting for. He slipped his hand into his pocket and took the prostigmin tablet Robin had given him into the palm of his left hand. He sneezed, pulling his handkerchief from his breast pocket in a well-rehearsed gesture with his right hand. At the same time, he quickly and unobtrusively dropped the tablet into Harvey's coffee. It would, Robin had assured him, be an hour before it took effect. To begin with Harvey would only feel a little sick; then he would get rapidly worse until the pain was too much to bear, before finally collapsing in absolute agony.

Jean-Pierre turned to the bar, gripped his right-hand fist three times and then placed it in his pocket. Stephen left immediately and warned Robin and James from the steps of the Casino that the prostigmin tablet was in Metcalfe's drink. It was now Robin's turn to be tested under pressure. First he rang the hospital and asked the sister on duty to have the theatre in full preparation. Then he rang the nursing agency and asked for the nurse he had booked to be waiting in the hospital reception in exactly ninety minutes' time. He sat alone, nervously waiting for another call from the Casino.

Stephen returned to the bar. Harvey had started to feel a little sick, but was loath to leave. Despite the growing pain, his greed was forcing him to play on. He drank the rest of this coffee and ordered another one, hoping it would clear his head. The coffee did not help and Harvey began to feel steadily worse. An ace and a king followed by a seven, a four and a ten, and then two queens helped him to stay at the table. Jean-Pierre forced himself not to look at his watch. The dealer gave Jean-Pierre a seven, Harvey another ace and the young man a two. Quite suddenly, almost exactly on the hour, Harvey could bear the pain no longer. He tried to stand up to leave the table.

'*Le jeu a commencé, Monsieur,*' the dealer said formally.

'Go stuff yourself,' said Harvey and collapsed to the ground, gripping his stomach in agony. Jean-Pierre sat motionless while the croupiers and gamblers milled around helplessly. Stephen fought his way through the circle which had gathered round Harvey.

'Stand back, please. I am a doctor.'

The crowd moved back quickly, relieved to have a professional man on the scene.

'What is it, Doctor?' gasped Harvey, who felt the end of the world was about to come.

'I don't know yet,' replied Stephen. Robin had warned him that from collapse to passing out might be as short a time as ten minutes, so he set to work fast. He loosened Harvey's tie and took his pulse. He then undid his shirt and started feeling his abdomen.

'Have you a pain in the stomach?'

'Yes,' groaned Harvey.

'Did it come on suddenly?'

'Yes.'

'Can you try and describe the quality of the pain? Is it stabbing, burning or gripping?'

'Gripping.'

'Where is it most painful?'

Harvey touched the right side of his stomach. Stephen pressed down the tip of the ninth rib, making Harvey bellow with pain.

'Ah,' said Stephen, 'a positive Murphy's sign. You probably have an acutely inflamed gall-bladder. I'm afraid that may mean gallstones.' He continued to palpate the massive abdomen, gently. 'It looks as if a stone has come out of your gall-bladder and is passing down the tube to your intestine – it's the squeezing of that tube that's giving you such a dreadful pain. I'm afraid your gall-bladder and the stone must be removed at once. I can only hope there is someone at the hospital who can perform an emergency operation.'

Jean-Pierre came in bang on cue:

'Doctor Wiley Barker is staying at my hotel.'

'Wiley Barker, the American surgeon?'

'Yes, yes,' said Jean-Pierre. 'The chap who's been taking care of Nixon.'

'My God, what a piece of luck. We couldn't have

anyone better, but he might turn out to be very expensive.'

'I don't give a damn about expense,' wailed Harvey.

'Well, it might be as high as $50,000.'

'I don't care if it's $100,000,' screamed Harvey. At that moment he would have been willing to part with his entire fortune.

'Right,' said Stephen. 'You, sir,' looking at Jean-Pierre, 'ring for an ambulance and then contact Doctor Barker and ask if he can get to the hospital immediately. Tell him it's an emergency. This gentleman requires a surgeon of the highest qualifications.'

'You're damn right I do,' said Harvey, and passed out.

Jean-Pierre left the Casino and called over his transmitter:

'Action stations. Action stations.'

Robin left the Hôtel de Paris and took a taxi. He would have given $100,000 to change places with the driver, but the car was already moving relentlessly towards the hospital. It was too late to turn back now.

James smashed the ambulance into first gear and rushed to the Casino, siren blaring. He was luckier than Robin. With so much to concentrate on he didn't have time to consider the consequences of what he was doing.

Eleven minutes and forty-one seconds later he arrived, leapt out of the driver's seat, opened the back door, gathered the stretcher and rushed up the Casino steps in his long white coat. Jean-Pierre was standing expectantly on the top step waiting for him. No words passed between them as he guided James quickly through the Salon des Amériques where Stephen was bending over Harvey. The stretcher was placed on the floor. It took all three of them to lift Harvey Metcalfe's 227 lb on to the canvas. Stephen and James picked up the stretcher and took him quickly through to the waiting ambulance, followed by Jean-Pierre.

'Where are you going with my boss?' demanded a voice.

Startled, the three of them turned round. It was Harvey Metcalfe's chauffeur, standing by the white Rolls Royce. After a moment's hesitation, Jean-Pierre took over.

'Mr Metcalfe has collapsed and has to go to hospital for an emergency operation. You must return to the yacht immediately, tell the staff to have his cabin ready and await further instructions.'

The chauffeur touched his cap and ran to the Rolls Royce. James leapt behind the wheel, while Stephen and Jean-Pierre joined Harvey in the back of the vehicle.

'Hell, that was close. Well done, Jean-Pierre. I was speechless,' admitted Stephen.

'It was nothing,' said Jean-Pierre, sweat pouring down his face.

The ambulance shot off like a scalded cat. Stephen and Jean-Pierre both replaced their jackets with the long white laboratory coats left on the seat and Stephen put the stethoscope round his neck.

'It looks to me as if he's dead,' said Jean-Pierre.

'Robin says he isn't,' said Stephen.

'How can he tell from four miles away?'

'I don't know. We'll just have to take his word for it.'

James screeched to a halt outside the entrance to the hospital. Stephen and Jean-Pierre hurried their patient through to the operating theatre. James returned the ambulance to the car park and quickly joined the others in the theatre.

Robin, scrubbed up and gowned, was there to meet them at the door and while they were strapping Harvey Metcalfe to the operating table in the small room next to the theatre, he spoke for the first time:

'All of you, change your clothes. And Jean-Pierre, you scrub up as instructed.'

All three of them changed and Jean-Pierre started to wash immediately – a long, laborious process which Robin had firmly taught him must never be cut short. Post-operative septicaemia formed no part of his plan. Jean-Pierre appeared from the scrubbing-up room ready for action.

'Now, relax. We've done this nine times already. Just carry on exactly as if we were still in St Thomas's.'

Stephen moved behind the mobile Boyles machine. For four weeks he had been training as an anaesthetist: he had rendered James and a faintly protesting Jean-Pierre unconscious twice each in practice runs at St Thomas's. Now was his chance to exercise his new powers over Harvey Metcalfe.

Robin removed a syringe from a plastic packet and injected 250 mg of thiopentone into Harvey's arm. The patient sank back into a deep sleep. Quickly and efficiently Jean-Pierre and James undressed Harvey and then covered him in a sheet. Stephen placed the mask from the Boyles machine over Metcalfe's nose. The two flow-meters on the back of the machine showed 5 litres of nitrous oxide and 3 litres of oxygen.

'Take his pulse,' said Robin.

Stephen placed a finger in front of the ear just above the lobe to check the pre-auricular pulse. It was 70.

'Wheel him through into the theatre,' instructed Robin.

James pushed the trolley into the next room until it was just under the operating lights. Stephen trundled the Boyles machine along behind them.

The operating theatre was windowless and coldly sterile. Gleaming white tiles covered every wall from floor to ceiling, and it contained only the equipment needed for one operation. Jean-Pierre had covered Harvey with a sterile green sheet, leaving only his head and left arm exposed. One trolley of sterile instruments, drapes and towels had been carefully laid out by the theatre nurse, and stood covered with a sterile sheet. Robin hung the bottle of intravenous fluid from a standard near the head of the table and taped the end of the tubing to Harvey's left arm to complete the preparation. Stephen sat at the head of the table with the Boyles machine and adjusted the face-mask over Harvey's mouth and nose. Only one of the three massive operating lights hanging directly over Harvey had been turned on, causing a spotlight effect on the protruding bulge of his abdomen.

Eight eyes stared down on their victim. Robin continued:

'I shall give exactly the same instructions as I did in all our rehearsals, so just concentrate. First, I shall clean the abdomen with a skin preparation of iodine.'

Robin had all the instruments ready on the side of the table next to Harvey's feet. James lifted the sheet and folded it back over Harvey's legs, then he carefully removed the sterile sheet covering the trolley of instruments and poured iodine into one of the small basins. Robin picked up a swab in a pair of forceps and dipped it in the iodine solution. With a swift action up, down, and over the abdomen, he cleaned about 1 square foot of Harvey's massive body, throwing the swab into a bin and repeating the action with a fresh one. Next he placed a sterile towel below Harvey's chin, covering his chest, and another over his hips and thighs. A third one he placed lengthways along the left-hand side of his body and a final one along the right-hand side, leaving a 9 inch square of flabby belly exposed. He put a towel clip on each corner to secure them safely and then placed the laparotomy drapes over the prepared site. Robin was now ready.

'Scalpel.'

Jean-Pierre placed what he would have called a knife firmly in Robin's outstretched palm, as a runner might when passing a baton. James's apprehensive eyes met Jean-Pierre's across the operating table, while Stephen concentrated on Harvey's breathing. Robin hesitated only for a second and then made a 10 cm paramedian incision, reaching about 3 cm into the fat. Robin had rarely seen a larger stomach: he could probably have gone as far as 8 cm deep without reaching the muscle. Blood started flowing everywhere, which Robin stopped with diathermy. No sooner had he finished the incision and stanched the flow of blood than he began to stitch up the patient's wound with a 3/0 interrupted plain catgut for ten stitches.

'That will dissolve within a week,' he explained.

He then closed the skin with a 2/0 interrupted plain silk, using an atraumatic needle. Then he cleaned the wound, removing the patches of blood that still remained. Finally, he placed a medium self-adhesive wound dressing over his handiwork.

James took off the drapes and sterile towels and placed them in the bin while Robin and Jean-Pierre put Metcalfe into a hospital gown and carefully packed his clothes in a grey plastic bag.

'He's coming round,' said Stephen.

Robin took another syringe and injected 10 mg of diazepam.

'That will keep him asleep for at least 30 minutes,' he said, 'and in any case, he'll be ga-ga for about three hours and won't remember much of what has happened. James, fetch the ambulance immediately and bring it round to the front of the hospital.'

James left the theatre and changed back into his clothes, a procedure which he could now perform in 90 seconds. He disappeared to the car park.

'Now, you two, get changed and then place Harvey very carefully in the ambulance and Jean-Pierre, wait in the back with him. Stephen, you carry out your next assignment.'

Stephen and Jean-Pierre changed quickly, back into their long white coats and wheeled the slumbering Harvey Metcalfe gently towards the ambulance. Once safely in, Stephen ran to the public telephone by the hospital entrance, checked a piece of paper in his wallet and dialled.

'Hello, *Nice-Matin*? My name's Terry Robards of the *New York Times*. I'm here on holiday, and I have a great little story for you . . .'

Robin returned to the operating theatre and wheeled the trolley of instruments he had used to the sterilising room, and left them there to be dealt with by the hospital theatre staff in the morning. He picked up the plastic bag containing Harvey's clothes and, going through to the changing room, quickly removed his operating gown, cap and mask and put on his own clothes. He went in search of the theatre sister, and smiled charmingly at her.

'All finished, *ma soeur*. I have left the instruments by the steriliser. Please thank Monsieur Bartise for me once again.'

'*Oui, Monsieur. Notre plaisir. Je suis heureuse d'être à même de vous aider. Votre infirmière de l'Auxiliaire Médicale est arrivée.*'

A few moments later, Robin walked to the ambulance, accompanied by the agency nurse. He helped her into the back.

'Drive very slowly and carefully to the harbour.'

James nodded and set off at funeral pace.

'Nurse Faubert.'

'Yes, Docteur Barker.' Her hands were tucked primly under her blue cape, and her French accent was enchanting. Robin thought Harvey would not find her ministrations unwelcome.

'My patient has just had an operation for the removal of a gall stone and will need plenty of rest.'

With that Robin took out of his pocket a gall stone the size of an orange with a hospital tag on it which read 'Harvey Metcalfe'. Robin had in fact acquired the huge stone from St Thomas's Hospital, the original owner being a 6 ft 6 in West Indian bus conductor on the No. 14 route. Stephen and Jean-Pierre stared at it in disbelief. The nurse checked her new charge's pulse and respiration.

'If I were your patient, Nurse Faubert,' said Jean-Pierre, 'I should take good care never to recover.'

By the time they arrived at the yacht, Robin had briefed the nurse on diet and rest, and told her that he would be round to see his patient at 11 am the next day. They left Harvey sleeping soundly in his large cabin, stewards and staff clucking attentively.

James drove the other three back to the hospital, deposited the ambulance in the car park and left the keys with reception. The four of them then headed back to the hotel by separate routes. Robin was the last to arrive at room 217, just after 3.30 am. He collapsed into an armchair.

'Will you allow me a whisky, Stephen?'

'Yes, of course.'

'Good God, he meant it,' said Robin, and downed a large Johnny Walker before handing the bottle over to Jean-Pierre.

'He will be all right, won't he?' said James.

'You sound quite concerned for him. Yes, he can have his ten stitches out in a week's time and all he'll have is a nasty scar to brag about to his friends. I must get some sleep. I have to see our victim at 11 tomorrow morning and the confrontation may well be harder than the operation. You were all great tonight. My God, am I glad we had all those sessions at St Thomas's. If you're ever out of work and I need a croupier, a driver and an anaesthetist, I'll know who to ring.'

The others left and Robin collapsed on to his bed, exhausted. He fell into a deep sleep and woke just after 8 the next morning, to discover he was still fully dressed. That had not happened to him since his days as a young houseman, when he had been on night duty after a fourteen-hour day without a break. Robin had a long soothing bath in very hot water. He dressed and put on a clean shirt and suit, ready for his face-to-face meeting with Harvey Metcalfe. His newly acquired moustache and rimless glasses and the success of the operation made him feel a little like the famous surgeon he was impersonating. The other three all appeared during the next hour to wish him luck and elected to wait in room 217 for his return. Stephen had checked them all out of the hotel and booked a flight to London for late that afternoon. Robin left, again taking the staircase rather than the lift. Once outside the hotel, he walked a little way before hailing a taxi to drive him to the harbour.

It was not hard to find the *Messenger Boy*. She was a gleaming, newly painted 100-footer lying at the east end of the harbour. She sported a massive Panamanian flag on her stern mast, which Robin assumed must be for tax purposes. He ascended the gangplank and was met by Nurse Faubert.

'*Bonjour, Docteur Barker.*'

'Good morning, Nurse. How is Mr Metcalfe?'

'He has had a very peaceful night and is having a light breakfast and making a few telephone calls. Would you like to see him now?'

'Yes, please.'

Robin entered the magnificent cabin and faced the

man he had spent eight weeks plotting and planning against. He was talking into the telephone:

'Yes, I'm fine, dear. But it was an A-1 emergency at the time. Don't worry, I'll live,' and he put the telephone down. 'Doctor Barker, I have just spoken to my wife in Massachusetts and told her that I owe you my life. Even at 5 am she seemed pleased. I understand that I had private surgery, a private ambulance and that you saved my life. Or that's what it says in *Nice-Matin*.'

There was the old picture of Harvey in Bermuda shorts on the deck of the *Messenger Boy*, familiar to Robin from his dossier. The headline read '*Millionaire s'évanouit au Casino*' over '*La Vie d'un Millionaire Américain a été sauvée par une Opération Urgente Dramatique!*' Stephen would be pleased.

'Tell me, Doctor,' said Harvey with relish, 'was I really in danger?'

'Well, you were on the critical list, and the consequences might have been fairly serious if we hadn't removed this from your stomach.' Robin took out the inscribed gall stone from his pocket with a flourish.

Harvey's eye grew large as saucers.

'Gee, have I really been walking round with that inside me all this time? Isn't that something? I can't thank you enough. If ever I can do anything for you, Doctor, don't hesitate to call on me.' He offered Robin a grape. 'Look, you're going to see me through this thing, aren't you? I don't think the nurse fully appreciates the gravity of my case.'

Robin thought fast.

'I'm afraid I'm not free to do that, Mr Metcalfe. My holiday finishes today and I have to return to California. Nothing urgent: just a few elective surgeries and a rather heavy lecture schedule.' He shrugged deprecatingly. 'Not exactly earth-shattering but it helps me keep up a way of life I have grown accustomed to.'

Harvey sat bolt upright, tenderly holding his stomach.

'Now you listen to me, Doctor Barker. I don't give a damn about a few students. I'm a sick man and I need you here until I've fully recovered. I'll make it worth your while to stay, don't you worry. I never grudge the money where my health is concerned, and what's more if it will persuade you, I'll make the cheque out to cash. The last thing I want Uncle Sam to know is how much I'm worth.'

Robin coughed delicately, wondering how American doctors approached the ticklish subject of fees with their patients.

'The cost could be rather high if I'm not to be out of pocket by staying. It might be as much as $80,000.' Robin drew a deep breath.

Harvey didn't blink.

'Sure. You're the best. That's not a lot of money to stay alive.'

'Very well. I'll get back to my hotel and see if it's possible to rearrange my schedule for you.'

Robin retreated from the sick-room and the white

Rolls Royce took him back to the hotel. In room 217 they all sat staring at Robin in disbelief as he completed his story.

'Stephen, for Christ's sake, the man's a raving hypochondriac. He wants me to stay on here while he convalesces. None of us planned for that.'

Stephen looked up coolly:

'You'll stay here and play ball. Why not give him value for money – at his own expense, of course. Go on, get on the blower and tell him you'll be round to hold his hand every day at 11 am. We'll just have to go back without you. And keep the hotel bill down, won't you?'

Robin picked up the telephone . . .

Three young men left the Hôtel de Paris after a long lunch in room 217, allowing themselves another bottle of Krug '64, and then returned to Nice Airport in a taxi, catching BA flight 012 at 16.10 to London Heathrow. They were once again in separate seats. One sentence remained on Stephen's mind from Robin's reported conversation with Harvey Metcalfe.

'If ever I can do anything for you, don't hesitate to call me at any time.'

Robin visited his patient once a day, borne in the white Corniche with white-walled tyres and a chauffeur in a white uniform. Only Harvey could be quite so brash, he thought. On the third, Nurse Faubert asked for a private word with him.

'My patient,' she said plaintively, 'is making improper advances when I change his dressing.'

Robin allowed Dr Wiley Barker the liberty of an unprofessional remark.

'Can't say I altogether blame him. Still, be firm, Nurse. I'm sure you must have encountered that sort of thing before.'

'*Naturellement*, but never from a patient only three days after major surgery. His constitution, it must be *formidable*.'

'I tell you what, let's catheterise him for a couple of days. That'll cramp his style.' She smiled. 'It must be pretty boring for you cooped up here all day,' Robin continued. 'Why don't you come and have a spot of supper with me after Mr Metcalfe has gone to sleep tonight?'

'I should love to, *Docteur*. Where shall I meet you?'

'Room 217, Hôtel de Paris,' said Robin unblushingly. 'Say 9 pm.'

'I'll look forward to it, *Docteur*.'

'A little more Chablis, Angeline?'

'No more, thank you, Wiley. That was a meal to remember. I think, maybe, you have not yet had everything you want?'

She got up, lit two cigarettes and put one in his

mouth. Then she moved away, her long skirt swinging slightly from the hips. She wore no bra under her pink shirt. She exhaled smokily and watched him.

Robin thought of the blameless Doctor Barker in Australia, of his wife and children in Newbury, and the rest of the Team in London. Then he put them all out of his mind.

'Will you complain to Mr Metcalfe if I make improper advances to you?'

'From you, Wiley,' she smiled, 'they will not be improper.'

Harvey made a talkative recovery, and Robin removed the stitches gravely on the sixth day.

'That seems to have healed very cleanly, Mr Metcalfe. Take it easy, and you should be back to normal by the middle of next week.'

'Great. I have to get over to England right away for Ascot week. You know, my horse Rosalie is favourite this year. I suppose you can't join me as my guest? What if I have a relapse.'

Robin suppressed a smile.

'Don't worry. You're getting along fine. Sorry I can't stay to see how Rosalie performs at Ascot.'

'So am I, Doc. Thanks again, anyway. I've never met a surgeon like you before.'

And you're not likely to again, thought Robin, his American accent beginning to fray at the edges. He bid his adieus to Harvey with relief and to Angeline with regret, and sent the chauffeur back from the hotel with a copper-plate bill:

> *Dr Wiley Franklin Barker*
> *presents his Compliments to*
> *Mr Harvey Metcalfe*
> *and begs to inform him that the Bill for*
> *Professional Services rendered is*
> *$80,000*
> *in respect of surgery and post-operative treatment.*

The chauffeur was back within the hour with a cash cheque for $80,000. Robin bore it back to London in triumph.

Two down and two to go.

13

THE FOLLOWING DAY, Friday, Stephen sat on Robin's examination couch in Harley Street and addressed the troops.

'The Monte Carlo operation was a total success in every way, thanks to Robin keeping his cool. The expenses were fairly high, though. The hospital and hotel bills totalled $11,351, while we received $80,000. Therefore, we've had $527,560 returned to us, and expenses so far have come to $22,530, which leaves Mr Metcalfe still in debt to the tune of $494,970. Does everyone agree with that?'

There was a general murmur of approval. Their confidence in Stephen's arithmetic was unbounded, although in fact, like all algebraists, he found working with figures somewhat tedious.

'Incidentally, Robin, however did you manage to spend $73.50 on dinner last Wednesday night? What did you have, caviar and champagne?'

'Something a little out of the ordinary,' admitted Robin. 'It seemed to be called for at the time.'

'I'd bet more than I laid out in Monte Carlo that I know who joined you for dinner, and I bet she shared more than a table with you too,' said Jean-Pierre, taking his wallet out of his pocket. 'Here you are Stephen, 219 francs – my winnings from the Casino on Wednesday night. If you'd left me alone in peace, we needn't have bothered with Robin's butchery. I could have won the whole amount back on my own. I think the least I deserve is Nurse Faubert's telephone number.'

Jean-Pierre's remarks went straight over Stephen's head.

'Well done, Jean-Pierre, it'll all come off expenses. At today's exchange rate, your 219 francs,' he paused for a moment and tapped out on his calculator, 'is worth $46.76. That brings the expenses down to $22,483.24.

'Now, my plans for Ascot are simple. James has acquired two badges for the Members' Enclosure at a cost of $10. We know that Harvey Metcalfe also has a badge, as all owners do, so as long as we get our timing right and make it look natural, he should once again fall into our trap. James will keep us briefed on the walkie-talkie and will follow the movements of Metcalfe from his arrival to his leaving. Jean-Pierre will wait by the entrance of the Members' Enclosure and follow him in. Robin will send the telegram from Heathrow Airport at 1 pm, so Harvey ought to receive it during lunch in his private box. That part of the plan is easy. It's if we manage to lure him to Oxford that we all have to be on our toes. I must confess, it'd make a pleasant change if Ascot were to work first time.'

Stephen grinned widely.

'That would give us much needed extra time to go over the Oxford plan again. Any questions?'

'You don't need us for part (*a*) of the Oxford plan, only (*b*)?' asked Robin, checking Stephen's notes.

'That's right. I can manage part (*a*) on my own. In fact, it will be better if you all remain in London on that night, well out of the way. Our next priority must be to think up some ideas for James or he might, heaven preserve us, even think up something for himself. I'm becoming very concerned about this,' continued Stephen, 'because once Harvey returns to America we'll have to deal with him on his own ground. To date he's always been at the venue of our choosing. James would stick out like a sore thumb in Boston, even though he's the best actor of the four of us. In Harvey's words, "It would be a whole different ball game".'

James sighed lugubriously and studied the Axminster carpet.

'Poor old James – don't worry, you drove that ambulance like a trooper,' said Robin.

'Perhaps you could learn to fly a plane and then we could hijack him,' suggested Jean-Pierre.

Miss Meikle did not approve of the laughter coming from Doctor Oakley's room and she was glad to see the oddly assorted trio leave. When she had closed the door finally on James she returned to Robin's room.

'Will you see your patients now, Doctor Oakley?'

'Yes, if I must, Miss Meikle.'

Miss Meikle pursed her lips. Whatever had come over him? It must be those dreadful types he had started mixing with lately. He had become so unreliable.

'Mrs Wentworth-Brewster – Doctor Oakley will see you now, and I'll have the pills for your trip to Italy ready for you when you come out.'

Stephen returned for a few days' recuperation to Magdalen College. He had started the entire exercise eight weeks before and two of the Team had succeeded far beyond his expectations. He was conscious that he must crown their efforts with something that would live on in the legends of Oxford long after his departure.

Jean-Pierre returned to work in his gallery in Bond Street. Since he only had to deliver one sentence at Ascot he was not going to be overtaxed, although part (*b*) of Stephen's Oxford plan kept him nightly in front of a mirror rehearsing his role.

James took Anne down to Stratford-upon-Avon for the weekend. The Royal Shakespeare Company obliged with a sparkling performance of *Much Ado about Nothing* and afterwards, walking along the banks of the Avon, James proposed. Only the royal swans could have heard her reply. The diamond ring James had noticed in the window of Cartier while he had been waiting for Harvey Metcalfe to join Jean-Pierre in the gallery, looked even more beautiful on her slender finger. James's happiness seemed complete. If only he could come up with a plan and shock them all, he would want for nothing. He discussed it with Anne again that night, considering new ideas and old ones, still getting nowhere.

But an idea was beginning to formulate in her mind.

14

ON MONDAY MORNING James drove Anne back to London and changed into the most debonair of his suits. Anne had to return to work, despite James's suggestion that she should accompany him to Ascot. She felt the others would not approve of her presence and would suspect that James had confided in her.

Although James had not told her the details of the Monte Carlo exercise, Anne knew every step of the planned proceedings at Ascot and she could tell that James was nervous. Still, she would be seeing him that night and would know the worst by then. James looked lost. Anne was only thankful that Stephen, Robin and Jean-Pierre held the baton most of the time in this relay team – but the idea that was taking shape in her mind just might surprise them all.

Stephen rose early and admired his grey hair in the mirror. The result had been expensively achieved the previous day in the hairdressing salon of Debenhams. He dressed carefully, putting on his one respectable grey suit and blue checked tie. These were brought out for all special occasions, ranging from a

talk to students at Sussex University to a dinner with
the American Ambassador. No one had told him the
colours clashed and the suit sagged unfashionably at
the elbow and knees, because by Stephen's standards
it was elegance itself. He travelled from Oxford to
Ascot by train, while Jean-Pierre came from London
by car. They met up with James at the Belvedere
Arms at 11 am, almost a mile from the course.

Stephen immediately telephoned Robin to confirm
that all three of them had arrived and asked for the
telegram to be read over to him.

'That's perfect, Robin. Now travel to Heathrow
and send it at exactly 1 pm.'

'Good luck, Stephen. Grind the bastard into the
dust.'

Stephen returned to the others and confirmed that
Robin had the London end under control.

'Off you go, James, and let us know the minute
Harvey arrives.'

James downed a bottle of Carlsberg and departed.
The problem was that he kept bumping into friends
and he could hardly explain why he was prevented
from joining them.

Harvey arrived at the members' car park just after
midday, his white Rolls Royce shining like a Persil
advertisement. The car was being stared at by all the
racegoers with an English disdain which Harvey mis-
took for admiration. He led his party to the private
box. His newly tailored suit had taxed the ingenuity
of Bernard Weatherill to the utmost. A red carnation

in his buttonhole and a hat to cover his bald head left him nearly unrecognisable, and James might have missed him had it not been for the white Rolls Royce. James followed the little group at a careful distance until he saw Harvey enter a door marked 'Mr Harvey Metcalfe and Guests'.

'He's in his private box,' said James.

'Where are you?' asked Jean-Pierre.

'Directly below him on the ground level by a course bookmaker called Sam O'Flaherty.'

'No need to be rude about the Irish, James,' said Jean-Pierre. 'We'll be with you in a few minutes.'

James stared up at the vast white stand, which accommodated 10,000 spectators in comfort and gave an excellent view of the racecourse. He was finding it hard to concentrate on the job in hand as once again he had to avoid relations and friends. First was the Earl of Halifax, and then that frightful girl he had so unwisely agreed to take to Queen Charlotte's Ball last spring. What was the creature's name? Ah yes. The Hon. Selina Wallop. How appropriate. She was wearing a mini-skirt that was a good four years out of fashion and a hat which looked as if it could never come into fashion. James jammed his trilby over his ears, looked the other way and passed the time by chatting to Sam O'Flaherty about the 3.20, the King George VI and Queen Elizabeth Stakes. O'Flaherty quoted the latest odds on the favourite at the top of his voice:

'Rosalie at 6:4, owned by that American, Harvey Metcalfe, and ridden by Pat Eddery.'

Eddery was on the way to becoming the youngest-ever champion jockey – and Harvey always backed winners.

Stephen and Jean-Pierre joined James at the side of Sam O'Flaherty's bag. His tick-tack man was standing on an upturned orange box beside him and swinging his arms like a semaphore sailor aboard a sinking ship.

'What's your fancy, gentlemen?' Sam asked the three of them.

James ignored Stephen's slight frown of disapproval.

'£5 each way on Rosalie,' he said, and handed over a crisp £10 note, receiving in return a little green card with the series number and 'Sam O'Flaherty' stamped right across the middle.

'I must presume, James, this is an integral part of your as yet undisclosed plan,' said Jean-Pierre. 'What I should like to know is, if it works, how much do we stand to make?'

'£9.10 after tax if Rosalie wins,' chipped in Sam O'Flaherty, his stub cigar bobbing up and down in his mouth as he spoke.

'Hardly a great contribution towards $1 million, James. Well, we're off to the Members' Enclosure. Let us know the moment Harvey leaves his box. My guess is that around 1.45 he'll come and look at the runners and riders for the two o'clock, so that gives us a clear hour.'

The waiter opened another bottle of Krug 1964 and began pouring it for Harvey's guests; three bankers, two economists, a couple of ship-owners and a distinguished City journalist.

Preferring his guests to be famous and influential, Harvey always invited people who would find it almost impossible to refuse because of the business he might put their way. He was delighted with the company he had assembled for his big day. Senior among them was Sir Howard Dodd, the ageing chairman of the merchant bank that bore his name, but which actually referred to his great-grandfather. Sir Howard was 6 ft 2 in, as straight as a ramrod, and looked more like a Grenadier Guard than a respectable banker. The only thing he had in common with Harvey was the hair, or lack of hair, on his balding head. His young assistant, Jamie Clark, accompanied him. Just over thirty and extremely bright, he was there to be sure his chairman did not commit the bank to anything he might later regret. Although he had a sneaking admiration for Harvey, Clark did not think him the sort of customer the bank should do business with. Nevertheless, he was far from averse to a day at the races.

The two economists, Mr Colin Emson and Dr Michael Hogan from the Hudson Institute, were there to brief Harvey on the parlous state of the British economy. They could not have been more different. Emson was a totally self-made man who had left school at fifteen and educated himself. Using his social contacts, he had built up a company specialising in taxation, which had been remarkably successful thanks to the British Government's habit of putting through a new Finance Act every few weeks. Emson was 6 ft tall, solid and genial, game to help the party along whether Harvey lost or won. Hogan, in contrast, had been to all the right places – Winchester, Trinity College, Oxford, and the Wharton Business School in Pennsylvania. A spell with McKinsey, the management consultants, in London had made him one of the best-informed economists in Europe. Those who observed his slim, sinewy body would not have been surprised to learn that he had been an international squash player. Dark-haired, with brown eyes that rarely left Harvey, he found it hard not to show his contempt; this was his fifth invitation to Ascot – Harvey, it seemed, was never going to take no for an answer.

The Kundas brothers, second-generation Greeks who loved racing almost as much as ships, could hardly be told apart, with their black hair, swarthy skins and heavy dark eyebrows. It was difficult to guess how old they were, and nobody knew how much they were worth. They probably did not know themselves. Harvey's final guest, Nick Lloyd of the *News of the World*, had come along to pick up any dirt

he could about his host. He had come near to expos-
ing Metcalfe in the mid-sixties, but another scandal
had kept less juicy stories off the front page for several
weeks, and by then Harvey had escaped. Lloyd,
hunched over the inevitable triple gin with a faint
suggestion of tonic, watched the motley bunch with
interest.

'Telegram for you, sir.'

Harvey ripped it open. He was never neat about
anything.

'It's from my daughter Rosalie. It's cute of her to
remember, but damn it all, I named the horse after
her. Come on everybody, let's eat.'

They all took their seats for lunch – cold vichys-
soise, pheasant and strawberries. Harvey was even
more loquacious than usual, but his guests took no
notice, aware he was nervous before the race and
knowing that he would rather be a winner of this
trophy than any he could be offered in America.
Harvey himself could never understand why he felt
that way. Perhaps it was the special atmosphere of
Ascot which appealed to him so strongly – the combination of lush green grass and gracious surroundings, of elegant crowds and an efficiency of
organisation which made Ascot the envy of the racing
world.

'You must have a better chance this year than ever
before, Harvey,' said the senior banker.

'Well, you know, Sir Howard, Lester Piggott is
riding the Duke of Devonshire's horse, Crown Prin-

cess, and the Queen's Horse, Highclere, is the joint favourite, so I can't afford to over-estimate my chances. When you've been third twice before, and then favourite and not placed, you begin to wonder if one of your horses is going to make it.'

'Another telegram, sir.'

Once again Harvey's fat little finger ripped it open.

'"All the best wishes and good luck for the King George VI and Queen Elizabeth Stakes". It's from the staff of your bank, Sir Howard. Jolly good show.'

Harvey's Polish-American accent made the English expression slightly ridiculous.

'More champagne, everybody.'

Another telegram arrived.

'At this rate, Harvey, you'll need a special room at the Post Office.' There was laughter all round at Sir Howard's feeble joke. Once again Harvey read it out aloud:

'"Regret unable to join you Ascot. Heading soonest California. Grateful look out for old friend Professor Rodney Porter, Oxford Nobel Prize Winner. Don't let English bookies stitch you up. Wiley B., Heathrow Airport". It's from Wiley Barker. He's the guy who did stitch me up in Monte Carlo. He saved my life. He took out a gall stone the size of that bread roll you're eating, Dr Hogan. Now how the hell am I supposed to find this Professor Porter?' Harvey turned to the head waiter. 'Find my chauffeur.'

A few seconds later the smartly-clad Guy Salmon flunkey appeared.

'There's a Professor Rodney Porter of Oxford here today. Go find him.'

'What does he look like, sir?'

'How the hell do I know,' said Harvey. 'Like a professor.'

The chauffeur regretfully abandoned his plans for an afternoon at the railings and departed, leaving Harvey and his guests to enjoy the strawberries, the champagne and the string of telegrams that were still arriving.

'You know if you win, the cup will be presented by the Queen,' said Nick Lloyd.

'You bet. It'll be the crowning moment of my life to win the King George and Elizabeth Stakes and meet Her Majesty The Queen. If Rosalie wins, I'll suggest my daughter marries Prince Charles – they're about the same age.'

'I don't think even you will be able to fix that, Harvey.'

'What'll you do with the odd £81,000 prize money, Mr Metcalfe?' asked Jamie Clark.

'Give it to some charity,' said Harvey, pleased with the impression the remark made on his guests.

'Very generous, Harvey. Typical of your reputation.' Nick Lloyd gave Michael Hogan a knowing look. Even if the others didn't, they both knew what was typical of his reputation.

The chauffeur returned to report that there was no trace of a solitary professor anywhere in the champagne bar, balcony luncheon room or the paddock buffet, and that he'd been unable to gain access to the Members' Enclosure.

'Naturally not,' said Harvey rather pompously. 'I shall have to find him myself. Drink up and enjoy yourselves.'

Harvey rose and walked to the door with the chauffeur. Once he was out of earshot of his guests, he said, 'Get your ass out of here and don't give me any crap about not being able to find him or you can find something for yourself – another job.'

The chauffeur bolted. Harvey turned to his guests and smiled.

'I'm going to look at the runners and riders for the 2 o'clock.'

'He's leaving the box now,' said James.

'What's that you're saying?' asked an authoritative voice he recognised. 'Talking to yourself, James?'

James stared at the noble Lord Somerset, 6 ft 1 in and still able to stand his full height, an MC and a DSO in the First World War. He still exuded enthusiastic energy although the lines on his face suggested that he had passed the age at which the Maker had fulfilled his contract.

'Oh hell. No, sir, I was just . . . em . . . coughing.'

'What do you fancy in the King George VI and Queen Elizabeth Stakes?' asked the peer of the realm.

'Well, I have put £5 each way on Rosalie, sir.'

*

'He seems to have cut himself off,' said Stephen.

'Well, buzz him again,' said Jean-Pierre.

'What's that noise, James? Have you taken to a hearing-aid or something?'

'No, sir. It's . . . it's . . . it's a transistor radio.'

'Those things ought to be banned. Bloody invasion of privacy.'

'Absolutely right, sir.'

'What's he playing at, Stephen?'

'I don't know − I think something must have happened.'

'Oh my God, it's Harvey heading straight for us. You go into the Members' Enclosure, Stephen, and I'll follow you. Take a deep breath and relax. He hasn't seen us.'

Harvey marched up to the official blocking the entrance to the Members' Enclosure.

'I'm Harvey Metcalfe, the owner of Rosalie, and this is my badge.'

The official let Harvey through. Thirty years ago, he thought, they would not have let him into the Members' Enclosure if he'd owned every horse in the race. Then racing at Ascot was only held on four days a year, jolly social occasions. Now it was twenty-four days a year and big business. Times had changed.

Jean-Pierre followed closely, showing his pass without speaking to the official.

A photographer broke away from stalking the outrageous hats for which Ascot has such a reputation, and took a picture of Harvey just in case Rosalie won the King George VI Stakes. As soon as his bulb flashed he rushed over to the other entrance, where Linda Lovelace, the star of *Deep Throat*, the film running to packed houses in New York but banned in England, was trying to enter the Members' Enclosure. In spite of being introduced to a well-known London banker, Richard Szpiro, just as he was entering the Enclosure, she was not succeeding. She was wearing a top hat and morning suit with nothing under the top coat, and no one was going to bother with Harvey while she was around. When Miss Lovelace was quite certain that every photographer had taken a picture of her attempting to enter the Enclosure she left, swearing at the top of her voice, her publicity stunt completed.

Harvey returned to studying the horses as Stephen moved up to within a few feet of him.

'Here we go again,' said Jean-Pierre in French and went smartly over to Stephen and, standing directly between the two of them, shook Stephen's hand warmly, declaring in a voice that was intended to carry:

'How are you, Professor Porter? I didn't know you were interested in racing.'

'I'm not really, but I was on my way back from a seminar in London and thought it a good opportunity to see how . . .'

'Professor Porter,' cried Harvey. 'I'm honoured to make your acquaintance, sir, my name is Harvey Metcalfe from Boston, Massachusetts. My good friend, Dr Wiley Barker, who saved my life, told me you'd be here today on your own, and I'm going to make sure you have a wonderful afternoon.'

Jean-Pierre slipped away unnoticed. He could not believe how easy it had been. The telegram had worked like a charm.

'Her Majesty The Queen; His Royal Highness The Duke of Edinburgh; Her Majesty Queen Elizabeth The Queen Mother; and her Royal Highness The Princess Anne are now entering the Royal Box.'

The massed bands of the Brigade of Guards struck up the National Anthem:

'God Save the Queen.'

The crowd of 25,000 rose and sang loyally out of tune.

'We should have someone like that in America,' said Harvey to Stephen, 'to take the place of Richard Nixon. We wouldn't have any Watergate problems then.'

Stephen thought his fellow American was being just a little unfair. Richard Nixon was almost a saint by Harvey Metcalfe's standards.

'Come and join me in my box, Professor, and meet my other guests. The damned box cost me £750, we may as well fill it. Have you had some lunch?'

'Yes, I've had an excellent lunch, thank you,' Stephen lied – something else Harvey had taught him. He had stood by the Members' Enclosure for an hour, nervous and pensive, unable even to manage a sandwich, and now he was starving.

'Well, come and enjoy the champagne,' roared Harvey.

On an empty stomach, thought Stephen.

'Thank you, Mr Metcalfe. I am a little lost. This is my first Royal Ascot.'

'This isn't Royal Ascot, Professor. It's the last day of Ascot Week, but the Royal Family always comes to see the King George and Elizabeth Stakes, so everybody dresses up.'

'I see,' said Stephen timidly, pleased with his deliberate error.

Harvey collared his find and took him back to the box.

'Everybody, I want you to meet my distinguished friend, Rodney Porter. He's a Nobel Prize Winner, you know. By the way, what's your subject, Rod?'

'Biochemistry.'

Stephen was getting the measure of Harvey. As long as he played it straight, the bankers and shippers, and even the journalists, would never doubt that he was the cleverest thing since Einstein. He relaxed a little and even found time to fill himself with smoked salmon sandwiches when the others were not looking.

Lester Piggott won the 2 o'clock on Olympic Casino and the 2.30 on Roussalka, achieving his 3,000th win. Harvey was getting steadily more nervous. He talked incessantly without making much sense. He had sat through the 2.30 without showing any interest in the result and consumed more and more champagne. At 2.50 he called for them all to join him in the Members' Enclosure to look at his famous filly. Stephen, like the others, trailed behind him in a little pseudo-royal entourage.

Jean-Pierre and James watched the procession from a distance.

'He's too deep in to climb out now,' said Jean-Pierre.

'He looks relaxed enough to me,' replied James. 'Let's make ourselves scarce. We can only get under his feet.'

They headed into the champagne bar, which was filled with red-faced men who looked as if they spent more time drinking than they did watching the racing.

'Isn't she beautiful, Professor? Almost as beautiful as my daughter. If she doesn't win today I don't think I'm ever going to make it.'

Harvey left his little clique to have a word with the jockey, Pat Eddery, to wish him luck. Peter Walwyn, the trainer, was giving final instructions before the jockey mounted and left the Enclosure. The ten horses were then paraded in front of the stand before the race, a custom only carried out at Ascot for the King George VI and Queen Elizabeth Stakes. The gold, purple and scarlet colours of Her Majesty The Queen's horse Highclere led the procession, followed by Crown Princess, who was giving Lester Piggott a little trouble. Directly behind her came Rosalie, looking very relaxed, fresh and ready to go. Buoy and Dankaro trotted behind Rosalie, with the outsiders Mesopotamia, Ropey and Minnow bringing up the rear. The crowd rose to cheer the horses and Harvey beamed with pride, as if he owned every horse in the race.

'. . . and I have with me today the distinguished American owner, Harvey Metcalfe,' said Julian Wilson into the BBC TV outside-broadcast camera. 'I'm going to ask him if he'd be kind enough to give me his views on the King George VI and Queen Elizabeth Stakes, for which he has the joint favourite, Rosalie. Welcome to England, Mr Metcalfe. How do you feel about the big race?'

'It's a thrill to be here, just to participate in the race once again. Rosalie's got a great chance. Still, it's not winning that matters. It's taking part.'

Stephen flinched. Baron de Coubertin, who had first made that remark when opening the 1896 Olympics, must have turned in his grave.

'The latest betting shows Rosalie to be the joint favourite with Her Majesty The Queen's horse Highclere. How do you feel about that?'

'I'm just as worried about the Duke of Devonshire's Crown Princess. Lester Piggott is always hard to beat on a great occasion. He won the first two races and he'll be all set for this one – Crown Princess is a fine little filly.'

'Is a mile and a half a good distance for Rosalie?'

'Results this season show it's definitely her best distance.'

'What will you do with the £81,240 prize money?'

'The money is not important, it hasn't even entered my mind.'

It had certainly entered Stephen's mind.

'Thank you, Mr Metcalfe, and the best of luck. And now over for the latest news of the betting.'

Harvey moved back to his group of admirers and suggested that they return to watch the race from the balcony just outside his box.

Stephen was fascinated to observe Harvey at such close quarters. He had become nervous and even more mendacious than usual under pressure – not at all the icy, cool operator they had all feared him to be. This man was human, susceptible and could be beaten.

They all leant over the rails watching the horses being put into the stalls. Crown Princess was still giving a little trouble while all the others waited. The tension was becoming unbearable.

'They're off,' boomed the loudspeaker.

As twenty-five thousand people raised glasses to their eyes, Harvey said, 'She's got a good start – she's well placed,' continuing to give everybody a running commentary until the last mile, when he became silent. The others also waited in silence, intent on the loudspeaker.

'They're into the straight mile – Minnow leads the field around the bend – with Buoy and Dankaro, looking relaxed, just tucked in behind him – followed by Crown Princess, Rosalie and Highclere . . .

'As they approach the six-furlong marker – Rosalie and Crown Princess come up on the stand side with Highclere making a bid . . .

'Five furlongs to go – Minnow still sets the pace; but is beginning to tire as Crown Princess and Buoy make up ground . . .

'Half a mile to go – Minnow still just ahead of Buoy, who has moved up into second place, perhaps making her move too early . . .

'Three furlongs from home – they're quickening up just a little – Minnow sets the pace on the rails – Buoy and Dankaro are now about a length behind – followed by Rosalie, Lester Piggott on Crown Princess and the Queen's filly Highclere all making ground . . .

'Inside the two-furlong marker – Highclere and Rosalie move up to challenge Buoy – Crown Princess is right out of it now . . .

'A furlong to go . . .'

The commentator's voice rose in pitch and volume.

'It's Joe Mercer riding Highclere who hits the front, just ahead of Pat Eddery on Rosalie – two hundred yards to go – they're neck and neck – one hundred yards to go — it's anybody's race and on the line it's a photo finish between the gold, purple and scarlet colours of Her Majesty the Queen and the black-and-green check colours of the American owner, Harvey Metcalfe — M. Moussac's Dankaro was third.'

Harvey stood paralysed, waiting for the result. Even Stephen felt a little sympathy for him. None of Harvey's guests dared to speak for fear they might be wrong.

'The result of The King George VI and The Queen Elizabeth Stakes.' Once again the loudspeaker boomed out and silence fell over the whole course:

'The winner is No. 5, Rosalie.'

The rest of the result was lost in the roar of the crowd and the bellow of triumph from Harvey. Pursued by his guests, he raced to the nearest lift, pressed a pound note into the lift-girl's hand and shouted 'Get this thing moving.' Only half of his guests managed to jump in with him. Stephen was among them. Once they reached the ground floor, the lift gates opened and Harvey came out like a thoroughbred, past the champagne bar, through the rear of the Members' Enclosure into the Winners' Enclosure, and flung his arms round the horse's neck, almost unseating the jockey. A few minutes later he triumphantly led Rosalie to the little white post marked 'FIRST'. The crowd thronged around him, offering their congratulations.

The Clerk of the Course, Captain Beaumont, stood by Harvey's side, briefing him on the procedure that would be followed when he was presented. Lord Abergavenny, the Queen's Representative at Ascot, accompanied Her Majesty to the Winners' Enclosure.

'The winner of The King George VI and The Queen Elizabeth Stakes – Mr Harvey Metcalfe's Rosalie.'

Harvey was in a dream world. Flash-bulbs popped and film cameras followed him as he walked towards the Queen. He bowed and received his trophy. The Queen, resplendent in a turquoise silk suit and matching turban that could only have been designed by Norman Hartnell, said a few words, but for the first time in his life Harvey was speechless. Taking a pace backwards, he bowed again and returned to his place accompanied by loud applause.

Back in his box the champagne flowed and everybody was Harvey's friend. Stephen realised this was not the moment to try anything clever. He must bide his time and watch his quarry's reaction to these changed circumstances. He stayed quietly in a corner, letting the excitement subside, and observed Harvey carefully.

It took another race before Harvey was half back to normal and Stephen decided the time had now come to act. He made as if to leave.

'Are you going already, Professor?'

'Yes, Mr Metcalfe. I must return to Oxford and mark some scripts before tomorrow morning.'

'I always admire the work you boys put in. I hope

you enjoyed yourself?' Stephen avoided Shaw's famous riposte, 'I had to, there was nothing else to enjoy'.

'Yes, thank you, Mr Metcalfe. An amazing achievement. You must be a very proud man.'

'Well, I guess so. It's been a long time coming, but it all seems worthwhile now . . . Rod, it's too bad you have to leave us. Can't you stay on a little longer and join my party at Claridge's tonight?'

'I should have liked that, Mr Metcalfe, but you must visit me at my college at Oxford and allow me to show you the university.'

'That's swell. I have a couple of days after Ascot and I've always wanted to see Oxford, but I never seem to have found the time.'

'It's the university Garden Party next Wednesday. Why don't you join me for dinner at my college on Tuesday evening and then we can spend the following day looking at the university and go on to the Garden Party?' Stephen scribbled a few directions on a card.

'Fantastic. This is turning out to be the best vacation I've ever had in Europe. How are you getting back to Oxford, Professor?'

'By train.'

'No, no,' said Harvey. 'My Rolls Royce will take you. It'll be back well in time for the last race.'

And before Stephen could protest, the chauffeur was called for.

'Take Professor Porter back to Oxford and then return here. Have a good trip, Professor. I'll look forward to seeing you next Tuesday at 8 pm. Great meeting you.'

'Thank you for a wonderful day, Mr Metcalfe, and congratulations on your splendid victory.'

Seated in the back of the white Rolls Royce on his way to Oxford, the car which Robin had boasted he and he alone would travel in, Stephen relaxed and smiled to himself. Taking a small notebook from his pocket he made an entry:

'Deduct 98 pence from expenses, the price of a single second-class ticket from Ascot to Oxford.'

15

'BRADLEY,' said the Senior Tutor, 'you're going a bit grey at the edges, dear boy. Is the office of Junior Dean proving too much for you?'

Stephen had wondered whether any of the Senior Common Room would think the change in the colour of his hair worthy of comment. Dons are seldom surprised by anything their colleagues do.

'My father went grey at an early age, Senior Tutor, and there seems to be no way of defying heredity . . .'

'Ah well, dear boy, you'll look all the more distinguished at next week's Garden Party.'

'Oh yes,' replied Stephen, who had been thinking of nothing else. 'I'd quite forgotten about that.'

He returned to his rooms where the rest of the Team were assembled and waiting for their next briefing.

'Wednesday is the day of the Encaenia and the Garden Party,' began Stephen without as much as a 'Good morning, gentlemen'. His students made no protest. 'Now the one thing we've learnt about our millionaire friend is that when we take him away from his own environment he still continues to assume he knows everything. We've now shown that his bluff can be called, as long as we know what's going to happen next week and he doesn't. It's only the same skill he used when promoting Prospecta Oil – always keeping one step ahead of us. Now, we're going to keep two steps ahead of him by having a rehearsal today and a full dress-rehearsal tomorrow.'

'Time spent on reconnaissance is seldom wasted,' muttered James. It was about the only sentiment he could recall from his Army Cadet days at Harrow.

'Haven't had to spend much time on reconnaissance for your plan, have we?' chipped in Jean-Pierre.

Stephen ignored the interruptions.

'Now, the whole process on the day will take about seven hours for me and four hours for you, which includes the time required for make-up; we'll need an extra session on that from James the day before.'

'How often will you need my two sons?' asked Robin.

'Only once, on the Wednesday. Too many runs at it will make them look stiff and awkard.'

'When do you imagine Harvey will want to return to London?' enquired Jean-Pierre.

'I rang Guy Salmon to check their timetable and they've been instructed to have him back at Claridge's by 7 pm, so I've assumed we have only until 5.30.'

'Clever,' said Robin.

'It's awful,' said Stephen. 'I even think like the man now. Right, let's go over the whole plan once again. We'll take it from the red dossier, halfway down page 16. When I leave All Souls . . .'

On Sunday and Monday they carried out full rehearsals. By the Tuesday they knew every route Harvey could take and where he would be at any given moment of the day from 9 am to 5.30 pm. Stephen hoped he had covered every eventuality. He had little choice. They were only going to be allowed one crack at this one. Any mistakes like Monte Carlo and there would be no second chance. The dress-rehearsal went to a second.

'I haven't worn clothes like this since I was six years old and attending a fancy-dress party,' said Jean-Pierre. 'We're going to be anything but inconspicuous.'

'There'll be red and blue and black all round you on the day,' said Stephen. 'It's like a circus for peacocks. No one will give us a second look, not even you, Jean-Pierre.'

They were all nervous again, waiting for the curtain to go up. Stephen was glad they were on edge: he had no doubt that the moment they relaxed with Harvey Metcalfe, they would be found out.

The Team spent a quiet weekend. Stephen watched the College Dramatic Society's annual effort in Magdalen gardens, Robin took his wife to Glyndebourne and was uncommonly attentive, Jean-Pierre read *Goodbye Picasso* by David Douglas Duncan, and

James took Anne to Tathwell Hall in Lincolnshire, to meet his father, the fifth earl.

Even Anne was nervous that weekend.

'Harry?'

'Doctor Bradley.'

'I have an American guest dining with me in my rooms tonight. His name is Harvey Metcalfe. When he arrives will you see he is brought over to my rooms, please.'

'Certainly, sir.'

'And one small thing. He seems to have mistaken me for Professor Porter of Trinity College. Don't correct the mistake, will you? Just humour him.'

'Certainly, sir.'

Harry retreated into the Porter's Lodge shaking his head sadly. Of course, all academics went dotty in the end, but Dr Bradley had been afflicted at an unusually tender age.

Harvey arrived at eight. He was always on time in England. The head porter guided him through the cloisters and up the old stone staircase to Stephen's rooms.

'Mr Metcalfe, sir.'

'How are you, Professor?'

'I'm well, Mr Metcalfe. Good of you to be so punctual.'

'Punctuality is the politeness of princes.'

'I think you'll find it is the politeness of kings, and, in this particular instance, of Louis XVIII.' For a moment Stephen forgot that Harvey wasn't a pupil.

'I'm sure you're right, Professor.'

Stephen mixed him a large whisky. His guest's eyes took in the room and settled on the desk.

'Gee – what a wonderful set of photographs. You with the late President Kennedy, another with the Queen and even the Pope.'

That touch was due to Jean-Pierre, who had put Stephen in contact with a photographer who had been in jail with his artist friend David Stein. Stephen was already looking forward to burning the photographs and pretending they had never existed.

'Let me give you another to add to your collection.'

Harvey pulled out of his inside coat pocket a large photograph of himself receiving the trophy for the King George VI and Queen Elizabeth Stakes from the Queen.

'I'll sign it for you, if you like.'

Without waiting for a reply, he scribbled an exuberant signature diagonally across the Queen.

'Thank you,' said Stephen. 'I can assure you I will treasure it with the same affection as I do my other photographs. I certainly appreciate you sparing the time to visit me here, Mr Metcalfe.'

'It's an honour for me to come to Oxford, and this is such a lovely old college.'

Stephen really believed he meant it, and he suppressed the inclination to tell Harvey the story of the late Lord Nuffield's dinner at Magdalen. For all Nuffield's munificence to the university, the two were never on entirely easy terms. When a manservant assisted the guest's departure after a college feast, Nuffield took the proffered hat ungraciously. 'Is this mine?' he said, disdainfully. 'I wouldn't know, my lord,' was the rejoinder, 'but it's the one you came with.'

Harvey was gazing a little blankly at the books on Stephen's shelves. The disparity between their subject matter, pure mathematics, and the putative Professor Porter's discipline, biochemistry, happily failed to arrest him.

'Do brief me on tomorrow.'

'Surely,' said Stephen. Why not? He had briefed everyone else. 'Let me first call for dinner and I'll go through what I've planned for you and see if it meets with your approval.'

'I'm game for anything. I feel ten years younger since this trip to Europe – it must've been the operation – and I'm thrilled about being here at Oxford University.'

Stephen wondered if he really could stand seven hours of Harvey Metcalfe, but for another $250,000 and his reputation with the rest of the Team . . .

The college servants brought him shrimp cocktail.

'My favourite,' said Harvey. 'How did you know?'

Stephen would have liked to say, 'There's very little I don't know about you,' but he satisfied himself with, 'A fortunate guess. Now, if we meet up at 10 tomorrow morning we can take part in what is thought to be the most interesting day in the university calendar. It's called Encaenia.'

'What's that?'

'Well, once a year at the end of Trinity Term, which is the equivalent of the summer term in an American university, we celebrate the ending of the university year. There are several ceremonies followed by a magnificent Garden Party, which will be attended by the Chancellor and Vice-Chancellor of the University. The Chancellor is the former British Prime Minister, Harold Macmillan, and the Vice-Chancellor is Mr Habakkuk. I'm hoping it will be possible for you to meet them both, and we should manage to cover everything in time for you to be back in London by 7 pm.'

'How did you know I had to be back by 7?'

'You warned me at Ascot.' Stephen could lie very quickly now. He was afraid that if they did not get their million soon he would end up a hardened criminal.

Harvey enjoyed his meal, which Stephen had planned almost too cleverly, each course featuring one of Harvey's favourite dishes. After Harvey had drunk a good deal of after-dinner brandy (price £7.25 per bottle, thought Stephen) they strolled through the quiet Magdalen Cloisters past the Song School. The sound of the choristers rehearsing a Gabrieli mass hung gently in the air.

'Gee, I'm surprised you allow record players on that loud,' said Harvey.

Stephen escorted his guest to the Randolph Hotel, pointing out the iron cross set in Broad Street outside Balliol College, said to mark the spot on which Archbishop Cranmer was burnt at the stake for heresy in 1556. Harvey forbore to say that he had never even heard of the reverend gentleman.

Stephen and Harvey parted on the steps of the Randolph.

'See you in the morning, Professor. Thanks for a great evening.'

'My pleasure. I'll pick you up at 10 am. Sleep well – you have a full day ahead of you tomorrow.'

Stephen returned to Magdalen and immediately called Robin.

'All's well, but I nearly went too far. The meal was altogether too carefully chosen – I even had his favourite brandy. Still, it'll keep me on my toes tomorrow. We must remember to avoid overkill. See you then, Robin.'

Stephen reported the same message to Jean-Pierre and James before falling gratefully into bed. The same time tomorrow he would be a wiser man, but would he be a richer one?

16

AT 5 AM THE SUN rose over the Cherwell, and those few Oxonians who were about that early would have been left in no doubt as to why the connoisseurs consider Magdalen to be the most beautiful college at either Oxford or Cambridge. Nestling on the banks of the river, its perpendicular architecture is easy on the eye. King Edward VII, Prince Henry, Cardinal Wolsey, Edward Gibbon and Oscar Wilde had all passed through its portals. But the only thing that was passing through Stephen's mind as he lay awake that morning was the education of Harvey Metcalfe.

He could hear his own heart-beat, and for the first time he knew what Robin and Jean-Pierre had been through. It seemed a lifetime since their first meeting only three months before. He smiled to himself at the thought of how close they had all become in their common aim of defeating Harvey Metcalfe. Although Stephen, like James, was beginning to have a sneaking admiration for the man, he was now even more convinced that Metcalfe could be outmanoeuvred when he was not on home ground. For over two hours Stephen lay motionless in bed, deep in thought, going over his plan again and again. When the sun had climbed over the tallest tree, he rose, showered, shaved and dressed slowly and deliberately, his mind still on the day ahead.

He made his face up carefully to age himself by fifteen years. It took him a considerable time, and he wondered whether women had to struggle as long in front of the mirror to achieve the opposite effect. He donned his gown, a magnificent scarlet, proclaiming him a Doctor of Philosophy of the University of Oxford. It amused him that Oxford had to be different. Every other university abbreviated this universal award for research work, to PhD. In Oxford, it was DPhil. He studied himself in the mirror.

'If that doesn't impress Harvey Metcalfe, nothing ever will.'

And what's more, he had the right to wear it. He sat down to study his red dossier for the last time. He had read the closely typewritten pages so often that he practically knew them by heart.

He avoided breakfast. Looking nearly fifty, he would undoubtedly have caused a stir amongst his colleagues, though probably the older dons would have failed to observe anything unusual in his appearance.

Stephen headed out of the college into the High, unnoticed among the thousand or so other graduates all dressed like fourteenth-century archbishops. Anonymity on that particular day was going to be easy. That, and the fact that Harvey would be bemused by the strange traditions of the ancient university, were the two reasons why Stephen had chosen Encaenia for his day of battle.

He arrived at the Randolph at 9.55 am and informed one of the younger bell-boys that his name was Professor Porter and that he had come to pick up Mr Metcalfe. Stephen took a seat in the lounge. The young man scurried away and returned moments later with Harvey.

'Mr Metcalfe – Professor Porter.'

'Thank you,' said Stephen. He made a mental note to return and tip the bell-boy. That touch had been useful, even if it was only part of his job.

'Good morning, Professor,' said Harvey, taking a seat. 'So tell me, what have I let myself in for?'

'Well,' said Stephen, 'Encaenia begins officially when all the notables of the university take a breakfast of champagne, strawberries and cream at Jesus College, which is known as Lord Nathaniel Crewe's Benefaction.'

'Who's this Lord Crewe guy? Will he be at the breakfast?'

'Only in spirit; the great man died some three hundred years ago. Lord Nathaniel Crewe was a doctor of the university and the Bishop of Durham, and he left £200 a year to the university as a Benefaction to provide the breakfast and an oration which we shall hear later. Of course, the money he willed no longer covers expenses nowadays, with rising prices and inflation, so the university has to dip into its own pocket to continue the tradition. When breakfast is over there is a procession and parade to the Sheldonian Theatre.'

'What happens then?'

'The parade is followed by the most exciting event of the day. The presentation of the Honorands for degrees.'

'The what?' said Harvey.

'The Honorands,' said Stephen. 'They are the distinguished men and women who have been chosen by the senior members of the university to be awarded Oxford honorary degrees.' Stephen looked at his watch. 'In fact, we must leave now to be sure of having a good position on the route from which to watch the procession.'

Stephen rose and guided his guest out of the Randolph Hotel. They strolled down the Broad and found an excellent spot just in front of the Sheldonian Theatre, where the police cleared a little space for Stephen because of his scarlet gown. A few minutes later the procession wound into sight round the corner from the Turl. The police held up all the traffic and kept the public on the pavement.

'Who are the guys in front carrying those clubs?' enquired Harvey.

'They are the University Marshal and the Bedels. They are carrying maces to safeguard the Chancellor's procession.'

'Jesus; of course it's safe. This isn't Central Park, New York.'

'I agree,' said Stephen, 'but it hasn't always been so over the past three hundred years, and tradition dies hard in England.'

'And who's that behind the Bedel fellows?'

'The one wearing the black gown with gold trimmings is the Chancellor of the University, accompanied by his page. The Chancellor is the Right Honourable Harold Macmillan, who was Prime Minister of Great Britain in the late '50s and early '60s.'

'Oh yes, I remember the guy. Tried to get the British into Europe but De Gaulle wouldn't have it.'

'Well, I suppose that's one way of remembering him. Now, he's followed by the Vice-Chancellor, Mr Habakkuk, who is also the Principal of Jesus College.'

'You're losing me, Professor.'

'Well, the Chancellor is always a distinguished Englishman who was educated at Oxford; but the Vice-Chancellor is a leading member of the university itself and is usually chosen from the heads of one of the colleges.'

'Got it, I think.'

'Now, after him, we have the University Registrar, Mr Caston, who is a fellow of Merton College. He is the senior administrator of the university, or you might look on him as the university's top civil servant. He's directly responsible to the Vice-Chancellor and Hebdomadal Council, who are the sort of cabinet for the university. Behind them we have the Senior Proctor, Mr Campbell of Worcester College, and the

Junior Proctor, the Reverend Doctor Bennett of New College.'

'What's a Proctor?'

'For over 700 years the Proctors have been responsible for decency and discipline in the university.'

'What? Those two old men take care of 9,000 rowdy youths?'

'Well, they are helped by the bulldogs,' said Stephen.

'Ah, that's better, I suppose. A couple of bites from an old English bulldog would keep anyone in order.'

'No, no,' protested Stephen, trying desperately not to laugh. 'The name bulldog is given to the men who help the Proctors keep order. Now, finally in the procession you can observe that tiny crocodile of colour: it consists of heads of colleges who are doctors of the university, doctors of the university who are not heads of colleges and the heads of colleges who are not doctors of the university, in that order.'

'Listen, Rod, all doctors mean to me is pain and money.'

'They are not that sort of doctor,' replied Stephen.

'Forget it. I love everything but don't expect me to understand what it's all about.'

Stephen watched Harvey's face carefully. He was drinking the scene in and had already become quieter.

'The long line will now proceed into the Sheldonian Theatre and all the people in the procession will take their places in the hemicycle.'

'Excuse me, sir, what type of cycle is that?'

'The hemicycle is a round bank of seats inside the theatre, distinguished only by being the most uncomfortable in Europe. But don't you worry. Thanks to your well-known interest in education at Harvard I've managed to arrange special seats for us and there will just be time for us to secure them ahead of the procession.'

'Well, lead the way, Rod. Do they really know what goes on at Harvard here?'

'Why yes, Mr Metcalfe. You have a reputation in university circles as a generous man interested in financing the pursuit of academic excellence.'

'Well, what do you know.'

Very little, thought Stephen.

He guided Harvey to his reserved seat in the balcony, not wanting his guest to be able to see the individual men and women too clearly. The truth of the matter was that the senior members of the university in the hemicycle were so covered from head to toe in gowns and caps and bow-ties and bands, that even their mothers would not have recognised them. The organist played his final chord and the guests settled.

'The organist,' said Stephen, 'is from my own college. He's the Choragus, the leader of the chorus, and Deputy Professor of Music.'

Harvey could not take his eyes off the hemicycle and the scarlet-clad figures. He had never seen a sight like it in his life. The music stopped and the Chancellor rose to address the assembled company in vernacular Latin.

'*Causa hujus convocationis est ut . . .*'

'What the hell's he saying?'

'He's telling us why we're here,' explained Stephen. 'I'll try and guide you through it.'

'*Ite Bedelli,*' declared the Chancellor, and the great doors opened for the Bedels to go and fetch the Honorands from the Divinity School. There was a hush as they were led in by the Public Orator, Mr J. G. Griffith, who presented them one by one to the Chancellor, enshrining the careers and achievements of each in polished and witty Latin prose.

Stephen's translation, however, followed a rather more liberal line and was embellished with suggestions that their doctorates were as much the result of financial generosity as of academic prowess.

'That's Lord Amory. They're praising him for all the work he has done in the field of education.'

'How much did he give"

'Well, he *was* Chancellor of the Exchequer. And there's Lord Hailsham. He has held eight Cabinet positions, including Secretary of State for Education and finally Lord Chancellor. Both he and Lord Amory are receiving the degree of Doctor of Civil Law.'

Harvey recognised Dame Flora Robson, the actress, who was being honoured for a distinguished lifetime in the theatre; Stephen explained that she was receiving the degree of Doctor of Letters, as was the Poet Laureate, Sir John Betjeman. Each was presented with his scroll by the Chancellor, shaken by the hand and then shown to a seat in the front row of the hemicycle.

The final Honorand was Sir George Porter, Director of the Royal Institution and Nobel Laureate. He received his honorary degree of Doctor of Science.

'My namesake, but no relation. Oh well, nearly through,' said Stephen. 'Just a little prose from John Wain, the Professor of Poetry, about the benefactors of the university.'

Mr Wain delivered the Crewian Oration, which took him some twelve minutes, and Stephen was grateful for something so lively in a language they could both understand. He was only vaguely aware of the recitations of undergraduate prize winners which concluded the proceedings.

The Chancellor of the university rose and led the procession out of the hall.

'Where are they all off to now?' asked Harvey.

'They are going to have lunch at All Souls, where they will be joined by other distinguished guests.'

'God, what I would give to be able to attend that.'

'I have arranged it,' replied Stephen.

Harvey was quite overwhelmed.

'How did you fix that, Professor?'

'The Registrar was most impressed by the interest you have shown in Harvard and I think they hope you might find it possible to assist Oxford in some small way, especially after your wonderful win at Ascot.'

'What a great idea. Why didn't I think of that?'

Stephen tried to show little interest, hoping that by the end of the day he would have thought of it. He had learnt his lesson on overkill. The truth was that the Registrar had never heard of Harvey Metcalfe, but because it was Stephen's last term at Oxford he had been put on the list of invitations by a friend who was a Fellow of All Souls.

They walked over to All Souls, just across the road from the Sheldonian Theatre. Stephen attempted, without much success, to explain the nature of All Souls to Harvey. Indeed, many Oxonians themselves find the college something of an enigma.

'Its corporate name,' Stephen began, 'is the College of All Souls of the Faithful Departed of Oxford, and it resonantly commemorates the victors of Agincourt. It was intended that masses should forever be said there for the repose of their souls. Its modern role is unique in academic life. All Souls is a society of graduates distinguished either by promise or achievement, mostly academic, from home and abroad, with a sprinkling of men who have made their mark in other fields. The college has no undergraduates, and generally appears to the outside world to do much as it pleases with its massive financial and intellectual resources.'

Stephen and Harvey took their places among the hundred or more guests at the long table in the noble Codrington Library. Stephen spent the entire time ensuring that Harvey was kept fully occupied and was not too obvious. He was thankfully aware that on such occasions people never remember whom they meet or what they say, and happily introduced Harvey to everyone around as a distinguished American philanthropist. He was fortunately placed some way from the Vice-Chancellor, the Registrar and the Secretary of the University Chest.

Harvey was quite overcome by the new experience and was content just to listen to the distinguished men around him – which surprised Stephen, who had feared he would never stop talking. When the meal was over and the guests had risen, Stephen drew a deep breath and played one of his riskier cards. He deliberately marched Harvey up to the Chancellor.

'Chancellor,' he said to Harold Macmillan.

'Yes, young man.'

'May I introduce Mr Harvey Metcalfe from Boston. Mr Metcalfe, as you will know, Chancellor, is a great benefactor of Harvard.'

'Yes, of course. Capital, capital. What brings you to England, Mr Metcalfe?'

Harvey was nearly speechless.

'Well, sir, I mean Chancellor, I came to see my horse Rosalie run in the King George and Elizabeth Stakes.'

Stephen was now standing behind Harvey and made signs to the Chancellor that Harvey's horse had won the race. Harold Macmillan, as game as ever and never one to miss a trick, replied:

'Well, you must have been very pleased with the result, Mr Metcalfe.'

'Well, sir, I guess I was lucky.'

'You don't look to me the type of man who depends on luck.'

Stephen took his career firmly in both hands.

'I am trying to interest Mr Metcalfe in supporting some research we are doing at Oxford, Chancellor.'

'What a good idea.' No one knew better than Harold Macmillan, after seven years of leading a political party, how to use flattery on such occasions. 'Keep in touch, young man. Boston was it, Mr Metcalfe? Do give my regards to the Kennedys.'

Macmillan swept off, resplendent in his academic dress. Harvey stood dumbfounded.

'What a great man. What an occasion. I feel I'm part of history. I just wish I deserved to be here.'

Having completed his task, Stephen was determined to escape before any mistakes could be made. He knew Harold Macmillan would shake hands with and talk to over a thousand people that day and the chances of his remembering Harvey were minimal. In any case, it would not much matter if he did. Harvey was, after all, a genuine benefactor of Harvard.

'We ought to leave before the senior members, Mr Metcalfe.'

'Of course, Rod. You're the boss.'

'I think that would be courtesy.'

Once they were out on the street Harvey glanced at his large Jaeger le Coultre watch. It was 2.30 pm.

'Excellent,' said Stephen, who was running three minutes late for the next rendezvous. 'We have just over an hour before the Garden Party. Why don't we take a look at one or two of the colleges.'

They walked slowly up past Brasenose College and Stephen explained that the name really meant 'brass nose' and that the famous original brass nose, a sanctuary knocker of the thirteenth century, was still mounted in the hall. A hundred yards further on, Stephen directed Harvey to the right.

'He's turned right, Robin, and he's heading towards Lincoln College,' said James, well hidden in the entrance of Jesus College.

'Fine,' said Robin and checked his two sons. Aged seven and nine, they stood awkwardly, in unfamiliar Eton suits, ready to play their part as pages, unable to understand what Daddy was up to.

'Are you both ready?'

'Yes, Daddy,' they replied in unison.

Stephen continued walking slowly towards Lincoln, and they were no more than a few paces away when Robin appeared from the main entrance of the college in the official dress of the Vice-Chancellor, bands, collars, white tie and all. He looked fifteen years older and as much like Mr Habakkuk as possible. Perhaps not quite so bald, thought Stephen.

'Would you like to be presented to the Vice-Chancellor?' asked Stephen.

'That would be something,' said Harvey.

'Good afternoon, Vice-Chancellor, may I introduce Mr Harvey Metcalfe.'

Robin doffed his academic cap and bowed. Stephen returned the compliment in like manner. Robin spoke before Stephen could continue:

'Not the benefactor of Harvard University?'

Harvey blushed and smiled at the two little boys who were holding the Vice-Chancellor's train. Robin continued:

'This is a pleasure, Mr Metcalfe. I do hope you are enjoying your visit to Oxford. Mind you, it's not everybody who's fortunate enough to be shown around by a Nobel Laureate.'

'I've enjoyed it immensely, Vice-Chancellor, and I'd like to feel I could help this university in some way.'

'Well, that is excellent news.'

'Look, gentlemen, I'm staying here at the Randolph Hotel. It would be my great pleasure if you could all have tea with me later this afternoon.'

Robin and Stephen were thrown for a moment. He'd done it again – the unexpected. Surely the man realised that on the day of Encaenia the Vice-Chancellor did not have a moment free to attend private tea parties.

Robin recovered first.

'I'm afraid that would be difficult. One has so many responsibilities on a day like this, you understand. Perhaps you could join me in my rooms at the

Clarendon Building? That would give us a chance to have a more private discussion?'

Stephen immediately picked up the lead:

'How kind of you, Vice-Chancellor. Will 4.30 be convenient?'

'Yes, yes, that will be fine, Professor.'

Robin tried not to look as if he wanted to run a mile. Although they had only been standing there for about five minutes, to him it seemed a lifetime. He had not objected to being a journalist, or an American surgeon, but he genuinely hated being a Vice-Chancellor. Surely someone would appear at any moment and recognise him for the fraud he was. Thank God most of the undergraduates had gone home the week before. He began to feel even worse when a tourist started taking photos of him.

Now Harvey had turned all their plans upside down. Stephen could only think of Jean-Pierre and of James, the finest string to their dramatic bow, loitering uselessly in fancy dress behind the tea tent at the Garden Party in the grounds of Trinity College, waiting for them.

'Perhaps it might be wise, Vice-Chancellor, if we were to invite the Registrar and the Secretary of the University Chest to join us?'

'First-class idea, Professor. I'll ask them to be there. It isn't every day we're visited by such a distinguished philanthropist. I must take my leave of you now, sir, and proceed to my Garden Party. An honour to have made your acquaintance, Mr Metcalfe, and I look forward to seeing you again at 4.30.'

They shook hands warmly, and Stephen guided Harvey towards Exeter College while Robin darted back into the little room in Lincoln that had been arranged for him. He sank heavily into a seat.

'Are you all right, Daddy?' asked his elder son, William.

'Yes, I'm fine.'

'Do we get the ice cream and Coca-Cola you promised us if we didn't say a word?'

'You certainly do,' said Robin.

Robin slipped off all the paraphernalia – the gown hood, bow-tie and bands – and placed them back in the suitcase. He returned to the street just in time to watch the real Vice-Chancellor, Mr Habakkuk, leave Jesus College on the opposite side of the road, obviously making his way towards the Garden Party. Robin glanced at his watch. If they had run five minutes late the whole plan would have struck disaster.

Meanwhile, Stephen had done a full circle and was now heading towards Shepherd & Woodward, the tailor's shop which supplies academic dress for the university. He was, however, preoccupied with the thought of getting a message through to James. Stephen and Harvey came to a halt in front of the shop window.

'What magnificent robes.'

'That's the gown of a Doctor of Letters. Would you like to try it on and see how you look?'

'That would be great. But would they allow it?' said Harvey.

'I'm sure they won't object.'

They entered the shop, Stephen still in his full academic dress as a Doctor of Philosophy.

'My distinguished guest would like to see the gown of a Doctor of Letters.'

'Certainly, sir,' said the young assistant, who was not going to argue with a Fellow of the University.

He vanished to the back of the shop and returned with a magnificent red gown with grey facing and a black, floppy velvet cap. Stephen forged on, brazen-faced.

'Why don't you try them on, Mr Metcalfe? Let's see what you would look like as an academic.'

The assistant was somewhat surprised. He wished Mr Venables would return from his lunch break.

'Would you care to come through to the fitting-room, sir?'

Harvey disappeared. Stephen slipped out on to the road.

'James, can you hear me? Oh hell, for God's sake answer, James.'

'Cool down, old fellow. I'm having a deuce of a time putting on this ridiculous gown, and in any case, our rendezvous isn't for another seventeen minutes.'

'Cancel it.'

'Cancel it?'

'Yes, and tell Jean-Pierre as well. Both of you report to Robin and meet up as quickly as possible. He will fill you in on the new plans.'

'New plans. Is everything all right, Stephen?'

'Yes, better than I could have hoped for.'

Stephen clicked off his speaker and rushed back into the tailor's shop.

Harvey reappeared as a Doctor of Letters; a more unlikely sight Stephen had not seen for many years.

'You look magnificent.'

'What do they cost?'

'About £100, I think.'

'No, no. How much would I have to give . . . ?'

'I have no idea. You would have to discuss that with the Vice-Chancellor after the Garden Party.'

Harvey took a long look at himself in the mirror, and then returned to the dressing-room while Stephen thanked the assistant, asked him to wrap up the gown and cap and send them to the Clarendon building to be left with the porter in the name of Sir John Betjeman. He paid cash. The assistant looked even more bewildered.

'Yes, sir.'

He was not sure what to do, except continue praying for Mr Venables' arrival. His prayers were answered some ten minutes later, but by then Stephen and Harvey were well on their way to Trinity College and the Garden Party.

'Mr Venables, I've just been asked to send the full DLitt. dress to Sir John Betjeman at the Clarendon Building.'

'Strange. We kitted him out for this morning's ceremony weeks ago. I wonder why he wants a second outfit.'

'He paid cash.'

'Well, send it round to the Clarendon, but be sure it's in his name.'

When Stephen and Harvey arrived at Trinity College shortly after 3.30, the elegant green lawns, the croquet hoops having been removed, were already crowded with over a thousand people. The members of the university wore an odd hybrid dress: best lounge suits or silk dresses topped with gowns, hoods and caps. Cups of tea and crates of strawberries and cucumber sandwiches were disappearing rapidly.

'What a swell party this is,' said Harvey unintentionally mimicking Frank Sinatra. 'You certainly do things in style here, Professor.'

'Yes, the Garden Party is always rather fun. It's the main social event of the university year, which as I explained, is just ending. Half the senior members here will be snatching an afternoon off from reading examination scripts. Exams for the final-year undergraduates have only just ended.'

Stephen observed the Vice-Chancellor, the Registrar and the Secretary of the University Chest carefully, and steered Harvey well away from them, introducing him to as many of the older members of the university as possible, hoping they would not find the encounter too memorable. They spent just over three-quarters of an hour moving from person to person, Stephen feeling rather like an aide-de-camp to an incompetent dignitary whose mouth must be kept shut for fear of a diplomatic incident. Despite Stephen's anxious approach, Harvey was clearly having the time of his life.

'Robin, Robin, can you hear me?'

'Yes, James.'

'Where are you?'

'I'm in the Eastgate Restaurant: come and join me here and bring Jean-Pierre.'

'Fine. We'll be there in five minutes. No, make it ten. With my disguise, I'd better go slowly.'

Robin paid his bill. The children had finished their reward, so he took them out of the Eastgate to a waiting car and instructed the driver, who had been hired especially for the day, to return them to Newbury. They had played their part and now could only get in the way.

'Aren't you coming home with us, Dad?' demanded Jamie.

No, I'll be back later tonight. Tell your mother to expect me about seven.'

Robin returned to the Eastgate to find Jean-Pierre and James hobbling towards him.

'Why the change of plan?' asked Jean-Pierre. 'It's taken me over an hour to get dressed and ready.'

'Never mind. You're still in the right gear. We had a stroke of luck. I chatted up Harvey in the street and the cocky bastard invited me to tea with him at the Randolph Hotel. I said that would be impossible, but asked him to join me at the Clarendon. Stephen suggested that you two should be invited along as well.'

'Clever,' said James. 'No need for the deception at the Garden Party.'

'Let's hope it's not too clever,' said Jean-Pierre.

'Well, at least we can do the whole damn charade behind closed doors,' said Robin, 'which ought to make it easier. I never did like the idea of walking through the streets with him.'

'With Harvey Metcalfe nothing is ever going to be easy,' said Jean-Pierre.

'I'll get myself into the Clarendon Building by 4.15,' continued Robin. 'You will appear a few minutes after 4.20, Jean-Pierre, and then you, James, about 4.25 pm. But keep exactly to the same routine, act as if the meeting had taken place, as originally planned, at the Garden Party and we had all walked over to the Clarendon together.'

Stephen suggested to Harvey that they should return to the Clarendon Building, as it would be discourteous to be late for the Vice-Chancellor.

'Sure.' Harvey glanced at his watch. 'Jesus, it's 4.30 already.'

They left the Garden Party and walked quickly down towards the Clarendon Building at the bottom of the Broad, Stephen explaining en route that the Clarendon was a sort of Oxford White House where all the officers and officials of the university had their rooms.

The Clarendon is a large, imposing eighteenth-century building which could be mistaken by a visitor for another college. A few steps lead up to an impressive hallway, and on entering you realise you are in a magnificent old building which has been converted for use as offices, with as few changes as possible.

When they arrived the porter greeted them.

'The Vice-Chancellor is expecting us,' said Stephen.

The porter had been somewhat surprised when Robin had arrived fifteen minutes earlier and told him that Mr Habakkuk had asked him to wait in his room; even though Robin was in full academic dress, the porter kept a beady eye on him, not expecting the Vice-Chancellor or any of his staff to return from the Garden Party for at least another hour. The arrival of Stephen gave him a little more confidence. He well remembered the pound he had received for his guided tour of the building.

The porter ushered Stephen and Harvey through to the Vice-Chancellor's rooms and left them alone, tucking another pound note into his pocket.

The Vice-Chancellor's room was in no way pretentious and its beige carpet and pale walls would have given it the look of any middle-ranking civil servant's office, had it not been for the magnificent picture of a village square in France by Wilson Steer which hung over the marble fireplace.

Robin was staring out of the vast windows overlooking the Bodleian Library.

'Good afternoon, Vice-Chancellor.'

Robin spun round. 'Oh, welcome, Professor.'

'You remember Mr Metcalfe?'

'Yes, indeed. How nice to see you again.' Robin shuddered. All he wanted to do was to go home. They chatted for a few minutes. Another knock and Jean-Pierre entered.

'Good afternoon, Registrar.'

'Good afternoon, Vice-Chancellor, Professor Porter.'

'May I introduce Mr Harvey Metcalfe.'

'Good afternoon, sir.'

'Registrar, would you like some . . .'

'Where's this man Metcalfe?'

The three of them stood, stunned, as a man looking ninety entered the room on sticks. He hobbled over to Robin, winked, bowed and said:

'Good afternoon, Vice-Chancellor,' in a loud, crotchety voice.

'Good afternoon, Horsley.'

James went over to Harvey and prodded him with his sticks as if to make sure he was real.

'I have read about you, young man.'

Harvey had not been called young man for thirty years. The others stared at James in admiration. None of them knew that in his last year at university James had played *L'Avare* to great acclaim. His Secretary of the Chest was simply a repeat performance, and even Molière would have been pleased with it. James continued:

'You have been most generous to Harvard.'

'That's very kind of you to mention it, sir,' said Harvey respectfully.

'Don't call me sir, young man. I like the look of you – call me Horsley.'

'Yes, Horsley, sir,' blurted Harvey.

The others were only just able to keep a straight face.

'Well, Vice-Chancellor,' continued James. 'You can't have dragged me halfway across the city for my health. What's going on? Where's my sherry?'

Stephen wondered if James was overdoing it, but looking at Harvey saw that he was evidently captivated by the scene. How could a man so mature in one field be so immature in another, he thought. He was beginning to see how Westminster Bridge had been sold to at least four Americans in the past twenty years.

'Well, we were hoping to interest Mr Metcalfe in the work of the university and I felt that the Secretary of the University Chest should be present.'

'What's this chest?' asked Harvey.

'Sort of treasury for the university,' replied James,

his voice loud, old and very convincing. 'Why don't you read this?' and he thrust into Harvey's hand an Oxford University Calendar, which Harvey could have obtained at Blackwell's bookshop for £2 as indeed James had.

Stephen was not sure what move to make next when, happily for him, Harvey took over.

'Gentlemen, I would like to say how proud I am to be here today. This has been a wonderful year for me. I was present when an American won Wimbledon, I finally obtained a Van Gogh. My life was saved by a wonderful, wonderful surgeon in Monte Carlo and now here I am in Oxford surrounded by all this history. Gentlemen, it would give me a great deal of pleasure to be associated with this famous university.'

James took the lead again:

'What have you in mind?' he shouted at Harvey, adjusting his hearing-aid.

'Well, sir, I achieved my life's ambition when I received the King George and Elizabeth trophy from your Queen, but the prize money, well, I would like to use that to make a benefaction to your university.'

'But that's over £80,000,' gasped Stephen.

'£81,240 to be exact, sir. But why don't I call it $250,000.'

Stephen, Robin and Jean-Pierre were speechless. James alone was left to command the day. This was the opportunity he had needed to show why his great-grandfather had been one of Wellington's most respected generals.

'We accept. But it would have to be anonymous,' said James. 'I think I can safely say in the circumstances that the Vice-Chancellor would inform Mr Harold Macmillan and Hebdomadal Council, but we would not want a fuss made of it. Of course, Vice-Chancellor, I would ask you to consider an honorary degree.'

Robin was so conscious of James's obvious control of the entire situation that he could only add:

'How would you recommend we go about it, Horsley?'

'Cash cheque, so nobody can trace the money back to Mr Metcalfe. We can't have those bloody men from Cambridge chasing him for the rest of his life. Same way as we did for Sir David – no fuss.'

'I agree,' said Jean-Pierre, not having the vaguest idea what James was talking about. Neither, for that matter, had Harvey.

James nodded to Stephen, who left the Vice-Chancellor's office and made his way to the porter's room to enquire if a parcel had been left for Sir John Betjeman.

'Yes, sir. I don't know why they left it here. I'm not expecting Sir John.'

'Don't worry,' said Stephen. 'He's asked me to pick it up for him.'

Stephen returned to find James holding forth to Harvey on the importance of keeping his donation as a bond between himself and the university.

Stephen undid the box and took out the magnificent gown of a Doctor of Letters. Harvey turned red with embarrassment and pride as Robin placed it on his shoulders, chanting '*De mortuis nil nisi bonum. Dulce et decorum est pro patria mori. Per ardua ad astra. Nil desperandum.*'

'Many congratulations,' bellowed James. 'A pity we could not have organised this to be part of today's ceremony, but for such a munificent gesture as yours we could hardly wait another year.'

Brilliant, thought Stephen, Laurence Olivier could not have done better.

'That's fine by me,' said Harvey, as he sat down and made out a cheque to cash. 'You have my word that this matter will never be mentioned to anyone.'

None of them believed that.

They stood in silence as Harvey rose and passed the cheque to James.

'No, sir.' James transfixed him with a glare.

The others looked dumbfounded.

'The Vice-Chancellor.'

'Of course,' said Harvey. 'Excuse me, sir.'

'Thank you,' said Robin, his hand trembling as he received the cheque. 'A most gracious gift, and you may be sure we shall put it to good use.'

There was a loud knock on the door. They all looked round terrified except for James, who was now ready for anything. It was Harvey's chauffeur. James had always hated the pretentious white uniform with the white hat.

'Ah, the efficient Mr Mellor,' said Harvey. 'Gentlemen, I guarantee he's been watching every move
we've made today.'

The four froze, but the chauffeur had clearly made
no sinister deductions from his observations.

'Your car is ready, sir. You wanted to be back at
Claridge's by 7 pm to be in good time for your dinner
appointment.'

'Young man,' bellowed James.

'Yes, sir,' whimpered the chauffeur.

'Do you realise you are in the presence of the
Vice-Chancellor of this university?'

'No, sir. I'm very sorry, sir.'

'Take your hat off immediately.'

'Yes, sir.'

The chauffeur removed his hat and retreated to
the car, swearing under his breath.

'Vice-Chancellor, I sure hate to break up our
party, but as you've heard I do have an appointment . . .'

'Of course, of course, we understand you're a busy
man. May I once again officially thank you for your
most generous donation, which will be used to benefit
many deserving people.'

'We all hope you have a safe journey back to the
States and will remember us as warmly as we shall
remember you,' added Jean-Pierre.

Harvey moved towards the door.

'I will take my leave of you now, sir,' shouted

James. 'It will take me twenty minutes to get down those damned steps. You are a fine man and you have been most generous.'

'It was nothing,' said Harvey expansively.

True enough, thought James, nothing to you, but everything to us.

Stephen, Robin and Jean-Pierre accompanied Harvey from the Clarendon to the waiting Rolls.

'Professor,' said Harvey, 'I didn't quite understand everything the old guy was saying.' As he spoke he shifted the weight of his heavy robes on his shoulders self-consciously.

'Well, he's very deaf and very old, but his heart's in the right place. He wanted you to know that this has to be an anonymous donation as far as the university is concerned, though, of course, the Oxford hierarchy will be informed of the truth. If it were to be made public all sorts of undesirables who have never done anything for education in the past would come trooping along on the day of Encaenia wanting to buy an honorary degree.'

'Of course, of course. I understand. That's fine by me,' said Harvey. 'I want to thank you for a swell day, Rod, and I wish you all the luck for the future. What a shame our friend Wiley Barker wasn't here to share it all.'

Robin blushed.

Harvey climbed into the Rolls Royce and waved enthusiastically to the three of them as they watched the car start effortlessly on its journey back to London.

Three down and one to go.

'James was brilliant,' said Jean-Pierre. 'When he first came in I didn't know who the hell it was.'

'I agree,' said Robin. 'Let's go and rescue him – he's truly the hero of the day.'

They all three ran up the steps, forgetting that they looked somewhere between the ages of fifty and sixty, and rushed back into the Vice-Chancellor's room to congratulate James, who lay silent in the middle of the floor. He had passed out.

In Magdalen an hour later, with the help of Robin and two large whiskies, James was back to his normal health.

'You were fantastic,' said Stephen, 'just at the point when I was beginning to lose my nerve.'

'You would have received an Academy Award if we could have put it on screen,' said Robin. 'Your father will have to let you go on the stage after that performance.'

James basked in his first moment of glory for three months. He could not wait to tell Anne.

'Anne.' He quickly looked at his watch. 'Six-thirty.

Oh hell, I must leave at once. I'm meant to be meeting Anne at eight. See you all next Monday in Stephen's rooms for dinner. By then I'll try to have my plan ready.'

James rushed out of the room.

'James.'

His face reappeared round the door. They all said in chorus: 'Fantastic.'

He grinned, ran down the stairs and leapt into his Alfa Romeo, which he now felt they might allow him to keep, and headed towards London at top speed.

It took him 59 minutes from Oxford to the King's Road. The new motorway had made a considerable difference since his undergraduate days. Then the journey had taken anything from an hour and a half to two hours through High Wycombe or Henley.

The reason for his haste was that the meeting with Anne was most important and under no circumstances must he be late; tonight he was due to meet her father. All James knew about him was that he was a senior member of the Diplomatic Corps in Washington. Diplomats always expect you to be on time. He was determined to make a good impression on her father, particularly after Anne's successful weekend at Tathwell Hall. The old man had taken to her at once and never left her side. They had even managed to agree on a wedding date, subject, of course, to the approval of Anne's parents.

James had a quick cold shower and removed all his make-up, losing some sixty years in the process.

He had arranged to meet Anne for a drink at Les Ambassadeurs in Mayfair before dinner, and as he put on his dinner-jacket he wondered if he could make it from the King's Road to Hyde Park Corner in 12 minutes: it would require another Monte Carlo. He leapt into his car, revving it quickly through the gears, shot along to Sloane Square, through Eaton Square, up past St George's Hospital, round Hyde Park Corner into Park Lane, and arrived at 7.58 pm.

'Good evening, my lord,' said Mr Mills, the club owner.

'Good evening. I'm dining with Miss Summerton and I've had to leave my car double-parked. Can you take care of it?' said James, dropping the keys and a pound note into the doorman's white-gloved hand.

'Delighted, my lord. Show Lord Brigsley to the private rooms.'

James followed the head porter up the red staircase and into a small Regency room where dinner had been laid for three. He could hear Anne's voice in the next room. She came through, looking even more beautiful than usual in a floating mint-green dress.

'Hello, darling. Come on, I want you to meet Daddy.'

James followed Anne into the next room.

'Daddy, this is James. James, this is my father.'

James went red and then white, and then he felt green.

'How are you, my boy. I've heard so much about you from Rosalie that I can't wait to get acquainted.'

17

'CALL ME HARVEY.'

James stood aghast and speechless. Anne jumped into the silence.

'Would you like a whisky, James?'

James found his voice with difficulty.

'Thank you.'

'I want to know all about you, young man,' continued Harvey, 'what you get up to and why I've seen so little of my daughter in the past few weeks, though I think I can guess the answer to that.'

James drank the whisky in one gulp and Anne quickly refilled his glass.

'You see so little of your daughter because I'm always modelling, which means that I'm very rarely in London.'

'I know, Rosalie . . .'

'James knows me as Anne, Daddy.'

'We christened you Rosalie. It was a good enough name for your mother and me and it ought to be good enough for you.'

'Daddy, whoever heard of a top European model

calling herself Rosalie Metcalfe? All my friends know
me as Anne Summerton.'

'What do you think, James?'

'I was beginning to think I didn't know her at all,'
replied James, recovering slowly. It was obvious that
Harvey did not suspect a thing. He had not seen James
face to face at the gallery, he had never seen him at
Monte Carlo or Ascot, and James had looked ninety
years of age at Oxford earlier in the day. He was
beginning to believe he had got away with it. But how
the hell could he tell the others at their Monday
meeting that the final plan, his plan, would be to outwit
not Harvey Metcalfe, but his future father-in-law?

'Shall we go through to dinner?'

Harvey did not wait for a reply. He marched on
into the adjoining room.

'Rosalie Metcalfe,' whispered James fiercely,
'you've got some explaining to do.'

Anne kissed him gently on the cheek.

'You're the first person who's given me the chance
to beat my father at anything. Can't you forgive me?
. . . I do love you . . .'

'Come on, you two. Anyone would think you'd
never met before.'

Anne and James joined Harvey for dinner. James
was amused by the sight of the shrimp cocktail and
remembered how Stephen had regretted that touch at
Harvey's Magdalen dinner.

'Well, James, I understand you and Anne have
fixed a date for the wedding.'

'Yes, sir, if it meets with your approval.'

'Of course I approve. I was hoping Anne would marry Prince Charles after I'd won the King George and Elizabeth Stakes, but an earl will have to do for my only daughter.'

They both laughed, neither of them thinking it was remotely funny.

'I wish you'd come to Wimbledon this year, Rosalie. Imagine, me there on Ladies' Day and the only company I had was a boring old Swiss banker.'

Anne looked at James and grinned.

The waiters cleared the table and wheeled in a trolley bearing a crown of lamb in immaculate cutlet frills, which Harvey studied with great interest.

'Still,' said Harvey, chattering on, 'it was thoughtful of you to ring me at Monte Carlo, my dear. I really thought I was going to die, you know. James, you wouldn't have believed it. They removed a gall stone the size of a baseball from my stomach. Thank God, the operation was performed by one of the greatest surgeons in the world, Wiley Barker, the President's surgeon. He saved my life.'

Harvey promptly undid his shirt and revealed a 4-inch scar across his vast stomach.

'What do you think of that, James?'

'Remarkable.'

'Daddy, really. We're having dinner.'

'Stop fussing, honey. It won't be the first time James has seen a man's stomach.'

It's not the first time I've seen that one, thought James.

Harvey pushed his shirt back into his trousers and continued:

'Anyway, it was really kind of you to phone me.' He leant over and patted her hand. 'I was a good boy too. I took your advice and kept that nice Doctor Barker on for another week in case any complications arose. Mind you, the price these doctors . . .'

James dropped his wine glass. The claret covered the tablecloth with a red stain.

'I'm so sorry.'

'You all right, James?'

'Yes, sir.'

James looked at Anne in silent outrage. Harvey was quite unperturbed.

'Bring a fresh tablecloth and some more wine for Lord Brigsley.'

The waiter opened a fresh bottle of claret and James decided it was his turn to have a little fun. Anne had been laughing at him for three months. Why shouldn't he tease her a little, if Harvey gave him the chance? Harvey was still talking.

'You a racing man, James?'

'Yes, sir, and I was delighted by your victory in the King George VI and Queen Elizabeth Stakes – for more reasons than you realise.'

In the diversion caused by the waiters clearing the table, Anne whispered *sotto voce*:

'Don't try to be too clever, darling – he's not as stupid as he sounds.'

'Well, what do you think of her?'

'I beg your pardon, sir?'

'Rosalie.'

'Magnificent. I put £5 each way on her.'

'Yes, it was a great occasion for me and I was sorry you missed it, Rosalie, because you would have met the Queen and a nice guy from Oxford University called Professor Porter.'

'Professor Porter?' enquired James, burying his face in his wine glass.

'Yes, Professor Porter, James. Do you know him?'

'No, sir, I can't say I do, but didn't he win a Nobel Prize?'

'He sure did and he gave me a wonderful time at Oxford. I enjoyed myself so much I ended up presenting the university with a cheque for $250,000 to be used for research of some kind, so he should be happy.'

'Daddy, you know you're not meant to tell anybody about that.'

'Sure, but James is family now.'

'Why can't you tell anyone else, sir?'

'Well, it's a long story, James, but it was quite an honour for me. You do understand this is highly confidential, but I was Professor Porter's guest at Encaenia. I lunched at All Souls with Mr Harry Macmillan, your dear old Prime Minister, and then I attended the Garden Party, and afterwards I had a meeting with the Vice-Chancellor in his private rooms along with the Registrar and the Secretary of the University Chest. Were you at Oxford, James?'

'Yes, sir. The House.'

'The House?' queried Harvey.

'Christ Church, sir.'

'I'll never understand Oxford.'

'No, sir.'

'You must call me Harvey. Well, as I was saying, we all met at the Clarendon and they stammered and stuttered and they were totally lost for words, except for one funny old guy, who was ninety if he was a day. The truth is that those people just don't know how to approach millionaires for money, so I put them out of their embarrassment and took over. They'd have gone on all day about their beloved Oxford, so eventually I had to shut them up and simply wrote out a cheque for $250,000.'

'That was very generous, Harvey.'

'I'd have given them $500,000 if the old boy had asked. James, you've gone quite white. Do you feel all right?'

'I'm sorry. Yes, I'm fine. I was quite carried away with your description of Oxford.'

Anne joined in:

'Daddy, you made an agreement with the Vice-Chancellor that you would keep your gift as a bond between the university and yourself, and you must promise never to repeat that story again.'

'I think I shall wear the robes for the first time

when I open the new Metcalfe library at Harvard in the fall.'

'Oh, no sir,' stammered James a little too quickly, 'that wouldn't be quite the thing. You should only wear full robes in Oxford on ceremonial occasions.'

'Gee, what a shame. Still, I know what sticklers you English are for etiquette. Which reminds me, we ought to discuss your wedding. I suppose you two will want to live in England?'

'Yes, Daddy, but we'll visit you every year and when you make your annual trip to Europe you can come and stay with us.'

The waiters cleared the table again and reappeared with Harvey's favourite strawberries. Anne tried to steer the conversation to domestic issues and stop her father returning to what he'd been up to during the past two months, while James did everything to get him back on the subject.

'Coffee or liqueur, sir?'

'No, thank you,' said Harvey. 'Just the check. I thought we'd have a drink in my suite at Claridge's, Rosalie. I have something to show you both. It's a bit of a surprise.'

'I can't wait, Daddy. I love surprises. Don't you, James?'

'Normally yes, but I think I've had enough for one day.'

*

James left them and drove the Alfa Romeo to Claridge's garage so that Anne could have a few moments
alone with her father. They strolled along Curzon
Street, arm in arm.

'Isn't he wonderful, Daddy?'

'Yeah, great guy. Didn't seem too bright to begin
with but he cheered up as the meal went on. And
fancy my little girl turning out to be a genuine English
lady. Your Momma's tickled pink and I'm pleased
that we've patched up our silly quarrel.'

'Oh, you helped a lot, Daddy.'

'I did?' queried Harvey.

'Yes, I managed to get things back into perspective
during the last few weeks. Now tell me, what is your
little surprise?'

'Wait and see, honey. It's your wedding present.'

James rejoined them at the entrance to Claridge's.
He could tell from Anne's look that Harvey had given
him the seal of parental approval.

'Good evening, sir. Good evening, my lord.'

'Hi there, Albert. Could you fix some coffee and a
bottle of Rémy Martin to be sent up to my suite?'

'Right away, sir.'

James had never seen the Royal Suite before. Off
the small entrance room, there is a master bedroom
on the right and a sitting-room on the left. Harvey
took them straight to the sitting-room.

'Children, you are about to see your wedding
present.'

He threw the door open in dramatic style and there on the far wall, facing them, was the Van Gogh. They both stared, quite unable to speak.

'That's exactly how it left me,' said Harvey. 'Speechless.'

'Daddy.' Anne swallowed. 'A Van Gogh. But you've always wanted a Van Gogh. You've dreamed of possessing one for years. I couldn't possibly deprive you of it now, and anyway I couldn't think of having anything as valuable as that in my house. Think of the security risk – we don't have the protection you have.' Anne stammered on. 'We couldn't let you sacrifice the pride of your collection, could we, James?'

'Absolutely not,' said James with great feeling. 'I wouldn't have a moment's peace with that on the premises.'

'Keep the painting in Boston, Daddy, in a setting worthy of it.'

'But I thought you'd love the idea, Rosalie.'

'I do, I do, Daddy, I just don't want the responsibility, and in any case Mother must have the chance to enjoy it too. You can always leave it to James and me if you like.'

'What a great idea, Rosalie. That way we can both enjoy the painting. Now I shall have to think of another wedding present. She nearly got the better of me then, James, and she hasn't done that in twenty-four years.'

'Well, I've managed it two or three times lately, Daddy, and I'm still hoping I shall do it once more.'

Harvey ignored Anne's remark and went on talking.

'That's the King George and Elizabeth trophy,' he said, pointing to a magnificent bronze sculpture of a horse and jockey with his hoop and quartered cap studded with diamonds. 'The race is so important they present a new trophy every year – so it's mine for life.'

James was thankful that the trophy at least was genuine.

The coffee and brandy arrived and they settled down to discuss the wedding in detail.

'Now, Rosalie, you must fly over to Lincoln next week and help your mother with the arrangements, otherwise she'll panic and nothing will get done. And, James, you let me know how many people you'll have coming over and I'll put them up at the Ritz. The wedding will be in Trinity Church, Copley Square, make sense, James?'

'Sounds wonderful. You're a very well organised man, Harvey.'

'Always have been, James. Find it pays in the long run. Now, you and Rosalie must get the details sewn up before she comes over next week; you may not have realised it, but I'm returning to America tomorrow.'

Page 38A of the blue dossier, thought James.

James and Anne spent another hour chatting

about the wedding arrangements and left Harvey just before midnight.

'I'll see you first thing in the morning, Daddy.'

'Goodnight, sir.'

James shook hands and left.

'I told you he was super.'

'He's a fine young man and your mother will be very pleased.'

James said nothing to Anne in the lift on the way down because two other men stood beside them in silence, also intent on reaching the ground floor. But once they were in the Alfa Romeo he took Anne by the scruff of her neck, threw her across his legs, and spanked her so hard that she didn't know whether to laugh or cry.

'What's that for?'

'Just in case you ever forget after we're married who's the head of this household.'

'You male chauvinist pig, I was only trying to help.'

James drove at furious speed to

'What about all your so-called background – your parents live in Washington and Daddy's in the Diplomatic Corps",' James mimicked. 'Some diplomat.'

'I know, darling, but I had to think of something once I'd realised who it was you were up against.'

'What in hell's name am I going to tell the others?'

'Nothing. You invite them to the wedding, explain that my mother is American and that's why we're getting married in Boston. I'd give the earth to see their faces when they discover who your father-in-law is. In any case, you still have a plan to think of and you can't possibly let them down.'

'But the circumstances have changed.'

'No, they haven't. The truth of the matter is that they've all succeeded and you've failed, so you be sure you think of a plan by the time you reach America.'

'It's obvious now that we wouldn't have succeeded without your help.'

'Nonsense, darling. I had nothing to do with Jean-Pierre's scheme. I just added some background colour here and there – Promise you'll never spank me again?'

'Certainly I will, every time I think of that picture, but now, darling . . .'

'James, you're a sex maniac.'

'I know, darling. How do you think we Brigsleys have reared tribes of little lords for generations?'

Anne left James early the next morning to spend some time with her father, and they both saw him off at the airport on the midday flight to Boston. Anne could not resist asking in the car on the way back what James had decided to tell the others. She could get no response other than:

'Wait and see. I'm not having it changed behind my back. I'm only too glad you're off to America on Monday.'

18

MONDAY WAS A double hell for James. First, he had to see Anne off on the morning TWA flight for Boston, and then he had to spend the rest of the day preparing for the Team meeting in the evening. The other three had now completed their operations and would be waiting to hear what he had come up with. It was twice as hard now he knew that the victim was to be his father-in-law, but he realised that Anne was right and he could not put that forward as an excuse. Nevertheless, he still had to relieve Harvey of $250,000. To think he could have done it with one sentence at Oxford. That was another thing he could not tell the rest of the Team.

As Oxford had been Stephen's victory, the Team dinner was at Magdalen College and James travelled out of London just after the rush hour, past the White City Stadium and on down the M40 to Oxford.

'You're always last, James,' said Stephen.

'Sorry, I've been up to my eyes . . .'

'Preparing a good plan, I hope,' said Jean-Pierre.

James didn't answer. How well they all knew each other now, he thought. In twelve weeks James felt he had come to know more about these three men than any of the so-called friends he'd known for twenty years. For the first time he understood why his father continually referred back to friendships formed during the war with men he normally would never have met. He began to realise how much he was going to miss Stephen when he returned to America. Success was, in fact, going to split them up.

James would have been the last to go through the agony of another Prospecta Oil, but it had certainly had its compensations.

Stephen could never treat any occasion as a celebration, and as soon as the servants had brought in the first course and left, he banged the table with a spoon and declared that the meeting was in progress.

'Make me a promise,' said Jean-Pierre.

'What's that?' asked Stephen.

'When we have every last penny back, I can sit at the top of the table and you won't speak until you're spoken to.'

'Agreed,' said Stephen, 'but not until we do have every last penny. The position at the moment is that we've received $777,560. Expenses on this operation have totalled $5,178, making a grand total of $27,661.24. Therefore, Metcalfe still owes us $250,101.24.'

Stephen handed round a copy of the current balance sheet.

'These sheets are to be added to your own folders as pages 63C. Any questions?'

'Yes, why were the expenses so high for this operation?' asked Robin.

'Well, over and above the obvious things,' said Stephen, 'the truth is that we've been hit by the floating exchange rate of sterling against the dollar. At the beginning of this operation you could get $2.44 to the pound. This morning I could only get $2.32. I'm spending in pounds but charging Metcalfe in dollars at the going rate.'

'Not going to let him off with one penny, are you?' said James.

'Not one penny. Now, before we go on I should like to place on record . . .'

'This gets more like a meeting of the House of Commons every time,' said Jean-Pierre.

'Stop croaking, frog,' said Robin.

'Listen, you Harley Street pimp.'

Uproar broke out. The college scouts, who had seen some rowdy gatherings in their time, wondered if they would have to be called in to help before the evening was completed.

'Quiet,' the sharp, senatorial voice of Stephen brought them all back to order. 'I know you're in high spirits, but we still have to get $250,101.24.'

'We must on no account forget the 24 cents, Stephen.'

'You weren't as noisy the first time you had dinner here, Jean-Pierre:

The man that once did sell the lion's skin
While the beast liv'd, was killed with hunting him.'

The table was silent.

'Harvey still owes the Team money and it'll be just as hard to acquire the last quarter as it was with the first three-quarters. Before I hand over to James, I'd like to place on record that his performance at the Clarendon was nothing less than brilliant.'

Robin and Jean-Pierre banged the table in appreciation and agreement.

'Now, James, we're all ears.'

Once again the room fell into silence.

'My plan is nearly complete,' began James.

The others looked disbelieving.

'But I have something to tell you, which I hope will allow me a short respite before we carry it out.'

'You're going to get married.'

'Quite right, Jean-Pierre, as usual.'

'I could tell the moment you walked in. When do we meet her, James?'

'Not until it's too late for her to change her mind, Jean-Pierre.'

Stephen consulted his diary.

'How much reprieve are you asking for?'

'Well, Anne and I are getting married on August 3rd, in Boston. Anne's mother is American,' explained James, 'and although Anne lives in England, it would please her mother if she was married at home. Then there'll be the honeymoon and after that we anticipate returning to England on August 25th. My plan for Mr Metcalfe ought to be carried out on September 15th, the closing day of the Stock Exchange account.'

'I'm sure that's acceptable, James. All agreed?'

Robin and Jean-Pierre nodded.

James launched into his plan.

'I shall require a telex and seven telephones. They'll need to be installed in my flat. Jean-Pierre will have to be in Paris at the Bourse, Stephen in Chicago on the commodity market and Robin in London at Lloyds. I will present a full blue dossier as soon as I return from my honeymoon.'

They were all struck dumb with admiration and James paused for dramatic effect.

'Very good, James,' said Stephen. 'We'll await the details with interest. What further instructions do you have?'

'First, Stephen, you must know the opening and closing price of gold in Johannesburg, Zürich, New York and London each day for the next month. Jean-Pierre, you must know the price of the Deutschmark, the French franc and the pound against the dollar every day during the same period, and Robin must master a telex machine and PBX 8-line switchboard by September 2nd. You must be as competent as an international operator.'

'Always get the easy jobs, Robin, don't you?' said Jean-Pierre.

'You can . . .'

'Shut up, both of you,' said James.

Their faces registered surprise and respect.

'I've made notes for all of you to work on.'

James handed two typewritten sheets to each member of the Team.

'You add these to your dossiers as pages 74 and 75 and they should keep you occupied for at least a month. Finally, you're all invited to the wedding of Miss Anne Summerton to James Brigsley. I shan't bother issuing you with formal invitations at such short notice, but I've reserved seats for us on a 747 on the afternoon of August 2nd and we're all booked in at the Ritz in Boston for the night. I hope you'll honour me by being ushers.'

Even James was impressed by his own efficiency. The others received the plane tickets and instructions with astonishment.

'We'll meet at the airport at 3 pm and during the flight I shall test you on your dossier notes.'

'Yes, sir,' said Jean-Pierre.

'Your test, Jean-Pierre, will be in both French and English, as you'll be required to converse in two languages over a trans-Atlantic telephone, and appear expert on foreign currency exchange.'

There were no more jokes about James that evening, and as he travelled back up the motorway he felt a new man. Not only had he been the star of the Oxford plan; now he had the other three on the run. He would come out on top and do his old pa yet.

19

FOR A CHANGE James was the first to arrive at a meeting and the others joined him at Heathrow. He had gained the upper hand and was determined not to lose it. Robin arrived last, clutching an armful of newspapers.

'We're only going to be away for two days,' said Stephen.

'I know, but I always miss the English papers, so I've brought enough for tomorrow as well.'

Jean-Pierre threw his arms up in Gallic despair.

They checked their luggage through the No. 3 Terminal and boarded the British Airways 747 flight to Logan International Airport.

'It's more like a football ground,' said Robin, stepping for the first time inside a jumbo jet.

'It holds 350 people. About the size of the crowds most of your English clubs deserve,' said Jean-Pierre.

'Cut it out,' said James sternly, not realising that they were both nervous passengers and were only trying to relieve the tension. Later, during take-off, they both pretended to read, but as soon as the plane reached 30,000 feet and the little white light that says 'fasten seat-belts' switched off, they were back in top form.

The Team chewed its way stolidly through a plastic dinner of cold chicken and Algerian red wine.

'I do hope, James,' said Jean-Pierre, 'that your father-in-law will feed us a little better.'

After the meal James allowed them to watch the film, but insisted that as soon as it was over they must prepare to be tested one by one. Robin and Jean-Pierre moved back fifteen rows to watch *The Sting*. Stephen stayed in his seat to be grilled by James.

James handed Stephen a typewritten sheet of forty questions on the price of gold all over the world and the market movements during the past four weeks. Stephen completed it in twenty-two minutes, and it came as no surprise to James to find that every answer was correct: Stephen had always been the backbone of the Team, and it was his logical brain that had really defeated Harvey Metcalfe.

Stephen and James dozed intermittently until Robin and Jean-Pierre returned, when they were given their forty questions. Robin took thirty minutes over his and scored 38 out of 40. Jean-Pierre took twenty-seven minutes and scored 37.

'Stephen got 40 out of 40,' said James.

'He would,' said Jean-Pierre.

Robin looked a little sheepish.

'And so will you by September 2nd. Understood?' They both nodded.

'Have you seen *The Sting*?' asked Robin,

'No,' replied Stephen. 'I rarely go to the cinema.'

'They're not in our league. One big operation, and they don't even keep the money.'

'Go to sleep, Robin.'

The meal, the film and James's quizzes had taken up most of the six-hour flight and they all nodded off in the last hour, to be woken suddenly by:

'This is your captain speaking. We are approaching Logan International Airport and our flight is running twenty minutes late. We expect to land at 7.15 in approximately ten minutes. We hope you have enjoyed your flight and will travel again with British Airways.'

Customs took a little longer than usual as they all three had brought presents for the wedding and did not want James to know what they were. They had considerable trouble in explaining to the customs officer why one of the two Piaget watches had inscribed on the back: 'Part of the illicit profits from Prospecta Oil – the three who had plans.'

When they finally escaped the customs official, they found Anne standing at the entrance by a large Cadillac waiting to chauffeur them to the hotel.

'Now we know why it took you so long to come up with something: you were genuinely distracted. Congratulations, James, you're entirely forgiven,' said Jean-Pierre, and threw his arms round Anne as only a Frenchman could. Robin introduced himself and kissed her gently on the cheek. Stephen shook hands with her rather formally. They bustled into the car, Jean-Pierre sitting next to Anne.

'Miss Summerton,' stuttered Stephen.

'Do call me Anne.'

'Will the reception be at the hotel?'

'No,' replied Anne, 'at my parents' house, but there'll be a car to pick you up and take you there after the wedding. Your only responsibility is to see that James gets to the church by 3.30. Other than that you have nothing to worry about. While I think of it, James, your father and mother arrived yesterday and they're staying with my parents. We thought it might not be a good idea for you to spend this evening at home because Mother's flapping about everything.'

'Anything you say, darling.'

'If you should change your mind between now and tomorrow,' said Jean-Pierre, 'I find myself available. I may not be blessed with noble blood, but there are one or two compensations we French can always offer.'

Anne smiled to herself. 'You're a little late, Jean-Pierre. In any case, I don't like beards.'

'But I only . . .' began Jean-Pierre.

The others glared at him.

At the hotel they left Anne and James alone while they went to unpack.

'Do they know, darling?'

'They haven't the slightest idea,' replied James. 'They're going to get the surprise of their life tomorrow.'

'Is your plan ready?'

'Wait and see.'

'Well, I have one,' said Anne. 'When's yours scheduled for?'

'September 13th.'

'I win then – mine's for tomorrow.'

'What, you weren't meant to . . .'

'Don't worry. You just concentrate on getting married . . . to me.'

'Can't we go somewhere?'

'No, you terrible man. You can wait until tomorrow.'

'I do love you.'

'Go to bed, you silly thing. I love you too, but I must go home, otherwise nothing'll be ready.'

James took the lift to the seventh floor and joined the others for coffee.

'Anyone for blackjack?'

'Not with you, you pirate,' said Robin. 'You've been tutored by the biggest crook alive.'

The Team were in top form and looking forward to the wedding. In spite of the transatlantic time dislocation they didn't depart for their separate rooms until well after midnight. Even then, James lay awake for some time, turning over the same question in his mind:

'I wonder what's she's up to this time?'

20

Boston in August is as beautiful a city as any in America, and the Team enjoyed a large breakfast in James's room.

'I don't think he looks up to it,' said Jean-Pierre. 'You're the captain of the Team, Stephen. I volunteer to take his place.'

'It'll cost you $250,000.'

'Agreed,' said Jean-Pierre.

'You don't have $250,000,' said Stephen. 'You have $187,474.69, being one quarter of what's been raised so far, so my decision is that James must be the bridegroom.'

'It's an Anglo-Saxon plot,' said Jean-Pierre, 'and when James has successfully completed his plan and we have the full amount, I shall re-open negotiations.'

They sat talking and laughing for a long time over the toast and coffee. Stephen regarded them fondly, regretting how rarely they would meet once, *if*, he corrected himself sternly, James's operation were accomplished successfully. If Harvey Metcalfe had ever had a team like this on his side instead of against him, he would have been the richest man in the world.

'You're dreaming, Stephen.'

'Yes, I'm sorry. I mustn't forget that Anne has put me in charge.'

'Here we go again,' said Jean-Pierre. 'What time shall we report, Professor?'

'One hour from now, fully dressed to inspect James and take him to the church. Jean-Pierre, you will go and buy four carnations – three red ones and one white. Robin, you will arrange for the taxi and I shall take care of James.'

Robin and Jean-Pierre left, singing the *Marseillaise* lustily in two different keys. James and Stephen watched them depart.

'How are you feeling, James?'

'Great. I'm only sorry that I didn't complete my plan before today.'

'Doesn't matter at all. September 13th will be quite early enough. In any case, the break will do us no harm.'

'We'd never have managed it without you. You know that, don't you, Stephen? We'd all be facing ruin and I wouldn't even have met Anne. We all owe you so much.'

Stephen stared fixedly out of the window, unable to reply.

*

'Three red and one white,' said Jean-Pierre, 'as instructed, and I presume the white one is for me.'

'Pin it on James. Not behind his ear, Jean-Pierre.'

'You look fantastic, but I still fail to see what the lady sees in you,' said Jean-Pierre. Although the four of them were ready to leave, they still had half an hour to kill before the taxi was due. Jean-Pierre opened a bottle of champagne and they toasted James's health, the Team's health, Her Majesty The Queen, the President of the United States, and finally, with simulated reluctance, the President of France. Having finished the bottle, Stephen thought it wise for them to leave immediately and dragged the other three down to the waiting taxi.

'Keep smiling, James. We're with you.'

And they bundled him into the back.

The taxi took only a few minutes to reach Trinity Church, Copley Square, and the driver was not unhappy to be rid of the four of them.

'Three-fifteen pm. Anne will be very pleased with me,' said Stephen.

He escorted the bridegroom to the front pew on the right-hand side of the church, while Jean-Pierre made eyes at the prettiest of the girls. Robin helped hand out the wedding sheets while one thousand overdressed guests waited for the bride.

Stephen had just come to Robin's aid on the steps of the church and Jean-Pierre had joined them, suggesting they took their seats, when the Rolls Royce arrived. They were riveted to the steps by the beauty of Anne in her Balenciaga wedding gown. Her father stepped out behind her. She took his arm and proceeded to climb the steps.

The three stood motionless, like sheep in the stare of a python.

'The bastard.'

'Who's been conning who?'

'She must have known all along.'

Harvey beamed vaguely at them as he walked past with Anne on his arm. They proceeded down the aisle.

'Good God,' thought Stephen. 'He didn't recognise any of us.'

They took their places at the back of the church, out of earshot of the vast congregation. The organist stopped playing when Anne reached the altar.

'Harvey can't know,' said Stephen.

'How do you work that out?' asked Jean-Pierre.

'Because James would never have put us through this unless he'd passed the test himself at some earlier date.'

'Good thinking,' whispered Robin.

'I require and charge you both, as ye will answer at the dreadful day of judgment when the secrets of all hearts shall be disclosed . . .'

'I'd like to know one or two secrets right now,' said Jean-Pierre. 'To start with, how long has she known?'

'James Clarence Spencer, wilt thou have this

woman to thy wedded wife, to live together after God's ordinance in the Holy estate of Matrimony? Wilt thou love her, comfort her, honour and keep her, in sickness and in health and, forsaking all other, keep thee only unto her, so long as ye both shall live?'

'I will.'

'Rosalie Arlene, wilt thou have this man to thy wedded husband, to live . . .'

'I think,' said Stephen, 'we can be sure that she's a fully fledged member of the Team; otherwise we could never have succeeded at Monte Carlo or Oxford.'

'. . . so long as ye both shall live?'

'I will.'

'Who giveth this woman to be married to this man?'

Harvey bustled forward and took Anne's hand and gave it to the priest.

'I, James Clarence Spencer, take thee, Rosalie Arlene, to my wedded wife . . .'

'And what's more, why should he recognise us when he's only seen each of us once, and not as we really are,' continued Stephen.

'And thereto I plight thee my troth.'

'I, Rosalie Arlene, take thee, James Clarence Spencer, to my wedded husband . . .'

'But he must have a chance of working it out if we hang around,' said Robin.

'Not necessarily,' said Stephen. 'No need to panic. Our secret has always been to catch him off home ground.'

'But now he's on home ground,' said Jean-Pierre.

'No, he isn't. It's his daughter's wedding day and it's totally strange to the man. Naturally, we avoid him at the reception, but we don't make it too obvious.'

'You'll have to hold my hand,' said Robin.

'I will,' volunteered Jean-Pierre.

'Just remember to act naturally.'

'. . . and thereto I give thee my troth.'

Anne was quiet and shy, her voice only just reaching the astonished three at the back. James's was clear and firm:

'With this ring I thee wed, with my body I thee worship, and with all my worldly goods I thee endow . . .'

'And with some of ours too,' said Jean-Pierre.

'In the name of the Father, and of the Son and of the Holy Spirit. Amen.'

'Let us pray,' intoned the priest.

'I know what I'm going to pray,' said Robin. 'To be delivered out of the power of our enemy and from the hands of all that hate us.'

'O Eternal God, Creator and Preserver of all mankind . . .'

'We're near the end now,' said Stephen.

'An unfortunate turn of phrase,' offered Robin.

'Silence,' said Jean-Pierre. 'I agree with Stephen. We've got the measure of Metcalfe, just relax.'

'Those whom God hath joined together let no man put asunder.'

Jean-Pierre continued mumbling to himself, but it didn't sound like a prayer.

The blast of Handel's Wedding March from the organ brought them all back to the occasion. The ceremony was over and Lord and Lady Brigsley walked down the aisle watched by two thousand smiling eyes. Stephen looked amused, Jean-Pierre envious, and Robin nervous. James smiled beatifically as he passed them.

After a ten-minute session for the photographers on the steps of the church, the Rolls Royce carried the newly married couple back to the Metcalfes' house in Lincoln. Harvey and the Countess of Louth took the second car, and the Earl and Arlene, Anne's mother, took the third. Stephen, Robin and Jean-Pierre followed some twenty minutes later, still arguing the pros and cons of bearding the lion in his own den.

Harvey Metcalfe's Georgian house was magnificent, with an oriental garden leading down to a lake, great beds of roses and in the conservatory his pride and joy, his collection of rare orchids.

'I never thought I'd see this,' said Jean-Pierre.

'Nor me,' said Robin, 'and now that I have, I'm not too happy.'

'Let's run the gauntlet,' said Stephen. 'I suggest that we join the receiving line at well-separated intervals. I'll go first. Robin, you come second, at least twenty places behind, and Jean-Pierre, you come third, at least twenty places behind Robin, and *act naturally.* We're just friends of James's from England. Now, when you take your places in the queue, listen to the conversation. Try and find someone who's a close friend of Harvey's and jump immediately in front of them. When it comes to your turn to shake hands, Harvey's eyes will already be on the next person because he won't know you and will want to talk to them. That way we should escape.'

'Brilliant, Professor,' said Jean-Pierre.

The queue seemed interminably long. A thousand people shuffled past the outstretched hands of Mr and Mrs Metcalfe, the Earl and Countess of Louth, and Anne and James. Stephen eventually made it and passed with flying colours.

'So glad you could come,' said Anne.

Stephen did not reply.

'Good to see you, Stephen.'

'We all admire your plan, James.'

Stephen slipped into the main ballroom and hid behind a pillar on the other side of the room, as far as he could be from the multi-storey wedding cake in the centre.

Robin was next and avoided looking Harvey in the eyes.

'How kind of you to come all this way,' said Anne.

Robin mumbled something under his breath.

'Hope you've enjoyed yourself today, Robin?'

James was obviously having the time of his life. After being put through it in the same way by Anne, he was relishing the Team's discomfiture.

'You're a bastard, James.'

'Not too loud, old fellow. My mother and father might hear you.'

Robin slipped through to the ballroom and, after a search behind all the pillars, found Stephen.

'Did you get through all right?'

'I think so, but I don't want to see him ever again. What time is the plane back?'

'Eight pm. Now don't panic. Keep your eye out for Jean-Pierre.'

'Bloody good thing he kept his beard,' said Robin.

Jean-Pierre shook hands with Harvey, who was already intent on the next guest as Jean-Pierre had, by shameless queue-barging, managed to secure a place in front of a Boston banker who was obviously a close friend of Harvey's.

'Good to see you, Marvin.'

Jean-Pierre had escaped. He kissed Anne on both cheeks, whispered in her ear, 'Game, set and match to James,' and went off in search of Stephen and Robin. He forgot his original instructions when he found himself face to face with the chief bridesmaid.

'Did you enjoy the wedding?' she asked.

'Of course. I always judge weddings by the bridesmaids, not the bride.'

She blushed with pleasure.

'This must have cost a fortune,' she continued.

'Yes, my dear, and I know whose,' said Jean-Pierre, slipping his arm around her waist.

Four hands grabbed a protesting Jean-Pierre and unceremoniously dragged him behind the pillar.

'For God's sake, Jean-Pierre. She's not a day over seventeen. We don't want to go to jail for rape of a juvenile as well as theft. Drink this and behave yourself.' Robin thrust a glass of champagne into his hand.

The champagne flowed and even Stephen had a little too much. They were all clinging to their pillar for support by the time the toast-master called for silence.

'My lords, ladies and gentlemen. Pray silence for the Viscount Brigsley, the bridegroom.'

James made an impressive speech. The actor in him took over and the Americans adored it. Even his father had a look of admiration on his face. The toast-master then introduced Harvey, who spoke long and loud. He cracked his favourite joke about marrying off his daughter to Prince Charles, at which the assembled guests roared heartily as they always do at weddings, even for the weakest joke. He ended by calling the toast for the bride and groom.

When the applause had died down, and the hub-bub of chatter had struck up again, Harvey took an envelope from his pocket and kissed his daughter on the cheek.

'Rosalie, here's a little wedding present for you, to

make up for letting me keep the Van Gogh. I know you'll put it to good use.'

Harvey passed her the white envelope. Inside there was a cheque for $250,000. Anne kissed her father with genuine affection.

'Thank you, Daddy, I promise you James and I will use it wisely.'

She hurried off in pursuit of James, whom she found besieged by a group of American matrons:

'Is it true you're related to the Queen . . .?'

'I never met a real live lord . . .'

'I do hope you'll invite us over to see your castle . . . ?'

'There are no castles in the King's Road,' said James relieved to be rescued by Anne.

'Darling, can you spare me a minute?'

James excused himself and followed Anne, but they found it almost impossible to escape the crowd.

'Look,' she said. 'Quickly.'

James took the cheque.

'Good God – $250,000.'

'You know what I'm going to do with it, don't you?'

'Yes, darling.'

Anne hunted for Stephen, Robin and Jean-Pierre, which was not an easy task as they were still hidden behind a pillar in the far corner. She was eventually guided to the spot by the subdued but spirited rendering of 'Who Wants to be a Millionaire?' issuing from behind it.

'Can you lend me a pen, Stephen?'

Three pens shot out for her use.

She took the cheque from the middle of her bouquet and wrote on its back, 'Rosalie Brigsley – pay Stephen Bradley'. She handed it to him.

'Yours, I believe.'

The three of them stared at the cheque. She was gone before they could even comment.

'What a girl our James has gone and married,' said Jean-Pierre.

'You're drunk, you frog,' said Robin.

'How dare you, sir, suggest that a Frenchman could get drunk on champagne. I demand satisfaction. Choose your weapons.'

'Champagne corks.'

'Quiet,' said Stephen. 'You'll give yourselves away.'

'Well now, tell me, Professor, what's the latest financial position?'

'I'm just working it out now,' said Stephen.

'What?' said Robin and Jean-Pierre together, but they were too happy to argue.

'He still owes us $101 and 24 cents.'

'Disgraceful,' said Jean-Pierre. 'Burn the place down.'

Anne and James left to change, while Stephen, Robin and Jean-Pierre forced down some more champagne. The toast-master announced that the bride and groom would be leaving in approximately fifteen minutes and requested the guests to gather in the main hall and courtyard.

'Come on, we must watch them go,' said Stephen. The drink had given them new confidence and they took their places near the car.

It was Stephen who heard Harvey say, 'God damn it. Do I have to think of everything?' and watched him look round his guests until his eyes fell on the trio. Stephen's legs turned to jelly as Harvey's finger beckoned him.

'Hey, you, weren't you an usher?'

'Yes, sir.'

'Rosalie is going to leave at any moment and there are no flowers for her. God knows what's happened to them, but there are no flowers. Grab a car. There's a florist half a mile down the road, but hurry.'

'Yes, sir.'

'Say, don't I know you from somewhere?'

'Yes, sir, I mean, no sir. I'll go and get the flowers.'

Stephen turned and fled. Robin and Jean-Pierre, who had been watching horrified, thinking that Harvey had at last rumbled them, ran after him. When he reached the back of the house, Stephen came to a halt and stared at the most beautiful bed of roses. Robin and Jean-Pierre shot straight past him, stopped, turned round and staggered back.

'What the hell are you up to – picking flowers for your own funeral?'

'It's only Metcalfe's wishes. Somebody forgot the flowers for Anne and I have five minutes to get them, so start picking.

'*Mes enfants*, do you see what I see?'

The others looked up. Jean-Pierre was staring rapturously at the conservatory.

Stephen rushed back to the front of the house, the prize orchids in his arms, followed by Robin and Jean-Pierre. He was just in time to pass them over to Harvey before James and Anne came out of the house.

'Magnificent. They're my favourite flowers. How much were they?'

'$100,' replied Stephen, without thinking.

Harvey handed over two $50 bills. Stephen retreated sweating, to join Robin and Jean-Pierre.

James and Anne fought their way through the crowd. No man in the gathering could take his eyes off her.

'Oh Daddy, orchids, how beautiful.' Anne kissed Harvey. 'You've made this the most wonderful day in my life . . .'

The Rolls Royce moved slowly down the drive away from the large crowd on its way to the airport, where James and Anne were to catch the flight to San Francisco, their first stop on the way to Hawaii. As the car glided round the house, Anne stared at the empty conservatory and then at the flowers in her arms. James did not notice. He was thinking of other things.

'Do you think they'll ever forgive me?' he said.

'I'm sure they'll find a way, darling. But do let me into a secret. Did you really have a plan?'

'I knew you wouldn't be able to resist asking me that, and the truth is . . .'

The car purred effortlessly along the highway and only the chauffeur heard his reply.

Stephen, Robin and Jean-Pierre watched the guests dispersing, most of them saying their goodbyes to the Metcalfes.

'Don't let's risk it,' said Robin.

'Agreed,' said Stephen.

'Let's invite him out to dinner,' said Jean-Pierre.

The other two grabbed him and threw him into a taxi.

'What's that you have under your morning coat, Jean-Pierre?'

'Two bottles of Krug *dix-neuf cent soixante-quatre*. It seemed such a shame to leave them there on their own. I thought they might get lonely.'

Stephen instructed the driver to take them back to the hotel.

'What a wedding. Do you think James ever had a plan?' asked Robin.

'I don't know, but if he has it will only have to bring in $1.24.'

'We should have retrieved the money he made from his win on Rosalie at Ascot,' mused Jean-Pierre.

After packing and signing out of the hotel, they took another taxi to Logan International Airport and, with considerable help from the British Airways staff, managed to board the plane.

'Damn,' said Stephen. 'I wish we hadn't left without the $1.24.'

21

ONCE ON BOARD, they drank the champagne Jean-Pierre had captured at the wedding. Even Stephen seemed content, although he did occasionally revert to the theme of the missing $1.24.

'How much do you imagine this champagne cost?' teased Jean-Pierre.

'That's not the point. Not a penny more, not a penny less.'

Jean-Pierre decided he would never understand academics.

'Don't worry, Stephen. I've every confidence that James's plan will bring in $1.24.'

Stephen would have laughed, but it gave him a headache.

'To think that girl knew everything.'

On arrival at Heathrow, they had little trouble in clearing customs. The purpose of the trip had never been to bring back gifts. Robin made a detour to W. H. Smiths and picked up *The Times* and the *Evening*

Standard. Jean-Pierre bargained with a taxi-driver about the fare to central London.

'We're not some bloody Americans who don't know the rate or the route and can be easily fleeced,' he was saying, still not yet sober.

The taxi-driver grumbled to himself as he nosed his black Austin towards the motorway. It was not going to be his day.

Robin read the papers happily, one of those rare people who could read in a moving car. Stephen and Jean-Pierre satisfied themselves with watching the passing traffic.

'Jesus Christ.'

Stephen and Jean-Pierre were startled. They had rarely heard Robin swear. It seemed out of character.

'God Almighty.'

This was too much for them, but before they could enquire, he began to read out loud:

' "BP announced a strike in the North Sea which is likely to produce 200,000 barrels of oil a day. The strike is described by their Chairman, Sir Eric Drake, as a major find. The British Petroleum Forties Field is one mile from the so far unexplored Prospecta Oil field and rumours of a bid by BP have sent Prospecta Oil shares to a record high of $12.25 at the close of business." '

'Nom de Dieu,' said Jean-Pierre. 'What do we do now?'

'Oh well,' said Stephen. 'I suppose we'll have to work out a plan for how to give it all back.'